Aethersmith

Book 2 of the Twinborn Trilogy

By J.S. Morin

Cover Art by Duncan Long
duncanlong.com

ISBN: 1939233062
ISBN-13: 978-1-939233-06-6

Dedication

To Kristin, who has been behind me all the way (pushing as needed).
I would never have gotten this far without you.

Kadris

1 - Imperial Palace
2 - Tower of Contemplation
3 - Solaran Estate
4 - Imperial Academy
5 - Army Headquarters
6 - Ralak Square
7 - School of Arms
8 - Tournament Grounds
9 - Benklear Estate
10 - Hallimere Estate
11 - Gardanus Estate
12 - Lurien Estate

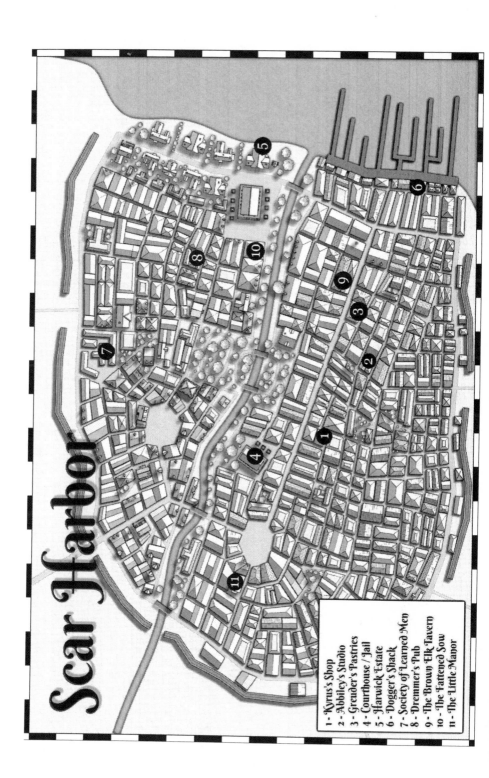

Scar Harbor

1 - Kyrus's Shop
2 - Abbicy's Studio
3 - Greuder's Pastries
4 - Courthouse / Jail
5 - Harwick Estate
6 - Dogger's Shack
7 - Society of Learned Men
8 - Dremmer's Pub
9 - The Brown Elk Tavern
10 - The Fattened Sow
11 - The Little Manor

Chapter 1 - Priceless

With naught but the faintest whisper of fabric, a shadow rendered in flesh crept down the moonlit corridor. The polished stone floors and vaulted ceilings that always made a chorus of echoes at the clop of leather-soled shoes lent no voice to soft slippers. Light from the nearly full moon poured in through the stained glass, turning red, gold, and green as each pane added its own hue to the otherwise colorless moonbeams, but the windows were high above, and cast their illumination only to one side of the hall—the other remained a haven for shadows.

The shadowy prowler crept among pedestals and glass cases that displayed various artifacts of Acardian history. There was a bust of Paillus Imarcos, the High Priest of Moloun who had originally commissioned the building as a cathedral to his god; a copy of the Writ of Establishment signed by General Tonald Duthford; a sword that dated back to the nomadic tribes that lived in the area some fourteen hundred years ago; and many other treasures whose value lay more in their history than their substance.

The prowler passed by these and many more. Curiosity was for the daylight hours, and lingering over valueless relics was pastime for the idle and the scholarly. There were exceptions among the exhibits. Not every case contained bits of metal or scraps of writing that were mundane in every way save for their age. There were items of far more intrinsic value elsewhere in the vast halls.

* * * * * * * *

Mulview tipped back in his familiar old chair, the wood creaking as he shifted position. His feet were up, crossed at the ankles on the worn oak desk that he shared with his cohort. His thick-fingered hands cradled a book, *The Fables of Fenmund*, as if it were made of fine crystal. Professor Darlingsworth had let him borrow it on condition it be treated gently, and Mulview had no wish to upset the curator. The book was filled with children's stories, but the old watchman pored over it as if it contained the lost mysteries of the Kheshi Empire. The book was fragile with age, its binding crackled as it was opened and pages past yellowing to the point where they were near to crumbling—but not quite so close that occasional handling was out of the question. Mulview was familiar with many of the stories, but not intimately. He would learn the tales as best he could, and recount them to eager little faces, too young to realize their grandfather was anything less than a master storyteller.

The room was quiet except for the turning of pages, the *snick* of knife on

1

wood as his fellow watchman Danberry whittled away the hours, and the ticking of a clock. It was lit by just a pair of lanterns, one belonging to each of the night watchmen, who each used theirs to light their own hobby-work. There was a pleasant whiff of freshly cut wood in the room, but it fared badly against the odor caused by long hours of men idling about within.

As he finished "The Prince's Dog," Mulview spared a glance at the clock; it was very nearly eleven. He would not have time to begin another story. He closed the book and set it carefully aside.

"What's this one to be, then?" he asked Danberry, peering across the desk at the misshapen hunk of wood he was bothering with his knife.

"A boat," Danberry said. "I got this bit o' wood on the small coin—fella said it floats in water no matter what shape it is. I figure to make the hull solid so's I don't need to worry 'bout makin' it too thin and pokin' a hole."

"Good idea. Smart friend ya got, Dan."

"I ain't said he was no friend, mind ya. Just a fella," Danberry returned, just a bit defensively.

"What? You got some fella sellin' shady driftwood or sumthin'?" Mulview asked, giving his friend a hard time of it.

"Naw, just don't wantcha thinkin' I gots friends what has connections or nothin'. Next thing I know, I gots every man o' the watch dogging me for short-coin deals."

Ding-ding!

A small clock, dangling from the wall by a single nail, stepped in to break up their discussion. It was a small, ugly thing, a cheap copy of the magnificent clock tower that rose majestically from the upper reaches of the very museum they guarded. There had been clocks before Cadmus Errol had built the tower, but the master tinker's landmark touched off a frenzy of popularity of the devices, which had spawned a small industry of cheap clock-makers.

"That thing right?" Mulview asked.

"Ya, I think. Bromny said he set it jus' this morn—by the bell," Danberry replied.

Mulview nodded, having suspected as much, but secretly hoping he had a bit more time off his feet. With a grunt of effort, he set his feet back on the floor and hefted himself out of his chair.

"Ah well, another round to be made. See you in about an hour," Mulview said and then sighed.

The two men took up their lanterns, and headed out into the museum, heading in opposite directions.

* * * * * * *

The prowler heard the footfalls echo across the massive central chamber of the museum, illuminated by the moonlight cascading down from the stained glass overhead. The soles of the watchman's boots made for a hard clacking sound that was easy to track back to its source, despite the acoustics of the former cathedral. The chamber was subdivided into aisles by silk ropes strung between short wooden posts. The watchman made his way deliberately up and down each of them.

The prowler worked out the pattern of the patrol, and used the displays themselves to shield against the watchman's sleepy gaze. It became a simple matter for the prowler to reach the true target for that night's work: the glass-enclosed cases that housed the royal family's heirlooms.

King Gorden was a humble man. It was a trait rare enough in common men, and rarer still among monarchs. But it was the age of the Progressive Reformation Movement, which Gorden supported. The king would lead, but the people chose their own destiny: elected parliaments, participatory governance, voluntary civic service. It was unseemly in such an age for the king to hoard such artifacts as his ancestors had accumulated over their centuries of rule. Thus for years, the king had commissioned scholars and artisans to clean and restore old jewels and artwork that had long moldered in palace cellars. When they were fit to display, they were sent to the museum so that the public might marvel at them during very reasonable public viewing hours.

That was fine for other folk, but for what the prowler had in mind, unreasonably late hours were the rule—and the fewer viewers, the better.

At the center of the rather large display of royal adornments was the official raiment of the office of the king: scepter, doublet, crown, and cloak. All had been worn by King Gorden at his coronation and not since. The king dressed as well as any well-heeled nobleman, but no better, and certainly not with the gaudy tastelessness of the merchant guild leaders.

Surrounding the royal raiment were numerous displays of similar regalia from earlier in the kingdom's history. Rings, crowns, necklaces, brooches, swords both ceremonial and those wielded by warrior kings, scepters, diadems, chalices, and censers. A fortune could be made selling any one of them, but the risk was too great. The pieces were famous, distinctive, and beloved. The reward alone for their safe return would exceed the price one might find for them among disreputable connoisseurs.

Coin was power, so it was said, but an indirect and often unreliable sort. The prowler's eyes unfocused, and saw a different sort of power. There, in the currents of aether, was a small beacon among the drab, mundane bits of diamond and worked gold. *Magic!* Among the old relics was one wholly unlike the rest. A bit simpler in design if not material, it was a gold circlet set with rubies across the front—or so it appeared to most eyes. In the aether, it took on a blue-white glow, standing apart from the indistinct forms of the non-magical items and the general swirl of wild aether that filled the rest of the chamber.

Turning, the prowler looked back across the museum and saw, highlighted in blue-white like the circlet, the Source of the night watchman. Man-shaped and leaking aether, that Source was the guard's life essence. All aether flowed from the Source, and all life depended upon the aether.

The watchman was wending his way to the main entrance on the back end of his rounds. Shaking away the trance-like state of aether-vision, the prowler returned to using normal sight. The circlet was boxed in a small glass case along with a handful of other jewels from its own era. Top, bottom, and all four sides of the box were of expensive clear glass, girded at the joints with thin edges of gilded steel. A quick check confirmed that it simply sat upon the display pedestal, with no lock or clamp or catch to hold it in place, just its own weight.

The dark-clad prowler took the case in two gloved hands. With care and steady nerves, those hands slowly lifted the glass from the pedestal.

Clang!Clang!Clang!Clang!Clang!Clang! ...

Blessed winds! the prowler swore mentally. *That crazy tinker must have rigged some sort of alarm for the museum when he was here to build the clock tower.*

It was too late for stealth, so the next logical step was distraction. The prowler took the glass case cover, and threw it as far as it was willing to fly, smashing to the floor with a crash loud enough to be heard clearly over the alarm bell. A quick glance revealed that there was a tiny, hidden catch that had been held down by the weight of the glass.

Eschewing the other finery, the prowler grabbed the magical circlet, and shoved it into a satchel. Light from a lantern was sweeping about the area, and the prowler dove for cover to avoid being spotted.

* * * * * * * *

Drat! The alarm!

"Danberry! Rouse the city guards! Now!" Mulview shouted.

Taking in hand the truncheon that he kept hooked at his belt, the stocky watchman set a well-practiced scowl on his face, and stalked back into the exhibit hall he had *just* finished checking. There had been false alarms before, but with the alarm making such a racket, the watchmen could hardly be taken to task for rousing the city guards; the lads probably could hear it from their barracks anyway, just next door.

Mulview swept the aisles with his lantern, seeking a glimpse of the intruder. Ungainly though he was, he tried to make his movements quick and unpredictable, to catch his quarry off guard.

"Aha, found you!" he cried.

The light from his lantern framed the prowler mid-scurry, showing a figure dressed head to foot in black cloth, with a hooded cloak of black pulled so low that there were slits to see through it.

"Whatever you've got there, thief, drop it and give yourself up."

They were good words, and practiced often in the heads of guards who seldom saw any real excitement in the course of their duties. The mere presence of guards was supposed to deter thieves, so actual thefts were a rarity. Thus it was with great disappointment that Watchman Mulview found that his order went unheeded.

The prowler kept low, and ducked behind displays, crossing rope barriers, and violating the sanctity of exhibits of priceless artifacts. Mulview did all he could to keep himself between the prowler and the doorway, but it was a lost cause. The portly guard had come too far into the exhibit hall to confront the thief, and was not quick enough afoot to backtrack and cut off the path of escape.

"Danberry! He's past me! This is no game; there's a thief escaping!" Mulview yelled before lowering his voice to curse himself thoroughly for being a creaky old man, too slow to run down thieves from behind.

Things had always gone much better in his daydreams.

* * * * * * * *

Clang!Clang!Clang!Clang!Clang!Clang! ...

"C'mon, lads! You heard 'im!" Danberry shouted at the regiment of glassy-eyed city guardsman he had just let in through the museum's main entrance.

The guards were unarmored, but wore short, heavily padded jackets with the Golis city sigil on them. They carried drawn truncheons but, unlike the museum guards, had short swords belted at their hips as well. Two took up positions at the entrance to prevent exactly the sort of error Mulview had just made in the main exhibit hall, and the rest followed after Danberry to sweep the museum for the thief.

* * * * * * * *

Clang!Clang!Clang!Cla—

Thank you, Merciful Tansha, the prowler prayed silently.

The alarm bell had either been shut off or had run down on its own accord. The sounds of booted feet—lots more than there ought to have been—were no longer drowned out by the blaring alarm.

Down one corridor then the next, the prowler stayed ahead of the encroaching boot-steps. Thoughts of escaping back out through the open-air courtyard were dashed when guards could be heard from that direction.

There are enough of them that they are splitting up and cutting off all the exits.

There was one exit, though, that they would not have thought of.

* * * * * * * *

"We've got 'im now, eh?" Danberry said to the group of five guards who had stayed with him as others had split off to seal all routes of escape. "He's heading up fer the clock stairs. Ain't nothin' up there 'cept fer clock bits and a fair view o' the countryside."

The thunder of the guards' boots rolled onward and quickened apace as they spotted the black-clad thief entering the stairwell as Danberry had predicted.

"We got him panickin', cuz he ain't got no other way outta here now," Danberry said. "No rushin' now. Stairs is a might tight, ya see. No point in breakin' yer neck runnin' now that he's caught."

Preceding Danberry up the clock-tower stairs, the guards filed up in a line. The stairs ran in a blocky spiral around the inside of the tower. It surrounded the great pendulum that hung down near to the ground, and as they got farther up, they saw a dizzying arrangement of gears, ratchets, cogs, belts, levers, and so forth. Light shone from above, both from the moonlight that entered through the clock face and from the oil lamps that lit the clock from the inside. Pipes ran up the inside walls of the tower, drawing kerosene from ground-level reservoirs. No one had to climb up the tower to keep the lamps lit; the upper reaches of the tower were seldom visited, least of all by the guardsmen.

Men were gasping for breath by the time they reached the landing at the top of the tower. The last few steps were tentative ones, due to both fatigue and the expectation of finding a cornered thief prepared to have one last go at defending his freedom.

"Huh?" Danberry wondered aloud. "Where'd he go?"

There were clockworks all about, but no proper hiding place. As guardsmen filled the landing all about him, Danberry looked up to see if the thief had climbed atop the uppermost gears, but there was no one there. Finally, he noticed that a small access door, used for cleaning the clock face from the outside, was unlatched. He pushed it open and stuck his head out, fighting back a wave of queasiness as he looked at the dizzying drop to the cobblestones far below. There was no place for the thief to have dropped to the museum roof, for the clock face was to the far end of the building, facing away from the roofline. Looking up and down, there seemed to be no footholds or handholds worth noting.

"Well, unless that fella's part bird, he's splattered all over Lords' Crossing. That's my guess. Betcha you'd see the body if'n it weren't for that blown lamp," Danberry said, pointing down at the road for one of the guardsmen who had stuck his head out beside him.

* * * * * * * *

In a rented room, several blocks from the museum, sat a huge bear of a man, with a shaggy black beard and an unkempt mop of greasy black hair that tried to hide the fact that he was balding at the top. A toothy yellow smile split his face as a satchel plopped down on the table in front of him.

"I heard the alarm from here. Anyone follow you?" the man asked.

"No, they're probably searching the ground outside the clock tower for my gory remains even as we speak."

The speaker was still dressed all in black, but now was unhooded. Jaw-length auburn hair framed a face smooth with the signs of youth. Her piercing green eyes met those of her associate directly, with no sign of deference or fear. She was tall, and thin of face and limb. The loose black outfit hid her modest curves and called into question her gender, but only when her face was hidden away as well; she was unmistakably beautiful.

Her associate reached into the satchel, and took out the circlet from within. He turned it over carefully in his hands. "I sort of expected something a bit fancier," he mused.

"Sure, Zell, let me just nick back into the museum and pick you out a nicer one. I figured you wanted a dressed-down magic crown that you could wear with your every-day rags. But I can take you down to Duke Street in the morning, and get you something that would go with a nice *fancy* crown," the prowler replied.

"Does it work?" the man asked, shrugging off her sarcasm out of old habit.

"Try it," she replied.

The man put the crown on. It looked ridiculous on his massive head, a thin ring of gold lost amid a tangle of sweat-glossed black hair.

"Whoa, is this what you always see?" the man asked as he slowly looked all about the room, especially lingering on the walls and floor. "I can see you quite clearly—and the two daggers you are hiding. I can even see Rakashi and Tanner in the next room, and the innkeeper downstairs."

"Glad you like it. *Now* can we get back on our way to Scar Harbor?"

"Sure, Soria, first thing in the morning."

Chapter 2 - Fighting the Tide

The sea thrashed, and the wind howled past Kyrus Hinterdale as he stood staring out into the approaching storm. His bare feet sank slightly into the thick-packed, muddy sand left by the receding tide. Kyrus had adopted the natives' custom of going about with no shirt in the tropical climate of Denku Appa, a remote equatorial isle that, for now at least, was his home.

Kyrus had seen many a storm, safe on dry land and huddled indoors in his homeland of Acardia. His thick northern blood was not so bothered by the cooler air this southern storm blew; in fact, it seemed a refreshing change from the often sweltering heat of the daylight hours of summertime on the island. If not for the steel-grey sky with its otherworldly look to it, the windblown rain trying to drive itself beneath his skin like a storm of nails, and the threat of the storm surge washing out the low-lying village, the day might almost have been pleasant.

Toktu, senior elder among the Denku, had told Kyrus that this storm did not look so bad as many the islanders had seen. Nonetheless, most of the Denku had retreated to more sheltered ground, taking refuge in some caves farther inland. Those who had remained behind wished to see a unique sight: their "spirit man" wanted to hold back the storm.

Kyrus had been using shielding spells as exercise for his Source. He had only learned of magic's existence a few months ago, and was trying to make up for a youth of lost opportunity. In the realm of Kadrin—which Kyrus saw through the eyes of his counterpart from the other world, his "twin" Brannis, each night instead of dreaming—a sorcerer would be trained from an early age, starting as young as eight or so with formal training. Kyrus had seen all the rudiments as Brannis had struggled through the early ranks of the Kadrin Imperial Academy of Sorcery before they finally gave up on ever making a sorcerer of him, despite his family's strong magical heritage. It seemed as if, joined by some mystical connection, their Sources were the inverse of one another. Brannis was a stone, almost entirely cut off from the aether; Kyrus found that it leapt to his call and flowed from his Source like a river.

For weeks, Kyrus had been wading out into the shallow waters near the tide line and practicing holding back the sea. At first, he had just tried stopping the lapping kiss of water that would tickle the toes of walkers along the beach. It amused him at first to see the water stop weirdly at an invisible barrier and crash lightly against it, as if he had fashioned a glass so clear it did not cast any distortion or glare to betray its presence. With practice, he was able to form his shield farther and farther out into the tide. He kept the shield arced so that the vast and cunning Katamic Sea did not simply sneak around the sides, and he stood close to the center of that arc, as it seemed easiest to keep an equal pressure of aether in all directions that way.

With the coming of the storm, Kyrus found both a test and a purpose. The Denku had taken him in when the notorious pirate Denrik Zayne had stranded him on their island after expressing concern about potential retribution in this world for the attack of Denrik's own twin on Brannis's homeland in the other. Kyrus had shared their food, lived in one of their homes, and had begun to learn their language. In return, he had been able to do nothing of use for them, save entertain with his magical tricks. Now, though, with talk of storm surges that might wash away part of the village, Kyrus intended to keep his new home safe from the storm.

* * * * * * * *

"He is brave, our spirit man," Tippu commented, crouched behind a palm tree in an effort to shield herself from the worst of the storm winds.

Her green-dyed hair was being played havoc by the storm winds. Clad in just a loincloth and a pair of necklaces—the latter doing little to either cover or protect her—she shivered against the cool, wet air that tore past her.

"Yes, very," agreed Kahli, her long, scarlet-dyed braids whipping behind her as the wind gusted. She huddled against Tippu's back both for warmth and the shelter of the wind. "And look, he does not even shake with cold."

"He is a northerner. Their winds are always cold. He sweats like a hunter even on mild days," said Gahalu, Kyrus's best friend among the Denku.

While the two girls had claimed Kyrus as their own and had been trying—with limited results—to woo him, Gahalu had been Kyrus's interpreter and guide on the island. Worldly by Denku standards, Gahalu had sailed aboard foreign ships, learned about distant lands, and picked up a few exotic languages, Kyrus's among them.

"This weather probably reminds him of home," Gahalu said.

"This is home now for him," Kahli insisted. "Look how he risks his life to defend it." She pointed to the bare-chested northerner, standing where the water ought to have been chest deep, with the seawater stopping eerily a few paces from him at well over head height.

"You said he was not spirit man among his own people, that they chased him off and wished to kill him. That does not sound like home. Home is where he is loved. Home is where he will have strong sons who will grow up to be hunters and elders and spirit men," Tippu said.

Despite his scrawny body and skin that refused to darken to the creamy bronze color the Denku felt looked healthiest, Kyrus was an object of desire and envy among the Denku women. Tippu and Kahli had gotten to him first and claimed him, but should he decide to send them away, others would be quick to fill their places.

Gahalu sighed and watched his friend fighting the Katamic. Kyrus spoke more to Gahalu than anyone else, even though he was picking up the Denku language quite quickly. He knew that Kyrus had other reasons for damming the tide, though he had no cause to think the lad was being less than selfless in this particular instance. It allowed him to strengthen his powers with the spirit world, and Gahalu knew why that was important to Kyrus.

Kyrus had explained that, with enough power, he could make himself disappear from Denku Appa and appear in his homeland of Acardia. There was a girl there, in Scar Harbor, that he missed very much, and he wished to return to her. He was too polite to shun Tippu and Kahli, and was smart enough to know that if he did, more would come after him, but he did not want them. Surely he had fallen prey to their charms—the two girls were not shy at all about their victories when speaking to the other Denku women—but he always seemed shamed by it after.

The Scar Harbor girl was like a shark, Gahalu thought: she had sunk her teeth into Kyrus, and he was not able to swim free of her. Gahalu found himself thinking like the elder that his grey hairs said he was becoming, meddling in the loves of the young. For all their inane chatter, he wished the two girls well in their quest to win Kyrus's heart. He did not want to see his friend go.

* * * * * * * *

I had expected this to be harder, Kyrus thought.

He was holding back a wall of water ten feet high and hundreds of feet long. He had struggled at first to get the wall shaped properly. It had to be wider than usual, and therefore could not be as far out to sea as he would have liked. He had abandoned his usual tactic of standing at the center of the arced wall, and instead stood close to it. With how long the wall needed to be to protect the village, to center it at the water's edge would have pushed it so far out that it would have had to be thrice the height and bear a much greater weight of water. As it was, Kyrus was hardly noticing the effort now that he had it stable.

Aether in, aether out.

Kyrus was drawing a small, constant flow of aether to keep up the spell. Aether was fortunately a resource in abundance on the island. Many of the native species produced admirable amounts of the stuff, and the sea life inhabited the area in such vast numbers that the supply seemed inexhaustible. With few sorcerers in his own world, the aether seemed to be all his for the taking. In his counterpart's world, sorcerers were common enough that such vast seas of aether were unheard of.

Kyrus knew that he ought to have felt like a mighty wizard of the fairy stories, but he knew the trick now. It was still wondrous, but he suspected that any sorcerer from Kadrin, brought into his world, would be able to manage much the same with the ready supply of aether at hand. More than that, though, with the more challenging effort of creating and stabilizing the wall now past, it was growing boring. Storms were not momentary things by and large, and this one had already been raging for hours. His feet were aching, and his back was growing sore from standing so long in one place.

Kyrus knew that he could sit down in the mud, or even recline, and still hold the wall intact just as well. He also knew that there were a dozen or more Denku who had trusted him enough to come out as close as the tree line to watch. Among them were all his closest friends on the island, as well as Tippu and Kahli. As much as their advances exasperated him, he did not wish to diminish himself in their eyes. A primal, primitive part of his brain insisted that the affection of pretty girls was important—and not to be jeopardized by sore feet or boredom.

* * * * * * * *

Kyrus took his midday meal at his post, holding back the storm sea. He had grown accustomed enough to the light work of holding the aether-formed wall in place that he felt safe performing other magics while he held it. He had chosen from among the multitudes of fish arrayed before him like a child's fishbowl, and plucked the Source from a tasty-looking specimen. Flat and tall, the green-and-yellow striped fish was shaped like the paddles the Denku used for their fishing boats, and as long as Kyrus's forearm. Gone limp as its life's essence was cleanly removed, the fish offered no resistance as Kyrus then levitated it over the invisible wall and into his waiting hands, frying it with aether as it floated the short distance through the air.

Kyrus kept a small knife at his belt—made of steel, it was a valuable gift from his Denku hosts—and used it to fillet the fish. He ate as he worked, never taking his eye long from the real task at hand as he continued to hold back a mind-boggling amount of seawater. When he'd had his fill, he threw what remained of his meal over the wall and back into the Katamic for other predators to finish off.

When the ache of his feet finally got the better of him, he quietly cast a levitation spell, just using it to lift himself up such that his heels barely brushed the muddy ground.

I wonder if this means I am beginning to think like a sorcerer, when levitation magic seems like the proper course of action, rather than sitting down and getting my trousers muddy.

* * * * * * * *

When the storm finally calmed, and the risk to the village had passed, Kyrus released the shielding spell. He was worn inside and out. It was the longest he had ever used his Source, certainly, and as best he could recall, the longest he had ever stood in one place.

With the storm clouds obscuring the sun all day, Kyrus could only guess how long he had kept up the wall, but he figured six hours at least. *Should anyone ever inquire about it one day, that is what I shall tell them, anyway.* The overcast sky allowed occasional breaks that let in the light of late afternoon. Kyrus just had no idea how early it had been when the storm began, having awakened to a deep grey ceiling of the world.

The freed surf washed around Kyrus's ankles as he turned back toward the village, and saw his audience rush down to meet him, finally feeling safe with the spirit man's strange magic no longer in effect. Too many of them talked at once for Kyrus to pick out more than a stray word here or there in the Denku tongue, which he only understood at a modest pace. When Tippu and Kahli saw him fatigued, and came to support him under each arm, he at least tried to focus on what they were saying to him, since he suspected it would have the most immediate bearing on his evening.

"We will help ..."

"... to ..."

"... house ..."

"I ..."

"... you ..."

There were too many words Kyrus was unfamiliar with, and they were both speaking too fast for him to separate the words and decipher them. He gathered that they were intent on helping him back to the little house he had been given, but beyond that, it was all gibberish to him. When Tippu took her long necklaces and slung them over his head as well as hers, he began to suspect that rest was not on his agenda for the evening.

"Hungry," Kyrus managed in Denku, one of the words he had made sure Gahalu taught him. "Sleepy."

Kahli seemed to understand the former at least and rubbed his stomach, nodding eagerly.

Hopefully with a full belly and a worn-out brain, I can fall asleep right after dinner.

* * * * * * * *

Gahalu stayed back from his friend as the crowd—and Kyrus's two amorous pursuers—escorted Kyrus back to the village. The Denku had much wisdom about the sea, but their people did not make up catchy little sayings the way so many foreigners did to help make them easy to convey. Thus it was a Feru Maru saying that stuck in Gahalu's mind as he looked at Spirit Man Kyrus: "No man can stop the tides."

Kyrus just had—and stopped a storm atop it. The young Acardian was seeking to increase his magical power so he could use it to return to his home. After what he had just witnessed, Gahalu did not expect it would be long before Kyrus would try to use his powers to leave them.

* * * * * * * *

Kyrus lay awake on his sleeping mat, unable to still his mind. Kahli curled against him under one arm and Tippu the other, slumbering softly. The bedding in the small stone house that some previous mainlander had built on Denku Appa had been lumpy and uncomfortable, so Kyrus had adopted the Denku custom of sleeping on the ground. His own head rested on a pillow made from a sand-filled sack, which formed a cradle shaped for the size of his head by many nights' experience; his two companions pillowed their heads on his chest. He felt badly for having used magic on the girls to lull them to sleep, but it was easier than arguing with them and kinder than spurning them. He owed Brannis a debt for having learned a sleeping spell for him to defend himself with. Even with the spell, the two of them still found alertness enough before drifting off that they had latched onto him.

Kyrus wore ruts in his mind with his mental pacing, wondering what to do with Tippu and Kahli. He could not sum them up on a ledger like some merchant, though he had tried. He did not dislike either of them—far from it. They were sweet and thoughtful, unfailingly attentive, and (he reluctantly admitted) alluring. They were cousins, he had discovered, but were as close as sisters and had always planned to share some hunter together. They never quarreled with one another, at least with Kyrus around. They just seemed so … young.

Kyrus was a young man himself, just twenty-two years old, and he would have been surprised if his two suitors were much younger, at least in years. Kyrus drew a distinction between young and youthful. The latter bespoke vigor, energy, and a brightness of spirit; the former indicated naivety, overexuberance, and a stubbornness born of a refusal to accept unpleasant truths. For all the times they were not trying to busy themselves with the bits he kept beneath his trousers, they seemed like young girls, playful and cheerful, irresponsible and oblivious to all that went on outside the focus of their vision. He would have liked to consider himself something of a philosopher for seeing the difference, but he knew he was splitting hairs in trying to indict the girls for traits he found himself drawn to in Abbiley.

Abbiley Tillman was somewhere back in Scar Harbor, the only girl Kyrus had ever fallen in love with. He loved the joy she took in the simple things in life, like the break of the sea against Acardia's rocky shores or the sights and smells of the markets when foreign traders came to town. She had little money and only a brother to call family, yet she did not let the cares of the world burden her; she carried on with a smile, and was always considerate of others ahead of herself. That was probably the key difference, as Kyrus saw it. As much as Tippu and Kahli doted on him, it was a greedy sort of love they showered on him. They wanted him for themselves, to be the spirit man's wives, to be the envy of the other girls from the village, to have their children possibly become spirit men one day themselves.

Thus he longed for Abbiley, who fell in love with him when he was a simple scrivener whose only claim to wealth was an old shop he had been given by his former employer as a gift (Kyrus had paid a pittance for it, for appearance's sake, but knew it for the gift that it was). He was resolved to return to Scar Harbor, outlaw or not, and marry her. They might have to live on the run—he hoped she would be willing to go—and there would be other complications to be sure, but they were not insurmountable, not with the magic he was learning.

Kyrus sighed, staring up at the ceiling of his little house as the sky outside gave way to the dark of night. The storm-churned Katamic stank of things normally buried deep under the water, and belched forth a cold, brackish wind. Kyrus was not bothered by the rank air that the sea coughed up, for the fragrance of Tippu's and Kahli's hair dyes filled his nostrils with scents of melon and spice. The unseasonable chill of the night's winds blew in through the straw-covered doorway, but Kyrus did not mind. The two Denku girls pressed tight against him for warmth, and the heat from their bare skin warmed Kyrus as well.

I have never even held Abbiley this close, Kyrus mused. *I think that is why they bother me at times. They take liberties I had thought to have reserved just for her. I will make amends. I have grown stronger, and soon enough, I will rip a path through the aether and step through it, leaving Denku Appa and arriving back home, if only for long enough to reclaim Abbiley.*

I wonder if she would like it here …

Kyrus thought his last thought before sleep claimed him, picturing Abbiley clad in Denku fashion, curled at his side instead of Tippu. He met slumber that night with a smile on his face.

Chapter 3 - Plans and Preparations

Steam rose from the sweating combatants as they circled each other in the palace courtyard. Two lads from the School of Arms with bared steel in their hands faced off against one young man in black sorcerer's garb, who stood half a head shorter than either of them. The smaller man was wielding a heavily padded wooden sword in both hands and appeared to be holding his own against the pair of younger fighters. The two lads worked well in tandem, continually trying to flank their opponent, who spun, slashed, and parried his way free of the traps they kept trying to lay for him.

"He seems to be improving, at least," Brannis commented, watching the practice session from afar.

He was sitting at a small table set outdoors on a ground-level terrace just off the courtyard, sipping warmed cider in the cold morning air. Brannis was Grand Marshal of the Kadrin Army, and wore his gold-and-quicksilver armor covered in a doublet with both the imperial sigil and his own Solaran house crest. Young for such a lofty position, he wore the surprisingly comfortable magical armor often to give himself the appearance of authority to match his station.

"His footwork is improving, and the technique is not the disaster it once was, but he lacks any strength behind the blows," replied Rashan.

Despite looking even younger than Sir Brannis Solaran, Rashan was an uncle of his, some five generations removed. Unlike Brannis, he was strong in aether. The empire had bred sorcerers for thousands of years to refine the hereditary aspects of what made for a potent sorcerer, and trained them at the Imperial Academy with the hope of teaching them the rest. Rashan Solaran was among the greatest successes of that endeavor. While sorcerers could be bred, warlocks were a chance occurrence—sorcerers gifted enough in their powers that they could use them safely amid the confusion and chaos of combat. Rashan was not only a warlock, he had learned the secret of immortality. After a century's absence during which he was believed dead, he had recently returned to the Empire.

"What do you expect? You may have been throwing him out into the practice yard daily this past season, but last autumn that boy had hardly lifted anything heavier than a quill. A body takes time to harden," observed Fenris Destrier.

A smallish, pudgy man with little hair left on his head, Fenris slumped round-shouldered in his chair as he cradled his own cider just below his face, letting the steam rising from it fill his nose with warm air. He could have used magic to warm himself, or at least keep away the chill—as a sorcerer of the Inner Circle, it would have been a scant test of his powers—but he did not wish to give the warlock the satisfaction of seeing him give in to a dislike of the cold.

"You have seen the reports," Rashan said. "Megrenn is readying for an invasion. We do not have a season to prepare; we have perhaps half a season if we are lucky. Iridan needs to be ready. He is just going to have to put in more of an effort. He does not have the luxury of a leisurely training regimen."

The warlock was shorter and slighter of build than his son Iridan, with long white hair the color of fresh snow and pale eyes that seemed to lack for any nameable color. For all the world, he seemed like a youth playing at being a warlock … until he spoke. There was a manner about him that carried energy, authority, and menace. He could make underlings uneasy just by inquiring about the weather.

"Want me to stand in for the boys, then?" Brannis offered, half-joking. "I would use a padded blade, of course."

Brannis smiled at the last bit. His own sword was rune forged, ancient, and powerful. It was named Avalanche, and virtually nothing could impede it when swung. Even gravity had little hold over it; for outside its sheath, it would hang suspended in air unless taken in hand. In battle, it cut through foe and fortification alike.

"You tempt me, Brannis, but no," Rashan answered. "You may be stronger than both those lads at once, but you are no dancing blade-master to be giving lessons. I promoted you for your brain, not your blade. If we were to be facing an ogre uprising, I would see the wisdom in preparing him against you, but the Megrenn fighters tend to be more nimble and skilled. Young as they are, both those boys fight more soundly than do you."

"He is taking too many blows against his shielding spell," Fenris said, gesturing toward Iridan with his nose so he did not have to remove his hands from the warm cup.

* * * * * * * *

The blow to his stomach had registered vaguely in Iridan's mind. He felt it not in the flesh, but in his sense of the aether. He was not harmed. He knew that the steel blades his opponents wielded would not hurt him so long as his shielding spell held; his swordsmanship was just not up to the task on its own yet.

Jafin and Moln had maneuvered Iridan directly between them, as they always tried to do. Iridan only had one sword and no shield, so he could only defend himself from one side at a time. Iridan watched their timing, and stepped quickly aside and out of reach of Jafin, launching a spinning attack at Moln, the better fighter of the two boys. The squires hated the attack, and used to remind him how foolish it was. Iridan knew that the knights favored a defensive, tactical approach to swordsmanship, waiting for an error by their opponent, and trying to force them into making one if none was forthcoming. Rashan had given

Iridan extensive tutoring on how a warlock ought to fight before turning him loose against the finest lads (aged fourteen summers or younger) of the School of Arms.

Iridan used his aether-vision instead of the light to see during combat. It filtered out all the non-essentials of color and background and inanimate objects, leaving him a full "view" all around him of aether, and he saw his opponents by their Sources. The drawback was that swords had no Source and were virtually invisible to him, but he had been learning to judge the path of a weapon by the way it was wielded: posture, momentum, fighting style ... all gave clues once one he knew how to interpret them.

Moln knew that he could strike a quick blow before Iridan completed his spin, but this attack was one he had seen before. The would-be warlock could take the hit on his shielding spell, and there would be no defense from Iridan's own attack if he did not devote himself to avoiding it. Typically Moln would either hop back out of reach, keeping his sword clear of Iridan's to force him to continue the spin or switch to a two-handed grip and meet the blow hard with a parry.

This time, Moln tried something new. He hopped back and lifted his sword clear, similar to how he often did, but he followed in immediately after the warlock's sword cleared him, and struck a quick blow down on the blade.

Iridan had been preparing to follow around and counter the attack that was already coming from Jafin at his back. Moln's blow was solid enough to force his sword down and cause him to stumble in his swing. Jafin struck him square in the back, hard enough to have cut his spine had he not been shielded by aether. Moln closed in quickly, and a blow to the temple turned Iridan's head to the side, dizzying and disorienting him.

"Enough!" Rashan shouted from across the courtyard. It seemed that he had seen all he needed to for the day's practice. "Good work, lads. The day is yours yet again." The warlock reached into a pouch at his belt, and removed two gold lions, tossing one coin to each boy. "You have earned it. Spend it well and I shall see you back here tomorrow morning."

The two squires gathered themselves up in presentable fashion and, once they had sheathed their blades, saluted the warlock, fist to chest. "Yes, Warlock," they replied in unison.

Rashan dismissed them and walked a few paces to where his son was on hands and knees waiting for the world to hold still enough to stand atop it.

"They are learning more than you are out here," Rashan said. "Are two of them too much for you? I could invite back just Moln for tomorrow's session, if you cannot handle Jafin and him together."

"They both have more experience at this than I do, and Moln is bigger than me," Iridan said, breathing heavily.

"That is the sorriest excuse you have used yet. I am trying to train you here, not puff your ego. If you had been armed and trained, you might not have been defeated by that Megrenn sorcerer at Raynesdark. You might have prevented the

Megrenn from obtaining the Staff of Gehlen," Rashan said.

"That's unfair. I was barely walking after exhausting myself defending the wall. A sword in my hand would not have made a difference," Iridan said, pushing himself up to his knees as he stood. He bent to retrieve his wooden sword.

"I disagree. You attack where your opponent is weak, defend where he is strong. You attacked from surprise and stunned him—I have no quarrel with that. But then you sought to defend yourself instead of finishing him. You allowed a more seasoned sorcerer to have his turn at attacking. He had one worry, and you allowed him respite from it to formulate an attack," Rashan said, having gone through the same argument with Iridan several times on previous occasions when he questioned his training.

"But I was undefended. A quick spell could have been the end of me, and—"

"Precisely why you need to learn to fight. Draw aether into your shielding spells from close range. Your draw is still stronger than most, and you could strengthen your own defenses while denying him aether—this needs to be second nature. All the while, you press him, in close combat. His spells must be cast quickly or done silently, and you may force errors. The warlock's trade is not so easy; few can manage to keep their wits clear enough to manage such a task while a sword is threatening their hide."

"But I—" Iridan began, but Rashan cut him off again.

"Speaking of your draw … Fenris is ready for you."

Rashan smiled mischievously. Iridan's swordsmanship lesson might have been done, but his day of training was not yet at an end.

* * * * * * * *

"Excuse me," Fenris muttered to Brannis as he rose.

They had both been watching the exchange between Rashan and Iridan, and Brannis knew that the warlock was ready for Fenris to take his turn with the boy. Ninety-four springtimes old, Fenris was now the senior member of the Inner Circle, excepting the warlock, whose birth was a matter for history books. Fenris's joints ached, his eyesight was not so strong, and he found his thoughts wandering more than they used to. For all that, his Source was strong and so was his draw.

The warlock's lackeys had worn Iridan down physically, and Brannis knew that it was now Fenris's duty to wear him down by the Source. Each day, it was the same routine, with small variations: practice at arms, then a draw against one of the Inner Circle. Rashan had made a mistake early in Iridan's training, and had followed up sparring against a lad of thirteen summers with a draw against a Third Circle sorcerer. While Iridan had been battered and bruised by his adolescent sword-fighting tutor, he had embarrassed the poor sorcerer he had faced. Ever since, he had only been matched against the Inner Circle.

So far, Iridan had shown that he could overmatch his great-great-great-great-niece Aloisha (eight summers his elder), the next youngest member of the Inner

Circle, and could give Thayl Greydusk an even match or even defeat him at times. Rashan had not wanted Iridan to have easy matches; he wanted to temper and reforge him. Iridan had not defeated Fenris in eight draws. He had not fared well against Caladris—Brannis's and Aloisha's uncle, and fifty summers Iridan's elder—in any of the twelve bouts they had. Dolvaen Lurien had drawn against Iridan just the once. A lowborn sorcerer from a bloodline not even accorded the status of "lesser," it was clear that Dolvaen had gained his position among the Inner Circle by skill and power, not patronage. The draw between him and Iridan had been brief, decisive, and humbling for the younger sorcerer.

Brannis watched as the old sorcerer made his way out into the courtyard to contest against Iridan. There was a temptation to stay and watch, just to see the result, but Brannis would take no enjoyment in it. Iridan was nearly guaranteed to lose, and Brannis was blind to the aether and thus could not even properly spectate the event. The two sorcerers would stand several paces apart and, upon command of whoever was judging the contest, they would each call upon the aether to see whose draw was more powerful. If neither was clearly stronger, they would be commanded to stop drawing and hold the aether they had drawn for as long as possible. Stored aether burned; the more a sorcerer held, the stronger the burning, and careless bravado could result in serious injury.

Brannis, alone at the table after Fenris's departure, rose to make his own exit. For all Brannis would see, it would be two sorcerers standing and staring at each other, until suddenly one was declared winner. The first clue to an aether-blind observer as to who was winning might be a blast of steam from the water basins into which the losing sorcerer would discharge his stored aether to signal his defeat. Brannis had better uses for his time, and many responsibilities. Even staying for the sparring was beyond what he had intended in visiting with Warlock Rashan.

Brannis had merely needed to give him the status of the reported Megrenn troop movements. As usual, the information was scant, received third- and fourth-hand from traders and travelers. The Empire's own information sources were scattered and ineffective. Long years of focusing on internal squabbles among the powers of the Kadrin Empire had left their foreign information sources undermanned. It was a constant annoyance to the warlock, and Brannis felt little better about it himself. Though Rashan had said nothing yet to Brannis, Kadrin's young marshal suspected that the old warlock had some plan to remedy that deficiency.

* * * * * * * *

Brannis spent much of the afternoon meeting with various officers and representatives of noble landholders who bordered on Megrenn. Troop strength and readiness discussions always discouraged him. The borderlands were better defended than the Empire's interior; with ogres, bandits, and raiding to contend with, they had to be. But none had the sort of standing army to contend with the reported numbers the Megrenn were amassing.

Brannis looked at the map of the continent of Koriah, laid out on its own massive table. Kadrin occupied most of the south, all of the east, and a bit of the northeast as well, wrapping cautiously around the ogre lands. Megrenn was tiny by comparison, a federation of city-states along the north coast on both sides of the Cloud Wall mountain range. It was a populous land for its size, but even at that, they had fewer than a tenth Kadrin's citizenry. What troubled Brannis was the vast expanse past Megrenn to the north. Across the Aliani Sea in every direction lay nations that traded with the Megrenn, providing weapons, food, sell-swords, and the exotic mounts that the Megrenn preferred over horses for their heavy cavalry.

Brannis picked up a small, painted clay figurine representing a stripe-cat with a rider. The green and brown stripes helped the creatures hide in their native jungles, far away in Elok, but would give them little advantage in the rolling plains and forested countryside that formed the Kadrin border with Megrenn. He looked at the rider sitting atop it, an afterthought with a tiny spear and shield, guiding the deadly beast with his knees. By accounts of the older knights who had seen them in person, the scale was correct—and daunting; the creature was more than head height at the shoulder. Brannis set it back down on the map just south of the Megrenn capital city of Zorren, where it represented a unit of actual stripe-cats that his spies had reported being based there. Brannis's map was littered with similar toy military units, helping his generals understand more intuitively where their forces and the enemy troops were arrayed. There was a log book so that any time figures were added, moved, or taken away, it was noted with the time and exact nature of the change in case the truth of any bit of intelligence be brought into question.

The map with figurines was inspired by something that Kyrus had seen once in the drawing room of the Society of Learned Men in Scar Harbor. It had been set up to depict the Battle of Garlow Falls, but that was not what had caught Kyrus's fancy. He had been fascinated by the tiny soldiers and horses, each representing a number of real ones that had been present at the battle. Forces had been arrayed across half of Acardia during that period of the Staltner Revolution, but with the aid of a hooked stick to slide the figures around, one of the professors had explained the battle to Kyrus in just a few minutes.

Brannis and his generals were now using the same technique to track all Kadrin troop movements and what they could learn of the Megrenn and their allies. A few local tradesmen had made the figures in short order and had done a marvelous job of rendering the various martial assets in exacting detail. Brannis only wished he had cause to purchase more of them, since they showed a rather embarrassing imbalance in strengths. The Megrenn had obviously planned and saved for this invasion for many winters; they probably borrowed coin as well, with a promise to repay in plunder. Kadrin could eventually build up to the point where the Megrenn army would fall to them by sheer numbers, but conscripts fought poorly, and proper soldiers took winters to train. It was one thing to show a man which end of a spear was which and drape a mail shirt over him; it was another to teach him not to break ranks the first time he saw an eight-hundred-gallon monohorn thundering toward him (in fairness, the proper response *was* a withdrawal action, which was distinctly *not* "running away").

The major problems Brannis saw were twofold. First, they were not going to be allowed the years needed to properly remilitarize the population and increase the standing army to the size they would need to repel such a force as the Megrenn were arraying against them. Were it not for the extreme aversion stripe-cats and monohorns had to the cold of Kadrin winter, Megrenn likely would have already attacked—so Brannis hoped for a long, cold winter to persist past the equinox.

The second problem was Jinzan Fehr; he knew too much. Like Brannis, Jinzan was aware of the other world, Tellurak, where technology was more developed and magic all but unheard of. Jinzan had already used that connection to barter the knowledge of cannon-making to the goblins in return for working units and an invasion of Raynesdark that also gained him the Staff of Gehlen. Surely at some point in the war, the Kadrin forces would once again be faced with cannons of Acardian design. Brannis also had no way of predicting what further aid the Megrenn sorcerer might import from Acardia or other lands of Tellurak (which Brannis had begun whimsically to think of as KyrusWorld).

The staff Brannis could do little about, but he could at least try to match cannon to cannon with Jinzan—figuratively at least. Brannis suspected that black-powder alchemy was probably too tricky to teach to the chemists and apothecaries in Kadris, atop the fact that Kyrus would have to reach mainland somewhere civilized to learn the exact recipes he would need. Sorcery might fabricate working cannons if Kyrus could find one to take measurements from, but that had the same problem of too little knowledge, too far from where it could be learned.

Instead Brannis had taken a different approach. The maps and clay soldiers were a small thing compared with cannons; let the pirate who was Jinzan's counterpart in KyrusWorld worry about those. Brannis had thought of a better source of ideas to import: fairy tales.

Tales of magic, monsters, and heroes existed in Brannis's own world, but he had begun to realize, once he thought of it, that they lacked the whimsy and imagination of those in KyrusWorld. It made sense, after a fashion. If a sorcerer heard a story of magic that sounded implausible, he would tell you six different ways that it was wrong, and could not happen as written. It stifled creativity and limited the boundaries that could be tested by imagination.

Brannis had dug through Kyrus's memories for inspiration and was drawing up plans of his own ...

* * * * * * * *

"I understand the decorum and omens involved in a winter wedding, but with the threat of Megrenn hanging poised at our throats, should we not perhaps move the date forward?" Shador Archon asked Rashan.

A tall, dignified Second Circle sorcerer, Shador sat next to his wife in one of the Imperial Palace's more private sitting rooms, sharing tea with their daughter's future oathfather.

"I hear your concern, but I feel better about waiting for springtime. Besides, every day we wait gives us more time to muster our strength. We will not strike first in this war; we may not even strike second. We must ensure only that we strike last," Rashan said, taking a sip of his tea mostly for appearance's sake. As an immortal (demon, in less flattering parlance), he had no need of food or drink, but then he supposed that no creature, mortal or not, truly required tea for any purpose but to sip it politely among company. It had a weak, bitter taste that he did his best to ignore.

"Would it not make sense to have our new warlock prepared for the inevitable war, with his marriage pact sealed and consummated?" Shador argued.

Aha, thought Rashan, *there is the heart of his argument. He wants a grandson in case Iridan gets himself killed in battle.*

"Rest assured, Iridan's preparations for the wedding will run in parallel with his training as a warlock. Every additional day of training makes him stronger for when I finally loose him upon the Megrenn," Rashan replied.

The warlock genuinely liked Shador. Had he known the man prior to his realignment of the Inner Circle, he would have promoted him in place of Brannis's sister Aloisha, who was rather sadly underprepared for her elevation.

The conversation shifted to more tedious matters of decoration, attendees, and other logistical arrangements. Rashan let his mind wander a bit, and allowed Ophelia Archon—a slightly older-looking version of her daughter, down to the aether-tinted reddish-gold hair—to dominate the discussion. Rashan wanted the event to carry all the pageantry and glamour of a royal wedding, but cared little for how that was managed. He objected only once, when the idea of Brannis acting as Iridan's oathkeeper was suggested.

"He may be Iridan's best friend," Rashan said, "and it would normally be expected, but I think in this circumstance, it may be better to bend tradition and find another friend of Iridan's to fill that role."

Rashan tiptoed around the subject that Juliana's parents would rather not have brought up: Brannis's former betrothal to their daughter. Rashan had never been able to extract from either of them just what had passed between them, but he expected that, around the age of thirteen, Brannis and Juliana had taken news of their arranged marriage rather well. Kadrin's new grand marshal still carried the girl in his heart, more so than Rashan would have preferred, given that the feeling seemed mutual. Brannis was rational in all other things, so it was readily forgivable, but Rashan feared to let the lad stand as oathkeeper all the same.

It was a seldom exercised post, harkening back to more tumultuous days of the Empire, when bloodshed rode on the success of marriage alliances between noble houses. The oathkeeper's duty was to see that the groom kept to his promise to wed his bride. In olden times, this meant dogging the groom's steps for a tenday or longer prior to the ceremony, but in present-day Kadrin, the duty amounted to just a day's shepherding and good-natured carousing. The houses of the major sorcerous bloodlines styled themselves after noble houses in this way, as in many others, and kept the tradition in their own weddings as well. Brannis, for all his apparent blunt and straightforward honesty, kept a merchant's tongue in his mouth. Leave him for a day with Iridan and Brannis might end up wedded to Juliana in his son's stead—such was the duty of an oathkeeper, to seal the pact between houses if he failed to ensure the groom fulfilled his oath.

"Perhaps that sorcerer who saved his life at Raynesdark—Faolen Sarmon," Shador suggested, seeming glad that someone else had put Brannis out of the discussion for oathkeeper.

Rashan knew that Shador and Ophelia both adored Brannis and had looked forward to having him for an oathson, but the complications between him and Juliana were awkward enough that they both were happy to have them clear of each other on her wedding day.

"Faolen is … otherwise occupied. Perhaps we can find someone he knew at the Academy," Rashan said. He had found the gifted illusionist Faolen to be surprisingly resourceful, and had already developed other plans for him that did not involve oathkeeper duties.

"I shall ask around a bit. Surely there must be someone else he was rather close with," Ophelia said. "Um, and I do not know quite how to bring this up, but there is one other matter I had wished to discuss with you."

"Yes?" Rashan leaned closer, intrigued by whatever matter seemed to be disconcerting Ophelia Archon, Third Circle sorceress and part of one of the most influential families in the Empire.

"Well, what of Iridan's mother? Will she … be attending?" Ophelia asked. "We are both quite curious to meet her."

Rashan Solaran stared wide-eyed, mouth parted slightly, struck dumb for lack of words for the first time in longer than he could remember.

"I had forgotten," he finally admitted at length. After a long pause, he added, "I will contact her shortly and inquire."

Have I really been enjoying my time here so much—political snake-handling and all—that I forgot all about her? Everyone except Brannis has probably been too frightened of me even to ask about her, and that was a season ago. Even Iridan seems to avoid the subject for some reason.

* * * * * * * *

Iridan shuffled across his bedchamber in the palace, where he had relocated after Rashan appointed him as the next Kadrin warlock. He was stiff and bruised despite the protection his shielding spell had granted him. If not for his father's intervention, the boys might have done him real harm. Dazed as he was from the blow to the temple, he would not have properly reinforced his protective magics before they struck again.

"Blasted urchins," he cursed under his breath, aware that no one was around to either hear him or be bothered by his mutterings. He had begun talking to himself more than he preferred, which was an easy habit to get into when few others would take up a share of the conversation on your behalf. Since Rashan had formally acknowledged Iridan as his son, and began training him as a warlock, people had looked at him differently.

Casual acquaintances no longer met his gaze when he passed them in the halls or out in the streets. Servants and guards snapped to his every implied order, even when he was merely making helpful suggestions. The sorcerers of the Imperial Circle at large treated him coolly and seemed offended by his rapid promotion. No less offended were the Inner Circle, who now were forced to call Iridan a colleague rather than an underling. None of them disputed his talent or potential, but the favoritism shown by Warlock Rashan for his newly acknowledged son rubbed them ill.

Among the many ways the latter had manifested itself was the very room he now occupied. With the charade of the false emperor exposed, there was no one to tell the warlock how best to allocate the palace's accommodations. Spending so much time there himself, the warlock had arranged for his son and the commander of his armies to move into vacant rooms. Despite being only several doors away from one another, Iridan hardly saw Brannis anymore.

"I wish Brannis were not so busy. I know he has an army to look after now, but at least he doesn't seem bothered by me being a warlock. He probably has the same feeling: being thrown off a cliff and told to fly, offending the birds as he plummets past them." Iridan shook his head.

He poured himself a glass of sweetened wine from a decanter left for him by his ever-attentive servants. He had dismissed them after arriving back from his morning practice session. It was only mid afternoon, but it was his fourth glass. It sped the passing of a long day, and dulled the aches in his body.

* * * * * * * *

That evening, in a different palace bedchamber, Brannis set aside his pen and ink, and took up a book entitled *To Anywhere*. After Kyrus's test against the Katamic Sea, Brannis felt he might finally be ready to try learning the transference spell contained within its age-yellowed pages. Like many of the books from the Circle's libraries, it had aged well due to magical means of preservation. Similarly protected, steel would last for entire eras, and stone was nearly eternal. Paper could be kept for hundreds of summers, but eventually would need to be rewritten and replaced. Annotations inside the front cover of the book indicated that it was the third copy of the book, and the inscription put this copy at over three hundred summers old itself.

Transference was one of the more difficult and dangerous spells of which sorcerers were widely aware. It literally took two identically sized chunks of the world, and exchanged them in space. Without special modifications (and why anyone would wish to further complicate such a spell was beyond Brannis's understanding), the chunks of space would both be spherical in shape, with one centered about the caster, and as large as the sorcerer had aether to make it.

The latter was one of the most obvious pitfalls of the spell. The book was nothing if not explicit in its warnings of the perils of the spell. Should the spell be cast without enough aether to fully surround the sorcerer, a rather grisly package might end up delivered to some far-flung destination: whatever chunk of sorcerer was on the inside of the sphere when it formed.

Another was the matter of where one ended up. As a part of the spell, the mind would be cast into the aether to find a place for the companion sphere to form. Traveling the world mentally could be dizzying and the landscape—rendered all in shades of blue-white aether—would look nothing like it would in the realm of light. A keen observer would be able to discern terrain and structures from the way the flow of aether was impeded by them, but they would not be obvious. Sources would be easy to spot, but without foreknowledge of to whom a Source belonged , many sorcerers would find it difficult to distinguish between a man or a woman, let alone identify one uniquely.

Brannis sighed. If Kyrus ended up missing his mark and burying himself below a mountain or deep underwater, he would be sorely pressed to save himself. Too high seemed the safer error, since Kyrus could at least levitate himself, but Brannis would prefer being no party to that, either.

"Doxlo intuvae menep gahalixviu ..." Brannis began, reading the chant from the book aloud as he pantomimed the gestures of the spell as it described them—intricate weavings of the fingers, with little motion of the rest of the body. The chant was long and tedious, exacting in pronunciation by the book's own admission and, above all, dangerous.

Kyrus would have to be very careful in practicing the spell, lest he injure himself horribly. Brannis, of course, had nothing to worry about from practice and Kyrus learned nearly as well from Brannis's work as from his own.

This is for you, Kyrus. You have earned it many times over. This is thanks for discovering Jinzan Fehr's plot and for forcing him to barter my life for his counterpart's own in your world. Thank you for letting me feel what it is like to use magic. And thank you for paying attention when your grandfather read you Captain Erasmus and His Flying Ship.

Brannis paused at the end of his third run-through of the transference spell chant, and looked at the papers he had set neatly aside prior to resuming his magical studies. Below a fanciful sketch of a sailing ship with feathered wings were pages of diagrams and annotations showing how and where wards ought to be carved to turn one of Kadrin's warships into an airship.

Chapter 4 - Traderous Intent

"As you see, sirs, this device is unlike any catapult or trebuchet," Jinzan said, gesturing to the gleaming brass cannon that sat in the grand foyer of his palatial home.

Gathered around him were a large number of men and women in various cultural dress. Dignitaries from all the far-flung lands that had shores upon the Aliani Sea had come to see Jinzan Fehr's great siege engine. They crowded around, jostling with unbecoming familiarity to get close enough to touch the strange weapon.

The cannon was of Acardian design, though Jinzan took full credit himself; none of those present were aware of the other world, as best he knew, and he enjoyed being thought a genius of destruction.

"It does all your missive said? It looks puny. I had hoped to see more," one guest said, a dark-skinned elder with thinning white hair who was a general in Narrack's army. He regarded the cannon with a skeptical eye.

"I assure you," Jinzan began, reaching over to a small table that held the remaining three cannonballs he had salvaged during his escape from Raynesdark and picking one up in his hand. The iron ball was engraved with simple runes to help it penetrate wards and to keep its shape after impact. It filled Jinzan's hand and weighed a bit more than two gallons. "This is going to fly from the open end with a speed twice that of a loosed arrow. I do not ask you to take this claim on faith. The demonstration this afternoon will prove its capabilities."

Jinzan allowed the group to gawk and paw at the cannon for a time, and he answered their questions and smiled more than he was accustomed to, acting like the merchant he supposed he had become. Megrenn was wealthy, in a peculiar sort of way. Despite few resources of their own, goods came into their ports at one price and left at another, with the difference ending up in Megrenn coffers. So many ships and caravans passed through that there was enough to keep the Megrenn citizenry fed, clothed, and supplied with luxuries that made life better ...

... like steel swords, mercenaries, and ferocious beasts, to finally repay the Kadrin Empire for their long winters of occupation. The Freedom War had put Megrenn far into debt, but those debts had been repaid. If the war to overthrow Kadrin dominance of Koriah was to succeed, they needed the coin to buy all those things they needed.

Jinzan was a sorcerer of great standing among his people, and his counterpart in the other world was a pirate. He was no merchant to haggle, barter and wheedle, eking each copper coin out of a deal. He was accustomed to taking what he wished, or having it given to him. But his people needed him, and he had reluctantly agreed to act the part, since no one else knew how the cannons worked as well as he did. He had scant gunpowder left and only the three cannonballs, durable though they might be. There had been only one other demonstration since his return from Raynesdark, for the rest of the Megrenn High Council. That demonstration had led to the missive that had been sent to all Megrenn's allies and trading partners.

They needed craftsmen, materials, and buyers for the finished weapons.

Jinzan hated seeing the things proliferate in his own world, but it seemed necessary to gain the cooperation of so many nations. In times of war, profiteering was a tradition, if not a noble or revered one. Soon Megrenn would find that fewer ships were willing to brave their ports, and the price of bringing goods to their wharves would increase. Some would blame the increased risk they faced, others the increase in demand for their goods. Some would go so far as to admit the real reason: "because you need it so badly that you will pay whatever we ask."

They were not so far gone yet. With only preparations underway for the main offensive, Zorren was not deemed to be a war zone by their merchant friends. That would change with the season. As the weather warmed to the south, in Kadrin's less forgiving climate, Megrenn would be free to bring their heavy cavalry to bear. The warm-weather beasts they had imported were ill suited to Kadrin in winter, but with the spring thaw, the balance of power would shift heavily to their favor. However, with the advancing of their war plans, the cost of doing business with the outside world would rise. Kadrin was a paltry naval power, but they had warships, and trading with Megrenn would put ships at risk of predation by them. Despite how little risk they actually took, merchants would still use the excuse to drive up their prices.

Jinzan was a sorcerer of fire, water, wind, and stone. The Megrenn High Council counted among their members a man named Varduk Steelraven. Varduk was a sorcerer of coins. Folk said that he could sell a man a gold hex—the six-sided coins the Megrenn mint turned out, along with silver squares and copper circles—and charge him two hexes for it. As minister of finance, Varduk had been responsible for Megrenn's economic success. He set taxes, tariffs, duties, and a hundred other means of controlling the flow of money. He worked coins like an expert glassworker, slowly and methodically forming a bubble of molten glass, shaping it to his vision, and sure-handedly skirting the edge of ruining his piece without ever doing so. It was the same with coin. Men saw what Varduk did and tried to emulate him, but always they were missing something: a deftness of hand, a keenness of timing, and the understanding of the roots of why men spent their coin or did not.

Varduk had seen the demonstration of the cannon and saw it not as a specially formed piece of cast bronze, but as a rather large pile of gold hexes. He had been the one who saw victory embodied in the cannon's novelty and utility. Jinzan was asked to sell its virtues to the visiting dignitaries and make them wish to own them. Jinzan was a patriot, and he hated the Kadrins as much as any of the Council. With some trepidation, he was persuaded to play the role of a street hawker.

"What price will you ask for these?" asked one of the more practically minded of the visitors.

"Ten thousand gold hexes and after the demonstration, you will consider it a bargain," Varduk spoke up from the back of the assembly, where he had been waiting to chime in once the discussion inevitably turned from show-and-tell to buy-and-sell.

* * * * * * *

The Fehr Estate had extensive gardens with lush green grass. Fruit trees and flower beds were scattered about in whimsical arrays, with trellis-covered walkways wending their way throughout.

The assemblage of foreign allies was congregated at one end of the vast central lawn, clustered on the breech side of the cannon. They had already taken a brief walk to inspect the mortared stone wall that had been built some three hundred paces distant. A trio of foreign-born sorcerers had been hired to inspect the cannon, the wall, and all the accoutrements that went along with the demonstration and to verify that there was no magic at work.

It had amused Jinzan to watch old men leaning against the wall with their shoulders and rapping soundly at it with walking canes. *You are the ones here to buy. You need convince none but yourselves. Perhaps as youths you might have truly tested the wall with such efforts, but you could not have toppled a wall of loose bricks.*

When everyone was settled into their seats in a great semicircle, with no line of sight to the target obscured, Jinzan went through the process of loading and readying the cannon. He was grateful to the goblin tinkers who had improved on the Acardian design when they made it. The pull-chain mechanism that sparked the powder was something he never would have thought of, and it made for a more predictable demonstration than lighting the cannon with a brand would.

"Honored guests, the moment you have all journeyed here to see. I give you the Fehr Cannon," Jinzan announced grandly, flourishing with his left hand as the right gripped the pull chain, facing his audience and not the target. With a quick motion, he tugged the chain.

Kthooom!

There were screams of surprise as the shock wave of sound tore through the spectators. Jinzan had given them no warning of the sound it would make: a deep, sonorous cracking that shattered the very air. Battle-hardened veterans had heard the blasts of arcane magic that some sorcerers used in battle, but those were a kitten's whisper when held against the sound of a cannon's report from three paces away.

Those steel-nerved enough to have kept their vision downfield on the target saw nothing of the projectile that flew from it, only its impact a heartbeat after the report. A great cloud of dust obscured the wall immediately, but as the wind slowly parted the stony curtain of debris, the wall could be seen to be in a sorry state. An arm's length thick, twice the height of a man and four times as wide, a massive chunk was missing, turned to rubble and dust, with the larger chunks presumably having fallen on the far side.

As the assemblage gaped at the stricken wall, Jinzan was already at work cleaning the bore. He did all the work manually so that none could accuse him of altering the cannon's performance through the use of magic even for something so simple as cleaning the gun. He also wished them to see how quickly it could fire a second shot. Once he had cleared the bore and reloaded it with powder, wadding, and one of the remaining two shots, he nudged the cannon's aim over just a fraction.

Taking up the chain once again, he deigned to issue a warning: "You may wish to guard your ears. It gets no quieter than the last." And with that, Jinzan pulled the chain again, wincing as he thought of the damage that was being done to his gardens.

Kthooom!

Jinzan knew enough of the showman's trade to understand that you do not demonstrate something against a challenging target. Build something impressive enough, but leave enough room for the result to be spectacular. The wall had stopped neither of the shots, and no doubt the cannonballs were now lying in some devastated flower bed.

"If you all will be so kind as to follow me, we shall have a look at the damage that we have wrought." Jinzan stooped to pick up the one remaining cannonball. "And we also have a bit of a puzzle ahead of us. Somewhere in the gardens, there are two more of these. Familiarize yourselves with the look of them, and let us see about finding where they have gone."

Jinzan then passed the cannonball around, and let everyone have a turn examining it. He had little doubt the shots would be easy enough to find; it was just more showmanship. Let them see the cannonball, and wonder that such a small thing had caused so much havoc.

At the head of the assembly as they walked down toward the wall, Jinzan smirked.

* * * * * * *

That same evening, after the various foreigners had departed with dreams of cannons in their eyes, Jinzan sat on his own terrace with a glass of Halaigh wine in his hand. He was accompanied by Varduk Steelraven and his wife Tuleen, as well as his own three wives, Nakah, Frenna, and Zaischelle. It was a small, reserved celebration of a great many promising deals ahead with the trade nations of the Aliani Sea.

They dressed warmly against the cool evening air, but the smell of the nearby sea made it pleasant despite a bit of chill. Down below in the gardens, Jinzan's children played with Varduk's. The children laughed and shouted, making the palatial estate feel homey rather than intimidating. Of all the sounds that Jinzan associated with Zorren, it was the one he had missed the most during his time away among the goblins.

"Listen to them down there," Jinzan remarked. "Did we make such riots at their age? I think not."

"Perhaps we did, and do not remember," Varduk answered. The black-bearded mercantile genius had known Jinzan for over twenty winters, when they had fought together in the Freedom War. There were few men in the world Jinzan knew or trusted so well.

"I think not. I think we laughed and shouted, true, but those are the sounds of freeborn children, who have never lived under Kadrin rule," Jinzan said. "There is no fear in them. There are no secrets to keep. Should any man take issue with their manner of dress or how they address some soldier, a magistrate will stand between them and brutal punishment, not some Kadrin lord. They could never tell you the difference themselves, but I hear it."

"Jinzan, you should drink more often. We can make a poet of you yet if you loosen your tongue more often," teased Nakah, Jinzan's second wife.

With the population of able-bodied men vastly depleted by the Freedom War, the Megrenn High Council had decreed that men might take two wives each, except for the Liberators. The Liberators were the heroes of the rebellion, and might take as many wives as they could find women who would have them. Despite their hatred for their Kadrin oppressors, they had learned the lesson that strong blood begets strong blood. Nakah Fehr was born in the faraway Painu Islands. Her father had been one of the merchant princes who threw in with the Megrenn when it seemed clear they would win their freedom. He had offered his eldest daughter as a gift to strengthen relations between Painu and Megrenn. Nakah had skin the color of walnut wood, with striking green eyes like a cat's, which stood out from her dark skin. In the sixteen summers since, she had barely aged in Jinzan's eyes.

"As you prefer," Jinzan replied, taking a large swallow from his glass, drawing a chuckle from his companions.

"What will the world be like, once Kadrin surrenders?" asked Tuleen Steelraven, a plump woman who ran a third of Varduk's trading empire for him. She had been a beauty in her youth, but traded the primping and preening of her vapid contemporaries for a life of ledgers and business dealings after her marriage. She loved her husband for teaching her his trade rather than expecting her to just tend to babes and look pretty.

"Better, once it has been watered in blood," suggested Frenna, Jinzan's first wife, though not his eldest. He had wedded her as a barely flowered girl, taking her into his protection after her parents died in the war. She had been heir to a large fortune and lands—on which they were now gathered—and the arrangement had been largely political. In no rush for heirs of his own, Jinzan had waited years before consummating their vows, leaving her in the hands of tutors, and eventually Nakah's care, before finally making a proper wife of her. He kept largely away from her in the meantime, not wishing to form too strongly the image of his wife as a child. She was a bitter one, though, Frenna was. Any mention of Kadrin reminded her of her slaughtered parents—it was, sadly, something she had in common with her husband.

"It will be better once the harmless, beleaguered peasants realize they have been freed from the yoke of the Imperial Circle and the noble houses," Jinzan corrected. Jinzan had lived in Kadris as a youth while training as a sorcerer. Possibly the most valuable lesson he had learned in his time there was that peasants were all largely alike. They worked, they fell in love, they raised families, and they died. If left undisturbed, they would do the same under any ruler who wished to claim dominion over their homes, in any part of the world where crops could push their way up through the soil or fish could be wrested from the sea.

"To the sword with all of them, then?" Varduk asked, goading Jinzan just a bit.

"By and large, I suppose. Most are too invested in the current system to embrace real change that would not have them pulling the puppet strings from safe in their fortresses. A few might see reason and join in truth, and not just say the words to keep their neck employed holding head to shoulders."

"What of the warlock?" Varduk asked. "Is that staff of yours enough?"

"The Staff of Gehlen is our best answer to that threat, yes. I suspect we will have a game of Guards and Cutthroats on our hands, and I do not know yet who will be who. Certainly it ought to be enough to overmaster any of the rest of their sorcerers, but I will always refrain from making assumptions where it relates to Rashan Solaran. One day, I think, fate will pair us across a battlefield and the river of history will be diverted to a new path." The warlock was a problem to be sure, but the staff ought to help with that. Jinzan was more worried about Kyrus Hinterdale and his counterpart. He knew of cannons as well, and might think of other inventions to bring to Kadrin from the other world.

He is too clever by far. Cannons were the best weapon I could think to bring, but that does not mean he will not match me. Who can say what pieces of Tellurak I might find cropping up among the Kadrins?

"Councilor Jinzan," one of the young pages of the estate interrupted the conversation apologetically. "There is a goblin to see you. He seemed polite enough, so I allowed him in to wait in the front sitting parlor."

"Hmm?" Jinzan disengaged his mind from the philosophical, and re-emerged in a more suspicious state. "Did the goblin give a name?" Goblins were not unheard of in Megrenn, and Zorren had a few small goblin enclaves. Jinzan suspected that any goblin calling on him personally was not local.

"Gut me if I know, sir," the page answered. "He understands Megrenn just fine, but I could not say he speaks it. He had a go of it, but it sounded like someone was hurtin' him, so I begged him to stop. If he had a name somewheres in there, I sure did not catch it."

Jinzan smiled at the irreverent page. Among his own people, it felt good to hear honesty for a change. He heard so little of it outside Megrenn borders. He suspected he would hear little from his new guest as well, given his recent experiences with the goblin folk.

* * * * * * * *

"You?" Jinzan's first word of shock greeted his guest.

Unafraid of assassins or other treachery, Jinzan had shortened the rest of his evening with his wives and guests, and gone to see the goblin visitor. He was a wizened little creature with grey-green skin and thin grey hair, sitting in a human-sized chair with his feet dangling halfway to the floor. He peered up at Jinzan through a thick pair of spectacles.

[Ha-ha, Sorcerer, I see life among your own kind treats you well. That is good,] K'k'rt greeted his one-time ally.

Jinzan understood goblin-speech perfectly well, and did not ever remember hearing the goblin butcher his own language. Until shortly ago, he had not known whether this goblin understood Megrenn or not. During his time among their people, Jinzan had spoken the more widely understood Kadrin dialect of human.

[I could not help but hear the sound of one of my cannons earlier today,] K'k'rt said. [It is good to hear that at least one was saved.]

K'k'rt was the goblin tinker responsible for converting Jinzan's sketches of an Acardian-style cannon into the working devices that had been used in the Battle of Raynesdark. Though the cannons had been successful, and Jinzan had escaped with the Staff of Gehlen, the rest of the battle had gone far beyond poorly for the goblin side.

"I did not know that any of your people survived the battle," was all Jinzan could think to reply. With the death of their dragon goddess, there was little hope for the goblins when faced with the demon the Kadrins had dredged up from somewhere in their history books. Rashan Solaran, by all accounts, had massacred the lot of them.

[Ha-ha, I do not hear any joy in your voice at finding that I am alive. How unsurprising. Still, I think you will be happy to see me before long,] K'k'rt said.

"Why would that be?" Jinzan asked, not bothering to dispute the goblin's suggestion that he was indifferent to K'k'rt's survival. The tinker was useful, but could be grating at times, with his flippant and condescending attitude; he was also too observant and too often correct, traits that annoyed Jinzan in others.

[I hear you need to make cannons,] K'k'rt answered, smiling a wide toothy smile. [I could probably be of some help.]

* * * * * * * *

While the rest of the children had been out playing, one of Jinzan's brood had slipped away unnoticed. Anzik Fehr was an odd boy who never fit in well with the other children. Many children learned to dislike sport, or their studies, or any subject they began to find tedious or difficult. Anzik disliked everything.

He did not throw tantrums or pout. He did not cause trouble. He did ... not. He did *lots* of not. Anzik looked at things, and seemed to think a great deal, but by and large did nothing. Sometimes he would refuse to take his lessons, only to be found later to be engrossed in the same book that his tutors had tried to get him to read. On the occasions he could be drawn into conversation, he seemed remarkably bright, as if all that he had appeared to ignore had been absorbed and tucked away in his mind.

Despite being just shy of eleven springtimes old, he would sometimes be found playing with blocks meant for children young enough to still soil themselves. He would ignore all attempts to persuade him to more appropriate activities, not even looking at those who spoke to him. Calls to mealtime might well have been spoken to the stones of the wall.

But magic was somewhat different. Anzik did magic. No one seemed to approve when he did, though. Jinzan had discovered when Anzik was very young that his son saw the aether all the time. It was a debilitating thing to a young child, seeing always what most folk cannot see at all. It must have been like living in another world from everyone else. But the time he spent looking there had given him insight, and made magic easy for him. While there seemed to be no malice behind it, his workings in the aether always seemed to cause mischief.

The worst was when one of the Fehr dogs died. Distant as he was with people, Anzik seemed almost on the level of the dog when they were together. The dog was old but playful, and it reacted simply to Anzik's commands in a way that people never did. He had been despondent when the dog had died. Days later, he seemed happy again. His mother Frenna had been relieved, but Jinzan had been suspicious. They had found the dog stationed out near the kennels, awaiting commands, animated from the dead by Anzik's magic. He had fixed his broken pet and been so proud. It crushed his spirit anew when Jinzan had destroyed it as an abomination, much more so than the beating and reprimands that had followed.

Thus it was no surprise that none of the other children had wished to play with him or even gave him a thought as they played. The governess who was looking after the children that night usually paid him little mind; none of his worst offenses had occurred during her watch.

Anzik had unrestricted access to the house, especially since he could see his way through most of his father's wards. Since Jinzan had returned, he had been watching for an opportunity to slip away for an extended time. He looked up at the Staff of Gehlen, warded away in a glass case, and smiled.

It looks so wonderful.

33

Chapter 5 - Sizing Up Foes

Dogger's Shack was among the worst ale-halls in Scar Harbor, and the owner, Dogger, liked it that way. The age-greyed wood of the walls and floors only got washed enough to get the occasional splatter of blood off, but the tables and chairs were always near to new, though of the cheapest make that could be found. Fights were regular to the point of almost being expected on a busy night, and the furnishings took a beating or were used in dealing one out. It was a place where a man with one eye and a few rotten teeth could go to drink with his social inferiors. The regulars ran the name of the place together as Doggershack, and could tell anyone who did not belong when they used two words to name it.

Foreigners were not unheard of in Doggershack, being right near the water where newcomers first set foot in Acardia after getting off the boat that brought them. Some stumbled in by mischance, often to their dismay. Others sought it out with purpose for the same two reasons the locals did: it was a place where ruffians might still find welcome and piss-poor ale still got a man drunk.

The door was jammed open with a bit of driftwood to keep the stink of the place manageable and let out the heat from hot, sweating patrons on a warm late afternoon. Folk came and went all day, so it took something more than passingly unusual to draw attention. The lot that entered that day qualified.

They were preceded by a woman, Kheshi by her look, with a short mop of yellow hair and a few tiny braids hanging to one side. Her eyes were so deep a blue that they looked nearly black; they flitted back and forth as she swept the room appraisingly before passing the threshold. She was tall, comely despite her stern look, with youthful, pale skin—probably even had all her teeth—and thin limbs. Her most womanly features were obscured by her leather armor, close fitted, but still vague enough to leave hungry eyes guessing at the shape beneath, and the loose black tunic thrown over it only made things harder on the lecherous eyes sizing her up like the day's catch. The armor was Kheshi styled, with a steel neck guard running from collarbone to collarbone with the front left open. Her arms were left bare. They bore no scars despite being left exposed by her armor, which might be taken as a sign of being untested in battle, if not for the tattoos.

Kheshi warriors of a certain mind-set had tiny circles along their upper arms. Each circle represented a coin left on the body of a slain enemy, ostensibly to pay whoever found the body for the trouble of disposing of it. It was not a tradition among soldiers, who might leave a wounded foe and never know his fate, or who might range about the field of battle for half a day, killing and avoiding death's pursuit. Of old, it was the sign of an assassin, so that none might mistake the crime for an accident or a fit of anger or passion. In more modern times, mercenaries wore the marks as a sign of prowess, some in the old way of the assassins who might even leave coins as tradition would dictate, while others would brazenly take on far more than they had ever killed. To wear Kheshi armor open-sleeved with dozens of the markings showing was a braggart's boast without even having to speak a word.

Gazes followed gazes, and men looked to see what had captured their drinking companions' attention. Nudges and low, ribald comments alerted the rest until nearly the whole of Doggershack was watching her. Having deemed the place suitable by whatever low standard she must have had, she turned her head to look back at her companions, and gave a sideways nod inside to beckon them.

First in behind the Kheshi girl was a tall, wiry Acardian with a sword at his hip. He had a face that looked permanently punched, with a large brow, flat nose, and a large chin like a small child's knee jutting below his mouth. He had a mean glint in his eyes and a languid ease to his movements—the sort that blustering youths try to imitate when they want to look tougher than they are.

Right behind him was a black-skinned Takalish warrior. He wore a patch over one eye, and had a scar running down the jaw on the other side, partly obscured by his beard. There was light aplenty in the taproom, otherwise his features would have been difficult to discern, with the black-on-black contrast of his skin, eye patch, and beard. The white of his one good eye shone starkly against the brownish green of the rest. If the men in Doggershack that night did not know that his long twin braids dangling down over his grey-trimmed burgundy tunic marked him as a warrior, the Takalish half-spear sheathed on his back made it obvious. The Takalish had decided that the bits of swords nearest the cross-guard were not worth the trouble of sharpening. Instead they decided to shorten the blade and lengthen the grip. The weapon was lighter than a greatsword, but with just as much reach, and their warriors had learned to use the lengthened handle to grasp the half-spear at different points to change the weapon's reach, striking force, and blocking ability. It was no weapon for a novice.

The last to enter was a hulking bear of a man. Not much taller than the Kheshi girl, he might have outweighed her thrice over. His greasy black hair and beard were wild and unkempt, obscuring much of his ruddy red face and making his wide blue eyes seem a bit unnerving; he had the look of a madman, and it was a convincing enough act to cause wariness, even if it turned out he was feigning. He wore a voluminous tarp of a sweat-soaked blue woolen tunic over a shirt of chain that looked to be custom-sized to his massive gut. He kept two swords at his hip: one looked expensive, with a jeweled pommel and cross-guard, while the other was shorter and more utilitarian.

The quartet was obviously well off by their gear and the jingle in purses as they walked in. Doggershack was a rough establishment, where a lot of bad things could happen to folk who walked about with too much coin on their person. However, being a rough establishment, it contained a lot of men who knew the difference between snagging an easy mark and getting run through trying to rob a coinblade.

The Kheshi girl headed straight for the bar, while the others bullied free a spot from a couple of dockhands who were not making full use of a table that sat four. The crowd parted for her, at least enough so that she might try to shoulder her way past those in her path, rather than confront them. There was no shortage of foul-smelling drunkards that would not mind even so little attention from her.

"I am looking for a man," she told the barkeep after sizing up none other than Dogger himself, working at the taps. She spoke Acardian well, but there was enough of a Kheshi accent that it made her sound exotic, with the drawn-out vowels and lyrical intonation.

A small chorus of volunteers spoke up immediately, vouching for their own manhood and offering credentials. One was even so bold as to take her by the arm and run a thumb along her kill-marking tattoos. "Pretty thing like you ought—"

The rest of the man's insights and advice were lost to the world as the Kheshi girl reached across, and grabbed his wrist. At the same time, she lifted her foot and gave a sharp heel kick into the offender's knee. As the knee buckled with a sickening crunch, the wretch screamed. The girl twisted his wrist until she was free of his grasp, and then used her newly freed arm to push him solidly to the ground, flipping him over the leg that had just kicked him. The lecher hit headfirst and lay there moaning until she twisted again, breaking his arm and setting him off screaming again. She let his arm fall limp and stomped down on his head, silencing him. Whether he was unconscious or dead, none could tell.

"Sorry ... reflex," the girl—Soria—said to Dogger.

"Some o' you lot, drag this feller outta here! If'n he's breathin', leave 'im out back. If'n he ain't, pitch him inna tha harbor. I'll gut any of ya's with a ladle if I get any truncheon sniffin' round here after 'im," Dogger ordered. Anyone who hung around Doggershack got used to it after a while. Dogger could not go two breaths without making some sort of threat.

Soria herself had never been to Scar Harbor before—possibly as a babe when she was too young to remember—but she puzzled out that "truncheon" must have been the local slang for the city guards.

"You look like you gots some coin. You better after that little stunt. Oughtta push those two pretty little ears o' yours t'gether fer that," Dogger said.

"As I was saying, I am looking for a man. His name is Kyrus. I heard he lived here in Scar Harbor," Soria said, ignoring the colorful image Dogger had just sketched out for her of her head squeezed flat until her ears touched.

"Ne'er met 'im. Set o' cannonballs danglin' from his yardarm fer sure, tho'. Nickin' off with the *Harbinger* like 'e did. Filleted his-self two truncheons was watchin' o'er him in the pokey, burnt down a ship and half the docks. Folks says 'e's a witch," Dogger spat. "I ain't fer knowin' spit about that. What I know's that fella you floor-stomped owed me fer thirty eckles in drinks and ain't paid up. I'm fer thinkin' you owe fer that."

"If you can't rein in your patrons, that hardly seems my problem. If he hadn't paid, you should have had someone search his pockets before dumping him in the Katamic," Soria shot back.

"Din't think of it at the time. I's more feared o' bringing truncheons inna the place about it than I was o' pickin' the pockets of some rough salt with his lamp blown out by a Kheshi bint with a leakin' spigot. I oughtta knock yer skull in and pass yous round like a hat at a jugglin' show to take up a collection," Dogger said.

Soria could not help herself, and laughed at the absurd thought.

"You're thinkin' this is a lark, eh Miss Mercenary Arm-twister? This lot's like fam'ly: they'd gut and clean ya if'n I says some Kheshi quick-hand was stiffin' me on a tab," Dogger said.

"I do. And I doubt it."

Dogger offered a rueful smile. "Heh, you might be right at that," he said and chuckled, taking a liking to a lass who could weather his worst storm and laugh about it.

* * * * * * * *

"The barkeep's a useless blowhard, but he knew where the witch worked. Apparently it turned into a bit of a gawk-spot, and everyone in town knows about it," Soria explained to her companions as she joined them at the table. She took the ale they had procured for her, and took a deep swig; arguing was thirsty work.

"It's somethin', at least," Zell said, then shrugged. "I was hoping for something more to go on than a building. Someone to talk to and question, that sort o' thing."

"Scar Harbor is big enough. There will be plenty of people to talk to. Someone will know him better than the barkeep at the first place we tried," said Rakashi, nursing his own ale. The Takalish was used to much stronger (and more flavorful) liquors, and he only pestered his ale to keep up appearances.

"Gotta say, Soria, the Kheshi look suits you better than Acardian," Tanner said as he looked her over playfully.

"Keep mentioning that every time and I'll need to start putting another little circle tattoo on," Soria said. She had been fending off halfhearted advances from Tanner since she had known him. It had disgusted her when she was a girl of fifteen and he was eight years her senior. Now it was just annoying. The jest had teeth, though; magical disguise or not, the count of circles on her arm was correct as best she remembered it.

"Ha! Get an eyeful," Zell said, then gave Soria a gentle backhand slap in the shoulder to get her attention. She broke her glare at Tanner and looked where Zell's attention had fallen.

Nailed on one wall of Doggershack were a number of sketches. There was writing below each, but across the taproom, it was too small to read, and the sketches too indistinct to identify anyone by them. Without saying a word, Soria stood and crossed the taproom. After the incident at the bar, no one got in her way.

They were bounty postings. She scanned through the pictures until she found the one she knew had to be there. Her heart quickened in her chest when she looked at it. The text below read: *Kyrus Hinterdale—Wanted for witchcraft, murder, and piracy. 300,000 eckles for his return.*

The words may have said it was Kyrus Hinterdale, but when she saw the crude picture, Soria muttered under her breath, "I found you, Brannis."

* * * * * * *

Soria had appropriated the sketch of Brannis (or Kyrus, as she would now have to struggle to remember), and shown it to the others. She had told none of the others of her suspicions that the reported sorcerer found in Scar Harbor had been Brannis Solaran back in Kadrin. She wanted to surprise everyone—and to make sure she was right. The picture had set her mind at ease on the last count, at least. Though the artwork was unimpressive, and it had been reproduced on a printing press, it was clearly him.

The four of them—Soria, Zellisan, Rakashi, and Tanner—had taken up rooms at a much nicer inn far from the dock district. Noblemen's estates might overlook the sea, but the closer you got to a working port, the seedier and more dangerous the accommodations became. For all their dangerous looks, Soria and her companions had the coin to spend on comfort and enjoyed using it.

Safely in her own room, she allowed her appearance to shift back to normal. Gone were the blonde hair and too-blue eyes. The skin on her arms returned to its smooth, unmarred state, with no tattoos and a shade darker than she had made it—a subtlety no doubt lost on the ruffians at the dock and the rubes in the city. Soria prided herself on thoroughness in her disguises, though, and took care in case one among the unwashed pack was worldly enough to tell northern Kheshi from southern.

The little braids in her hair she had woven that morning on the ride to town, and rather taken a liking to. The brown beads woven into them stood out less against her natural auburn color, so she doubted anyone would mistake her for the same girl who had stormed through Doggershack. The armor was her own, Kheshi made and well molded to her form in the years she had owned it. It left her arms free to fight, and acted as more of a safeguard in case her magical shields were ever lacking, or she was caught unawares. *That* would certainly be noticed should she go about clad in it in Scar Harbor as Soria Coinblade, rather than her Kheshi alter ego. She stowed the armor away until they were ready to leave the city.

The accent she had used had taken no magic, nor any special acting on her part. She had spent much of her youth in Khesh, and spoke Kheshi better than her birth language of Acardian. She could drop the accent when she had to, but it took effort, and she slipped up when flustered. Usually she did not bother to try to hide it, since many foreigners found it charming.

Weary and sweat caked from traveling and wearing armor about, Soria took advantage of the amenities available at a nice inn like The Little Manor, and had one of the maids draw her a bath. She tipped the lass a twenty-eckle coin and made the girl's day. The water was hot, and Soria was intent that it remain so. It might not draw suspicion in Kadrin to have a cold bath drawn and heat it to taste by means of aether, but in Acardia, she waited the extra time for the girl to bring the water hot. Should it begin to cool, Soria planned to use enough aether to keep herself warm a long time.

She soaked in the little tub for hours, until her legs cramped and her bottom began to lose feeling from sitting on hard metal for too long. It was well past midnight, but Soria was accustomed to late nights, and not yet sleepy.

As she relaxed, she unfocused her eyes, drifting into aether-vision, and seeing the world in swirling blue-white aether, with little Sources all about, slumbering. The aether being less than compelling enough to hold her interest, Soria let her mind drift a little more loosely, and slipped past the aether-vision to watch through Juliana Archon's eyes.

* * * * * * *

Rakashi drew curious glances as he walked the streets of Scar Harbor the next morning, after splitting off from the rest of the group. They had gone their separate ways after scouting the neighborhood around the witch's shop, and talking to his neighbors for leads. Takalish were not unheard of in Acardia, but visibly armed folk always drew more attention, even that of the constables that roamed the city like watchdogs on an over-large estate. Many Takalish merchants brought their goods to Acardia through Scar Harbor, and some had even settled in the city. The merchants wore flashy clothing, bright jewelry, and funny little hats (to Acardian thinking at least) that told the enlightened shopper what guild they were affiliated with. The conservatively dressed Takalish with the eye patch and war braids bore watching.

He walked about the city, passively taking in the sights he had never seen before, as it was his first time in Scar Harbor. He had a task to accomplish, but there was almost no chance that the sorcerer they were looking for was still in the city, so the urgency to find him was scant. It felt good to be away from the others for a while. He loved them as brothers and sister, but they were often loud and rash. Rakashi preferred time to think before speaking and to speak before acting. Soria was the worst in that regard. She thought quickly and felt that it gave her leave to act on any whim, counting on her wits—or at worst, her magic—to save her.

Rakashi made his way generally in the direction of the Society of Learned Men, but wended his way via side streets and thoroughfares that bore only the slightest hint at his destination. Tanner or Soria might have done the same out of some paranoid sense of diversion, and Zell would almost certainly not have taken such an oblique route at all, but Rakashi liked to see the world he lived in, not just survive it and profit from it. He looked into shops to see what sort of things the Acardians liked to buy and how they dealt in business. He met the gaze of passersby with a slight nod and a hand to his chest, the standard Takalish greeting between strangers who have nothing to discuss. He even stopped on two occasions to give five-eckle coins to beggars and inquire after their health.

By the time he had arrived at the Society of Learned Men, it was a proper time to take lunch. After introducing himself to the society's manservant as a traveling scholar, he was invited to luncheon with Professor Honothan Whitegull, whom Kyrus Hinterdale's cobbler neighbor had claimed was a patron of the scrivener's shop from time to time.

"It is so rare for us to have armed guests at the table, Rakashi old boy," the professor commented. Stooped and gaunt, with a fluffy fringe of white hair about his head, he was hardly one to be commenting on his guest's age.

"I travel much. Just as a merchant ship carries cannons or a diplomat travels with men at arms, so I carry my half-spear. One day, I may have a nice position in a university, as you have here in Acardia, but I must earn my way first. And just like a merchant or a diplomat, my travels may take me places that are not so friendly," Rakashi said.

"Might I have a look at it?" Professor Whitegull asked politely, peering over Rakashi's shoulder at the handle of his weapon.

"Of course," Rakashi replied smoothly, drawing the blade and setting it down gingerly next to the professor's plate. He was not normally of a habit of handing over his weapon in an unfamiliar setting, but no man who served cucumber and minced-pork finger sandwiches as lunch was a threat to take up his blade against him, no matter his age or apparent infirmity.

The old man gave the half-spear an appraising look and ran a fingernail across the blade to see the mark it left. "Very nice. Very nice. Good workmanship coming out of Takalia these days, it seems. You keep a good edge on it too. Looks about a dozen years old, to judge by the condition of the leather on the grip. It ought to last another dozen at least before it needs any serious repair."

"I use it gently. I have never killed with it." Rakashi indulged in the pleasant lie to keep the luncheon more congenial. Not every non-warrior was comfortable in the presence of one who had killed. "Twice in my travels I have been accosted, but never have I had the misfortune to shed my attacker's lifeblood. Most of the nicks and marks you see upon it are from practice. It takes years to learn to use a half-spear well, and the learning keeps the body in good health."

"So what then brings you to Scar Harbor, sir?" Professor Whitegull inquired.

"I am looking for a man named Kyrus Hinterdale," Rakashi told him, glad to have the professor broach the change of subject so that he had a proper reason to bring up his search. "I have heard that you did business with him."

"Hmm, a bit, yes. Mostly with his former employer, though—Expert Chartler. Kyrus seemed like a good enough lad. You know ... quiet, bookish, professorial … one of my own kind, so to speak." The professor chuckled lightly at what he must have found to be an amusing observation. Rakashi did not patronize him by pretending to understand the jest, but merely listened respectfully. "Anyway, that whole witch business was a bunch of poppycock! Magic does not exist. If folk were less inclined to their cups, there would be fewer troublemakers claiming it did."

Rakashi nodded through the professor's little tirade, as if to agree with all he was saying. With the aether-vision in his patched eye, however, Rakashi could not help but notice that the drawing room in which they ate contained no fewer than three items imbued with aether. The Society of Learned Men were either better collectors than they realized, or someone among them was more "Learned" than the others.

"Well, whether he is a witch or not, I hope to find him. I would very much like to meet a witch if they exist. If they do not, I would like to see what sort of man would earn such a reputation," Rakashi said.

"Be a bit off, by most folks' reckoning, and have the misfortune to be around some odd happenstance that a drunken mind might not wrap itself fully around. By my best conjecture, in the absence of any personal connection to the facts, that is most likely what befell Expert Hinterdale," Professor Whitegull pontificated—pontificating being a special privilege of academia.

Satisfied that he would find little of practical use in speaking with the professor, Rakashi instead spent the afternoon in a stimulating discussion of foreign politics.

* * * * * * * *

Zellisan had eaten a hearty breakfast in the common room of The Little Manor, but was intent on another morning meal with his choice of investigative subjects. The witch had apparently been friendly with one of the local bakers, and Zell was planning to sample his wares if he got naught else from his assigned task.

Greuder's Pastries was a tidy little establishment, not a bad walk from where he had just parted ways with the others. Apparently the Hinterdale fellow was a regular customer and friend of the proprietor, so Zell was going to see what he could learn about him.

Business was brisk; there was room to move in the little shop. There were tables filled with late breakfasters and a small line waiting at a counter to purchase sweets to take away. They were city folk, peasant merchants, and tradesmen from the look of them, with night workers predominating the lot of them, if Zell was any judge. A large man to begin with, Zell stood out all the more for being armed in a bakery in a rather safe little Acardian seaport. The docks might have had pretentions of roughness, but the interior portion of the city stank of sweets and flowers.

Zell played nice and waited his turn in line. Despite a number of customers in front of him, it did not take long before he made his way to the front. There was an admirable efficiency to the operation; he hoped the food was admirable as well.

"What would you like today, sir?" the baker asked when Zell was left with none between him and the counter.

"You know a fellow named Kyrus Hinterdale?" Zell asked, skipping to his reason for coming without preamble.

"Haven't got any of those today. Try a scone, perhaps?" the baker replied without pausing so much as a heartbeat.

"You Greuder, ain't ya?" Zell said, not to be dissuaded by an impertinent baker.

"If I'm not, I've been doing him quite a favor running his bakery all these years," Greuder replied. "Now are you going to buy something? I have customers waiting, you know."

Zell glanced over his shoulder, and noticed that there were indeed people who had come into the shop behind him while he was not paying attention. It was the sort of mistake that could get him killed in a place like Darkwater or Marker's Point, but Scar Harbor was the sort of place that lulled one with its idyllic seaside charm. The name made it sound a bit rough at the edges, but the "scar" it referred to was just a sandbar that cut through the harbor on maps and looked a bit like a facial scar—if you were a cartographer or navigator with too much imagination who stares at maps all day, seeing in them shapes and objects like children do pointing up at the clouds.

"Give me two of those little puffy ones, and two of the twisty ones. Oh, and I'll have one of them big cream-topped ones, too." Zell picked out whatever looked tastiest, a hard task since it all looked and smelled wonderful. He waited a breath until Greuder was busying himself about wrapping up his order, then set back in on his main line of questioning. "So you know this fellow Kyrus the Witch, or don't ya?"

"You another purveyor of justice for hire, then, I take it?"

"Close, but way off," Zell answered, not even realizing the paradox. "You're a friend of his, I hear, so I think I can give you the back alley on this one. I'm a coinblade, and I could use a fellow like him, if rumors be true. Only a madman would go chasing a witch if he meant to do him harm. So either this Kyrus is a witch—and I'd be crazy to tangle with him if he was—or he isn't, and I got no use finding him or trying to hire him. So now since I'm playing cards-up with you, how 'bout you tell me this: you think he's really a witch like they say? If'n he is, any help you can give me findin' him is no trouble to him. Either he likes my offer or he doesn't; no one is takin' a witch to jail twice. Even once is probably fool's luck."

Greuder gave Zell a hard look. He was near to Zell's size, but not quite, and there was far less hard muscle under his own fluffy outer layer than the coinblade's. "Eighty-six eckles, sir," he replied evenly.

Zellisan fished in his pockets, and slowly counted out no less than two hundred eckles, then a few more for flair, and slapped them down on the counter. Greuder started to hand him his purchase, but noticed that Zell was not removing his hand from atop the coins.

"It was a simple enough question," Zell stated, looking Greuder square in the eye with as little menace as he could manage to keep from mustering.

"All right then, yes. I think Kyrus pulled the hat down over our eyes and was a witch all along. He was a good lad, though ... amiable, pleasant, thoughtful, bit of a wit to him. Never had I heard a word against him until suddenly they said he was a threat to everyone. Do I think he attacked constables who sought to arrest him? Of course! Back a spinster's lap cat into a corner, and it will remind you that it still has claws; it is your fault for forgetting, and provoking it. It defended itself the only way nature provided. If they had left Kyrus alone, he would still be working at his shop, bothering no one."

"Fair answer. Sounds like a man who could use a new home, somewhere folk respect that everyone's got claws o' their own. Where you think he might head, in case someone wanted to see about offering him work?" Zell asked.

"I doubt Kyrus has ever been outside Acardia before," Greuder said, then sighed. "If he has any sense in him, he should find a nice quiet place to make himself a new home, and never be heard from again, at least not as Kyrus Hinterdale. If he has somewhat less sense, he might have headed to Golis; his mentor lives there now as scribe to King Gorden. I could see why he might try to have him intervene with the king.

"Of course ... if he has no sense at all," Greuder amended, looking away as if pondering, "he might sneak back to Scar Harbor to whisk away his lady."

"Your friend always been the sensible sort, would ya say?" Zell asked, smiling amiably.

"Thoughtful, perhaps. Smart as a kick in the shin. But sensible? Couldn't rightly say."

* * * * * * *

Of course he drew the docks. It was the most dangerous assignment of all the places they meant to ask around about Kyrus Hinterdale. Zell looked toughest of all of them, and Rakashi was no clean-bladed virgin, but Tanner had magic to fall back on if things turned that special reddish version of "ugly." He was no proper sorcerer like Soria, but he could manage to cast a shielding spell in the morning—out loud, since he could not manage silently like she could—and keep it going weakly as he went about the day. He would be fine so long as he did not doze off or become too distracted by something and let it lapse, and if he got into trouble, he could draw a bit of aether to strengthen it.

Soria, that quick-talking horse merchant! She should be the one down here badgering longshoremen, Tanner groused internally. Anyone could walk around the docks as they pleased and not worry too much. It was when you started asking lots of questions that you had to watch for knives out of the corner of your eye. *She wouldn't even have to threaten or bribe 'em, more than likely. Pretty thing like her can just lick her lips and sway her backside, and this lot'd tell her anything and not know it.*

Tanner caught himself, and tried to remember to leave Soria's backside out of his thoughts. Her little threats used to be cute when she was a lass. He would comment on her womanly assets, or "accidentally" walk in on her in the bath. He was getting the growing impression, though, that his leash was being pulled taut and that the next thing he said that offended her might be his last. That fellow in the bar had not been half so forward as Tanner had been on more than one occasion and she nearly killed him. It was as friendly a warning as he was likely to receive from her.

He eased himself into his task by making casual talk with a few of the locals. They were a pathetic lot, and were more informed about parochial matters than what transpired in the greater world around them, despite working at one of the major entry points for foreigners visiting Acardia. They had all heard of the trial of Kyrus the Witch, though, and one even claimed to have been there, but none had heard of him since his escape from jail. It seemed to be common wisdom down by the waterfront that Kyrus had fallen in with the notorious pirate, Denrik Zayne. Zayne had escaped the New Hope penal colony shortly before Kyrus Hinterdale's trial, and was unaccounted for, up to the point a navy ship was commandeered under bizarre circumstances. Folk claimed that the witch had used magic to swing a gangplank about, knocking navy sailors into the harbor as they fought to reclaim their vessel. Then one of the ships nearby had been set ablaze, burning a fair bit of the piers with it.

Tanner was impressed. If half what the longshoremen told him was true, then this Kyrus fellow was a true sorcerer. Soria knew her business when it came to magic, but she trusted to her fists or daggers when trouble came, not fire and telekinesis. It sort of raised the question of just how Kyrus Hinterdale had gotten himself stuck in jail in the first place. He was either new to sorcery—which would have made the feats described to Tanner all the more impressive—or he had been trying to avoid confirming everyone's suspicions that he was a witch. Of course, it was also possible that the longshoremen were having a lark with him, spouting fisherman's tales when it was nothing but a simple daring raid on an understaffed navy frigate.

Tanner finally found some more worldly sea-folk to talk to. Many offered ill-mannered suggestions about his parentage, gender, looks, or skin, but a few were willing to talk over free ale, which Tanner grudgingly supplied. He had a better plan than asking about some accused witch whose fame likely ended at the water's edge. Instead he talked to them about the pirate.

"Ya. Zayne. I heared of him," one thick-tongued mongrel garbled in response to his query. The man chewed some pungent mash of roots that bulged one side of his mouth. "He crew his new ship in Marker Point. I think of going too, but … ahh … bad leg, see?" The man flexed one leg as if to prove it gimpy, but Tanner could see nothing wrong with it.

Coward or liar, more like. Tanner did not challenge him, though.

"They say where he was headed from there?" Tanner asked.

"No' tha I heared. Was a big powder 'splosion. Burned down lotta houses.

Lotta ships left afta that. Zayne ship left too. Nobody like to stay and get blame, maybe," the man said.

"How'd they know it was a gunpowder and not just a fire?" Tanner asked. He had a hunch.

"There was a big *boom*. No lamp oil or cookin' fire make a boom when it burn," the mongrel answered.

Maybe Marker's Point ought to be the next place we look, Tanner thought. If he could burn down ships, maybe Kyrus Hinterdale could burn down houses, too. *I'm startin' to wonder if this fella is gonna be worth the trouble he causes if we* do *convince him to join us. Winds, maybe we don't wanna take the chance of him not caring much for our offer.* Tanner did not like the idea of fighting a real sorcerer.

* * * * * * * *

Why did I do this to myself? Soria asked herself for at least the dozenth time as she strolled across Scar Harbor with a tranquil, aloof smile painted over her face. *I should have traded with Rakashi; he's more delicate with these sorts of things anyway.*

"Soria Coinblade" had been left behind at The Little Manor, and she had gone as "Darlah Silverweave" instead. Darlah was far from her favorite persona, but it was one that seemed appropriate for the day. She wore long, honey-blonde tresses, tumbling front and back of her shoulders in ringlets, and had turned her eyes a striking blue. The curls were from a ratty old wig she kept for long-haired disguises, magically tinted to whatever look suited her purpose; it was a comfortable bit of her disguise, having had it for years. The dress was less comfortable. Juliana was accustomed to dresses, but they felt weird and awkward to Soria, Darlah, and any other names she cared to take. Her muscular thighs rubbed together for lack of the proper undergarments to accompany her attire— she was not a pack mule to be carrying all that fine ladies would wear as she traveled. The warm spring breeze tickled the tops of her bosoms, which were left open for the world to see in ways that armor never would, nor her traveling gear.

There were times when Soria looked into a mirror before going out in disguise, and could feel no connection to her reflection. Kji-Tala, her southern Kheshi persona, had never seemed so alien to her as Darlah, whom she had copied from a Hurlan nobleman's daughter that she met once. Bright blue eyes looked unreal to her. Dark, Kheshi eyes had looked at her most of her life, and her own darkish green ones looked back at her often enough in reflections. Her figure seemed foreign to her as well. Her muscled arms lay hidden below a wispy layer of delicate pink fabric, and the lacings of her dress pulled it tight at her waist, making her hips seem wide when she really had very little of them to speak of. The low cut in the front, and some trick in the making of expensive dresses made it appear she had the bust of a grown woman, rather than a newly flowered maiden.

She had almost changed her mind before leaving The Little Manor. *I lie better than any of them do. I can just say I got no useful information, or make up some banal blather and take a strong liking to some lead one of them turns up.* In the end, though, curiosity drove her out into the streets dressed as a lady of wealth and style (the latter being more a hope of hers, with little fashion sense of her own to count upon).

Soria purchased a parasol from a little boutique on her way. With only a small handbag to carry, her hands itched for something to do, and she knew it would not be ladylike, whatever her idle hands did while she lost track of them. She was liable to end up cracking her knuckles or tugging at the awkward-feeling bits of her dress, possibly something worse.

Doubts nagged at her as she crossed the city. *It does not mean anything. I would bet heavy coin that Brannis did not even know of the connection until just recently. Whatever his twin did, he did on his own. "What works in one world, works in the other."*

She reminded herself of the Rules of the Twinborn, as taught to her by Rakashi. She had known of Juliana since they were little girls together, but if Brannis had just met his twin, it would take time for them to learn from each other. Soria sat a horse better than any Kheshi-raised city girl had a right to. Juliana would give a good accounting of herself in a Takalish dagger fight, despite being a spoiled princess of a sorceress. If someone were to shout "Juliana" across a crowded room, Soria's head would turn. It would only be a matter of time before Brannis and his twin shared the same bond.

Soria kept on wrestling with her own thoughts, and decided thrice to turn back, only to find that her legs had dutifully kept her on a steady course as her mind had wandered halfway to Kadrin and back. She finally arrived in front of a studio door. A painted sign above showed a brush and palette, colorfully painted. The sign was not carved at all to stand against weather and still proclaim its message as wind and rain faded and wore the colors; it was a sign of a cheap sign.

Nothing to be done but to do it, she told herself firmly.

Soria knocked on the door. She heard muffled voices from inside, followed by footsteps. If it were not already squished tight by her dress, her stomach would have clenched with nerves.

"Good morning," a comely young girl answered as she opened the door.

Celia! The thought struck Soria like an arrow to the heart, but the sensation passed. *No, but close enough, I think.* Celia Mistfield had been newly appointed as one of Juliana's least favorite people, ever since she had turned up after the Battle of Raynesdark and started trying to woo Brannis away from her. The girl was built the same as Celia, at least: middling height—certainly not so tall as Soria—but with an ample bosom and hips that did not need a tailored dress to prove their presence. She had the same dark hair and blue eyes, but Celia's face was more angular. Celia's eyes were also less bright and more cunning than those of the young painter who had just greeted Soria.

"Good morning," Soria returned in kind after a pause that was just on the borderlands of awkwardness. "I understand that you are an artist. You have been recommended," Soria spoke airily, and with as Acardian an accent as she could manage. Her brain was feeling just a touch fuzzy and she hoped it was piloting its course well enough without both hands upon the wheel.

"Please, come in. I shall just be a short while longer. I have a sitting this morning, but I can get you a chair if you don't mind waiting."

The artist—Soria knew her name was Abbiley Tillman, but stubbornly refused to acknowledge the fact—was saccharinely pleasant in her manner. Her voice sang better in conversation than Soria or Juliana could manage in song when truly trying. Soria tried hard not to hate her.

She followed the artist inside the studio, and took the proffered seat once it had been dusted off. Soria folded up her parasol and set it point down against the floor like a cane, holding it with both hands lest her idle habits embarrass her. She made a concerted effort to unclench her jaw, which she had not intended to clench in the first place, working it side to side a bit when no one was looking in order to relax the muscles of her face.

The studio had one other occupant, a gentleman of perhaps thirty years of age, dressed in his feasting-day finest. He was seated upon a small wooden stool near the window, well illuminated by the morning sunshine. He was a dashing fellow, with curling hair that hung to just below his jaw and that framed a face with bright brown eyes and a determined nose. Halfway between Soria and the gentleman was a canvas showing a striking likeness of him, rendered in colored oils.

"Tomas Harwick, my lady. It is my pleasure," the gentleman introduced himself when he noticed Soria looking at him. He was smiling as he said it, apparently taking her casual interest for less-than-casual interest, or at least being in the habit of often thinking such, and reacting flirtatiously by rote.

"Darlah," Soria replied, startled from her mind's wandering to the point where she caught a bit of Kheshi in her own introduction. Composing herself quickly, she tried again. "Darlah Silverweave."

"Feel free to have a look around as you wait. If you like, you might even assure Mr. Harwick that his portrait is nearly finished," Abbiley—the artist—said, not turning from the canvas to which she had returned and resumed her work. "I have not let him see it yet. It is unseemly for a man to see himself half-finished," she jested, smiling.

Merciful One, dimples!

Soria let her eyes sweep around the small studio. Every space along the walls was taken up by paintings, not hung, but rather leaning against the walls. Most were portraits, but a few landscapes and seascapes were mixed in. On a whim, and with nothing better to occupy her time, Soria looked into the aether. The dashing Mr. Harwick seemed ordinary enough as Sources go, and the artist girl seemed robust and healthy, but nothing special. She noticed a necklace that the girl wore. It was some cheap jade thing that they sold far and wide in Khesh and shipped by the crate to foreign lands where they would fetch better prices. It was the sort of stuff jade-workers gave their apprentices to practice on. The artist was wearing one that had a bit of aether in it.

Where did you learn to do that little trick, Brannis?

After an uncomfortable half hour of forcing herself repeatedly to try to relax, the sitting was finally at an end. Tomas Harwick was overjoyed at his likeness and promised to send a servant by to collect it later that day. Soria had muttered some platitudes to keep in character.

"So, Lady Silverweave, thank you for waiting. How may I be of service?" the artist asked cheerily.

You can tell me where Brannis is and save me the trouble of beating the information out of you!

"I was hoping you might paint a simple portrait for me," Soria said instead. She reached into her handbag and removed a scrap of paper. It was the bounty notice of Kyrus Hinterdale, with the written part at the bottom torn off, leaving just the sketched image. "I have made inquiries and I have come to understand you knew the subject of this crude likeness."

Soria saw the girl's smile falter. "Aye, milady. Put it away please, if you would not mind so much. I could paint Expert Hinterdale from memory well enough, should I wish to. If you do not mind my asking, what is he to you?" the artist asked.

Aha! The first sign of jealousy, eh? He was mine before he knew you existed.

Soria had done her scouting, though, and had everything prepared. "My father is a dear friend of Expert Davin Chartler, to whom Expert Hinterdale was once apprenticed. I understand that they were quite close, and Expert Davin has taken hard the awful news to have come out about Expert Kyrus. The portrait would be a gift to him."

Abbiley's suspicious demeanor melted like chocolate left under the summer sun. "Oh, that is so kind of you."

I have a talking duck I can sell you as well, Soria thought. *How does this girl run a business being this naive?*

"Have you any news of Expert Hinterdale that you could share? Any word at all might be some comfort," Soria crooned, hamming up her performance now that she realized how easily the girl was taken in.

"No, but if you must know, he did admit to me that there was some truth to what they accused him of," the girl said sheepishly. "Not that I believe for a moment that he meant anyone harm, of course."

"If you believe he is a witch, why would you not believe he killed two men and escaped with a pirate?" Soria prodded, having heard the same rumors and tales as most folk about the night Kyrus made off with one of the navy's finest ships, reportedly in the company of Denrik Zayne.

"I am sure he had nothing to do with that," the artist girl said, raising her voice. "He might have escaped, but he did not do the rest of that awful stuff."

"I think it just might be possible that you did not know him as well as you thought. If you truly ever loved him, he could tell you that all that happened is true, and it would change nothing. Consider for the moment that every bit of what people say about him is true. Consider that he killed men who wished him ill and took the only means of escape at hand, making allegiance with a pirate. Could you still love him?" Soria pressed, forgetting to keep the Kheshi out of her

Acardian. Abbiley seemed disinclined to notice.

"Kyrus isn't like that! He told me that he had dreams of being a knight," Abbiley said.

"Then he wishes to be like that. That is the sort of thing knights do." Soria stabbed the verbal dagger into Abbiley's heart. Feeling a twinge of remorse, she made a small alteration to her plan. She took some coins from her handbag. "Here is a thousand eckles," she told Abbiley, having no idea how much portraits cost and guessing that it ought to be enough. "Have the finished work sent to Davin Chartler, care of the palace in Golis. Paint Kyrus as you remember him, not as you have discovered him to be."

Soria was sweating and dizzy when she left the studio. She had never expected the girl to have any useful information about Kyrus Hinterdale's whereabouts, but once she had learned that Kyrus had courted her, Soria had to meet her.

You obviously learned some things from my Brannis, Mr. Hinterdale; you are not figuring out magic all on your own, I would wager. You also obviously have a lot left to learn from him, though, if that girl was the best you could find here.

Chapter 6 - Unfettered

"You sure you oughtta be doing that?" Tod asked, a note of concern in his voice as he peered over his companion's shoulder.

"You gotta listen close, I think. He says what he means, real exact like," Jodoul replied, twisting a thin metal rod into the end of the little lock. "He gave us the coffer and said there was thirty lions in it. We find the goblet, we get it back, he says. 'I do not care how; just do what you need to do.'" Jodoul mimicked the warlock's voice as best he could. "We gotta get our goal, see, and he won't care what we did."

"I don't think that meant breakin' his coffer," Tod said.

"What's a coffer? Bit o' wood and iron. He wants that goblet what got stole from the cupboards where they keep the fancy stuff for them feasts. I'm getting the idea that Warlock Rashan ain't the sort to muck about on small stuff like a broken coffer. Besides, how we gonna spend the thirty lions finding it if it's locked up inside? We ain't even counted it."

"I'm pretty sure gold goblets is small stuff when you're emperor," Tod said, attempting to bring some perspective to the conversation. "And how you figure he might short us on just thirty lions? Prob'ly got himself a whole cellar full o' little coffers like that, filled with lions."

"He ain't emperor, he's regent," Jodoul said, breaking out in a grin as the lock gave way and the coffer popped open. The coffer contained thirty gold lions, just as promised. "Let's go buy us some answers."

The two spent a good portion of the day talking to old acquaintances of the less savory variety. Few men got conscripted into the army if they had a stable trade and enough coin to do all their business in the marketplace. Neither Tod nor Jodoul had been much for apprenticeships or day labor. Tod was from Naran Port originally, and had earned much of his coin at dice and reselling "lost" valuables at a small profit. Jodoul was from Kadris, and used to run errands for the sort of ruffians that thought they had elevated themselves above the less "sophisticated" class of scum. That was before a misplaced delivery had run him afoul of his former employers, and he sought refuge in the spear-and-mail of the Imperial Army as a volunteer; the army never frowned on willing conscripts.

Most folk who had known either of the two had been well-enough informed to know that they were working for the warlock, so getting anyone to talk candidly ate into their supply of the warlock's lions rapidly. They spoke of old times and common friends, inquired after the health of relatives and offered condolences when hearing of former comrades who had not survived their last job. When the subject turned to practical matters, suddenly a man who had once known where half the goods in the city were heading would not so much as admit to seeing the sun yesterday—"The sun? Never seen it. You got the wrong guy." It was not that Tod and Jodoul were armed. Their short swords and daggers would avail them little if anyone really wanted them brought to harm. It was that they were now playing for the side of the law.

At length, they found someone who did not know who either of them was, and they were able to at least learn that the goblet had been fenced through someone named Derrel Three-Finger. Then the three-fingered thief had sold them the name of his buyer for five lions, leaving them eighteen after their fruitless efforts chatting with former associates. They were looking for Foxblade.

"Rotten luck. What say we head north, maybe throw in with Megrenn?" Tod jested.

Foxblade was head of the Grey Hoods, who ran an unfair share of Kadris's less reputable enterprises.

"Naw. Anything goes, right?" Jodoul asked. "I got an idea." He beckoned for Tod to follow him.

Tod paused for a moment, brow furrowing in thought. "I got a better one."

The two exchanged suspicious glances, daring the other to divulge his idea first.

In the end, neither told his plan, but they went off together preparing for them nonetheless. They were already near enough to markets that Jodoul's side trip was short. He purchased some smoke vials, caltrops, and a small jar of mint jelly.

"All right, you got me," Tod admitted. "I see what ya might want the smokies and caltrops for, if'n you're thinkin' this is gonna be a snatch 'n' run. I'll be sliced six ways if I know what the jelly's for though."

Jodoul had them duck into a side alley where there were fewer eyes about. He drew his dagger and dipped it in the jelly. "Stuff looks like spider venom stuff the Olaks use, if ya spread it on thin. My old man showed me once. To most folk, it'd just seem like jelly, but a smart fella like Foxblade'll know about spider venom." Jodoul dipped his finger in the jelly and put it in his mouth. "Tastes loads better, don't cost hardly nothin', and won't rot yer finger off if'n you nick yourself."

Tod glanced down the alley in both directions, gave a little half smile, and knelt down to pry up a pair of cobblestones from the streets. Keeping his back to the main thoroughfare, he drew his own blade and scratched at the surface of one of the stones, then the other. He then drew a small flask from inside his coat, and upset it over the two stones, washing them clean of dirt with his fingers. There was a strong smell of alcohol.

"Hey now! That's a waste o' good firewine," Jodoul protested.

"Aww, cram it," Tod replied, not looking up from his work. "I'll pinch some more when we get back to the palace, leastwise if'n we live."

Finding Foxblade was not so difficult. He had folk all over Kadris working for him, from the dockside to the markets and back again. It was easier bribing one of his underlings to get a meeting than it was to find out about the goblet in the first place. Tod nabbed a street mouse aged no more than ten winters, and told him he would get dragged to the warlock himself if he did not lead the way to the thief's lair. Folk were scared of the warlock, seeing as he had executed three members of the Inner Circle as traitors and the Inner Circle was a bunch that none wanted to cross. Considering Tod and Jodoul still both wore imperial uniforms, the threat seemed likely enough; the warlock had his hand in far more of the city's affairs than previous rulers had ever seemed to. Reluctantly the boy led them down to the sewer level of the city.

Kadris's sewers were a thoroughfare in their own right. Despite magical wards preserving the buildings, the city was over six thousands summers old, and had been rebuilt in whole or in part a number of times. The ground beneath the great metropolis was not entirely firm, and over time the city slowly sank; it was hundreds of summers before anyone would notice a change, but the city's forefathers had hundreds to spare. As the city was pushed down into the soil, buildings were filled in, streets walled off and turned into new sewers, and new construction would proceed atop. Thus, when Tod and Jodoul walked down what appeared much like the siding of a main road, it most certainly once had been exactly that.

Various groups made their homes in the layers underneath Kadris. The level more immediately below the city's surface was foul, but largely habitable. Its streets were wetted with filth, and runoff from storms, but many buildings of the lower levels had been cleared out and repurposed, sharing the underworld with the cellars of more respectable establishments on the topside, and often having passages leading from the world of merchants to the world of thieves—and only the foolish saw the two as such different creatures. Brothels, gambling dens, smugglers, mercenaries, assassins, and simple thieves shared space below, with room enough that territorial disputes were rare.

The largest hazard faced by the subterranean citizens of Kadris were the wardkeepers. The sewers and sub-structure needed maintenance, and the Imperial Circle sent sorcerers about to make sure nothing got too badly out of shape. Folk who lived below got to learn which wardkeepers would share an ale or friendly conversation and which ones were best not to trifle with. By unspoken agreement, the wardkeepers were off limits to all manner of harassment; the last time one had been so much as wounded in the sewers, a dozen sorcerers and a hundred guardsmen had been dispatched to clear a wide swath of the tunnels of all inhabitants.

They saw no wardkeepers, though, as the young thief led them through the meandering underground city. Folk occasionally passed on one dark errand or another, in both the literal and figurative sense. Torches and lanterns dotted the streets here and there, along with bits of magic for light, but mostly they found their way by vague shadow. Tod was surprised the boy had not tried to bolt and lose himself in the darkness; there would have been little recourse for the two guardsmen if their little guide managed to get more than a pace away and quickly change direction. The stone streets echoed with their footsteps, which would make it nearly impossible to track him by sound. Combined with the darkness, the boy was only a quick twist free of Tod's grip from vanishing on them.

After a time, they came to a building that had once been part of the tournament grounds some several hundred years earlier. While the exploits of knights, archers, and gladiators would have taken place in the open air, all about the grounds themselves were seating for spectators, preparation areas for competitors, armories, storerooms, kitchens, stables, and offices for administrators. Foxblade's Grey Hoods had excavated out most of the old structure for their own use as a headquarters. While the thieves' reputation was dark and sinister, the spot they made for themselves as a home was anything but. Once they were let inside, Tod and Jodoul were met with a comforting amount of light and a strong scent of incense that did a fair job masking the smell of human filth, both from the sewers and from the residents of the Grey Hoods' abode.

The monolithic guards within the main hall took over escort duties from the rather relieved juvenile street-thief. There was a brief mention of a warlock and a message, and two grumbling Grey Hoods took them within Foxblade's sanctum. Mention of the warlock scared folks. No one was sure quite how far he would go to dispatch petty nuisances; the dark parts of the city were quieter than in the days before his coming, taking care to remain out of even his peripheral vision. Tod and Jodoul knew that the mention of who sent them likely saved them a knife in the gut, and they followed Foxblade's lackeys through the complex, grateful for their uniforms that day.

Foxblade's offices had once been the retreat for the royal family when they were in attendance at tournaments. Outdoor competitions were most often held in the warm summer months; such traditions had changed little since the ancient tournament grounds had been the center of Kadrin festivities. Another fact that had changed little over the centuries was that as one grew more powerful and influential, one grew less tolerant of being stranded out in the summer heat. The suite of rooms was lavish, though aged. Hand-painted stonework was chipped and flaking, but still showed splashes of the color and beauty of an older Kadris.

Foxblade himself sat behind a much newer desk of dark, polished oak. He was a pudgy man, with chipmunk cheeks and eyes twisted into a permanently annoyed and suspicious expression. He wore a grey square of cloth tied about his head to obscure his (likely receded) hairline. His fat fingers sported rings of gold and silver, with many colors of jewels among the stones they held. He puffed absently at a pipe made from the twisting horn of a ram. It was hard to picture him as the nimble sell-sword who had earned the nickname "Foxblade."

"Spit it. I don't have all day. What's this about the warlock havin' a message for me?" Foxblade demanded without preamble. If not his body, at least his voice seemed both quick and sharp.

"He sent us here, yeah," Jodoul replied, stalling as his eyes scanned the shelves about the room to see if he could spot the stolen goblet among the myriad gaudy trophies the thieves had stored all around the room.

"You boys gonna try my patience?" Foxblade snarled. "I don't care if you work for the warlock or not. Nobody wastes my time."

"Well, there's two things, ya see," Tod said. "First off is a small matter of a pinched goblet from the palace. He's wantin' that back. Sent us with coin, mind ya, fer yer trouble." Tod was trying very much to sound like the street-savvy urchin he had grown up as. He felt himself almost forcing it, having noticed that hanging about first soldiers and then imperial guardsmen had been elevating his speech a bit.

"You mean to tell me that Rashan Solaran gives a pile of rat scat about a stolen goblet?" Foxblade sounded incredulous.

"A bit, yeah. Not so's as he'd send us down fer it, mind ya, but while we's here, he made a point o' mentionin' it. Naw, real reason we's here is he wants to talk to ya," Tod bluffed, hoping that he did not look as nervous as he felt. He could feel his stomach twisting and the room felt much hotter than when they had arrived just a moment earlier.

"Hah. Warlock wants to see *me*?" Foxblade asked, but looked all around the room where his guards and advisors lurked, eavesdropping openly. "Catch this load o' vomit! Thinks I'm gonna march myself up to the warlock and talk to him. I'd be on the end o' his blade afore—"

"Naw, you don't needs t' go nowheres," Tod interrupted, reaching into a pocket and taking in hand the cobblestone he had scratched false runes upon. He reached up and—

"What're you—" Jodoul began, but Tod warned him away with an gesture.

"Naw, fair's fair an' all. You done the last three and more'n paid back yer debt," Tod said, hoping that Jodoul would take the hint and shut up. Tod finished raising the stone to his forehead and held it there, just between his hairline and eyebrows.

"Greetings, Foxblade," Tod spoke, using his best imitation of Rashan's voice. He had always thought he did it better than Jodoul's impression, which had given him the idea in the first place. He tried hard to keep his expression neutral as he spoke, unlike his more animated natural demeanor.

"What's this now?" Foxblade replied, startled by the sudden introduction of a magically controlled thrall to the conversation, conveying words in the warlock's own voice, it seemed.

"I am Rashan Solaran, Warlock of the Empire, High Sorcerer, and the blood-stained right hand of the emperor." Tod hoped he either remembered that bit all correctly, or at least that Foxblade knew it no better than he. "You are Foxblade, once known as Harton Mrull, leader of the Grey Hoods and orchestrator"—Tod knew the warlock liked using big words like that one—"of more than his share of trouble in Kadris."

"Hey, I am a valuable mover of coin in Kadrin and we're no worse—and a lot better—about it than the noble houses. If you—"

"Enough," Tod interrupted, hoping that he was not pushing his luck beyond reason. If he were to get run through for his ruse, it would not be for lack of gusto. "Spare me your perspecations. It is not the trouble you cause that interests me, but the things that you hear in the perpetration of your dealings. I want to know what happens in Kadris and I want you to find out for me."

"Wait. You're trying to hire me?" Foxblade sounded skeptical.

Jodoul had a hand in his pocket, fiddling with the tiny smoke vial in case things went badly. The opportunity to bluff their way through with a jelly-poisoned blade had wandered off the road a few lies back.

"You misunderstand. I do not intend to pay you; I am recruiting you into the service of the Kadrin Empire." Tod wanted to get around the idea of having to explain why they were now paying coin to the Grey Hoods. Besides, it was much the same argument Rashan had made to him when pressing him into service as a guard at the Tower of Contemplation, though his job involved a modest salary. "Let us just say that while in service to the Empire, certain deeds may go overlooked … certain deeds that I may start becoming disconcerted with should you turn down my offer."

"Umm, what would that involve, exactly?" Foxblade was sweating. He clearly had little desire to work for the warlock, but even less desire to be thought to be working against him. He was happy being entirely ignored by the warlock, the Imperial Circle, and anyone with more blades at their command than he did for that matter.

"Plots, alliances, the movement of aggravated amounts of coin," Tod explained, trying to think what Warlock Rashan might possibly want with a gang of thugs that mostly ran protection shakedowns and petty-theft jobs. "If you know these tunnels, you know that there is one that runs beneath the palace kitchens. You will meet me there personally at midnight on each date that ends in five."

"Well, I guess," Foxblade responded meekly. He was unaccustomed to being confronted. Normally he would have killed a man who spoke to him thus, or at least ordered someone to do so on his behalf. Yet he seemed unwilling to risk harming the warlock's lackeys.

"Oh, and see that these imbeciles are sent back with that goblet. I tend to all details, large and small. Do not become a detail," Tod finished and then took the stone from his forehead. "Sorry," he apologized to Jodoul. "Weren't me sayin' it. He was callin' me one, too, so's it's not like I was havin' a jape at ya."

"If you just hand over that goblet, we'll be on our way, fellows," Jodoul said, taking over the conversation from a relieved Tod.

They left shortly thereafter, goal achieved.

* * * * * * * *

"Excellent work. I am proud of both of you," Rashan complimented them, goblet in hand. "There is a small gathering tomorrow morning just after sunrise. You two shall attend. You have earned it. We will be gathering in the emperor's suites."

Jodoul whistled. "Sounds fancy. We gotta dress up at all?"

"No. Your uniforms will serve," Rashan replied, turning to leave.

"Hey, don't you wanna know how we got the goblet?" Tod asked after him.

"I told you when I gave you the task that I did not care how you went about it. If I now ask of you how, you might think that in the future you will have to answer such questions as well, which I do not want," the warlock replied, pausing just long enough so he could finish before leaving earshot of the two guards.

"Umm, well, just be expecting a visit from the leader of the Grey Hoods night after next at midnight, beneath the palace kitchens. He works for you now as an informant," Tod shouted after Rashan, who did not turn, but closed his eyes, lowered his head, and chuckled beneath his breath.

* * * * * * * *

Tod did not belong in the emperor's chambers. Every scrap of fabric, every little plate, every odd little trinket decorating an alcove was worth more coin than he would ever earn in a lifetime. He sat next to Jodoul on a divan and tried not to touch anything, even trying to keep from putting his full weight on his seat.

Around the room, some of the other guests appeared uneasy as well. A hairy ogre of a man dressed in a peasant's feast-day best stood trying to avoid leaning against the wall he stood next to, the painted image of Emperor Tameron hovering over him disapprovingly. A reedy thin man with a merchant's look to his eyes kept his hands folded in his lap as his eyes bought and sold each item in the room. A stunning young sorceress dressed in black sat perched at the edge of her chair, studiously ignoring the rest of them. The one who seemed most at ease, aside from their host, was the long-haired dandy of a sorcerer—nearly as pretty as his female colleague—who lounged in a high-backed chair with gold arms.

"Welcome, all of you," Rashan greeted the assembly. "Some of you may have some inkling of why I have called you all here, but not all. You should know that you all have one thing in common: you have each passed a test I have set out for you.

"When I returned to Kadrin, I found that it had been left in a shambles. Our armies had grown soft and shrunken to the point where Megrenn now stands at our borders awaiting the spring thaw to attack. The emperor was revealed to be nothing but a puppet of aether, controlled by the Inner Circle and a few key lackeys. The nobles began quarreling as soon as they found out that there was no clear successor to Emperor Dharus and I spend hours a day listening to them petition for bastards, eighth cousins, and outright frauds to ascend the throne. I found the highest positions in the land filled by arrogant, comfortable imbeciles and ruthless, conniving traitors. Against these foes I had little: a few chance companions and my kin. I was entirely certain of neither.

"But this is where you come in, all of you. I have taken your measure and learned you for your strengths and faults. For every one of you, those faults could have cost you your life, had another sort of man come in my stead. You are rule breakers, truth benders, opportunists, and by some measure, traitors yourselves. I not only cast you free of these rules that would threaten your very lives should you come under the power of someone other than myself, I cast you free of all rules entirely.

"You are now my Unfettered. You answer to no law but my orders. The tasks given to you were given with the understanding that I cared not how they were completed. This will be the manner of future assignments as well. If you must steal, cheat, kill ... whatever you need to do, do it. Should you get caught by any Kadrin, demand to see me. I have already alerted all the noble houses and the army that all such requests must be honored. If any besides you Unfettered use this privilege, I will deal with them individually.

"One other thing I ask is this: that nothing be withheld from me. I do not slay underlings for failure, or for bearing ill news, nor do I vent anger against those who disagree with me. I value loyalty and honesty. Deal with your enemies how you like, but deal truly with me and you will never have to fear.

"Does anyone have any questions?" Rashan paused, waiting for his carefully rehearsed speech to sink in.

"So ... you mean, you don't care what we do?" Jodoul asked slowly.

"So long as you do what I tell you, all else does not concern me. Allow me to suggest something. I notice that most of you seem uncomfortable in these lavish accommodations. That is ridiculous. There is no living emperor to offend and I just told you I do not care what you do. Go ahead and break something," Rashan suggested.

No one in the room moved.

Rashan frowned. "Like this, see?" The warlock moved to one of the glass-paneled doors that led out to the wintry cold of the balcony. With one finger, he poked a pane hard enough to break it, shattering both the glass and the eerie silence that fell over the room each time he stopped talking. "Now one of you. I will not force you, but feel free."

The pretty sorceress reached out to a porcelain vase on a small table next to her and gave it a gentle shove. It toppled to the floor and smashed into a thousand pieces, each piece likely still worth more than a gold lion. She winced at the sound, but Rashan clapped.

"Well done. Everyone, this is Celia Mistfield, Fifth Circle. Her task was to prevent Sir Monfred Halleigh from keeping his appointment to present his case for imperial succession. He did not appear at his appointed time for an audience and has not yet petitioned for a new one." Rashan looked around the room expectantly.

The huge man by the painting of Tameron turned and regarded the dead emperor's likeness, then gently lifted it by the bottom of the frame with one finger, loosing it from the cord by which it hung. The man's finger was not enough to balance the portrait and it toppled sideways to smash on one corner against the floor.

"Tameron was the least favorite of the emperors I served and that likeness of him brought me no fond memories," Rashan proclaimed, beaming. He was clearly enjoying the little acts of vandalism he was inspiring. "I present you Sanbin Colvern, a weaponsmith from Raynesdark. His task was to forge a weapon from a dragon's tooth, a feat he has not only achieved, but duplicated. I shall not go into details now, but it is quite a tale in its own right. Now who would be next?"

Jodoul leaned forward to reach an exquisite crystal decanter filled with an amber liquid. He unstoppered it and took a sniff. Nodding in approval, he poured it sloppily across a half dozen small matching crystal goblets until there was none left. Then he took the empty decanter and casually dropped it over his shoulder to smash on the floor as he lifted one of the goblets to his lips.

"Marvelous. Our brandy connoisseur is Jodoul Brect, one of my personal guards in the Tower of Contemplation. He and Tod Hellet ..." Rashan paused for a moment and looked at Tod, who took a moment to pick up on his cue. Tod then snatched up the stopper to the decanter, and pitched it through yet another pane of the glass-paneled door, prompting Rashan to continue his introduction. "He and Tod navigated Kadris's underbelly to find and retrieve an object stolen from the palace."

Not waiting to be prompted, the lounging sorcerer casually tossed a small wire cage containing a beautiful songbird across the room. "Catch," he called out to the thin nervous man who had heretofore avoided contact with anything in the room. Aghast, the man lunged to catch the bird, which was just close enough for him to reach before it crashed to the floor. He caught nothing but air, however, and knocked over a display case of ornamental daggers in the attempt. The bird cage, being nothing but an illusion, disappeared entirely.

"Wonderful. Full credit to our resident illusionist, Faolen Sarmon, Third Circle. Should anyone tell you that the smuggler ship *Song of Night* ran aground due to rough seas or a drunken helmsman, he is lying. As for his cat's-paw in the destruction of that display of daggers, meet Aelon Beff. Aelon also fought at the Battle of Raynesdark as part of the militia. He was a great help in finding a trading company that does business both here and in Megrenn. We had need of such men.

"Other than the items that would be irreplaceable, it would likely cost the Empire thousands of lions to repair the damage we have just done here. I never liked this sitting room, and since my previous tenure, it has only grown a hundred winters uglier in my eyes. Once I leave you, I suggest you acquaint yourselves with one another and feel free to continue ravaging these tasteless furnishings. Before then, though, there are two matters. Firstly, any questions you might have ..." Rashan waited expectantly.

"We passed your tests. Did all? Were there others who failed and if so, what became of them?" Aelon asked.

"Fair questions, both," Rashan replied. "In fact, no. Not all whom I tested were successful. Through no action of mine, two died and the rest returned to whatever duties they held before, with no blight in my eyes."

"Did everyone accept your offer?" Celia wondered.

Rashan smiled. "Nearly all. One suggested I attempt a rather painful anatomical contortion when presented with my offer."

That drew chuckles from everyone.

"And is he still alive, too?" Celia followed up.

"I brought no harm to anyone I tried to recruit. That is one thing you are simply going to have to see for yourself over time. I am not wanton or capricious in how I bring violence, even to those I may dislike. Fail me and I trust that you will learn from your failure. I do not like failings, but I understand how they can be taken to advantage. Killing those who fail or dissent is utter foolishness," Rashan said. It bothered him how history had taken the detailed nuances of his life's work and painted over them with a thick brush, turning him into a caricature. It would take time, he knew, to alter those perceptions.

"Any others, besides us?" Faolen queried, having some inkling as to another who might be kindred to them.

"It would have been more kind to let another puzzle that one out, Faolen, but since you ask: yes. You are all familiar with Sir Brannis Solaran. His is the example you are following. With few allies in the present-day Empire, I turned to Sir Brannis to lead the army. I gave him four sorcerers and a decrepit garrison to defend against a host of goblins that was undercounted by nearly half. I consider the unexpected presence of the dragon and my intervention to roughly cancel one another when deciding how he handled that assignment; and let me assure you that without Sir Brannis, I would very likely not have survived facing that dragon. I have since given him almost entirely free rein within the Empire and I am confident that we are the better for it," Rashan explained, gushing about the leader he had handpicked for his armies. "He is working on something remarkable, he tells me. I look forward to his surprise."

* * * * * * *

Celia strode down a dimly lit stone corridor in the lower levels of the palace. Ahead of her, Brannis strode purposefully along, trailing his cousin Danilaesis in his wake.

He is making this hard on me intentionally! Celia thought. *Danil can manage at a half run and has the energy to keep pace thus. He wants me to give up.*

His sword Avalanche bounced along at his hip, but Brannis wore no armor. Traveling about in the safety of the Imperial Palace, and not on any official business as far as she could gather, he had forgone his golden armor. She had always found him dashing and handsome in that armor, but she found she was enjoying seeing his body less obscured by metal as she trailed behind him, eyes drawn to his backside.

"So it's really done, Uncle Brannis?" Danilaesis asked eagerly, looking up at Brannis from close enough to trip him as they walked. Just seven summers old and the son of Brannis's uncle, Caladris, Danil had apparently been involved in the little side project Brannis had been working on in secret. The boy was too smart for his own good (or anyone else's), and stronger in aether than either Celia or Brannis had realized.

"Yes. You just need to fill it one last time and it should hold aether on its own after that," Brannis answered, then continued just loud enough to be heard: "If I got it right, anyway."

"So what is it that you have been sneaking off to do all season?" Celia demanded from a few paces behind them, struggling to keep up with the rapid pace of a long-legged knight and an energetic young lad while wearing formal robes and heeled slippers.

"Since it is too late for anyone to find out now: making wedding gifts," Brannis replied, not turning back to look.

"You went to all that trouble to hide from me just to make gifts for Iridan and Juliana?" she asked. "Did you think I was going to spoil a surprise or something?"

"No, not really. You barely know Iridan and if either you or Juliana ended up floating facedown in the sewers, I would suspect the other," Brannis replied, stopping in the hall so that she could hear him clearly. "Mostly I wanted a bit of privacy and to prove I could slip free of your leash any time I wished."

"That's not fair, Brannis," Celia shot back, hurt by the implication.

"I know that Rashan assigned you to keep me from causing trouble with the wedding. I had that figured as far back as Raynesdark. You are not bad company when we both manage to forget that, but I have an excellent memory in general," Brannis said.

"Except when you're drunk," Danilaesis piped up, interrupting the grown-ups' conversation. Celia blushed immediately.

"Brannis, what have you been telling him?" she demanded.

"Telling him? Nothing. Danil's the nosiest boy I have ever known and we were at the family's estate that night," Brannis said.

"I cast a quick shield for privacy and everything," Celia protested.

Danilaesis laughed. "That's why I got curious what you were hiding. Brannis's door never has any shields or wards on it. He wouldn't even be able to let himself in." And he laughed anew at his own joke. "Besides, that shield was *so* bad. You must have wanted to keep mice out or something, cuz it wasn't going to stop anything smarter."

"I can only imagine what harm we caused his delicate—"

"Danil, you want to tell Celia here where babies come from?" Brannis asked solemnly, trying to keep a straight face.

"She doesn't know?" Danilaesis sounded puzzled.

"It would seem not."

"Well, you see—"

"No! I know. I know," Celia cut him off quickly.

"It is from Axterion looking after him so much. The old codger is too old to remember what is appropriate for a seven-summer-old to know about, so he tells him everything," Brannis explained. "He is about as innocent as the door guard to a brothel, and it surprises me at times too." Danil just grinned. He liked knowing things he was not supposed to know. "I am sure he will be very popular when he starts at the Academy this autumn."

"Someone else should be looking after the boy, then, I would think," Celia said.

"If you are volunteering, just clear it with the warlock first. I do not know that you can act as nanny for both of us. He wore the nerves of two esteemed governesses to tatters before Axterion took to watching him, so the old man must know a thing or two about how to raise young boys. I would just leave it alone if I were you.

"Now, if we are done with the subject, I have a busy day planned," Brannis finished. He started down the hall again without waiting for Celia to respond.

He always has a busy day planned! she thought. *He wears himself down to the nub every day, with hardly a moment unspent.*

Rashan had commissioned the forge for his own secret project over a hundred winters ago: the forging of Heavens Cry. It was well built and had been easily refurbished for making Brannis's gifts.

Sitting on a stool by the bellows was Sanbin Colvern, whom Celia had recently met, and whom she was not aware Brannis knew at all. He had a black-bladed sword across his knees and was polishing it with a cloth.

"All finished, Marshal. All but the boy's part, anyway," Sanbin said.

The burly smith did not acknowledge Celia at all, which was more than she could say for herself. She had given an audible gasp upon recognizing him. The three visitors gathered around to admire the blade as Sanbin held it up for inspection. It was smooth and razor-edged, with finely carved runes etched into the surface, only visible when the light caught them just so, being black on black. It curved slightly all down its length, a stylistic choice reminiscent of the dragon's fang from which it had been made. It even retained the length it had originally had in the mouth of Nihaxtukali, the mighty dragon they had slain at Raynesdark more than a season ago; it would be a greatsword to Iridan, too long for even Brannis to wield properly with one hand.

Celia leaned in close to examine the runes. "I do not recognize these. I mean, I know the individual runes, but none of the patterns make sense."

"The stone folk showed me. I paid them enough in dragon bones and scales to rebuild five cities. I insisted as part of the bargain that they show me how to work the stuff ourselves, considering how resilient it all is. Try to imagine forging a sword when the ingots are impervious to fire. Well, Sanbin had that very problem given to him by the warlock, and came to me for help," Brannis explained, smiling with pride. "Well, the stone folk use special acids to etch runes into the bone. They create wards to soften the bone to the point where it can be worked with a hammer. After it gets flattened out, they hammer the runes out of it and it hardens again. Once they get that going, they etch the softening runes on one side and the runes they want the finished blade to carry on the other. They then fold the piece, sealing the finished runes inside, before the blade is flattened again and the process is repeated."

"Would that not destroy the runes within, as the material is stretched?" Celia asked, curious and impressed. She had not expected to come down to a forge in her formal attire, having caught Brannis shortly after leaving the meeting of the newly chartered Unfettered, but she was already finding the trip worth the taking.

"They thought of that, of course. Every layer has protections for the runes, so they stay intact as the blade is folded and flattened," Brannis answered.

"And Danilaesis's part in all this?" Celia asked. "More secrecy?"

"Hardly. He has kept the secret well, I will grant, but I needed someone with a strong enough Source to empower the runes—someone not busy about a dozen other tasks. I had tried a few sorcerers I could pry free from Dolvaen's oversight, but none could manage. I went to Axterion to ask advice and he recommended Danil. I had no idea how strong he was already," Brannis said. "He has done a wonderful job."

Danilaesis smiled, looking that peculiar mixture of innocent and smug that only young children can manage.

"How hard can it be? Most sorcerers do a stint as wardkeepers at some point in their career, unless they are well connected. You could have just asked me, you know," Celia said to Brannis. It seemed silly to her that he would involve a seven-summer boy when more competent help was so close at hand.

"Go ahead. Try it," Danilaesis said, grinning at her.

"Oh, no. I could not. You have already worked so hard on it. It would not feel right," Celia demurred.

"Oh, it's all right. I'll still get to do it," he replied sweetly.

Arrogant little imp. I will show him.

Celia took the blade from Sanbin's hands, and focused her aether into it. She felt the flow seeping into the blade, but it slowed the farther into the runes it went. It was like pulling back a bowstring: easy at first, but growing harder rapidly the farther it was drawn. Before long, she gave up and the aether spat harmlessly back out.

"You can try again if you want." Danil smiled, enjoying seeing her fail.

"Just finish it, Danil," Brannis interrupted. "We have a lot to do today and it is not getting done while you and Celia play at this."

He must feel like he is watching two children instead of one, Celia realized. *Why am I competing with a little boy?*

Celia set the blade down on a work table, and Danilaesis laid his hands on it. Celia shifted her vision into the aether to watch. When she did so, she noticed that Danilaesis had a Source stronger than just about anyone she had met. Usually a Source was not fully matured until puberty or thereabouts, so either the boy was well ahead of his peers, or he was destined for great power. Iridan,

Caladris, Dolvaen, Jinzan ... the dragon ... she had seen stronger Sources, but never on one so young.

Danilaesis furrowed his brow in concentration, seeming serious for the first time she had seen all day. Aether flowed into the blade, slowing as it went, but never coming to a stop. After a few moments, the runes sprang to life, glowing blue-white against the black dragon-bone metal.

"That was harder than the daggers," Danilaesis observed sagely, turning to his elders for approval. He turned back to the blade before any of them could say anything, though and picked it up by the handle.

"Danil, be careful!" Brannis shouted.

Whooom. Whooom. The blade cut through the air effortlessly. Brannis, Celia, and Sanbin took cover.

"Uncle Brannis, try to block with your sword," Danilaesis called out.

Brannis kept his head low and did no such thing.

"Danil, put that down right now, before you hurt someone," Brannis ordered. Of all the people in Kadrin who would jump to obey an order from the Grand Marshal of the Imperial Army, Danilaesis was far down the list, in Celia's mind.

"I helped make it. I just want to try it before you give it to Uncle Iridan," Danilaesis said, slamming the blade clean through the work table he had just been using. "Oops."

Danil realized he had overstepped caution by a wide margin. It was all sunshine and roses to say you just wanted to try something, but once you smashed a piece of furniture to pieces, you lost a lot of credibility with the "I have it under control" argument. Danilaesis set the sword down on the floor and stepped back from it.

Brannis took three angry steps across the room and picked up the blade, examining it for damage. It had picked up a bit of grime, but was unharmed. Brannis took a cloth when Sanbin proffered it and began cleaning Iridan's sword.

He has a war to run, and a wedding to prepare for, yet here he sits, cleaning a sword, Celia thought. It was going to be a long day. *Still, it was impressive to see it work.* She could not help noticing the grin on Brannis's face, carefully turned so that Danilaesis could not see. *I bet he wishes he had been the one to try it.*

* * * * * * * *

"Marshal Brannis!" came a shout from across the docks. "Marshal Brannis, I need a word with you." The shouting voice belonged to Dolvaen Lurien, to whom Rashan had ceded the day-to-day operation of the Imperial Circle. Brannis had been waiting half the afternoon and well into the evening for Dolvaen to arrive while he oversaw the final preparations. He had not invited the second-highest-ranked sorcerer in the Empire, but had arranged for matters to require his attention ...

Brannis turned from the plans he was studying, and looked to the self-made sorcerer of no bloodline at all. Nearby, one of the Imperial Navy's ships swarmed with activity. Carpenters, riggers, shipwrights, and sorcerers bustled about anxiously. It was well past the time that they usually broke off from working, and went for their evening meal, but they were so close to completion. None wanted to miss the spectacle that everyone had been picturing since Brannis had recruited them for his plan, so they worked past sundown in the growing cold of night on the waterfront.

Brannis hailed the sorcerer as he drew to a more polite distance that did not require shouting such that the whole Kadris seaport could hear him. "Fair evening, Sorcerer Dolvaen."

"Fair evening, yourself," Dolvaen replied brusquely, a note of annoyance in his tone. "What is the meaning of this? You asked for sorcerers, and I assigned four to help you in your mysterious project. I find that you have eleven working for you now."

"In practical terms yes, but technically, no. You assigned me four, and indeed they have been helping me admirably. But you see ... those four had subordinates, so technically seven of those eleven are merely working for the other four," Brannis reasoned. He had suspected that some of that logic might fail to make a pressing case, but he had been using the subordinate sorcerers for days and had gotten plenty of use from them in the meantime.

"You cannot cut eggs in half with *me* to double them, Sir Brannis. I have fielded complaints of wards in need of repair or aether having gone unanswered for days. You are crippling the wardkeepers, and have one of my best rune-carvers unavailable for lucrative jobs that I cannot just pass off to lesser artisans. This was not meant to be a permanent assignment, nor had I intended that you press more than the four assigned to you into service," Dolvaen spoke quickly, likely having organized the diatribe into a neat little speech on his journey from the tower. He had managed to give Brannis no opening to interject until he was finished.

"You do have a point. My apologies. Perhaps I can send my cousin Danilaesis to help shore up your numbers. I have found him to be quite adept," Brannis told Dolvaen. Then he turned back to the ship, and called up to one of the sorcerers on board: "Krogen, is she ready to test?"

"Aye aye, captain!" the sorcerer responded, making an attempt to sound nautical.

"What have you done to that vessel?" Dolvaen asked. "The rigging is a mess, you have cargo netting everywhere, and I do not even see what you have done with most of the sails. What sort of seafaring monstrosity have you got my wardkeepers working on?"

"Why ... none at all," Brannis replied simply, and waited.

There was a rumbling sound and a creaking of protesting wood. Slowly, the ship rose. Seawater ran off her sides to make a small sloppy rain into Kadris Harbor until even the keel was free of its aquatic medium. All the workers on board rushed to the sides of the ship, looking down at the docks as they ascended. There were hoots and cheers as even sorcerers past fifty summers found childlike glee in the sensation of flying.

"Take it around the harbor once, and set her back down," Brannis ordered Krogen, shouting up at the vessel now well above them, grinning as broadly and as proudly as any aboard.

Brannis and Dolvaen watched as the vessel made a circuit of the airspace around Kadris Harbor, using just one small sail and a magically created wind to power them. Another sail was set fore to aft to act as a rudder. Dolvaen stared in silence.

As the ship settled back down in the water, Brannis leaned close to Dolvaen. "This is how I intend to deal with the Megrenn cavalry and siege weapons."

"I will find as many sorcerers as I can spare and put them at your disposal."

Chapter 7 - Testing Phase

Kyrus watched Gahalu stare down at the chessboard. The dark and light squares were fashioned from the woods of the acacia and ebony trees that grew on Denku Appa. Kyrus had made it with his magic, along with two armies of pieces that had once been tide stones and seashells. Gahalu claimed to have seen chess pieces and heard of the game during his travels, but the sort of folk he had sailed with were not the sort to play the game themselves.

"I take your knight with my knight," Gahalu said, removing one of the stone figures from the board and replacing it with his own knight.

Kyrus made a show of studying the board. He had been teaching Gahalu to play, but mostly it was the conversation, and a bit of a feeling of home that he appreciated. So much of Denku Appa was strange to him that his favorite game was a welcome reminder of the place to which he longed to return. He had been teaching many of the Denku how to play, mostly elders and older children. The hunters respected the spirit man, but found his game too slow, its concepts too abstract. None of the Denku posed any challenge for Kyrus, but he enjoyed the leisurely pace and the chance to see his pupils improve and face off against one another. Kyrus had seen five moves he thought Gahalu might make, and knew what he would do against any of them; he was merely giving Gahalu a break from the task of considering his own moves, and to allow the two of them to talk as he awaited the spirit man's play.

"Toktu seems worried these days. More cares than an elder should have in good times, I think," Kyrus commented. As scattered as his Denku was, Kyrus could tell by the elder's body language that there was something bothering him.

"The tide. He says he wonders now if you are a spirit man or just a spirit. No man can hold back the tide. Maybe a spirit could," Gahalu answered Kyrus's unspoken question.

They both knew it was Kyrus's magic that was the cause of concern. Tricks of fire and levitation were fun for the villagers. Being able to turn wood and stone into trinkets and toys seemed harmless. Stopping a sea storm that should have at least washed into the low-lying parts of the village was different. As benign and benevolent it may have been, it bespoke a power that they had not realized their spirit man possessed. Hadku, the last spirit man, had blessed newborns and painted protective spells on the hunters who went into the jungles; it was nothing that could be seen working. It worked quietly, subtly. It was not the frightening power that Spirit Man Kyrus had shown.

"He has just never heard of a man who could do it before. Now he has. Everything is impossible until someone has done it," Kyrus answered. It was a play on a Kadrin saying: *"Everything is possible, and someone has done it."* It was an easier position to hold in a world with a vast history of magic that spanned back longer than anyone could remember.

"Why did you do it?" Gahalu asked. "To break the saying? To see if you could manage it? The storm was not so bad. No one was in danger if we had just waited inland until it passed. We could have rebuilt anything that was damaged or swept to sea. We have done it before. More were in danger from this storm because they wanted to be close and watch."

"Your hunters hunt the little boars that run around all over the island," Kyrus said by way of reply. "Are they difficult to kill?"

"Young hunters kill them all the time. They are only dangerous if you do not have a spear or do not know how to use it properly. They weigh half what even the youngest hunters do. You could probably kill one with no magic, Spirit Man."

"They taste wonderful, too. There are enough of them that you would hardly need to hunt anything else to feed the village, even if the fishermen's nets came back empty," Kyrus added, and Gahalu nodded his agreement with the sentiment. "So why does Gaktu wear a necklace of panther teeth around his neck? Why does he tell anyone who will listen about the scars on his arm, and how he got them?"

"To prove he is a good hunter. He wants to be first hunter when Fannu becomes an elder," Gahalu said.

"And is he a good hunter? Should he be first hunter after Fannu?" Kyrus pressed.

"I think so," Gahalu said, then nodded after considering for a moment.

"I doubt he learned to be a good hunter by killing little boars," Kyrus said. "He fought panthers and crocodiles and whatever else he could find in the deep jungle. Well I am no hunter, but I will not become a better spirit man by playing with cooking fires and lifting children in the air for their amusement."

Kyrus took his queen and captured the knight Gahalu had just moved. The board was thinning of pieces, since when Gahalu was pressed to make a move, he tried to capture anything he could.

"So ... now you can stop the sea itself. What more do you need to prove?" Gahalu asked. He moved one of his bishops to point at Kyrus's queen.

"No. Try again." Kyrus pushed Gahalu's bishop back where it had come from. "I could have taken it with my queen and you did not have it protected. And it is not a matter of proving. It is a matter of practice and control. I have more I need to learn before I am ready."

Gahalu glared at his reprimanded bishop. "Why are queens so strong in this game? I never heard any stories where a king is so weak and his queen is stronger than all his soldiers."

Kyrus could not help but think about Iridan and Juliana. "Not all kings are mighty warriors, and not all queens are delicate flowers. I admit, though, it is probably less common that way."

Kyrus managed to draw the game out a while longer. Gahalu needed practice more than a thrashing and Kyrus did not want to demoralize his friend. He really wanted to find someone who was a worthwhile opponent, rather than merely a student, but he knew that he would have to be on the island a long time before that would ever come to pass.

* * * * * * *

Kyrus managed to find some time to himself that afternoon. He had learned to keep his clothing from being left behind when he turned himself incorporeal and had slipped through the wall of his house and into the jungle when no one was watching. Eventually they would grow curious and come looking for their spirit man, but for a while Kyrus had bought himself privacy and a bit of safety for any who might have been curious enough to spy on him. What he was dealing with were forces he understood poorly and was still struggling to control.

There was a small stretch of beach well outside the normal Denku wanderings that Kyrus had taken for his practice with the transference spell. It was on a small inlet, too rocky to make a good spot for putting fishing boats into the water. There were little tidal pools all along the water's edge, teeming with tiny sea animals, from barnacles to crabs. The tidal pools had been threatened by the storm's fury as well as the Denku village, but Kyrus's protection had not extended so far from where his hosts made their homes. The aquatic inhabitants had been violently displaced by the strong tides and massive waves, and even days later, things were only beginning to show signs of recovery.

Kyrus had spent part of the previous afternoon practicing a slight variant of the transference spell. He had used it to create tiny spheres only a handspan in width that he could create in one spot and make appear a few feet away. The variant was a bit more complex than the version he intended to use to travel home to Acardia, but far safer to practice, since he was not actually moving his own body when he did it.

Kyrus's next step was one that he considered crucial in his quest. *"Doxlo intuvae menep gahalixviu junumar tequalix ferendak uzganmanni dekdardon vesvata luo."* Kyrus weaved his hands through an intricate set of gestures, envisioning it as a rune he was painting in the air with his fingers. He kept track of each line of the rune as he created it, each finger leaving its own trail of fire in its wake in Kyrus's imagination as he challenged his mind to keep the memory of the rune's path in proper order.

A short way from where Kyrus stood barefoot in the sand, a small scavenger crab walked by, oblivious to the adventure upon which it was about to embark. A shimmering sphere of opaque aether enveloped it without warning, along with a few good handfuls of the sand around it. Kyrus felt the flow of aether quicken as he envisioned a spot a few paces down the beach as the sphere's destination, and then let the spell go. The sphere disappeared, leaving a perfectly smooth scoop taken out of the beach. At the intended destination, nothing.

Kyrus looked about and saw a shadow that did not belong. Ducking and glancing hurriedly upward, he saw the crab and a loose collection of sand plummeting down at him. Fortune smiled on the little scavenger crab as Kyrus managed to quickly catch it with levitation, and set it gently down on the beach near where it had begun its magical journey.

Well, that could have gone worse. Still needs work, though. Kyrus could easily forgive a bit of missed aim on his own journey, especially with his ward to protect him in the event of a fall, but he knew that he needed more practice.

Never did he harass the same creature twice, but Kyrus tried a dozen more times before finally being satisfied that he could reliably send a crab, sand piper, or seagull to whatever location he wanted.

"That was wondrous!" Tippu exclaimed, breaking Kyrus free from his introspection as he considered the results of his final sand piper relocation. "Send me!" The Denku girl was squealing with excitement. Kyrus's lesser magics had become accepted among the island's inhabitants, and even if it was still strange to them, the awe and wonder had lost their edge. This making of things disappear in one place and appear in another was enough to renew the sense that their spirit man was still beyond their understanding.

"What are you doing here? And no, it is too dangerous to send you." Kyrus tried to sound stern, but it was a tone he still thought sounded hollow coming from him.

"The bird is fine. I want to go," Tippu insisted. "Now, before Kahli finds us. I want to go first." Kyrus assumed that the two of them had split up to search for him, but did not want to sidetrack the conversation by asking for details on why the near-inseparable pair had separated.

"You are too big. I need to try more times." Kyrus wished he had a better vocabulary in Denku to better argue his point, but was consigned to battle with the armaments he had and not those he wished for. "I maybe hurt you. No."

"You try again. Make it bigger this time and I watch," Tippu countered, undeterred.

Kyrus was glad that through days of complaining and pleas to have them repeat themselves, both Tippu and Kahli had simplified their choices of words to the selection of Denku that Kyrus had learned. It helped that the two of them had been in no small part responsible for his learning the language.

"Fine. Stay back and do not speak." Kyrus hoped that maybe seeing it a few more times (along with his likely setbacks) might assuage her interest in becoming an experimental passenger on the ill-fated magical ship, *Guess and Try*, that Kyrus was currently captaining.

"Doxlo intuvae menep gahalixviu junumar tequalix ferendak uzganmanni dekdardon vesvata luo." Kyrus sought no passenger, but instead ripped a man-sized scoop of earth from the ground not far from them. Hoping to put a bit of a scare into the girl, Kyrus gave a rather larger share of aether, even beyond what increasing the size of the sphere required. He pictured in his mind not a spot a few paces

distant along the beach, but a spot well out over the water, in front of him such that Tippu's eyes would spot it easily as she watched him and the opaque sphere he created.

Sploosh!

A great mass of sand and the packed earth well beneath it splashed noisily into the Katamic. Kyrus turned to Tippu. "Do you still want to try?"

Tippu frowned at Kyrus. "Try again," she insisted.

Kyrus repeated the spell, but this time there was a great crash in the foliage behind them as Kyrus dumped the sand in the sparse jungle not far from the water's edge.

"Try again," Tippu said, unwilling to give up on her hope of trying the spell voyage herself.

Kyrus began to grow annoyed. *Who does she think she is, anyway? Ordering me around like I am hers to command. She is not my wife, though she wishes she was. She is not an elder. Even Gahalu I would not allow to tell me what is right and wrong to do here on his island.* Kyrus decided to rid himself of Tippu for a while.

It was a small change. There was a part of the gesture for the spell that directed the location of the originating sphere; that was all that was needed. *"Doxlo intuvae menep gahalixviu junumar tequalix ferendak uzganmanni dekdardon vesvata eho."*

Kyrus vanished.

Tippu at first though he was playing a joke on her, but she did not find him and then returned to the village greatly worried. In his place, there had briefly been a giant sphere of seawater, which immediately crashed to the ground, leaving a flooded pit with a handful of colorful (and confused) fish.

* * * * * * *

The world of light disappeared in an instant. Kyrus had seen the world of aether before, but it looked different, cut off not only from his coexistent vision of the light, but also from the shackles of his physical body. His view shifted with the faintest whim, disorienting him without a solid frame of reference to ground his vantage point.

He could make out a rough mass of Sources that he figured were the jungle trees and one human one that was probably Tippu. His own form stood immobile within a cage of aether, a hollowed husk with no Source in it at all. He was cut adrift, Source from body, and was venturing forth without the fleshy home his Source had inhabited since long before he had been aware of it.

Kyrus perceived little motion among the Sources he saw; time was slowed to the point of nearly stopping. He tried to stop and watch some single Source for a time to check his assumption that time was still passing, but his thoughts would not hold still enough for him to make such a painstaking observation. He flitted about like a hummingbird bereft of its innate navigator, his attention drawn to something only to find that he had sped to it as quickly as he could form the thought.

A sudden chilling feeling pervaded Kyrus's discorporate form. His movements began to slow; his vision started to grow hazy. *Aether. I must be using up what I had drawn.* Kyrus called to the aether. It responded sluggishly, like an ocean of honey oozing toward him, grudgingly heeding his summons, where normally it snapped to his call as a gale wind. The syrupy aether invigorated him as he drank it in, more aware of its feel as he had no bodily distractions to dilute the experience.

I cannot stay in this form indefinitely. I need to find a place to reform and emerge into the world. Someplace Tippu will lose sight of me.

Kyrus was a bit uncertain of the geography as related to the aether. It was not the same as seeing the aether overlaid upon the world of light, as he had grown so accustomed to seeing it. The ground was as permeable to aether as was the air, or the sea for that matter. Air would have been fine had he not wished to hide upon his re-emergence, but water suited his purpose better. Kyrus watched until he saw what was either a flock of birds or a school of fish, and settled upon the latter being most likely. He moved to within their midst, and willed the aether sphere and the inert Kyrus within to come to him. Once it had surrounded him, he released the magic.

Kyrus had but a fraction of a second to gulp air as the temporary pocket that came with him from the beach collapsed under the weight of the Katamic. He fought down the panic as the weight of the water crushed in on him suddenly, and was thankful for the protection of his tattooed ward that his ribs were not crushed as well. He was much farther below the water's surface than he had expected.

Though not a strong swimmer, Kyrus was still adept at silent telekinesis magic and he used that to yank himself up to the surface. He gasped for air and saw that he was staring out to sea. From behind him, he heard frantic shouting from the beach.

Wonderful. Kahli found Tippu and they both just noticed me.

Kyrus began a slow, resigned swim to shore.

* * * * * * *

"I hear your training went poorly today," Toktu commented, taking a bite from a spit of boar, and passing it on to the next reveler. It was the evening of the equinox, which was one of the many days the Denku took for feasting. All along the beach, festive fires were lit and the islanders danced, sang, and shared both tales and drink.

"I need more practice. I will do better," Kyrus responded. He sat not far from the elder, who was widowed and had no wives to attend him with the fawning attention Kyrus studiously ignored from Tippu and Kahli.

"I am told that Tippu asked you to use your magic on her," Naknah added. She was another of the elders, as well as Tippu and Kahli's common grandmother. She looked much like Kyrus would have imagined either of them to look had they been left for long years in the sun to dry. She was darker skinned, but it had a greyish cast to it; it did not shine or glisten as Kyrus's companions' did, and her curves had receded to sharp angles covered by sagging skin. Her head she kept clean shaven in perpetual mourning for her long-dead husband. "I thank you for showing wisdom by telling her 'no,'" she said.

"Thank you." Kyrus nudged the inattentive Tippu, who was curled at Kyrus's side, eating a hollowed mango that had recently been filled with liquor. "Do you hear your grandmother? Listen to her when you would not listen to me, next time." Kyrus paused a moment, uncertain whether that came out quite right. The point seemed lost on Tippu anyway, who looked up long enough to nod in the way that children learn when they are required to agree with their elders: insincerely, but with feigned deference.

"How much longer do you think until you are ready?" Gahalu asked.

It was a question that hung in many minds, but the Denku struggled to bring themselves to broach the subject with Kyrus. It seemed such an impolite question from all angles. By asking it, they admitted they were pondering his departure, which made them seem poor hosts. By telling him they wished him to stay, they imposed upon him selfishly. Mostly, it seemed, they just wished that Kyrus would change his mind after a time and decide not to go at all.

"You got your magic to work, at least a little," Gahalu said.

"Not long. I was not ready for a long go (the best word Kyrus could think of for a journey). A little more practice. A plan to find home and I go." Kyrus nodded. "I mean to come back," he stated, "once I find the one I left. I want to bring her here. This is a good place. Good home."

"Did you tell them that?" asked Kappi, another of the elders, nodding toward Tippu and Kahli.

"Each night when I came here, more times than I counted. I stopped. They do not listen," Kyrus explained.

But they were listening. Kyrus had felt them tense when he mentioned the girl he had left back home. Abbiley was a sore subject with them. Kyrus had explained about her when he first arrived—that she was the one he wished to be with and that he longed to go home to see her. They had insisted that he was better off with them, making every effort to supplant this mystery foreigner in Kyrus's heart.

The feast lasted long into the night. The Denku were experts at merriment and hard drinkers for the most part. Kyrus had learned his lesson and managed to drink little, despite vessels of various sweet-smelling drinks being passed to him. His head was clear as he made his way to the secluded stone house that was his home for whatever little time he would remain among the Denku. With his success on the beach, he was confident that his time in paradise was nearly at an end, at least until he could return with Abbiley.

In his footsteps followed a rather less-sober Tippu and Kahli, who leaned on one another for support. He could not follow their slurred, hushed conversation in a language he only somewhat knew, but he could tell they were not happy with him. He ignored them as best he could as he entered the house.

"You cannot leave," Kahli said deliberately, in the manner of a drunk who realized she is drunk and wished to make herself understood to someone less so.

"I told you too many times," Kyrus began, and Tippu put a hand over his mouth.

"She is not finished saying," Tippu stated, nodding to her cousin to continue.

"Ya. No, you cannot leave. I am carrying your baby," Kahli finished, nodding for emphasis and awaiting Kyrus reaction.

Kyrus looked hard at the younger girl. She was perhaps two years his junior, yet seemed such a child at times. She was desperate to keep Kyrus, no matter the cost. He could see the tears welling behind an indignant mask, accusing Kyrus of paternity to leash him to her side. She was hoping, no doubt, to put truth to it before he saw through her ruse, but it was the seeing that was her problem.

"Kahli. You cannot lie to me. My eyes," Kyrus pointed to them, "are spirit man's eyes. I see life. If you had a baby, even a tiny one, growing in you, I would see it."

"No, it is very new and you will—" Kahli began, but Kyrus cut her off with a gesture. It was not a conversation he ever expected or hoped to have. He wished it were Brannis in his place.

How would Brannis handle this? He would never have let it carry on this far. He managed to refuse Juliana in his bed and send her back to her own and he loves her more than anyone. I let two girls who were little more than strangers to me share my bed and constantly scheme to seduce me. Brannis would either have sent them away immediately or shared an evening or two with them and let some other lucky girls have their chance, I would wager. He would be envied by the hunters and the other Denku men and gossiped over by half the women, but he would never have let himself become the pet of two little wisps of girls who act like spoiled children.

Kyrus had paused long enough that Kahli was about to begin speaking again. "Go," he finally spoke and pointed out the door of his house. His tone left no ambiguity about his meaning. Tippu, crouched down next to Kyrus, tried to curl up to him to avoid being lumped together with Kahli, but it was for naught. "You, too. Go."

As the two sullen girls departed his house with tears in their eyes, Kyrus knew he had finally done the right thing with them. He cast a shielding spell over the open doorway, and threw his sleeping mat up onto the bed where it belonged.

Kyrus knew that the old familiar method of Acardian sleeping would avail him little; it was to be an awkward night's sleep. Being in the right would not assuage his conscience from the hurt he had given Tippu and Kahli; it was his own fault for allowing them to become so attached. He also knew that it was the first day of springtime in Kadrin and Brannis was set to have a lousy day as well.

Chapter 8 - Pursuits

The reflection stared back at Soria from a handspan away, upper lip curled back, examining her teeth. They stood straight as pickets, evenly spaced, ideally proportioned to her face. As she watched, they gradually turned just the slightest shade whiter, undoing the damage of a few weeks' neglect. With a finger, she pulled at the corners of her mouth to see the more reclusive teeth in back and below, touching them up just a tinge as she went.

That artist girl has peasant teeth. Mine would never have looked like that even if I had no magic to fix them.

Soria had taken up the rather Kadrin habit of "guiding" her appearance through the subtle use of magic ever since Juliana had learned the tricks of it at the Academy as a young girl. Unlike Juliana, Soria had no mother to shepherd her as she practiced, nor to keep her pretty as a babe before she was old enough to manage it on her own.

Soria's mother had been a priestess of Tansha the Merciful One, traveling the world with Soria's father to spread the joys of the goddess's blessings. Their untimely deaths in Khesh had landed Soria in the care of the Tezuan Sun, an ascetic order that raised orphans and trained them to carry on in their traditions. Soria could neither picture her parents nor remember their names. The ascetics at the temple knew only her parents' business in Khesh. Of her origins, all she had was the tale of their deaths: murdered, robbed, stripped of any trinket or document that might have given clues to trace them to their homeland. Her parents' killers were ruthless and cold-blooded, but not monstrous. Their greed demanded nothing that involved the killing of a child not yet four years old.

Taken in by responsible but dispassionate folk in the ascetics of the Tezuan Sun, Soria had disconnected herself from the waking world. She sleepwalked through her days to play as a princess in the magical world of Kadrin in her dreams. She had taken Ophelia Archon to be her mother, much more real in her dreams than her own mother had become in her childlike memories, which had faded past hazy to become only memories of memories. Soria had loved it when Juliana had her hair colored fanciful pinks and violets as a young girl, and was saddened each morning when she awoke to find her own mundane looks staring back at her from the washing pool.

Soria worked her lips about to limber them again after the stretching she had given them, then wiped her wet finger on her tunic. She leaned in close to the aether-formed mirror she had fashioned and gave a big, toothy smile. *Perfect*, she thought, but had little enthusiasm behind that thought. It felt unnatural—not the magical enhancement but the smile itself. Soria's smile was impish, sly, even wicked at times, but never like the goofy, vapid look she had just seen. Pretty though it might have been, she could not get her eyes to bolster it properly; it was a smile for show and she knew it. It was the sort of smile Juliana would be needing shortly ...

Soria shook her head to clear that image from her mind. The less she thought of her wedding in Kadrin, the better off she would be.

Her preening was no reflection upon the other world at all; she wanted to look her best when she finally tracked down Brannis (or Kyrus, or whatever name he wished to use in her world). She had met his counterpart's paramour, and knew whom she was liable to be compared with. Soria scrunched up her face and gave a disgusted huff.

Stepping back from the aether mirror for a moment, Soria pulled her tunic off and threw it carelessly on the bed. The captain's cabin was modest, but it was the best that the *Yorgen's Bluff* had to offer and Soria's troupe had paid more than sufficiently to commandeer it for their voyage to Marker's Point, as well as a room for Zell, Tanner, and Rakashi to share. Soria wanted her privacy and there were occasions when her contentious friends knew she would not be argued with; sleeping three to a cabin was preferable to a bloodied nose or broken arm.

Using a bit of well-practiced telekinesis, Soria reached under the overlapping layers of her tailored leather armor and undid the clasps. It was made so that there was no way for a weapon to reach any buckle or binding. All those were tucked safely underneath. With the armor loose about her, she pulled it over her head much the same way she had done with her tunic, though more carefully, mindful of the metal edges of the neck guard. With the sweat-dampened inner lining away from her skin, there was a pleasant and refreshing chill to the air. She removed the leather leggings as well and then walked barefoot back to the mirror.

She knew she looked much less like Juliana when comparing more than just faces. Though the same height and general build, the two bodies had been treated far differently in their young lives. Juliana was thin, pale, and looked like her arms and legs were brittle as wicker. Soria had the body of an acrobat, with each muscle carefully carved upon her skin and no bit of wasted flesh anywhere. She was also darker skinned, not from any quirk of birth, but from being far less sheltered from sunny days and outdoor labors—in fact, the only reason she had bothered wearing her armor at all was that, by the captain's request, she had tried to stop being a distraction to the crew.

She wore nothing but underbreeches and a cloth wrap that encircled her chest. The latter was a quintessentially Kheshi garment, considered suitable for public wearing in the warmer climes. Kheshi women were far less sheltered from day labor than the comparatively pampered ladies in the northlands. While the well-to-do might flaunt their curves and act as living decorations for their menfolk, more active women found them burdensome, and ascetic warrior women more so than most. Easily thrice her body length, the cloth bound up her womanly assets and kept them out of her way when fighting. Ever since her first flowering and the accompanying changes that went with it, Soria had quietly been grateful to have been sparingly endowed. She saw the contortions that some of the more buxom sisters went through to keep their bosoms from interfering with their movements—thicker, wider wraps than hers, bound so tightly it was painful just to look at.

Reluctantly Soria untied the wrap where the two ends met and began unwinding it. She felt self-conscious, despite her assurance that she was alone, as well as silly, vain, and … inadequate. As she surveyed her reflection, she could not help but compare herself to Kyrus's woman. *Peasant teeth, but udders a cow might envy*, she thought bitterly, turning sideways and pushing her breasts up to try to envision them larger. *Is that what Brannis really likes? Celia's are bigger too. I mean, he never mentioned it, but we were so young back then.*

Juliana had done a little here and there to get hers to fill out a dress a bit better; "silly" and "vain" were concepts that fit well with her life. Soria had always lived more practically. She had always seen attracting men as a means to an end—and not the one the men hoped for—but had gotten by on charm and attitude. She could be as forward as a tax collector, and few men could defend themselves against such brash advances. But her ends were information, access to valuable objects … or murder. Brannis's twin she wanted to keep, and that meant more than just befuddling that dumb part of the male mind that hid behind a codpiece for long enough to get what she wanted.

With another sigh, she let her little companions flop the short distance back to where they belonged. *I will worry about that later. I can judge Brannis's reaction before I go messing about, changing how my armor fits*, she reasoned. *Maybe once we are rich enough to retire like royalty, I won't mind so much. If his twin is as good a sorcerer as he is not, we ought to be able to conquer ourselves a nice little corner of the world for our very own.*

Retrieving a clean wrap from among her belongings, Soria recomposed herself for venturing out on deck.

* * * * * * *

It was evening by the time Soria met Zell and Rakashi at the bow of the ship. Tanner had been recruited for a Crackle game in the crew quarters, but the sailors were wary of the huge mercenary and the Takalish who wore war-braids and a half-spear. The two of them were passing a bottle of brandy back and forth, taking swigs as if it were cheap wine as they conversed.

"We'll make the Point tomorrow, maybe midday," Zell said. "Captain doesn't think we'll have any trouble with the weather."

"No. I would think not," Rakashi replied thoughtfully. "The clouds in front of us look placid."

Indeed, the reddish-grey wisps in the sky looked far from threatening in the direction they traveled, south and east. The sun hung low in the sky to the starboard side of the ship, and a second sun danced beneath it, reflected in the water of the swelling sea.

"Evening, boys," Soria called out as she approached, swaggering across the deck. She was wearing her tunic thrown loosely over her wrapped chest—a compromise between modesty and a desire to let her sweaty armor air out before putting it back on in the morning.

"Done teasing the crew, are you?" Zell chided her, knowing that she cared little whether men eyed her, so long as they kept to just that.

Despite her scant attire, the sailors aboard the *Yorgen's Bluff* had initially been wary of her "bodyguards" when she came aboard. When it became apparent that none of them were either her lover or particularly watchful of her, they had grown bolder. Rakashi had to take a few aside quietly and warn them—not of anything he would do, but rather that none of her three companions would protect them from her should she take offense.

"I like having a cabin of my own, but I need the air," she replied, settling in next to them, leaning against the ship's railing.

"Well, it's gonna be a cool night if you're planning on being out here a while, 'specially with just that flimsy thing to cover you. Care to knock a swallow off the top, to keep the chill away?" Zell handed her the bottle.

The label was Takalish, but nothing they had brought aboard with them. She could barely read any Takalish, but it seemed to claim it was from Khetlu. Whether that was a distillery or a town, she knew not, but she had never heard of it. She took a sniff.

"No, not tonight," she stated, pushing it back into the big man's hands. "Stuff's strong enough, for sure. Few turns at the neck of that and I'd have no trouble sleeping tonight."

"Big day tomorrow," Zell said in a transparent effort to sound positive.

He knew as well as anyone that she was not eager for Juliana's wedding. Because he was captain of the House Archon guards, Juliana had appointed him as her oath guardian without anyone thinking much of it. For the past week, leading up to the wedding itself, they had been nearly inseparable. It was his job to make sure nothing untoward happened to Juliana before she was married. Like the position of oathkeeper, the job was largely ceremonial, but in Zellisan's case, he was chosen so that Juliana could have someone to complain to about it in two worlds.

"I have no intention of falling asleep tonight," Soria said. "She's on her own this time."

Soria felt petty and a bit guilty about leaving her twin—her other self—alone at such a time, but bearing witness was nothing she wanted a part of. She would have memories of it afterward as if she had been there, so all she would really miss would be the visceral feeling of being locked up in a marriage she had not wanted. *Oh, and I will get to miss the wedding night as well. No great loss there.* Juliana had taken Iridan into her bed a handful of times, first when drunk, then with a vague intention of whipping him into some semblance of a man before she married him.

"Long night, then. Want me to wait up with you?" Zell sounded uncharacteristically sympathetic.

He was not half the grizzled warmonger he presented himself as. He kept up a good ruse, but they had known each other too long for such a facade to hold up against real emotion. He was the first to have discovered Juliana's gift for seeing into the other world, a common guard in House Archon's service who inquired about the strange, troubling dreams that woke his six-summer-old charge crying in the middle of the night. He had taken the fragmented story and his own knowledge of the other world and taught the young Juliana how being twinborn worked. Eventually, when she was old enough to be on her own, he sought Soria out in person.

"No, I know you are looking forward to the whole loud, shiny, flowery mess. Go ahead and get to it. Get an early start," Soria told him. She came close to telling him to reacquaint himself with Brannis, but she wanted to keep their quarry's identity a surprise. For all the rest of them knew, Kyrus Hinterdale was just another potential recruit, albeit one with exceptional promise, if he was the sorcerer he was rumored to be.

"Fine by me, then. Just don't get too down, you hear me? It'll work out okay." Zell gave Soria a perfunctory hug, and lumbered off to the cabin he shared with Tanner and Rakashi.

"I will keep you company if you like," Rakashi spoke quietly, as if hesitant to interrupt her thoughts.

She found him so unlike the other two. When forced to share accommodations, he was the one she bunked with. He had taken a wanderer's oath, which both freed him and bound him. While away from Takalia, he would father no children, nor would he spill the blood of his own people. By swearing the oath, he was free to pursue his travels free from the other moral restraints of Takalish life. He was free to flaunt the laws of other nations—at his own peril of course—and bring no dishonor on himself. Soria found it a strange custom, but it was for that reason that she trusted him to tend her wounds and knead sore muscles loose without fear of him taking advantage.

"If you drank half what was missing from that bottle, I don't know that you have much say in the matter," she joked.

"I did not."

Even with Zell, whom she had known most of her life, she tried to maintain her air of toughness. Somehow she did not mind so much if Rakashi saw her cry.

* * * * * * *

The crowd gasped as a gout of flame billowed from the magician's fingers. He was an older gentleman, distinguished and genteel in manner, with the boyish looks accentuated by grey hair rather than given lie to by it. That grey hair hung loose about the magician's shoulders and snapped smartly to a point at his bearded chin. He wore a black dress coat that would not have looked out of place if worn by a magistrate and he covered his hands with white gloves. A flat-topped silk hat sat not upon his head, but rather waved about in one hand while the other gesticulated with a pointed stick.

"Now, before I move on to my next trick, I would like to demonstrate that this hat is empty."

The magician, known professionally as Wendell the Wizard, held the open end of the hat out toward the audience that gathered all about him a few paces away. He had commandeered a sizable chunk of plaza space in Marker's Point and people were packed in and around the merchants' stalls to get a better view of him.

A few hecklers in the crowd complained that they would not be able to see if there was anything shady with the hat.

"Suit yourselves," Wendell said, "but toss it back when you are satisfied. I have nothing to fear from its close examination."

With that, Wendell threw the hat into the crowd. It was grabbed and rumpled and generally mistreated as a dozen denizens of the rough port city gave it a thorough once-over. Amazingly the hat was returned in serviceable condition.

"Now, if you will all stand back and prepare yourself for a sight that will shock and amaze you …

"*Huaxti janidu deldore wanetexu elu mulaftu sekedori puc'anzu margek lotok junubi,*" Wendell chanted ominously, slowly waving his wand about in the air, tracing supposedly mystical patterns in the air with it. At the end, he tapped the wand twice on the brim of the upturned hat. Tucking the wand inside a coat pocket, he reached one gloved hand into the hat and drew out a dove, displaying it to the crowd in the palm of his hand with a flourish of his hat. The tiny little creature shook its feathers and beat its wings a few times, then flew off.

The crowd hooted and cheered. Wendell the Wizard smile and bowed a little, turned to a different section of the crowd and bowed again. Then a curious look passed over his face. His hat jerked about in his hand, seemingly of its own accord. The magician stopped his bowing and investigated, looking down into the hat as if it were a good deal deeper than it appeared. Reaching into it again, he drew out another dove, releasing it into the air with a disgusted harrumph. After a brief pause, the hat moved about a bit again, and Wendell withdrew another dove, then another, then another. Soon doves were streaming out of the hat, to the delight of the crowd.

Several of the doves, not content to fly off, returned to attack their former captor. They flapped about as Wendell dropped his hat and devoted his efforts to swatting them away. The crowd roared with laughter. Soon Wendell switched to snatching the birds out of the air and hurling them away from him. First one bird, then another … but they would just circle back around to attack him again. The crowd soon realized that the hurled and returning birds were making a circular circuit of the air just over their heads, returning at regular intervals and evenly spaced out—Wendell the Wizard was juggling birds!

As his grand finale, Wendell quickly snatched up his hat from where it had fallen and started catching the birds with it. Once he had recaptured all the juggled birds, he put two gloved fingers to his lips and whistled.

"All right, boys, get back in. That is all for tonight's show."

And with that, all the birds that had flown away and not stayed to be juggled returned in a storm of feathers, diving headlong straight into the hat. The crowd cheered and applauded.

"Thank you. Thank you, all." Wendell handed the hat to someone in the first row of bystanders. "If any of you cares to look for those birds, toss in a coin. If you find one, you can keep all the other coins you find."

* * * * * * *

The Wendell Dumark who departed the plaza was better financed than the one who had entered it. With men knowing his name, and with a bit of coin in his pocket, he was able to make friendly inquiries about the whereabouts of one Captain Denrik Zayne, noted patron of the mystical arts, if Acardian authorities were to be trusted on the matter.

Wendell was interested in meeting the infamous pirate, but he was more interested in meeting the Acardian witch he kept company with. There was more to that story than folk were letting on, Wendell was convinced, and he knew that he wanted to be the one to assemble the puzzle and see what it was before anyone else. There was profit to be had in such knowledge—in coin perhaps, but in other, more valuable currency for certain.

The *Fair Trader* had sailed for the east by all accounts. It was a chance meeting with an elderly former crewman of Captain Zayne's who had given the key bit of information, though: Zayne had a particular fondness for a little island known as Denku Appa that lay along that course.

It took all the money Wendell had earned in the plaza, and most of his savings, but he managed to convince a ship to take him to Denku Appa as a stop well out of their way to Khesh.

Wendell did not know that the maneuver put him a day's pursuit ahead of Soria and her companions, looking for the same man.

Chapter 9 - Staffing Issues

Jinzan fidgeted in his seat, an endeavor he was little familiar with. He was seated at the hexagonal stone table of the Megrenn High Council, listening as each of his fellow Councilors gave their report on the state of their preparations on the eve of the invasion of Kadrin. He was not looking forward to the prospect of his own. While there was no petitioner to the Council, leaving the sixth side of the table vacant, the five High Councilors were far from alone. Desks and tables ringed the walls of the room, where assorted functionaries listened and recorded. Even casual comments made in the Council chamber were recorded for posterity and more than a few in the room had little purpose there but to write the land's history as it occurred. Others there ensured that orders were carried out with all practical haste. Troop deployments could be relayed by lieutenants who waited near the chamber's doors. Requests for information were often returned by the end of longer meetings. Rumors could be spread throughout the city before the Councilors adjourned for their midday meal—whether they intended such rumors to be spread or not.

Council meetings were thus half rulership, half theater. Had Jinzan been alone among his old friends, he could have borne their censure quietly and deservedly. It was an embarrassment lying in wait for him, though, with the crowded Council chamber. His only hope to avert a public loss of face was that the situation resolved itself before it was his turn to present the readiness of the kingdom's sorcerers for the war.

"The blockade will be in place by the morrow. Any ships that wish to reach Kadris are going to have to venture a long way out of their course to bypass our ships," Varduk Steelraven reported. Twenty years earlier, he had become de facto admiral of the rebellion's navy. When none of the Megrenn back then knew anything of ships but fishing and trade, Varduk had pieced together a functioning navy out of trade ships and secondhand castoffs from other kingdoms' fleets. Ever since, he had overseen both Megrenn's sea trading and their navy, though he left the actual sailing to much younger men.

"It will not do much, but it is prudent, I suppose. We will need the blockade much closer to Kadris before they feel any real pain from it," said General Kaynnyn Bal-Tagga, the Megrenn Minister of War. Once the face of the rebellion, she had been a ferocious beauty who commanded the stripe-cat cavalry that had done so much to help free Megrenn. Reckless and wild, she inspired both the men and women of the rebellion and most of the men were willing to die for the chance to bed her. Her close-cropped hair was white now, still teased with ointments into a forest of short spikes like she had worn in her youth, and it stood out starkly against her deep brown skin. Her once muscular body had grown thick and soft, covered in a layer of flab that she attributed to the prosperity that had come following the rebellion. The breasts that once numbed the reason of her troops had grown huge and sagging, having nursed six children of her own and a dozen fosterling orphans in the early years after the war. She adorned herself in gold and silks instead of armor, but her spirit was as fierce as the day she first charged headlong into the Kadrin garrison as they drilled in the practice yard—the first strike of the war. If any were to embody the rebellion in the hearts of Megrenn, it was Kaynnyn "Bloodstorm" Bal-Tagga.

"In time. The war will not be quick and we must have the long view of it," Varduk replied. "We start with the periphery, just as you plan for the land war. Ultimately we will have to lay siege to Kadris, but that day is a long way off. Their strength is concentrated there, and we will not dislodge it by direct action. We must whittle away at their borders and draw their strength out to us. They have more troops than us—more sorcerers, too—but they have far more land to defend with them. We just need to track their movements, and wait for the opportune time to pick them apart."

"Speaking of troop deployments, Narsey, how are the Kadrin forces looking?" General Kaynnyn asked.

"They are scrambling to prepare for our attack. It looks as if they are prepared to concede border territory," Narsicann Tenrok answered. The only other sorcerer besides Jinzan to sit among the High Council, Narsicann oversaw Megrenn's web of spies and informants. Less gifted in open warfare than was Jinzan, Narsicann concentrated more on defending Megrenn from magic than inflicting his own on others. While Jinzan had been trained among the Kadrins after they decided—foolishly—that Megrenn was integrated sufficiently into the Empire, Narsicann kept his magic secret from their occupiers his whole life. "They have already evacuated many of the less defended towns, leaving token forces that I expect will flee as we approach. I think we shall find the resistance much heavier once we get farther inside their borders. Munne, Garsley, Pevett, Reaver's Crossing ... all seem to be receiving reinforcements."

"What news from Kadris?" asked Feron Dar-Jak, Megrenn's Interior Minister and the only member of the High Council who was not one of the Liberators. He had taken over for the great General Ashton Sweely, who had been an old man when the rebellion started and who had served Megrenn well into early senility before retiring to spend his last few years at leisure with his great-grandchildren. Feron had fought in the rebellion as well, but he had earned his position largely based on his valuable service under Sweely in the Interior Ministry.

"Not much of import. We have lost three sneaks and four informants trying to gain access to substantive information on their military plans. That demon is too quick to kill anything that smells wrong to him. I would bet good coin he kills three by mistake for every one of ours he gets," Narsicann said. "We know that they are having a major wedding planned for the first of spring—the demon's avowed son and some Archon heiress."

"As always, pomp and self-congratulation comes before practical matters." Jinzan could not help chiming in. He had intended to keep quiet until his turn to report on the state of the sorcerers and his cannons. *Why can I not just let such matters lie? Stupid. Stupid!*

"To our advantage," Varduk observed, drawing nods from Narsicann and Kaynnyn.

"For that day at least, we ought to know the whereabouts of the demon and many of the Inner Circle," Feron observed. "Would that not be the best day to make our first real strike?"

"The frosts have not broken yet over much of Kadrin. Their lingering winter is saving them from our stripe-cats for another tenday. I have monohorns ready to assault Temble Hill on the first of springtime—which is tomorrow I must remind you, Feron," Kaynnyn said curtly. She never respected Feron's position on the Council, though she knew it was inevitable that the Liberators would someday need successors. She just did not like the fact and resented him meddling in her planning.

"Perhaps Jinzan can duplicate his little transference trick and take some remote city himself? With the demon preoccupied, it seems almost a shame to let the opportunity pass. After all, what better use to test out the Staff of Gehlen?" Feron suggested.

"Are you mad?" Narsicann broke in.

Good. He can save me from having to say much the same and sound like a coward, Jinzan thought.

"After all that Jinzan went through to secure it?" Narsicann said. "It is the key to our defenses against Kadrin's sorcerers. Wherever the wielder of that staff is, we will have an advantage against any opponent. We cannot risk losing it with something so chancy as a transference spell."

Not what I had in mind, Narsey. Your concern for my safety is touching as well.

"All right, all right," Feron said. "No need to flay me in the Council chambers over it. Consider my suggestion withdrawn. Anyway, it is about time we heard from Jinzan about the sorcerers' readiness. Is everything in order for the invasion to begin?" Feron inquired, giving Jinzan a simpering smile in the hope that he had given him something to brag about and ease the tension he had caused.

"Well ..." Jinzan paused and drew a deep breath. "Not quite ..."

* * * * * * * *

Elsewhere in Zorren ...

Small hands fumbled with the latch of a stable door. One hand simply was not enough, at least not for a boy of ten springtimes. Anzik tucked the Staff of Gehlen awkwardly under one arm and used both hands to spring the door open. It was a task that could easily have been accomplished with magic, but Anzik had not thought of that. His first instinct was to open the door using his hands and that thought stayed lodged in his mind until he was finished with it.

They will look for me. I took Father's staff. My staff now. They will look for me. Hide. Need to hide.

It was hard to concentrate. Anzik had to keep reminding himself where he was, what he was doing. The voices were badgering him again. He knew that if he concentrated on the task at hand, he could wait them out and they would stop for a while.

The door creaked only a little as Anzik pushed his way through, not daring to open it wide and draw attention. *Be quiet. Horses make noise. Quieter than a horse and they will not hear me. If they do not hear me, they cannot find me. Quieter than a horse. Quieter than a horse …*

Anzik settled himself in an empty stall in the back, paying scant attention to the horses that occupied the half-full stable. He could see in the aether, looking through the walls, that the stable boy was just outside. It was an enclosed stable, well vented but with full walls on all sides. It seemed like a good place to hide.

Anzik had been hiding for days, moving from one place to another. He knew that he had stolen his father's staff. He knew that meant he would get in trouble when he was found. *I just need to hide long enough to grow up. Everyone says I will be more powerful than Father when I grow up.*

"Stop it! I'm not hungry!" Anzik clutched his ears, trying to block out the voices, but it was in vain. "I just ate. I took pies from the market." He could not reason with the voices. The voices told him to eat. They told him to open his mouth, to just try a little. Sometimes the voices blathered on about nonsense, which was easy to block out. When they got insistent, sometimes he had to just give in to make them go away.

Anzik opened his mouth, keeping his eyes clamped shut and hands pressed over his ears. He felt something warm and mushy in his mouth, and then felt a spoon. He closed his mouth and felt the spoon pull out. The mush was not unpleasant, tasting of potato and carrot, and Anzik swallowed it. He opened his mouth again and another spoonful followed the first. He knew from having lost the battle with the voices that once was never enough. When it finally stopped, the voices went quiet.

Anzik opened his eyes and fell back into a pile of hay. His mind was quiet. He was sweating, breathing quickly, but he felt free. After a few moments to compose himself, he took stock of his surroundings with a clearer head. He had wandered into one of the wealthier parts of Zorren, where someone had money and land enough to have their own stable within the city. Zorren sprawled with bustling markets filled with people and warehouses stacked with trade goods, intermixed with tiny orchards, walled estates, and public parks. There were hardly any people about where Anzik had stashed himself. There was a stable-boy, a groom, and a half dozen horses—though those probably did not count as people.

Anzik was exhausted. His newfound freedom had made him bold, and he had fought against the voices longer than usual, but had not prevailed. Most often, he would block them out, losing himself in whatever task he could find, then placate them quickly when they became too intrusive.

I bested Father. I will best the voices, too. Maybe tomorrow.

Anzik wanted to sleep. It was only midday, but both his mind and body felt used up. Running away was hard work.

I should disguise myself, in case they look in here while I sleep. I cannot let them see me here. Something innocuous … Maybe just make the hay pile look a bit larger than it had been.

It was easier to think when the only thoughts in his head were his own. Even at home, it seemed rare to have a truly quiet moment, with so many other people around.

Anzik needed no gestures or words for his magic. He had been seeing how his father and the other sorcerers did it since he was a babe. He could get the aether to respond much more easily than they. Mimicking what the aether did when they commanded it was, for Anzik, child's play.

He began to draw in a bit of aether for a simple illusion. Few in Megrenn were well versed in the art, but after Anzik had seen it, it had become one of his favorites to practice, causing no end of strife in the Fehr household. He wanted to ensure that the spell would last the length of his nap at least, so he drew in a bit more aether than he normally would have for a simple prank.

The Staff of Gehlen threw things amiss. Still barely having tested the artifact's power, Anzik unintentionally called on the staff's draw to augment his own. Amplified many times over, the aether was sucked toward the staff like the funnel of a cyclone. Anzik's persistent aether-vision saw a vortex forming around him as his draw sped beyond his control. Horses whinnied in terror, feeling their very life forces being wrenched at and the nearest one to Anzik's stall fell over dead before he could stop drawing in aether.

Anzik felt the roiling power thrashing about within his Source. It was the most he had ever held at once, but it was not foremost on his mind.

I broke the horse. I scared the horses. The horses made noise. They must have heard. They will come to look. They will find me. I need to hide. No. I need to fix the horse. How? Is it really dead? I pulled out its aether; maybe I can just put it back.

Anzik's vision was keen enough that he could make out the hollowed remains of the horse's Source. Carefully, he directed much of the aether back where it had come from, filling the Source like a vintner filled bottles. The Source did not look quite healthy when he finished, but the horse obeyed his silent command to get to its feet.

Somehow the other horses could sense something wrong with their comrade. The one in the next stall, bearing a placard that identified it as "Snowflake," began to panic and try to break free of her confinement.

No! Stop that! They will come look!

Anzik panicked. It was no good fixing one horse if the rest were going to give him away. He looked around at the contagious fear among the residents of the stable, and then back to the horse he had just "fixed." Thinking quickly, he pointed the staff at the panicked horse and deliberately drew its Source dry of aether. The creature fell limply to the ground, its muscles flaccid and unresisting.

That set off a general panic among the rest of the horses, beasts intelligent enough to realize there was something horrifically wrong. Anzik silenced the rest of them as well, and his head swam as the vast wave of aether crashed down over his senses. He stumbled to the nearest empty-Sourced horse and refilled it, easing the pain of too much stored aether. Each horse he fixed made him feel a bit better, both in eased pain and eased worry.

With the ruckus he had caused, it was too much for Anzik to have hoped that he had not drawn attention. Behind him, he saw a small human Source approaching the stable: the stable boy.

"Hey now. What's wrong in there?" the lad called out as he approached. "Skunk got inside with ya or somethin'?"

The horses were all quiet and gathering themselves up on their feet again, but the boy had heard too much already. Anzik's eyes turned toward the stable door, waiting for the boy's image in the aether to merge with the light, to see him as a person rather than just a Source.

He was a boy about Anzik's own age, perhaps a summer or two older, but bigger and with the healthy look of a lad raised in fresh air.

"Hey! What are you doing in here, scaring my horses?" the boy demanded.

I am sorry. I will go. Please do not tell anyone I was here. Anzik meant to say it aloud, but the words only echoed in his own head. His tongue felt like a sack of flour in his mouth, limp and heavy.

"I asked you a question, kid. What you doin' in here with my horses?" the stable boy persisted, approaching threateningly.

Anzik held the Staff of Gehlen clutched close to his body, but it did not seem like much of a weapon in Anzik's hands, scrawny as he was.

Nothing! I did not kill them! They are fine, see? Anzik's eyes widened as the stable boy was not accepting either his apology or his excuses. He took a step backward. *Please leave me alone. Please!*

"Fine, then. Looks like I get to pound ya."

They were the stable boy's last words. When Anzik fled the stable, he left his would-be assailant standing mutely, staring at one of the horses, slowly leaking unhealthy aether.

* * * * * * * *

"Curse you, Jinzan!" Narsicann scolded, a rarity in open Council. "You should have told us as soon as it went missing."

"I had hoped that I would be able to retrieve it discreetly before it became an issue requiring the Council's attention," Jinzan responded defensively.

"How long has the boy been gone?" Kaynnyn asked, sounding concerned. "I cannot imagine Anzik on his own in Zorren."

"Nor could I, until now. I am finding myself impressed with his resourcefulness, despite the inconvenience he is causing," Jinzan admitted.

Anzik had always been possessed of more promise than usefulness. *He has a Source that burns like a little bonfire and a draw many adult sorcerers would envy. He casts nearly all his spells in his head and sees aether as clear as daylight. If the latter had not driven him to the edge of madness as a young child, he might have become a warlock one day.* Jinzan still held out hope for his son, despite all practical evidence that he was a lost cause, but it was not his job as a father to give up on Anzik.

"What if someone has already taken him?" Narsicann asked. "Did you think of that when you decided not to enlist help looking for him?"

"No, but I remembered his pet dog." There were uncomfortable looks shared about the table. They all knew that the boy had dabbled in necromancy recently. "I preferred to send folk he knew and would recognize. He is young and naive, more so than even most boys his age. He might be taken by treachery, but I would like to think that if there had been brute force involved, we would have felt the aether rock under the force of him using that staff to defend himself."

"Not all of us notice such things, Jinzan," Varduk commented somberly, trying to diffuse a potential argument to get the conversation back on course.

"If he truly tried to use it to its fullest extent, you might," Jinzan said. He had felt the awesome power when he had transferred himself halfway across Koriah after the Battle of Raynesdark, using the staff's draw to give him the aether he needed.

"If they have been turned to undead puppets, so be it. That staff needs finding. We will be cautious and they will bring no harm to the boy, but we cannot let it wander loose in the city," Narsicann ordered, looking over his shoulder to see that one of his assistants nod to him in understanding and hasten off to carry out his command.

"Now that we have something being done about that missing staff, I thought of another question for you, Narsicann," Feron piped up cheerily, trying to lighten the dour, contentious mood that was threatening to cast a pall over the remainder of the meeting.

"Yes?"

"You mentioned that you had lost men in Kadris. Does that mean we have none now, or are there still assets we can avail ourselves of?" Feron asked. "I have this idea, you see—"

"The ones left are untethered," Narsicann interrupted. "They have general orders, but do not report back on any schedule, and are left to their own resources. It is safer for them if they do not have our people trying to contact them. As such, I have no count of exactly how many are left, or where they are now, but they are men and women I trust completely and whose loyalty I do not question. Save your suggestion for when we have new recruits to send in; I will not try contacting any of our current spies in Kadris."

"Ooh, up to anything mischievous?" Feron grinned. Jinzan was spared the council's scorn as it turned to Feron and his insipid questions.

"Since word could not reach Kadris in time, I suppose there is no harm in revealing that there is a plan in place to coincide with the first day of springtime,"

Narsicann relented, trying to placate the simpering fool of an interior minister. Feron was brilliant in his own work, but he was so bothersome at Council. Everyone just wanted him to shut up so they could finish.

"Something for a wedding, perhaps?" Feron pressed.

With no further business requiring attention, a quick glance among the other four members ended the High Council's session by mutual agreement, leaving Feron's question unanswered as they got up simultaneously and left. A few chuckles from the outskirts of the room followed their departure, many from Feron's own underlings.

* * * * * * * *

"How long will it take us to get there?" Though he looked like a trader from Gar-Danel, he spoke with Faolen Sarmon's voice. He sat up front in the wagon, next to the driver. A team of four horses—fine, strong animals, native to western Megrenn—pulled them along.

"Three days, at this rate," replied a man who sounded—but did not look like—Aelon Beff. Faolen's magic was making them appear as foreigners so that they did not attract undue attention as they trekked northward to Megrenn territory. The wagon, the horses, and the clothes they wore were taken from actual Gar-Danel traders that had the misfortune of being in Kadrin at the time Aelon had been assigned by the warlock to find them a cover story. The goods they carried in trade were plundered from the *Song of Night*, which Faolen's magic had fooled into plowing into a sandbar.

"So many people on the road. You would never think that we were on the very threshold of war," Faolen commented. Kadrin citizens streamed southward, seeking safety in the heartlands. Megrenn and other foreigners ambled alongside Faolen and his companions on their way north, to Anywhere-But-Kadrin, the continent's most popular place for anyone not of Kadrin blood.

"Dunno 'bout that," Jodoul's voice came from the back of the wagon, where he and Tod diced as best they could on the bumpy road. "Folk know what's good fer 'em. War ain't it."

"Yeah. It's like them huntin' dogs what can smell fear, 'cept in reverse," Tod observed sagely.

Faolen furrowed the brow of his borrowed face, unable to follow the analogy as it was spoken, but understanding what Tod probably meant.

"So once we got that staff, then what?" Jodoul asked.

"I do not expect to have that question troubling us for some time yet," Faolen replied. "Like as not, it is either under lock and ward, or in the hands of that sorcerer who stole it in the first place. The opportunity to gain it may take some time in the arranging."

"Or we might just all die tryin'," Aelon suggested, keeping an open mind about their options.

"In the meantime, we will worm our way into their confidences however we can manage. If we cannot make a play for the staff immediately, we can find other ways to disrupt them and divert them," Faolen continued.

I travel with three who barely speak Megrenn, and speak it with a Kadrin accent, not a Gar-Danel one, Faolen thought. *I must remember that they are the expendable ones here— my cover. I must retrieve the staff and bring it safely back to Warlock Rashan. Barring that, I must see it destroyed. I will save their lives if I might, but I must not risk my mission by it.*

Faolen looked to Aelon and the two rough scamps that gambled in the back of the wagon. He did not *dislike* them or anything …

Chapter 10 - First Strike

The ground rumbled as they advanced, beating a slow, irregular rhythm. Iron plates as thick as a man's thumb rang against one another, covering the enormous beasts they protected like insect shells. Perched atop his walking mountain of flesh and iron, General Hellmock peered through the tube of the farseeing lens, and tried to confirm his scouts' reports.

The High Council had ordered a coordinated assault to begin on the first day of springtime, but they had not been privy to the reports he had been given. Kadrin forces were marching to reinforce Temble Hill, his intended target for the invasion's first strike. The city was reported to be nearly deserted, with the peasants fleeing to the interior of the Empire with whatever they could carry. They were staffed with their normal garrison and the city would normally be fine to hold off a siege for a few days until help arrived. That was why they sent the monohorn cavalry.

Three hundred monstrosities lumbered along under Hellmock's command, the largest such force in the Megrenn Alliance. Ten thousand infantry supported them, with regiments from most of the kingdoms of the alliance represented. Two thousand archers were along as well, but they would play a larger role in holding the city once it was taken. Hellmock's army did not have any siege weapons in the traditional sense—not even any of Councilor Jinzan's new weapons, which Hellmock quite admired—but the monohorns had provisions that rendered those optional.

With the prospect of facing a larger force if he delayed, Hellmock took it upon himself to order the attack a day early.

* * * * * * *

On the walls, spotters had been watching the approaching Megrenn force uneasily. Temble Hill had prepared its soldiers to be ready to defend the Empire, as they were on the front lines of its defense, but drilling in the practice yard with spears and shooting arrows into hay bales was unlike the prospect of facing a charge by monohorn cavalry.

"They are getting close. This looks like the real thing," Colonel Polarch called out to the archers along the battlements. "They would not risk entering our range if they did not intend to continue forward. Bows to the ready, men. Await my command."

All along the walls, soldiers and knights ended what respites they had been taking and got to their feet. There were four hundred of them left in the city. The rest had gone south to escort the peasantry to Munne, which was better prepared to withstand Megrenn's army. Once they had seen the peasants safely removed, they had been told to turn north and head back to Temble Hill. If all was going to plan, their return was what had prompted the Megrenn to attack early.

* * * * * * * *

"Looks like many of the ones up on the wall are knights, sir." Lieutenant Carva handed the farseeing lens back to the general. "Maybe close to half."

"They must see us with monohorns and know that the fighting will be within the city gates soon, no matter how many archers they put up there. The knights just want a better view in the meantime," General Hellmock said.

The monohorns were armored to stop ballistae, so arrows were nothing to them; even the eyes of their ponderous helms were shielded with mesh cages too tight for an arrow to slip through. The creatures did not see especially well to begin with, so the obstructed view was no great loss.

Carva and Hellmock watched as a crew worked with a mobile crane to lift a great battering ram onto the yolks of two pair of monohorns. The device was the closest they came to a proper siege engine and they brought but one with them. That one was more than enough, according to the logistics officers who had to manage the massive, unwieldy weapon. Four docile monohorns stood by as two dozen infantrymen swarmed about them, the footings of a small construction site. The caged eyes of the monohorn helms had solid cups that could be raised and lowered to blind the creatures completely. So long as they went uninjured, being blind caused them to freeze in place; aeons of evolution had made them instinctively fearful of loose footing and not seeing where they were walking. It made the work safer if the beasts kept still.

Once the ram was in place, Hellmock ordered the advance. The monohorns with the ram took the fore, and the bulk of the heavy cavalry followed a short distance behind. Monohorns were not swift beasts, but they could work up to a brisk pace with enough room. They were also not agile beasts, being somewhat more nimble than turtles—elderly turtles at the least. However, what they lacked in speed was more than compensated for in their titanic strength and near imperviousness to most weapons. They carried hundreds of gallons of armor on their backs, and riders as well, without showing the least burden. Strip the armor off and their hides could still turn aside many sword blows. The four with the ram were larger than average specimens and barely slowed by a ram that must have weighed a thousand gallons.

The Kadrins did not even bother them with many arrows as they closed the distance to the gates.

* * * * * * * *

"Off the wall. We're done," Colonel Polarch ordered. "Light the ropes and mount up. Get to the south gate. Your lives depend upon it." The colonel then followed his own advice and slid down a ladder to ground level.

All around him, men were untethering horses that had been set waiting for them in the streets. There were enough for every man to make his escape if they hurried. The Megrenn force was hurrying to arrive in the city before Kadrin reinforcements could get there, and had not taken the time to surround the city with even a token force prior to attacking. Marshal Brannis's plan had counted on that.

On the wall and in the city just inside it, catapults filled with fist-sized rocks stood ready to be fired. They had all been rigged with oil-soaked ropes and piled with kindling. When the long length of rope finally burned through, the catapults would fire and then be set afire. The rocks would slow the monohorn charge and might incidentally kill a few if they lost their footing at a full run.

As he mounted his white mare, Colonel Polarch looked to the city gate. The runes that normally reinforced it had been scratched to ruins, leaving the gate nothing but a thick wooden barricade. It would stand against the Megrenn ram as well as a wicker basket might against a smith's hammer. Though it would cost him his life to stay, the colonel wished he could be there when the monohorns crashed through that gate …

… and into the massive pit dug just beyond it.

Colonel Polarch spurred his mount, and galloped for the southern gate, near the rear of the organized retreat. He grinned wickedly when he heard the crash of splintered wood and the great bellowing screams of the monohorns. By nightfall, his force would meet with the "reinforcements" coming up the road toward them, and they would all make for Munne to make a stand in earnest.

Chapter 11 - The First of Springtime

Iridan plodded down the halls to the practice yard. He knew that this being his wedding day would offer no reprieve from his warlock training—he had asked. The world seemed a bit fuzzy, but he hurt less than he had before a half bottle of wine had eased his searing headache and made the soreness in his shoulders and hips—a remembrance of the previous day's beatings—easier to ignore.

He squinted his eyes, and blinked hard against the intrusion of bright daylight as the sun shone low in the sky when he exited the palace. He saw his father and his opponents for the morning waiting for him, as well as more curious onlookers than were usually permitted to watch his training. Jafin and Moln had been replaced days ago as his antagonists; he had gotten the better of them a few times too many for Rashan's liking. The new boys were almost fully trained, carrying the title of squire officially. Bairn and Kolm were their names and Iridan had taken an instant dislike to them.

"Morning, little warlock," Kolm called out to him. He stood more than a full head taller than Iridan and was close to Brannis's size, though he had not finished filling out his body with muscle the way Brannis had.

"We won't be having it easy on you. No weddings going on in the yard," Bairn added. Bairn lacked the size and reach of Kolm, but he was the stronger fighter of the two. "We'll keep from bruising the important bits, though, eh?" He turned and winked to Kolm.

Braggarts. If Rashan was not here to protect you, I could turn you to ash and you know it.

Ever since the two of them had taken over his arms practice, Iridan had been limping his way to bed each night. Unlike with the younger boys, Iridan could not wait for these two to make mistakes; they did not make any that he could notice. Rashan had picked from among the best at the School of Arms. Iridan wondered whether he would begin facing veteran soldiers if he survived long enough to beat these two. With the beatings he had suffered at their hands, though, he wondered if he would make it.

"Enough talk. Arm yourselves and get to work," Rashan snapped. Iridan had noticed that the warlock spoke differently depending on his audience. Privately he was friendly, thoughtful, and soft-spoken. Around the Inner Circle, he was an orator, projecting confidence and weaving tapestries of logic and rhetoric. Among lesser underlings, especially soldiers, he was short-tempered, all business, even rude.

Iridan took up his sword, hardwood covered in padding. He looked at Kolm and Bairn with their bared steel, and thought it unfair. *They are better swordsmen than I am. They are both stronger than me. I still ache from yesterday's training. I have no patience for this nonsense this morning.* Iridan had enough troubles weighing on his mind already.

Kolm struck first, a probing thrust that Iridan batted away as Bairn circled to get around him. It was much like the tactic Jafin and Moln had used against him, but more polished in its execution. Iridan spun to meet the attack he knew would be coming from his flank, parrying it just in time to be struck from behind as Kolm recovered and lunged for him. The attack struck Iridan's shielding spell, but he felt it.

Kolm followed up with an overhand chop that caught Iridan in the shoulder before he could get his sword up. The padded blade struck a glancing blow against Kolm's arm, but did nothing to disrupt the squire as he pressed the attack.

As Iridan tried to defend himself from Kolm's onslaught, he saw Bairn in his aether-vision, closing from behind. Iridan dove to the side and rolled, but the maneuver had not surprised his opponents. They pursued quickly and were upon Iridan as soon as he gained his feet.

At least they are both in front of me for now.

He tried to mount a counteroffensive, but Bairn handily stopped his two-handed downward hacking attack with just his one-handed blade. Kolm's blade struck him hard in the chest as Bairn used the momentum of Iridan's strike to force his blade away from where it could parry the attack.

"You are not even trying," Rashan called out from the edge of the yard, where he was seated and talking with a group of sorcerers and nobles. After his admonishment, the warlock turned his attention back to the conversation.

Rage bubbled up in Iridan. *He wasn't even watching when he said that. He's just goading me.* Iridan drew in a bit of aether. *If he's going to complain no matter what I do, I will at least save myself the beating I will take.* Rashan's rules included never using magic on his practice opponents, but technically he was not going to use it *on* them.

Iridan's muscles surged as he infused them with aether. It was not quite magic, as such, but similar to a surge of adrenaline. As with any aether directed inside a sorcerer's body, there was risk to it, but if Iridan was to become a warlock, then risk would be his lifelong companion. The next cut of Kolm's blade hit air and Iridan skipped sideways faster than the squire could anticipate. As Bairn followed with a slash of his own, Iridan's blade hummed through the air, meeting the steel sword head on and nearly wrenching it from Bairn's grasp. He launched an attack of his own at Kolm, repeating the same overhand strike he had tried against Bairn, but with the force of an ogre behind it.

Kolm tried to parry the blow, but had not the strength to divert it. His sword was swept out of the way as the padded practice blade crashed into his collarbone with a crunch. The young squire cried out in agony as he crumpled to the ground.

Bairn had already recovered and was trying to take Iridan from behind. Iridan whirled and used the advantage of his longer weapon to catch Bairn in the ribs before he could make an attack of his own. So swift had Iridan's blade been that the squire could not even get his sword in the way in time to slow it. The blow lifted him from his feet, and threw him two body lengths to the side, where he fell unmoving.

Iridan was panting with exertion and exhilaration. *I beat them. Maybe I cheated, but I won. In a real battle, that is all that matters.*

"Much better," Rashan called out, clapping in appreciation as he excused himself from his guests and walked toward Iridan. "I waited nearly a full season for you to realize that. You did not use a bit of aether on them. Well done."

"You are not angry with me?" Iridan asked. "That *was* cheating."

"Your goal was to best them with swords and to learn how to fight. You have seen the futility of fighting purely defensively and took that lesson hard," Rashan said. "One day soon, we will sort this mess out and have an emperor again. You will serve him. When that day comes, you must understand that results matter, not methods. If you are given a goal and a bunch of rules, worry about the goal. If you cannot achieve it within the rules, break them. There are no punishments for warlocks who take matters into their own hands to get done what needs doing. Emperors will cluck their tongues and tell you to listen better next time, but they will forget such trespasses much more quickly than any failure. They *need* to know that anything they wish done, they have but to give the order. The ones that learn wisdom find out that sometimes those orders necessitate unpleasant messes. They learn then to limit such orders to true needs, rather than whim. You wish them to think of you as an attack dog, not a caged songbird."

Iridan looked pensive as he left the yard, given a reprieve from drawing against Dolvaen, who was acting as his oathkeeper for the wedding. Instead Iridan retired to his chambers to try to relax and refresh himself for the noontime ceremony. It would be the last quiet respite he expected to have for some years hence.

A soldier was sent to bring aid for the fallen squires, but it was for show. Rashan knew from ages of experience in battle that neither would survive the wounds Iridan had inflicted.

* * * * * * * *

"We are going over the ship with polish and cloth now, sir," Captain Drecker reported. "All else is as ready as we know how to make it, considering this is new to all of us. I expect once we see it in the field, we will have suggestions on how to improve it."

The captain was as ambitious and capable a man as Brannis could find in Kadrin's neglected navy. With islands of ice to their south, Kadrin fleets largely patrolled the waterways for smugglers and ventured out to the waters off the eastern shore mainly as escorts. Fully self-sufficient within its borders, Kadrin played little in the affairs of Veydrus's naval powers. Their navy was tiny for an empire so vast.

"Very well," Brannis said. "There will be men with flags up on the palace roof. When they signal, just loop around a few circuits, let the trumpeters play their fanfare, and head back to port. Exchange those musicians for bowmen and be off as soon as possible thereafter. Avoid flying near the palace as you leave the city, so as not to disrupt the feast."

"Aye, sir. We are fine for show, but none want to see us actually working. Is that about the right of it?" Drecker was a plainspoken, direct man.

"Something like that. Same with me, I suppose, at least for today." Brannis was clad in fine raiment, befitting his station. He wore black silk under a sleeveless short-coat that bore the Solaran crest, along with grey hose that did little to keep his legs warm. The first day of springtime though it was, Kadris was very far south. "No armor for me today. Too gaudy, the warlock said, and I cannot disagree. I would prefer fewer eyes on me today than I usually draw."

"No trouble about that today, I'm thinking, sir," Drecker replied. "I was just a boy when Emperor Dharus was wed and I do not recall this much fuss."

"Well, I think you were probably put on your father's shoulder to watch the parade and little more. Of course it seemed less than it was. This time you get to be a part of the show—and see how much time we waste on it that could be better spent preparing to fight Megrenn at Munne," Brannis said.

"Well, these things seem a bit more frisky than a ship at sea and faster than any vessel that has set in water. We draft nothing but fog now. Unless we run amiss, two days ought to see it in Munne," Drecker said.

"On the subject of running amiss ... do not fly over the wedding site. Aim wide of it and circle the perimeter. If anything goes wrong, I do not want trumpets, musicians, or—I daresay—ships, falling onto the guests," Brannis said.

"Anything you should be telling me about these that I don't know?" Drecker asked. Brannis could not tell if his suspicion was feigned or if he was masking real concern.

"No, I think you were already aware that these are the first of their kind, that I drew them up from plans I saw in a dream, and that I dropped out of the Academy before learning proper rune theory." Brannis smiled reassuringly. "What could go wrong?"

* * * * * * *

Rashan was surrounded by a pack of ravenous functionaries, pestering him with last-moment details that "absolutely required his personal attention." The wine steward did not have enough of the chosen vintage for everyone at the feast—could they switch, or should they have two different ones? The Archons had decided to bring more of their household servants and now outnumbered the Solarans by some fifty guests—should some be seated among the Solarans or would it be best to just leave the sides imbalanced? Some Fifth Circle sorcerer brought news via the speaking stone in Munne that Temble Hill had been taken the previous night—should they relay any new orders? A young knight had been sent to inquire about the circumstances of the deaths of two squires earlier in the morning. The blood-scholars wanted his seal on the wedding documents.

"Bring up the second vintage. Half the guests could not tell a Tameron vintage from horse piss. ... Just let the unaffiliated guests balance the seating. ... Marshal Brannis has that situation under control. All is according to his expectations. ... It was an accident in training. Please pass my sympathies on to their families, and see that they want for nothing. ... I have not seen my personal seal in over a hundred winters. Make do for now; I will not hold up the ceremony for such nonsense."

Rashan paused, causing those keeping pace with him to jostle one another in an effort not to walk into the warlock. There was a faint, familiar tingling in the aether. Rashan smiled.

"You are all dismissed. You may bother me again after the feast tonight."

The functionaries knew better than to argue—many had replaced men who had lost their posts for doing so—and hastened to remove themselves from the warlock's presence.

The warlock ducked quickly into a nearby vacant room. The tingling sensation grew stronger, and before him appeared a female form—roughly Rashan's size, with smooth skin the color of a fawn's fur and tangled green hair that fell to the tops of her plump breasts. From beneath her hair curled two delicate horns, shaped like a ram's, but thinner. She was clad in a simple, strapless gown of diaphanous white and nothing else; her tiny bare feet hung just above the floor, with the tips of her toes just touching. Her overlarge brown eyes gulped in Rashan's image and she smiled.

"I was beginning to think you were not coming, Illiardra," Rashan said, returning the smile.

He was always impressed with her command of aether. The thunder of his own transference spell was enough to shake buildings—wasted aether, but impressive to the peasantry who knew no better. Hers took only herself, not a scoop from the world about her, and she could avoid alerting a sleeping dragon should she appear next to one, so subtle was the disruption is caused. Had he not been waiting on her appearance, he might have missed it himself.

"I considered not coming. You grow arrogant when everything you plan works out as you hope. But I am too curious to meet our son and see what sort of man he has become. It seems amazing that he is grown already," Illiardra replied. She floated over to a wall as she spoke and felt along it with a thin hand, trying to get a sense of the place in which she found herself.

"Time passes quickly out here. Blink and you could miss a lifetime. I imagine it to be even worse for your kind. Even your mortals can live ten human lifetimes," Rashan said, moving closer to her. "It is good to see you. I must say, though, that your appearance is inappropriate for the ceremony. You should alter it before I introduce you."

"I am not so ignorant of mortals, you know. I wore this for you. I have missed you, it seems." Illiardra met Rashan's gaze from a handspan away.

"I meant these." Rashan ran a finger gently along one of her horns, tracing the curve slowly and deliberately. "And these as well." He brushed aside her mop of hair and revealed ears too long for a human her size, reaching halfway to the top of her head and dropping just slightly. "Iridan does not know."

"I will meet our son later. For now, I seek only you," Illiardra answered, letting her gown puddle quietly upon the floor.

* * * * * * *

A gaggle of servants fussed about Iridan, adjusting things that looked fine by his eye, polishing the metal bits of his warlock attire, and just generally being a nuisance about his person. He reached through the throng to retrieve a decanter of brandy and took a swig straight from it.

"There will be time enough to drink at the feasting," Dolvaen chided him from across the small room, where he sat dutifully watching over his charge in the capacity of oathkeeper. He bore no love for the warlock; the favor was to Iridan himself, despite the warlock making the request. Iridan had always been one of his favorites, a shining light among the lowborn at the Academy. Dolvaen had fought the same battles in his youth, having to be twice as good as his blooded peers to achieve even half the respect they got. It was a blow to Dolvaen to discover that his successor as champion of the unblooded sorcerers was of Solaran blood, from a strong branch of the line thought lost in the Battle of the Dead Earth.

"Well, unless the drinks at the feast will bear magic enough to calm my nerves *now*, I think this will work best," Iridan joked, taking a second pull from the decanter before setting it back down again.

I killed those two boys this morning, Iridan thought. *I can't see how they could have survived those wounds. He knew it ... but he was happy. Was he just going to keep finding harder and harder opponents as I improved, until I lost my temper and used magic to win?*

Iridan drew a deep breath, drawing a clucking sound from the very proper little man who was trying to get his tunic straightened.

So I marry Juliana in an hour or so. A few days and I will be sent off to the battlefields, ready or not. I think I can manage to survive a few days on my own with her. Maybe if I return home a war hero, she will take me seriously.

Iridan had been of a mind to refuse the arrangement, but Rashan had seemed quite set on it, since Juliana was a more proper match than any unwed girl in the Empire.

I don't know that she'll ever love me, not like she does Brannis, but at least maybe she will learn to respect me. I am a warlock *now, by the winds! I should not have to put up with her bullying anymore. I am not eight springtimes old anymore,* Iridan told himself, building up anger like a wall, one brick at a time.

One of the attendants muttered a quiet spell, and ran her fingers through Iridan's hair, shaping it in a dashing, side-swept style. "The wind might muss it now, and it will go back likewise afterward, Warlock," she told him. He had not caught her name, but she was dressed in Sixth Circle formal garb.

And I thought being wardkeeper was trivial work for a sorcerer. I should have counted myself lucky not to have been grooming grooms. Now that I am powerful, I need to remember not to look down on peasants—not even peasant sorcerers.

* * * * * * * *

A few doors down the hall, Juliana sat on a small, velvet-cushioned stool and fumed. She had been angry with herself since she had awoken. *Spit on you, Soria. Why do you get to sit out this whole fiasco while I have to slog through it?* It was less the feeling that Soria had abandoned her, staying awake the night through to keep from watching the wedding, than it was envy that she could not do likewise. *There is nothing bad about Iridan, all things considered. I know he has a sense of humor. He is polite and well positioned; I will want for nothing, just as it was growing up, maybe even more so.* She tried positive thinking to cheer herself.

It was the first time that Soria had abandoned her in a long while, not so much as peeking through the veil of worlds to watch her through her own eyes. The last time had been on her last Ranking Day. There had only been four of them left and it had fallen much the way she had expected—just as it had the previous two years. She knew that she either had to throw her match or face Iridan in the final draw. She preferred to come in third-ranked than lose to Iridan, and threw a match before having to draw against him. Soria had hated that decision, and it was one of the few major disagreements the two of them had. Juliana hated the reminder that they were only *mostly* the same person and not just the personas she adopted in each world.

A tugging at her hair snapped her back from her mind's little momentary escape. Two older servants were weaving her hair through some silly fan-like contraption perched atop her head. *I must look like a peacock,* she thought sourly. Apparently her mother had worn the same piece at her own wedding, nearly forty springtimes ago. She did not know what her mother had done to deserve such a fate, but she quietly suspected that she had done enough to vex her own mother during her short life to have warranted the ridiculous accessory as a small vengeance.

After all, the entire day seemed bent on causing her embarrassment. *I pictured this day a thousand times as a little girl. It never looked like this.* When she had been very young, the groom had been some indistinct prince or knight—they seemed so much more dashing than sorcerers—in her daydreams. She started fixating on particular boys she liked as she matured into considering the actual prospect of marrying some*one*, and not just "getting married," finally settling on Brannis as the object of her fantasies.

She had not been put into her gown yet. Old ladies were still fussing over its fold and making sure there were no blemishes on it. Instead she sat in just a light slip, barefoot and bored. Everything would be dressed onto her, she would have little to do with the process, but stand up, move a limb here or there upon request, and try to keep from mussing anything. In the meantime ...

Juliana reached quietly into the aether, and lifted a wineglass from a small table laid out for the servants to pick from. It was a long morning, and there were to be no breaks for the staff until the ceremony was underway. There was nothing fancy about the vintage they were provided, but Juliana was no snob when it came to fermented grapes. "Some barefoot peasant stomped on these; how refined can it possibly be?" she had once argued to her father after spilling a valuable vintage.

"Milady, hold still," one of the old ladies complained from above as she tilted her head back enough to down a swallow of wine.

"This will go a lot faster if I have something to occupy myself," she countered.

"Aye, maybe for you, your ladyship," the old woman shot back. Juliana chuckled. She always preferred older servants. Beyond a certain age, they lost that obsequious veneer that got lacquered onto them wherever it was that servants were trained. You could actually talk to them without having them all agree with every inane thing you said: "Yes, milady, the sky is much too blue today." "Of course, milady, I will bring your morning feast out to the stables." "Milady, I would be delighted to take your pony to the market to let her pick out her own apples."

Juliana paused a moment in her musings. *I was a rotten little thing. No wonder Mother wants me to wear this silly hair-thing. I probably deserve it.*

When her hair was finally done, they had her stand to begin assembling her dress around her. The weight and size of her peacock's crest made her head wobble strangely as she moved. It only felt right when she kept her movements slow and her head steady.

Aha! Now I see. If I do not keep dignified, the thing will pull my hair. Devious …

The gown was all white satin, with gold trim and embroidery. It covered from the tops of her breasts clear down to the floor, hugging her slender torso and billowing out like a bell to hide her skinny legs. If she held her arms straight out, she could make a long band of bare flesh from fingertip to fingertip across her collarbone, but that was about all that was left untouched upon her.

Some young lass (who was probably ten summers her senior and expert in life extension) came and reddened her lips, darkened her eyelids, and brightened the whites of her eyes. Juliana usually took care of her cosmetic magics herself, but the young sorceress was versed in making brides appear stunning even when viewed from half a jouster's tilt away.

At last, she stepped into her slippers. They were the plainest part of her wardrobe, chosen for comfort in standing for extended periods rather than looks—the only kindness they had done her all day, by Juliana's reckoning. The length of her dress would hide them entirely. She had always wanted to wear heeled slippers on her wedding day, but she towered over Iridan as it was, they told her. She had then offered to go barefoot and was met by stern, disapproving looks.

She sighed. *Maybe when married life wears on me, I can see if Brannis could be convinced to take a mistress. The man is not made of stone.*

* * * * * * * *

Captain Varnus Coldlake cut an impressive figure as he stood guard over the door where Juliana dressed: a hulking mass of muscle wrapped in polished silver armor (which bore real, functional runed steel beneath the surface) and baring a heavy steel greatsword, gleaming as it sat point-first against the black marble floor shot through with veins of green. Hard, ice-blue eyes scanned the corridor in either direction, clearing a path around him that servants and guests alike steered clear of. Though of a mind to wear a beard through the cold season, he was clean-shaven for the wedding, his weathered face finally getting the same view that his shiny, waxed pate normally got after a winter of being entombed in greasy black hair.

It was a proud day for Varnus. While he was not to be the center of attention, he would be just slightly off-center, in full view of everyone worth knowing in the Empire. His position with House Archon was secure. His low birth limited his options for advancement anyway, but he liked the idea of being known. Juliana had done him quite the favor in naming him oath guardian. It was a ceremonial position to be sure, harkening back to the days when a treaty might ride on the continued virginity of a noble daughter up to the point of her wedding night. The thought was that a trusted knight would guard the honor of a lass of fourteen summers or so, lest anyone overpower and defile her. They had not anticipated in that bygone era that the hereditary sorcerous bloodlines would take up the idea and parade a soldier around with a sorceress of twenty-and-three autumns under the pretense of her needing his protection.

Still, Varnus honored the tradition, keeping anyone from entering the room. At length, there was a knocking from within, and he took the key from around his neck and unlocked the door. Even with one in six guests being a member of the Imperial Circle, they used a mundane lock and key as tradition would have it.

Juliana emerged, prettier than he had ever seen her, despite the funny fan thing they had done with her hair. She smiled up at him self-consciously, seeking approval.

"You look stunning, Lady Juliana," he offered. There were days when he had trouble keeping her and Soria separate in his head, but today was not one of those. He could not envision Soria wearing such finery (without being in disguise, at the least).

Varnus sheathed his blade and offered Juliana his arm. It was his honor to escort her to the ceremony while his Archon house guards kept the halls clear as they made their way to the expansive front lawns of the palace.

He could feel the tension in Juliana as she walked along beside him. She usually had such an ease about her, doing what she wanted, when she wanted. Being paraded about at the center of an event she would much rather have avoided entirely, she was trembling.

She manages to look happy enough. Most folk wouldn't know the difference. Hope she can keep the act up all day. That Iridan doesn't seem like a bad sort. Perhaps he'll grow on her.

When they exited the palace doors, they were greeted with a massive cheer from the assembled guests gathered upon the lawn. He handed the bride off to her father, who escorted her down an aisle in the middle of the throng, so that more of the attendees might see her, and brought her back again. Iridan would have already done the same before their arrival, escorted by his mother.

The mother was a curious woman, Varnus noted. She was petite and looked young enough to have been Iridan's sister—with him the elder brother, at that. She wore her hair a gaudy green color, unlike the more tasteful blondes and deep blacks that most Kadrin sorceresses preferred, or even the more exotic reddish-gold that Juliana and Lady Ophelia fancied. Her eyes seemed just a bit too large for her face as well. Juliana said she had heard Iridan's mother was immortal, but had no other information about her. She stood out from the warlock at her side, dressed in a plain white shoulderless gown of humble design. It contrasted with her creamy brown skin, making her look foreign among the fair-skinned native Kadrins. Iridan obviously took after his father's looks.

With the pageantry out of the way, the blood-scholars took over. Bookish sorts by nature, they seemed to thrive on being called away from their recordkeeping duties to finalize the marriages their order arranged. Varnus paid scant attention to the names they gave, or the fables they recounted, or the history they invoked. It was dry, meaningless stuff, meant to lend dignity and weight to the art of picking out which two sorcerers got to rut in order to advance the breed. It worked the same with pigs, horses, or hunting dogs. Everyone knew it, but few folk spoke of it in earshot of a Circle member. They knew it too, according to Juliana. The blood-scholars' words were meant to remind them of their duty, of the upside, of being bred like cattle …

In the crowd, Varnus noticed Sir Brannis, the brawny knight standing out in both garb and build among his family on the Solaran side of the center aisle. He pitied the poor lad. *He's got the weight of the Empire on him, with the warlock over one shoulder and General Sir Hurald Chadreisson hovering over the other, waiting for him to fail so that he can retake command of the army. Juliana ought to have married him instead. Would have made her happier, anyway. Seemed like an upstanding one, for a Solaran, even before the knights got hold of him.* He had barely known Brannis, remembering him more as a boy of fourteen summers who had courted Juliana at the start of their doomed engagement. Protective as Varnus was of Juliana, he approved of the boy; he could be trusted to put himself between her and a sword blow.

* * * * * * * *

At length, the meat and gristle of the ceremony began. While the earlier pronouncements had been for the guests as much as the couple, the blood-scholar turned his attention solely to Iridan and Juliana. "Iridan Solaran, Warlock of the Imperial Circle, I call on you to make a binding oath. Swear before all present … will you guard Juliana Archon against all harm?"

"I swear it," Iridan replied solemnly.

"Will you place Juliana Archon's needs before your own?" the blood-scholar asked.

"I swear it," Iridan answered.

"Will you disavow all other claims against your wealth, your lands, and your heart, that Juliana may share equal claim of them?"

"I swear it," Iridan replied. His possessions were meager and his heart unclaimed by any other.

"Will you raise your children under the guidance of the Imperial Circle, strengthening the Empire by joining your blood with hers?" the blood-scholar continued.

"I swear this as well," Iridan stated.

"Then swear your oath to your betrothed and pledge your life to her," the blood-scholar instructed.

Iridan turned to face Juliana. His voice caught in his throat for just a moment as their gazes locked. He saw in her eyes a trapped sort of fear that described his own feelings far more eloquently than he could have hoped to with words.

"I swear, before all gathered here, that I will join my life with yours. I will share your joys and comfort your sorrows. I will father your children and teach them strength and wisdom. I will stand by your side until the day of my death and wait for you beyond." Iridan managed to get through it all without his voice breaking, but they were the hardest words he had ever spoken. They were oppressively heavy words whose weight he could barely stand to carry. He could only hope that he would live up to them.

The elderly blood-scholar nodded approvingly. He had no doubt seen more reluctant couples than the two before him and had heard poorer oaths.

"Juliana Archon, Sorceress of the Sixth Circle, I call on you to make a binding oath. Swear before all present ... will you guard Iridan Solaran against all treachery?"

"I do swear," Juliana replied, inadvertently slipping up and mixing in the Kheshi vows that Soria had learned.

Hold it together, Juliana, she told herself. *Everyone is watching.*

"Will you place Iridan Solaran's needs before your own?" the blood-scholar asked.

"I swear it," Juliana replied, allowing herself a tiny sigh of relief at getting it right on the second attempt.

"Will you disavow all other claims against your wealth, your lands, and your heart, that Iridan may share equal claim of them?"

"I swear it," she lied.

"Will you raise your children under the guidance of the Imperial Circle, strengthening the Empire by joining your blood with his?" the blood-scholar continued.

"I swear this as well," Juliana agreed.

"Then swear your oath to your betrothed and pledge your life to him," the blood-scholar instructed.

"I swear, before all gathered here, that I will join my life with yours. I will share your joys and comfort your sorrows. I will bear your children and teach them loyalty and compassion. I will stand by your side until the day of my death and wait for you beyond," Juliana recited.

Just words. No magic to them at all. They only have the power I allow them to have. They probably should have had Iridan pledge the loyalty part, though.

"Now, if you will clasp hands ..." the blood-scholar requested. They complied, reaching out tentatively for one another. Juliana's hands were damp with sweat. She noticed his were shaking. "By the authority of the Kadrin Empire and her regent, I declare you wedded. May your union last a hundred springtimes."

The crowd waited, hushed and expectant. She knew what was expected of them, and they came together shyly, Juliana bending down to bring her face level with Iridan's.

Everyone is watching, she thought. *Just do it and be done with it.*

Juliana closed her eyes, and pictured Brannis as their lips met, hearing the eruption of cheering from the crowd as they kissed.

Their kiss broke off with a start as a trumpeting call blared from high above. Three sailing ships sped through the sky above, circling their wedding guests and playing a fanfare. The gleaming hulls were freshly painted light blue and white, matching the midday sky. Trumpeters lined the railing that faced the crowd, wearing alternating tabards of Solaran yellow and Archon green. The crowd cheered anew at the sight, and Iridan and Juliana were spared the intense focus on them as gazes turned skyward to take in the spectacle.

A parting gift from the crews of your new airships, Brannis? Juliana mused. *You have always known what to do to make me feel better.*

* * * * * * *

Varnus had worried that Juliana would "get a bit of Soria in her," as he called it when she acted without regard for anything but her own interest. To his relief, the ceremony went much as planned. His eyes keep sweeping through the crowd, looking for trouble in the habit of one who had spent most of his life as a personal guard.

It was his training that perked up his senses as he noticed a flinch in Iridan's mother. Something had caught her attention, though she showed only the barest hint of distraction. It was enough to set Varnus on edge, to the point where his hand strayed to his sword hilt. The guests' attention was drawn away from the palace steps, and even the warlock's attention was on the skies above, when a man appeared out of nowhere behind the warlock.

Naked but for a loincloth, and covered in painted runes, he carried a wicked-looking runed dagger in one hand, poised close enough to lunge for Warlock Rashan. The assassin's eyes widened as he made his strike, unprepared for the warlock's reaction. Rashan spun, catching his assailant by the wrist and twisting, forcing the man to the ground. In the span of a heartbeat, the man was thrashing futilely on the ground, with the warlock's small, booted foot pressed to his throat.

Only a few had taken notice of the attack, and Rashan cast a quick illusion over the strange assailant to hide him from the unobservant among the crowd. Brannis's sword hand had not even reached the hilt of Avalanche before all had been rendered safe by the warlock's actions.

"You are nearly done. Pay this no mind and finish, if you please," Rashan told the blood-scholar who had been one of the few either close enough or circumspect enough to have noticed the disturbance amid the fanfare.

Rather than orating on the future that Iridan and Juliana were to be expected to share together, the blood-scholar wisely made a few brief remarks and adjourned everyone to the feast as soon as decorum allowed. The warlock kept his attention on the speaker, allowing his would-be assassin just enough air to breathe to keep him alive.

It was an awkward end to a wedding, but it was better than Varnus had expected.

* * * * * * * *

Rashan threw his attacker to the floor of a small storage room a level below the palace's main floor, where he had dragged him immediately following the ceremony. The paint from his body had smeared the floors all along the way, leaving blood mixed in as well, as not all of the palace's floors were polished smooth (and certainly not the stairs to the servants' levels).

"So you were sent by the Megrenn, I assume," Rashan began. "I admit I am impressed at your boldness and your skill at stealth. I did not notice you until it was almost too late."

"One demon I was prepared to kill. Two, I was not ready for," the man confessed. His accent sounded familiar to Rashan, but a hundred winters of exile from the mortal world had muddied dialects in his absence. "I do not know what strange magic stripped my spell from me, but I think it was not your own."

"Yes, take pride that you fooled me at least," Rashan conceded. He looked the dagger over appraisingly. "You were dead the moment you used this thing, you know. It would have sucked your Source dry in an attempt to destroy mine." Rashan paused a moment, concentrating his attention on a few key runes, then studying his attacker's Source. "It might have worked, too."

"I was glad to die to rid the world of you," the man proclaimed. "I would have been a hero."

"Well, hero, take heart that I have little thought to keep you alive for information. As one warrior to another, if you tell me where you would like your body sent, I will see it returned to your people," Rashan said.

Someone is going to pay for this, Rashan thought. *And one life is not going to suffice.*

The man studied the warlock's face, but found it impassive, betraying no insight to the demon's thoughts. "Truly?" he asked warily.

"You will be dead before the first course of the wedding feast is over, whether you tell me or not. The only difference is whether I send your body home or feed it to whatever lives down in the sewers these days. I have neither the patience nor the inclination to torture. It is the idle amusement of a sick mind, and no proper pastime for a warlock," Rashan bluffed.

Come now, put a name to your homeland for me. I will bring your body to them, of course. I would hate for them all to die confused, with no explanation for my anger at them.

"Hu'nua. It is a small island in the western half of Gar-Danel," the man admitted. "Do you know it?"

"I do."

"Thank you, demon. Die well, and soon," the assassin closed his eyes and resigned himself to his fate.

* * * * * * * *

Brannis could not help glancing down the long feast table, to where the bride and groom shared the head. Off in another part of the palace grounds from the ceremony, they supped out of doors in the new springtime air. Fires blazed all about, warring with the stubborn vestiges of a winter too bold to retreat upon its celestial expiration. A fire a few paces behind him was enough to warm Brannis against the worst of the afternoon breezes. He wondered whether his proximity was by good fortune or design. A great many sorcerers feasted that day and all but the least among them could protect themselves against such paltry inconvenience as weather.

Juliana looked gorgeous, preened to display her beauty, rather than flaunting it as she often did. Brannis understood the difference and obviously so did whoever styled her gown and jewelry. *She is trying so hard. That toothy grin is not hers, though. I have seen every smile she has.* Brannis wondered what it would have been like in Iridan's place. It had been on his mind the whole of the ceremony, including the point where he would have drawn his blade to protect Juliana against the would-be assassin. Brannis took another long swallow of his drink. The ale was weak, to keep the feast going longer and to moderate the drunkenness of the guests as the night wore on.

"When will they get their gifts?" Danilaesis asked, seated next to him. He had kept quiet through the wedding, for which Brannis had been thankful, but apparently the reprieve was at an end.

"Not likely until tomorrow. They must have gotten hundreds and the feasting will last all night," Brannis replied.

"Not all night, Grandfather said. They—" Danilaesis began but Brannis cut him short.

"No! Stop right there. I know and I know you know. I do not need to hear it," Brannis told him. He glared over the top of Danilaesis's head at his grandfather. "Did you really need to tell him all that?"

"What? The truth? Of course not. I could lie to him like his father and blather on about babies popping in from the aether. I could tell him women have the same bits as men beneath their robes and that they get married because they love each other. But then he goes and finds out different and thinks us all liars. Well, he shall know his grandfather will tell him true and that is worth something," Axterion said, not quite facing Brannis as he spoke. The ancient wizard was nearly blind and used aether-vision to get by. With his weak Source, Brannis was hard to see either way.

I sometimes wonder if you enjoy being thought senile, old man. You get away with far more than if more folk realized your wits were mainly intact.

"So you would tell him about torture and rape, necromancy, that sort of stuff, should he just ask?" Brannis tried to make his stubborn old grandfather see where such roads led.

"Nasty stuff, all of it. Wonderful stories, though, if you have a mind for it. Better to be repulsed by it early than build up curiosity for years. Brannis, my boy, you were always good about it, but do not forget that the truth is always the best path. Do not let that seventy-first great uncle of yours, or whatever he is, convince you otherwise," Axterion said.

Brannis turned his attention back to his meal, tiring of trying to reason with Axterion. The old man had been High Sorcerer before his years caught up to him and left him using all his power to hold onto life, with none left for working magic. He was a veteran of too many arguments to count, and refused defeat even when logic sided against him.

"Pardon me," Brannis heard a voice in his head. His eyes widened in surprise. He looked furtively up and down the table to see who might have tried to get his attention. *"My name is Illiardra, Iridan's mother. I have not yet had the chance to make your acquaintance. I sense that your Source is not strong enough to reply, so merely listen a moment. When the dancing begins, which ought to be shortly, ask me to dance. I wish to speak with you."*

Brannis looked down to the head of the table again, but not seeking Juliana for once. He saw the strange immortal whom Rashan had brought to the wedding. It was clear she was not human, as least insomuch as Rashan was no longer human. She appeared as she wished, by agency of whatever magic she chose to use.

Brannis waited until the music changed from peaceful melodies for dining to boisterous songs for dancing. As couples made their way to a nearby stone terrace to dance, Brannis approached the warlock's consort (he realized he had never asked their relationship, or whether Iridan was born a bastard). She seemed otherworldly, much less similar to human than Rashan was. The warlock kept his appearance as it had been in his own youth. Illiardra had been much less bound in her choice of form.

"My lady, I am Sir Brannis Solaran, Grand Marshal of the Imperial Armies. Might I have the pleasure of a dance?" Brannis was glad that many of the folk at the table had already adjourned to the dance floor, including the newly married couple. The guests had not made a fuss over it, considering the circumstances, but the warlock had not yet appeared at the feast. Word had spread about the assassin that had tried to kill Rashan, and everyone seemed to assume he was off somewhere dealing with the matter. Most had a "better him than me" attitude about the whole thing. It was a more jovial atmosphere without Rashan around, anyway. In truth, many were scared of the warlock's mere presence.

"I would be delighted, Sir Brannis."

Illiardra extended a hand, and allowed Brannis to help her to her feet. She weighed almost nothing. It felt like he was helping a cloud rise from the seat she had occupied.

She rose from the ground as they danced, lest the vast difference in height make both the steps and the conversation awkward. They drew curious glances, but mostly due to the unfamiliar face in the large clique that was the Imperial Circle and their families. Floating in the air was simple magic, not enough to impress jaded old eyes.

"So tell me about my son," she asked. She bounded and twirled along with Brannis so expertly that her eyes never left his as she spoke. "Rashan spoke highly of you and said you were the best of Iridan's friends. Why then were you not his oathkeeper?"

"It is a long story, but I was once betrothed to Juliana Archon. I suppose Rashan wanted to guard against me doing something silly and romantic. Iridan and I have been friends since the Academy. I was there until I was fourteen summers and they gave up on me ever showing any promise. I used to protect him from Juliana when we were all little. She used to beat him."

Brannis was not sure why he chose to introduce Illiardra to her son that way. *Maybe because that seems to sum him up so well. He always needed protecting.*

"And now Rashan wishes to make him a warlock. Perhaps he thinks to toughen him by foisting his tormentor upon him as a wife. My, what changes a few seasons can wreak," she said, then laughed. It was a melodic laugh, with a smile that seemed so much more at ease than Juliana's fake one.

"Well, that was fourteen winters ago," Brannis commented.

"A whiff of fragrance from a petal as it falls from a rose. That is the length of fourteen winters," Illiardra said softly, looking deep into Brannis's eyes. "Do you have any idea how old I am?"

"By your looks, twenty springtimes and no more, but I know better. You are immortal and choose whatever appearance you wish. By your words, I would guess you are closer to Rashan's age," Brannis ventured. Mortal women were so sensitive about age, he did not want to risk angering her by guessing any older than that.

Rather than taking offense, she laughed. "My dear Brannis, you are so tactful. You wish not to offend me, but miss the mark by kingdoms. I was old when Kadrin was founded, a little city-state in the wilderness, carved out in the shadow of the elder woods and brash enough to name itself an empire. I knew Gehlen, whose staff your people seem to have misplaced, and mighty Tallax, two thousand winters dead when Gehlen was born."

Rashan being two hundred and forty-two summers old was a hard thing to grasp at times. He was a creature of a different age, who lived in a much different

Kadrin from the one that now stood. He had no reason to disbelieve Illiardra's claim, ludicrous though it seemed on its face, but the span of summers defied Brannis's comprehension.

"Tallax was a real man?" was the best response Brannis could muster out of the information he had just absorbed. "I was taught that he was just a legend."

"Oh, he was a legend, for certain, but a real man as well. Your ancestors used to claim his blood ran within them. He never unlocked the secret to immortality, but kept alive over seven hundred summers on life extension alone. All that is true," Illiardra said.

"And his Source?" Brannis asked, his love of history brimming to the surface. "Was it as strong as the stories said?"

"It is so hard to compare such things, especially across so many years. But men in that age said that his Source hurt to look upon," Illiardra said. As the music slowed, the couples dancing did as well. Illiardra drifted lower and closer, and rested her head against Brannis's chest. "Brannis, your obvious love of history is endearing to one who has seen so much of it and finds too many who care not. That reason is why I so seldom visit the mortal world. It seems so foreign and unwelcoming. I had come to visit Rashan, and to meet my son.

"When I look in my son's eyes, I see disbelief and denial. I saw how he looked to the guests at the wedding. The couple that we sent him to be fostered with were there, and I saw in that look the love a son bears for his mother. I bore Rashan a son, but I did not mother one. Iridan fears me and what I represent: a mother he never knew and a heritage he does not understand. So my son avoids me, and my Rashan has gone off. He used a transference spell shortly after the ceremony, and I could not see far enough to know where he went. Brannis, you are a clever boy. Where might he have gone?"

Brannis could think of only one option when he thought of Rashan: vengeance. "Did he ever tell you of his philosophy, to let none live who have tried to harm him?" Illiardra nodded sadly. "I can only surmise that he found out who sent that assassin, and is laying waste to whatever city they might be in."

"He can be so thoughtful at times. He was always full of vigor and ideas. He did things. He did not just wonder aloud about them, as so many of our kind fall into the habit of. But he has this killing lust within him as well, that try as he might, he could never overcome. Now, it seems, he has stopped trying entirely, and is giving in to his base need to spill blood. He left without even telling me, leaving me alone among strangers, with a son who denies me in his heart."

Brannis did not know what to say to that, so he wisely said nothing. He allowed the neglected immortal to spill her sorrows upon his doublet and continue talking as they floated about the terrace in time with the music.

"We have each lost someone today, someone who was already gone, but whom we could not let go. Rashan has no special claim on my heart. I am not his wife nor his concubine. Juliana is now wed to another, no longer seemly to dream of. Let us spend this night in each other's comfort." She lifted her head and looked up at him. Her eyes brightened when they met his and she smiled. "I have always preferred younger men."

* * * * * * *

The next morning, Brannis strode down the halls from his room to the practice yard, where he expected the warlock to be, if indeed he had seen fit to return from whatever burning city he had likely left in his wake. He was wearing his armor again, a precaution he felt more than justified by the assassin's attempt on Rashan the previous day. He was far less equipped to defend himself than Rashan. Without his armor, he was ripe to be killed should Megrenn send someone to end his life.

Despite Illiardra's assurances that Rashan had no hold over her, and that she had no intention of mentioning their liaison, he approached the warlock with some trepidation. Any servant who had seen them could have reported them adjourning to Brannis's chambers for the night; none would believe that they had talked for hours until Brannis fell asleep from exhaustion (and perhaps just a bit of magic). *Rashan always figures out too much for the amount of information he has.* Any hint of a tryst and Brannis's life would hang on whether Rashan was the jealous type. Brannis did not like his odds on that wager.

As he walked along, he saw someone approaching from one of the side corridors. He stopped short, recognizing Juliana's distinct form—forever etched into his psyche—out of the corner of his eye. Her hair was a disastrous mess, not just uncoiffed, but snarled and tangled. Her black Sixth Circle robes hung loose about her thin frame, not cinched at the waist as she usually wore them, and she had her armed tucked into the opposite sleeves, hugging them close to her body. What really drew Brannis attention was her face: wickedly reddened on one side, with a swollen knot beneath the eye that would surely turn purple with a bit of time.

Juliana backed up a step tentatively as Brannis rushed over to her, her eyes widening as if unsure of what to do.

"What happened?" Brannis demanded, sounding both concerned and angry at once.

"We argued. It just … happened. Everything is fine." Juliana's voice trembled. "I was just on my way to ask Rashan if Iridan can skip his training today."

"Iridan did this to you?" Brannis asked, trying to keep calm so as not to sound like he was blaming her.

"I said something I shouldn't have," Juliana protested but Brannis shook his head.

"That is no excuse," Brannis told her. "Go see someone about that lump." Brannis strode off in the direction she had just come from, moving at twice the pace and with far less uncertainty than he had felt when preparing to approach the warlock.

* * * * * * *

"Brannis!" Juliana called after him. "I can look after myself. You do not need to 'save' me!" she shouted as he grew too far to converse with at any lower volume. She drew a deep breath and loosed it raggedly.

It is nice to know he still cares. She would have felt a bit better had Brannis not had a hand on Avalanche's hilt as he rushed off to defend her honor. *If my children grow to be tall, strong, and brave like him, I will just have to say they take after my father ...* (Shador Archon was not so different in frame from Brannis, even if he lacked the muscle) ... *instead of their own.*

She continued on to the practice yard where indeed she found the warlock awaiting Iridan's arrival. He sat with her new oath-uncle Caladris as the portly sorcerer took his morning feast.

"Iridan will not be coming down for practice this morning," Juliana interrupted them, startling Caladris with her quiet, timid approach.

"My dear girl, what happened?" Caladris asked.

"Nothing. I am fine," she answered.

"It was a long while ago, but I got married too—twice you know—and that is not a typical result." Caladris tried to keep the mood light, but Rashan was intent on darkening it.

"Iridan did that." Rashan did not even form the observation as a question. He scowled as he inspected Juliana's injuries.

"I pushed a bit too far. I know I sometimes do not think before saying things that might be hurtful. I started it," Juliana said, but Rashan was apparently indifferent to her explanation.

"I will have to have a talk with that boy," he growled. Caladris quietly excused himself in the opposite direction as Rashan made to leave the yard.

"You are just as bad as Brannis," Juliana muttered beneath her breath, but had not counted on the warlock's excellent hearing.

"Brannis saw you like that?" Rashan demanded, his eyes widening. The warlock took off at a run.

When he was gone, Juliana quietly pulled her hands out of her sleeves. The knuckles were raw and bloody. *Soria, are you watching today? If you are, tell me how you manage not to ruin your knuckles.*

* * * * * * *

Rashan saw the door to Iridan's chamber wide open, with a pair of the palace guards flanking it. Whatever orders they might have been given, Brannis was authorized to countermand. He rushed past them to find Brannis standing next to a pool of blood.

"What did you do?" he shouted at Brannis, torn as to whether he should chastise the general of his armies or just slay him where he stood.

"It was not me." Brannis turned to face the warlock, clean of any blood. The warlock came around the side of the bed to see Iridan curled up on his side, a bloody pillow propped under his head and a blanket over him. His face was a gory mess.

"Perhaps I ought to reconsider which of them to train as a warlock," Rashan commented.

Chapter 12 ~ Aftermath Examined

The cobblestones were blackened, even melted in places. The charred remains of buildings stood about the edges of the devastation, but toward the middle, only buildings with stone foundations showed any signs of having existed at all. There were signs of recovery, though, for the residents of that particularly downtrodden neighborhood of Marker's Point. A few ramshackle buildings had been put up, while real work was being done to replace others.

"How far across would you say it is, one side to the other?" Soria asked, her eyes sweeping the scene. She wore her Kheshi persona. In a place like Marker's Point, looking as if you invited trouble was paradoxically the best way to avoid meeting it. It also saved her the trouble of either hiding or drawing strange looks for her Kheshi accent.

"A hundred paces across, I'd say," Tanner offered. "Maybe a hundred and fifty."

"Hmm, closer to two hundred, I think," Rakashi ventured. "You have a long stride, my friend."

"Well, I'm not measuring with yours. What sort of fool counts using his guess at someone else's stride?"

"So, black powder, or aether?" Soria asked. She nodded in the direction of the helm that Zell was carrying. Zell donned the helm and looked about the burned streets.

"Aether," Zell stated. They had concealed the stolen crown inside the helm, wrapping it in cloth and sewing it to the leather liner that cushioned the wearer's head. "It all looks ... scratched up. I don't know how else to describe it, but it stands out for certain."

"So ... what, then?" Tanner asked. "We have a warlock running around here, incinerating buildings. I don't think I care to meet him. If he knows his stuff, what would he want with a bunch like us? We'd be small timers to him. If he can't control his aether and *this* is what happens," he gestured to their general vicinity, "I don't know that it would be safe traveling with him."

"I think Tanner's right, Soria," Zellisan added, taking the magical helm off and nodding. "This one is too dangerous. We do well enough for ourselves that I don't see the risk being worth it."

"Really?" Soria asked sardonically. "You are both turning squirrel on me now that we are getting close to our quarry. Some warriors you two are. How about you, Rakashi?"

"I think it is time you told us who we are following. You know something, I think, that we do not," the clever Rakashi answered.

Soria eyed him steadily, watching for a sign that he would relent, but he met her glare stoically. "Fine," she replied. "But not out here in the open."

* * * * * * * *

"So, if Rakashi's right, you have some reason to think this Kyrus fellow will join us," Zellisan postulated, taking a swallow of a thick dark ale.

They had picked out an upper-class tavern for their discussion, *The Ale Exchange*. It served mainly ship owners, financiers, traveling noblemen, and the assorted retainers such men brought with them. It also attracted coinblades of various ilk, so their weapons were not entirely out of place.

"Speak Kadrin while we are here, just in case," Soria instructed in Kadrin. "If anyone looks like they are paying attention to what we say, we will have to kill or capture them."

"He's that important, this person we are looking for?" Rakashi asked, speaking Kadrin with a Takalish accent. It was not his native tongue, but he spoke it well.

"Yes. And use no names. A garbled conversation with a proper name mixed in stands out, if the name is the only familiar word," Soria said.

"Now you're just being paranoid. Anyone who knows the name must be able to understand the rest, wouldn't you think?" Tanner objected. He was waiting on the steward to bring up a bottle of Takalish apple liqueur that Rakashi had suggested. Watching Zellisan and Soria already enjoying their ales was making him impatient and irritated.

"Fine, then," Soria relented. "I do know who this Kyrus Hinterdale is, or at least quite strongly suspect. I got the clue I needed at Raynesdark, when—"

"Skip it. Tell the story later, just give us a name," Tanner cut in, looking around distractedly for the steward.

"You have no sense of drama," Soria complained. "When I was at Raynesdark," she picked up, ignoring Tanner's complaint, "I saw the Megrenn sorcerer who stole the Staff of Gehlen. He did not recognize me, but he knew Brannis by sight. Brannis knew him as well, addressing him as Captain Zayne."

"Wait, so that pirate is a twinborn Megrenn sorcerer?" Zellisan asked. "Small wonder he has been so successful."

"Yes, those were cannons he used at Raynesdark. He taught the goblins to make ones like those a ship would carry. I saw a few of them before the warlock had them melted down," Soria said.

"I see ..." Rakashi stated, having surely already skipped ahead to her conclusion.

"Yes, well, this sorcerer knew Brannis as well, and he called him Kyrus." Soria finished her little tale, and Tanner and Zell gaped at her.

"No wonder you're so hot to find him," Zellisan joked. "I had wondered if you would follow through on the whole wedding arrangement, and now I see why you did. You are just going to find yourself a new Brannis."

"Ha-ha," Tanner said. "I've been wanting a chance to cross swords with this new grand marshal of ours. Can't exactly march up to him in Kadris and ask for a sparring match, though."

"Mind you, he is still the same man we have been tracking. He is a scribe in Tellurak, not a knight, and I do not think he has known that he is twinborn for very long at all. Four months ago, it seems, he was playing with light and telekinesis spells. Three months ago, he needed help to free himself from a non-aether-proof prison cell, but managed to burn a ship down in the harbor. A week after that, he destroyed a chunk of Marker's Point. On the road to Raynesdark, Brannis had brought along books of magic. Oh, he said they were to figure out how best to use the sorcerers he was assigned, but Brannis is too clever by half. He was teaching this Kyrus some proper spells so he would not have another incident like Marker's Point."

"How can you be so sure of all that?" Zell seemed more curious than skeptical, knowing Soria to be rash and reckless, yes, but she was far from stupid.

"I know him too well. Most of us had some help in figuring out how being twinborn worked, and all of us were much younger than two-and-twenty when we first learned our dreams weren't dreams. Brannis seems to have puzzled out much of it on his own, or gleaned it from Captain Zayne. But availability of the libraries in the Tower of Contemplation is too valuable to pass up. As Sixth Circle, even I was not allowed in most of those, but because Brannis seems to have found favor with the warlock, he has free run of the place," Soria said. "If you discovered magic in Tellurak, and knew of no one in Veydrus whom you could trust with the twinborn secret, how much better could you have it than being able to access every book in Kadris at your leisure?"

"Yeah, but if that was him with Zayne and Zayne is Megrenn on the other side, how do we know we can trust either of them?" Tanner asked. "Maybe he plays both sides. You say he's so clever, maybe he has you fooled, too."

Soria frowned, crossed her arms, and leaned back in her chair. "I bet my life that he will not side against me."

Rakashi appeared to be about to say something, then paused, distracted. He sat with his back to the door, but with his patched eye he saw in the aether. Direction mattered little. "You said that pirate's name too many times, I think. Someone just left furtively. I think our pirate quarry has ears with coins in them."

Zellisan swore under his breath. Soria threw a backhanded slap that jarred Tanner's shoulder. "Paranoid, huh?"

"I lost track of him in the crowds outside. There are too many people here and he was not so distinctive," Rakashi said.

"What now?" Tanner asked.

"Nothing," Soria replied. "At least, nothing we were not about to do anyway. We know the pirate sailed months ago and his ship has not returned. Safe to say, we will not meet him in person. Whatever lackeys he paid to inform on troublemakers dropping his name in public will pose little threat."

"Yeah, but who will they be telling about us?" Zellisan asked. "The pirate might have the kind of coin that could buy a few of the Tide's Watchmen. That might get us stranded here."

"Deal with the problems we know about," Soria said. "We aren't the sort to get pushed around, after all. If our little parrot talks to someone, and gets the pirate's hired knives to come looking for us, at least it will be a lead. In the meantime, we ought to split up and spend a lot of coin with the sort of folk a pirate might deal with. They may not take open bribes for information on someone as dangerous as the pirate, but we might loosen tongues if we buy their wares first."

"Anything in mind?" Zellisan asked. "I don't go to market with pirates much. What would they buy that a common man wouldn't?"

"How should I know? Be creative," Soria responded.

Zell just rolled his eyes. "Nice to know we're in good hands, eh?" Zellisan leaned over to Tanner and spoke loudly enough to ensure Soria still heard.

"Well, you two will go together," she told the mock conspirators, "and Rakashi will come with me."

"Why do I get saddled with the big oaf?" Tanner complained. "If we have to run, I'll have to hold up and wait for him, and that means a lot more sword work."

"Well, with how well that helm shows the aether, Zell ought to be able to walk around with it on and not trip all over stuff you and I cannot see without light. Rakashi can see both at once, so both pairs can keep an eye to the aether," Soria reasoned.

"What good'll that do us?" Tanner asked. "We aren't looking for a bit of magic; we're looking for a person, if he's even in the Point anymore. How would you expect to pick him out when every market has a thousand folk in it?"

"Tanner, your Source split to the Tellurak side. Mine split fairly evenly with Juliana's, maybe a bit in her favor. Zell's a dim candle in both worlds, and Rakashi is much stronger in Veydrus. Brannis's source is like the glow of a firefly. If this Kyrus is running around laying waste to whole city districts, you can bet that his Source will stand out like an ogre walking among the common folk around here."

"Makes sense," Zellisan said, though he was a bit sensitive about the subject of his weak Source and preferred not to discuss it. "And unless he looks a lot less like Brannis than you would expect, I ought to recognize him if I take the helm off. He ought to know my face too, just seeing it ... recently ..." Zell trailed off, not wanting to remind Soria about Juliana's wedding, and the little "incident" afterward.

Soria shot him a glare, but made no comment on the slip. "We will meet back at the ship an hour before sunset. If there is any night work to be done, I would rather plan it anew. We might be best hanging together after dark."

"Well I'll be flogged. She *does* have a sense of self-preservation," Tanner joked. "Only had to take comin' to the Point and having a pirate's hired ears catch a sniff of her."

"No," Soria shot back, "I don't trust you after dark because there are more brothels here than inns. If I ever have to identify your dead body, I would rather it be clothed."

Tanner could think of no clever response, so they parted ways in silence, one smug, two amused, and one consternated.

* * * * * * *

"I don't want no trouble," were the first words out of the shipper's mouth as Soria and Rakashi approached. He was Janza, by his look: scraggly grey hair framing a puffy, round face pocked by scars of a pimpled youth long decades ago. He carried a slate in one gnarled hand and held a chalk in the other. While all about men bustled with barrows filled with sacks of wheat flour or carried kegs of cheap ale, the shipping master merely watched and recorded.

"Excellent. Troubles make business go less smoothly," Rakashi replied, smiling broadly at the shipper. "I am Rakashi dar Fandar and it is business I am seeking today."

"And who's the lass?" the shipper asked suspiciously. Soria still wore her Kheshi persona, complete with tattooed kill markings. It was not the sort of sight most folk found comforting.

"My bodyguard," Rakashi answered, smiling serenely. Carrying his half-spear in a sheath on his back and built like a warrior, Rakashi did not look like the sort of man to need a bodyguard.

The shipping master eyed Soria warily, but turned his attention back to Rakashi. "What sort of business? I am a busy man. Nothing moves through this warehouse without me knowing about it."

"I am looking for a shipment of cinnamon cherry liqueur," Rakashi said. "My employer's ship was attacked by pirates and the spirits were plundered."

"I don't deal in pirated goods," the shipper replied testily. "If that's all you are concerned with, then I have no business with you."

"You misunderstand me. My employer has a very valuable customer whom he would much like to keep happy. I do not care where I find a replacement, but I must see that his customer receives the goods he has purchased. Even if we lose money this time, we wish to keep the customer's business for many years to come. So if you know of any such liqueur, whether it has come through your warehouse or not, I would be willing to pay generously for such information," Rakashi said. He reached into his coin purse, pulled out a thousand-darshi coin and handed it to the shipping master. The darshi was a small unit of currency, but a thousand of them acting in concert could secure the services of the best whores in Marker's Point, or purchase a bottle or two of the aforementioned liqueur.

"What's this for?" the man asked, narrowing his eyes and pocketing the coin before any talk of returning it came up.

"A pittance for your time," Rakashi answered. "Should you know anything about where such cargoes might find themselves, I would be more than generous." He patted his coin purse, making sure that the heavy leather pouch jingled loudly enough to convey just how much coin he was carrying.

"Well, there's a dock—that I never have cause to frequent, mind you—where I hear Zayne's people have set up their operation. If it was Captain Zayne's ship that took your employer's shipment, that might be a place to find it. If not, it might be a good bet to find a replacement.

As they walked away ten thousand darshis poorer, Soria muttered to Rakashi, "It's a good thing we have plenty of coin."

"We will not for long if we spend like this. But then again, it is only coin and we may have more whenever we wish. If Kyrus Hinterdale truly is your old lover from Kadrin, any impediment to our wealth ought to be gone once we have his aid."

Well, Soria thought, *I still have to figure out how to convince Brannis that bridgandry and mercenary work are respectable occupations. One problem at a time, though.*

* * * * * * * *

"What are you thinking, Tanner?" Zellisan sounded exasperated as Tanner held the pistol up close to his eye, examining it as if he possessed either a craftsman's eye for workmanship or an artist's appreciation of fine detail.

"I always wanted one," Tanner said. "I mean, I'm as good as any fella you want to put against me when it comes to swords, but what good's a sword when some drunk whoreson with a pistol can put a lead ball through your gut at twenty paces?"

"Thirty, I would say, with the one in your hand," the bespectacled pistolsmith corrected him. "Accurately, that is. The shot will go much farther, but accuracy is the byword when it comes to pistols. You do not want to miss your mark and have to clean and load it while some unruly gentleman is rushing to stab you before you can do so."

"Maybe I could buy myself two of them, then," Tanner reasoned. "Have the other ready if'n I happen not to hit the fella I was aimin' at."

"Many do, sir. I assure you, many do. Many dangerous men carry a pistol tucked in their belt. Carrying two or more is a sure sign of someone who intends to use one, though. Only a fool would trifle with such a man."

The pistolsmith no doubt smelled a sale that would let him close up shop for a week, if only he could draw Tanner a picture of himself as a man who commanded fear and respect.

"What if you can't hit a ship at ten paces, let alone a man?" Zellisan butted in, needling Tanner, who to the best of his knowledge had never fired a pistol in his life.

"I realize you jest, sir, but if you mean to ask what does one do if two shots is not enough?" The pistolsmith seemed to know his trade, and the crafting of weapons was only the half of it. The rest was the art of selling them once made. "At some point, only a very large man can keep putting more pistols in his belt."

He paused to allow Tanner a brief chuckle in Zell's direction. "For a more refined marksman, I do have a special piece."

The pistolsmith went to the back of his shop, and brought back a small, polished mahogany case. Tanner and Zellisan both crowded around to get a good look as the wiry little man opened the case. Inside was a queer-looking pistol, which had a sort of thick wheel stuffed in just above the trigger. It was smaller than the other pistols that the pistolsmith had shown them already, with a thinner barrel and shorter handle—though the latter was of sleek, polished ivory.

"Fancy handle but a bit of an ugly runt of a thing, ain't it?" Tanner commented to Zellisan.

"Yeah, what's that bit there do?" Zell asked, pointing a finger at the thick metal wheel at the trigger end of the barrel.

"This is an authentic piece from Cadmus Errol's workshop, made by the master's own hand. He has made a dozen or so, though now I understand his assistants have begun making more of them. You load this pistol with six shots, and each time it fires, it brings a new shot into line with the barrel." The pistolsmith pulled a pin and the wheel twisted out away from the rest of the weapon. With the flick of a thumb, the wheel spun effortlessly with a reassuring whirring sound. With a snap of the wrist, the pistolsmith locked the wheel back into place. He pushed and pulled to show that the wheel was once more securely held, then pulled the pin again and showed inside it.

"It takes special shot that has a powder charge already attached to it," the little man said, then took a small, pointed metal shot out of a different case stowed under the counter. It had a brass band around the non-pointed end, and a flat back. "I know, it looks strange, but it will hit what you aim at from fifty paces and you have six shots before needing to reload."

"Impressive," Zellisan said, but he was more impressed by seeing yet another of Cadmus Errol's creations. Soria had told him of the alarm system the Mad Tinker had set up in the museum in Golis, and any folk who had traveled widely had seen one or more of his clock towers. It seemed that the mechanical mastermind was delving into weapons as well.

"Ahh, I see your angle. You make coin sellin' shot I gotta buy from you," Tanner hedged, trying to set himself up to negotiate a good price. He wanted that pistol, and if he had to buy his ammunition from Marker's Point, so be it.

"Sadly, no. The master has his workshop churning them out like horseshoes. I have crates of the things, ready to sell, and I am far from the sole distributor of them." The smith shook his head. "I suspect in five years I will no longer be selling my own pistols anymore, just reselling the ones that Errol's workshop produces. Whatever it is you do for work, sir, pray that Cadmus Errol does not take a fancy to trying it."

An hour later, Tanner was walking at Zellisan's side, a Cadmus Errol pistol tucked in the front of his pants and a baldric laden with pre-powdered shots slung crosswise across his body. Despite the magical shield he cast each morning and the runed blade that bounced at his hip, sharp enough to bite into stone, it was the pistol that had cost him two hundred thousand eckles worth of trade bars—ten times what one of the ones made by the master's assistants would have lightened his purse by—that made him feel dangerous.

* * * * * * * *

"We are being followed," Rakashi said, leaning close to Soria as they walked, keeping his voice low so that they might not be overheard.

"How many?" she asked. She knew better than to request any more detail than that. Rakashi was watching behind them in the aether and his vision was nowhere near keen enough to determine age or garb, or what they carried.

"Two," Rakashi replied without turning to look at her. "We picked them up just after we left the warehouse."

"Do you think that shipper sent them?" Soria wondered aloud, turning down a side street to get away from the crowded main thoroughfare to somewhere she might be able to look back and check out their pursuers.

"Stranger things have happened, surely," Rakashi joked, "but I think not. I believe we merely stopped there for long enough that whoever was looking for us had time to find us."

Soria saw a stack of crates that had been delivered to a woodworker's shop, and ducked behind them. She grabbed Rakashi roughly by the arm, and dragged him behind cover as well. She crouched low and shifted her own vision into the aether to watch the men through the wood of the crates. Luck was with her, and the crates contained nothing with a Source of its own; no chickens, fresh lobster, or potted herbs were left blocking the sight lines of the narrow road in the aether.

As the two men neared, walking slowly and obviously wary of their vanished prey, Soria allowed her vision to revert to the light as she leapt from her concealment. Rakashi followed her lead, drawing his half-spear fluidly as he took up a position behind her. It was not the most gentlemanly of fighting arrangements, but he had learned through experience that being between Soria and her enemies was hazardous. Soria grabbed the closer of the two by the wrist, pulling and twisting to force him down and off his balance. She fell with him and atop him, rolling across his back to launch a kick at the back of his companion's knees. The blow struck true, and both men were on the ground before they could react to defend themselves. Soria continued her roll until she had regained her feet, one pursuer still held in her wrist-lock. Rakashi put the point of his half-spear to the base of the other man's throat.

"Fine day for a walk, good sirs," Soria greeted them sweetly in Kheshi.

Given the men's lightly bronzed skin, dark eyes, and dark hair, it was an easy guess as to their homeland—the northern part of Khesh where the native blood was mixed thickly with foreign. Neither of them had reacted to the fight like a trained warrior, though both carried knives at their belt. It was said that in Marker's Point, even midwives carried a blade, and that reputation was better deserved than most visitors realized. Still, a knife could only do so much from its sheath. The two Kheshi snoops bore lazy blades that had never left theirs to defend their owners.

"Please, do not kill me," begged the one Rakashi held at spear-point. "We mean no offense."

"You were interested in Denrik Zayne. Our master, he, too, is interested in Zayne. He would like to meet you and your friends," said the man whose arm Soria was wrenching.

"To what end?" Rakashi asked calmly, pulling the half-spear's point away from his captive's throat just a finger's breadth.

"Maybe to hire you," was the reply.

Soria and Rakashi exchanged a glance. Soria shrugged. Rakashi nodded. It was the best lead they were likely to find.

* * * * * * * *

"My thanks for sparing the lives of my servants. They are both clumsy and unwise," Parjek Ran-Haalamar greeted them that evening at his tiny palace on the seaside of the island chain, facing the sunset. Few could afford to excavate the rocky outer rim of the islands, giving such locales instant prestige among the residents of the Point. Parjek bore no noble title, for Khesh was miserly with such hereditary honors, having fewer noblemen than Acardia despite fifty times the population of those northern traders.

"They made no move for their weapons. I had the luxury of mercy." Soria spoke for the group as the four of them stood before the Kheshi shipping magnate. She looked curiously about the room as she spoke, admiring the opulent imported marble stonework as it contrasted with traditional Kheshi woven straw mats, which were sold in bulk in every market the Kheshi traded with.

"Quite so," Parjek agreed disinterestedly, giving the impression that his interest in his men's lives was feigned out of politeness. "Now I understand that you have some sort of interest in a pirate named Denrik Zayne?" He waved a hand dismissively at Soria to forestall the answer she was about to give. "No, no, I know you do. I have an interest in him as well. I have lost two ships to him now. This is most obviously not good for my business. My customers expect their shipments to arrive. Storms may sink a trader's ships, and send the cargo to a soaking grave, but what can be done about a storm, hey? You find good captains and hope they are better than the storms they see. Ahh, but pirates? My customers do not like hearing that some pirate now has their wares."

"So you want us to hunt him down for you?" Soria asked, raising an eyebrow. She had really hoped to find out about Brannis's (or Kyrus's) whereabouts through more oblique methods rather than dealing with Denrik Zayne directly. Aside from the very real possibility that he would recognize her from their encounter at Raynesdark, he might very well be a threat in her own world.

"No. I wish to bait a trap for him. I have another ship setting sail, laden with valuable goods. Hmm, for the sake of discussion, let us call them mangoes. I am too well known to ship my mangoes in complete secrecy, so word escapes even before the ship leaves port. Pirates love mangoes, because they are easy to carry, easy to sell, and quite valuable," Parjek explained.

"And when he attacks your ship, we catch him and kill him? That about do it?" Tanner quipped.

Soria and Parjek both glared at him. Soria was supposedly their leader, or she had told Parjek as much, at least. It undercut her authority to have her underling interrupt the negotiation of the deal.

"That ... roughly outlines the plan ... yes," Parjek continued. "However, I need to know that I pay for good fighters. My coinblades must be able to overpower the boarding party that Zayne sends aboard, and then to take the fight to his own ship. You," he said, looking at Soria, "who take 'Coinblade' as a surname even, I hope to see some evidence that you are worthy of the name. By your dress and manner, you are Tezuan Sun trained. I have two Tezuan bodyguards myself."

And at the mention, two formidable-looking men stepped in from a side room. They were both Kheshi, with close-cropped yellow hair and muscular bare arms—pure-blooded southerners—exposed by the same design of armor that Soria wore. Neither was as tall as she was, but they were more stocky of build.

"Meet Jovin and Daar-Ben. They will be among those on the bait ship with you, should you pass my test," Parjek said.

"What test?" Soria asked, narrowing her eyes at the Kheshi merchant prince.

"It is easy for a Kheshi lass to buy armor and call herself a Tezuan Sun disciple," Parjek answered, his hands worrying at one another under her glare. "You need not win, of course, but you must convince Daar-Ben that you really are Tezuan. No blades, no killing, this is merely to confirm you are who you claim to be."

Soria fought to keep a smirk off her face. *If only you knew ...*

Managing to keep her composure, Soria turned to face her would-be opponent. She cracked her knuckles as she let her vision fade to the aether. Though she had not been told which of the two Kheshi was to be her opponent, she knew immediately. The one to her right was the stronger of the two by his Source and was the easy choice to test her skills. Drawing from her own Source, Soria worked a straightforward telekinesis spell.

The one whom she had guessed to be Daar-Ben stood still, dark eyes widening as he tried to adopt a formal Tezuan sparring stance. Soria knew, though, that he now felt as if he had been buried in sand, his limbs held tightly in place. He could wiggle a bit, but was otherwise held fast.

"Daar-Ben, step forward and face her," Parjek ordered impatiently when his guard had not made a move after a moment. "What are you waiting for?"

"Do you yield?" Soria asked him, looking him squarely in the eye. She had always hated being asked that question ...

* * * * * * *

The children knelt in orderly rows on the rough stone floor of the courtyard in the Temple of the Sun. They were ordered by age, then by skill, with the eldest students at the front and the strongest of each age toward the middle. Soria knelt in the very center of the fourteen-year-old disciples, as she had knelt in the center position of the thirteen-year-olds the year before. The Parting of Ways had come yet again, along with another chance at freedom.

She kept silent, unmoving, respectful. She had learned to stopper the emotions that had gotten her into so much trouble in her ten years as a Tezuan Sun disciple. They boiled inside her, but she had become more careful about how often they showed themselves. It allowed her to watch the formal proceedings with just the hint of a smile betraying her intent.

One by one, the students twenty years aged were called before Mother Stina, the highest-ranked of their temple. One by one, each learned their fate. By their skills and their conduct during their training, each had been evaluated and the masters had figured out how best they would serve the temple. The honored few were taken on as full Brothers and Sisters of the order. Those would teach and lead as the successors of the temple's legacy. Others were assigned as gardeners, cooks, or other servant positions. The temple allowed no outsiders and certain tasks were better suited for adults to oversee, rather than the young disciples. Those chosen for such roles were rarely surprised, as their later years had groomed them for specific specialties. Another group was sent away from the temple. They would be expected to use their skills to earn money, most of which would be sent back to the temple to pay for their meager needs. It was the only source of income the ascetics had.

Soria was impatient. She knew her fate and six years seemed too long to wait. She would never belong in the temple. Juliana's eyes saw more of the world each morning than Soria's had since the temple had taken her in. There was a world beyond the walls, and Varnus had promised to show it to her. He was waiting in Delfar for her, just an hour's walk from the Temple of the Sun. All she had to do was earn her freedom to leave.

"Are there any who would challenge their fate?" Mother Stina asked after the last of the assignments was handed down.

They were the words Soria was waiting for.

"I challenge my fate!" Soria proclaimed, standing and addressing Mother Stina directly. As far as she could recall, it was the first she had spoken to the Mother of the temple aside from apologies and excuses for her behavior.

"Your fate was not chosen today, young Soria," Mother Stina replied serenely.

"That is what I challenge. I want my fate settled," Soria countered and she began to walk forward, picking her way through the neatly ordered rows of her fellow students.

She stopped a few paces from the elderly Tezuan ascetic. The two women locked gazes. The younger was clad in nothing but the loose black pants that all the students wore and the cloth wrap the girls wore about their chests. She was barefooted, bare armed, but wore a look of determination like armor. The elder wore a robe of silk the color of saffron, which shone in the early morning light. She wore sandals beneath the robe, and walked with a staff that was a badge of authority more than any sort of aid. Her wrinkled face kept a serene look in place, but her dark eyes betrayed a hint of annoyance. Soria had a rather inimitable ability to annoy Mother Stina.

"Your fate is to spend six more years learning humility and patience," Mother Stina spoke coldly, never taking her eyes from her petitioner.

"I challenge that, too," Soria shot back.

There were gasps from among the onlooking disciples and even a few of the instructors. A few mutters were heard, but Mother Stina's gaze quickly swept the courtyard, and all was silent again, save for the morning calls of the birds.

"So be it. If you would challenge me, then do so," Mother Stina declared.

Soria fought back a grin, gritting her teeth and pursing her lips.

Many years, one or more of the disciples challenged the fate they were assigned. Few ever managed to actually oppose Mother Stina. She would stare at them until they changed their minds and yielded, never having so much as taken a fighting stance. Soria had paid closer attention the last year, when Ronmo had objected to being sent out rather than being installed as a fighting instructor as he had wished. She had seen the rudimentary telekinesis that the old woman used, holding her opponent in place with the power of her sann—what the Tezuan called aether or Source—they did not understand the two separately. Juliana had spent a good deal of time helping Soria find out how to counter such a trick.

"Do you yield?" Mother Stina asked.

Her manner suggested the mere question was a formality. Soria watched in the aether as the tendrils of Mother Stina's spell wove themselves around her. Soria's Source was stronger than Ronmo's had been, and was not held entirely immobile. Fighting the spell, she brought her hands up in front of her, palms facing Mother Stina. With a quick jerk, she spread her hands, severing the spell's connection to her. She continued the motion into a Tezuan fighting stance. Mother Stina seemed the tiniest bit surprised, but accepted that she would have to fight Soria to enforce her edict. The old woman let go her staff, which balanced perfectly on end, demonstrating her skill and control.

Soria saw through that little trick as well. She reached out in the aether, and loosed the staff from Mother Stina's spell as well. It clattered to the ground. and Soria could not stop herself any longer. Her lips curled into the mischievous grin that had accompanied so many of the troubles she had gotten herself into during her years at the Temple of the Sun.

Mother Stina took the small disrespect for what it was, and leapt to the attack. No follower of the Tezuan way was unschooled in combat; age and experience often triumphed over the strength and speed of youth. The old woman flew through the air with her body outstretched, one foot leading in a kick. Soria ducked the blow and spun to face Mother Stina as the old ascetic landed behind her. Soria slapped aside two punches, a kick, another punch; Mother Stina thought to overwhelm an undisciplined defense. Soria kept her aether in check, her Source balanced. She took aether to where it was most needed within her body: legs to speed her footwork, forearms to absorb impacts … hands to deliver blows.

While Soria had started out on defense, she merely wanted to put on a show for the watching throng of disciples and instructors. Her first punch was faster than Mother Stina imagined a disciple could throw. It caught her squarely in the chest and took her from her feet. Mother Stina hit the ground as fluidly as any ascetic among them could manage, landing in a roll and popping back to her feet immediately. Soria could tell the blow had hurt her, though. A few murmurs began again among the disciples, but this time Stina was in no position to silence them.

"No, I do not yield," Soria finally answered.

Mother Stina was more cautious in her second onslaught, keeping her defenses up while making attack after attack. She tried trips and feints, punches, kicks, and elbows. She tried to grab Soria to throw her. Nothing worked. Soria was too fast, her Source speeding her movements by skilled direction of the aether within it.

Finally one blow aimed at Soria's face struck cleanly. Soria had made no attempt to block, dodge, or deflect it. Even with her own sann to strengthen and protect her, Mother Stina broke her hand against the shielding spell Soria enacted. Juliana had learned to cast them two seasons before, and Soria had been practicing them almost nonstop ever since.

As Mother Stina recoiled in pain from the unexpected impact against something she had not seen, Soria grabbed the wrist of her broken hand. She pulled down and across her body, bringing Mother Stina's stomach and her own knee into solid contact. As the old woman doubled over, Soria brought her free hand across and stuck a blow to Mother Stina's jaw. The Tezuan Mother's control of her sann kept her teeth in her mouth, but a spray of blood and spittle spread across the stone floor.

As Soria twisted her arm, and forced her to the ground, to all appearances preparing for a fatal blow, Mother Stina spoke up.

"I yield," the old ascetic croaked though bloodied lips. "Begone and never return, you rotten, ungrateful child."

"Thank you. That is all I wanted," Soria replied, letting go the old woman's arm. To the rest of the assembly, she said, "Should I encounter any of you in the world out there, we will be as strangers. There is no past between us. I am starting anew. Friendships I may remember, but I leave all grudges here. Any who seek to do me harm or take my freedom again, remember this," she said, pointing to where Mother Stina lay.

That night, she changed into some traveling clothes at the inn where Zellisan was staying. She met his friends Tanner and Rakashi. They did not care that she was not Kheshi born, like so many of her fellow disciples had. They spoke Juliana's language to her, until she re-learned the forgotten Acardian of her infancy. They treated her like a friend.

* * * * * * * *

"What do you mean 'yield'? You have not even begun to fight him yet!" Parjek objected.

"I yield," Daar-Ben whispered hoarsely, short of breath as Soria's spell held his chest tightly. A heartbeat later, he slumped forward, coughing and gasping to recover his breath as Soria released him. She turned her attention back to Parjek.

"Satisfied, Daar-Ben?" she called out over her shoulder, watching Parjek as she did so.

"Yes. Master, she is Tezuan," Daar-Ben confirmed between ragged breaths.

"What nonsense is this?" Parjek demanded. "I ordered to you test her in combat, not stare at her and lose your composure. You ought to be ashamed of yourself."

"Master, it is a Tezuan technique that is beyond me. My muscles stiffened and I could not move." Daar-Ben begged his master's forgiveness. "Please believe me."

"Jovin," Parjek turned his attention to his other guard. "You fight her, then. See if you can actually attack her, unlike cowardly Daar-Ben."

"No, Master. With respect, I will not," Jovin answered, bowing slightly in deference, despite his insubordination.

"Fine. If you will not fight a girl, prove yourself against the large one. This is your test, though, not his. If you will not fight this one, I will dismiss both of you from my service," Parjek snarled.

"Of course, Master. I hope to redeem myself in your eyes," Jovin replied, obviously relieved to be fighting the giant Zellisan instead of the tall but wispy Soria. "No helmet or blade, but you may wear the rest of your armor," he told his opponent.

Zell grunted a reply, handed Tanner his helm and sword, and stepped forward to meet his opponent. He was a full head taller and twice the man's heft but, he had seen Soria fight, and was wary of another with her pedigree. He took up a brawler's stance, crouched just slightly, chin tucked, hands raised in loose fists with his forearms framing his face. He could tighten a fist to punch, but was ready to grab as well; grappling seemed likely to favor him, should the chance present itself.

Soria and Tanner exchanged looks. By a system they had worked out over years of traveling and gambling together, they settled on a wager without so much as a word or hand signal. Tanner favored the Tezuan fighter for two thousand eckles. Soria gave him two-to-one odds in Zell's favor. Soria had never been able to manage a mind-speaking spell silently, so they had developed other ways to communicate surreptitiously. They had no real worry about their host and prospective employer learning about their wager, but whoever was found to be betting against Zellisan would find themselves on the wrong side of a very large man's temper should he find out.

The two opponents circled, each feeling the other out. Jovin shot quick punches and kicks at Zellisan to test the big man's reaction time. Zellisan threw jabs to find his range, and move close enough to hit the smaller man. Zell had little formal training in Tellurak, but had been in many brawls, stretched across decades back to his youth. His Kadrin training included some hand-fighting, but he had never kept up with it, seeing as he always had a blade near at hand.

Jovin landed a kick that Zellisan caught on his forearm, taking it full force to protect his head. His mail coat spread the blow's force, and probably kept his forearm from breaking.

He doesn't hit like Soria, though. Must not be able to do that thing with the aether that she says she does.

Jovin tried to follow up with a similar attack, but just feinted as Zellisan hopped back quickly. Zell threw a pair of quick jabs, purposely pulling them short, hoping to confuse his opponent about his reach and draw him a bit closer.

Jovin tried the high kick again, but it was another feint. Zellisan predicted it, and moved forward instead of back. Both men ended up surprised as Jovin's quick follow-up kick connected with the side of Zellisan's knee, and Zell managed to grab hold of Jovin's upper arm. Zell grunted in pain as his knee nearly buckled beneath him; Jovin let out a quick yelp as the larger man followed up by putting his other hand to Jovin's stomach and lifting him off his feet.

"Enough!" Parjek shouted, just as it looked like Zellisan was going to hurl the Tezuan bodyguard headfirst to the marble floor like a spear. "You have both satisfied my curiosity. I wish to lose no men before the trap has even been baited."

Zellisan gave the Kheshi man a curious look, then shrugged and set him down on his feet.

"My apologies if I have injured you," Jovin said.

"Hmph, I've had worse," Zell replied, favoring the leg heavily.

"Daar-Ben, I give you another chance," Parjek said to the other Tezuan. "You do not get another opponent. You fight or you find a new master."

"It is not worth losing your job over," Soria told him mildly, stepping toward the Kheshi she had defeated once already.

"Please forgive me, mistress." He bowed to Soria and found he was able to take up his fighting posture.

Soria did not mirror it, nor take any stance at all. She merely stood and nodded her readiness to Daar-Ben, who approached her cautiously. With the first tentative punch, he was done in. Channeling aether through her muscles, Soria reacted more quickly than any opponent Daar-Ben had ever faced. She grabbed him by the wrist and yanked him forward right into a side kick, which Soria buried low in his stomach. The blow was hard enough to lift the man from his feet. He wore hardened leather armor, and was trained to tighten his core muscles when hit, but still had the wind knocked out of him. Soria kept hold of his wrist and drew him forward as his legs and lower torso went back, resulting in a cringe from the spectators when he landed spread out flat as he hit the straw mat on the floor.

Soria released his wrist, and Daar-Ben struggled to his hands and knees, again desperate for breath.

"You are hired," Parjek informed her.

Chapter 13 - Nighttime in the Aether

The jungle undergrowth rustled at Kyrus's passing. There was just enough starlight passing through the treetops that he was able to find his way without stumbling around by aether-vision alone. Accustomed though he was to watching in both, he was going to have his fill of seeing aether soon enough, and wanted to enjoy the light a while longer, scant though it was in the predawn hours.

His slumber had been restless, first from seeing the aftermath of Iridan and Juliana's post-marital brawl, then more persistently due to his own worries about the thought of what he was about to undertake. *Juliana is fine. Iridan is going to be fine. How will I fare, when someone thinks back to me on the morrow?*

Kyrus had thrown on his old tunic, an odd feeling after becoming so used to baring his chest like the Denku natives. He knew he would be wanting it when he arrived in Acardia, though, so he kept it with him. The northern air would be pleasant enough, but not so much so that he would shun the protection that a good layer of wool would afford. The sea breezes were cut down by the jungle trees, but it was not so warm before dawn out of doors; it was better than forgetting about the tunic later.

Kyrus bent low to place a palm-sized stone on the ground. It was adorned with runes he had carved the previous day and infused with aether. The runes did very little, but they were easy to see in his aether-vision. He looked back at the path he had taken, peeking into the aether briefly to align the stone he had just set down with the ones that were already in place. The Denku had little in the way of navigational equipment, but Kyrus was fairly certain his line was good enough to get him to Acardia, if not straight to Scar Harbor.

The first hints of dawn peeked above the horizon, and Kyrus continued to lay his stones. He had a satchel filled with them, and was going to lay them as far as he could, until he ran out of stones or island upon which to place them. It was quiet and peaceful; the earliest risers among the Denku were the fisherfolk and they would not be heading into the jungle.

Will I miss this place? There is the same salt in the air back home, but it smells of fruit and flowers here, not just brine. Winter will come soon, and Denku Appa will scarcely notice the difference, while I stomp through drifts of snow to buy ink for four months of the year in Scar Harbor. It will be good to hear Acardian spoken by native tongues again, though, and to have a few spiced crescents, even if I must sneak into Greuder's in disguise. I think, though, that if I can have Abbiley with me, I can be happy anywhere.

Kyrus placed another stone, smiling to himself.

* * * * * * * *

Kyrus's satchel was nearly empty by the time Gahalu found him, late in the morning. The weight of the stones had been wearing on Kyrus's shoulder, and he was glad to be nearly done with his task. The burden of saying his farewells was not so easily shed, though.

"What are the stones for, Spirit Man Kyrus?" Gahalu asked, suspecting the answer based on the direction he had traveled in following them.

"The spirit world is dark," Kyrus explained. "I will be going far and lacking for landmarks. I want to be sure of my course before setting off across the Katamic. The stones will shine in the spirit world, giving me a heading to follow."

"So your time with us is at an end?" Gahalu ventured, watching as Kyrus placed another of his beacon stones, and checked it against the long line he had already placed.

"Yes. Today I will make my journey. My short trials on the beach have been going much better. I can control it well enough now that I think I will be safe even for so long a distance."

"How soon?" Gahalu asked him.

Kyrus felt as if his heart had already departed the island, and he began to miss his friend before he had even left.

"We can walk back to the village. I will take a midday meal, say my farewells. Then I will gather what little I will take with me and be on my way," Kyrus said. "I do not intend to be away for too long. Days certainly, perhaps months, but I expect to return when I am able."

"Once you have found your woman and convinced her to join you here?" Gahalu guessed, following as Kyrus stood and began the walk back to the village, his satchel empty.

"That is my plan. I have a few others I wish to visit as well, whom I have wondered about in my exile from Scar Harbor. With the manner of my leaving, my reputation must be in a shambles and I do not wish that to be the last impression my friends and family have of me. I will visit my parents and any of my siblings who are still living nearby. I will see my baker friend and my old mentor who now works for the Acardian king. I will see my old colleagues, perhaps, as well. I dare not linger, though. I was still thought a criminal when I left and though I could defend myself, I have no wish to cause strife by my return."

"You will be missed," Gahalu replied.

The farewell meal was an emotional affair. Kyrus had not realized how deeply he had affected the lives of the Denku. Their previous spirit men had been advisors and wise men, but had never shown them such vivid demonstrations of the power of the spirit world before. The Denku had grown more devout by Kyrus's presence among them, and it pained them to see him go. Many of the womenfolk wept openly; Tippu and Kahli could not even stay long enough to make their good-byes to him personally, running off sobbing from the small feast.

Men drank in tribute to him, but Kyrus had to refuse to join them. He explained that strong drink would cloud his powers, and make his trip dangerous. The hunters did not know how the spirit man's powers worked, but understood well enough the impairments that liquors caused, and accepted his polite refusal.

As Kyrus stood to make his way to the spot he had plotted for the start of his trip, the Denku crowded around, hugging him and touching him. They shook his hand in the Acardian tradition he had shown them. They clapped him on the back and wished him a safe journey. Kyrus accepted all the kind words and gestures, but was already beginning to block them out as he cleared his mind in preparation.

This is it, he thought. *Time to go home.*

* * * * * * * *

"Doxlo intuvae menep gahalixviu junumar tequalix ferendak uzganmanni dekdardon vesvata eho." And the world of light went dark as Kyrus finished the incantation.

Sources abounded on the island, but the beacons he had runed stood out as clearly as the moon in a starry sky. He drifted toward the first of them deliberately, keeping his pace slow so that he did not whiz past and lose his way. From the first stone, he headed to the second and from the second to the third. There was no sense of up or down, left or right in the void he found himself in, as a disembodied Source loosed in the aether. He could spin himself around and not feel dizzy, though disorientation would be certain.

Without those stones, I could never have aimed my way to Acardia.

The stones did not give the sense of a straight line the way they did as he laid them out that morning, confirming to Kyrus that they were going to keep him to his heading better than his free-floating senses could have managed. Confident that he was on course, he increased his speed.

This is amazing! I always knew Tellurak was round, but I think I can see it in the slight arc of the stones' path.

Kyrus passed by stone after stone until he saw the end of his guiding beacons. Steeling himself, he passed the last of them and kept his heading as steady as he could manage. *Here goes nothing …*

Kyrus shot through the aether like a cannonball. He passed through the remaining Sources on the island in a blur, and found himself in a sparse wilderness, as if leaving a dense fog to find himself in a light mist. *The Katamic,* he realized. *It must be much less densely populated in the deep waters away from the islands.*

He knew from his experiments that his sense of time was accelerated while using the transference spell. He had probably just been enclosed in the sphere of aether a moment ago, by the Denku bystanders' reckoning.

Kyrus held his attention dead ahead, not daring to veer for fear of losing his way. It was dark all about him, with just occasional breaks for a Source here and there.

I wish I could see in the light while traveling like this. The view must be singularly compelling, flying over the water as fast as I must be going.

Time passed and Kyrus began to worry. *How long have I been gone? It feels like hours, but I have no way to know. I wonder if I can gain altitude to see farther, like a lookout would at sea. I would be much happier with some sight of a congregation of Sources.*

Kyrus moved upward as he went, judging as best he could without a physical sense of his orientation. The gambit paid no reward, though, save to aid the dark, nagging portion of Kyrus's brain in its attempt to convince him that he had gone astray. There were no large groups of Sources to be seen that would indicate a town, coastal shallows filled with fish, or even forests. Kyrus looked all about—and immediately knew his mistake.

I just lost my heading.

He could not keep his "body" still and just turn his head to look around; his body was back on Denku Appa. He had no sun or other landmark to guide himself by. Turn to the left and then back to the right; he had no way to tell if he had gone back to facing exactly the same direction.

Kyrus made his best guess, but he knew he was unlikely to find Scar Harbor or any part of Acardia except by sheer chance. Instead of certainty of direction, he settled for speed. *If I cannot find where I wish to go, I ought to at least get somewhere—and fast.* There was no telling how long he would be able to sustain the amounts of aether he was spending. He would find the first settlement he came across and reorient himself from there.

With a ferocious speed, Kyrus tore across the aether. There was naught around him but darkness and the ambient aether, long since departed from any Source. He was finding nothing. At the speed he imagined he was going, he ought to have crossed half the world.

What if...

The possibilities were beginning to stand and call the roll. What if he had gone up too far and was above the clouds? What if he was below ground, having mixed directions of up and down? What if some outside force was blocking his aether-vision and there were Sources all about? What if Tippu and Kahli had moved his beacon stones so he would get lost and have to return to Denku Appa?

Worries were pushed aside. *Whatever went wrong, I need to get somewhere soon.* The signs of fatigue were beginning to present themselves. He was feeling slower. His Source was beginning to ache just a bit. Kyrus renewed his efforts to draw in aether and pressed onward.

* * * * * * * *

Back on Denku Appa, the mood of Kyrus's well-wishers shifted. The mixture of sadness and solemnity that had marked their spirit man's departure was replaced by terror.

They had cautiously withdrawn a ways from Kyrus's sphere of aether, but many stayed to watch the strange magic whisk away their friend. It had seemed harmless enough at first, but then the magic began to claw at them. Few Denku had ever felt the touch of magic before Kyrus's arrival, and the friendly little magics he had used on them for their entertainment had been gentle and unthreatening. But the magic sphere that encased Kyrus and obscured their view of him was trying to draw the spirit right out of them, greedily attempting to devour their essences.

Men and women alike screamed and ran. A brave few, including Toktu and Gahalu, withdrew beyond the sphere's effects and then turned back to watch. The jungle undergrowth, and even the trees, leaned toward that sphere as if a gale wind blew in its direction. The greenery nearest to it browned and blackened, dying right before their eyes.

* * * * * * * *

Stay calm. The book said I could try navigating by feel as well. Home should feel familiar. I need to find a familiar feeling somewhere out in that void, and follow it back. Whether that takes me to Acardia, or back to my own body, I can make do.

Kyrus came to a stop and paused. He was still drawing gluttonous amounts of aether, but it would avail him nothing if he could not find a destination before running out of aether or burning himself out due to exhaustion. There were no distractions except those in his own mind, and he fought those down. He felt silly, wasting his time hoping that some path would open itself before him, when he could be getting *anywhere* with some haste, if only he moved.

At length—a length he had no way to judge other than by guessing at his level of fatigue—he felt something. Whether it was intuition or delusion, he thought he felt something. It was the best he had to go on. He focused his attention on that feeling and gave every bit of his mental effort over to heading in that direction.

The feeling had been so faint at first as to have been easily mistaken for a panicked mind turning optimism into false hope, but as he went, Kyrus felt more certain of his course. He drew harder and harder upon the aether, feeling that he was running out of time before he exceeded his own limits. His mind began to scream for him to stop.

In the distance, Kyrus saw Sources. He could discern little due to the fantastic rate at which he approached, but he could at least tell that it was a cluster of Sources and he could feel himself in there among them.

Back to Denku Appa, it seems, Kyrus thought ruefully.

Having no momentum as a disembodied Source, he parked himself at the Source-less Kyrus he found there, going from hurtling at incomprehensible speeds to a full stop quicker than the blink of an eye. The sooner he returned to the world of light, the better.

* * * * * * * *

Kyrus's senses snapped into reality accompanied by a sensation of falling. The sand beneath his feet gave way. He had just enough time for a brief, startled yelp before hitting the ground, slamming down onto his back on the fortuitously soft sand he had brought along with him.

Huh?

Kyrus looked up and saw neither sun, nor stars, nor any bit of Denku Appa he had recognized. He was in a softly lit room of green and black stone, looking up through a transference-spell-sized hole into the room above it.

He checked himself for injuries, giving the world an unobserved moment to discretely sort itself out, and start making sense. He had landed awkwardly, twisting a knee and wrist in the fall, but nothing at all serious; his ward must have been drained in transit. He patted at his head, feeling for lumps and checking his fingers to see if they came away bloody, but his body seemed largely intact. Kyrus's mind was about done, though. It had clearly had enough. Kyrus lost consciousness.

* * * * * * * *

"Welcome to Kadris." A strange but familiar voice above him roused Kyrus from his slumber. "I have warded us in. You are safe here for now, so we can talk."

"What? Where?" Kyrus tried to formulate questions as his eyes fought to focus. A few blinks brought Rashan Solaran's face into view hovering over him.

"First, two rules: you will have to go by 'Brannis' for however long you are here, and you will have to speak Kadrin. I cannot have you wandering about speaking Acardian," Rashan informed Kyrus.

Daring to turn his attention back to his surroundings, Kyrus pushed himself up onto his elbows, and looked around the room. The accommodations were entirely familiar to him, though he suspected that those in the room from which he had fallen would have been even more so ...

The spell had taken out parts of four rooms: the one he had actually centered the transference spell on, along with a chunk of the adjoining room, as well as the two rooms below those.

"How did I get here?" Kyrus asked in Kadrin, the familiar sounds tripping up his novice tongue.

"That was awful. Practice losing the accent before you give yourself away. Try whispering if you must talk to anyone else in the meantime; it will make the accent less obvious. As for an answer to your question: the transference spell that Brannis has been practicing at night, combined with reckless idiocy, the luck of Fate's own children, and a Source and draw that would shame a dragon," Rashan commented. "For all it is worth, I am rather astonished myself. I had not thought it possible to breach the veil of worlds like that." The demon looked Kyrus over appraisingly.

"This really is Kadris?" Kyrus asked.

"Oh, you had best not be a simpleton! We started with that. Yes, you are in

Kadris, in the Kadrin Empire, on the world of Veydrus. Brannis is one of the smartest lads I have ever met, and I am going to be needing you to be just as clever. You certainly did not manage to come all this way on muscle power." Rashan took hold of Kyrus's scrawny arm in one hand, then let it flop back down to make his point.

"How far did I travel?" Kyrus asked, managing an original question.

"Measured how? In miles, leagues, fathoms, yards, cubits, furlongs? I have not the slightest notion. I doubt very much that any such terms even apply. I have no concept of how far Tellurak is from here, or which direction it would be," Rashan said, appearing flustered in a way that Kyrus could not recall Brannis ever seeing him.

"I found my way here by feel. Give me the night to recover and I will set things right tomorrow," Kyrus promised, feeling distinctly in the wrong.

I am trespassing in the Imperial Palace, which I have also damaged. I have also essentially kidnapped their grand marshal.

"No. I shall have none of that. Count yourself lucky to be alive. Until a more thoughtful, rational means of controlling this power of yours presents itself, you will be staying here and taking Brannis's place," Rashan said.

"But ... I am not Brannis. I look nothing like him!" Kyrus protested.

"Nonsense. You are as good as a twin brother to him if we make allowances for your obviously less vigorous lifestyle. You will take to bed, exhausted after an ordeal of an experiment you conducted, through which you finally unlocked your Source's true potential. It has sapped your strength and vitality, but you have finally achieved what Gravis Archon predicted at your birth," Rashan said, apparently thinking through his plan aloud.

"It seems a bit premature, I think. I doubt anyone would call his prediction true, just based on having a useable Source now. He predicted Brannis would be some great sorcerer of his age," Kyrus said.

"As much as I hate having to make Gravis Archon look prescient, everyone will think it is true," Rashan told him. "Do you really have no concept of how strong a Source you have?"

"The one person who commented on it mentioned that it was stronger than average," Kyrus offered. During his time with Denrik Zayne, the pirate captain had looked at him using aether-vision and said as much.

"Well, someone either has a gift for understatement or is nearly blind in the aether. They said that the ancient sorcerer Tallax had a Source that shone with the fury of the desert sun, that it hurt just to look upon him in the aether. As we have been talking, I have been looking at you only in the light—something I hardly ever do—because I was getting a headache looking at your Source," Rashan said.

Kyrus said nothing. He did not know a proper response.

"Oh, but I did notice something before you awakened." The warlock poked Kyrus in the shoulder where the tattooed ward was inscribed. "It clearly identifies you as a fortified wall, though I suspect that there is some taxonomic error at work here. In any event, Brannis does not have a tattoo and neither should you. It has been strengthening itself off your Source since you got here. Draw the aether back out of it and I will remove the ink."

"I have been meaning to ask someone about that. *Is* it harmful to have wards placed directly onto the skin like that? I was told it was ill advised, but I seem none the worse for it, and it has been very useful." Kyrus hoped to finally get a definitive answer to that nagging question.

"Yesterday I would have said so. It would be like covering your flesh in ticks, or leeches. Seeing it on you, though, it is like a tick on a monohorn. I doubt you would notice it, though in some small way you will be better off without it. Once I remove it, I will want you to shave as soon as possible. I will keep folk away from you until you have acclimated a bit, but you need to *be* Brannis. Brannis was clean shaven as of last night."

"Do I really look that much like him otherwise?" Kyrus was dubious.

"Of course you do. It just works that way. Now I have many other matters to attend to, and I will have thoughts of what to do with you distracting me through all of them. If I do not see to them, rumors will escape reasonable control, and may start a panic. Among other matters, I am sure many residents of Kadris thought we came under Megrenn attack. Your spell shook the city."

Rashan took a surprised Kyrus under the arms, and lifted him up to the room above.

"One last question, then, before you remove this ward. You know about both worlds. Does that mean you have a counterpart in Tellurak as well?" Kyrus asked.

"Brannis," Rashan emphasized the name, "I am two hundred forty-two summers old. If I ever had a counterpart like you, who from your world has ever lived remotely so long?"

Chapter 14 - A Lack of Success

Rashan sat silently in his seat at the head of the Inner Circle. The guards in the Tower of Contemplation had been instructed to inform the rest of the Inner Circle that Warlock Rashan would explain matters just once, when all had arrived. Eight of his colleagues sat in matching silence, awaiting the stragglers in awkward fellowship.

Warlock Rashan did not drum his fingers, or stir in his seat. He did not look about or even blink. He thought, and he had much to think about.

It would be useful having Brannis around. His plans for the war seem sound. His airships have great promise. I did not even ask his twin's name—but then, I cannot slip and call him by it if I do not know it. But if his twin has the sort of mind he does, I will take the one with a Source such as I have never seen. So much potential ... So much danger ...

If he can "accidentally" breach the aether and cross between worlds, what other havoc could he cause? I need to teach him some proper spells and train him as a sorcerer before all Kadrin finds out.

The eleventh member of the Inner Circle to arrive stirred Rashan from his reveries.

"We are all here but Iridan. Where is your son?" Dolvaen asked. He had taken on the role of speaker for the rest of the Circle in dealing with the warlock.

"He will not be joining this session. He escorted his foster parents home, and I gave him leave to spend a day or so with them. I felt it best if he had time to gather himself," Rashan informed them.

"Very well then. Start by explaining what happened in the palace last night." Dolvaen rarely stood on formalities. Despite the fact Rashan was fairly certain the man hated him, Rashan found himself liking the peasant-born sorcerer.

"Since you are intent on bluntness, I will match it. It was Brannis. He finally unlocked his Source," Rashan said.

"What?" Aloisha Solaran gasped, merely the first to put voice to her surprise.

"I know not the details of how he managed it, but the quake that shook the city last night originated in his bedchambers. He opened some sort of rift into the aether. His room and the ones adjacent are missing some wall and ceiling. The desk he was working at is gone, as well as his sword and armor, which he was wearing at the time. As best I can tell, he was sucked in as well, but managed to escape," Rashan explained, having given the lie a bit of thought before the Inner Circle convened.

"That is ghastly," Caladris exclaimed. "Is the boy all right?"

"He is the worse for wear, but seems not to be permanently damaged. I think time may have passed strangely within the void. He seemed wasted as if famished by long illness, but he could not have been gone more than a few moments as time passed here. He has little recollection of the rift itself," Rashan said.

"Is this rift a danger still?" Dolvaen asked, ever practical.

"So long as I can convince Brannis not to try whatever trick he used to create it in the first place, I believe we are safe. I found no trace of the rift as I left him."

"Hmph, no curiosity anymore, eh? Concerned for your own hide?" Fenris needled Dolvaen, a friend he had always considered overly cautious. "Did it work?" Fenris grinned. The old sorcerer had asked after Brannis for years while he was at the Academy, wishing to see a truly powerful sorcerer in the Empire before he died.

"One might safely venture that opinion," Rashan said. "I have yet to witness him work any magic, but his Source is impressive, putting it mildly. Once he has rested up a bit, I intend to see what he can do with it. It is what the lad has wanted all his life. It would be a shame not to put him to the test." Rashan grinned.

"Got something in mind for him, then?" Caladris asked. "You look to be ruminating on something wicked. Tell us."

"Oh, I think I will save a surprise for later, presuming all goes well with Marshal Brannis's recovery. But I think time has come to attend to the real business we had planned for this morning. Shall we?" A stack of parchment sheets flew from Rashan's desk, and whisked themselves across the Sanctum, one to each in attendance.

Rashan gave them a moment to peruse the contents. He watched faces to see reactions and was not disappointed.

"Admirable that you have it down to three, but is this truly the best of the lot?" Caladris asked, holding up the list he had just read.

"Agreed. I had hoped for something people could gladly support. After that coronation of a wedding two days past, I half expected Iridan's name to top the list, but these are scant better," Dolvaen scoffed, waving a hand at his copy dismissively.

"It might in fact be true that there is a closer heir within the Empire," Rashan allowed. "Some poor, scared lad out there may wish to have nothing to do with succession and the plots and intrigues of court life. His folk may have sheltered him and humored him and we will hear naught of him ever. It could also happen that some poor, slovenly seneschal has misplaced enough of his lord's documents that a rightful claim was unable to be verified. But, good sirs, I would like to remind you that there was a conspiracy amongst this very assemblage here," Rashan swept his arms wide to indicate those present, "who actively sought out and culled the imperial line. I worked with what was left over, and these three are the best of them."

"This first one here, it seems out of place," Fenris commented, and several heads bent back to review their copies. "He is illegitimate. It even says so on your list. Explain that."

"The other two are legitimate, but their claims both branch back to Escelon the Fourth. Sommick Highwater was a bastard of Liead's line and two emperors less removed from Dharus. We lose Liead's blood, and Tameron's, if we skip back past them to a branch from Escelon," Rashan pointed out.

"Well, that is all fine on its own, but an illegitimate heir carries all manner of problems," Dolvaen said. "The people will not like the scurrilous break in lineage. In addition, you always have questions about the legitimacy of even an illegitimate claim. Once you break with officially kept records of noble births, who is to say what may have been forged?"

"Sommick Highwater swore to the veracity of the documents. I would accept the word of one descended of Liead's blood," Rashan countered.

"Bah, you beg the question. You cannot run us around by the ear like ink-fingered schoolboys with your tricks of logic. If Sommick Highwater is not royally descended, what would his word be worth?" Dolvaen snapped back, irritated that Rashan would try such a meat-fisted word play to convince them.

"I see it in his face, in his build. Five generations have not bred Liead's manner out of the line. I see little enough of Escelon when I look at Marnus Tollfury and none when I look at Brennen Hawkfield. I wish to re-establish the imperial line, not just continue it. We need the best and strongest of royal blood, not the cleanest," Rashan argued. There were few times when the cynical warlock showed genuine fervor for anything but bloodletting, but his service to the emperor's line was one of the exceptions.

"So you think that Sommick Highwater would be a better emperor than the other two, then?" Fenris asked. "Seems a good enough thought, if all other factors weight the same."

"No. Mistake me not, all three are vapid, spoiled slackwits. We might have made a proper emperor of any of them if they were younger, but none were brought up to handle the burdens and responsibilities. No, whomever we anoint will almost certainly be a disastrous emperor, and it will be our penance for allowing it to get to this point, just having to deal with him. You all allowed this to happen, knowingly or not, and I left the Empire to its own ends for far too long. It will take at least a generation to stabilize the dynasty, but we must begin soon, and from the best stock available," Rashan said.

"It is an interesting thought, this talk of dynasties. When this search began, I had higher hopes for an heir," Sonnin Tenruvin commented. He was quiet among the Inner Circle, and spoke seldom. When he did, it drew attention. "What if we were to install a new dynasty?"

"It would cause open rebellion!" Caladris exclaimed. "Even the lengthy search had a few noblemen gnashing their teeth and loosening swords in their sheaths. Appearances aside, we all know there are divided opinions among the Circle and even amongst ourselves. Who is to say we would not get dragged into a civil war even with Megrenn practically standing before the city gates?"

"I agree it is a poor idea, though I doubt it would be as bad as you describe," Rashan answered. "The Empire is vast enough that many do not yet see the Megrenn as threats. They expect the problem to be dealt with at the expense of marching a few troops off to join the cause. Civil war would bring death to their own homes, and few would act without a preponderance of support from the Inner Circle."

"And if some enterprising nobleman sided with Megrenn? A favorable peace with the promise of a new, more accommodating dynasty?" Dolvaen pondered. "I would support the bastard claim before ever agreeing to a new dynasty. The 'why' might be justifiable, but the 'who' would lead us to ruin."

"Aye. Whom would we choose, if it came to it?" Caladris wondered aloud.

"No! Do not even put a name to that thought," Dolvaen warned, leaping to his feet. "If word leaves this chamber of a favorite, we could well start a war as surely as if we had named an emperor to start that new dynasty. It would be the same sides, but a different man in power until it was ended."

"Please, settle down. No more talk of dynasty change. We ought to decide from among the three candidates," Rashan said as he attempted to rein in the meeting. "Once we have a name, I can have the court popinjays arrange a coronation ceremony. It will be good for the Empire, for the peasants and nobles alike, to see the matter of succession resolved."

"And you would step down as regent?" Dolvaen asked, arching an eyebrow skeptically.

"Assuming that is the wish of the new emperor, of course," Rashan replied with a shrug. "You think I enjoy the nonsense I must deal with running the Empire myself? Not a one of you would trade places with me, and you know it. I have a war to fight, and a child running it. Brilliant though Brannis may be, I will need to take a more personal interest once the real slaughter begins."

When the Inner Circle took a vote on the matter of the best claim, it split three ways almost equally. With four votes each for Sommick Highwater and Brennen Hawkfield, Warlock Rashan's vote carried the victory for Liead's bastard thrice-great grandson.

* * * * * * *

Juliana sleepwalked through her morning routine. She had taken her morning feast when the servants bringing it awakened her. She dressed in everyday garb: a half-robe over a tunic and breeches, with comfortable boots fit for riding or long walks and the harness for her dagger sheaths. It was a departure from the finery she was being prodded to wear now that she was respectably married, but she supposed that she was just not feeling that respectable.

Warlock Rashan had requested a meeting with her, once he had finished his Circle business for the morning. She was not sure what he wanted, but she had plenty of theories. *He looked at me strangely after seeing what I had done to Iridan. I have been stared at by men aplenty and his was a stare I cannot place. It was not lechery, plainly. It was not anger, which my new oathfather rarely deigns to hide. He seemed neither amused nor approving. Perhaps it was an appraising stare. Were a ship to be viewed by a prospective captain, would it have seen such a look?*

With Iridan gone to his foster parents' home, and no official business to attend to, Juliana decided to take stock of the wedding gifts they had received. There was a set of matching crystal goblets, chased in gold. Someone had given them a runed candelabra—the sorcerer's equivalent to handmade pottery. There was a pair of matching saddles with a note saying they were from Iridan's cousin Aloisha. There was …

… there was a trio of wooden boxes. The largest one, long and narrow, bore Iridan's name. The two smaller boxes—one stacked atop the other—bore the name *Juliana Solaran*. It was an odd thing to read. Seeing her own new name there looked out of place.

I always knew that would be my name one day, but not this way.

She opened the first and was surprised to see a dagger within. Black as slate, the blade was not cold to the touch as steel would have been.

Dragon bone. This is one of Jadefire's teeth!

Juliana picked up the blade and tested it in the air. It had more heft to it than was apparent by looking at it, but did not seem to slow her handling of it. Suspicious, she looked into the aether and was unsurprised to see it aglow. Many of the gifts the couple had received shone in the aether as well; it was a consequence of inviting the entire Imperial Circle to the wedding. Continuing in aether-vision, she saw that the other of her boxes held another dagger, and Iridan's contained a sword. They stood out from the trinkets and keepsakes that formed the bulk of their gifts for having much stronger concentrations of aether. These were not runed weapons, but true rune-forged blades!

She noticed in the bottom of the box that there was a slip of parchment. It bore a single word: *Freedom*. Replacing the dagger in its box, she opened the other and found a similar weapon. It was not identical, feeling lighter in her hand, having a slight curve at the tip, but it was no less wondrous or formidable. There was a note in the second box as well. It read *Adventure*, but she could see more ink showing through from the back side. She turned it over and read:

One day, long ago, I promised you a bridal gift. You thought I would promise you jewels or a horse, or some tangible thing. Instead I promised I would give you a life of freedom and adventure. Despite my failing, I had hoped to make some small amends. I hope they may offer you the protection I no longer can.

Also, think of names for them that you might share with others. Keep their true names for yourself, and do not keep these notes.

The note was unsigned, but she never doubted its origin. She knew what she would name them before she set the notes aflame and scattered their ashes in the fireplace.

* * * * * * * *

She had to poke holes in the ends of her sheaths to fit them, but the two new daggers nestled at her back, tucked beneath her tunic. The weight and size would take getting used to, and she would certainly have to get new sheaths made for their size before she carelessly injured herself on the exposed tips. Juliana had no illusions about how much good they would do her if Rashan was truly angry with her, but their presence was reassuring nonetheless.

As she walked through the palace's halls, no one greeted her. The ones that visibly took note of her made efforts not to be acknowledged. Side corridors suddenly became preferred routes, conversations became *much* more engrossing and servants about their tasks grew quite admirably focused upon them.

So none of them are certain where I fall in the warlock's graces, either. Rumors must be throughout half the Empire by now about my little spat with Iridan. I wonder if they are afraid of me personally, or of incurring Rashan's anger if they associate with me.

The room she was to meet the warlock in was a storage cellar on the lower level, which was never a good sign in Juliana's (or Soria's) experience. Whatever he wanted with her, he wanted it kept private. Rashan preferred most of his work to be veiled from public view, she knew, but rumors of what befell in those clandestine meetings ranged from the bizarre to the ominous. Some believed he had enthralled the minds of half the folk in the palace and several of the nobles. A few maintained that he was plotting to eliminate the rest of the Inner Circle, and take complete control of the Empire. Juliana suspected that he was a suspicious old curmudgeon with more plots afoot than she would ever begin to unravel.

The door was slightly ajar when she reached the appointed room. Like everything on the servants' level, it was plain and unadorned, though the surrounding walls and floor were still of the same black marble as the rest of the palace architecture. As she pushed it in, she saw that the room was largely empty, save for a few barrels and empty crates piled against one wall. Atop one of the barrels sat Rashan Solaran, his feet dangling well off the floor from his humble perch.

"I am a busy man, so I would hope to keep this brief." Rashan waved a hand and the door closed behind her.

Juliana whipped around and slipped into aether-vision, seeing that the door was shielded as well. It was not a strong shield; she might be able to break it if she had to run.

"Privacy. Do not worry, I have no intention of harming you, oathdaughter. You may have come within a hairsbreadth of killing your new husband, but that hairsbreadth was crucially important. I saw something that I could not see in the regimented confines of the practice yard. He thought himself safe out there, but not when he angered you," Rashan said mildly, slipping off the barrel to his feet.

"He hit me first," Juliana hedged warily.

"Indeed. I cannot imagine he was given any reason to do so," Rashan joked, giving a half smile. "You have as sharp a tongue as anyone has dared use in my presence. I doubt you kept it in check with just Iridan present. Care to share what you said to provoke him?"

"Not especially, no," Juliana replied.

There was something odd about Rashan's manner ... something in his stance.

In one swift motion, the warlock drew Heavens Cry and leveled it in Juliana's direction. Before the blade left its sheath, Juliana had already silently raised a shielding spell, drawn both her new blades, and leapt back a pace.

Rashan laughed, lowering his blade before returning it to its sheath. "*That* is precisely the reflex that Iridan lacks. He seems to be making fine progress in the practice yard. His Source and draw are fearsome, and he learns new spells quickly. What he cannot do is react surely under pressure, when action needs to precede thought. He aether-burns himself trying half measures, just as he did yester-morn. I have half a mind to train *you* as a warlock in his place. You have nowhere near the raw strength of aether, but you are a warrior at heart. I hope to find out soon whether Brannis is or not."

"Brannis? What do you mean by that? He is a warrior. You saw him at Raynesdark and in Kelvie Forest," Juliana responded, confused as to what Rashan meant. She was breathing heavily, still poised ready to defend herself.

"Actually I met him after his major encounter with the goblins in Kelvie, but that is not the point. Prowess with a blade in the heat of battle is not the same as keeping the calmness of mind to use magic," Rashan said.

"What are you talking about? Brannis can't use magic and everyone knows it," Juliana said, exasperated. "If you are still holding some hope of his suddenly developing a Source stronger than a candle, you have a long wait ahead of you."

"Oh my ..." Rashan mused. "No one told you?"

Juliana made sure her puzzled expression made it clear that no one had.

"That quake that shook half of Kadris last night was Brannis," Rashan said.

Juliana's puzzled look grew a perplexed aspect.

"The quake?" Rashan said. "The one last night?"

Rashan seemed to be prodding for some sign of dawning recognition in his oathdaughter's eyes, but was finding none.

"I sleep soundly." She shrugged. "What did I miss?"

"A quake shook the palace and half the city felt it. Everyone knows Brannis has been studying old books of magic—the new airships are a testament to that—but he seems to have figured out a way to unleash his Source," Rashan said.

"Unleash it? You could tie that sorry little thing to a chair leg with a bit of yarn and it would be held fast," Juliana joked, though she never would have voiced that opinion so flippantly had Brannis actually been present.

"Oh ... not anymore," Rashan said. "I have shielded off his room and a few adjacent ones damaged in the incident, so none has been in to see him yet as he recovers from the ordeal—and, yes, he is worse for wear but will be fine. Once you see for yourself, you may understand what your grandfather predicted all those years ago."

"Really?" Juliana remained unconvinced. "Brannis? The same Brannis who could not light a firefly's arse in six winters of trying at the Academy? That Brannis?"

"That one, yes. I have little notion of how much he has retained from his years there and how much he has gleaned from his more recent studies, but I suspect he has just enough knowledge to be terribly dangerous right now. I have the rooms shielded to prevent him bringing down half the palace trying some other fool experiment," Rashan huffed.

"You are afraid of him?" Juliana wondered aloud, instantly regretting it.

Winds, Juliana! Think before saying things like that!

"No, not afraid." Rashan waved away the notion dismissively. "I may be the only one *not* in danger around here, excepting Illiardra, if she has not yet departed. I am concerned that the commander of all Kadrin's armies may be more a danger to us than Megrenn at the moment." Rashan paced back and forth as he spoke, clearly bothered by the prospect.

"If he is really that strong, would that not be a good thing? I mean, it is Brannis, after all. He will catch on quick enough," Juliana said, trying to sound hopeful. The prospect of Brannis being a sorcerer was … complicated.

Now? she thought. *He picks* now *to finally become a sorcerer? Eight forsaken winters after he gets himself kicked out of the Academy and ruins our betrothal? He has some explaining to do.*

"Oh, of that there is no doubt. I intend to see what use he can be, and see to what sort of use we can put him. If he can keep the war running smoothly, though, I will satisfy myself with that," Rashan said.

"Do they ever? Run smoothly, I mean? Wars." Juliana stumbled over the question, her mind pulling itself in six direction at once. She was worried about Brannis. She was mad at Brannis. She was still wondering what Rashan had planned for her. She worried that she slept too soundly for her own good. She was trying to carry on an intelligent conversation. She was wondering when Iridan would be getting back, and how she was going to face him after their confrontation.

"None has yet, but I still think this one has a chance." Rashan smiled, breaking the tension a bit. "Now if you will excuse me, there are a great many noblemen I have to go upset." The warlock unraveled the shielding spell that had sealed them in the room and seemed about to leave when he paused. "Oh, and I know that Brannis had a hand in making those daggers. Did he happen to give them names?"

"Yes," Juliana answered. "Their names are Duty and Honor."

One answer, one comment. Both true.

Noting that she still held the blades in hand, she self-consciously returned them to their hidden sheaths.

"That boy thinks too much," Rashan commented as he departed, chuckling.

* * * * * * * *

"Fo how'f evfeybody beem?" Iridan slurred to his foster mother across the sturdy oak kitchen table of the house he grew up in. The swelling in his face had gone down, but it would take time to regrow new front teeth. Iridan had taken the wagon ride out to the countryside on the seat next to his father, but his mother had ridden in back, bundled up in blankets to keep warm in the early spring air. They had barely had a chance to talk.

"Well, Dabby'll be married in the fall; you'll come out for that, war permittin', I s'pose?" Ma Korian asked. Iridan nodded in reply; it was easier than talking. "Hadon's joinin' the army; says that bein' your brother got him into the regular army 'stead of them conscripts. They'll train him up a proper soldier. Meren is takin' over more'n more 'o the farmin' now that Pa's back gives him trouble— drives the oxen and ever'thin'. Ailie is expectin' sometime in the summer; she lives in Pevett now with that man 'o hers. Writes more often'n you do, though." She gave Iridan a playful glare.

"Fahwee, Ma," Iridan apologized, frowning at his own inability to speak.

His father saw his dismay. "Aww, ya still talk better'n Hadon, an' he's got all his teeth still. Leastwise ya can grow 'em back. Us reg'lar folk hafta just live 'thout 'em if'n we lose 'em," Pa Korian reassured Iridan. "Them wood swords ain't toys."

Iridan had not the heart to tell them it was Juliana who did it to him. He had blamed an accident in the training yard the morning after the wedding. They had left Kadris before the rumors of what really happened began to seep in amidst the lies Rashan put out. The warlock had wanted to deflect signs of strife in the new marriage.

"We'll have porridge 'stead o' stew tonight. No tough bits to gnaw through. Sure'n be easier'n chewin'," Ma promised.

Would I talk like them, had I not gone off to the Academy? Iridan wondered.

The practice of magic required precise diction, at least until a sorcerer reached the point of casting spells with no diction at all. All the students had proper enunciation beaten into their heads, sometimes literally.

If I had just kept quiet about my magical powers as a boy, could I have just lived out here, met some nice shy local lass, and settled in to raising barley and milking cows? It felt so … right sleeping in my own bed last night.

"Aww wight, Ma," Iridan managed. "Buh I godda go bag affa dinnew. Twaining tomowwow."

"So soon? That war-looker ain't much for recup'ratin' ya, is he?" Ma scolded Iridan in lieu of having Rashan present to chastise. They had only spoken to the warlock briefly, prior to the ceremony.

"Gomma be a wawlog," Iridan said.

Yes, Iridan thought to himself with a sigh, *a wawlog …*

· * * * * * * * ·

Why am I doing this? Juliana asked herself as she headed for the warlock's chambers. She did not expect to actually find Rashan within, but that was not the cause of her confliction. *She has as much reason to be angry with me as Rashan does but that does not mean she has overlooked it as well. Still, if anyone can get me past that thrice-cursed warlock's wards, it would be her.*

Juliana arrived at the door out of breath. She had not been aware of the haste she had been making in her journey across the palace and up three flights of stairs. She took a moment to compose herself and calm her breath. She attempted to knock on the door, but it opened as her knuckles were about to rap against the wood.

Of course she knew I was out here.

"Come in, child," a lyrical voice beckoned from within, "and do not worry yourself. I am not half the monster Rashan is and he saw fit to leave you alive."

It was not the most reassuring greeting she had ever received, but she had certainly heard worse. Juliana stepped into the room with her oathmother. Illiardra sat languidly on the sill of one of the room's massive windows, a hefty tome open in front of her, floating unsupported save by aether.

"I suppose you must want to know how it happened ..." Juliana began, attempting to break the ice before asking favors.

"Not really. The details may remain a mystery, though it is plain as to how it generally befell. He is Rashan's son much more so than mine. His timidity and meekness are a result of his upbringing—more that dreadful Academy of yours than the hearty peasant folk we fostered him with—but the rage that lies beneath is his father in nascent form. You are here to ask a favor of me. Do not deny it; I have seen this scene played out a thousand times with different actors and different favors to ask. Speak, and when you are done, I will have a favor to ask in return," Illiardra spoke, not allowing Juliana a word of her own, despite a few halfhearted tries at interruption.

"I want to see Brannis. I heard there was some sort of accident that opened his Source or something like that. Rashan said he would recover, but I want to see him," she told the ancient demon who looked so like a young maiden. "Can you get me past Rashan's wards and back out again without him knowing?"

"Yes," Illiardra answered softly, smiling as if to herself.

Juliana looked around, confused. "What? That is it? What of the favor you wished in return?"

"It is no hurry and I would have asked it whether or not you needed my help. I will tell you afterward. Come here, child, and take my hand," Illiardra said.

Juliana regarded the wizened old creature in her nubile, youthful form, with green hair and eyes a bit too large.

She is my oathmother now. If I want to see Brannis, I need her help.

Juliana reached out and took Illiardra's offered hand. It was cool to the touch, like wood or stone rather than flesh, but smooth as a baby's skin.

* * * * * * * *

Juliana found herself in another room. There was no sensation of movement. She felt nothing in the aether. She was just suddenly somewhere different, standing with her hand still outstretched to where Illiardra had been just the blink of an eye before. Juliana took quick stock of her surroundings. It was still the distinctive black marble of the palace all around her, and what looked to be a bedchamber. A massive hole was scooped out, exposing the adjacent room and two immediately below those; it was an eerie sight to be sure.

Curled beneath the bedclothes was a Brannis-sized figure, which she presumed to be Brannis. The sort of demon who could transfer her through Rashan's wards was certainly clever enough to put her in the right room. More cautious than was her typical custom, Juliana took a quick look into the aether.

She had wanted to confirm that she was indeed surrounded by Rashan's shielding wards, and to have a peek at Brannis's shiny new Source, like sneaking a look at her age-day presents a week early. She gasped, and cried out at the unexpected pain in her aether-vision when she saw Brannis's Source.

Merciful Tansha, have you begun granting Brannis's wishes as well, or did Grandfather work his prophecy from beyond death?

She was forced back into normal light vision to avert the headache she felt coming. Her gasp stirred Brannis in his bed, but did not wake him.

Well, he seems to be as sound a sleeper as ever, at least. She walked quietly over to the bedside, and sat down next to Brannis, seeming not to disturb him at all. *He looks pale and gaunt*, she thought as she brushed the hair back from his face. *What happened to him?* The question hung in her mind, but it did not hang long before her impatience shouldered it aside. She shook him gently by the shoulder.

"Brannis ... Brannis, wake up," Juliana spoke just above a whisper. Brannis stirred again, but did not wake. "Brannis, I may not have much time. I wanted to see you and find out what happened to you."

Brannis's deep, even breaths caught up short in a snort as Juliana shook him a bit more vigorously. He opened his mouth as if to say something, then stopped himself and closed it again. His eyes blinked open, gazing into Juliana's when he was finally able to focus them anywhere.

"What day is it?" Brannis whispered, speaking each word separately and slowly. He sounded weak and exhausted.

"Springtime third," Juliana replied. "You cannot have been asleep too long since Rashan left you. How do you feel?"

"Tired. Confused. Such ... beautiful ... eyes," Brannis replied, smiling weakly.

"Well," Juliana replied ruefully, "you had your chance and botched it. If you had that Source in you all along, you waited a season too long to reveal it. What *did* you do?"

"Not ... entirely ... sure. Think I had ... adventure." Brannis sounded as if his wits were not quite sorted within that head of his. She thought she might have caught a hint of Acardian in his accent, which might clue anyone who did not already know that he was twinborn. Juliana stroked his face gently with her hand, distracting him until he stopped even trying to talk.

"Well, Rashan said you were in a bit of rough shape after whatever it was that happened to you, but he expects you will be fine. I had to see for myself, though."

She leaned down and kissed him, lingering far longer than was probably proper for a recently married woman. Her hands ran along his body, finding scant muscle and more prominent ribs than she had been expecting.

* * * * * * *

Kyrus said nothing, head swimming with dredged-up adolescent memories of times Brannis had spent together with Juliana. He knew that nothing he said was going to avail him. Atop that, anything he said might give him away as an imposter if he was not thinking clearly.

"I had hoped that you were not quite so enervated by your ordeal as you are. I wish we could have made better use of the little slice of privacy we have gained here, but truly I am relieved that you were not harmed any worse," Juliana said, then lay down and nestled against Kyrus. The two lay together in silence until Illiardra came to fetch Juliana and they made their good-byes with another kiss. Juliana seemed not to care if her oathmother saw.

This is going to be a lot more trouble than Tippu and Kahli, Kyrus thought before allowing slumber to reclaim him and his exhausted mind.

* * * * * * *

"So you have had your indulgence," Illiardra spoke to Juliana as the two sat on the high balcony of Rashan's chamber, looking out over Kadris. "I trust everything was to your satisfaction?"

"Brannis seemed a bit strange. I don't know what happened to him, but he has yet to collect all the pieces of himself, and put them back the way they belong. I had intended to press him for details, but he just seemed so ... exhausted. Brannis is usually so full of energy, I did not know what to say to him like that," Juliana replied.

"So instead you just kissed him?" Illiardra smiled with amusement. Before Juliana could begin defending her actions, Illiardra chuckled. "Worry not. Rashan has told me about your marriage customs. You and Iridan were arranged. You did your duty in marrying. It does not erase loves you already carried in your heart. It never will. Have a care how you conduct yourself. Much is expected of you, oathdaughter." Illiardra chuckled at the last word, as if finding the concept absurd.

"You are just amused? You do not worry about Iridan?" Juliana wondered aloud, her inner censor as awake and alert as she had found Brannis.

"I am an awful mother," Illiardra admitted. "I gave up my babe before he was old enough to remember me and hardly gave him another thought. Had Rashan not contacted me about the wedding, Iridan might have died of age before I thought to inquire about him. He is mortal and will remain so. I am immortal and hope to remain so. Our paths were never meant to twine tightly to each other. I have but one boon I would ask of you, to satisfy whatever motherly obligation I might have."

"This is the favor you intended to ask of me?" Juliana asked, leaning close, wondering what Illiardra could want of her.

"Yes. I would ask that you do what you might to see that Iridan does not turn out like his father," Illiardra implored, her doe-like eyes fixing on Juliana's.

"I will do what I can," Juliana promised.

It was her fear as well, and she could already see the signs, the similarities. Iridan might not have the vicious nature that Rashan possessed, but it might yet lurk below the layers of meekness, of worry, of self-doubt, and of humility that lacquered his mind—a painted veneer that all who knew him saw, but which could be chipped away to reveal the base metal beneath: the true Iridan, whatever it might be.

"Thank you. Oh, and one last thing before I go: Iridan is almost entirely his father's son, but there is some of me in him as well. In whatever children you bear him, be mindful that they may be more fey than even two such sorcerers might be expected to conceive."

And with that cryptic farewell, Illiardra was gone.

Chapter 15 - On Holiday

It was easily the strangest place Brannis had ever awakened, to the point where even pondering the second strangest seemed pointless. No larder, no hay field, no dank wilderness cave could compare to being tossed an unfathomable distance through the aether to awaken at your own writing desk, and find it perched on a lonely bit of black marble floor, surrounded by a sandy beach and watched by an awestruck assemblage of people from another world. Brannis glanced around warily, working his mouth to rid it of the gummy feeling after just awakening and rubbing at his eyes.

Wonderful. I hope you know how to run a war, Kyrus, because you just bought yourself one with that little stunt.

Brannis took quick stock of what had been brought along to Denku Appa by the transference spell. The black marble with greenish veins was clearly from the palace wall and floor, carved out in a spherical chunk. The desk and chair he had fallen asleep at were wholly intact. There was an undisturbed inkpot and several sheets of parchment, and a small number of books of magic. He had fallen asleep with his armor on, something he had done the two nights running since the assassination attempt at the wedding. The gauntlets that went along with Liead's armor hung from a hook at his waist, and the helm was underfoot where he had left it—no bit was missing. Avalanche was sheathed at his hip, the tip resting on the floor. In short, he was prepared for being ambushed in the night by a Megrenn assailant.

I am not sure what countermeasures I could have prepared against my idiot twin dumping me on a tiny island in the middle of the Katamic Sea on Tellurak.

Despite his spiteful inner monolog, Brannis had begun to consider that Kyrus was the smarter of the two of them, spending more of his time in books while Brannis spent more time with a sword in hand or a horse beneath his rump. As the curious Denku approached, he could barely understand a word of what they said.

"(babbling noises) you? (indistinguishable yammering) Kyrus? Say (something something) name," a score of Denku spat questions at him along similar lines. He knew he probably knew most of the words, but his own ears were untrained, and were not picking them apart from amid the stream of foreign sounds he was hearing.

"Talk slow. Please," Brannis requested, standing up from his chair. If things went badly—and he could envision several ways in which it could—then he did not want to be at a disadvantage by being seated.

One of the elders held his arms out to his sides and gestured for the rest to quiet down. Brannis recognized him as Toktu. In fact, Brannis could put names to most of the Denku present. It was a strange sensation, the feeling of familiarity with sights his eyes had never seen, with scents his lungs had never breathed in. Brannis had been awakened as soon as the transference spell had been completed, so he had no idea how Kyrus was getting on in Veydrus or if he was having the same experience there.

"Who. Are. You?" Toktu obligingly spoke very slowly for Brannis's benefit. "Where. Is. Spirit. Man. Kyrus?" The latter question had a hint of worried desperation to it. The Denku elder suspected something had gone wrong.

"I am Brannis," Brannis explained. "I am ... Kyrus's ... spirit ... brother." Brannis struggled for words in a language he barely knew to explain a concept he did not fully understand himself.

There were muttered conversations among the gathered Denku, but Toktu remained respectfully attentive as Brannis fought to make his explanation.

"Kyrus go (Brannis winced, knowing that was not the right verb tense) ... to spirit world." Brannis gestured, pointing vaguely to the sky and out to sea. "He go out (*Blast it, what is the past tense of 'go' in Denku?*) ... other place. My home." Brannis poked himself in the chest. "Kyrus took ... part ..." Brannis gestured to the bit of imperial palace stonework that was brought along with him, outlining it with his hands. "... and send it here."

"So ... Where. Is. Kyrus?" Toktu asked, clearly not *quite* sure what his strange visitor was trying to convey. There was general unease among the villagers. They had expected a good-bye, but the horrific vortex at Kyrus's parting, followed by the arrival of Brannis, was something entirely different. They were not sure what.

"Home. My home." Brannis pointed to himself.

"Do you speak Spirit Man Kyrus's language," Gahalu called out in Acardian, hoping to bridge the cultural gap so that his people could find out what went wrong with Kyrus's parting.

"Yes," Brannis managed in Acardian of his own, the first time he had used the language. It was familiar as an old song he had heard since childhood, but he had never sung it before.

With Gahalu's help, Brannis and Toktu were able to discuss the details of Kyrus's spell and how it went wrong. The Denku were distraught that Kyrus was not home in Acardia as he had hoped, feeling that his departure from Denku Appa was all for naught.

* * * * * * *

The little stone hut was homey enough, and he recognized it, but Brannis hoped it would not be his for long. Brannis carefully piled the books he carried in a corner. None but he would be able to read them, but nevertheless, he did not want the Denku taking custody of them. The four tomes were all instruction on magic and belonged in the libraries of the Tower of Contemplation in faraway

Kadrin. It was hard to fathom that he was not currently on Veydrus, a fact that would have seemed impossible were it not his current state. Magic made all things possible, they said, but certain life constants *seemed* less mutable than others.

He took his helm off, and set it down atop the pile of books. He had no need of it, and had only worn it because it was easier than finding a free hand to carry it. Brannis might have pressed one of the Denku into service helping him, but he supposed they were a bit afraid of him and the otherworldly objects he brought with him.

Brannis slumped down onto the sleeping mat, elbows on knees, with a rattle of armor. *What am I going to do here? I belong here as much as Kyrus does in Kadris, which is to say: not at all. I still have a war to fight back home. Kyrus had better sort this out quickly.*

Brannis stood up again, unable to sit calmly and uncomfortable sitting on the ground in his armor, magically fitted though it was. He paced the small dwelling, aware of the murmurings outside that indicated the Denku were watching for him to emerge.

I could live here among them, as Kyrus did. Once he figures out how he did whatever it was he did, he can undo it and get me back on Veydrus where I belong. In the meantime, what? Fresh sea breezes and the company of those two lasses he was too shy to enjoy? I may be forced to … if Kyrus takes overlong and I cannot find a way to a civilized part of Tellurak.

Brannis began stripping off his armor as he formulated a plan. The island was hot enough that none of the natives wore more than the barest of clothing, and he had the distinct feeling that they were wary of the demonic-looking gold-and-quicksilver plate he was wearing when they first saw him. He needed to get on the next ship to visit the island, whenever it might arrive—he had to be ready at any time. Not only would wearing the elaborate armor scare the Denku, it might make the ship's crew think he carried a lot more coin than he actually had. Brannis had a small coin purse with a dozen or so Kadrin lions. There was no exchange rate between those and any Telluraki (Tellurakan? Tellurakish? Brannis had no idea how to properly name something belonging to KyrusWorld) currency. They were pure gold, and large enough to be worth a tidy sum, but hardly the sort of wealth a man with the armor he wore would have.

Clad in nothing but the loose garment he wore beneath his leg armor, Brannis buckled his sword belt back on. Avalanche was not going to leave his side at any time, if he could help it. It was not that the Denku were a threatening lot, but a select few of them had personal property issues, and very little sense or responsibility. Avalanche was dangerous enough that he could not risk anyone toying with it out of curiosity. The rest of his gear he piled in the corner with his other belongings. He would need something to pack it all in, but for now he had one other task that was more pressing.

When Brannis emerged from the hut, a throng had gathered. If dozens had gone to see Kyrus off, hundreds awaited Brannis's exit, nearly the entire village. Brannis waved amiably and headed back to the beach where he had arrived. The crowd parted for him, but followed his progress.

There is no way I will get privacy to do this. I will at least impress them, if not frighten them, but if a ship comes, I will not be able to explain it away.

The crowd held back as Brannis approached the odd structure that errant magic and happenstance had conspired to construct on their beach. It was a semicircular wall, standing there like some sculptor's impression of a sunset, rendered in black marble. It bisected a circular section of matching floor, with the side containing Brannis's desk and chair being the largest by far, and Brannis's chair was its center point. Brannis hauled the heavy desk off the marble and onto the sands several paces back toward the jungle and his hut, careful not to set a leg down on his bare feet. He did likewise with the chair, though it was far easier to move. He would enjoy the exotic furnishings while he was on Denku Appa, and their presence would not be any more odd than the incongruous little stone hut was in the first place.

The black marble abomination, however, was another matter.

Brannis drew Avalanche from its sheath slowly, turning to the Denku and calling to Gahalu, "Let them know to keep back. I just cannot leave this strange wall here."

Brannis took a gentle swing, and passed the blade through the wall. There was a crushing of stone as the wall rocked a bit, and gave way before the inexorable sword as it struck. The Denku were shocked, Gahalu included, but remained well back and safe from the destruction as Brannis continued chopping up the wall. Brannis worked carefully, never swinging the sword more vigorously than he would a full tankard of ale.

As the Denku villagers watched in fascination, Brannis leveled the wall and began breaking up the floor as well. There was empty space below, except for where the wall had continued on down to the floor below back when it was part of the Kadrin Imperial Palace. Kyrus had taken far more sand from Denku Appa when he had left than he had sent marble to replace it. Brannis was glad of that. In fact, he had counted on it. Once he had a pit filled with large rubble, he jabbed the blade down repeatedly to break it up further. With no other real pressing business to draw away his attention, Brannis spent hours turning the wall into gravel, and then knocked loose sand from around the edges of the hole to cover it.

What was left looked like a puckered scar in the beach head. In time, wind and tide would erase all evidence of Brannis's handiwork, but even before then no one would ever have thought that there had once been a wall from another world standing there.

* * * * * * * *

Brannis awoke in the late afternoon after a long nap. He had been relieved to see that Kyrus had suffered no major disasters yet in Kadris, and that Rashan was working to keep the swapping of Brannises a secret. *I suspected that demon rat knew more than he let on, ever since I set off for Raynesdark and dropped that tidbit about cannons. He did not ask what one was or show any reaction at all. He left me to wonder whether he understood what a cannon was or whether he was just willing to let the odd term pass unchallenged out of expedience but now I know which it was.*

One annoyance from his quick trip to watch Kyrus back in Kadris was that Rashan had forbade attempting the spell again until they understood how it had happened. He had gone so far as to indicate he would help Kyrus to learn how to control his Source. The prospect of Kyrus learning proper magic without Brannis having to read him bedtime stories out of the Tower of Contemplation's libraries was a welcome relief. Brannis had enough to work on between reading reports, devising strategies for the war with Megrenn, sketching designs for airships, and learning how to rune-forge weapons in the style of the stone folk. When he thought about it, it was amazing he had time to spare for breathing amidst all that.

I suppose I will learn whether I spread myself too thinly when the reports all come back with losses on the battlefields, airships begin falling from the skies, and that rune-forged sword snaps in Iridan's hand when first he wields it in a real battle. It would be just his luck.

Brannis was somewhat surprised to find that he had slept undisturbed. At the least, he had expected to find Kyrus's two little imps curled up nearby. Brannis poked his head outside the hut, and saw that Gahalu was sitting with his back against the wall, keeping the others away.

"You are awake. Good. You have a small problem," Gahalu told him, climbing to his feet and brushing sand and dirt from his legs.

"You mean in addition to being stranded here because Spirit Man Kyrus cannot aim his magic?" Brannis hoped he did not offend Gahalu by slighting the Denku's "spirit man," but he felt he had a rather special privilege in that regard, being his twin. "Any new problem is going to have to get in line behind that one."

Gahalu chuckled. "As I said, a small problem. Gaktu wants to challenge you. You are an outsider, uninvited, and showed great strength when you broke that rock thing that came with you."

Gaktu? Brannis searched his memories to place a face with that name, which sounded familiar. *Ahh, the hunter with the necklace of panther teeth,* he recalled.

"It did not belong in this world. If a ship comes, I want them to find nothing but a lost traveler looking for passage to the mainland. I want no mysteries to make them wary of me. So why does Gaktu want to challenge me? If everyone saw what I can do with that sword, why would he want to fight me?" Brannis wondered.

"To prove he is the best hunter. A panther's claws will cut a man's neck with one swipe. A boar's tusk will open his gut. A hunter lives by avoiding the weapons of his prey. The more dangerous the prey, the more the hunter proves himself. Gaktu is one among many who are saying you are a spirit who escaped the spirit world when Kyrus left. To kill a spirit would have his name told in stories long after he is dead," Gahalu explained, putting a hand on Brannis's shoulder.

"The Denku revere the spirits," Brannis protested. "Why would he be honored for killing one? And besides, I am no spirit. I am a man, like you, or like Kyrus. I am just a man far from home."

"I believe you are a man, and no spirit. And, yes, we revere the good spirits. They are not saying you are a good spirit."

* * * * * * * *

Brannis stood across an empty expanse of the village center, perhaps a dozen paces, and stared down his opponent. He had considered donning his armor, and allowing the Denku hunter free rein to jab ineffectually at him with a spear, but thought better of it. If he were to do that, he would never be able to take off the armor while he was on the island, lest they wait to catch him without it for a rematch. Avalanche was still sheathed at his side; Brannis did not want to kill Gaktu if he could help it.

"You want kill me," Brannis called out, feeling a tad more comfortable with Kyrus's knowledge of Denku than when he had arrived, sleepy and disoriented. "I say you are killer of men, not hunter."

"Words will not save you, spirit," Gaktu shouted back, loud enough to ensure everyone gathered to watch heard him.

"You kill strangers. I do not kill hunters." Brannis sat down on the ground. "Spirit Man Kyrus is my brother. I do not kill his friends."

"Coward."

"Friend," Brannis corrected.

"I have no spirits for friends. If you do not fight, I will just kill you." Gaktu advanced threateningly at Brannis, who could not be certain whether the Denku hunter was bluffing.

"Fine, then." Brannis scrambled to his feet and drew Avalanche swiftly from its sheath.

"Your slow blade is no match for my spear!" Gaktu boasted before all.

Oh, Brannis realized, *he saw me swinging it slowly so I did not send shards of rock everywhere.* Brannis grinned, holding his sword out lazily in guard position, letting it drift back and forth at approximately the speed he had used to break the marble wall.

Gaktu was cautious. Hunters lived longer lives when they made sure of their prey's limits before striking. The Denku hunter made short jabs with his spear, testing Brannis's reflexes. It was all Brannis could do to avoid letting his instincts take over and take a real swing in his defense.

Not yet, Brannis thought. *Not yet.*

When Brannis judged that Gaktu had made just the right sort of strike, a straight thrust that reached just inside Avalanche's reach, he sprang into action. The sluggish, drifting sword became a blur of motion faster than Gaktu could react to. The first swipe chopped the tip off the spear. The second halved its length. As Gaktu stumbled backward in surprise, Brannis deftly cut between his wide-spaced grip and left his opponent with two short, splintered sticks in his hand, each the size of a tent stake.

Brannis punched out with the cross guard of the sword, pulling the blow just as it connected with Gaktu's chest. It was still enough to take the hunter from his feet and deposit him jarringly on his back.

"I win," Brannis stated.

He sheathed Avalanche, making it clear that he had no intention of fighting to the death. Then he offered a hand to help Gaktu rise, but the hunter's pride—and ribs—were too badly hurt to accept. That was something Brannis could understand, until he saw the look Gaktu gave him. It was filled with fear and hatred, and was more than Brannis could ignore.

Reaching down as Gaktu cowered and tried to defend himself, Brannis grabbed the necklace Gaktu wore and snapped the leather thong. Letting it hang by one end, the panther teeth slid off and fell to the dirt all around the defeated hunter.

"You are not ready to be first hunter when Fannu becomes elder," Brannis told Gaktu, loudly enough for everyone to hear. "Fannu can tell what is prey and what is friend."

That should have been "who," but I think they understood me.

* * * * * * *

Brannis dined by his hut that night, on a bowl of fish and mango stew that Gahalu brought to him. It was tasty, with a sweet saltiness so prevalent in Denku cooking, but a far ride from the feasting that had accompanied Spirit Man Kyrus's arrival.

"You made enemies today," Gahalu told him, sitting by Brannis's side as the itinerant knight ate his supper.

"Gaktu is no more an enemy now than when he first tried to kill me," Brannis reasoned, talking around a mouthful of stew. If Brannis had any thought of the rudeness of speaking with a full mouth, it was mitigated by the fact that he was hungry and a new spoonful of stew replaced each that was swallowed with little break between.

"You broke his necklace. You shamed him," Gahalu explained. "You had beaten him. You could have left it at that."

"You should have seen the look in his eyes when I offered him help standing. It made me angry. He made a fool's mistake and I made one in turn." Brannis sighed. "I could have killed him, if that was my way, and I thought giving him his life ought to have earned me his thanks. Would I have made fewer enemies if I had killed him instead?" Brannis asked, genuinely curious as to the Denku custom on ending challenges.

"Perhaps. You certainly would have made one fewer," Gahalu joked, trying to ease the mood. "But I think perhaps to simply have walked away may have been best. He could not challenge you again without looking foolish, and if he attacked you by surprise, he would mark himself as a coward."

"Well, I have made enemies before. Hopefully I can mend that garment over time. I like to have a clean conscience. I sleep well. I think any man who lives his life right should and I would not want to lose that," Brannis said, staring vaguely off into the jungle rather than at his companion.

"Well enough," Gahalu said, rising to his feet. "One other thing. The fishermen pulled ashore with word of a ship on the horizon."

Brannis perked up. "A ship? Is it headed this way?"

Oh, Kyrus, your timing could not have been worse. Another day or two and you might have gotten off this island and back to Acardia, instead of Kadrin.

"It fights the wind, but yes. The night will be too treacherous to land without help. I doubt they will even get close enough tonight to try. Get sleep and take your leave of us in the morning, if they will have you. I think it would be best if they will take you. Spirit Man Kyrus never caused this trouble you brought," Gahalu said, seeming colder toward Brannis than he ever had seemed to Kyrus.

"Well, do not let them leave without me," Brannis joked, informing Gahalu that he knew how Kyrus had come to be stranded on Denku Appa in the first place.

"Have no worry. Toktu will be just as happy with you gone. He liked Spirit Man Kyrus, but I do not think he would go to any effort to keep *you* here, spirit or not."

* * * * * * *

Brannis had thought to get one night of peaceful sleep all to himself before departing on the morrow, but the thought was not destined to last. Giggling outside his hut broke him free of that drifting place where the mind waits idly for slumber to overtake it. His thoughts instantly went to Tippu and Kahli, Kyrus's seductive little admirers. He almost had to grudgingly admire their persistence, but he quickly realized there were more than just two awaiting him outside.

Brannis took their bait and rose to see what was transpiring without. There were a dozen or so girls, clad in … Well, by any Kadrin standard of decency, essentially they were *not* clad, except in the most nitpicking sense. They wore loincloths, beads, and bracelets, but Brannis saw it as a tawdry brothel turned inside out to deposit their wares in the sparse jungle. The Denku all dressed vaguely such, from old crones to fishermen, but intent made all the difference to Brannis's way of thinking. The thoughts of the giggling throng were plainly written in eager eyes and coy smiles.

Interestingly enough, Brannis saw no sign of either of Kyrus's nemeses among the group. Quite possibly, they were the only unwed girls from the village not present. The nervous, conspiratorial whispers ceased when they saw Brannis emerge from the hut, becoming a cacophony of shrill, incomprehensible Denku language that Brannis only guessed at the meaning of by context.

Brannis held up a hand in front of him and was grateful that the gesture to stop was universal enough for Denku to have adopted it. The girls' propositions, questions, and promises slowed to a halt as they waited for Brannis to say something in response.

"Wait here," Brannis told them.

They looked confused, but none wanted to give offense and upset him. There was a competition of sorts afoot and Brannis meant to settle it cleanly. He took a rock with something resembling a point and drew a long line in the dirt in front of the girls. By gestures, he got the point across that they were to line up along it.

"I pick one girl. I pick, not you. Understand?" Brannis asked. Heads nodded obediently and enthusiastically. One girl started babbling a question, but Brannis cut her off with an imperious gesture. "Not you." He pointed back toward the village. "Go."

The rest of the girls kept quiet as thieves as Brannis made his way up and down the line, making a show of looking them over. "I will pick one girl tonight. Any girl I do not pick, no argue. Understand?" Again, there was nodding.

As Brannis inspected them, one by one he sent them back to the village, never giving a particular reason, but leaving the impression that they had failed some test, were lacking a certain something he craved. Most bore the rejection with resignation. A few cried softly—their own doing, by Brannis's logic.

At last, he left himself with the shyest, least annoying of the girls—possibly the youngest, though he would have been hard pressed to divine her age. She stood rigidly at attention, not lifting her gaze to meet Brannis's.

Brannis lifted her chin, and looked her in the eyes when he spoke to her. "At home, I have a girl I love. I choose her. Tonight, if you be quiet, you can sleep in the hut. Tomorrow, I leave on a boat. You can tell other girls anything. Make a good story." Brannis smiled gently. He had no further trouble falling asleep that night and made a young Denku girl the envy of her friends.

Chapter 16 - Hide and Seek

"He was about yea high." A soft and fluff-faced tavern keeper held a stubby-fingered hand at chest height. "Hair a bit darker than hay, mayhaps. Built like a stick, but then so many boys are at that age, eh?" The man tried a bit of humor but it fell short in the face of the three very serious men to whom he was speaking.

"What did he carry with him? What was he wearing?" Jinzan Fehr asked in a low voice. He was dressed in the garb of the night guards to attract less attention as he made his way about the city. Black lacquered mail and doublet, dark grey hood and trousers. The truncheon and short sword at his belt were as useful as horseshoes on a monohorn, but he carried them to complete the disguise. He made no secret of his identity to those he encountered, but as one of the Liberators, he drew greetings and well-wishes as he walked down any street. For his purposes, that would have been counterproductive.

"Little lad was all in his feast-day best—'cepting of course he prob'ly dresses like that most days, being yours and all. He was scuffed and dirty like he'd been out playin' in the streets. Had himself a walking stick, fancy as beat all. Carried it around like a parade banner, though, he did, usin' both hands and keepin' it away from his body, like so," the keeper replied, mimicking the manner he described.

"Did you speak to him, or try to apprehend him?" Jinzan persisted. He was not angry with the tavern keeper, but a hint of desperation in his voice might have led one to think that he was.

"No, High Councilor. I heard the rumors of folk turnin' up dead and kept my mouth shut. Made like I didn't see him at all. He looked right at me—but not in the eye—and just kept on about whatever business he had. Never said a word or nothin'." The nervous keeper pulled a bar rag from his pocket and wiped at his brow.

"Where did he go from here?" Jinzan asked, staring intently at the keeper across his own bar. It was the first fresh sighting they had found in days and he could ill afford to squander it. The animate dead they had been finding in Anzik's wake were less than helpful when it came to answering questions.

"He rummaged a bit in the kitchen and left out the back way. I went straight to find a guardsman after that," the man half-pleaded.

Jinzan did not wait to make an apology for scaring the man, who had done no wrong. He strode to the door and stormed through into the kitchen. "For your help," one of Jinzan's similarly garbed companions said, leaving a weighty purse of gold on the bar. They were there to aid High Councilor Fehr in whatever way he required, including smoothing over the feelings of distraught informants.

The kitchens were dark, save for the starlight that came through the open window. Jinzan lit the room like daylight with a quick gesture. A stack of bowls had been upset, and there was a puddle of thick, brown broth on the floor near the stew pot. Jinzan looked into the pot and saw that the ladle had been left in carelessly, covering it with cold stew, handle and all.

At least he is remembering to eat, even if he is acting a pig about it.

Jinzan walked out the back door and into the narrow back alley behind the tavern. There was no sign of any boy. It was late night even by Zorren's cosmopolitan standards, with even the drunkards and whores abed. The only sounds were the far-off rush of the Santar River and the caterwauling of a cat in heat. When his two companions emerged from the tavern to join him, Jinzan picked a direction and took off, trusting to luck in the absence of a solid lead to follow.

They had come so close.

* * * * * * * *

Shadow to shadow, Tod made his way over to where Jodoul had hidden himself. "What sort of cat was that supposed to be? You thinkin' that's what a dead one would sound like?" Tod whispered sarcastically. The two were dressed plainly in dark greys and browns. Both were from a school of skulking that liked having answers to angry questions about why one might be nosing about in the dark. None of the answers to those questions bore as much credibility when the answerer was dressed in nothing but black. It was a suspicious color, and not a lot better for hiding than the dark drabs they had chosen instead.

"Worked, dinnit?" Jodoul snapped quietly. "They just went off that way, but I think they were guessin'. They seemed all hot and eager headin' in, like they was owed money from some fella in there. They come out slow, look around a bit, wander off. Think the kid bobbed 'em again."

"Well, we can sneak after 'em rest o' the night and hope that sorcerer don't get wind of us up his breeches, hopin' he gets lucky, or we can head back and tell Faolen 'n' see if he's got a better idea," Tod suggested, clearly favoring the latter option. Neither of them relished the thought of tailing a sorcerer of the renown of Jinzan Fehr. They had never heard of him back home, but everyone in Megrenn knew his name. The trouble with sorcerers was that they could see out the back of their heads and even through walls with their magic vision; one could never be certain when they would try looking.

"Yeah, let Faolen run around chasin' famous sorcerers if he likes. I'll run the docks and card-halls all night every night if'n he wants me to, but I'm not fer sticking my neck under an axe on the chance we get lucky the night they stumble on the kid," Jodoul said.

The two kept to the alleyways and backstreets of Zorren as they departed, safe from death at the hands of the Megrenn magic for one more night.

* * * * * * * *

"Yeah, looks like they lost the scent of him," Jodoul explained. "Kid musta gone through, though, 'cause they had a sure hurry headin' there in the first place. If'n they'd have gotten nothin', they'd have come back out the way they gone in."

Faolen looked down at the huge table around which the four of them gathered. Upon its surface was Zorren, rendered in miniature by Faolen's magic. It had started days ago as a crude copy, based on a paper map they had brought with them from Kadrin, but as they learned more of the city, it grew more detailed and more accurate. Many of the houses were still just little boxes with roofs, but the buildings they had studied bore more detail, especially the ones that Faolen had seen personally. The ships in the harbor bore tiny names scrawled upon their sides, keeping track of the comings and goings of Megrenn's merchant and naval fleets. The beautiful granite structures near the center of the city were the headquarters of the Megrenn High Council, the royal palace, the tournament grounds, and the Hall of Emissaries, where foreign lands housed their diplomats on a semi-permanent basis within Megrenn. Also rendered in greater detail were a number of seemingly random lesser buildings, whose roofs Faolen had turned red, breaking with the otherwise faithful—if incomplete—rendition of the city.

"High Councilor Fehr would not have stopped there in such haste had a sighting not been reported. I will mark it anyway, just to be safe." Faolen waved a hand over that portion of the city, and the roof of the Pickled Swine Tavern changed, along with a few details as Tod and Jodoul had described the building to Faolen earlier. There were two glassed and shuttered windows flanking the door, a back entrance to the alley, and a fanciful sign depicting a pig poking its head up out of a barrel.

Aelon shrugged. "If there's any melody to this song, I can't hear it. Lad seems to be running around the city on a lark. Could it be these Megrenn are having it on with us?"

"No. If they knew of us, I suspect they would have just killed us and been done with it. Chained in the dungeon at the very least. They have nothing to gain from leading us on a merry chase in their capital, with one of their High Councilors keeping out of the war atop it," Faolen reasoned.

"Well, figure it like this," Jodoul began, trying to make himself sound erudite. "The little fella starts at home, see?" Jodoul pointed to the Fehr estate in the northwest of the city, on a hillside with expansive gardens and a view of the Aliani Sea. "Then they find dead horses and a stable boy here." He pointed again. "A dockworker here." He pointed to a warehouse near the harbor. "A butcher and his apprentice. A librarian and some old scholar. A fisherman and half his crew. A greengrocer but not his wife or daughter. A pair of city watchmen. A Safschan caravan master and eight of his guards," Jodoul summarized, giving everyone a knowing look to add to the suspense. "The lad's lookin' for food and good places to hide. Think about it: warehouse, stables, library, caravan … all great hidin' spots. The rest he got somethin' to eat."

Aelon looked to Faolen and rolled his eyes, keeping Jodoul at his back. "I must get up front," Aelon said. "It's dawn and who knows, we might see a customer today." They had rented a storefront to work from, and ostensibly to sell the wares they had brought with them from Kadrin. While names like "The Mysterious Shop of Wonders," "Things from Kadrin," and "Exotic Goods" seemed like fine names for attracting business, Faolen had overruled them all. They called their shop "Marod's Goods" at Faolen's insistence, as he deemed it about the least likely name he could think of to attract neither unwanted business nor suspicious attention from authorities. They had a crude sign painted up on the short coin, just black paint on a plain wooden plank. The humble and boring facade kept away most; it was Aelon's job (in the role of the eponymous "Marod") to dissuade any stalwart shoppers who made it past those safeguards. Aelon spoke pidgin Megrenn, drove hard bargains, and made no attempt to win over any would-be customers.

Tod and Jodoul lingered as Faolen stared dreamily at the city model. They had no real business to attend to and no good excuse save fatigue for wanting to take their leave. It was not technically a military hierarchy, but since leaving Kadris, Faolen had been very clear about who was in charge. Faolen had not given them any further orders, nor permission to leave.

"Hungry. Yes," Faolen said, half to himself. After a long pause, he continued. "But not hiding—at least that is not his first thought. Stables, docks, caravans … He wants to escape the city but has failed each time. And he cannot be hiding in these places for long, since the bodies have been discovered quickly enough. He must have some other place he is taking refuge."

"Like where?" Tod asked. "Sounds like he got chased out of some good spots already."

"Has anyone considered the sewers?" Faolen asked, cocking his head curiously.

"Yeah, a bit," Jodoul replied. "It'd be the kinda place I'd have hidden if I was ten summers and runnin'. But nobody said anything about seein' dead folks standin' around down there."

"Only three sorts of folk make a habit of walking the sewers," Faolen observed. "Crews who keep them in working order, thieves, and guards who go down to protect work crews from thieves. I shall need you two to—"

"No problem, already ahead of you. Me and Tod ain't makin' enough coin at the export racket; we want some easy gold. I'll ask around and see what turns up, if any of them are talkin' about dead thieves in the sewers."

"Very well. I will make my rounds of the brothels," Faolen replied, straight faced and all business.

"Hey now! That don't seem fair," Tod replied.

"Jodoul noted that the boy left the grocer's wife and daughter alive. So far he has only killed men and boys. Brothels are also places known for harboring the sort of women whose maternal instincts may not be entirely fulfilled. They might take pity on a runaway. He might not take it into his head to kill them," Faolen said with a shrug.

Jodoul gave Faolen a hard, suspicious look but said nothing. *Gut them sorcerers. Can't win, fightin' 'em with words.*

* * * * * * *

Anzik blew a frustrated sigh that flipped a lock of his filthy hair out of his eyes. *Why does everyone try to grab me? Podley seemed so nice that time Mother brought us to see the Delamis.* The footman stood smartly aside the door of the Delami family carriage, just the way Anzik had remembered him. He seemed to belong that way, dead or not, so Anzik had put him there after reanimating him. *Maybe they will not notice … for a while.*

The carriage house had seemed large enough—and cluttered enough—that he might have hidden there a night or two. If the carriage had been readied to leave, he might have tried sneaking aboard to see where it got him. Alas, it appeared the carriage would be going nowhere; the one who put people in it was dead and Anzik did not intend to stay around to make him carry out his job.

The back of the carriage house opened onto a narrow road. Anzik poked his head out to make sure no one was around, even though he could see in the aether that there was not. It seemed like the thing heroes in the fairy stories did when hiding, so he thought he ought to as well. He darted across the narrow road to an even smaller one—more a man-width gap than a proper street. It was well that no one watched him go, as the sight of an awkward, scrawny boy trying to "dart" while carrying a staff half again his height might have given cause to laugh. Anzik hated being laughed at.

With barely a thought, a wrought-iron grating in the ground rose up, revealing an iron-runged ladder. Tucking the Staff of Gehlen under one arm, Anzik climbed down into the sewers.

The grate settled itself back down with a faint grating of metal on stone.

* * * * * * *

Jinzan sat in the foyer of his home, slouched across the arms of a velvet-upholstered chair. He looked haggard and scruffy. Unshaved stubble threatened to turn into a proper beard if left wild much longer. His eyes were red-rimmed from lack of sleep. A stink of sweat and manure wafted off him from days spent chasing reports of his son in stables, alleys, and warehouses. He had slept little, interrupted by new reports every few hours throughout the day, at his request.

Why did you have to choose now *to show signs of competence?*

Anzik had always been bookish, if he was indeed much of anything. He was often willfully ignorant of his surroundings, but had an enviable amount of focus. He acted however he wished much of the time, not out of unruliness, but rather obliviousness to the requests the world made of him.

All about Jinzan were Megrenn agents of import, all as haggard as he. They had run themselves to exhaustion chasing the elusive Fehr child. Normally a runaway would be no match for the forces the High Council could bring to bear, but few young boys possessed such innate gifts with aether as Anzik, nor did they carry a staff meant to swing the pendulum of power between the Megrenn Alliance and the Kadrin Empire. The boy was simply proving himself to be too clever to be trapped, and too well armed to be confronted.

If I send more men after him, Anzik will be found but Anzik will kill them. If I wait for him to return, the war will not be so kind as to wait for me. I began it. I must fight it. I also cannot allow the boy free rein to kill at will in the alleys and stables of Zorren while I wage war.

Jinzan closed his eyes and rested his forehead in the palm of his hand. *I must find a way inside that twisted little mind of Anzik's and find a way to bring him home.*

Jinzan was glad to have shielded his eyes with his gesture, as tears began to well in their corners. "Leave me some respite. I must think," he managed to order without his voice breaking. He heard the shuffling of feet and mutters of obeisance as his subordinates left him to his solitude. Silently, he began to weep.

... but I do not know my own son well enough.

* * * * * * *

Small splashes played around two pairs of boots, echoing in the dim light of the Zorren sewers. The conduit was arched and only man-height at the center, where a channel was cut down the middle to carry a flow of water. Small walkways ran along the sides, but due to the curvature of the masonry, a full-grown man could not walk upright along the sides.

"Cleanest sewer I ever saw," Tod commented. "Ain't even no rat dung or stains."

"Folk don't live hereabouts is why," Jodoul replied. "I'm sure'n it's an arse-brown mess in the districts. This all is just runoff from the rains and such. Prob'ly be dry in a couple-few days if'n there ain't another rain. I'll be hunkerin' over on the sides if'n we get to some such as that."

"Aww, you gone soft on me? I mucked Naran Port's sewers durin' a Founding Day festival once—twice the folk in the city as ya see most days. The water was like pudding and—"

"Yeah, yeah, stuff it. I don't need to hear nothin' 'bout what we're lucky we ain't stompin' about in," Jodoul said.

He held up a hand suddenly and both men stopped. There was banter aplenty during a long, boring assignment, but both had the good sense to go silent when either got the slightest hint of trouble. The light that came down from the occasional grating to the streets above was just enough to see such gestures by.

"I hear someone up ahead," Jodoul whispered, leaning close to Tod's ear. Tod nodded. They heard, faintly but growing steadily louder, a rhythmic clacking. It sounded like wood against stone.

No bodies had been found, but Tod and Jodoul had found that the sneaks and drifters of Zorren had become wary of the sewers of late. The trail of bodies around the city had spooked them and more good sense than real information had given them cause to suspect the tunnels below the city. They assumed anyone who had evaded detection for so long must have been making some use of them. The clacking sound was both promising and ominous.

"We should run," Tod said softly, taking Jodoul by the arm. "That kid's a killer. Let's get to Faolen, make it his problem." Tod gave a tug, but Jodoul resisted, shrugging free of Tod's half-hearted grasp.

"Naw, kids ain't no killers, even if'n they kill. This one's a runaway. Ain't you never run away when you was a lad?" Jodoul replied, a plan slowly coming together in his mind.

"Yeah, but I never had me one o' them kill-staffs, neither. Might'a settled some scores right quick if'n I had."

"Runaways need friends," Jodoul reasoned, staring down into the darkness of the passageway where the clacking sound was growing clearer.

"Live friends is good," Tod replied. "You make a friend. I'll be off and get Faolen. Best o' luck, Jo." Tod made a careful motion to extract his feet quietly from the water, then darted softly down the walkway, crouched at the waist.

Jodoul swore under his breath but held his ground. He was a gambler. He was also a coward. There were times, though, when a pot is so large that even a coward's eyes become clouded. *If'n I get that staff back for Warlock Rashan, I'll be rich as I want to be. I'll have whatever I ask, I know it.*

"Hey boy!" Jodoul shouted in a whisper when he began to hear soft footsteps of leather shoes mixed in with the tapping of wood against the walls of the sewer. "You need some help?"

"Who are you?" the voice was high-pitched, as Jodoul would have expected of a lad too young to shave. It was not a fearful voice but a curious one. It made no pretense of avoiding the notice of those who might have heard through the sewer gratings.

"A friend. My name is Jo," Jodoul replied, not raising his voice but ceasing to whisper.

As the boy continued to approach, he passed beneath one of the gratings, where Jodoul got a good look at him. He was a ragged, dirty thing, dressed in ruined finery. A skinny lad at his best, he looked hungry atop it. He was short enough to walk the sides of the sewers comfortably, but the staff he carried was too tall to hold upright. He had allowed it to bang carelessly against the wall in time with his gait.

"My name is Anzik. You do not work for my father, do you?" Anzik asked. The question sounded innocent the way he asked it, but Jodoul suspected that being a known associate of Jinzan Fehr right then might be an invitation to a restless death.

"Naw. I'm not from around here. I ran away too, like you," Jodoul responded. Tod might have been the better of the two of them at confidence schemes, but Jodoul had run away more times than he could count when he was a boy.

The boy looked at him strangely, cocking his head to one side. He had stopped approaching. "You do not want to catch me, take me back to my father?" he asked.

"'Course not. What you need is a place where you—" Jodoul began, but stopped when the boy suddenly dropped the staff with a clatter and clutched the sides of his head.

"Not now! Stop it! Be quiet!" Anzik shouted, squeezing his eyes shut and shaking his head. He covered his ears.

"I'm sorry, I didn't—" Jodoul babbled, thinking Anzik's commands were meant for him.

"I don't want a bath! Leave my shirt alone!" the boy ranted.

"I won't make you take a bath. I swear," Jodoul promised, his heart racing. He looked to the staff on the ground and wondered if he stood a chance to get to it before the boy could recover his senses and retrieve it.

"Not you! The voices." Anzik looked up at Jodoul from his hands and knees.

The boy's mad as monkeys! No wonder no one's caught him yet. Prob'ly been killin' voices in his head and catching up real folk instead. Aww, arse me, Tod had the right of it, runnin' like a little maid.

Anzik picked up the staff and stood, not bothering to brush the grime from his pants or hands. "What kind of place do you know?" Anzik picked up their conversation where he had interrupted Jodoul.

Jodoul's thoughts spun circles. *Maybe I can wait for another fit to come on him and run for it. Maybe if I just run now, he won't do nothin' to me. Maybe I can still reason with him despite those voices ... he ... hears.*

"Hey there, Anzik," Jodoul ventured. "I think I know someone who could help with those voices you hear. A smart fella who won't give you to your pa."

* * * * * * *

Faolen's daytime tour of Zorren's brothels had been enlightening, but not in any way that would help with the search for the lost Fehr boy or the Staff of Gehlen. The night ladies were as frightened of the lad as anyone in the city, and none admitted to having seen him, even when asked by one who appeared in the guise of a Megrenn officer, as Faolen had. He had learned, however, that he was unlikely to spend any coin at the establishments he had visited. He remembered the women he had seen ... and shuddered.

It was near to dusk when he arrived back at Marod's Goods, having taken a small meal at a street vendor. The streets had been growing quieter the past several days, Faolen had noted. The monstrous child on the loose had scared the common folk enough that many had locked themselves indoors at night, and kept clustered in groups in the daylight. No one had yet been killed openly in public, but that did not comfort those who needed to travel to and fro along lightly traveled streets.

Faolen paused before entering their shop-front hideout. As his eyes adjusted to the aether, he scanned the inside of the building to see who was within. He carefully navigated one of the alleys aside the building to look into the back room, as his vision was not strong enough to view the whole of the interior from out front.

Just Aelon and Tod, by the look of it. I hope nothing has befallen Jodoul.

"Welcome back," Aelon greeted him at the door as he entered. "Go and talk to Tod. He has news for you, and has been plucking his head bald waiting for you to return."

Faolen misliked the way that sounded. Aelon was nervous, but he preferred to hear whatever news from Tod directly. Aelon followed him into the back room.

He entered the back room cautiously, and was ambushed by Tod. "We found 'im! He was in the sewers. Jo and I went down, see, and we heard him. Then I says 'We should go tell Faolen,' and Jo says 'Naw, I got an idea,' and I says 'Best o' luck, I'm fer gettin' to Faolen,' and so's I did."

Faolen pulled up short as Tod had rushed up to him, and stood within breath-smelling distance of him. There was no scent of drink upon him, but Tod did smell vaguely of sewage, though a quick inspection did not show him to have been dunked in the stuff.

"Where is he?" Faolen asked simply.

"Over by the center o' town, where the arse-brown don't flow much. Kid prob'ly had the sense to stay to the nicer parts so's he didn't give his self away with the stink."

"Where is *Jodoul?*" Faolen emphasized. Information about the boy was well and good, but he only had so many accomplices with whom to catch him.

"Last I saw, he was plannin' to talk to the kid." Tod shrugged, his gaze wandering to the floor. "Prob'ly dead. I warned him we weren't the ones to stop him; you was. He thought he knew better."

"I did."

They all turned as Jodoul entered from the front.

"Boy's gonna be headin' here soon as it's dark," Jodoul said, "so we best be ready for 'im."

"How'd ya manage that piece o' magic?" Tod asked, incredulous, slapping Jodoul on the shoulder in congratulations—and chastisement for making him think Jodoul had died a vain death by the dangerous child.

"Kid needed someone to trust. I think I was the first one he ran into what wasn't mad at 'im or tryin' to catch 'im," Jodoul said. "Kid's also got a noggin more twisted 'n' a ship's riggin'. Got's 'im some voices in 'is head, buggin' 'im like no one's business. I says I know a fella who can help." Jodoul smiled at Faolen.

Strong in magic. Voices in his head. Oh, Jodoul, you have no idea how right you were. Faolen smiled in return.

"Let us prepare for him, then."

* * * * * * * *

The little shop had a back door. For a legitimate business, it might have been used for taking deliveries, and the comings and goings of the staff. Faolen and his companions had barred it so that visitors could only enter through the front, leaving it as an escape route only. As Faolen and Jodoul sat waiting, the bar was now leaning against the wall and the door stood open just a crack.

"Remember, leave us as soon as you have made your introduction. I want you and Tod covering the two exits. If you hear anything befall in here that makes you believe me dead, shoot him as he exits. There is some risk that he might have a shielding spell, and kill you, but if I am dead, it may be your only chance at the staff. If he exits but nothing has gone wrong in here, leave him be. It may take time to win his trust," Faolen said, going over the plan aloud with Jodoul for roughly the fifth time.

Jodoul nodded, then cocked his head as if realizing something. "Hey, what if he don't make lots o' noise killin' ya? How am I s'posed to know if'n yer dead then?"

Faolen furrowed his brow. It was not a pleasant prospect, to say the least, but Jodoul had the right of it. If the boy was killing merely with the draw of the staff, two unschooled ruffians like Tod and Jodoul would likely not feel the disturbance in the aether as even a modest sorcerer would. Faolen stood, and began rummaging through the crates left lying about the back room of the establishment. He found a crystal decanter, and hefted it in his hands, liking the feel of it. He found some twine as well.

Faolen set the decanter on the edge of the table, and tied the twine through the looping handle it bore. The other end he looped around his wrist with a short length in between. "There. If I fall to the floor, the decanter will as well, hopefully shattering loudly enough to wake you and Tod from your slumbers outside," Faolen joked, preferring to jest over his potential death rather than consider it seriously.

"Yeah, that oughtta do it." Jodoul nodded. The two proceeded to wait in nervous silence for the killer child to arrive, if indeed he actually intended to arrive at all.

Jodoul paced. Faolen sat still and quietly, trying to compose his thoughts: *If only it is true. This could go much better than I had ever hoped. It will be delicate—*

A noise outside had Faolen shifting his vision quickly into the aether. Outside was a small Source but a powerful one. It had to be Anzik Fehr. Something the boy carried made a wake in the aether as it passed through, but was otherwise indistinct. Most objects of magic shone in the aether; the Staff of Gehlen drew the stuff in upon command. It did not release its hold except by the will of its wielder.

Faolen let his vision resume in the light as the boy tentatively entered the shop. He looked just as Jodoul had described him: small, slight, and entirely unthreatening, unless you knew what the staff he bore was capable of.

"Hello, Anzik," Jodoul greeted him with nervous cheeriness. "This is my friend. His name is Faolen."

Faolen had judged the risk too high to be lying to the boy ... much. If he was a clever one, he would catch them in any slip. Their lies needed to be subtle and few.

"Nice to meet you," Faolen ventured politely, smiling disarmingly.

"You are old." Anzik frowned, looking intently at Faolen.

Faolen's eyebrows raised in mild surprise. *Well now, I had not even thought about that casual little lie.*

"None of us wishes to be old. Would you want to give up being a boy to become an old man?" Faolen asked.

As he did, he let slip an illusion he maintained habitually, with hardly any thought anymore. His hair greyed at the temples and retreated slightly. His skin lost some of its boyish luster, and grew a few wrinkles about the eyes and brow. Life extension had done well by him, but he hid its deficiencies behind a layer of illusions that were hidden from view even in the aether, though apparently not to such keenly observant young eyes.

"Who are you?" Anzik asked. Having already been introduced, he could only assume the boy meant more than his name.

"A friend of Jodoul's and someone who can help you," Faolen replied, picking the most promising of truths to share. "Jodoul can wait outside and guard us, to make sure we are not taken by surprise. I want us to be safe here."

"Yeah, I'll be just outside a ways, got it?" Jodoul said, taking up a short bow and quiver and heading for the back door, leaving the two sorcerers, young and old, Megrenn and Kadrin, alone to discuss their problems.

"You do not want the staff?" Anzik asked suspiciously, once Jodoul had left. "You will not tell my father where I am?"

"I will not tell your father where you are, I assure you. As for the staff, think of it as gold," Faolen said. "Have a seat with me and I will explain."

He gestured to the empty chair that Jodoul had left vacant for all his pacing. The large table that had earlier shown the expanse of Zorren was now just barren. Anzik clutched the staff warily in both hands, and accepted Faolen's offer of a place to sit.

"Gold has value and men use it to trade," Faolen said. "Dishonest men kill for it, steal it, do whatever they can to get it. Honest men trade and barter. They sell goods they make. They exchange it for services they offer. It is the way of the world. Sometimes men who have no gold need to barter instead. A man with bread but no gold can fill his belly, but will go thirsty. A man with ale but no gold can quench his thirst, but go hungry. If the two meet, with no gold between them, they can still meet both their needs by trading some ale for some bread," Faolen lectured. It was a speech he had spent an hour working out in his head.

"I see," the clever boy replied. "You want to trade the staff for helping with the voices."

"Yes, but I am an honest man. I will not take it from you. I will not demand it from you. I will help you with the voices, and when we have taken care of them, I would hope that you would give me the staff in payment," Faolen told him. He looked right at the boy, but Anzik did not make eye contact, preferring to look down at his lap.

"Can you really make them stop?" Anzik asked after a pause.

"Yes. When I was a boy, I had the same problem. A kindly man helped me and I intend to help you the same way."

"How?" Anzik asked meekly. "Father tried to make the voices go away, but he could not."

"First, I need to find where the voices are coming from. Then I will go there to stop them directly. I cannot stop you hearing them; I must stop them trying to speak to you," Faolen explained.

"They are in my head. I hear them there. Everyone knows they are in my head," Anzik whined, frustrated that Faolen seemed not to understand how the voices worked.

"No, they are not. If I stand across the room and shout to you, I am not in your chair. That is merely where you are when you hear. Just as you can see in the aether things that others are incapable of seeing, you hear what others are incapable of hearing. The voices are someplace, and I must find out where to go to stop them."

"I don't know, then," Anzik complained, sniffling. "No one talks to me about the voices. Even Father hardly does anymore."

"Ask the voices, then," Faolen told him. For the first time, Anzik looked up and met Faolen's gaze. "Ask them and tell me what they say."

"How do I do that?" Anzik asked, looking away again.

"Ask the question in your head. Ask it out loud, so you hear it in there, just as you hear their voices. You have your own voice in your head. Make it heard," Faolen instructed him. He felt an echo of his own past. He did not remember the words, but he had received similar instructions once, many summers ago.

Anzik shut his eyes tightly, concentrating. "Where are you? Where are you?" the boy repeated under his breath.

"You need to get a name for the place. Use their words, not your own," Faolen advised softly.

Anzik did not make any acknowledgment, but changed his mantra. "What do you call your place? What do you call your place?" Faolen noted with extreme interest that he had switched to speaking Acardian.

"Are they saying anything back?" Faolen asked eagerly.

"No! I will not be quiet! Tell me what to call this place!" Anzik shouted in Acardian.

"Easy. Easy. Shout in your head, not with your mouth," Faolen cautioned.

Anzik was breathing hard, exerting himself mentally. His eyes snapped open and he looked up at Faolen distantly. "Pious Grove Sanctuary," Anzik said, stumbling a bit over the Takalish words he was mimicking, clearly without understanding them. He looked as if he had been awakened from a nightmare.

Faolen took the shaking boy in his arms and hugged him tight. "It will be all right. I know where to go now to make the voices go away."

"Anzik!" a voice outside shouted. "Anzik, please come home!" The boy curled tighter against Faolen, seeking his protection. "Anzik, I forgive you! I just want you safe! Anzik!"

"I can help hide you from your father as well." Faolen worked a bit of simple illusion to dim the boy's Source from aether-vision. "If you do not use the staff, this spell will keep you from his notice for a few days. I take no payment until I have kept my end of our deal, do you understand?"

Anzik nodded.

"Staying here may be dangerous. I will tell you when it is safe to return. Go. Hide. Try not to hurt anyone until I have the chance to help you quiet those voices," Faolen told him.

Loosed from Faolen's embrace, the boy did not speak another word, but left by the back door, staff in tow. The voice, presumably belonging to a desperate father, continued, but grew distant.

Faolen looked to the decanter, perched unsteadily on the edge of the table, where it had slid when he thoughtlessly took Anzik in his arms. He untied the decanter, and looked for something to pour the contents into. He needed a drink.

Chapter 17 – Bait and Switch

The wooden planks beneath his feet swayed slowly, rocking back and forth as the *Frostwatch Symphony* masqueraded across the Katamic in the guise of a merchant ship. A day earlier, the ship had been loaded with mindroot, Kheshi silks, and several casks of Simmeran Sunset, one of the priciest Takalish brandies gold could buy. Shortly before putting to sea, longshoremen had hastily unloaded the mindroot and silks. The brandy was kept aboard in partial payment to the coinblades who had taken the place of the offloaded cargo.

Zellisan sat in the hold with a dozen of his new compatriots, waiting for the ship to be attacked. Parjek Ran-Haalamar had hired twoscore guards for his bait ship, counting on Captain Zayne's informants in the trade city to have already marked the *Frostwatch Symphony* as a target. If they reached Zayne's hunting grounds before word of the exchange, the pirate would walk into a trap that he thought was his to spring.

"Ain't learned me to swim anyway. Why not wear mail, am I right?" one of the other coinblades remarked, trying to break the grim mood with conversation. He was a scraggly man, all arm and leg, with an egg of a face and a week's unshaven scruff covering it. His posture suggested a military career to Zellisan, who knew the type all too well. Boring assignments, petty tyrants for commanders, and meager pay. Soon enough, any man good enough with a blade or bow starts wondering how much more coin he could pocket working for himself. A few even went through with it.

"Me, I swim just fine," Zellisan replied after an awkward silence that no one else seemed inclined to break. "You'll see me strippin' to my skivvies fast enough, if'n I go in that water out there." He smiled, scanning the hold for signs of anyone with a sense of humor, or at least the bravery to show it.

The men in the hold were the ones who would fight armored upon the deck, once the ship was boarded. They were to hold the middle ground, and keep Zayne's pirates from gaining the helm, defending the ship's captain. Almost to a man, they had agreed to keep well away from the railings, lest they plummet to a near certain death in the Katamic, pulled under by the weight of the steel they wore.

* * * * * * *

"Open this thing up a little wider. I can't breathe in here," a bare-chested Feru complained, a note of rising panic and frustration in his voice.

A sliver of bright daylight shone in through the wooden door, just enough to cast the inside of the crate into a stark contrast of light and dark that kept the eyes from fully adjusting to either. They were crowded inside with just a common bench to sit on and not enough room to stand. Sweating bodies rubbed uncomfortably together. Stowed weapons poked neighbors. The air was hot and more humid than the fresh sea air just outside. The door to the crate was disguised from the outside to look like any other side of the wooden box. It had leather hinges on the inside that let it swing wide open, and a rope handle to let the occupants pull it closed tightly to complete the disguise. Until pirates were sighted, they were leaving it open just a bit to get more air and alleviate the heat.

The Feru coinblade reached out for the dark-skinned hand that kept custody of that handle. Before he could wrench that hand away from the door, another hand had a finger to the man's throat. "Sit down," Rakashi commanded sternly. "There is air enough to breathe. The fear is in your mind. Do not shame yourself with cowardice just before a battle." The Feru man grabbed for the finger at his throat, but the hand it belonged to shoved him roughly back toward his seat. In the cramped confines, he was not welcomed back gently.

"Who put you in charge here, anyway?" someone else asked snidely. Apparently the Feru man was not the only one growing impatient with the accommodations.

"I am not in charge. I am just following the orders given by the captain, the man who will tell Parjek Ran-Haalamar who gets paid and who does not. No man on this ship is strong enough to defy all these hired blades." Rakashi spoke the truth carefully, for he rather suspected that there was a woman who could. "Thus we will follow our orders. The door does not open more than to allow a fist through."

Glares met Rakashi's answer. Rightly or wrongly, they went unnoticed, lost to the glare from the taunting sunlight.

* * * * * * * *

"I don't like having ya up here, or on the ship at all, ya know," Captain Rangelord groused, not so much as looking in the direction of the object of his ire.

"You've mentioned it a time or two," Soria commented dryly, standing next to him by the ship's wheel. It was late afternoon, and with *Frostwatch Symphony* heading south, the sun was slowly beginning its descent to their starboard side. "But if the pirates attack with the sun at their backs, it will be any time now. This is the best view besides the nest." She had said much the same that morning, when the expected attack would have come from the east, with the rising sun.

Tanner had won a contest that morning just after they set sail, and proved he had the best eyes of the bunch. That had earned him the honor of being the one to watch from up on high, in the crow's nest. Soria did not begrudge him his victory, but neither would she accept being stuffed in a box or stowed in the hold as the rest of them had. Instead she watched and waited, giving vague license to the crew to go on about their work around her without actually getting out of their way.

"If you weren't a woman, I'd—"

"—end up feeding the sharks," Soria finished for him, but not in any way as the captain had intended. "There is a reason I commanded three times the sum of the others for this job. When this battle is won, you will see why."

"Tez-u-won Master—or Mistress I oughta say," the captain spat on the deck. "Sack o' fish feet, that's what that's worth. Got folk scared of 'em cuz they can fight without a blade. Well, them pirates'll have blades and you'll see what's what. Not sure how ya snookered a man like Parjek Ran-Haalamar, but ya won't fool me."

"Listen here, root-peddler," Soria warned. "You've got a half dozen of your crew that could likely captain us back to shore somewhere. If you have a problem with me, I don't mind settling it."

Soria was not so foolish as to think that the mindroot Parjek Ran-Haalamar and his associates offloaded would not be sold elsewhere. Trading in mindroot was a high crime in almost any place with a functioning government. When inhaled, it was a potent and addictive hallucinogen, vile enough to warrant universal disdain, though that was not the use that kings and governors feared. When ingested, it reacted with the stomach's fluids, and killed horrifically in just moments. That was the sort of thing folk took a really strong stance against. Pirates, thieves, assassins, and—to a lesser extent—coinblades like herself, were all unsavory types that respectable folk kept away from. Poison-sellers were a level of scum below even those, and Soria might have considered doing the world a service being rid of a few, had she not a more immediate need of them for transportation to a meeting with Denrik Zayne.

* * * * * * *

The tiny speck on the horizon could have been anything. It might have been the peak of a mountain on some island he had yet to spot. It might have been a whale, or a shark, or some other sea creature breeching. Scale was impossible to judge due to the vast distance Tanner could see through the spyglass he had been given. From a wooden bucket built around the central mast of the ship, he had a splendid vantage, but no experience in spotting ships. The ship was staffed with a miser's crew, or some real sailor would have sat watch. It mattered little to Tanner's thinking, since the whole idea was to be found by Denrik Zayne, and not the other way around. He had taken the job just for the novelty. He had traveled many a time across the Katamic without ever having so good a view.

The motion of the ship made it difficult to keep the long, tubular contraption of aligned lenses pointed where he wanted to look. It was Tanner's first time using a spyglass as well, since he was a mere passenger on all his previous voyages, and there was little call for the things on land. Fiddling with the lenses to keep his vision from blurring vexed him. Had he any real talent for magic, he would have used that instead of the troublesome device.

"Ship!" he called down to the captain, when finally he was able to discern white sails against the pale blue of the horizon sky. "Way, way off in front and left of us, that way." He pointed when the captain looked up. It was hardly the most nautical of exchanges, but Tanner got the necessary information relayed.

Captain Rangelord took up his own glass, and confirmed the sighting as they drew close enough to see it from the quarterdeck. It was too far to tell much about it, but it appeared that it was heading west, across the course the *Frostwatch Symphony* was following. It was also far enough to the port side that it would pass quite close to them. The captain took the wheel, and turned it gently to steer them just a bit eastward of their previous heading. It was a common enough maneuver on the open seas, if one captain had no wish to parley with another, to veer to pass behind another ship instead of meeting it.

Captain Rangelord returned to his spyglass and watched. Most ships would think nothing of their change in course; a navy ship might investigate, had they any reason to suspect smugglers or pirates. A troubled ship or one bearing a message might have enough need of parley to turn to intercept. And of course there were pirates. Pirates most certainly would not let such an opportunity slip away just behind them.

Through a trick of the eye or a calming wind, the vessel in the distance seemed to slow; Captain Rangelord saw no change in their sails. As they drew closer, he recognized the ship's profile in the water and the cut of its sails, and knew it for an Acardian vessel. It was a frigate, but an older design than the *Fair Trader* that Zayne sailed.

"Rot it," the captain swore softly.

One way or another, if that ship tried to board them, be they Acardian sailors or pirates, their only option was to repel the boarders and take their ship. There was no way the Acardians would tolerate a ship such as the *Frostwatch Symphony* trolling the waters with a hold full of coinblades, looking for ships to plunder, pirate or no.

When the second vessel deemed the time right, they swung around and openly made straight for the *Symphony*. Captain Rangelord spun the wheel hard, taking evasive actions. As prepared as his mercenaries were for being caught, the trap would not be so convincing if they gave up without resistance.

Breaking her silence as she had stood watching the vessel approach from the forward railing of the quarterdeck, Soria called over to the captain: "They are dropping their colors and raising the blacks."

Rangelord looked briefly her way before he pulled out his spyglass once more to get a look at the ship's flags. In her eyes, he caught a glimpse of an eagerness that sat ill with him. In his experience, a gleam in the eye before a battle was the mark of a murderer, not a fighting man—or fighting woman, he amended mentally. Any sensible sort, hoping to live, win, and collect a purse afterward, had the sense to have his guts curl up inside him when about to wade into a clash of swords, knives, and pistols.

Through the spyglass, he saw something that he was not sure how to take.

On the one hand, the Acardian ship had raised a black flag emblazoned with a white "Z," the simple sigil Zayne had used for years. On the other, it was clearly not the *Fair Trader* that had left Marker's Point some months ago. Rangelord had seen it and marked it well, and this was not that vessel, unless his eyes were betraying him.

"Wretched whoreson has himself a fleet."

* * * * * * * *

The *Frostwatch Symphony* had a wide, rounded hull, excellent at hauling cargo for a ship its size. The wide beam and deep draft kept it stable in the water, and made for a safe, seaworthy vessel. It also made it slow. It was ideally suited to being caught and so it was.

As the two ships came close, the crew abandoned their posts and grabbed belaying pins. This gave them the appearance of desperate men, determined to die fighting, rather than surrender to the questionable mercies of the pirates of the cheekily named *Merciful*. The pirate ship sidled up to them without firing a shot, and threw grappling hooks, snaring the *Frostwatch Symphony* and drawing the two ships together. The *Merciful's* railings were lined with armed men, bristling to leap the gap and sink their blades into the outnumbered crew of their prey ship. For their part, the men with belaying pins backed away from the rails.

When the first dozen or so set boot to deck, the captain sprang their trap. "Now!" he shouted in Kheshi, a language most of the coinblades spoke, whether natively or from having traveled. The large crates on the deck sprung open and cramped, sore, irritable, and well-armed men poured out. Men thundered up the stairs from the holds below. From the *Merciful*, surprised but undeterred men continued their crossings over to the *Symphony*.

Amid all those men, one woman reached back, pulled two blades from their hidden sheaths, and leapt into the heart of the fray. At first, Soria's bold charge had gained her the advantage of surprise, allowing her to bury her blades into two pirates before they could react. The black lacquer on her blades concealed runes she had carved there herself, leaving only the razor edges gleaming, bare steel. It was crude work by the standards of Veydrus, but stood her in good stead punching through mail and plate on Tellurak. Blood ran off them like red waterfalls.

Freed from his duties keeping one of the crates closed, Rakashi drew forth his half-spear. As coinblades from Khesh, Feru Maru, Acardia, and a dozen other tinier places swarmed the deck of the ship, it was the Takalish warrior who gave men pause. The half-spear was an uncommonly used weapon, worse than either a sword or a spear in the hands of a novice. In the hands of a master, it was versatile and deadly. Rakashi's first swing was with both hands near the pommel, taking advantage of having a longer reach than anyone else in the melee to land the first blow. The leverage of the blow was too much for the cutlass that tried to parry it, and the blade buried itself in the chest one of Zayne's pirates via his collarbone. One of the man's comrades, seeking an opening, tried to make short work of Rakashi, but the Takalish master let go the hilt with one hand and dropped to the deck, ducking beneath the handle half of his weapon and letting the blow land there instead. He tangled his legs between his opponent's feet and tripped him as he regained his own footing. Freeing his blade from the dead pirate, he gutted the stumbling one and moved to look for more opponents.

Toward the center of the deck, Zellisan waded among the mercenaries as they formed some semblance of a military line. It was no neat row of troops, but rather an instinctive formation made of men who knew that, so long as you kept your allies to your left and right, you need only worry about what lies before you. The pirates fought well together, though, and had an advantage of numbers.

From high above, a shot cracked, splitting the air above the ferocious din of the battle raging on the deck of the *Frostwatch Symphony*. Tanner's new plaything was guarding against any unwelcome odds he saw his companions facing. The pirates had pistols as well, and shots volleyed between the swaying deck of the ship and crow's nest high above. Tanner felt safe enough, given what the pistolsmith had told him of the accuracy of the thing and his shielding spell in place. His Errol pistol felt easy in his hands. With a good eye and a feel for the roll of the waves, he was mainly hitting his targets. Tanner was a soldier by trade; seeing a battle from an archer's view was a new experience. He rather liked it.

✳ ✳ ✳ ✳ ✳ ✳ ✳

Where is he? Soria thought angrily … hungrily.

Men with blades thrice the length of her dagger were giving her wide berth after seeing half a dozen men dead by her hand, but she was more concerned with searching their faces than engaging them. They were more than obligingly not rushing to cross blades with her, either.

Zayne should be here somewhere. If he did not board, he must still be on his ship.

Soria had thought little enough of the ship's name—had not even really paid attention to it. They were at sea to catch a pirate and they had: one flying Zayne's sigil and everything. That it might not be his own *personal* ship had not crossed her mind. She assumed that she would see a face quite similar to one she remembered from the mines of Raynesdark, stealing the Staff of Gehlen.

Zayne's men had firm hold of the area where the ships met, but Soria did not let that deter her. She killed two more and kicked a third over the railings, leaving a path to make the leap to the *Merciful*. A shot reported from just behind her. Soria felt her shield reverberate and then a shock of pain shoot through her back, but it was fleeting. There was a sting left in its wake, but the pistol shot had not quite pierced her shield.

Stupid things are worse than arrows. Too fast and too small. Rakashi's half-spear would be easier to stop, she groused to herself. She paused just long enough to renew the aether of her shields from her own Source, then made the leap across.

The eager among the pirate crew had made the crossing already. That left the reluctant, the cautious, and the slow remaining on the *Merciful*'s deck. She scanned what she could see of the ship as men backed away from her, weapons drawn.

"Where's Zayne?" she demanded loudly in Acardian, hoping the pirate might even hear her himself, even if his crew would not reveal him. Unsurprisingly, none spoke up and she knew most had understood her.

Soria had been watching in normal light so that she could identify Denrik Zayne by her memory of what his twin looked like. She switched to the aether, which let her see all around her, and waited for an opportunity to present itself. She turned slowly, looking at each man and watching him shrink from her. She lurched the opposite direction in a feint and smiled as three men nearly tripped over one another to get out of her way. A quick look over her shoulder, and another man hastening to get out of her way made the mistake she was looking for.

With a quick snap of her wrist, a dagger flew. The unfortunate man she had picked out instinctively tried to deflect it with his cutlass, but it was aimed to miss high regardless. The dagger sank into the mast he had backed into, a handsbreadth above his head, and the free hand that had thrown it was twisting his sword arm before he could recover. A forearm jammed itself under his chin, forcing his head against the mast, and the blade Soria still held was just brushing his throat.

"Where is Zayne?" Soria snarled, meeting him eye to eye, though her own gaze appeared to look right through him until she shifted back into the light to see him better.

"This … This ain't Zayne's ship. I … I … I mean it's Zayne's ship, but he don't sail it. We just work fer him is all," the frightened man babbled.

"Who is captain here, then?" Soria demanded, addressing the ship at large and not just her captive.

Soria heard two clicks. Pistols were uncommon among decent folk, but she had been around enough of the other sort to recognize the sound of the hammer of one being cocked. Slowly she turned her head to see who held them.

"I am," replied a man with sun-browned skin and dark, slicked-back hair. He smiled as he spoke with an ease that bespoke confidence and curiosity about the visitor his ship had received. "I think you can stop one shot but just barely. Two … I think maybe not?" he asked, as if posing the question more theoretically than the two pistols aimed for Soria's head suggested. "We get so few visitors here, it would be a shame to make a habit of putting holes in them. Especially pretty visitors."

"Who are you?" Soria asked, trying to keep her accustomed "demand" out of her tone.

He may be right. Two might be too much and I don't relish even one hitting me in the head, shield or no shield.

"I am Robbono Stalyart, captain of the *Merciful*, proudly sailing under Denrik Zayne's banner. I am also a man who sees things others do not. Three times I will ask this: who are you?" Stalyart responded, bowing his head slightly in introduction, but taking neither his eyes nor the aim of his pistols from her.

"Soria Coinblade," she said, wondering what he was playing at—and he clearly seemed to be playing. There was something distinctly flippant about his attitude that made her think this Captain Stalyart was not taking her entirely seriously as a threat.

"Ahh, a Kheshi warrioress with no family name. Instead she takes on a false one, like her false hair, false eyes. Without those, who are you?" Stalyart prodded, chuckling.

His men were slowly making their way away from Soria, back to where their captain could offer some protection, real or perceived. Soria released her hold on the pirate she had pinned, and freed her second dagger from where it was stuck in the mast before deciding on an answer. The man was useless as a hostage anyway.

"Just Soria, then, I suppose. Acardian by birth but orphaned in Khesh and raised there. If you are done with distractions, I need to find someone. If Zayne isn't here, then maybe you can answer me," Soria said.

She took a deep breath as if to steady her nerves, and averted her gaze. Slipping back to aether-vision, she checked the Source of this Stalyart fellow. His was hale and healthy, stronger than most, enough so that she might have difficulty corralling him with a telekinesis spell. It might be enough for her to spoil his aim, though, should the need arise. The battle still raged aboard the other ship, occupying most of the crews of both ships, and on the *Merciful*, only the captain appeared to be armed with more than a blade.

"Aha! You claimed to be seeking Captain Zayne, but it is someone else you are looking for." The pirate captain laughed aloud. "I have your story figured out, I think, but I would hear one detail from you and your reason. Tell me, in truth, who you *really* are and why you seek the twin of Brannis Solaran, then we may be able to deal."

Soria's eyes widened. "You know where he is?"

Stalyart nodded.

"You could take me to him?"

Stalyart cocked his head innocently and shrugged, but said nothing.

"I am Juliana Archon," she replied in Kadrin. "Where is Kyrus Hinterdale?"

"My terms are these: win this ship for me, and I will take you to him, and grant safe passage back to the mainland, if you desire. I think this battle goes badly. You can change that, I think," Stalyart said.

Zayne's pirates or root-peddlers from the Point. Same scum, different pond, but this Stalyart knows where Brannis is.

"Deal."

* * * * * * * *

Zellisan grunted in exertion as he parried another heavy blow. The fellow he was dueling was one of the few opponents he had ever faced who had both a reach and strength advantage on him. The brute had carved up a handful of the *Symphony's* coinblades before engaging Zell and was now pressing him as well.

The man was not a graceful fighter, but was young and vigorous, making up in ferocity what he lacked in technique. Zellisan could tell that the pirates were losing men, though, and if he kept his current foe at bay long enough, someone would come free to help kill him. Zell was well past the age of caring who got the glory blow to end a fight, or objecting to dishonorable tactics in what had many similarities to a formal duel. In the end, they wanted one another dead and he was rather indifferent as to how the other fellow met his end, so long as he lived through the battle.

"Change of plans! Switch sides!" a high voice bellowed over the clash of swords, screams of the injured, and occasional reports of pistol fire. It spoke Kadrin.

Oh, for the love of . . .

Zellisan blew an exasperated breath, made a feint to draw his opponent's defenses up, and quick-stepped back away from him. Each of the hired blades aboard the *Frostwatch Symphony* had been given a purple ribbon to tie around his upper arm. In the chaos of battle among two crews of mongrels, they wanted some way to tell who was on whose side. Zellisan slipped his sword under his own ribbon and cut his away.

"Sorry, friend," he apologized to his opponent. "Looks like I finish up this one on your side."

The big man appeared unconvinced, but Zellisan gritted his teeth, and cut down two unsuspecting former comrades who had not yet realized the betrayal.

Little princess, you vex me sorely at times. You had best hope Rakashi goes along; he likes these little stunts of yours even less than I do.

It was not the first time one of Soria's plots had them changing sides mid battle, and he knew better than to toss vinegar in her stew.

* * * * * * *

These are the things that love makes us do. Would I do any less if the quest were for my own beloved? Rakashi knew the desperate need Soria felt for finding this Kyrus fellow, the twin of her twin's love. She could content herself in Veydrus if she could find contentment in Tellurak. Rakashi had never heard of such a thing happening among the twinborn, but he supposed that the bonds of marriage existed separately in each world. To carry on an affair in such a matter felt unseemly, but he could not rationalize the feeling with any sound reasoning. *"This world is not the other world." I taught her that myself.*

The crew of the *Frostwatch Symphony* were traders in death spices. Their employer, Parjek Ran-Haalamar, was a blight in Rakashi's eyes. The pirates might have been no better, but they were certainly no worse.

Rakashi used the flat of his blade where he found it convenient, and set about laying into his former associates. He was willing to test the name of the pirates' ship and see if there was mercy to be had after the battle. Some among the hired blades might have been worthy of it.

"So these three are yours?" Stalyart asked, touring the deck of the prize ship he had captured.

Soria, Zellisan, Rakashi, and Tanner stood amid the pirate crew who were rounding up the few survivors who had surrendered, as well as the ship's original crew. The rest of them were largely unhurt, but Tanner was limping. He had read in a storybook once about a pirate who slid down a sail using his dagger to slow his fall. Tanner's runed blade had cut through the *Symphony*'s mainsail as if it had been made of parchment instead of sailcloth.

"Yes, just these three and myself," Soria answered.

"And you, sir. What is *your* name here?" Stalyart addressed Rakashi directly.

"I am known as Rakashi dar Fandar," Rakashi replied. "You look older here."

Stalyart laughed. "I am older. I have not seen you in many years." He clapped the Takalish warrior on the shoulder. "The girl should have sent you to negotiate. We could have shared a drink while the rest fought."

"Wait, you know each other?" Soria asked Rakashi.

Rakashi was the only one of the four of them who did not live in Kadrin, and only Tanner had met him on the other side. They knew he was from Safschan, but Veydran politics were of little concern to them, even should they find themselves on opposite sides of the war between Kadrin and the Megrenn Alliance.

"Yes, for many years, though not for many years," Rakashi replied cryptically. "We held a common cause once and aided one another. I feel better now about your plan, since I know whose head to cut off should we be betrayed." Rakashi smiled at Stalyart, who took the threat in stride, his own smile never faltering.

"Well, this ship is in good enough shape to sail. We can make repairs to the main sail once we are in calm winds or when we reach our destination. Someone throw the rest of those coinblades in the water, but not the crew. We will let them sail their own ship," Stalyart ordered.

"Hey!" objected one of the aforementioned survivors from among the dozens of hired blades who had been brought on board. "How 'bout some o' that mercy. I'll fight for ya, work for ya, pay a ransom if ya put me ashore. C'mon!"

"Ahh. You make a common mistake, I am afraid," Stalyart explained. "I once sailed with Captain Denrik Zayne when his ship was the *Honest Merchant*. Once, when we captured a ship and took its cargo, their captain said, 'You claim to be a merchant? Your ship's name is a lie.' Zayne replied, 'It is the ship whose name is *Honest Merchant*. My name is Denrik Zayne and I am a pirate.' So you see, it is the ship that is merciful, not I. My name is Robbono Stalyart, and I am a practical man."

Stalyart was merciful enough, though, that he allowed the condemned men to remove any armor or clothing they wished, and he was dropping them in the water along a major trade route. There was a chance they might be rescued before drowning or being eaten.

"Where are we heading?" Soria asked as they headed back to the *Merciful*. She had hardened herself to killing long ago, but tried not to be wanton about it. The callousness of the pirates condemning men to the sea with some faint whiff of hope for rescue sat poorly with her. Her die was cast, though, and she had to see how it fell.

"Denku Appa," Stalyart replied. He looked Soria over appraisingly: tall, fierce, driven, and beautiful with her natural green eyes and auburn hair displayed once more. "I think you will not like it there."

Chapter 18 - A True Beginning

A cold, patchy grey-white blur rushed past them, obscuring all vision. The men on deck were bundled against the elements as if it were the dead of winter, and not early springtime. The winds were of their own making, not any natural current of the air. Krogen would not be able to keep them at such a pace for long, but they needed to keep their speed up for their next maneuver.

The cloud they flew through turned wispy as they reached the end of it, before giving way entirely, and bathing the crew of the *Thunderstorm* in crisp, clean sunshine. Below them spread the majesty of the north Kadrin landscape, verdant hills with blossoming wildflowers, plowed farmland with endless furrows planted for the summer harvest, and an army camped about the hillside city of Munne.

Munne was not a beautiful city. Viewed from on high, it looked like an ugly blemish on the pastoral wonder of the countryside, a block of grey and brown buildings surrounded by high walls that rose and fell as they traced the contour of the dozen or so hills that constituted the city's geography. Bridges spanned the Sweetwater River that cut the city in two. Others occasionally joined hill to hill over less hospitable terrain or connected buildings at heights other than ground level. Bridges and walls were Munne's defining features, other than the hills it sat upon. With naught but a fifth of Kadris's population, it still counted itself among the Kadrin Empire's larger cities.

While Munne was not a great prize of artistry or architecture, the army that camped all about it was far more colorful and diverse. There was the monohorn cavalry that had made the sacking of Temble Hill so easy, camped before the rest of the Megrenn forces like a shield of thick, tough hide. Native Megrenn infantry spread across the plains, settled into brightly colored tents, with cook fires burning. The large, black tents held sorcerers from Ghelk, few in number, but safe behind wards if the scouts' tales proved true. Safschan had sent horsemen and bowmen, but the vexing contribution of theirs was the stripe-cats: hulking felines larger than horses and faster in short bursts, with claws and fangs that would send many Kadrin soldiers to their pyres before the war would end. If possible, worse still were the rock-hurlers.

The goblin-made devices were impossible to defend against, and the *Thunderstorm* and her two sister ships—the *Cloud Maiden* and the *Dragonhawk*— had devoted much of their efforts to harrying them and their crews. At Marshal Brannis's insistence, Munne's defenders had filled empty grain sacks with gravel, dirt, sawdust, and anything else they could find and piled them before the walls. Between the airships' efforts, the sacks dispersing the effects of the Megrenn siege engines, and Munne's hilly geography hampering the monohorns, the city continued to hold out.

"Sorcerer Krogen, prepare us to dive!" ordered Captain Drecker, shouting over the shrieking wind. "Port side, prepare to rake the stripe-cats as we pass!"

With all the other efforts of the Megrenn forces held at bay, the arrival of the stripe-cat cavalry—the pride of Safschan and an integral part of the Megrenn Rebellion twenty-one winters ago—was cause for serious concern.

"Aye, sir!" Krogen shouted back.

The *Thunderstorm* pitched forward, giving the crew a spectacular panoramic view of the siege far below. Archers scrambled to catch hold of the high netting that kept the crew from falling over the ship's railings. Once situated, they took hold of the net, each gripping both it and their bows with their left hand while drawing with the right. Though Drecker had given no specific order, men at the aft of the ship were opening crates of blacksmithing debris: worn shoes, rusted plows, spare ingots, and the like. The airship was traveling at a terrific speed, and even without aiming, the flotsam would play havoc among the encamped forces.

The ground rushed up at them. Captain Drecker felt his stomach clench. A man of the sea, he had ridden out storms that had pitched his ship thusly in times past. Ever before, there had been water before him, and the promise of another wave. It was a grueling ordeal at sea, but there seemed to have been so much more room for error then than with the Munne countryside hurtling toward them with no promise but a messy demise should they fail to pull up in time.

"Hard to port! Level us out!" the captain screamed. His stomach dropped into his boots as the *Thunderstorm* pulled out of its dive a dozen paces above the battlefield and no more. It was the closest they had come to hitting the ground in the eight times they had tried the maneuver. Either they were getting better at it or they had narrowly averted disaster. Captain Drecker had yet to decide which.

As the ship banked hard, the deck pitched precipitously beneath their feet. The archers at the port railing were facing nearly straight down as they began firing, their boots jammed firmly to the deck by the force of their turn. They passed their targets too quickly to survey what damage they had wrought, but between the twoscore archers and the spilled iron scrap, they must have left a mark upon their adversaries.

Archers screamed and shied away from the railings as a riderless stripe-cat leapt at the ship. Its claws caught in the netting, jerking the ship in the air before cutting through the heavy ropes. It took no order for Krogen to pull them up and begin their climb to escape retributive fire from the ground.

Kthooom.

Something whistled past the *Thunderstorm*. Captain Drecker did not need two guesses as to what it might have been.

"Get us up and out of here, *now!*" he ordered. "The frolicking whoresons have managed to aim the blasted things *up*."

I hope those dratted iron balls rain back down on their own lousy heads, Drecker thought.

Kthoom.

The captain saw a blur as the second shot whizzed past.

Kthoom—CRACK!

"Turn us back to the city. Get us up to cloud level, on the double!" Drecker ordered.

He did not see the damage. Had they been at sea, a hit below the waterline was sure to sink a ship unless the damage was miniscule. There was no chance of that with the Megrenn weapons. Warded as the ship's hull was, it was suited to turning aside arrows and spears, not the iron balls the Megrenns' goblin weapons threw. Fortunately the worst they could take on was air, which seemed harmless enough, so long as no one fell out through the hole.

"Krogen, *up*, I said!" he shouted again.

"It's no good, sir," Krogen said into the captain's ear, stumbling into the man as the ship lurched. "Those runes were damaged. We aren't even going to have the *up* we've got for much longer. It has been a pleasure to know you, sir."

"Indeed." Captain Drecker solemnly took the sorcerer's offered hand and shook it.

The ground hurtled toward the *Thunderstorm* once more, Megrenn troops scattering at their approach. This time, they did not pull up.

* * * * * * * *

Commander Stotaala Bal-Kaynnyn eased her stripe-cat through the throng that surrounded the downed Kadrin airship. Soldiers fell over themselves to get out of the beast's way. With the tight-packed groups that wanted to get up close to the wondrous ship that had been harrying them for days, there was only so much room to give. The stripe-cat found its footing with a grace that belied its bulk.

The commander was wearing a shaggy, hooded fur jacket over her leather armor, dyed to match the brown-and-green striped pattern of her mount. Had the Kadrin weather been akin to her native Safschan, she would have painted her skin to match instead. Pressed against Katiki's back, she would be hard to discern for archers or sorcerers looking to remove the beast's rider. She would much have liked to press herself against Katiki's back, and nuzzle against her warm fur. The Kadrin idea of springtime was a farce, colder than the deepest winter she had ever known back home, or even visiting her mother in Zorren.

She made a circuit of the wreckage, with two of her fellow stripe-cat riders helping to keep the bystanders back. She was no sailor, but she had traveled by ship. What had crashed from the sky was very much a ship. *What odd magics the Kadrins work against us,* she mused. *They lack the strength to stand against us, so they try to lift their boats above us like archers' towers in the sky.*

Blood and broken bodies spattered the tall grasses amid the wood, rope, and sailcloth that had once been a ship. She considered dismounting to have a closer look, but decided to let others examine the wreck.

Too cold here. I will stay with Katiki. Like the other stripe-cat riders, she spent much of the day in her saddle. Her legs were strapped securely to the sides of her mount, her strong thighs squeezing and twisting to guide the well-trained animal. The act of dismounting took either great flexibility to reach all the buckles and straps, or one or more assistants. She took meals from the saddle, and sometimes slept atop her mount as well, burrowing into the thick, luxuriant fur for warmth and comfort. Katiki would grow restless if she was away from her for long. She was bonded to the great cat, raising her from a kitten the size of a mastiff. Katiki sensed her moods, and could read her thoughts just a bit—enough to obey Stotaala unhesitatingly, but not so much as to understand plans. It was a welcome defense against intrusive magic as well, as Kadrin sorcerers were known to bewitch beasts to defy their nature.

"Pull all the bodies from the wreck and lay them out. Search for orders, logs, journals, rank insignia, personal belongings—especially ones with names or sigils on them," she ordered, directing Megrenn troops as if she were their commander. Since none of higher rank in the greater alliance army were around, obeisance was hers.

The count went amiss somewhere beyond forty. That was the point where partial bodies became problematic, and double-counting might have begun. The worst news was that only one on the ship wore any garment indicating membership in the Kadrin Imperial Circle. *I had hoped to find ten aboard, to make a ship fly like a hunting bird. Ten fewer among the Kadrin sorcerers would be cause to celebrate. One less feels hollow. If one sorcerer can make a ship fly, how many more will we see?*

"Find some chunk of that thing with Kadrin runes on it. Send it over to the Ghelkans to examine," she added.

They managed to shoot the thing from the sky. Let them pick at its bones to see its workings.

* * * * * * *

With one Kadrin airship felled, the other two beat a hasty retreat for the city. They seemed to have realized that the Megrenn reinforcements meant that the forestalled attack would be resumed. Their last chance to own the field had just ended.

Stotaala took the spear and shield her spearmaidens handed her. Twelve and nine summers they had and awaiting kittens of their own. The elder, Shaminai, might be riding to war beside her in just two summers. Though weaker with arms than older girls, or the few young men among the stripe-cat riders, control of the beasts was paramount in battle. While Stotaala's spear was deadly, Katiki would kill twelve or fifteen men for every one that died on her spear. Riding the great cats was a task for the young. It took supple limbs and a healthy back to sway with the stripe-cats as they walked, and when they ran, it took a skill not to be thrashed about, even with the rider's legs strapped in. Even Stotaala's legendary mother Kaynnyn had not made it to her thirtieth winter before retiring from the cavalry.

A trumpet sounded, and the ground rumbled beneath Katiki's feet. Despite their ineffectiveness attacking uphill against the city's defenses, the monohorns were leading the advance. The behemoths would provide cover against the archers and sorcerers on the walls as the stripe-cats and infantry made their advances.

A series of high-pitched whistles pierced the air. Stotaala could not hear them, but rather felt them through her bond with Katiki, whose ears were far more sensitive than her own. General Felana Haliff, Stotaala's commanding officer, had signaled the stripe-cat cavalry to begin their own advance.

Perched high atop her mount, Stotaala still could not see above the monohorns as she trailed the monstrous cattle in their advance. The terrain around the city was flatter than the city itself, but still rolled a bit. She felt nothing but disdain for the monohorn riders as their mounts slowed and sped based on the grade. *The brutes just pull to the left and right. The beasts go whatever pace they find easy.*

They were in no rush. Arrows rained among them, but the cover from the monohorns made the passage less risky, at least as battlefields accounted such things. They conserved energy for the assault on the walls.

Katiki lurched to the side suddenly, narrowly avoiding freshly dropped monohorn dung. *I cannot wait to be out from behind these foul animals. They reek of manure and grime.* Had other, more genteel officers caught a whiff of Stotaala away from her mount, they might have thought much the same of her. She and Katiki were one, though, and the smell that the stripe-cat had was invisible to her nose.

No thunderous reports were heard from the goblin siege engines. They were being held in reserve in case the Kadrin airships made another appearance above the battlefield. Thus, when the whistles blew to signal the charge, they were heard across the plains.

Katiki needed no prodding. She sped forth, shooting between two shielding monohorns as if they stood grazing. Stotaala swayed in time with her stripe-cat's bounding gait, pressing her torso as flat as she could manage while still keeping a tight grip on spear and shield. She peered up as best she could, but knew that until they reached the wall, she was best off leaving their path to Katiki's discretion and staying sheltered against her back.

Bowmen, who had been patiently awaiting the Megrenn army's arrival at the base of the hilltops, opened fire in earnest. Arrows filled the air, occasionally snagging in thick fur, but rarely doing serious harm to the stripe-cat cavalry as they advanced. Stotaala felt one graze her leg, but the sting would not hinder her unless it started bleeding badly.

Thunder echoed in the air under a clear sky. Roars of wounded cats answered back. *The Kadrin sorcerers have decided to join this battle. They must respect our charge. They know we mean to enter their walls.*

The sound of hooves hammering the landscape caused Stotaala to lift her head to see what was happening before her. Munne had opened both its inner and outer gates, and raised its portcullis. Kadrin knights had emerged and were riding hard, lances leveled. It was foolish bravado. *Perhaps they think to die better here with lance and horse, than fighting within the city, sword against claw and spear.* A futile gesture though it may have been, Stotaala respected the choice. It was the choice of a warrior to meet his fate with his life's blood pooling with that of his enemy.

The world stopped making sense. Stotaala's vision went dark and spots swam before her eyes. She heard nothing but a high-pitched whine in her ears. She had a drunken feeling, like the world was wobbling beneath her. Instinctively she clutched Katiki's fur for support, her spear forgotten, and her shield flopping loosely from her forearm. A massive weight briefly mashed her against Katiki's back, forcing the breath from her lungs.

As her vision cleared, Stotaala saw one of her sisters leap over her. The stripe-cats were meeting the Kadrin knights. Some pulled short to bat away lances and bite at horseflesh, others leapt the cavalry formation to attack from the rear. Stotaala sat dazed in her saddle, atop a raggedly breathing Katiki who was trying to drag herself to her feet. Katiki seemed badly hurt, but certainly alive and with spirit left to try to fight on. Stotaala was sure she had broken ribs when Katiki had rolled over the top of her.

She watched as the battle passed her by. The knights were dispersed quickly enough by the stripe-cats, and left for the second wave of the Megrenn advance to finish off. The stripe-cats reached the wall, five times the height of a man, and leapt atop it.

* * * * * * * *

"*... and once the stripe-cats entered the city, the defenses unraveled. Lord Grenorn and his family were evacuated on the* Dragonhawk, *and the* Cloud Maiden *is making ready to depart with as many of the senior sorcerers and knights as they can fit aboard it. I am taking it as my duty to remain behind until the last possible moment and destroy the speaking stone before it falls into Megrenn control. Until then, I will report as I am able.*"

Rashan scanned the report, hurriedly scribbled by one of the speaking-stone attendants who were listening for news from the Battle of Munne. "Get word back to that messenger. Tell him to surrender the stone to the highest-ranking Megrenn he can. Have him tell them I wish to speak with them. Under no circumstances is he to allow that stone to be destroyed."

"What are you thinking?" Dolvaen asked. He was sitting across the desk from Rashan, getting updates as they became available. It was a nervous, tense, maddening sort of waiting. Kadrins were fighting and dying across the Empire as the border war expanded. Munne was a major city, though, the first real conflict since Raynesdark, and it was about to fall.

"Dolvaen, see to it that the wards on the future emperor's chambers are secure and treble the guard, then meet me at the speaking-stone chamber," Rashan replied, speaking quickly as his mind formulated a plan.

"To what end?" Dolvaen seemed suspicious. Aside from a rage-addled killing sojourn after the assassination attempt at the wedding, Rashan had not left the capital since his return from the Battle of Raynesdark. Ever since the new emperor had been selected, the man had been under constant guard, and Rashan was loath to leave the vicinity of the palace for fear of assassins.

"I do not abide well," Rashan answered, apparently all the explanation Dolvaen was likely to receive.

Once he had seen to the warlock's instructions, and secured the emperor's safety, the senior non-demonic member of the Inner Circle sought out his superior. As promised, Rashan awaited him in the speaking-stone chamber. At least, he was there as he said he would be. Rashan was not waiting.

The warlock had his hands on the stone, lost in thought. The conversation, with whomever was on the other end in Munne, was brief.

"Back out of the room. When the spell resolves itself, see to the safety of our own sorcerer, if I manage to get him, and kill or capture anyone else who comes along," Rashan ordered hurriedly. A sphere of opaque aether enveloped the warlock, the speaking stone, and a good chunk of the room as soon as Dolvaen retreated.

A few breaths later, the sphere disappeared. A speaking stone much like the one that normally occupied the room was situated in the middle of the room. The floor was set unevenly, as the chunk of Veydrus snatched from Munne was set just a bit differently from the chunk exchanged from Kadris. Three men stood about it as well. The one in black robes looked astonished and relieved, reacting with impressive presence of mind to dive past the looming Sorcerer Dolvaen Lurien, who was already chanting.

"*Fetru oglo daxgak sevdu wenlu.*" Dolvaen's fingers wove runes in the air before him, culminating in an imperious pointing gesture. Both the Megrenn sorcerer and general, by their attire and insignia, were fried from within as Dolvaen's lightning tore into them. There was a brief flicker from about the sorcerer, as a ward gamely tried to protect its owner before giving up in defeat.

"What just happened?" the Kadrin messenger wondered aloud as the smells of ozone and burnt flesh mixed in the air.

"Warlock Rashan just took a holiday, I think," Dolvaen replied dryly. "I imagine he may wish to speak to you upon his return. I will have someone find you quarters and fresh garments. If you have not soiled yours, you are a better man than I."

Dolvaen's heart pounded in his chest. He had not cast a spell with deadly intent in over twenty winters. The war had suddenly turned real for him.

* * * * * * * *

"I wish I had dared stay longer," Rashan opined. "But there is only so long I can justify being away when I hold responsibility for not only the stewardship of the Empire, but also the soon-to-be-emperor's life."

"You enjoyed yourself, though, did you not?" Dolvaen probed. The warlock had been nearly giddy upon his return. "I killed two men, and I felt like vomiting afterward, the stench hit me so. It was all I could do to keep my composure in front of that sorcerer you saved. His name is Arrin Heartstone, by the way ... one of mine." Rashan understood that Dolvaen meant a sorcerer from a nothing bloodline. They were a pet cause of his. Rashan thought it to be one of the man's few real flaws, akin to children who try to adopt each stray or wounded animal they find as a pet.

"I cannot deny the thrill. A dragon among horses, feasting at leisure and slaughtering for the sport of it? Who would not revel in such dominion? Alas, these were not goblins, and there were real sorcerers out there among the Megrenn host. If one of them were to have been carrying the Staff of Gehlen, I might not have made it back at all." Rashan had reappeared in the palace gardens, and ordered some guards to haul the Tower of Contemplation's speaking stone back indoors, and stow it somewhere safe. Rashan had managed to get back to the one he had brought with him before working a second transference spell.

"Aye, it will be a game of two hunters, you and this sorcerer of theirs who has the staff. Whoever finds himself in the wrong place at the wrong time is done for. Thus a stalemate as each fears to act," Dolvaen reasoned. "Excepting tonight's adventure, of course."

"I saw the carnage I left in my wake, but I know the risk I took. I shall avoid repeating that folly. What I need are more *weapons*. We cannot face the Megrenn with their beasts and their alchemical magic if we do not counter with magic— real magic, not the stuff those Third and Sixth and Fifty-fifth Circle sorcerers out there were playing at," Rashan ranted. He was growing frustrated and agitated. Dolvaen leaned ever so slightly away, just in case.

"But Iridan just is not ready yet. I should have raised the boy myself. He avoided the trap of arrogance and entitlement too well. He lacks confidence and ruthlessness," Rashan continued on.

"Well, I hear that Brannis's newly discovered Source is rather impressive," Dolvaen joked. Potential or no, it took years to train a sorcerer, let alone a warlock.

"Oh, I have already decided that I will test our new Brannis to see what he is capable of. No worry of that ..."

Chapter 19 ~ Competitive Advantage

Kyrus awoke to find that the wards that had surrounded his bedroom had gone away. He could see the Sources of a pair of guards standing outside the door, but suspected that they were there to keep others out, not keep him within. At the foot of his bed floated a message—not the paper and ink sort, but Kyrus understood its meaning clearly enough. It was a wooden chest that he remembered from Brannis's past and atop it lay a wooden sword.

Kyrus got up and lifted the lid of the chest, finding as he suspected he would, a suit of Brannis's old armor. It was simple, battered, and smelled strongly of the light oil that kept it from rusting in storage. He—or rather Brannis—had not worn it in years. It was a suit that had fitted him well enough when he had commissioned it, but he had been a lad then, fully grown but not filled out. Had Brannis tried to put it on, there would have been fist-sized gaps at the sides, had the straps even reached to buckle it on. Kyrus's face curled into an annoyed sneer as he realized it would likely fit him just fine.

No, Kyrus decided. *I will not play this morning's game. He can give me a proper order if he wants me to obey. Brannis thought to match wits with Rashan, pass all his little tests and see through his ruses. I will hold things together here best I can, for now, but I will send him back his grand marshal as soon as I am able.*

Of course, I should still go see what he wants of me.

* * * * * * * *

"A fine morning for a friendly sparring match," Rashan commented despite the cool, rainy weather that few would have chosen to describe as any sort of "fine." "I see you have not dressed for it, however."

Kyrus wore one of Brannis's outfits. It hung loose about him, just as Brannis's old too-small armor would seem to have been his size.

"I heard rumors in the halls on my way down here that Iridan returned late last night," Kyrus said. "You can spar with him this morning, instead of me. I still do not feel quite up to swordplay yet." Kyrus looked about, noticing that a larger number of spectators than usual had turned out to watch the practice session. Nearly the whole of the Inner Circle was in attendance. There were a number of other prominent members of the Imperial Circle as well, not to mention a few knights, the hangers-on at court, and a number of noblemen that were in the city for the impending coronation. Some were down around the outskirts of the courtyard. Others looked down from the balconies surrounding it.

"I had not expected to be your opponent this morning. I had expected you to be Iridan's." Rashan smiled to him. "Iridan!" the warlock shouted out into the courtyard, where Iridan was conversing with his new oathfather. "Look who is up and about."

"Brannith!" Iridan called out, smiling and revealing a handful of half-regrown teeth, giving him the look of a schoolboy. He jogged over to see his friend. "I had heard about your acffident." Iridan paused, rolled his eyes in frustration and tried again. "Ac ... ci ... dent. You all wight? You wook wike you been rung out wike a woffcwoff."

Kyrus frowned, fairly certain that he had just been compared to a damp rag. Did everyone in Acardia think of him thus as well, and just never said anything since they had no expectation that he ought to be otherwise?

"I ought to be fine, Rashan tells me, though I have seen better days." Kyrus tried to keep in character as best he could. In truth, he felt fine. He had slept well, for despite an unfamiliarity about it, the bed was finer than any he had slept in. His dreams had reassured him as well. Brannis would find passage off Denku Appa unless something odd befell him, and he had even rid himself of the attentions of the island girls.

Why had I not thought of that? he wondered.

"I had ffought Raffan was joking, or toying wiff me when he threatened to pit you againfft me thiff morning. Now I see that I could probabwy knock you over wiff a bwoom," Iridan joked, clearly enjoying seeing a Brannis that he might be able to defeat in a fight.

"Well, as I had no other opponent prepared for you this morning, and Brannis is not going to oblige, perhaps we will skip the sparring this morning ... unless of course you would prefer to challenge *me*," Rashan offered.

Iridan took a half step back away from his father, clearly not amused by the prospect. There was no trick to be used against Rashan, no clever ploy to find victory against some foe he fought on unequal ground, using only his skills with a blade lest he render the contest moot with fire or lightning. Iridan shook his head, enthusiastically declining.

"Very well then. Get out there, and I shall send you an opponent from among our esteemed spectators for this morning's draw." Rashan smiled, shooing Iridan out into the midst of the courtyard. Kyrus noticed that four extra basins had been placed around and filled with water. Kyrus wondered whether Rashan might finally think Iridan was ready to face him. He looked about to see who else might be chosen.

Dolvaen was on one of the upper balconies, gazing down. Iridan had never bested him, and he had long said that he thought Rashan would require that of Iridan before he ever drew against the warlock himself. Caladris was talking with Shador on one of the low terraces—Caladris at least was a possibility, though Shador might acquit himself well if it was him. The rest of the Inner Circle were *all* there, he realized. Perhaps Iridan would be facing more than one ...

Kyrus felt a nudge at his back. "Go get him," Rashan whispered.

Kyrus's eyes widened and his knees went weak. *Not me!*

His only experience in a draw was the one time Brannis had done it in his final days at the Academy. Brannis had felt like he had showed up to a horse race with a child's toy stick horse for a mount, and Kyrus remembered the feeling vividly. Brannis had never even been able to watch a draw, and now Kyrus was being thrown in against Iridan, who was working his way through the ranks of the Inner Circle—and near as Kyrus could figure would rank around fourth or so among them, were they holding to the Academy's method of determining such.

Kyrus sleepwalked to the middle of the courtyard, his thoughts running to escape the crowd of curious eyes that pursued him. *He wants to see what I am made of. I just told myself I would not get caught up in his tests. I refused to don Brannis's armor. And now here I am. I wonder if I had sparred, would I have been spared this, or would it have been even worse, being roundly thrashed by a "warrior" that Danil could probably best?*

"Is thiff a joke?" Iridan called out to Rashan. "I heard about hiff acffident and his Ffourff, but reawwy? Try him againfft ffomone from ffe Academy, wike you did wiff me and ffordfighting."

"Just look at him," Rashan called back.

Kyrus blushed, knowing that everyone was now probably ogling him in the aether. He could only wonder what they were seeing, but when he scanned the crowd, he saw people blinking away their aether-vision, or squinting at him with pained expressions—even though squinting the eyes did nothing to help when viewing the aether.

"You see," Rashan stated. "Now prepare yourselves, both of you."

Rashan paused a moment for them to compose themselves as they readied for the draw. Iridan looked wary and was not looking straight at Brannis—or Kyrus—at all. Kyrus felt ill with nerves. It was un-Brannis-like of him but he could not help himself. He had nearly seared his skull dry in his first attempts with aether. *I knew nothing of what I was doing.* He had lost control in Marker's Point and destroyed a neighborhood. *I was panicking then but this is just a game, a practice ... I will be safe.* He had drawn the Source right out of men. *They were thugs, right beside me; these are sorcerers and Iridan is the closest, ten paces away.* He had burned down a ship, but that just proved he was just a firehurler. *This is not about skill; it is about power and endurance. I held back the sea. I can do this!*

"Draw!" Rashan commanded, and Kyrus was shaken from his musings by the curious feeling of aether rushing *away* from him. Kyrus had been using his draw for months, but it was the first time he had ever experienced anyone else fighting him for control of the aether. Startled and a bit disoriented, Kyrus made an attempt to pull back.

There was really no trick. Iridan was not pulling very hard at it, and Kyrus matched him. *You have always been a good friend, Iridan. Thank you for starting out going easy on me for my first try.* As Iridan gradually increased his draw, so did Kyrus, keeping them as evenly matched as he could. Kyrus could not tell how long they had been at it, but watching in his dual aether- and light-vision, he noticed something he was unprepared for: Iridan was struggling.

"Hold!" came the call from Rashan. Instantly the even flow of aether to the two combatants turned into a torrent flowing solely to Kyrus. It took a moment, but Kyrus collected his thoughts, and stopped his own draw as well. He looked on in dismay as he could see the strain on Iridan's face. A light rain fell, but Kyrus could tell Iridan's brow was wet with sweat as well.

I feel nothing, Kyrus realized. *This aether is no burden at all. I must have had tenfold as much passing through me on the Denku Appa beaches when I walled off that Katamic Sea storm, and tenfold that when I sent myself here.*

Kyrus swallowed, wondering what he ought to do. Though he had never watched draws, he understood the etiquette. Iridan had let off a show of force the first time he had claimed victory at the Academy's tournament; doing more than just blowing steam from the basins was gloating. Worse yet was to do nothing afterward. Holding onto one's aether beyond the end of the contest was a sign of contempt. Kyrus could easily have managed such a feat, he knew.

Four basins, the four on Kyrus's side of the courtyard, shattered as superheated steam exploded from them. Kyrus went to one knee, as he had seen other defeated sorcerers do, swaying slightly and breathing heavily. Steam erupted from Iridan's shortly thereafter, the victor making no further claim of dominance over his vanquished opponent.

Iridan walked unsteadily over to Kyrus, and offered him a hand up. "Well fought, Bwanniff," he congratulated Kyrus. Kyrus muttered something gracious back, and the two of them went off to a corner where a table was set with refreshments to replenish them after their match.

* * * * * * * *

At the edge of the practice field, greedy, immortal eyes fixed hungrily on Kyrus. Conversations broke out all about him, discussing what they had just seen: a raw talent that had just given Iridan, a fine duelist in his own right, all he could handle. But Rashan had watched more carefully.

"You noticed too, I assume." Caladris kept his voice low, so that only the warlock heard him. Rashan nodded slowly. "Nice enough lad, that Brannis, but I would not want to cross him. I certainly would not step in against him in a draw after seeing that." Caladris chuckled softly. "Think you could best him?"

Rashan did not respond.

* * * * * * * *

Juliana's fingers caressed the page as she read. The book was well over one hundred summers old, and not preserved at all by magic. It *felt* old, much more so than the heavily protected works that were given to the children studying at the Academy. There were treatises on basic aether theory and the early history of the Empire that were over a thousand summers old. They had been handled by ten-summer-old boys throughout their entire existence, and yet they did not seem so old as the book she perused.

The Warlock Prophecies, its title proclaimed it. It was a simple enough description but that was not what had drawn her to it. It was the book that Illiardra had been reading, the one she left floating in the air when she vanished the previous night. Juliana had no way to be sure, but she suspected that it had been left for her to take. Though she had flipped through it, and read several sections, she had marked the page Illiardra had left it on.

> *Four tongues Wise,*
> *Four tongues Foolish,*
> *Four tongues False.*
> *False whispers in Foolish ears will doom the Wise,*
> *And the False shall rule with a crown of chains.*

Juliana was not sure what was meant, exactly, but if it was left as a message for her, she suspected what it might. Twelve tongues in total probably meant the Inner Circle, especially if the author truly was a warlock. If the prophecy was meant to tell about Rashan's return to the Empire, it implied that the three conspirators he executed were among the "Wise." It would also seem to say that he was one of the "False," though the crown of chains was still a bit opaque to her.

A knock on her door startled her, and she hastily shut the book, leaving it facedown with the spine toward the wall so that the title was not easily seen.

"Come in," she called out.

"My pardon, Sorceress Juliana," one of the palace messengers apologized. "The regent has requested your attendance in the lower levels."

"Tell him I shall be down directly," she replied.

Gut that demon! I had thought that Iridan returning and Brannis's condition would be enough to distract him. Rashan has entirely too much attention to spread around if he can still spare it in my direction.

"I will wait outside. I am to escort you there personally. Please be prompt; the regent is waiting," the messenger instructed, then excused himself, closing the door behind him.

Juliana sighed. She took several books off the bookshelf, and hid *The Warlock Prophecies* in the rear, placing the removed books back in front of it. She stepped back and gave the shelf an appraising look. She pulled a few more books off the shelf and replaced them as well, just so that the one section was not the only one to have been disturbed.

She moved to the mirror to see whether she was fit for public viewing. As she smoothed her hair into less of a tangle, she saw a disheveled bed behind her in the reflection. It was a testament to the fact she had not yet left her chambers that morning, for as soon as she left, servants would sneak in and tidy everything up properly.

Iridan had returned the prior night, quite late. She had been asleep but awakened when he entered the room. It was dark, so she just remained

195

motionless and listened, not even turning to the aether to see him properly. She heard him change out of his travel-stained clothes, and realized he was planning to stay. He had not even realized she was awake until he climbed into bed next to her. He did not seem surprised, just shy. The only thing he said was "I am sorry," to which she had answered, "Me, too." They had curled together as they fell asleep, sharing each other's warmth in an unspoken agreement that they would both try to make things work between them, though it was rather likely Iridan and she had different ideas of how that would play out.

Since she was going to see the warlock, it was likely she would be seeing either Iridan or Brannis—quite possibly both of them. She wanted to look good in any event. Once she was satisfied she had done her best toward that end, she swept out of the bedchamber, trailing the messenger in her wake.

"Where are we meeting the warlock?" she asked, not bothering to slow her pace or look back. The messenger was just an annoyance.

"The dungeons," was the reply.

Juliana's stride faltered but she kept on following the messenger.

* * * * * * * *

"What are we doing down here?" Kyrus demanded.

He, Iridan, and Rashan were in the lowest level of the palace dungeons, a desolate, deserted warren of stone passages, lined with cells. It was lit with a dim, angry, red glow that Kyrus knew to be magical and not the light of the demonic furnaces it tried to resemble. The world Brannis knew looked so different to Kyrus's eyes, with the added depth of seeing all that was magical for what it truly was.

"We are waiting for one more," Rashan replied, looking at neither Kyrus nor Iridan as he stood with them.

"And then what?" Kyrus pressed. He was not liking his surroundings and liked being kept in the figurative dark more than he disliked the actual shadowy darkness he found himself standing in.

"I would like to say that you have learned a little patience, but she is almost here," Rashan commented dryly.

Iridan said nothing. He was not in a mood to be stepping into an argument involving the warlock, even if Brannis was one of the few to ever come out on the winning side against him.

The messenger departed with a bow as soon as Juliana had gotten within sight of the warlock. Kyrus had studiously avoided paying her too much attention as he lay in his supposed sickbed, but now he had no such excuse. She looked like every dream Brannis ever had of her, with her reddish-gold hair and bright, mischievous eyes shining green. He had to shake himself mentally to stop from filling in the missing details that her clothing hid. *She is Brannis's, or Iridan's now, I suppose. She is not for me. There is a book in Rashan's office that tells of the eligible sorcerers for marriage and I was ruled out. I cannot be hers, could never be hers, will never be hers.* The thoughts rang hollow; he could not deceive himself. Those decisions had been made when Brannis had shown no signs of talent—of magical talent at least.

"What is this all about?" Juliana demanded to know. She was among the scant few to dare using that tone with the warlock. For whatever reason, he allowed her continued transgressions to pass unchallenged.

"Well, now that we are all here, I only have to explain this game once," Rashan began.

"Game?" Juliana asked. "What game?" She had saved Kyrus the trouble of asking the same thing.

"I have before me the three best, unrealized talents that I know of in the Empire. I am not saying the most talented, mind you, but rather the ones whose ultimate potential I am least sure of. Today we are going to take a step closer to finding out just what I have in the three of you," Rashan explained, sounding like a lecturing instructor from the Academy, which Kyrus supposed he was, or at least once was.

"You don't have me at all. I told you as much already, or don't you remember?" Juliana snapped.

"This is different. That was for my personal service, this is for the Kadrin Empire, and there is no refusing such service, unless of course you would prefer to live elsewhere," Rashan informed her, darkly.

Kyrus (largely via Brannis) had never been able to quite round up the way Rashan could put such a dreadful weight behind his words. He was like an actor or an orator; when he wanted to convey an awful fate, he needed no awful words by which to do it. All three of them understood thoroughly that refusal was not an option.

"So what is the game?" Kyrus asked, trying to get them back to the task at hand and away from veiled threats and apparently unsettled old arguments.

"A simple one to explain," Rashan told them, beginning a slow walk down the cell-block corridor. "And a less simple one to succeed at. I believe you all have the potential for success, though I suppose it is unlikely any of you will achieve it. You will each go inside one of these cells." Rashan led them down to where the doors were no longer made of iron, but of stone, hinged with magic.

"Wait a moment, those are the—" Iridan objected, or began to.

"The warded cells. Yes. Step inside a moment and I will explain the rest. One to a cell, mind you. I do not care who goes where. There are five cells and three of you, so take your pick."

Rashan handed a waterskin to each of them, and shooed them in. Iridan went in sullenly, resigned to yet another hopeless task set before him by his father—and after his morning had begun so well. Kyrus paused a moment, and considered objecting, but his mind was already working at the problem before it had even been explained. He stepped in warily but without complaint.

"No way. I'll take a failing mark right now, if you please," Juliana protested.

Kyrus had never seen her look so apprehensive—he had never seen her at all actually; it had always been Brannis, but he had not seen such a sight, either.

"Oh, nonsense." Rashan grabbed her by the arm, and marched her inside. His grip was like stone. Kyrus knew he was a demon, but it always seemed incongruous how strong he was, and it had caught him off guard again. Scrawny as she was, Juliana looked like she ought to have been able to shrug off the boyish warlock. She did not try to follow him back out, but Kyrus heard her breath coming quickly even from his own cell.

"Now all you need do is get out after I have sealed the doors," Rashan said. "You all have given me some reason to think you might manage it. Juliana, you have a strange way with drawing aether that may help you deal with the runes' own draw. Iridan, you are excellent with runes yourself, and you have the most control among the three of you. Brannis ... Well, let us just say that I think you just lack the motivation to show your capabilities. This ought to motivate you. Now if any of you manage to get out, just come find me; I will not stand here waiting. If any cannot manage their own exit, I will return in five days' time."

At that, three doors slammed shut and sealed, the runes that kept sorcerers trapped springing to life.

* * * * * * * *

Five days? He cannot mean that, Iridan thought. *This is a test of patience. I can wait him out.* Iridan had heard about the secure cells in the dungeons, though he had never worked on them personally. He sat himself in the center of the cell, where he knew the pull of its draw to be weakest, feeling it gnawing at the edges of his Source and trying to keep from his mind that it felt like flies swarming about him, drinking his blood a fraction of a drop at a time.

* * * * * * * *

You deceitful son of a whore! Juliana had made a leap for the door at the last moment when Rashan told them that it would be five days before he came to release them. She beat a hasty retreat when the draw of the walls began to claw at her Source. She had never felt anything so powerful from so close. She had kept well back from Jadefire, but it was like what she would have imagined a dragon's draw to be like. Even the Staff of Gehlen had not felt like it was trying to burrow into her Source to drink from it, the way the cell's runes did.

Planting herself on the floor in the middle of the room, she was able to reduce the effects on her Source enough that she could meditate. It was something Soria had done rarely since leaving the Temple of the Sun. Juliana had meditated in the Tezuan manner only a few times ever. Still, calmness and ease of mind were things she badly needed to recover. Tezuan techniques were all she could think of to manage that.

In the dark, wandering the avenues of her own mind, she lost all sense of time. She hungered a little by the time she felt calm enough to address her problem rationally, so she supposed it had been a few hours. She vaguely recalled the ground shaking a bit once while she had been in her meditative trance, but she could think of no daily event to match it with that could help her mark the time. They were too far down for it to have been the kitchen staff or the goings-on at court, and anything else she could think of would have been farther still. She decided to worry about it once she was free.

Her aether-vision was acute, but the runes on the walls were writ small, at least the most important ones. It was at least a three-tiered rune structure, she could tell. Large runes had smaller runes carved within their thick lines, and those in turn had runes carved within them as well. The problem was that she could not get close enough to them to make out the details of the smallest ones without hurting herself. She could fight back against the cell's draw, but only barely and not for very long. She could easily kill herself trying, if she was not careful.

She pursed her lips, and carefully reached behind her, drawing one of her new daggers. It was the heavy one, not the fast one; she never remembered which name went with which. She held it out at arm's length in front of her, watching to see if the cell walls devoured the aether from it. Nothing. She leaned forward, braving the milder effects of the cell's draw to dangle the blade farther yet into the dangerous area. Nothing.

Smiling in self-satisfaction, she looked in the area of the door for a point in the runes that seemed vulnerable. Not finding any obvious weaknesses, she picked a target arbitrarily, and loosed the dagger as hard as she could. It cracked against the wall satisfyingly and ricocheted away. Juliana crawled over and grabbed it before hurrying back to the center of the cell again.

Once she had calmed herself again after the harrowing scramble into the cell's draw and back again, she examined the wall to see what damage she had caused. *Well, there is a chip missing. A day or so and maybe I can break a rune, if my aim is good and I can keep hitting the same spot. Still, that is better than five.*

She threw the dagger again.

* * * * * * * *

This is my fault. Had I just drawn as hard as I could earlier, he would not have felt the need to test me—to test us—like this. Brannis had heard Rashan's tale about escaping from the very cells in which he was now trapped, but Kyrus knew little else about them. The runes were intricate, and covered nearly every surface in the cell. They had a bit of a draw of their own, keeping the cell dry of stray aether.

Kyrus noticed initially that the cell seemed to be trying to draw from his Source as well, but he could hold it back with a bit of effort. With a chagrined chuckle, Kyrus could not help but liken the effort to ignoring the need to urinate; it was a minor biological annoyance that could be set aside with a bit of effort, and maintained without having to concentrate on it.

Unaware that his companions were having a rougher go of it in their own cells, Kyrus stood close and examined the runes in great detail. It was fascinating. He had studied the stone folk's runes, which layered themselves within folded metal, and found the runes-within-runes concept to be a variant with similar intent. Unfortunately, without a year or three to study them, he doubted he would puzzle their workings out from the inside.

The runes keep the door closed. My task is to get out. Runes need aether. Kyrus stretched, and shook out limbs that had grown stiff as he had been largely stationary—for how long he could only guess—as he lost himself in thought examining the cell's workings. *Time to find out who has the stronger draw, Wall, me or you.* While Kyrus had not worked out everything about how the runes worked, he realized that for it to have its own draw, it had to be an open structure; there were ways to pull the aether back out.

Kyrus put his hands on the wall next to the door. Taking a deep breath, he drew as hard as he could, as he probably should have when facing Iridan in the courtyard. All the aether that his Source normally gave off was sucked back in instantly, denying the cell its continued sustenance. As Kyrus drew, the cell groaned in protest, a low, pained resonance as its workings were abused, and aether dragged through it the wrong way as if ripping prey free from a shark's angled teeth.

It did not take long before the glow of the wards in Kyrus's aether-vision began to flicker and fail. When it seemed it had failed completely, he stepped in front of the door, and released the aether all at once. A few moments later, he picked himself up off the floor, dazed, where the blast had left him. He had channeled the aether directly away from him, just firehurling, with no thought to trying to harness it in any sort of spell. He knew of no spell that he could have handled with so much aether anyway.

The door was gone, along with some of the surrounding wall, and bit of the floor as well, the edges of the vaporized region still glowing red, and dripping molten stone. Gone as well was the door of the cell opposite his, thankfully unoccupied. There was a channel though the far wall of that cell, and into the unworked stone beyond. Kyrus walked across to the other cell, choking and coughing at the cloud of soot hanging in the air, and looked into that channel. He thought he could see an end to it, fifty or so paces in, but the glow was dimming, and he was not so curious as to venture in to look.

Kyrus gave some thought to freeing Juliana and Iridan, but decided against it. *They'll be happier figuring it out on their own. I would not want to free them just before they manage it themselves. I will return in the evening if they have not gotten out by then.*

Following his instructions, Kyrus headed off to track down Rashan.

* * * * * * * *

"I rather suspected you might find your way free of those cells, Brannis," Rashan congratulated him upon seeing him approach. "So tell me, what trick did you use to get out?" He was seated in his office in the Tower of Contemplation when Kyrus finally found him. He had been attended by a number of functionaries dealing with logistics of the impending coronation, but Rashan dismissed them as soon as he saw Kyrus approaching.

"No trick. I just outdrew the wall, and melted it with hurled fire," Kyrus said.

Rashan laughed out loud. "You have a better sense of humor than the other Brannis ever did. I am going to enjoy having you around."

"It was no joke. You only have four of those cells now," Kyrus replied. "And I would not get too used to me being around. Once I figure out a way to find Tellurak again, I will be going back."

"Hurled fire? If you think that is a solution to a problem like those cells, you have as much business trying transference spells as an ogre does playing the dulcimer," Rashan snapped. "I have no idea how you managed to find your way to Veydrus or how you managed to survive channeling that much aether to make the trip. I would suggest you put any notion to trying that trip again far back into the reaches of your mind. Thank fate, gods, or what have you, for the luck that you survived it once, and do not tempt them again. With the power you have, someday you may unravel that mystery but for now, you are just a firehurler."

"You are speaking of winters, not days," Kyrus spoke softly, almost to himself despite addressing the warlock.

"Tens of winters, more like," Rashan corrected. Kyrus swallowed, finding a sudden lump in his throat. "Come upstairs a moment. I wish to demonstrate something for you." Rashan stood, and headed up the stairs to the Inner Sanctum.

Decades. I will learn life extension. Abbiley will grow old. Davin will pass away. If I ever make it back, what would I be going back to? In decades, what would Brannis be returning to, an old man, suddenly and mysteriously bereft of magic? If I cannot manage to return rather soon, I may not end up making the trip at all.

Kyrus blinked back his inner monologue long enough to remember that he ought to be following Rashan. He headed up the stairway after the warlock.

"This chamber is warded against violence, so it ought to be a bit safer. None of the others are around right now, so it is just the two of us," Rashan said, standing in the middle of the room. "Come down here."

Kyrus silently levitated himself down to the bottom of the chamber, where guests of the Inner Circle would present themselves. Rashan watched, shaking his head.

"It is like watching a blacksmith swing his anvil at a hammer to make horseshoes. I cannot fathom the amount of aether you waste with that shabby technique of yours. We shall work on that later but for now, a demonstration of the worthlessness of hurled aether," Rashan said. Kyrus saw a shielding spell spring to life around him. "Even the simplest of shields thwarts it. You may have been able to destroy a wall with it, once you drained it of aether." Rashan shook his head, still incredulous about Kyrus's claim. "But any construct of aether will stop it entirely. Now … if there is any mishap, stray fire ought not hurt anything in this room, due to the wards."

"But I thought the wards prevented all violence within the Sanctum," Kyrus said.

"Only in the Academy texts and the half-copper tours of Kadris. I killed Gravis Archon in here, and the wards did little enough to save him. The wards

protect the Inner Circle; they do not protect against those so powerful as we."
Rashan looked meaningfully at the hole in the wall, still unrepaired after a season
in power. The warlock had left it as a symbol, a warning. "Now go stand over
there, and hit me with everything you can manage—just hurled fire, mind you."

"Fine," Kyrus agreed. He walked over to the supplicants' entrance to the
chamber and turned. He drew in some aether, and hurled it right at Rashan as
fire. As promised, it turned harmlessly aside against his shield.

"Well now, someone thinks he is being *clever* again. You are not going to
believe me until you see your *best* effort fail. Now try again, like you mean it! I
was going to let Iridan and Juliana out of those cells in time for dinner tonight,
but if you continue to try my patience, I just *might* leave them down there the
whole five days," Rashan snarled, goading Kyrus with what he hoped was an idle
threat.

Despite seeing through the barb, Kyrus felt his heart begin to pound, and the
edges of his vision grow fuzzy. *So I am stranded here on Veydrus, most likely. I will
never see Abbiley again? It falls to me to protect Juliana, just as Brannis would. Brannis, if
you are watching right now, take care of Abbiley for me. Make her happy.* Kyrus drew hard
against the aether and Rashan's eyes widened in shock.

A moment later, there was a second hole to the outdoors in the Tower of
Contemplation, and the regent of the Kadrin Empire had been jettisoned
through it. It had passed through from the lower Sanctum wall, through the
warlock's office, and to the open sky beyond.

Kyrus walked to the edge of the hole with growing trepidation. He had hoped
to spend his anger against the warlock's shield. It had not occurred to him that
he would shred that shield, and blow the warlock through the building. He
looked around to the palace grounds below, and saw Rashan, charred and nearly
naked, rising unsteadily to his feet. In the aether, Kyrus was very interested to see
that wisps of aether rose from the warlock's exposed Source. As he watched, the
aether flow slowed and ceased. The charred flesh regenerated itself. A makeshift
wardrobe of aether formed about him.

Rashan walked unsteadily to the base of the tower, and looked up at Kyrus.
"I stand corrected," Rashan called up to him.

"I am sorry, I did not mean to—"

"No, no. It was my fault underestimating you. We will speak of it again, but I
think I ought to head down to the dungeons, and see about releasing the newly
married couple. Not sure what I was thinking … was no point locking them up
as well …" Rashan trailed off, and then wandered away.

Kyrus found himself alone in the warlock's office. Mischief was uncommon
to his nature, but there was a heady feeling welling up in him, making him bold.
He found a particular book, one that he had come to hate. It was a book of
names—names of sorcerers and sorceresses. He found the entry he sought with
little trouble: *"Brannis Solaran. (F) Maruk Solaran, (M) Lyphaela Solaran (Sharniss),"*
the whole of which had been crossed out with a double line, accompanied by a
notation in a different handwriting: *"UNSUITABLE."* Kyrus took up a quill and

ink—his preferred weapons—and crossed out the *"UN."*

Chapter 20 - Reacquaintances

There could be no mistaking: Kyrus Hinterdale was actually Brannis Solaran. Wendell had been on the first ship to land, but he had panicked, and thrown on a false face before he had been recognized. He had been nervous enough approaching a neophyte sorcerer, but finding one he knew had spooked him.

I need to talk to him. I cannot let caution deter me. I have to find him alone, and introduce myself properly. It is Brannis, after all. How much danger could there be? I owe it to Jurgin to take on an apprentice to carry on his teachings but I no longer need this Kyrus. He was a bad idea from the first but he was all I had.

Wendell had not been blessed with as strong a Source as his twin Faolen. He had little recourse beyond simple trickery should he get himself in trouble. He had made a long habit of identifying and avoiding other twinborn. There were troubles with the knowledge of two worlds, and not everyone was so mild in their interests in the connection between them. Jurgin had told him tales about twinborn that set themselves up as warlords or gangsters, even just run-of-the-mill mercenaries. They used the skills they learned in Veydrus to act as hawks among the chickens of Tellurak. Wendell's skills were useful—extremely useful—but he would not be able to put himself on equal terms with a Veydran sorcerer, should one be found on Tellurak.

I should tell him about the boy. I do not need Brannis's twin as my apprentice but I could have his help in securing the twin of Jinzan Fehr's son. It is in the Empire's interest that I get hold of the Staff of Gehlen, even if I must buy it with service in this world.

Wendell resolved to approach Brannis's twin, and reveal himself. He took a long, shuddering deep breath, and walked to the door of his cabin. He put his hand to the handle but the door would not open. His hand would not let him.

But he is incredibly powerful. What if he does not care for what I have to say? He may want peace here, safe from the Kadrin Empire and all the burdens he faces there. If he sees me as intruding, I could not imagine he would have any trouble reducing me to ash, and sprinkling me over the ship's railing, never to be missed. I could not even report the crime to Warlock Rashan without seeming a madman, and any vengeance would just as surely get me killed, successful or not. Brannis Solaran is too well placed to act against.

Having resolved not to cross the twinborn sorcerer with the mysteriously weak Source, Wendell sat down on the edge of his bunk. He sat in stillness for a time, but soon found that his leg had been bouncing up and down, belying his nerves.

I am being paranoid, he admitted. *He is Brannis Solaran, whatever he is called in this world, as surely as I am Faolen. He will know me. He will share common cause with me. I might need to abduct the boy, and I could enlist his aid. I could get messages to Kadris via him. He could arrange aid with no one questioning his authority or whence his knowledge came. I would be a fool not to take this opportunity for the gift it is.*

Wendell stood again, and strode over to the door, yanking it open before any part of his body took the opportunity to voice an objection. The plan worked, and he was freed from his prison of hesitation, for better or worse.

* * * * * * * *

"You do look familiar, now that you mention it," Brannis replied. The wizened magician looked like someone he knew, but Brannis, for all his memory for the written word, numbers, dates, and magic runes, was awful with faces. Worse, Kyrus had never been one to socialize much. There were likely folk all throughout Scar Harbor who knew him by sight, but whose names the scrivener had never attempted to learn.

"If you are wracking your memory, let me give you a hint to jar loose any spare thoughts from the corners of your psyche. I traveled with you once, a few months ago, by horse. There were five of us." Wendell knew that if that hint did not give him away entirely, this Kyrus Hinterdale was almost certainly not fully aware of Brannis. It seemed impossible how closely the two resembled one another, though. He had seen his own and Faolen's reflections in enough mirrors over the years to know myriad differences, even before life extension separated their apparent ages by a decade or more: a cut that scarred just a bit, a shade deeper tan in the warm months, fingers calloused from working sleight of hand versus ones that did no work at all. Kyrus Hinterdale looked exactly like he had remembered Sir Brannis looking when last he had seen him.

Brannis's eyes widened. "Faolen?" he guessed, sudden recognition spreading across his features. He looked the magician up and down. Wendell noticed how his eyes were drawn to the grey hair, the wrinkled features.

"Indeed. Here, though, I am Wendell the Wizard, worker of parlor tricks for coin. Faolen is off in Zorren at the warlock's behest, but here I have crossed paths with you, and only partly by coincidence," Wendell replied, glad that Kyrus and Brannis were aware enough to make introductions a simple matter of an exchange of names, with no need to delve into the mystery of the connection of worlds.

"What do you mean, 'partly'?" Brannis inquired. Wendell knew for certain then that he had the right man. Brannis was ever one to pick out the bit to question, needing to satisfy his curiosity above nearly all other concerns.

"Well, I had heard of your exploits. I tracked you down hoping to take you on as an apprentice. Two things had been obvious: you were vastly powerful, and you were dangerously unschooled in magic. I am growing old, and I have a debt to repay my old master. I must pass on his teachings so that his legacy will live on. It seemed a long-odds wager, but I had hoped to find a bewildered young sorcerer in need of mentoring. I had no idea it was *you* I was seeking out."

"Would that have made a difference?" Brannis wondered.

Wendell marveled that Brannis's twin was so single-minded. There were a thousand questions he might have asked, but he doggedly pursued his first line of questioning, and would continue until he had been answered to his satisfaction. He had overheard him do the same thing to Warlock Rashan, and had nearly laughed aloud as he twisted the slippery-tongued demon's words to get around Rashan's constant evasions.

"I think so, yes. I had even considered bypassing this opportunity, even after paying dearly for a ship to fetch you off that island. You see, twinborn are troublesome creatures. Not all of them are quite the same person in both worlds. Circumstance and the age they awaken, so to speak, to their knowledge, can affect how much they differ. From what I can infer, you are new to this knowledge, but if you do not mind me saying, you are the very image and equal of Brannis Solaran," Wendell remarked.

You have no idea, Brannis thought, smiling vaguely enough that he hoped he gave nothing away.

"So why did you, then?" Brannis asked. "There must be some reason. You must realize now that I have no need of a master. I have access to any resource in the Empire, with only a few limitations. I have even learned a trick or two from Rashan."

"Why would Rashan teach you spells? He must know you cannot cast them. What does he think it accomplishes?" Faolen asked, ignoring Brannis's question.

"Well, for starters, I seem to have been able to ... move ... my Source to the other world. You will find that I am not terribly capable as a sorcerer here now, and that I am quite a bit more so back home." Brannis's expression did not betray it, but he knew he had slipped in calling Kadrin "home." He hoped Faolen—or Wendell, as it were—had not noticed.

"Are you serious? I realize your Source is weak, or appears so at the least, but I thought it a mere curiosity that it so closely resembled Brannis's shabby Source—no offense. No, this is a jape you are having at me. I am too much the magician to take a tale like that at face value. You have some hidden trick to make your Source look weak. I cannot see it, but I can do much the same when I need to," Wendell rambled, throwing up a wall of skepticism against Brannis's best "plausible" lie. It obviously needed work.

"Would you believe that I worked a transference spell, and managed to wind up switching places with Brannis?" Brannis ventured. Wendell said nothing. He just raised an eyebrow, crossed his arms before him, and shook his head slowly.

"How about this one? I have no idea what I am doing. I cannot even see my own Source. I have pieced together a few workable spells out of books from the Tower's libraries, but I cause havoc wherever I use them. For the time being, just assume I am a non-sorcerer; I will not risk burning the ship down while at sea," Brannis tried.

"I can accept that one for now, I suppose, but I will get you figured out. Not to worry." Wendell winked at him. "Now since I know you are just going to ask again anyway, I will answer your earlier question. I came to see you because I think you can help me."

"With?" Brannis pressed.

Wendell was truly a showman, dramatic flair worked its way into his everyday speech, it seemed. He also drew things out, such as the pregnant pause he had just left hanging between them.

"I have found Jinzan Fehr's son," Wendell concluded, smiling as he revealed his wondrous news. Brannis seemed less than overwhelmed.

"Do you need me to tell Rashan or something?" Brannis guessed. "I did not know the boy was even missing. Is this somehow related to your search for the Staff of Gehlen? Are you trying to kidnap the boy to trade for the staff?" Brannis could hardly disguise his disgust at the last notion.

"No, not yet." Wendell paused a moment to replay in his mind the order Brannis asked his questions. "Yes. Certainly not."

"All right, then, what does this mean, and how do you think to involve me in it?" Brannis relented, taking the bare, literal answers to his badgering as chastisement.

"Well, first off, his son is like us, I have discovered. The boy hears voices in his head. They think him mad, but I was afflicted much the same as him in my youth. My old master, Jurgin, knew the signs, and helped me separate the two worlds in my mind. I know where the boy is, and I intend to pass the gift along to him as well. It will be a better continuation of Jurgin's teachings than taking you on as an apprentice ever would have."

"Very noble of you, certainly. How does this relate to the staff? Is this just a side project for this world?" Brannis was thinking up questions faster than Wendell could answer them. If there was some remote corner of Tellurak that was overflowing with answers because they had run short of questions to pair them with, Wendell suspected Brannis's twin would be to blame.

"The boy stole the staff. He has been leading half the snoops and sorcerers of Zorren on a merry chase for days. He has been using it to kill folk who have tried to apprehend him," Wendell said.

"But not you," Brannis put in, playing along with Wendell's drama. Wendell appreciated the opening left to him to continue the story in his own fashion without being sidetracked by yet another question.

"No ... not me. I bargained with the boy. I offered my help," Wendell continued. His eyes had an almost manic earnestness to them. "I will get my apprentice in this world, just as I promised. In the other, I will have the staff when he is ready to give it to me."

"You are assuming that the boy keeps it long enough for you to win him over. Eventually they are going to catch him and get it back, I would think. You may have hours, maybe days. They could have it back now for all you know," Brannis said. He did not like Wendell's plan, it was clear. And why not? It counted on a young boy with a powerful weapon outmaneuvering half a city's dedicated defenders. Like them or not, the Megrenn showed every sign of being a competent people in the execution of their affairs, both financial and military. The plan was no certain thing.

"A risk, yes. But it is the risk of getting the staff from him or losing it and having to try again; weigh it against an attempt to wrest the staff from him by force or trickery, when failing means death at his hands. I will take the former. I would also have your help," Wendell said.

"And my part would be...?" Brannis let the statement hang half asked as a question, awaiting the final detail to be supplied by Faolen's twin.

"I am an old man, and a poor one. I cannot buy his release from the refuge where he is cared for. I cannot take him by force. My magic *might* allow me to sneak him out unnoticed, but I do not wish to chance it. My best resource is my voice, and what words I can think to arm it with. I fear I may not talk my way around this problem. If I can, all for the better. If not, I could use the sort of help you might provide."

"You need me for my muscle, is that it?" Brannis scoffed. While Wendell could well imagine Brannis storming Pious Grove Sanctuary, he had expected to find Kyrus Hinterdale, noted scrivener and weakling, and possibly dangerously unstable witch. Seeing the brawny lad before him had come as a surprise.

"So to speak, yes. We can work out details on the voyage there. I had not the time to ponder options that included you. I only just discovered what I have stumbled upon. With a bit of time to think, I am sure we can manage a solid plan," Wendell said.

"So where is it that the boy is being kept?" Brannis asked, wondering where he might be heading, should he consent to accompany Wendell.

"Takalia."

* * * * * * *

The cards flicked through the air, once, twice, thrice around the table, until each player had their allotment. Stalyart's practiced wrist had sent them unerringly into tiny piles, around obstacles of coin and drink. Soria was immediately suspicious of anyone who showed such skill in handling cards. It was the sort of thing you saw from dockside grifters and back-tavern hustlers. If she had thought upon agreeing to play that they were merely seeking to feel one another out, and pass the time, she knew better now.

"Barkin' wonderful," Tanner groused, folding even before the communal cards were shown at the middle of the table.

Two of Stalyart's crew, whose names Soria did not care to learn, threw their cards down as well. The skinny one said nothing; the one smoking the pipe somehow managed to say even less.

Stalyart threw in a small bet, enough to move things along, but not seem a bully. "Four hundred eckles," he said, throwing in what seemed to be a proper amount. Soria was not interested in the accuracy of tiny sums like that.

Zellisan scratched at his stubble as he studied the cards in his hand. "I call," he said at length, tossing in a like amount.

"Raise," Soria said immediately. She selected a stack of coins, and shoved it toward the pot without counting it out. It might have been two thousand eckles. It might have been twenty-five hundred. She was sure it was enough of a raise to get the pirate captain's attention.

The rest of the pirates abandoned their cards. Rakashi did nothing; he had not deigned to join the game. He disliked the pirates as much as any of them, but was less shy about expressing it. He would not share either table or games with them, given the option.

Stalyart looked at her, studying her face. Most Crackle players avoided making eye contact with an opponent who was considering their play, fearful of giving themselves away, whether bluffing, trapping, or merely not wishing their opponent to know whether they were trying any deception at all. Soria met the pirate captain's gaze, though, locking stares with him. The man was older than her and, by grace of years, had likely seen more hardened men in his day than she'd had the opportunity to meet. The dark brown orbs reached out to her bright green eyes, and tried to force them to yield up her secrets. Her face was impervious to his scrutiny.

"I fold as well," he admitted after long consideration.

Zellisan followed suit, and Soria blinked away her aether-vision so she could see her winnings.

A shout from outside the cabin interrupted the game as the cards were being dealt for the next hand. Someone knocked hastily on the door, opening it before any response was received.

"A ship!" one of the crew yelled to those inside.

"What sort of ship?" Stalyart asked curiously, his dour, stern face resuming its animation as he was distracted from the card game.

"The best kind, sir," the man said, then grinned, showing a mouth half full of yellowed teeth.

"Excellent. Signal our prize ship to hang back, then begin pursuit. I will be there in just a moment," Captain Stalyart ordered. He took his tankard, and drained the contents in one giant swallow. The costly Takalish spirits went down smoothly, for all their potency.

"Hey, sit your ass back in that chair, Stalyart," Soria commanded. "We are heading to Denku Appa. No detours. No distractions. No delays."

"My pardon, lady," Stalyart apologized. "I would only have assumed that you would wish to stop any ship we saw. This is not a tradeway, very much not. We are not traveling very fast, so we would not have caught up to anyone sailing in the same direction as we. Anyone out here ought to be coming *back* from Denku Appa."

"What are you saying?" Soria demanded. "That you think Kyrus might be on that ship?"

"It may be that some smuggler wished to be very much far from the places other ships go. It would not be the first ship to travel thus. But more likely, I think the ship returns from the island we are heading to. It may be a coincidence, but I would think you would want to investigate it, to be certain," Stalyart said.

"And if it is not ... you stand to take a second ship as plunder," Tanner offered.

"Oh, no. That is not the case, my friend." Stalyart smiled. "We plan to take it for plunder either way. Everyone wins, you see."

Soria glared suspiciously, but could not find a hole in his logic before having to relent.

* * * * * * *

"Pirates!" came the call from on deck, loud enough for all to hear. The crew scrambled about the ship, changing their course, and trying to find as much wind as the gods and spirits could provide. Few pious men took to a life at sea, but devotion always peaked during storms and pirate attacks.

Belowdecks, Wendell rushed to find Kyrus Hinterdale. Old and fragile though he seemed, sailors shouldered past him with all the concern shown a street peddler during a riot. The scent of panic hung heavier in the air than even the odors of sea air, sweat, and pitch could overcome.

"Kyrus, we have to do something. *You* have to do something," Wendell clarified upon barging into the cramped little space they had housed Brannis in. This was just the sort of thing that he hated about being so weak in the aether: being at the mercy of those with more strength of arms.

"Working on it," Brannis replied, rummaging in the trunk he had brought aboard with his possessions. He heaped piece after piece of Liead's armor onto the bed until he had found all of it. Wendell looked on in puzzlement.

"This armor looks just like the stuff Brannis wears ... remarkably so. Where did you get this?" Wendell asked.

"Just shut up and help me get into it. I can manage it on my own, but it goes quicker with help," Brannis snapped. He stripped out of his tunic and breeches, and began pulling on the aether-forged armor.

Wendell seemed dazed as he handed pieces of the suit to Brannis, and helped with the more awkward pieces. Every time Brannis donned a part of the armor, it shrank and sized itself to fit him perfectly.

"This is remarkable," Wendell said. "You ... You have copied it marvelously. How did you manage it?"

"Depends which version of my story you would like to try believing. Either I am a master craftsman and aethersmith, able to duplicate priceless artifacts of magic just a few months after learning to keep a light spell from getting stuck on the end of my finger; or I am an overly gifted fool with a poor enough sense of direction to get lost and miss the entire *world* I was aiming for with my attempt to escape Denku Appa using a transference spell," Brannis said as he secured the demon-faced helmet to his head. "Have your pick, or worry about it later." He reached again into the trunk, and buckled on his sword belt. It felt reassuring to have Avalanche at his hip, pirate attack or no.

Wendell looked long and hard at him. The pieces were fitting too well—not just of the armor, but of the puzzle before him—and he was seeing a picture he had not been able to reconcile until he saw them all put together.

"Brannis?" Wendell ventured. "Is it *truly* you?"

Brannis nodded. "We can talk more when we have driven off these pirates."

"Wait," Wendell said as Brannis was about to head to the deck. "They might hit us with more cannon fire if you look too dangerous. That armor can stop grapeshot, I would imagine, but the rest of the crew will not be so lucky. If they board us without feeling threatened, you can better ambush them."

Wendell's gaze swept about the tiny room, finding nothing remotely useful aside from the bed linens. He gave a shrug, and tore them from the bed.

* * * * * * * *

"You will board," Stalyart told Soria as they closed in on the outmatched merchant ship. Men were lining the rails of the *Merciful*, like dogs straining against their chains, waiting to be loosed on their helpless prey. "If Kyrus is aboard, you will need to keep him from turning my ship into cinders. I will take you to where you need to go, but the pledge of safety must run both ways."

"No deal. You fight your own boarding actions. I will send Zell to look for Kyrus; he would know him by sight. I am not letting you put me off your ship until we have Kyrus with us. Tanner and Rakashi stay with us too. Neither would know Kyrus's face, and they are not here to bloody their hands for you," Soria answered back. Actually, she guessed that Tanner would be able to pick out the twin of the grand marshal by his face, but he had not known Brannis as well as Zellisan, nor seen him as recently. Tanner was just a middling officer, without regular interaction with the high command. He saw the army's commanders in parades and atop podiums, just like the commoners.

So Zellisan waited at the railing with no armor save for his helm and buckler. He was not a young man, and disliked the idea of leaping the gap between ships once the grapples had pulled them together, no matter how close they got. Even in mild seas, the boats could sway together, crushing anyone who was in the water between them—or so he imagined at least. Zellisan was not much of a swimmer to begin with. The ache in his injured knee made the prospect of plummeting into the Katamic seem more likely than normal for a man north of forty-five and stout of frame.

"You turn sides this time, I'll gut ya myself," Zell heard from near his right shoulder. He turned to see the mountainous man he had dueled with on the *Frostwatch Symphony* the day before. The threat seemed to carry more teeth in it when spoken from so close, with no armor to stop a hidden blade from sliding through his skin.

"Bah, mind yer own backside. I'll mind mine," Zell grumbled in reply. He watched as the merchant ship came closer—or rather as the *Merciful* gained on them. He reached up under his helm, and grabbed the corner of a handkerchief that he had stuffed beneath it. Tugging it free, the helm settled properly onto his head.

The world grew another dimension. His aether-vision overlaid the world of light, disorienting him at first, as he adapted to the magic of the crown concealed within his helmet. He saw Sources aplenty, from the strongest to the weakest among the crews of the two ships. The only one that stood out as distinct from the rest was Soria's, shining brightly among the rabble. A few, like Rakashi and Captain Stalyart seemed more than typical as well, but nothing on the ship they pursued seemed extraordinary.

Well, there is nothing but to see this out, he thought glumly, *but it does not look like they have anyone aboard with the kind of Source that Kyrus Hinterdale must have.*

It appeared that despite being an unarmed vessel, the merchant ship, bearing the name *Fontinue*, was going to try to repel their boarding. Crewmen had armed themselves with belaying pins and a scattering of blades, but there was one cloaked figure who stood out among them. His blade was a warrior's weapon, bared steel glinting in the sunlight, the ship's glimmer of hope. The man's bulk beneath his coverings suggested that he wore plate beneath, else he was the size of the hulking brute who stood at Zell's side.

Must have had some knight aboard as passenger. Must have insisted on making a stand of it. Blasted fool is going to get good men killed when Stalyart might have spared them if they had given up.

* * * * * * *

Brannis stood waiting, his makeshift disguise giving no cause for alarm as the *Merciful* drew to grappling range. It was not the *Fair Trader*, as he had feared, but the chatter of the crew suggested that it was known to be one of his ships. Denrik Zayne had been doing quite well for himself while Kyrus was stranded on Denku Appa.

It seemed he had wasted Wendell's time in obscuring the glow his weapon and armor gave off in the aether. It was good to know he was up to such a task, since circumstances might call for it again if they were to encounter gifted twinborn. He had wondered if Zayne would have been so eager to engage the ship, had he seen Brannis there, looking just as he had during the Battle of Raynesdark.

The crew of the *Fontinue* stood back from the railings as the pirates' grappling hooks took hold, and lashed the ships together. Brannis had been pleased at how well trained they were, and how smartly they snapped to obey his commands. It seemed that some men, either by selection or training, were malleable in the hands of a man who took command as second nature. The sight of him towering over them in his golden armor, and carrying a massive broadsword could only have helped his cause.

As the first of the pirates swung themselves over the railings, Brannis gave the signal to attack. "Get them!" he shouted, having had little time to prepare more elegant signals or tactics. Twenty fighting men, most of whom would not have been described as such by any commander on land, faced four times that number of hardened killers.

But the *Fontinue* had its secret weapon. Brannis met the advance head on. He hated killing men. Goblins and ogres were different enough that he could turn off that portion of his mind that could empathize with them, at least long enough to cut them to pieces in the heat of a battle. For all their monstrous actions, Zayne's pirates were still flesh and blood not so dissimilar to his own.

He thought back to the wall at Raynesdark, when wave upon wave of goblins and their wolf mounts swarmed him. The torrents of blood and gore had washed his blade as Avalanche smashed through them like they were merely glass pitchers filled with the stuff. Not wanting a reprieve of that scene, he pulled his blows. He swung lazily at his opponents, sweeping them before him with irresistible force. Invaders were knocked to the deck with broken bones or forced over the railings and into the warm waters of the southern Katamic Sea. Some were slain, surely, but none so gruesomely as he knew his sword was capable of.

The fighting spread as Brannis's presence was not ubiquitous. Wherever he fought, the defenders prevailed. Elsewhere the pirates were advancing and gathering their strength. Men of the *Fontinue* died—perhaps valiantly—but they were dead all the same. The well-scrubbed wood of the deck pooled with blood. Brannis saw that his gentle tactics were going to get his new comrades wiped out. He saw one man about to be run through, and bisected his attacker with a quick swipe of Avalanche. He winced at the gruesome mess it caused, but knew it had to be but the first of many.

* * * * * * *

From the quarterdeck of the *Merciful*, Soria watched the battle along with Captain Stalyart. Her eyes fixed on Zellisan, following him as he waited his turn to make the crossing. She saw him standing there, his unease at going into battle unarmored clear from his demeanor. She felt a pang of guilt. *If I trusted that the three of them could ensure Stalyart's cooperation, I could have gone myself.* She knew better than to trust any pirate—especially one she had so baldly threatened—to keep to any bargain without a figurative blade to his throat. She was the only one who she could be certain could keep one there.

On the poor, defenseless merchant ship, the crew was being overwhelmed. They had one warrior among them, who seemed to have anchored a portion of the defense, but he would not be enough, it seemed.

Zell had made the crossing, she saw, when she sought him out once more. He held his blade bared, but had not made any effort to engage the crew. He looked around, searching for any sign of Kyrus Hinterdale.

Suddenly the battle took a turn. The bulky, clumsy warrior became an agent of death itself. His cumbersome blade, which had seemed so slow as he waved it before him, cut through the air with the speed of a whip. Blood flew, and bodies were torn asunder. The oncoming pirates took notice, and tried to keep well back from the knight, whose golden armor had begun to peek from beneath his coverings as his movements came quicker and more sweeping.

"What sort of fiend have we cornered?" Stalyart wondered aloud, watching the slaughter of his men even as they took over much of the deck by force of numbers. Those odds were steadily declining, however, in the face of their devastating opponent.

Soria did not answer. Her heartbeat quickened in her chest, watching the movements of the knight in the golden armor as he tried almost singlehandedly to fight off the whole of the boarding party. She had seen a slaughter like it once before, watching the fighting on the wall at Raynesdark. She had been much farther away then, but the scene was eerily similar. It did not yet register with her that Avalanche ought to have been safely sheathed at Brannis's side back in Kadris—she had heard the tale of it being lost along with Brannis's suit of armor in his "incident" but she had been distracted by too many other things to give it much thought. It did not even occur to her at that moment that she was looking for a shy, bookish scrivener who had developed a talent for sorcery.

She could only think one word, and it came to the fore as she noticed that Zellisan was caught in the path of destruction.

"Brannis!" Soria shouted as loudly as she could.

* * * * * * *

Brannis blocked off the part of his heart that cursed him as a monster as he ended life after life. *Innocents or pirates, men must die this day and I can see to it that the choice is just.* Blood sprayed and entrails sloshed about the deck in a wet, sloppy mess. He wished he was Kyrus, that he could just lift up the pirate crew and hurl them a thousand paces out into the Katamic.

The pirates were not retreating yet, as such, but they were fleeing his path. Wherever he turned, pirates suddenly tried to be elsewhere. Their stumbling escapes might have been comical in other circumstances. Brannis continued to find where pirates were pressing the *Fontinue*'s remaining living crewmen, and to lend them deadly aid. He took any pirate who came within reach of his blade and saw to them along his route.

"Brannis!" the cry carried over the sound of the battle.

No, it could not have been. But it was. He knew the voice too well; it played itself over and again in his mind as he recalled his happiest memories.

Brannis scanned the pirates' ship, and saw a female figure, clad in armor, standing near the ship's wheel. He also saw a familiar pirate, one of Zayne's men: Robbono Stalyart. The two were arguing, or at least carrying on some heated discussion.

From near his feet, and just shy of being cleaved in twain before he had heard his real name called, one of the invaders spoke to him: "Grand Marshal," the man spoke in Kadrin, "we were looking for you. Juliana was."

"Fall back! Everyone return to the *Merciful!*" he heard Stalyart's voice ordering. Battles broke off as Stalyart's men obediently began an orderly withdrawal from the ship.

"I am Varnus Coldlake, captain of the Archon house guard. Around here, they call me Zellisan, or Zell," Zellisan continued in Kadrin, smiling as he regained his feet. "She goes by Soria here, but I rather think she would not mind you calling her Juliana."

Despite the press of bodies as the *Merciful*'s crew swarmed the railings back to their own ship, one person managed to fight through the tide of bloodied men, and make the trip the other way. Brannis has just enough presence of mind to return Avalanche to its sheath before a leaping Juliana—or Soria—crashed into his arms. He caught hold of her by the waist, noticing as he did, the toned, muscular physique and the slightly more drab auburn hair, as well as the fact she seemed a bit heavier than the Juliana he had last held in his arms. But it was the eyes that removed every bit of doubt from him; they were eyes that he could see any time he wished, just by closing his own.

They spoke not a word, but their lips met. A hunger, left too long unsated, found a feast spread before it. There was no force in all of Tellurak that cared to keep them apart. Brannis lost himself in memories of kisses they had shared in another world, in a small, sheltered corner of it that had allowed them, for a time, to see a future together. That future had been snatched from their hands, their destinies rewritten by whatever force had seen fit to allot the dragon's share of the twins' Sources to Kyrus instead of Brannis.

If men watching from the deck of either ship had felt inclined to hoot or call out, or comment upon their bared affections, they kept it well to themselves. They had seen the blood of too many of their fellows gushing forth in the wake of those two. And though their eyes might only have seen one another, all others could not help but notice the wash of gore and flesh they stood amid.

"You have no idea how much trouble I went to find you here," Soria said, beaming when drawing her first breath while parted from Brannis's lips.

"You have no idea the lengths I have gone to be here," Brannis replied. "I think we will have time aplenty for tales, though. Which ship will we be taking?"

"Whichever we want, of course," she said, then smiled lopsidedly. All seemed to have been put to rights in her world. There was no problem that seemed to matter anymore; all would be fine, with Brannis around.

* * * * * * *

Brannis looked at his cards, and found them worthless. He threw them into the middle, and took up his tankard in their stead. The ale that Stalyart kept aboard was top tier, much better than Zayne had kept on his ship. Brannis considered for a moment that Kyrus's palette might have different tastes than his own, but decided that Stalyart just had more class and a better appreciation of strong drink.

It had been Brannis who had pointed out to everyone that they really ought to be in charge of the disposition of the ships instead of Stalyart or his crew. The *Fontinue* had been sent on its way with generous reparations for the damage and casualties they suffered. Coin could not buy back the lives of the men who perished, but it could make their widows comfortable, and allow the captain to hire on new crew. Stalyart had been irritated at the loss of so much of his ill-won treasure, but seemed to have known he had been let off lightly by Soria and her friends, who had been more concerned with swift transport than with justice.

"So, Captain Kyrus, where are we heading off to?" Tanner asked.

Brannis had learned that Tanner's twin was one of his officers, stationed off in Naran Port. To the best of his recollection, he had never met him before, though with the size of the army, he could not be expected to know everyone. He made a point to look into the service record of Tanner's twin, though, both to check the character of Juliana's companions and for possible promotion; it was always good to have loyal men placed well.

Brannis chuckled. "I am not captain. I just happen to have one under my boot for now. Sorry if I cannot be a bit more accommodating, Stalyart, but last time I was on a ship with you, I got marooned."

"This was nothing personal, I assure you. Captain Zayne was merely wishing to avoid bloodshed," Stalyart responded. Being good sports, they had allowed the captain and his first mate into their game, a man by the name of Crispin.

"His own, no doubt," Zellisan commented. Not Varnus, Brannis knew. The old guard at the Archon estate had been a familiar face since Brannis had begun visiting Juliana at her family's home when he was courting her. Varnus or one of the other guards often accompanied them when they went riding—if they had not snuck off. Sorcerers might have been untouchable in the Empire, but their children still warranted protection from kidnappings and such when they traveled alone.

"We will sail for Takalia, then I think we can give Stalyart his ship back, assuming no betrayals between now and then," Brannis said. He looked around the table for signs of disagreement but found none.

"I will ensure he complies," Rakashi commented from his post by the door. The Takalish warrior disdained games of chance, but chose to stay close by his comrades. "He knows I can find him in Veydrus."

"Tiiba, you wound me," Stalyart feigned indignation lightheartedly. "You know I keep to my word when I give it. I am just a miser of promises, so I have few to keep. I swear I will not harm any of you, or take you anywhere but where I am instructed to go. I am no fool, and I wish my ship back. See that keeping promises runs both ways, Tiiba, because I have friends in Veydrus too. Remember who Captain Zayne really is." Stalyart grinned.

"Um, should we be talking about this in front of this person?" Wendell asked, indicating Crispin. It was an unwritten law among twinborn—as all "laws" for their kind were—that matters of the other world were kept well away from the ears of the one-worlders.

"Bah, Crispin is my half-brother. He has heard all this talk. It is so much gibberish among madmen to him. Besides, who would he tell that would find any use from such tales?" Stalyart said. He seemed far too at ease for Brannis's liking, considering the circumstances.

"I call," Soria commented, bringing attention back to the game at hand. She was well into her third tankard, and her eyes spent more time aimed at Brannis than the cards. The needs of their circumstances aside, Brannis was feeling much the same.

Juliana had always been a proper young lady, elegant and refined, with an acerbic tongue and a wild streak kept carefully in check among polite company (which, Brannis had noticed, she did not consider Rashan to be). Soria was that wild streak unchecked. While Juliana took her adventures in small bites—rides in the countryside, hanging about in dockside taverns—Soria was living the life he could only imagine Juliana wished she could.

It agreed with her. Her slim body was toned like a dancer's, her skin lightly bronzed. He liked her hair cut short, though it would take a bit of getting used to the color. He knew Juliana kept hers up with magic like nearly every sorceress; Soria's color was likely what Juliana's would have looked like if left to its own ends. There was an ease about her manner that Brannis only occasionally saw from Juliana, when they had been free of judgmental eyes.

"Where is the head?" Brannis asked, realizing that he had taken too much ale, and needed to relieve himself of it.

Stalyart frowned skeptically, as if the question were ludicrous. "To the bow. That is where we keep the front of the ship, before you ask that, too."

Brannis excused himself from the table, where his small pile of Kadrin coins had nearly run itself to ruin. Kyrus had not been much of a Crackle player, but at least he was able to cheat to win. Brannis had just been guessing at the game, and staring into Soria's eyes over his tankard.

Rakashi followed him out of the captain's cabin, where they had been playing. Brannis did not know what to make of the Takalish twinborn, suspecting that he was not fighting for Kadrin on the other side, and likely allied against them. There was an odd separation of politics between the worlds that he was going to have to learn to understand.

"Sorcerer Kyrus, a moment if you will?" Rakashi asked politely, putting a hand on Brannis's shoulder.

Brannis had changed out of his armor once it was clear that Soria and her companions had the ship well controlled, thus Brannis could feel the warmth of the man's hand through the fabric of his tunic.

"I am no sorcerer, but of course. Just a moment first ..."

Brannis returned from the head to find Rakashi staring out at the twilight sea. There was a calmness about him that almost seemed wistful. Kyrus knew little of the ways of Takalish warrior-scholars, and Brannis was finding this one an intriguing introduction to them.

"Kyrus, you are a man known to many on the other side. You have a reputation, even among your enemies, you know," Rakashi began. "I would know what kind of man you are, and your intentions as regards Soria. Are you the warlock's thrall, or just a man fighting the war his people find themselves drawn into? Are you the sort of man who gets rescued by a pretty girl, and takes her to your bed, or do you truly care for her? I am not blind. I see the looks between you."

"In Kadrin, I take on the burdens I am given. As for Juliana, I have loved her since I was a boy. Beyond that, it is our own business. I think here, away from Kadrin politics and meddling, that bit matters—to me at least, and I suspect perhaps even more so for her."

The door to the captain's cabin opened, and Stalyart and his brother emerged. Stalyart once again looked irritated, though being put out of his own quarters seemed enough of a slight to warrant it. Close behind them followed Zellisan and Tanner. Wendell emerged a moment later, carrying his hat in both hands, piled over with coin. Despite making him play with his sleeves rolled to the elbow, and half of the players having aether-vision, the street magician had cleaned them out. Soria was the last one remaining within.

"Kyrus, I think you know as well as I what she has in mind," Rakashi commented. "But for all her bravado and swagger, I very much believe she is a maiden; she does not let men close to her. If you are not gentle with her, we will have a quarrel."

Brannis smiled wistfully at the cabin door, left slightly ajar in invitation. "We have played this out once before, she and I. I think your reminder might better have served her ears than my own. She needs no protection from me."

When the door to Stalyart's cabin closed behind Brannis, a crude, hastily scratched ward flickered to life, ensuring their privacy for the evening.

Chapter 21 - Sharing Secrets

Juliana was nearly skipping through the halls of the palace the next morning, her evening with Brannis in the other world being a memory just hours old. Iridan had not been in her bed when she awoke, though he had been when she had fallen asleep. Her only tiny worry was that she had given some hint of her actions in Tellurak as she slept. *A dream is a dream, unless you are not a dreamer yourself,* she reasoned. Even if she had talked in her sleep, she could hardly be held at fault for it. She was certain Iridan was stuck in Veydrus.

Her destination had not been far from the chambers she shared with Iridan. The wards nearly glowed in the light, making Kyrus's room simple to find, even had she not known where to look for it. Juliana knocked softly on the door, hoping not to draw attention to her visit. Unfortunately the ward kept the knock from making any noise at all.

From its concealed sheath, she drew Freedom, having assigned the name to the heavier of her daggers that had seen her through Rashan's ordeal the day before. When he had come to let her and Iridan out of the cells, he had found her collapsed and nearly insensible, but she had broken the wards; the door had been unlocked, and only awaiting the return of her strength before she would have left under her own power. She took Freedom, and jabbed at the door with it, hard, watching in the aether for a reaction. Wobbly waves shuddered through it, like poking a finger into the still water of a wash basin. It gave no sign of relenting before her attack, but it served better than knocking with her fist.

After a moment, the ward relaxed and the door opened. Juliana snuck inside before a surprised Kyrus could react—or object. She shut the door again behind her. She felt the rush of aether past her as the ward sealed them in together.

"Fair morning, my love." She grinned mischievously at him, throwing her arms around his neck, and kissing him passionately. "Guess who *you* are not?" She still held him close by, her fingers laced behind Kyrus's neck. She was still smiling at him.

"By the winds, girl, how did you ever find me out?" Kyrus deadpanned in reply before his own face split wide in a grin to match her own. He could not help himself; she was infectious.

"I admit, a bit more muscle looks good on you, but I suppose, given that you have met Soria, that I am not one to cast aspersions regarding idleness." Juliana giggled. "You had an outlandish tale, but the alternative was even more so, until I saw for myself. Even when I first saw Brannis, I thought perhaps I had discovered where your sword and armor had ended up. The plate hid your physique well enough, and Avalanche would be just as deadly in the hands of a scrivener as a knight, I supposed."

"And my appearance?" Kyrus offered. "Not enough of a giveaway?"

"Of course not. I was looking for Brannis all along. I was hoping to identify you by his look, and I found him. I was, perhaps, a bit blinded by desire for you. All I saw was my Brannis. I didn't stop to think that probably was not what I should have found."

"So when was it that you realized?" Kyrus asked. They had taken so little time to really talk in Tellurak. There was more privacy to be had behind his wards than Soria's paltry ones. Even without aether-vision, Brannis had been able to tell that her runes were shabby.

"You sure you want to know?" Her grin spread a bit wider. Kyrus chuckled but nodded. "Well, you may not even have known about them, but you have the tiny little scars on your back—Well, Brannis does at least. They do not look like anything, but you can feel the little raised lines where they differ from the skin around them. I made those, years ago." Kyrus blushed. Juliana laughed out loud. "I should check to make sure you don't have them, too. I would feel silly if you had them as well, and that other Brannis over there had gotten a matching set by coincidence."

She moved her hands to the hem of his tunic, and grabbed hold.

* * * * * * *

Oh, I am a lucky fool. A bad friend, though, but perhaps I can find some way to make amends.

Kyrus was exhausted. Juliana napped peacefully on his chest. There were a hundred things he ought to have been doing, and eventually Warlock Rashan would be looking for him. The wards at the door might thwart him, or they might not. Kyrus's wards were simple, but well formed and powerful. Whether he was kept out or not, whether he could see within or not, eventually the wards would have to be lifted for Juliana and him to emerge.

Things seemed so much simpler now in Tellurak than they did in Veydrus. The Imperial Circle's arcane policies had parted them but had no provision for going back and righting that miscarriage of justice. Juliana and Iridan had wed. Brannis had been there to hear the vows exchanged; they were pledged for life, not the convenience of the emperor, the warlock, or certainly not for some unschooled sorcerer who was not even officially a part of the Imperial Circle, however powerful his Source might be.

Dark thoughts drifted idly through Kyrus's head as he watched the serene, sated beauty playing out on the face that rose and fell with his breathing. *I could kill him,* Kyrus pondered. *Strong as everyone says he is, he would hardly put up a fight, I think. If hurled fire can wound Rashan like that, I would need no other weapon against him. Or I could get him killed in battle. He seems to come close every time even without effort; just send him to the battlefront and wait, try again if I must. It is my duty to send men to die, to choose whose sacrifice benefits the Empire.* Kyrus shook the thoughts away. *No, I could never do it. I can only think thus when I ignore that it is* Iridan, *not some nameless, faceless suitor of my love. Her husband, my best friend. Never. Might that I could convince him to give her up. It was never what he wanted. With my emergence as a sorcerer, I am no longer an embarrassing match. Maybe I could approach Shador to see about it.* Kyrus knew that was not going to work. An alliance with the warlock's son was too politically valuable to abandon; he might have chanced it before the wedding had occurred, but there would be too much fallout from the dissolution of the union.

He turned his attentions back to Juliana herself. He watched her, and she pillowed upon his chest. He felt her breath on his skin. He saw her eyelids flicker. *Are you watching Soria's mischief as you nap?* he wondered. She could probably hear the beating of his heart.

Juliana stirred a bit, stretching and arching her back, working the sleep out of her muscles. Her eyes opened sleepily, drawing a smile from Kyrus, which she matched. She planted a kiss on his chest, then another, working her way up to his lips one kiss at a time. She wrapped her arms around him. When she rolled over, Kyrus found himself pulled atop her. He was helpless to resist.

I can stop this any time I want to, he told himself.

He could not want to.

* * * * * * * *

Rashan paced the hall, fuming. *No Iridan. No Juliana. No Brannis.* Iridan's absence at morning practice had been his first annoyance. The boy had been furious at Brannis after being released from the sorcerer cells in the dungeon. Hearing that Juliana had managed all of her escape save for leaving the cell had stung. Seeing the blatant destruction Brannis had wrought upon the cells and surrounding dungeon had both awed and shamed him. *He knew that Brannis had thrown their draw. How could he have not, if he was capable of outdrawing the wards in those cells?*

It had taken all his persuasion to keep Iridan from running off to confront Brannis about his deception. Once word got around Kadris of Brannis's feat of power in the dungeons, everyone else would know that Iridan had won their draw by sheer force of pity. Eventually Juliana had promised to see to calming him and they had retired to their chambers. *I hope she did not kill him and dump his body in the sea,* Rashan mused darkly. Iridan had warded their door too well for him to spy on them within. That same ward made him think that Iridan must have released it to leave; Juliana was strong, to be sure, but not to the point of breaking Iridan's wards—*Unless perhaps she used that dagger again to destroy them physically,* Rashan muttered in his head.

Rashan waited. He stared at the door to Brannis's chambers, impatient but preferring to wait, and see who emerged—and in what state—rather than barge in and betray his presence (or worse, attempt to barge in and fail).

Worry crept into the warlock's thoughts, winning a long battle of attrition against his anger and annoyance. *What if something has gone terribly wrong in there?*

Could Iridan and Brannis's imposter have dueled within? Did Brannis try to enact his escape with another attempt at a transference spell? The explanations seemed implausible. Iridan was angry with Brannis, but should have held no illusions about trying to fight him. Had Brannis tried to get back to Tellurak, Rashan would have felt even a failed attempt reverberating in the aether.

Rashan waited. Paranoia crept into his mind once more. *This could be a trap, a ruse, a diversion. What if the wards were sealed from the outside? What if no one has seen them by some other coincidence or trick, and the room was left for me to puzzle over while they hatched some plan or other?*

Stop it, the warlock ordered himself. *This is the path to madness!* Rashan stalked down to one of the disused sitting rooms on the floor, and procured for himself an easy chair. Setting it up just outside Brannis's door, he flopped down into it to wait out whoever might be inside.

"Warlock Rashan!" a call came from the far end of the corridor. A thin stick of a young man in a messenger's uniform approached him, handing him a rolled sheet of parchment tied with a ribbon. Had it been a matter of true import or secrecy, it would have been sealed with wax or in a case. Rashan was bored, though, and welcomed whatever mild diversion the missive would supply.

Airships 5 and 6 are confirmed functional. All runes tested. New designations: Starflower, Eagle Wing. Flying crews have been assigned. Awaiting orders and supplemental personnel.

Sorcerer Uthgern Fernwall, Fourth Circle

Rashan read it over thrice, brief as it was, before it hit him. "Where is the fourth airship? Why is it not mentioned?"

"Your pardon, Warlock, but the *Aether Hammer* set sail—if that is the term—this morning, first light," the messenger replied stiffly, uncomfortable with the warlock's attention fixed on him. Little did the lad know that Rashan would as soon harm him as smash a dish because he disliked a meal; it would have been a childish response, mindless destruction perpetrated on one undeserving of blame.

"By whose order?" Rashan asked. He had guesses, but wished to hear confirmation.

"I was not told, Warlock," the messenger replied, cringing but not backing away.

I really, really *must do something about this reputation of mine.*

"Understood. Carry on," Rashan said, then dismissed the relieved young man.

There is at least one answer I will be pleased with, one I will care little for, and one that someone just may have to die for.

* * * * * * *

Later, too much later by Rashan's reckoning, the wards relaxed and the door peeked open. Before it could slam shut again, Rashan thrust it open with his magic.

"Well, oathdaughter, how good of you to freshen up before rejoining the day. I hope the marshal of all Kadrin's armies has not kept you from any important business this morning." Rashan's words dripped venom as he strode into Brannis's chambers. He saw the fresh-scrubbed skin, and smelled the masculine scent of the bath salts the palace staff kept stocked in the rooms of the male residents.

"Not at all, but it seems we kept the Imperial Regent from his charge of running the Empire," Kyrus butted in, protecting Juliana from the warlock's direct attention. He was still straightening his tunic, and buckling on his sword belt, decorative though he considered the weapon.

"Oh, you had best have a good explanation for this, Brannis," Rashan growled. "I spent half the morning awaiting your presence."

"Sounds like something you could have delegated. I had no appointment this morning. You like direct answers, despite rarely being one to give them. You want my explanation, there she is." Kyrus pointed to Juliana. "Simplest explanation works the best at times. Perhaps you saw the little note I made in your book?"

Juliana looked puzzled, not aware of Kyrus's petty vandalism.

"What have you done with Iridan?" Rashan glared at one, then the other of them.

"He is your problem each morning," Juliana put in. "I have him at night, and the rest of the day is his to do with as he pleases. He was gone when I woke this morning, so I had assumed he was at practice."

Rashan took pause a moment. "One of the new airships is missing, the *Aether Hammer*. What do you know of this?"

"It was expected to be ready at any time. I did not order it away. The *Aether Hammer*, *Starflower*, and *Eagle Wing* were going to be ordered to perform reconnaissance around Munne to check for Megrenn's next move," Kyrus replied, more curious now than irritated at the warlock's rude entrance. Somehow, after the prior day's encounter, he could not bring himself to feel quite the same note of unease in Rashan's presence.

"My suspicion, naturally, is that Iridan is aboard. What was his demeanor when last you saw him?" the warlock asked, forgetting to make clear to whom he spoke.

"A bit nervous. You were about to throw him in a cell," Kyrus answered innocently, not willing, in some obstinate portion of his mind, to realize that Juliana ought to have seen him much later than that.

"Exhausted," Juliana answered. "I think he took his anger, and found that fine line between being afraid of me, and trying to ..." she trailed off. She did not turn to look at Kyrus, her eyes losing their focus aimed off somewhere roughly in the direction of Rashan. She did not blush often but must have realized she was turning red.

"I find myself realizing that I have no idea what you do to occupy your days,"

Rashan commented, sparing her the awkward silence she had dropped in their midst. "Whatever is it, go off and see to it."

Juliana did not have to be told twice. She left quickly, not looking back at either of them.

They waited in silence for a moment after she left. With a slight gesture, Rashan pulled the door closed. "It is you she should be ashamed of, not Iridan," Rashan commented mildly. Kyrus could not tell if it was accusation, wistfulness, or resignation; perhaps it was a combination of the three.

"Well, I mean, that is to say, he is her husband now, after all," Kyrus said. "Certain things ... were bound to happen, I suppose. I had not really, I mean I did not—"

"Shut up," Rashan interrupted. Kyrus ceased his babbling. "I cannot abide idiocy, and I know you are better than this. If you have something to say for yourself, then say it."

"She was always supposed to be mine," Kyrus said calmly, collecting himself.

"Your betrothal was terminated. She was promised to Iridan and wed. It is too late to change that now," Rashan replied, as if lecturing.

"Wrongly. She was meant to be *mine*! You waited and waited for Brannis to turn out to be some great sorcerer, for his promised talent to manifest itself. You were waiting for him to turn into *me*! I am here now, and your impatience has taken her from me. It was never supposed to have been Brannis; it was supposed to be me. I do not know what merit Gravis Archon's prediction may have had, but I was there, lost in the wrong world. I was dragon-walking among the tortoises, never seeing my own reflection to tell the difference between me and them. I belonged here. I belong with *her*." Kyrus was out of breath at the end of his rant, and could feel a bit of aether built up inside him; he had not even realized he was drawing it.

"But you were not here. We—I had no way of knowing you would come. There is a war to be fought, an emperor to crown, an empire to put to rights. I had no time to waste. Iridan needs to be fighting to truly be a warlock. Unprepared as he is, he must leave the nest, and I must throw him out if needs be; though it looks as if he had taken that step on his own. If there is to be a wedding, there needs to be an heir. If a warlock goes off to war, there is some urgency involved in begetting that heir. *If* you must feel anger, direct it my way; I am used to unjust anger. Neither of them has done anything wrong in this, excepting what you and Juliana have just done. See that this was a one-time occurrence, and pray that her first child is not tall as a tree with brown hair," Rashan warned. "Then we can put this behind us, and continue our machinations. I still have great plans for you, *Brannis*."

"Shador is my size and coloring," Kyrus muttered under his breath, knowing full well that Rashan would hear him. He got no response save for a warning glare.

"Come by my office tonight. I have much to attend to this day, and no further time for nonsense." Rashan turned and left the room, with Kyrus unable to think of a pithy reply to send him off with.

"You would not think it was nonsense if she was yours." *Yes, that would have done nicely, just a moment ago,* Kyrus thought in the direction of the closed door.

* * * * * * * *

Kyrus had taken a few meetings with his generals, read some reports and written others. He had given new orders to the garrisons defending the border cities of Dolok, Sharefield, Weiselton, and Thinbrooke, in the event that one of them was the next target of the Megrenn main host. He had taken a few more books from the Tower of Contemplation libraries to read in the evening. He had considered seeking out Juliana to smooth things over with her—he was not upset with her at all—but thought better of it. *Brannis and Soria can talk it over in the morning,* he reasoned.

Atop his mount, Kyrus was on his way to see about the preparations on the two remaining airships that had not yet left the harbor, when he was approached by a messenger. Unlike most of the messengers he received, this one was neither one of his own men from the army, nor part of the palace staff. He wore green and blue, chased in gold trim; it was not garb he recognized, to his chagrin. *I ought to know every one of the houses in the Empire, both noble and sorcerous. Brannis did not devote enough effort to studying such things. I should try to do better.*

"Marshal Brannis." The man reined his horse to a stop just to the side of Kyrus's path. "A moment, if you would."

Kyrus took hold of his own horse's reins, and pulled up gently. *Cursed thing,* he swore to himself when the animal did not slow as quickly as he had wished. *Brannis had a much better feel for these beasts. My thighs will ache from merely riding across town—worse should I have to stop suddenly again.*

"Yes, who are you?" Kyrus demanded, setting the man aback.

Ooh, I guess should have recognized the livery, he chided himself.

"Klarmont Dryrock, sir, of House Lurien," the man informed him formally. "Sorcerer Dolvaen would like to meet with you."

Kyrus was more intrigued than worried by the offer. Sorcerer Dolvaen had been nothing but polite to Brannis, and Kyrus had noticed no difference when he met the man himself for the first time—as Kyrus, that is.

The sorcerer kept a modest estate in Kadris. His was only called a "House" at all because of his personal standing. His own blood descendants were not fit for Rashan's little book of matchmaking for the Imperial Circle; it took at least four generations telling true with sorcerous blood to gain that privilege. Dolvaen had grandchildren at the Imperial Academy, but it would be *their* children who would win the distinction for "House" Lurien.

The estate itself was tidy and well cared for. The sorcerer had great wealth of his own, by virtue of his standing in the Inner Circle, sufficient to maintain the thirty or so rooms Kyrus judged it to have by the look it presented to the street. Kyrus—or rather Brannis—had only met the sorcerer's wife in passing. She had taken on his name upon their marriage, and he could not recall what it had been before; certainly it was some lower family. Chaura Lurien had always seemed pleasant enough, though, and did nothing to dispel that impression when she greeted Kyrus at the door. She looked older than the sorcerer, though he suspected that it was just a lesser talent for life extension that he was noticing. She had the look of a woman in her late fifties, with hair gone nearly all to grey and a light ashen tone to her skin. She seemed to make no attempt to disguise her age, unless she was using some trick Kyrus could not see in his split aether-light vision.

"Marshal Brannis. Thank you for taking this meeting on such short notice. Please, do come in." She ushered Kyrus through the white marble archway and through the foyer. They climbed the open stair to the mezzanine level, where she brought him to a double door. "My husband is waiting for you inside. I will send one of the servants along in a bit with some refreshments."

"Thank you," Kyrus replied. He had considered asking what the meeting was about, but then thought better of it. Had Dolvaen wanted him to know from someone else, he would have left an order to that effect.

Kyrus briefly studied the wards on the doors. They were as well crafted as any he had seen in Kadrin, which admittedly was a small sampling, since Brannis had largely seen them as background decoration, and not taken much note of them. He could not see inside, which was a good sign, since everyone seemed rather taken with all his raw magical talents; he had no reason to guess his aether-vision was less than superlative.

"Come in, Brannis. Do not just stand there gawking at my wards," came a voice from within. Kyrus smiled sheepishly, and pulled at the door handle, which obliged him.

The study was large but looked functional. While many wealthy men kept studies for entertaining or show as much as real work, Dolvaen's was ill kept and cluttered. A panoramic vista of the estate's back garden was obscured by a chalkboard on a wooden stand, a cloak rack, and bookshelf that looked to be a late addition to the room's design. The desk behind which Dolvaen sat was strewn with papers and books inter-stacked with each other. Piles of books cluttered nearly every surface of the room, from the little tables that were meant to display decorative artwork or sculptures, or merely set a drink upon, to all the chairs and the low chaise. As Kyrus took in the scene, the stack that rested on one chair nearest the desk rose, and cleared a spot for Kyrus to seat himself.

"Have a seat, my boy. There is much to discuss and little enough time," Dolvaen began crisply, his manner suggestive of a freight master trying to get a ship loaded before the tide went against him. Kyrus took the offered seat.

"What is this about? You do not normally have me here for meetings." Kyrus left the implied question hanging in the air beyond the actual one.

"Frankness it is, then. Firstly, if anyone asks, I wanted to personally report that Iridan stole—no, make that commandeered, since I suppose he was within his rights—the *Aether Hammer* shortly before dawn this morning. The ship's assigned sorcerer, Jaines Hiessens, remained aboard, as did the crew that had already been picked for it." Kyrus noted that Dolvaen did not refer to ships as female, like so many of the nautical sorts were wont to. "We do not know the destination or intent of Sorcerer Iridan, nor, as near as I can gather, was he acting under any authority but his own."

"I can vouch for the latter. Neither I nor Warlock Rashan gave any such order. The warlock was rather put out this morning in looking for Iridan, in fact," Kyrus said.

"I never doubted such. That is just the story that you must remember should anyone ask you later what we discussed. I wished to speak to you personally—and privately—due to the sensitive nature of who was involved. Understood?" Dolvaen asked. He seemed to be in a great hurry for something.

"Thus far, yes. What is it that we will really be discussing, then?"

"Rashan Solaran's regency of the Empire," Dolvaen stated.

Kyrus's blood ran cold.

Rashan knows he has enemies within the Empire working against him. Dolvaen must be one of them. No ... if he is involved, he must be leading them.

"To what end?" Kyrus asked in a forced monotone.

"Brannis, you see him as much as anyone. You know he is unstable. Can you deny it?" Dolvaen asked, staring down Kyrus in what appeared to be an attempt to force an affirmative.

"Volatile, perhaps, but predictable. He consistently works for the best interest of the Empire." Kyrus found himself defending Rashan, even though he questioned the warlock's actions constantly. He could not understand why he did so reflexively.

"Best interests? He has but one true skill, and he is not using it at all. Munne has fallen to Megrenn, and he sat in Kadris bartering favors to get his pick of emperors. In a tenday or less, we will put a crown on some jumped-up bastard of his favorite emperor from the good old days when he razed cities for amusement and enraged all of Koriah—by the winds, half of Veydrus would have declared a holiday had Loramar killed every last one of us."

"He worries that if he leaves to go fight the war, like he did in Raynesdark, that the conspiracy will take further control over the Empire. He already thinks those days he spent fighting off the goblin army and dealing with the aftermath cost him support, and allowed dissent to solidify behind his turned back," Kyrus said. Paranoia was always easier to justify after the fact, once you had rooted out all the secret plots against you. It seemed that Rashan was no fool in that regard.

"Do not mistake me. I do not call him a fool. A madman, a megalomaniac, a liar, and a usurper I will call him—but not a fool," Dolvaen replied.

Kyrus was starting to enjoy the exchange; it was falling into a free-form debate. He was matching wits with one of the best sorcerers in the Kadrin Empire, and it appeared that the stakes were to be: "I see, you have convinced me, sir."

I see it now, why I am defending him. I drew the short lot. I started out on Rashan's side by default, since I owe him my position. If I concede Dolvaen's points, I concede the argument.

"Whom has he usurped?" Kyrus asked. If he was to lose in the end, as he now suspected he must, since many of Rashan's actions were inexcusable, at least he would play out his side of the debate. "There was no emperor at the time. As warlock, he was highest rank in the Empire."

"A warlock who abandoned the Empire for a hundred winters. He lost all claim to any position of authority when he left Kadrin to our fate. I admit there was no true emperor, but the Empire had been prospering under our guidance. Magocracy is so much more stable a system than consolidating power in one man chosen by birthright, and possessing no qualification beyond the pedigree of the seed that begot him," Dolvaen said, having gotten to his feet and begun pacing as he spoke.

"Tradition?" Kyrus answered meekly in reply.

"So you have been playing at this, have you? You know as well as I that the Empire would be better off run by the Inner Circle than entrusted to the whim of that ennobled rapscallion Rashan plucked from the dung heap. There *is* no royal line anymore. If you want tradition, tradition would say that there needs to be a new dynasty. This time, though, that dynasty will be the Imperial Circle."

"Why come to me now? Why should I not just tell Rashan? Better yet, why not kill you myself as a traitor?" Kyrus carefully kept his tone neutral, posing the question as a hypothetical, rather than a bald threat.

"The same reason you can even ask that question today. Had some puffed up knight from a sorcerous bloodline made veiled threats against me like that, they would be finding charred bits of him from here to Zorren. But rumors spread, Brannis. Your little escape from the sorcerer cells in the dungeon and your altercation with the esteemed warlock in the Sanctum yesterday—even the minor cataclysm that accompanied the discovery of your newfound power—all show that you have more power than any of us have seen before," Dolvaen said solemnly. "It may well come to the point where the future of the Kadrin Empire rests on your conscience. Whether you become a monster like Rashan and take his place, or throw him down and let reason govern the Empire."

"Both those scenarios involve me confronting Rashan," Kyrus observed, pointing out what appeared to be an obvious flaw in Dolvaen's logic.

"I suppose the third option ought to be mentioned: he kills you," Dolvaen added. "You admit he is paranoid. You know he kills when he is uncertain of his course. How long can you expect to work by his side, growing in power each day as you learn to control that monstrous Source of yours?" Dolvaen asked.

"But ..." But Kyrus had nothing to follow that "but." Kyrus could not disagree with Dolvaen's logic.

"I think we have talked too long already," Dolvaen said. "If anyone noticed your absence, it may seem suspicious. However, one last thing before you leave ..."

* * * * * * *

Kyrus spent the remainder of the afternoon working on sketches for new airships, based on an idea he had. Brannis had made good use of the stone folk's dragon-working techniques to make weapons. He wanted to see if the same principles could be applied to making armored ships. They would look like hideous monstrosities of steel, armored like knights but in the shape of a ship, impossible to float upon water. If he could fold runes into those plates, though ...

It warranted thought—and lots of planning and figuring. The rune structures would be vast, covering not only the surfaces of the airship, but layers beneath those surfaces as well. Old, sea-kissed wood could hold a rune, but nowhere near so well as steel. The new ships would bear wards strong enough to turn aside cannonballs, if he could only find someone with a Source strong enough to ignite a rune structure so large and intricate. Kyrus grinned. *About time I saw some use of this Source of mine, beyond playing at Rashan's tests.* There were other uses he could put it to, but he wanted to bury Dolvaen's warnings deep in his mind. *With the shielding spell Dolvaen showed me, I should be safe enough from Rashan, at least while I am vigilant.*

The thought of Rashan reminded Kyrus that he had been invited to the warlock's offices in the Tower of Contemplation. It was unusual for Rashan to make any sort of social plans, but it had certainly sounded like one when he suggested it. Most often if the warlock wanted Kyrus (or Brannis), he would send word by messenger, and the implication was that the timeframe was "now."

All along the walk to the tower, Kyrus wondered what sort of mood he would find the warlock in. Rashan's moods were as shifting as the Katamic: never quite calm but ranging from "pleasant enough" to "evacuate to higher ground," often with little notice or time to react.

The door was open, and waiting for him when he arrived, which in and of itself was unusual for Rashan's doors. He was the sort who seemed to think that doors ought to be closed when not being actively traversed.

"Come in, Brannis." The warlock's voice sounded a bit different than normal as Kyrus heard him call out as he hesitated briefly outside.

Kyrus stepped carefully into the office, wondering what was amiss but unable to quite grab hold in his thoughts as to what it was. The chalice in Rashan's hand gave him a clue.

"Are you drunk?" Kyrus wondered aloud, arching an eyebrow.

"A touch, perhaps. Just a touch. Please come in, have a seat." Rashan motioned to a comfortable-looking chair that had not been there Kyrus when had last seen the office. In fact, Kyrus noted, a fair bit of remodeling had been done, including the repair of the holes through its walls.

As Kyrus took the offered seat, the door swung shut behind him and the usual wards sprang to life. "I did not think that would be possible for a demon," Kyrus noted, prodding Rashan for an explanation.

"Takes more effort, I suppose, letting alcohol take its course upon me, but I needed a bit of respite. Too many things happening, even for me to deal with all at once, I think," Rashan explained. He seemed more human than he ever had before. "But never mind about that. I think it is about time we got to know one another, not-Brannis."

"You ... want me to have a drink with you, then?" Kyrus asked.

Rashan laughed. "Not hardly!" The warlock stood and, going against what he had just said, took up a matching chalice for Kyrus. He picked up a decanter, and poured a white liquid into it.

"You just said you did not want me to drink with you," Kyrus protested as the beverage was pressed into his hands with slightly less crispness and efficiency of motion than Rashan was wont to display. Kyrus lifted the chalice to his nose and sniffed.

"Sweetmilk," Rashan said, then smiled at him. "Last thing the Tower needs is more holes in it, am I right?"

Sweetmilk was a treat given to good children at bedtime. It was warmed goat's milk sweetened with honey. Kyrus had never tasted it himself, but Brannis had loved it as a boy—as had near to every child in the Empire whose parents could afford to waste honey on bedtime treats.

"It is delicious," Kyrus commented upon tasting it. "Thank you."

"One of the many pleasures of Veydrus that I thought you might enjoy, Brannis. There was no equivalent in Acardia, last I was there," the warlock spoke quietly, the first explicit admission Kyrus had heard from him regarding Tellurak.

"So you were from Acardia, then?" Kyrus asked, wondering how far Rashan would be willing to open up to him.

"Indeed. Born in Udur, did business out of Golis largely, traveled the world until I got too old for that sort of nonsense. I had a thought for a bit of fun tonight, Brannis. I have come to understand that I will not have you as an underling for very much longer. It is time we became partners in this endeavor. I have found myself thrust unwittingly into the role of being the brains and wisdom behind the Empire; I was always the muscle, so to speak. You ... You are the sort whom I could leave behind to run things while I go out to play at war. But ... ahead of myself." Rashan shook his head. "The fun part ..."

"Yes?" Kyrus asked. Rashan might have been drunk, or he might have been faking it, but his words were a far cry from the scenarios that Dolvaen had painted.

"I would like to get to know you, and I will tell you a bit about myself in return. Where in Acardia is it that you were from?" Rashan asked, smiling mischievously.

"I was born on a farm outside Scar Harbor a bit. I apprenticed there and inherited my master's shop. I guess that is as good an answer as I have got," Kyrus replied, seeing no harm in it.

Rashan set his chalice down on the desk and stood, walking carefully to the middle of the office.

"Huaxti janidu deldore wanetexu elu mulaftu sekedori puc'anzu margek lotok junubi," the warlock said as he painted the air with his fingers. Brannis had once seen Rashan work a spell out loud to show him how it was done. This time, a pair of

illusory, ghostly hands remained in the air where Rashan had held them when he began the spell. From each finger, a colored line trailed in the wake of Rashan's own fingers as he motioned through the spell. When he finished, a tangle of lines floated in the air.

Off to the side of the room, a scene appeared in the air. Kyrus saw cobblestone streets and horse-carriages. He recognized the Society of Learned Men and the courthouse where his trial had been held. The view flowed, as if they were viewing the scene through a lens, and Kyrus saw houses and shops with unfamiliar signs outside, though he noticed that Dremmer's Pub was still there in Rashan's memory. The scene meandered about the city for a time, with Kyrus lost in a sense of wonder that he had thought simple magic had ceased to be capable of for him.

"Your turn," Rashan spoke softly from behind Kyrus, snapping him from his reverie as the illusion faded. The glowing diagram of the spell hung in the air, awaiting him. "Do you remember the words?"

Kyrus shook his head, and the runes spelling it out appeared in the air just above the snarl of colors he would have to trace. It took him five tries, but Kyrus finally managed the spell for himself. He laid out a vista of his own for Rashan, showing the view of Scar Harbor as he remembered it. He pointed out his shop, Greuder's Pastries, the Brown Elk Tavern, and a dozen other places, including the wharf he had burned down.

The two stayed up into the late hours trading scenes from their memories. Kyrus showed Marker's Point and Denku Appa to Rashan. He even managed to work in a bit from the mines of Raynesdark as best he could from Brannis's memories. In return, Rashan showed him the Battle of the Dead Earth, attending the birth of Liead the Only, and the draw where he had killed his grandfather.

"I am sorry about yesterday," Kyrus apologized, feeling like he had taken undue satisfaction in his injuring of Rashan.

"It was my own fault underestimating you. Although, technically that was cheating," Rashan commented.

"How do you mean? I just hurled fire, like you told me to," Kyrus responded, confused.

"Well, that is why I take much of the blame. What you threw at me was not fire but dragonfire," Rashan explained. Kyrus's eyes widened. "Hurled fire mixed with raw aether. You expelled it faster than it could ignite. I have no idea how you managed it without the physiology to back it up, but it was the same stuff dragons breathe. I could have wound up just like my grandfather: killed in a thoughtless, youthful show of power.

"Worthless, stupid kid, I was," Rashan said. "My grandfather was not a good man but he was not so bad as to deserve an end like that, either. Had I been unlucky in emperors, I might have been killed that day for what I had done. Instead ..." He gestured to himself as if to say "Everything else happened."

"I did not expect regrets from you, of all people," Kyrus mused, smiling companionably at the warlock.

"Regrets? I can show you regrets." The warlock chuckled without mirth. An image appeared in the air between them, a vision of loveliness with honey-blonde ringlets and soft brown eyes. She might have been eighteen summers—or years, depending which world she was from—old.

"She is very pretty. Who was she?" Kyrus asked, assuming that as a regret, she probably qualified for the past tense.

"A girl I loved, a long time ago. The first one where I could finally tell the difference between love and simple lust. Everything seems like love until you really, truly find it; after that, you can see all your other silly dalliances for what they were."

"What became of her?" Kyrus asked.

"Age. Eventually it gets them all." Rashan sighed. "How about you? Did you have a girl back in Scar Harbor, before you got swept up in your little adventure?"

Kyrus just smiled in reply, and began his own illusion. As it took shape, he was pleased that he could still recall Abbiley's face clearly enough to paint it for Rashan. He had worried that the time they spent apart would have dulled his memory, left it somehow less vivid.

Rashan smiled, and nodded sagely. The warlock then took another pull on the decanter, having abandoned the pretense of using a chalice some time ago. "What was her name?"

"Well, I have no reason to believe she is anything other than still 'is,' but her name is Abbiley," Kyrus stated, but he was surprised to see Rashan perk up.

"What was that you said?" the warlock asked, still clearly inebriated.

"Abbiley. That is the girl's name. Why do you ask?" Kyrus inquired, wondering what possibly could have prompted such a reaction.

"Try mentioning that name to Celia sometime." Rashan chuckled. "But you cannot tell her I was the one to mention it."

As Kyrus walked back to his room shortly afterward, he could barely keep his eyelids up. Sweetmilk was wonderful at helping children sleep. In larger quantities, it worked as well on adults. *I have to remember to ask Celia in the morning,* Kyrus thought, fighting to keep the task in his head as his thoughts became heavy. *Of course, if Juliana is in my room waiting when I get there, I give it a coin flip at best that I do not recall it.*

* * * * * * * *

Iridan stood at the prow of the ship, wind whipping past them at a rate that was alarming most of the crew. The sails were stretched taut, and the captain had been forced to ask him to ease his wind spell lest he tear the ship apart.

I will never be a real warlock practicing with wooden swords in the palace courtyard or contesting draw after draw with old men. I will go out and make myself a warlock ... or die. The thought sobered him some, acknowledging the very real possibility that his rash action would lead to an early death. There would be no Brannis to look after him, no Faolen to hide him, no Rashan to train him. He would be on his own.

The realization that not only was Brannis now a sorcerer, but stronger than him by leaps and bounds galled him. Brannis had been his friend since they were boys, but he had grown up in Brannis's shadow. Brannis had been taller, stronger, more popular, from a better family (or so he had believed at the time). When Iridan came into his own magically, he had found some measure of equality with Brannis, a way he could be the strong one, the important one.

If I do not act soon, Brannis will take my place. Rashan is already acting as if Brannis will become a warlock as well, even though he showed all the finesse and skill of an ogre with a needle and thread.

"We are coming upon Munne soon, Warlock Iridan," the captain informed him, shouting above the wind. "What are your orders?" The man might not have liked his orders, but Iridan at least appreciated that they were followed.

He had begun to forget that he outranked nearly everyone, having his company predominated by Rashan and Juliana. She at least ought to have obeyed his orders, but feeling along his newly grown teeth with his tongue reminded him of the reality of that dynamic. *I would pay dearly for Brannis to teach me whatever trick he uses to keep her in check*, he thought sourly. *Perhaps motherhood will temper her disposition.* Iridan had thought to see about getting her with child before he departed, but he found himself acting out of anger at Brannis instead. Brannis might have had everything he ever wanted, but Iridan still had Juliana.

"Go higher, well above the clouds. I do not want a repeat of what happened to the *Thunderstorm*, Captain," Iridan ordered. He reached behind him, to the hilt of Dragon's Whisper, sheathed at his back. It should have given him comfort, a wedding gift from his best friend, but he could not find it. *You can just do everything now, can't you, Brannis?* The blade had been given the name "Sleeping Dragon" when he received it, but Iridan thought it might have been a subtle jab at his as-yet untapped depths of skill as a warlock. He had chosen the new name by the quiet swishing it made as it sliced through air … or wood, stone, or steel.

The crew were puzzled by Warlock Iridan's order, but obeyed. The ship's assigned sorcerer, whom Iridan was unfamiliar with, and whose name he had not bothered to ask, guided the ship higher as they neared the city. The cold night air grew frigid, and breath came shorter as the air thinned in the higher altitude, but Iridan was not concerned. *It will only be for a little while.*

"Captain, take the ship back to Kadris and receive new orders," Iridan shouted, feeling a bit dizzy yelling in the thin air.

"What do you mean, sir?" the captain asked but stopped short as Iridan put a foot up on the railing, and leapt over it.

The captain rushed over to the side of the ship to look down, and just caught a glimpse of Iridan in the starlight, disappearing down into the clouds.

* * * * * * * *

"What news of the killer?" a lyrical voice asked in a perfect tenor. The speaker appeared as a bronze-skinned young man, clad in nothing but a knee-length kilt. He could have been sixteen or eighteen winters if looks were to be believed. Those looks were liars.

"He is as he ever was," Illiardra replied with a sigh. She had resumed the form she had first greeted Rashan in, with her elongated ears and delicate horns. It was no more the form she was born to than was her companion's, but it was the one she preferred.

The two immortals stood in a glade surrounded by towering pines, and lit by nothing but starlight. The trickle of a brook was the only sound besides their voices; no crickets, no owls, no wolves called the vale home.

"Shall we tell the others, then, and make his banishment official?" her companion asked.

"I would just as soon not speak of him again, nor trouble the others with such unpleasant talk. He will have no thought of returning, and if he ever does, that will be the time to bear ill news," she replied.

"And what of your son?" asked the bronze-skinned man, who was not so young.

"Rashan wished for a son to carry on after him, and do better than he had done. For love of him, I went along and bore him a son, but Iridan is no son of mine. He is as much his father as a boy can be; I gave little to nothing of myself. I fear he is destined for the same fate. The work of the gentle, kindly folk we fostered him with is being undone, and I do not expect it will be repaired."

"That is indeed tragic. If you ever need someone upon whom you can unburden your troubles, I am here." The bronze-skinned man winked slyly.

"Perhaps in a dozen seasons or so. First I ought to watch the fruits of my folly as they rot from the tree," Illiardra replied.

"How morbid. Really, I cannot fathom the fascination you have with that place," the bronze-skinned man scoffed, referring essentially to everywhere else besides where they were.

"Become a woman for three seasons, and bear a child. See then if your attitude remains the same," she challenged.

"Hmm, an interesting thought," the bronze-skinned man commented, giving it some consideration.

Chapter 22 - The Enemy Within

The sun rose over the city of Munne. Many of the Kadrin peasants who called it home had somehow not expected it to. Smoke drifted up from some of the buildings, but came from chimneys, not the structures themselves. All was not well, but it was far better than they had feared. Some folk went to work that morning as if nothing had happened; most did not. The streets were hardly quiet, for soldiers in unfamiliar blue uniforms patrolled them in numbers, more for something to occupy themselves than out of any need for occupying the city.

The few remaining Kadrin troops who had finally surrendered had been led from the city. No one had told the population just where those soldiers had been taken or what had been done with them.

Soldiers spent the day knocking on doors and searching homes. They took anything that seemed likely to be used as a weapon, but were surprisingly restrained. Tailors' scissors and cooks' knives were allowed to be kept; even butchers' cleavers were permitted. Swords and axes were confiscated, as were any bows found among the residents' possessions.

In the wealthy districts of the city, merchants with gold stashed in every cupboard and under every floor board fretted about their coin; most did so in vain. Those with tinges of noble blood in their lineage—something they were usually all too proud to claim—found their homes looted but their lives spared. Those merchants lucky enough to have friends in Megrenn were permitted to pack their belongings, and leave the city and seek asylum there.

The lesser nobles who engaged in no real trade, but lived on the wealth of their lands, were gone; no one knew where. Lord Grenorn had escaped, along with most of his relatives, aboard one of the Kadrin airships. Monohorn teams were busily tearing his estate to rubble, the great beasts hauling heavy chains wrapped around the support pillars or merely butting their armored heads into the walls.

The day passed peacefully, if uneasily, for the peasants in occupied Munne.

* * * * * * * *

Night fell, bringing with it a sense of normalcy, after a fashion. Common folk who would be at work all day felt trapped within the walls of their homes, with hostile troops all about outside. Those same folk felt protected when the darkness came, and those same walls surrounded them.

A curfew had been put in place, requiring all civilians to stay indoors after dark. It had been shouted at every major street corner by a strong-voiced lad who spoke Kadrin well enough, despite a strong Megrenn accent. The peasants were generally happy with the arrangement, wanting no part of the darkened streets with Megrenn all about.

The peasants were not the only ones within the city walls.

The night had deepened to its fullest as clouds suffocated the moon. That was when the fires began. The first blaze started in the Kadrin barracks, where Megrenn troops had settled, though the structure was nothing remotely adequate to house the whole of the occupation force. Normally someone would have thought to stop it, but it continued to burn. Few woke to see it, mainly those close enough to hear the clash of steel and the screams of men and beasts from the vicinity.

The second fire started in the winter stores, giant warehouses near the marketplace where dried fruits and salted meats were packed in during the mid-autumn months, and that kept the city fed through the lean months of winter. Though springtime had come, the stores were far from empty, having been well provisioned with the prospect of war hanging over them all winter. Now the reserves of food were cooking uncontrolled. It was not the only food in the city, but it represented half a season's worth of sustenance for whomever held it.

The third conflagration was in a residential neighborhood. More folk took note of that fire, as homes burned and peasants took to the safety of the street, curfew or not.

* * * * * * * *

"What does he want at this uncivilized hour?" Councilor Fehr demanded of the man who had wakened him from the little sleep he had been able to find.

Jinzan was dressed in a knee-length nightshirt and his boots, with several days' stubble upon his face. His eyes were parted but little, taking offense at the glare of the lantern the messenger carried. The light made him look sinister; the combination of boots and nightshirt made him appear ridiculous. The murder lurking in his eyes kept the messenger from commenting on either.

"He said there was urgent word from Munne," the messenger replied crisply, pointedly ignoring the Councilor's dishabille. By his manner, they might have been meeting in the Council chamber and not the hallway outside Jinzan's bedroom. "I have the helm. A porter is waiting with it in the foyer, upon your leave."

Jinzan muttered under his breath, but reminded himself that it was Narsicann that had ordered them to awaken him. He was the one deserving Jinzan's ire, not the poor night-duty messenger he had collared into carrying out the order.

"Very well," he said. Narsicann might be many things, but frivolous was not counted among them. If there was word from Munne that Narsicann felt Jinzan needed to be made aware of halfway to dawn, he would hear it for himself ...

... and if it did not please him, he would scribble himself a note so that he would remember in the morning—after returning to a much-neglected bed—to flay Narsicann for bothering him.

Jinzan lighted the foyer as he descended the stairs, choosing a soft blue color that was easy on eyes that had been adjusted to the dark. He saw the porter—a stocky, stiff, nervous-looking fellow—with a warded lockbox. Still in his nightclothes and boots, Jinzan walked over, and quickly disabled the runes. It was a simple matter, since he was one of the few who were permitted the helm's use.

The helm he took out was gold wrought, plain in design, but covered in complex runes. Megrenn only had two of them. As he donned the helm that had been delivered to him, Jinzan wondered to whom he would be speaking.

"This is Councilor Jinzan Fehr," he thought, pressing his words out into the aether by force of will. *"What is this urgent news?"*

"Councilor Fehr, this is Dembeck Drall, Tourmaline Mystery, servant of Ghelk. We have had multiple disturbances this night. There is a Kadrin force somewhere within the city," a voice in the helm replied. There was no tone to it, no timbre, just a tinny, echoic sound, bearing intelligible speech. It could have been anyone on the other end, so long as they had the power to use the obstinate devices. Jinzan had heard of Dembeck Drall but did not know him well. He had to take it on faith that the man was who he said he was.

"This is war, Dembeck. Did you expect they would all flee and leave you the city? Hunt them down and kill them or take them prisoner, if it suits you. I did not need to be awakened for this." Jinzan attempted to convey his irritation, but knew it was unlikely to have carried over well through the farspeech helms.

"We believe it is Rashan Solaran," the voice added.

"Again?" Jinzan asked.

The demon had appeared via transference spell, stealing the speaking stone from Munne's Tower of Grace as they tried to parlay using it. He had killed a hundred or so troops, including a handful of sorcerers and two generals—three if one counted General Tarrakan, who had been sent off presumably to Kadris when the spell brought Rashan Solaran. The demon had retreated shortly thereafter, taking the Kadris speaking stone that had come with him. Jinzan sorely wished Megrenn had such devices at their disposal. They were beyond his ability to create, however, so they would have to make do with the helms the Ghelkans had so thoughtfully supplied.

"Fires burn across the city in small pockets. None has seen him yet and survived the encounter," the voice of Dembeck Drall answered. *"This is bad for morale."*

"I will send reinforcements," Jinzan reassured him, breaking off the connection.

"Do you know where the blade-priests are staying while they are in Zorren?" Jinzan asked the messenger as he removed the farspeech helm, and returned it to its box.

"Yes, Councilor," the man replied. "They are staying at Councilor Varduk's estate, as his guests."

"Bring them here. Do not rush them, just convey that it is urgent, and that they should be prepared to depart the city shortly afterward. They will come at their own pace, regardless of any prodding," Jinzan ordered. "If possible, do not rouse Councilor Varduk. Just leave word of the blade-priests' departure for him to receive in the morning. There is little he could do to help between now and then anyway." He turned to the porter. "I have no further need of that helm tonight. Return it to Councilor Narsicann's home, and then get yourself some sleep. Oh," he added as an afterthought, "if you can make enough noise to awaken the good Councilor, you will find a small addendum to your pay."

The man grinned, and winked his understanding to Councilor Fehr. Jinzan kept his expression neutral except for the barest hint of a smile.

* * * * * * * *

In a darkened alleyway behind a coopersmith's shop, Iridan Solaran sat with his back to the wall, trying to catch his breath. Dragon's Whisper lay across his lap, smeared with partially wiped-off blood. Iridan found himself in much the same state. He was covered in blood and sweat—the latter largely his own, the former entirely not.

He was terrified, exhausted … and exhilarated. *Death stalks me at every turn. All blades and claws seek me. None has yet to scratch me! Every foe falls before me. I cannot say what trick my father used to hold me back in practice each morning but those beardless lads he sent against me were thrice the challenge these Megrenn weaklings are. Brannis, I forgive everything I thought about you. This sword is wonderful!*

Already dressed in black as his warlock attire had him, he had become a nocturnal hunter. He had thought back to all the histories he had studied to think of targets to attack, and had simply thrown himself headlong against them. *One firestorm set the whole barracks ablaze. It was so much easier than at Raynesdark. All that practice drawing has paid off as well. My Source is still fine,* Iridan thought. He was brimming with aether, litte enough that he could still hold it safely for a long while, but sufficient for incinerating any patrol that might stumble upon him as he rested.

They had already come upon him once. The house where he had tried to find shelter for the night had instead raised the alarm. Iridan was not sure why they had sided against him, but he had managed to fight off three stripe-cats and a score of soldiers. When he had set one of the great cats on fire, it had thrashed about wildly, knocking into a row of houses, and putting them to the flame as well. Iridan had hidden, and waited for more of the occupiers to arrive to battle the flames before they spread, but Iridan had ambushed them as well.

They are Megrenn houses now anyway, he reminded himself. *This is war, and I am in occupied territory. I have to think like a soldier now.* He had not hurt any of the peasants, so far as he knew, but he had not been paying such close attention to their fates.

Iridan had been finding that not paying attention to certain details made everything so much easier. He had stopped looking down at the bodies of the men and beasts he killed. *It is just meat now, lying there, is it not?* He had blocked out the sounds of the screaming as best he could manage. *Just like sleeping through a thunderstorm, once you realize it cannot hurt you.* He had ignored the fates of the people he was fighting for. *I can worry about a few here or there, or I can try to save all of them. The choice is obvious.* He ignored the gore that splattered about and got all over him. *Like playing in the mud as a boy. It will wash off.* The smell was harder to ignore, the coppery scent of blood and the sick, cloying, smoky scent of burned human. *I will get used to it, in time.*

Once he put that all past him, it was just his skills and guile against his enemies'. He was winning. He felt strong, in control. Iridan realized that he was smiling. *This is fun, in a way.*

* * * * * * * *

Jinzan had shaved and dressed by the time the five Safschan blade-priests had arrived. Among Megrenn's major allies, Ghelk held the most magical power; Safschan could not find one sorcerer among them for every ten Ghelk counted. Megrenn herself had a third the populace of Safschan, but possessed thrice their wealth. For all that, though, Safschan was the real force in the alliance's army. Their stripe-cat cavalry had already shown well in the conquest of Munne, and now it was time to see another of their contributions to the cause.

Five of them were arrayed before him, standing in a neat line in his foyer. The blade-priests waited in identical poses, feet spread just wider than shoulder width, knees slightly bent, arms crossed before them. The leader stood at the center, a half pace forward of the rest; he would be the only one speaking without being directly addressed.

The leader of the blade-priests was a well-built man, not brawny like many knights or the men who wrangled monohorns, but with a lean, balanced body like a tumbler. His hair was shorn close, so as not to give any advantage to his enemies. He wore blue-and-gold garb of leather and silk intermixed. It protected some critical areas, but largely left the arms unencumbered. Like all blade-priests, he carried a rune-blade sheathed on his back. The long-hilted swords were legendary for their versatility and the ferocity of the men who bore them. The leader stood out from his men in one unusual way: his eyes did not match. One was a brownish green; the other was a scant contrast of two shades of white. The white eye did not follow Jinzan as he approached, like the green one did.

"Master Tiiba, thank you for coming on short notice and at this unseemly hour. I do apologize," Jinzan greeted the men. Strong as he was, he was still wary of the power the blade-priests wielded. While none of them could hope to stand against him in a purely magical encounter, while within theoretical reach of those rune-blades, he was at best on equal footing.

"You would not have done so if there was not cause, I am confident," Tiiba replied. He sounded neither sleepy nor annoyed by the summons. It was better than Jinzan could have said for himself, earlier that night.

"Of course. I have received a report that there is an insurgency beginning in Munne. The sorcerer who made the report, a Ghelkan named Dembeck Drall, believes that the demon, Rashan Solaran, is at the heart of it. There were strikes this very night against our forces, and we need to act quickly to counter this threat.

"There are very few options we have at our disposal for dealing with a warlock. Until such time as we recover the Staff of Gehlen, you priests are the best option we have," Jinzan told them. There was no point in putting up a pretense before the blade-priests. They were as unlikely to object to the order as they had been to being awakened hours before dawn.

"You pay us a great deal of respect, Councilor. The privilege of facing a great monster such as Rashan Solaran is no small gift. There have been few warriors of such renown," Tiiba responded. "I will relish the opportunity to destroy him myself."

"Do you think you five can handle him?" Jinzan asked, skeptical but hopeful. He wanted the honor of killing Rashan himself, but more than that, he just wanted the demon warlock dead. Without the Staff of Gehlen, he did not like his own chances.

"No, Councilor, I do not. But war is a tricky thing. Sometimes fortune favors the righteous. More often, it just favors the lucky." Tiiba smiled. Jinzan could not help but chuckle. He had not expected an attempt at humor from a Safschan blade-priest.

Jinzan studied the man a moment, seeing a warrior born and bred. Tiiba's father had been a blade-priest, and his grandfather before that. The priests took no wives but fathered children out of duty to the order. Girl children would be raised by the mother's family; boys fostered with the mother until the age of eight, when they were given to their fathers to train as the next generation of priests. Tiiba had been fairly young for the Freedom War but he might have served, Jinzan reasoned.

"Where were you, during the war?" Jinzan asked. It was a common pleasantry among those who had lived long enough to see Megrenn throw off Kadrin rule. Most veterans of the war loved nothing better than to brag of their exploits.

"My father left me behind in Safschan when he sailed for Zorren," Tiiba began. "But he never forbade me. I found myself passage on a stripe-cat vessel, bringing cavalry for the war. I fought in three nameless battles before earning my blade in the Battle of Boots."

Jinzan knew of the battle, though he had been closer to the main fighting around the capital. The Battle of Boots was a nighttime ambush by Kadrin forces desperate not to be responsible for letting Megrenn slip from the Empire. They had stalked barefoot into a Megrenn campsite after their sorcerers killed the sentries without raising the alarm. There had been few survivors, but the Megrenn force had prevailed. Upon tracking back to the Kadrin camp, many of the men had taken the unused boots of the Kadrin soldiers as trophies.

That was the sort of man he was sending to his death: a hero. Jinzan hated command at times.

Chapter 23 - Choosing Teams

Brannis awoke to a swaying sensation that reminded him instantly that he was on a ship. A warm, heavy pressure on his chest turned out to be Soria using him for a pillow. It was such a strange feeling, an echo of Veydrus following him; Kyrus had found Juliana in much the same way when she shared his bed.

The captain's quarters had windows facing out the rear of the ship, and two port-holes to either side, covered with glass. Pale light streamed through, but it was plenty bright enough to see by. Brannis turned as best he could without disturbing Soria's sleep, and looked outside. The sky was flat grey; a ceiling of clouds hung over the Katamic. It might have foretold a coming storm or it might have just been a cloudy day, Brannis could not say. Either way, he was neither sailor nor sorcerer; there was naught he could do to help even if it was to be a storm. He settled back in and waited until his love awakened.

After a time, she stirred. By the time she came fully awake, Soria found Brannis's arms wrapped tight around her. She relaxed and just allowed him to hold her for a time. Despite the very strange reality that she had only just met him the day before, Soria felt as if she had known Brannis all her life. Through Juliana's memories, she nearly had.

"Good morning," Brannis spoke softly, brushing a lock of hair away from her face.

"Mmm," she cooed back. "Good morning, Kyrus," she made a point of remembering the name that he used in Tellurak.

"You do not have to call me that outside of the crew's hearing. Once we are rid of them, you may as well just call me Brannis from now on. Kyrus Hinterdale is a wanted criminal," Brannis said. "I still find it odd calling you Soria, Juliana."

She stretched, one limb, one joint, one muscle at a time, squirming about in Brannis's embrace as she worked herself awake for what seemed to be a conversation steering its way clear of insipid pillow chatter. "Think of it as playacting. You are who you are, whatever you are called. The difference between Kyrus and Brannis is only as wide as you make it out to be. You *are* Kyrus, Brannis."

"You of all people should know better than that. You have met us both now, though Kyrus is doing much more playacting than I am. You can see the differences," Brannis argued.

Soria worked her way free of Brannis's grasp, and propped herself up on an elbow, looking down at him. "I know *better than* better than that, actually. You are fit and strong, and Kyrus looks like a strong wind would carry him off; that's superficial. If he spent years in the practice yard working with sword-masters, traipsing about in armor, and generally living like a knight, he would look just like you."

"Yes, but no amount of study can make my Source anything like his," Brannis countered.

"Well, that is one key difference with twinborn. Your Sources might be like the sun and moon—a new moon at that—but they are your own, at least. The two parts of the split Source seem to be what bind a set of twins together, from what I have been told, at least. It is in here that is the same, though." She tapped Brannis on the forehead.

"Well, that is where you are wrong," Brannis quickly replied. "We do not think alike or act alike. Kyrus is playing at being me, and probably only getting by at it because they are all so confused about the sudden change in him."

"You two boys don't think alike, huh?" Soria asked sarcastically, looking meaningfully at the two of them in bed together. "Kyrus had not met Juliana before a few days ago, but certainly remembered her well enough to betray Iridan's trust to have her. There are prettier girls in the Empire, I figure; so why me?"

Brannis had no ready answer for that one. Soria pressed her advantage while he struggled to find one.

"And how about you and me? You *know* I am not Juliana, at least not the way you thought of Juliana, but I am close enough. I know all the words to convince you I am. I remember little details neither of us would have told from when you tried courting me years ago. You were so adorably chivalrous about it, treating me like your lady when you were barely old enough to grow fuzz on your face, and call it a beard."

"But it is not like that with me and Kyrus," Brannis protested. It was not much—not anything really—but it was all he could think of.

"It will be. Soria and Juliana have been aware of each other since I was a little girl," Soria explained, hurting Brannis's brain by referring to herself in the third person by two different names in the same sentence. "It takes some getting used to. You have been aware of Kyrus for how long, a season, perhaps two? When we were searching for you, I found out your trial had been held on the fourteenth of Gladewatch, which was about a season ago. How long had you known by then?"

"Oh, maybe a week or so, I guess, truly. Thinking back on it of late, I think I had a vague awareness for years that I had just never paid much attention to." Brannis suspected that talking to Soria and Juliana was going to be confusing if she insisted on mixing months with seasons or other similar misuses of Telluraki and Veydran standards.

"Give it time. Someday when you talk about Kyrus, you will find yourself referring to him as 'I,' even in your own head." Soria smiled down at him. "Whether you choose to call me Soria or Juliana, or any other name you like, you will think of me as Juliana. That's fine. It's all the same to me." Her smile turned mischievous as she continued. "And I think Juliana has had just about enough talking for now." She leaned down and kissed him.

To her faint surprise, she found herself being lifted gently but firmly into the air and off of Brannis as their kiss concluded. She was a fair bit heavier than Juliana, with actual honest-to-goodness muscle on her frame, but Brannis still hoisted her up as if she was filled with straw.

"Kyrus has not," Brannis joked. "There will be time enough for that later, and plenty of it, mind you. There is nothing in this world to keep us apart. You work where and when you choose. I am a fugitive, if anyone ever makes the connection between me and Kyrus, at least; even at that, I think we ought to be able to keep at bay any trouble from that front. For now, though, things are going on that need attention."

"Well, if I had any doubts about you being Brannis, you certainly have shattered them." Soria sighed. She twisted in his arms, breaking his careful hold on her, and collapsing faceup into the crook of his arm. "If you insist on being all practical, go ahead."

"I need to know about these companions of yours. If I am going to be trusting them with secrets of two worlds, there are things I will need to know," Brannis began.

"What sort of things?" Soria asked with an irritated huff. Brannis surmised that she hoped they would be short things and few of them.

"Well, you gave me the 'we are surrounded by pirates' version last night, but I would like to know who they each are, in *both* worlds. What is their story, how long have you known them, what is it they do, how well do they fight? That sort of thing," Brannis said.

Soria turned to look Brannis in the eye, and when she saw no hint that the conversation could be forestalled, she took a deep breath and began. "Well, you know Zellisan is Varnus, so he ought to be easy enough to explain. I met him as a girl in Veydrus, and as a fifteen-year-old here. He has been nearly as much a father to me as Shador Archon has been. There may be no blood relation, but he was always there, and my father rarely was. He guarded me for a shift each day of my young life until I went to the Academy, and any time I was home after that. Merciful One, he was the one who found me in hysterics, and called for a midwife to calm me down after my first moonflow scared me witless. Around here, he spent some time in the Acardian army before leaving for better coin as a mercenary. He tried the 'noble blade' routine for a while, but there wasn't enough work in it, so he got himself mixed up settling scores for one group of scum against another. It wasn't exactly knightly stuff, but it was keeping the wolves fighting amongst themselves at least. Eventually he gathered up a little group of fighters who were twinborn, and they were able to make some real coin at it.

"Those twinborn would be Tanner and Rakashi. I never did get the story of how *those* two met, but it somehow involved a duel as far as I could gather."

Soria paused for a moment as if trying to remember something. "Anyway, Zell took over as their leader, and in addition to earning coin, they looked for magic stuff. It seems that twinborn have been polluting Tellurak with magic for centuries, at least, and some of the stuff is still floating around here and there. They figured if they armed themselves with enough magic, they could carve themselves out a little fiefdom somewhere, and live like royalty."

"So how did that work out?" Brannis asked.

"It's still working out. None of us is ready to hang up our blades yet, but we could buy a bit of land in any kingdom we wanted. I have enough trade bars on me now to buy this ship," Soria bragged, and then giggled as Brannis made an exaggerated search of her for them. "Well, *with* me, I meant. Anyway, we have a fair bit of magic among us as well, enough that we do not get pushed around by anyone without some connection to Veydrus and the ability to fight back with magic of their own."

"Are there many of you—of us—around?" Brannis asked.

"Enough, I guess. I mean, we are still a tiny minority, but there are enough that you need to watch yourself letting slip details of Veydrus around here, and of Tellurak back there. You should always be more careful around sorcerers. Zell is the exception; one of every pair usually has magical ability. For you, it is Kyrus."

"I guess you are the opposite side of exceptions?" Brannis guessed.

"Yeah, Juliana's fingers get a lot more practice at spells, but I could manage most of what she does. I concentrate on silent casting, since anything overt might cause trouble if I got found out. You saw how that goes, with the whole witch trial," Soria said, once again fluidly mixing Brannis up with Kyrus.

"Is that why you did so poorly in the Academy? You had all the talent you ever needed. You could have been Fourth Circle by now if you ever tried," Brannis prodded. Juliana could have been a top student if she had shown the interest that Brannis had.

"I guess so. I never really thought about it like that at the time. I was just suspicious in general. Getting held back a year was embarrassing, so I tried a bit more after that, but I never really cared to devote my whole life to the Imperial Circle. I just sort of got carried along," Soria mused. Brannis wondered how often she fell to introspection. He would have brooded for years over his own failings if that had been his path through the Academy. In fact, he had brooded over his failings, insomuch as being devoid of talent was a failing.

"What about the others?" Brannis knew Juliana always hated getting caught up talking about herself, so he did her the favor of changing the subject. He would learn about Soria's past when she was ready to tell it. It was not *her* that he was worried about.

"Well, Tanner is Tanner, I suppose. It is his Kadrin surname he uses: Tanner. First name is Elmin but he hates it, so he just goes by Tanner," Soria said. "I suppose he has to answer to it in the army, so he had to keep that bit at least."

"What is his name in Tellurak?" Brannis asked. He felt like a pest, interrupting her to pick at details, but one day he might have to make inquiries about the man, and knowing his given name could prove useful.

"Dunno," Soria admitted. "I only got the 'Elmin' bit out of him betting on the outcome of a street brawl in Khesh. I tried to get his Acardian name out of him over a game of dice, but I didn't win that time."

"What was your stake?" Brannis asked, teasing her.

"A kiss," she admitted. "Only one he's ever gotten, and I stopped trying to weasel his name out of him after that. I only gamble for coin now, not secrets. You're welcome to try him, though. I'm sure you've got plenty of secrets to barter."

"I can do better than that. I'm his senior officer in Kadrin, remember?" Brannis chuckled. "I can get him the post of his dreams, or make his life miserable. If I decide I want to know, I have plenty of leverage."

"Just promise me I can be there to watch if you try the 'miserable' route." Soria grinned. "Even if it's a bluff, the look on his face ought to be worth it."

"Fine. Deal," Brannis agreed.

"When we thought we were still chasing Kyrus around, Tanner mentioned something about wanting to duel him. He may still have some thought of it. We dissuaded him by pointing out that it wouldn't be a fair match, since Kyrus was ... you know ... sort of a weak, skinny, bookish sort," Soria managed with barely suppressed laughter as she teased Brannis. He glared at her, but since they were both more or less looking up at the cabin ceiling, it lacked the intended effect. "Since you're not Kyrus, he may still want to try you."

"Do I need to worry?" Brannis wondered. He knew he was not the greatest technical swordsman, but he held his own well enough.

"Use Avalanche and you should be fine, so long as you're well armored. That suit you have with you will be plenty," Soria joked.

"That good, is he?" Brannis asked.

"Yeah," she replied. "He and Rakashi used to spar more often, years ago. It was something to see. Rakashi really knows how to use that half-spear of his, but Tanner would still win almost every time. If you ever see Rakashi without his shirt on, you'll see dozens of little scars; they used to duel to first blood."

"What about Rakashi, then? What is his story? The rest of you, I can see how you got mixed up together, but how does a Takalish warrior fall in with Acardian coinblades?"

"Rakashi fights for the sake of fighting. He won't brawl like some drunk but he'll cross blades with anyone who'll have at him. Tanner used to be like that in a way, too. With Tanner, he was just an arrogant kid who was great with a blade. I thought he had mostly grown out of it, but the way he's been going on about that new pistol of his, and how that's what warriors will be in a few years, I wonder whether that's true anymore. For Rakashi, the fighting is some sort of spiritual thing. He doesn't get mad when he fights, he just does the best he can, to test himself."

Brannis said nothing. It confirmed something he had been worried about since they had first introduced him to Rakashi. He had been privy to every bit of information the Kadrin Empire had about Megrenn and their allies. He had studied the Megrenn Rebellion and the tactics they had used. Rakashi had to have been trained as a blade-priest.

"He doesn't talk much about himself," Soria continued. "He thinks a lot. He likes to look at nature when he thinks, saying it helps him keep his perspective about his own problems. He likes to look at the sea or the mountains, to show himself how small he really is. I know what he's trying to say but I don't quite understand it. I was raised in a Tezuan temple; they taught us that there is more within us than outside us. You can explore the whole of the world if you lived long enough, but if you lived a thousand years, you could never finish exploring your own mind."

"I should ask Illiardra about that one. She might be able to settle it for you," Brannis joked. "She is over ten thousand summers old."

Soria turned over, and pushed herself up to look Brannis in the eye. "She worries me," Soria said. "When she sent me though Rashan's wards to see you, it was so easy. It was like no magic I had ever felt … I actually didn't feel it at all. She was reading this book, too. It was filled with prophecies—dark, evil stuff, mostly."

"I would like to see that book," Brannis told her, trying hard to keep it from sounding like he was giving her an order, though that was just what he was doing. "But can you please stop talking about Juliana and Kyrus as if they were us? It is confusing."

"I remember all that happening. You remember it too. What's the difference?"

Brannis frowned. Soria smiled, and settled back in next to him.

"One other thing about Rakashi …" Brannis said.

"Yes?"

"You mentioned that Tanner was a match for him. What about you?" Brannis asked. "Have you ever dueled with him?"

"He said he wouldn't hit a woman," Soria answered. "I agreed, he wouldn't. It was one of the first times I really ever saw him laugh but we didn't fight. If it ever came down to it, though, he wouldn't stand a chance. I am a Tezuan master, in the way they never believed possible. They talk about aether and Source in their own terms, but they don't understand them like we Kadrins do. I am the closest thing they've seen to a warlock." Soria chuckled, shaking her head at something she just thought of. "You know, for as much as I loathe my oathfather, I understand what it is like having free rein to do what you want because no one can tell you otherwise."

"If that was true, why did you want to find Kyrus to recruit him for your little band of coin-seekers?" Brannis wondered aloud.

"Because it was you, silly. I knew since Raynesdark that you were out here somewhere, and the whole Kyrus thing just seemed too good a gamble to pass up. Once I saw the wanted posters of you in Scar Harbor, I knew for sure," Soria claimed. "Oh, and by the by ..." She whacked him, hard, right on the stomach. Brannis winced, accompanied by a startled grunt. "You are dense as stone at times. I had dropped hints from Kadris to Raynesdark to see if anything would seem familiar. Half the trail songs I sang were from Tellurak."

"I thought I might have recognized some of them, but could never quite get past how awful your singing was," Brannis said, then snickered. Soria pulled one of the pillows from the bed, and hit him with it. A minor skirmish ensued, and Brannis emerged victorious, with Soria laughing helplessly under his onslaught of feather-filled pillows.

"Are you hungry? I just realized I am." Brannis panted as he caught his breath after the mock fighting, and laughing he had just done. Soria nodded in the affirmative. They both found clothes, and went to see what the *Merciful* had lying about for a breakfast.

* * * * * * *

The food was better than Brannis had expected. While he was still unused to the cuisine of Tellurak, extensive trading seemed to have led to more diverse fare. He had eaten more than his share of preserved meats in his day, but the pork sausage was spiced with something he could not name. They ate out on the deck of the ship, the six of them, Brannis's new crew in Tellurak: himself, Soria, Wendell, Tanner, Zellisan and Rakashi. The rest of the crew stayed well away from them as they worked.

With the noise of the sea, and the fore of the ship all to themselves, Brannis thought it safe enough to discuss his plans, now that he was confident that he had one. It felt odd to Brannis that everyone had deferred to him so readily. Soria had been their leader—except for Wendell—and since she seemed content to let Brannis choose their path, the rest had gone along.

"All right, everyone," Brannis said. "I have decided what our next moves are going to be. Wendell has business in Takalia. Once we make it to port, that will be our first priority. Since it may be a delicate endeavor, I think it would be best to keep the numbers to a minimum. Therefore I think it would be best if Zellisan would accompany him." Brannis looked to the hulking older man for confirmation. What he saw was a mixture of puzzlement and acceptance. Zellisan had been a wanderer with none, but his companions to answer to for a long time, but back in Veydrus, he was a soldier at heart.

"To what end?" Zellisan asked. It was not the sort of response a marshal expected from a soldier, but without a solid command structure to back him out on the Katamic, Brannis supposed that Zellisan had grounds enough to question him.

"Well, Wendell has to go; it is his errand, after all. Of the rest of us, you are the best suited to act as a bodyguard. I know you are suited to it, and experienced as well. I have no worry at all, putting Wendell's safety in your hands," Brannis told Zellisan, hoping that the vote of confidence in him would make the sting of being shipped off with the rascally magician a little less painful.

"Are you certain you would not rather accompany me yourself, Sir Brannis?" Wendell asked, leaving his preference exposed for all to hear. "With that sword and armor, none would stand against you. That is just not the sort of magic one finds lying about in Tellurak."

"I am flattered that you would take my protection over Zellisan's, Wendell. I have other business to attend to, though, which takes me in another direction. Besides, I think that I would be hard pressed to keep it to just the two of us," Brannis replied, giving a grin and a meaningful glance Soria's way.

"Right on that count. I spent months tracking you down. I'm not letting you out of my sight," Soria said, not giving the slightest hint of joking. There were a few chuckles anyway, at her manner.

"I will be heading to Kyrus's home, Scar Harbor," Brannis said. "When he— I, I suppose—fled, I must have left a cataclysmic mess in my wake. I want to go back, and tie off a few loose ropes, set a few things to rights. There are a few things I need to look into as well, none of which I can send another to do in my place."

"Sure thing. I'll be glad to help," Tanner said, nodding, "just as soon as you untangle that knot of a plan, and explain it again. If that was supposed to be something to work on, I missed where you said what we were doing."

"Well, the 'we' part is a bit of a different story, but I was purposefully vague. While Wendell is just on personal business, I have some sensitive matters to see to, which I do not feel safe enough discussing on Stalyart's ship. Once we book passage out of Takalia, I will go into more details," Brannis hedged. In truth, it was quite the opposite. Wendell was working some scheme he had only half-explained, but he was clearly working on an elaborate plan to get the Staff of Gehlen. Either that, or he was using such a plan as a ruse for some even deeper plot. Either way, Brannis wanted as little attention drawn to it as possible, from Stalyart, as well as Rakashi.

"So we're just gonna end up in a circle after all this?" Tanner asked, clearly unimpressed with the plan. "We just came from there a week or so ago. I'm gonna get dizzy. Hey, how 'bout after that, we head on over to Marker's Point, then maybe see if we can shave a day off our time from last trip."

"Well, I am glad you hate my plan," Brannis joked, drawing glances away from Tanner's direction and toward himself. "Because I have a different task for you." Brannis gave a wide smile that did not seem to reassure Tanner in the least.

Tanner turned his head, and looked sidelong at Brannis. "What's that?"

"You get to stay and keep an eye on Denrik Zayne. You are Kadrin's new ambassador to Megrenn."

Tanner's jaw dropped. He stood there gaping at Brannis as if he had just see him sprout a second head.

"Brannis, you can't just abandon him with these pirates!" Zellisan objected.

"He's right, Brannis, that's not fair at all," Soria said, sounding concerned about the prospects Tanner had of surviving on his own among the pirates. "He doesn't deserve that."

"Deserve? We are a few days yet from Takalia, so you have time to think it over," Brannis told Tanner. "But I think once you do that, you are going to find yourself enjoying the prospect. Denrik Zayne made me an offer of an ambassadorship, but he could not trust Kyrus's magic. Tanner will fill that vacant role, and there will be no threat of him burning down the ship. Admittedly, with Kyrus, there was always that concern."

"So you're sayin' I get to play at pirate, with the official status of ambassador to protect me?" Tanner asked, seeming to warm slightly to the idea.

"They make good coin, stock better ale than most taverns, and you would likely be spared any of the real work of running the ship. As for 'official,' well, I do not know how official we can possibly make it, but you will be protected by mutual interest in keeping open a line of communication. Sorry to say but you are not valuable enough to make a hostage of, nor dangerous enough for him to fear. You get to fall in between, under the category of 'too useful to kill,' which is a good place to be," Brannis said. He felt like he was tipping Tanner over the edge, past his objections.

"I'll think about it. Might not be the trick coin it sounded like when you first mentioned it," Tanner conceded.

Brannis knew at that point that he had won; Tanner was just saving face by not admitting he was swayed so quickly. He would let the question linger a bit before making his decision known. Brannis had been picking up on the way Rashan maneuvered people, and had seen the warlock elicit the same reaction from a number of nobles and Inner Circle members. People more or less all functioned the same, and anyone with pride and at least a nominal ability to refuse would prefer to make it seem like they had come to the decision on their own. Either way, it served Brannis well enough.

"Since I will be heading to Scar Harbor, and I assume by her earlier comment that Soria will be coming as well, that just leaves you, Rakashi," Brannis said, continuing his allotments of personnel with the one he was least sure of. "You can choose whether you come with me and Soria, or stay with Tanner and head over to Denrik Zayne's ship when I convince Stalyart to deliver him. Of course, you could also choose your own path. I have no authority in Kadrin that I could hold over you, so you are free to do what you like."

"Takalia is my homeland. Perhaps it would be best if I were to escort Wendell and Zellisan," Rakashi offered placidly. His manner gave no indication of duplicity, but Brannis had seen far better than him at subterfuge. He would choose to distrust Rakashi's motives until he had taken his own stock of the man. Soria's trust carried some weight, but that was loyalty to her, not any general regard for Kadrins.

"No. Wendell is taking Zellisan with him and no one else. If you wish to return home, I will not stop you, of course, but Wendell's family business is his own to keep to himself or not, as he chooses. One bodyguard is enough," Brannis informed Rakashi.

"Yes," Wendell said, "if I were as adept here as I am back in Kadrin, I might do well on my own, or even if I were a younger man. However, if I must accede to the effects of age, I would prefer involving as few outsiders as possible in my family's affairs," Wendell contended, thankfully picking up on Brannis's wish for Rakashi to stay away from whatever plan he was working on between Takalia and Zorren.

The Takalish warrior brushed aside the rejection as if it were of no concern. "Very well then. I will accompany you and Soria."

"That settles it, then." Brannis clapped his hands once, signaling the finality of the assignments. "We have until we get to Takalia to work out any further details. Now I just have to go have a conversation about Tanner."

* * * * * * * *

"Ahh, Kyrus, you wonderful madman!" Captain Stalyart laughed uproariously when he heard Brannis's plan. "I think I just might start believing those tales I keep overhearing that you are actually Brannis Solaran. First you cheat Denrik Zayne, then threaten him, and when he shows you mercy by leaving you in paradise, you have your friends in Kadrin arrange your rescue." Stalyart paused a moment, realizing that it sounded very much like the plan he had followed to free Denrik from Rellis Island. Shaking this off as a coincidence, he continued. "Now you are free, and the first thing you do is to try to get one of your assassins near to Captain Zayne."

"He is no assassin. He is a swordsman and a coinblade," Brannis argued. "And you should have been one of the first to realize I was not actually Kyrus; you saw me not so very long ago. How many men can fill out a suit of armor so quickly, short of eating himself to ruinous girth?"

"You travel with a man who cheats at cards better than any I have ever seen. I have no idea his trick, but I know he was not winning fairly. And you ... you had the potential to be a remarkably strong sorcerer. Even if the tale of your magical adventure were false, I would have to guard against deception by your own magic," Stalyart reasoned.

"Well, since you might as well warn Zayne, it is Kyrus he will be matching wits with. I am also receiving proper training in magic from Rashan Solaran," Brannis bragged. "As for my 'adventure,' it was an accident, and I am making the most of my situation here. Had I known so many of my own had twins on this side, I would have tried something like this all the sooner. I had hoped that Captain Zayne would view Tanner's presence as a compromise; he gets his ambassador, and does not have to risk either me accidentally torching his vessel or deciding that I would be best off with him dead, and tearing his Source out."

"Well, maybe you are Brannis and maybe you are Kyrus. To be quite honest ..." Stalyart began, then trailed off, changing his mind mid-sentence. "You know, there is a fanciful old map in my quarters—perhaps you have seen it more recently than I—that is decorated along the margins. It shows the whole of the world as men once saw it, ending a bit east of Takalia and a bit west of Acardia, with nothing between them—as if the world were not round and no man had set foot on Elok. The edges show serpents and devils, whirlpools and mermaids; there are even dragons there. If ever there were a man who might find his way off the map, and find the land where dragons live, I suppose I would have to think of Kyrus. He is too strong for his own skills—a hazard to friend and foe alike."

"I am not sure quite how to take that, but in any event, my offer stands. You have until we reach Takalia to decide but I think it works to everyone's benefit. Jinzan gets a line of communication with Kadrin. You get to do Zayne a service. Tanner gets to play pirate. I get some time with Soria without him around, constantly watching her." Brannis smiled.

Stalyart nodded slowly in understanding. "This is the man who wrings Denrik Zayne's neck at chess, I remember," Stalyart congratulated him. "I see now, you are a man who moves men as chess pieces. It is a noble tradition, you know, among generals. A good tactician, whether on a chessboard, a battlefield, or at sea, knows that he must place carefully each of his pieces, not just the important ones. Battles are won and lost because a small piece was in just the right place when it was needed."

"Something like that." Brannis shrugged.

"And pawns are meant to be used and discarded, when they serve their purpose best in death," Stalyart observed ominously.

"I do not intend that Tanner is being sacrificed, you know. If I thought Zayne was going to kill him—if he could, mind you, the man is a demon with a blade from what I hear ..."—Brannis immediately regretted his choice of words, but there was nothing to be done about it—"... then I would not send him at all."

"Denrik Zayne is a man who thinks freedom is worth dying for. He understands that to make Megrenn free was a great thing, and worth the risk to himself. He sees freeing Kadrin much the same way. He would like to see the people free, and your nobles and sorcerers ground to dust beneath his boot for how you behave. For all those noble thoughts, he would think nothing of sacrificing a pawn to advance his ends. Would you not do the same?" Stalyart asked.

Brannis found himself wondering about the dashing swashbuckler, whether there was more to him than met the eye—and not just his eye for detail or quick wit. He did not know the man well, but was seeing for the first time that he was perhaps a bit of a philosopher. "I would. I have a job to do, and sometimes I have to order men to risk their lives based on my plans. Munne fell despite my efforts. We gave up Temble Hill as a diversion and a trap, knowing it would never hold, but I sent a lot of men to Munne who died because of it. They died trying to keep Munne free, but it fell anyway."

"The tragedy is that they died for freedom but never had it to begin with," Stalyart said.

"How do you mean? Of course they were free," Brannis said. He suspected deep down that he knew the gist of what Stalyart's argument would be, and hated himself for it.

"Free? What would have happened if a soldier had said 'No, I will not fight. I wish to go home,' and he did so?" Stalyart asked, but he did not wait for Brannis to answer. "I will tell you that he would be called a deserter. I do not know your custom for such matters, but I suspect he would be killed or thrown in a dungeon. That is the Kadrin way. A Megrenn soldier would be called a coward. They would take back any weapons and armor he had been given, any provisions the army had provided. It might mean that he walked home naked, begging at farmhouses for food, but it would be his choice. That is a free man."

"It sounds much the same. He would likely die of starvation as no one would feed a known deserter, or he might turn to brigandry. He is not really any better off than the Kadrin deserter, except the Kadrin would get a cleaner, quicker death," Brannis said. No army would hold together long should there be no punishment for desertion. Megrenn merely made it unpalatable in a different way than Kadrin did.

"You really cannot see the difference?" Stalyart asked innocently, shaking his head. "I had hoped that maybe you would see more clearly, but the rot that the Empire brings has corrupted you as well, I see. Too much power, too close to the top, to see how little freedom there really is. The Megrenn will fight for real freedom. They have gotten their own, and they will bring it to Kadrin. They are even willing to die for it.

"And that is where we differ, the Megrenn and I," Stalyart stated, reminding Brannis that Gar-Danel was allied with Megrenn, not a part of it. "I am willing to kill for my freedom. I am even willing to kill for someone else's, if the right situation comes. I will not die for my freedom, though; that is the height of folly."

"A lot of men die for their freedom. Entire wars are fought over it," Brannis said.

"Freedom is the ability to choose your own path. The dead do not have that choice any longer," Stalyart noted.

Brannis could not argue the point. He merely made a note of it in the back of his mind, wondering if someday knowing that Stalyart valued his life over his freedom could be put to use. Brannis found himself conscious of reducing the person of Stalyart to a chess piece in his mind. He was a part of a much larger game than chess, and it was a game where the players had to be constantly learning more of the rules as they played. He had just discovered one of the rules for moving Stalyart.

Chapter 24 - Forging Chains

The room had a military smell to it. The air was fresh and crisp from the window he had opened, but it could not overpower the heavy scent of leather oil and steel that saturated the building. Brannis had spent less and less time at the army's headquarters as he became embroiled in the politics at court, and in Rashan's schemes. Kyrus had gone a step further in his brief tenure as Brannis's replacement, never having set foot in Brannis's office until that morning. General Sir Hurald Chadreisson had emptied the room of many of the accoutrements of command. The desk was bare, and the rack of scroll canisters was empty as well; scouts' missives had been redirected to Brannis's suite at the palace. The personnel records had been moved to some major's office (Kyrus had already ordered them returned). The large map he had been using to track the Kadrin deployment, and reports of Megrenn forces had been removed, but the little statues were left strewn across the table. Monohorns and stripe-cats lay with their feet up in the air, Megrenn infantry swept into a pile. The Kadrin forces had been bunched at one end of the table, all together, but someone had at least taken the care to leave them standing upright.

Kyrus had awakened with a plan, conceived largely by Brannis, but with which he wholeheartedly agreed. He sat at Brannis's desk with stacks of officers' files at his left hand, and a pile of blank parchment to his right. With a quill in hand, he was going to rearrange the army just a bit.

In all the files, there was one name he was looking to find: Elmin Tanner. Soria had told him that Tanner was assigned to Naran Port, so it would not take a great deal of searching to find him or his file. What Kyrus needed was to find enough other officers to reassign to cover the inclusion of Tanner among them. His pretense would be sending more of the senior leadership of the army out into the field, and bringing the inexperienced ones back to Kadris to get them logistical training, and vet them for higher positions, as the army was destined to grow in size as the war effort took hold.

Kyrus spent a good portion of the morning arranging for promising middling officers to be brought to army central command, and assigning irascible old veterans to apply their oft-touted expertise where it could be more immediately used: on the battlefront with Megrenn. He looked for men with unusual skills and circumstances. Ronnad Darkhorse was accounted one of the best archers in the Empire; he would train recruits at the School of Arms while in Kadris. Sir Hanliy Garlent's career had foundered after a falling out between Lord Jomon and his son; he would get a chance to prove himself. Elmin Tanner was an arrogant sword captain who had been reprimanded on occasion for insubordination. Well, he would be a project, certainly, but "Sir Brannis" really could use a good sword instructor. Kyrus smiled.

He picked a half dozen other officers who he thought could avail themselves of a change in locale, and found plausible assignments for them as well. *Do other commanders make these sorts of assignments as well? It would certainly explain the grousing among the men of nonsensical orders coming from the top levels of the army. I had always thought they were just looking to place blame for things that inconvenienced them, and had no clear purpose from their viewpoint. I had never considered that the orders were as capricious as those men had claimed. The maligned wisdom of the downtrodden, I suppose.*

Kyrus looked over the sad, empty table from which Brannis had plotted their defense against the expected Megrenn invasion. His first thought had been to get the map back from wherever it had been taken, but then he remembered the spell Rashan had shown him the night before.

"Huaxti janidu deldore wanetexu elu mulaftu sekedori puc'anzu margek lotok junubi," Kyrus intoned, carefully weaving his fingers through the complex motions the spells required. As he did so, he could picture the colored lines hanging in the air that the warlock had provided for him to trace with his fingers.

The table transformed. The glossy wooden surface turned rocky and brown, and the edges turned to water, outlining the continent of Koriah as best Kyrus could remember it from maps. Giving in to fancy, he let the water cascade off the edges like a waterfall, in a small tribute to Stalyart, and his ideas about old maps. Kyrus approximated the locations of the Cloud Wall and Stone Talon mountain ranges, and they rose from the continent like erupting teeth of stone. Using those mountains as a guide, he set about creating rivers and lakes, forests, roads, cities, and towns as best he could remember them. He knew the scale and proportion were awful—he would have to retrieve the map to consult it, at the least—but certain locales he was more familiar with were likely accurate enough for tactical use: the vicinity of Kadris, Raynesdark, the ogrelands, Kelvie Forest. The little figurines representing the armies floated up out of the illusory map at Kyrus's command. He was going to place them where reports had last claimed them to be, but then redirected them over to a bookshelf, where he set them down safely out of the way. Upon the topography of the map appeared the forces of Kadrin and Megrenn, and all their allies, in fine detail, though not to scale.

Kyrus spent much of his morning reading through reports, and making alterations to his map accordingly. He also got hold of his original, flat, paper map, and adjusted his aether-constructed one until it matched as exactly as he could make it. From his limited experience in such things, he judged that the construct would last several days before needing to be reinvigorated with aether. While he was away, the illusion of falling water, some little waves crashing against the coastlines, the flow of rivers, and some swaying of the trees and prairie grasses would continue on their own. Kyrus thought a moment, and added some clouds above; those would continue to laze across the continent on their own as well. The rest of the map would be unchanging except by the application of aether by a sorcerer.

Kyrus left orders for some of the officers to study the map, and make note of anything they were aware of that was based on outdated intelligence or erroneous reports. He had not spent nearly enough time digesting every report that Brannis had received to ensure the map's complete accuracy, but it ought to have been close enough for military strategists to work from.

There was one last order he wanted to send. It really ought to have been a request. He wanted to offer a position to someone who was not under his command. For that matter, the position he intended to fill was neither vacant, nor under his purview. It would be a test of the leeway that Rashan allowed him, but he rather expected that it would work. The captain of the palace guard was sixty-three autumns of age, and no longer the hard-eyed sentinel he had once been. The man managed the palace guards well enough, but lacked vigor, fire, and the ability to provide much protection by his own sword anymore. Kyrus somehow suspected that it would not be too difficult to convince Varnus to accept the position.

* * * * * * * *

Kyrus left the army headquarters shortly before noontime. It was a warm, mild day of the sort that southern Kadrin rarely got so early in the season. He should have been glad of the fact, but found that it only reminded him that the exotic cavalry of the Megrenn would be all the more comfortable; the blue skies and sweet-smelling breezes were lost on him.

He made for a home he had scarcely imagined he would have to visit. Celia Mistfield had so dogged his steps since their return from Raynesdark that he half-expected that he could merely look over his shoulder to find her. Ever since Iridan and Juliana's wedding, however, she had left Brannis in peace. Now Kyrus set about actively seeking her out. He had needed to ask one of the palace messengers that morning just to find out where she lived; he had never thought to ask.

Rashan may be playing at something. I cannot risk it, though; the bait is too tempting and he knows it. A drunken demon? Even one-quarter in his cups, he ought to have been more politic than to drop such a juicy morsel accidentally. He had some motive and I will not divine it without speaking to her. The warlock's sudden recognition when Abbiley's name was mentioned suggested that it was not the first time he had heard it. *Was it feigned or a genuine reaction?* Kyrus could not tell.

He had not, in fact, found Juliana awaiting him in his bedchambers the night before. It would have been well past impulsive, even for her, to antagonize Rashan again so soon. With the peace of a solitary pre-slumber, Kyrus's sleepy mind had wandered its way back through the conversation between himself and the warlock. What details he had given, what tricks might have been played on him, what sort of motive he might have had for deception—all sloshed about in his mind like the water in a carelessly carried bucket; most had fallen out.

The sweetmilk had helped him to a wondrously restful night's sleep, but he recalled little of the detail of his deliberation. He had no reason to suspect the warlock of poisoning him or drugging him; the effect of sweetmilk was tried out on children from the age of two summers clear through to … *How old am I now, twenty-two summers?* Kyrus shook his head at his foolishness. It was as good as wine for putting you out cold for the night, but with no hangover afterward, and more importantly, no violent, drunken outbursts while awake and under its influence.

When he arrived at the modest home that had been provided for Celia, Kyrus knocked at her door, standing smartly at what he thought was military attention as he awaited a response from within. He studied the door, noting its construction and estimating how sturdy it was as a defensive bulwark; he had no intention of assaulting the place, but his preoccupation with military planning since his arrival in Veydrus was beginning to leak into his thoughts more and more.

"Good morning, your lordship," a young maid answered the door. She was pretty in the plain sort of way that even rather ordinary girls are at a certain age; flush in newly found womanhood, and not yet worn out by a life of work and childbearing. Her sleeveless grey dress was cut thigh-length, with plain trousers showing beneath them. Brannis would have thought nothing of it, having been around such garb all his life, but Kyrus found it cynical. The dress was a mere covering for work clothes: arms bare for washing and scrubbing, no long skirts to catch on things, trousers for kneeling for truly lowborn tasks.

"I am here to see Sorceress Celia," Kyrus informed her, brushing aside his thoughts on the class system evident in Kadrin. He had too many other matters to worry about right then.

"Milady is not in the house. I can prepare tea and tarts for you, if you care to wait for her, or you may return in the evening," the girl replied with all deference, not even looking Kyrus in the eye.

"Where can I find her now?" Kyrus asked. He did not have the sorts of days that permitted waiting in Sixth Circle sorceresses' sitting rooms.

"I do not know, your lordship," came the reply. It sounded honest enough; she was just a maid, not privy to all Celia's affairs. Had she been better dressed, he might have taken her for a ladies' maid, and not the cleaning sort, and his expectations of her knowledge would have been more demanding.

It was then that Kyrus noticed something subtle in the aether. The girl's Source was hiding it partially, but there was some sort of aether construct about her. The girl squirmed and blushed under Kyrus's scrutiny but voiced no complaint.

At length, Kyrus spoke to her. "Do you know that someone has put a spell on you?" he asked bluntly. He had no reason to worry about offending her. Had that been his aim, he would have known better than to stare at her so long to begin with.

"Of course, my lord," she replied, her voice a tiny thing, as if she were trying to keep her answer a secret from her own Source.

"To what end?" Kyrus asked, annoyed that Celia—or possibly someone on her behalf—had enspelled the poor girl. He had not puzzled out the exact nature of the spell, but he could not see any protective effects in evidence. He suspected that the girl's ignorance was not entirely of her own making.

"It was a condition of my employment, your lordship," she confessed.

Kyrus seethed. Taking commoners as thralls was a time-honored—and widely condemned—practice among sorcerers. The Imperial Circle expressly forbade it, and Kadrin law made it a crime punishable by banishment. It was in many ways worse even than the practice of necromancy, since not everyone was convinced that the suffering evident in the bodies of the dead was felt by the individual whose consciousness had once inhabited that body. Thralls were worse than slaves, with no freedom even in their own minds.

"Who cast this spell on you? Just give me a name, and I will be on my way." Kyrus focused on the construct and it shattered, spilling its aether loose and succumbing to his draw.

"Thank you, your lordship, but I have no name I can give you. I remember the fact of it, but I can recall no details. I may as well remember events from before I was born, it is such a blackness in my mind," the girl explained, relieved but worried that she was not able to provide what her benefactor wished to hear.

"I will find out by other means. Until then, if Celia returns, tell her to report to me immediately," Kyrus ordered.

"If I might beg your pardon, my lord, but what name should I give her?" the girl asked diplomatically.

Of course! I am growing arrogant indeed to expect that the whole of the Empire knows me by my face, especially since I only somewhat look like Brannis.

"Brannis Solaran," Kyrus lied. He was getting good at it.

* * * * * * * *

Kyrus was in his office in the palace when Celia arrived, per his orders. Kyrus had been going over the plans for his newest airship with Sanbin, who had become his own private smith of late. The sword-maker would be helping to construct a hull made of folded, runed metal, similar to the construction of the dragon-tooth weapons they had made together; the process looked to be easier and quicker using steel.

"Sanbin, if you would excuse us," Kyrus told the smith.

Sanbin swiveled a neck that looked too thick for such a movement, and saw the arrival of Brannis's tag-along shadow. He gave a knowing wink when he turned back to look Kyrus way. "I have plenty o' work fer keepin' me busy a while. No worry on that account." He took up the sheaves of parchment with Kyrus's drawings and runes on them, and packed them in a neat bunch.

Kyrus waited for Sanbin to exit and Celia to take his place across the desk from him. He studied her a moment as she stood there, wearing a green dress with white fabric showing at the tight-laced bodice that hugged her form. She was of a height with Abbiley, and built just like her, buxom and curvy, not so painfully thin as Juliana seemed at times. Her hair was darker but that was no hard thing for a sorceress to change. The face was smoother, her teeth straighter and brighter. *They take the girls at the Academy aside, and teach them all those vain tricks, though.* He could not honestly rule it out.

The other matter could wait. He would not let such abuses of magic pass, but it was a subject that required less delicate handling than the one that was foremost on his mind. "I had a long talk with the warlock last night," Kyrus began noncommittally. He watched for signs of a reaction from Celia, but saw nothing but earnest curiosity (possibly feigned, in the long tradition of humoring long-winded superiors).

"And?" she prompted when Kyrus did not continue after a pause she deemed a bit too long. Kyrus wanted to see her mannerisms in all forms, looking at them in a new light, comparing them to his memory of Abbiley.

"We talked about a great many things, things I had quite frankly never expected to hear from him. We talked about distant lands and people in our pasts—his from much further ago than mine. At one point, I mentioned a name and he suggested that I mention it to you." Kyrus allowed himself to wander just a bit, to make her impatient. It was working.

"What name? Brannis, I know you are important around here now, but that does not mean you should fritter away at other people's time. I have work to be getting to, and a meeting I am going to be late for," Celia said.

"Abbiley," Kyrus dropped the name in front of her, to see what she would do with it.

"That forsworn bastard! What else did he tell you about my dreams?" Celia demanded, her nose scrunched up in disgust. Her face was reddening as well, Kyrus noted.

"Tell me? Nothing? I brought the name up, and he thought I ought to mention it to you. Tell me, what does it mean to you?" Kyrus asked, trying to keep his tone neutral and inquisitive, rather than the eager and interrogational it was steering toward on its own.

"I started having recurring dreams after Raynesdark. I figured I had just seen enough horrors there and in Illard's Glen that I just needed to see something mundane and comforting every night; my sleeping mind was making it up for me, like some sort of cure for nightmares," she explained.

"How does the name come in?"

"That is the name they called me by in the dreams: Abbiley Tillman," Celia stated simply, as if it were not germane to the heart of the matter. She seemed not to realize how much it mattered to one heart.

I never told him her family name, Kyrus realized. *Or did I? Did I slip and let loose that key bit of information, and forget I had done it? I know I had wanted to hold it back in case of such treachery as this may be.*

"Do you remember any details of these dreams? People, by any chance?"

Kyrus pressed. Celia gave him a funny look, growing suspicious of his questions.

"Why are you so interested all of a sudden, Brannis?" she asked.

"Just humor me, if you would." Kyrus tried being reasonable, to see if that would get him just a bit farther.

"I do not remember details very well," she said. "I have a brother, Neelan, or something. That is the only one that comes to mind. Is this what you brought me here for, to ask after my dreams? They are just dreams, Brannis."

"Rashan told you that?" Kyrus asked, filling time as his brain absorbed the blow it had just taken.

Neelan really is her brother's name. I never gave that up. I hardly remembered it before she said the name but that was it. Perhaps it was too much to hope for her to remember me, if it has truly only been since Raynesdark.

"I did not need to be told whether my dreams were really dreams. I had asked him in case some magic might have been at work. I had assumed two things, both of which turned out to be wrong. First that he would be of some use in telling me what might be happening in my head; the second, that he could be discreet about it."

"I will not keep you any longer from your other engagements." Kyrus tried not to stumble over the words. He needed time—time he was not going to have with Celia in his office—to sort through his thoughts.

I do not know how, but Rashan managed to arrange for Abbiley's twin to be set right before me. Whatever scheme he is playing at, it seems he might really have found her.

"Good. Caladris is a bit more jovial than Rashan, but he still dislikes being kept waiting." Celia seemed relieved for the change of topic, and being given leave to depart. She turned for the door.

"You are working for Caladris now?" Kyrus called after her. He had not delved into the matter of the enspelled maidservant, but he now had a better candidate, it seemed, for that particular conversation.

"You were my last assignment for Rashan for the time being. Now that Juliana is safely married off, he does not have to worry that you will ruin the wedding," she said, then grinned impishly back at Kyrus. "So he loaned me out to Caladris as an assistant. It ought to help my career ... assuming I can actually get to my meetings with him on time."

"Fine. Be on your way, then. Just tell the old man to stop by and see me this evening. I do not expect he will object, and as he is Inner Circle, I have no authority as such, but you can tell him it is an order, if it comes to that," Kyrus told her.

Celia was a trifling sorceress, resourceful and clever, but lacking real power. She certainly had not cast the intricate spell he had seen on that maid. Caladris likely knew who had, though, even if he had not done so himself. The high likelihood of the latter gave Kyrus latitude to bully Brannis's uncle a bit.

"I will try *not* to let him think it is an order, if you do not mind. You play a dangerous game provoking him, you know. You might be able to get away with such transgressions now, Sir Dragon-Source, but the rest of us have hides to keep intact." She smiled at him again, flirtatiously he thought this time, and strode off to her meeting with his uncle.

Dangerous game? You have no idea, Abbiley.

* * * * * * *

"This had best be worth my time, Brannis. I had planned to dine with your aunt for the first time this season," Caladris huffed as sat down across from Kyrus.

Kyrus had taken one of the small sitting rooms that were scattered throughout the residential portion of the palace for their meeting. He wanted it to be more cordial than an interrogation from across his desk; there was always the chance that Kyrus's guess about Caladris's guilt was wrong.

"How is Aunt Fia?" Kyrus asked, proud that the name of Brannis's perpetually ailing aunt Fiadora came so readily to mind that he could mention it casually without having to wrack his brain.

"Awful as always, of course. The cough gets worse by the season," Caladris grumbled. Fiadora was his second wife, and if matters kept their course, he would be looking for a third by the next winter. "You did not call me here for that, though. Of all the audacity, I might add! Celia had to tell me that you had 'ordered' me to attend you, as if you had any authority to do so!"

"Then why did you come?" Kyrus asked, pouring a glass of wine for Caladris and another for himself.

Rashan's temperance efforts … ha! Kyrus snickered mentally.

"Curiosity, I must say. A character flaw, I know, but one to which I am nonetheless a slave," Caladris admitted.

Oh, is it to be one of these conversations? Kyrus wondered. *Celia must have noticed that "Brannis" had freed her lady-servant and told him.*

"So out with it, then," Caladris said. "What is so important that you are issuing commands to the Inner Circle?"

"I had business with Celia earlier today, and visited her home to find her. She was not there, and the maid who answered her door seemed to have been under a peculiar charm," Kyrus began. "Celia is not well known for her expertise in … well, anything magical, so far as I can tell. She has a sharp wit but a Source as dull as a horseshoe."

"Oh, look who has grown snobbish now that his own Source can re-light the sun on a moonless night. She is clever and resourceful; that has always been more useful than a strong Source. You yourself showed that well enough getting Rashan's attention," Caladris spoke quickly, as if it were a line of logic that he had practiced before a mirror prior to meeting with Kyrus.

"That is neither germane nor entirely accurate. I became far more useful to Rashan once I unshackled my Source. Celia, though, is just a pawn here; someone else tampered with her servant's mind," Kyrus said, steering them back to the matter at hand.

"Is that really all that you brought me here for, Brannis?" Caladris sounded exasperated. "I had truly hoped that was a pretense for a more interesting conversation. I thought that maybe you were beginning to grasp the subtler side of politics. Alas, the claws of the knighthood are sunk deep in you: 'Do what is right, and you shall never sleep light.' Awful rhyme, childish sentiment."

"So you admit that you were a party to this mind-control magic?" Kyrus asked, surprised to have gotten even a tacit admission so quickly.

"Admit? Admit what?" Caladris asked in return. "That I do my job, do it well, and do not sleep any the worse for it, despite what your knightly comrades would have you believe? I am tempted to leave you to ferment on the subject a while, and be about my evening, but I think I have some duty to see this righted."

"I did not entirely follow that. Are you going to undo the damage you have done to the girl?" Kyrus wondered aloud.

"Damage? Nonsense, the girl is fine, I am sure. This sort of magic is used all over. It is subtle; you cannot see it with all the aether used about the palace unless you know what to look for. Now that you do, pay attention to the chambermaids, porters, rat-catchers, and the like. We cannot find trustworthy, honest, loyal folk for every position needed to run the Empire. The magic keeps them from spreading secrets they were not meant to hear, or bringing violence against their betters."

Kyrus sat mutely for a time, letting all he had just heard process itself in his head. He thought back to something that Denrik Zayne had said to him once. *"... your people suffer for the rule of the powerful houses—noble and sorcerous alike—and I intend to see them free to live as Megrenn do ..."*

"You are beginning to understand," Caladris spoke after a time. "There are measures in place to see that events do not pass beyond our control. It is *we* who are in charge of the Empire: Rashan, myself ... even you, I suppose. The warlock suspects some conspiracy against him, and I feel in my bones that he has the right of it. There are a scant few who are loyal to him; most just serve the Empire, and would turn on him at the first hint of vulnerability. He has never been well liked. He was always too brutal, too ruthless, too focused on twisting emperors to do what *he* wished. Only a few of us stand well and truly behind him. You would do well to count yourself among them. Do not let our methods put into question our rightness or our conviction. If there ever comes a time when we must choose sides over the course of the Empire, remember that House Solaran is on Rashan's side."

"I will remember," Kyrus answered flatly. He was not sure he understood, but he had just seen a glimpse behind the curtain of the puppet show. Colorful cloth characters had turned out to be filthy, drunken old men, playing at civility for an audience.

"Oh, get over it, Brannis! Mind wards are simple and harmless—a mild unpleasantness that keeps the world running. You ought to understand that, being a soldier. By the winds, the world is full of necessary unpleasantness, the sorts of things that you are glad someone else did, but would rather not either do or see: butchering calves, cleaning and dressing battle wounds, the … the … the whole process of childbirth." Caladris found himself rambling, and paused a few breaths to compose himself. "Just content yourself that the proper controls are in place, and keep your eyes wide in the aether as you walk the palace. You will see more now that you know what to look for."

"I will," Kyrus promised. Caladris drained his wineglass and took his leave, allowing Kyrus time to mull his revelations.

The emperor? Kyrus realized after sitting, pondering, for a time he had not tried to count. *Could they be controlling the soon-to-be emperor the same way?* Kyrus was not certain just then that the conspiracy that Maruk Solaran, Gravis Archon, and Stalia Gardarus died for was not being replaced with another just as sinister.

* * * * * * * *

"None may enter," the guard informed Kyrus as he approached the door to the chambers of Sommick Highwater, the man who would be emperor in a few days' time. "Warlock Rashan's orders."

"Those orders were not meant for the likes of me," Kyrus replied. "I would prefer to abide by the niceties, have the wards released for me, and for you two men to stand aside." The guards held halberds crossed ceremonially in front of the door. It was a poor tactical position, intended less for defending the doorway, and more to imply that they were really not letting you in without a fight. A sorcerer was stationed nearby, idling away the hours ogling the chambermaids as he minded the door wards to let food and drink be delivered. "However, I will be going in to see the emperor-in-waiting regardless of how it befalls."

It might have been the polite, casual tone he used that convinced them that he was unconcerned about their ability to block his passage, or the knowledge that Rashan would deal with any fallout from the incident in his own fashion should "Marshal Brannis" have overstepped his authority, but the sorcerer unwarded the door, and the guards stood aside to let him pass. Kyrus gave them all close scrutiny in the aether, shutting out his light vision briefly to better see any aether constructs that might be about their persons. None were afflicted like Celia's maid had been.

"Marshal Brannis, how wonderful!" Sommick greeted him once the door closed behind Kyrus. "I have been shut up in here for far too long with no visitors, but Warlock Rashan said it would not be safe to have visitors, but—"

Giving lie to the statement Sommick seemed about to make, Kyrus suddenly felt a sharp impact against the shielding spell he had kept constantly active since learning it. Reflexively, Kyrus drew more aether and reinforced the shield. Something flickered where the stabbing sensation had originated, and a man appeared, dagger in hand, trying to stab him in the back. He was "dressed" just like the assassin at Iridan and Juliana's wedding, naked but for the elaborate runes painted all across his body, and carrying a runed dagger. Brannis had been the one to see the wedding-day assassin, so Kyrus was mildly surprised to note how strong this one's Source was.

The man cried out wordless surprise, and drew back. A moment's panic passed through his eyes before he turned his attention to the would-be emperor, and made a lunge for him.

The assassin never made it halfway there. A vice-like grip closed about him as Kyrus's silent (and probably spectacularly inefficient) telekinesis spell took hold. Kyrus noted with a detached curiosity that the aether within the man's Source rushed to and fro as he struggled against the spell that held him; he might as well have been encased in stone for all he was able to move.

Kyrus checked to see that Sommick Highwater was unharmed. The successor to the throne was speechless with shock, but in all ways physical, he was whole. Kyrus remembered to look him over for signs of magical tampering, and discovered to his relief that all was well. *For all their other crimes, at least Rashan and Caladris are not planning to mind-control their way to power over the emperor.*

"If you will excuse me, Your Highness—I might as well begin calling you that, I suppose—I think I must deal with this matter presently. I am sorry my visit was so brief," Kyrus excused himself. He left by the door he came in, startling the guards and sorcerer who waited for him outside. They shouted questions after him, and rushed inside to check on the well-being of Sommick Highwater. Kyrus did not answer and continued down the corridors, the assassin towed telekinetically behind him, wrapped in a coverlet from the emperor's bed.

* * * * * * * *

There were just three of the cells left, but Kyrus was well aware of their location within the lowest level of the palace dungeon. Shortly into their journey down, he had realized that his prisoner could not breathe for how tightly he was being held. Kyrus had recast his spell and gripped the man by the limbs alone, allowing his chest room to expand and contract enough to draw breath. The man had not spoken a word.

Kyrus left the blanket for his attempted killer as he dumped him unceremoniously into the middle of one of the sorcerer cells.

"What you do with me?" the man asked, his Kadrin accented by a language Kyrus did not know well enough to identify. The paint obscured his features and made his appearance—such as it might have been in his natural state—difficult to discern. He could have been thirty or forty winters, by his voice, which was gravelly with worldly wear.

"Me? Nothing. This is one of those things that I will be glad for someone else to do, but which I would rather not see," Kyrus informed him. The look on the man's face before the door slammed shut between them was wide eyed with fear.

Good enough for him. Better than he probably deserved after trying to kill me—oh, and kill the emperor, too, I suppose.

* * * * * * * *

"So what are you going to do?" Juliana asked, smiling. "You going to like having a new boss in two worlds?" She sat across a small table from Varnus in an empty room in the Archon Estate.

Varnus scratched his chin, and twisted his face up as he pondered. "I guess this must have been his plan all along, sending me off with Faolen's twin. Makes a certain amount of sense, I suppose. Faolen's all the way out in Megrenn with no way to communicate. Brannis is pretty clever. How come we never thought of it?"

"Don't know that it ever came up. We travel together. Really, this will be our first time truly being apart since I met you," Juliana mused thoughtfully, her gaze wandering upward as if trying to see into her own thoughts.

"'Spose not," Varnus agreed. "Can't say I like the idea of quittin' on your family, though. It's been years and years." Varnus could not quite recall just how many it had even been. He had been a young man when he entered the Archon family's service and he was no longer a young man.

"Well, like it or not, we're getting caught up in politics and warfare. I think my father will understand; palace guard captain is undeniably a promotion, and refusing to let you leave his service would cast us in a bad light with the regent," she reasoned.

"... who is also your father now," Varnus continued on her behalf. He knew she was not fond of the warlock, but there were certainly perks of being his oathdaughter.

"Oathfather, that is. I can be glad I wasn't sired by that madman," Juliana spat. There were times that Varnus got to see a bit of Soria in her, when they were the only two around. She seemed so much happier when there was no expectation of propriety placed on her.

"Oh, he may be ruthless but I doubt he is a madman. Those are just slanders that build up when someone unlikeable has been gone a while," Varnus said, waxing philosophical, at least by soldiers' standards.

"Oh, I think I have reason to believe he just might be," Juliana stated cryptically.

* * * * * * *

By the time Kyrus's day allowed him the peace to return to his room for sleep, he was past exhaustion, and into the realm of activity normally left to the animate dead. The stir the assassin had caused had kept him up well past midnight answering questions from Rashan, Dolvaen, Caladris, and many others whose authority was far surpassed by their persistent curiosity.

The door swung shut behind him as if by its own accord, though Kyrus had gotten used to doing it with magic, and had been the cause that time. He reactivated the wards that granted him privacy, and lit a soft blue glow to see by as he changed into his nightclothes.

Upon doing so, he noticed something on his bed, cast oddly in the surreal bluish light. It was a book. Its cover proclaimed it *The Warlock Prophecies*. Kyrus opened it, and flipped through a few pages to see what it was about. A slip of paper fell out.

You should read this. He wrote it. —SC

The note was written in Acardian. "SC" could only have been "Soria Coinblade." "He" most assuredly meant that Rashan was the warlock mentioned on the cover. Kyrus let the note slip from his grasp and fall toward the floor. It never made it to the stone, however, turning to a puff of ash on the way down. The ashes made their way neatly to the fireplace.

I can stay up a while longer, I suppose.

Chapter 25 - Meanwhile

A light rain wetted the air of Zorren, warm and smelling of the turn of spring. The scent was not quite enough to hide the fragrance of brine wafting off the Aliani Sea. The seagulls—dense, stubborn birds that they were—circled the harbor anyway, looking to pillage the treasures of the fishing boats as they returned with the morning's catch.

"Stuff this," Tod griped, wiping his mouth on the back of his sleeve, and passing the flask over to Jodoul. "How we supposed to get anywhere now?"

Jodoul shrugged in reply, already taking a swig.

"I mean, we all come up here together, you think we'd have … you know … finished up together," Tod continued. He gave his friend a lost, plaintive look.

"Not the first time we got done by someone didn't need us no more," Jodoul replied, licking his lips clean of the Halaigh wine they had been drinking. He upended the flask, and watched for any sign of further liquid to emerge, but the flask was empty.

"I mean, we done our part, right? We got the kid to come see him. We oughtta have gotten looked after a bit better, I think. That's all," Tod continued.

"Deserved better. Yup. Deservin' didn't do us no good, though," Jodoul agreed. "I reckon we gotta figure the rest out on our own."

"Rest of what?" Tod asked, a note of hope sounding in his voice.

"I ain't dead. Neither are you. Rest of livin' through this whole mess, that's all."

"You got some kinda plan?"

"Yeah," Jodoul answered, declining to elaborate.

From their vantage on one of the low rises north of the city, they watched as a transport ship unloaded. Scores of dark-skinned Narrack soldiers filed down the docks and into the city: Megrenn reinforcements.

Tod waited for a time, watching Jodoul for signs that he might volunteer his insights. Jodoul's gaze hung obstinately on the small military procession, ignoring his compatriot's quizzical look.

"What is it?" Tod asked when he could stand waiting no longer.

"You ain't gonna like it," Jodoul told him, still staring off into the distance.

"Anything's gotta be better than moping around waiting for some Megrenn to sniff us out and hang us," Tod countered. "Spit, even walking back home would be better, taking our chances that the army don't see us."

At that, Jodoul turned and glanced sidelong at Tod with a half smile.

"What? What's that look for?" Tod asked.

"We're enlisting."

* * * * * * * *

The shushing hiss of steam drowned out any hope of conversation for the brief moment it lasted. Chains clattered through pulleys in rhythmic jerks as workers hauled something out of the chest-deep bath. The thing that emerged took on a sinister look in the reddish lighting of the foundry as water ran off it in a mass of small waterfalls, revealing a yellowish-brown metallic surface. Zorren was the first city in Megrenn to have a proper goblin foundry.

The bronze cannon barrel that they proceeded to set down on a pair of wooden cradles bore some resemblance to the works of art the goblins had brought to Raynesdark, but only so much as a child's drawing approximates the human form. It was ragged and irregular, with a pitted surface.

"Leave that one to cool. Now next one," K'k'rt directed, his voice stronger than it had been in many winters from having spoken so much Megrenn of late. He still used a megaphone to make himself heard over the din of the workers, but they snapped to obey when they heard him.

The goblin tinker trusted the workers to perform such a simple task without his aid, and walked about the rest of the workshop to see how things progressed. An ox-driven rig of leather belts and wheels was spinning one of the cannon barrels axially while a pair of human workers ground and polished the surface. A similar contraption was set up for reaming the bore, with a human working at the inner surface with a file, and one of K'k'rt's few goblin workers taking measurements, and directing the work. Woodworkers put together carriages, made ramrods, and helped repair and replace the numerous wooden fixtures that were used and battered throughout the workshop. A smaller table in one corner was surrounded by goblin artisans who were casting the small components of the pull-chain sparkers using a crucible the size of a teacup.

"How are today's deliveries?" asked Lieutenant Daimin Kladds, K'k'rt's nemesis, the Megrenn Alliance Army's junior assistant logistics officer. The title "junior" denoted rank rather than age, for Lieutenant Kladds was bald and greying in the moustache. The human was always disrespectful of K'k'rt on his frequent visits, standing close and towering over him. His own workers had been trained to either speak to him from three of their paces away or to go to a knee to talk to him.

"There will be twelve today," K'k'rt promised. He had begun with eight per day as his quota, but as the workers improved, he got more and more out of them. He hoped to be up to fifteen per day within the tenday.

The junior assistant logistics officer harrumphed, but had no grounds for complaint. K'k'rt met his deadlines without fail, and the quality was approaching what his own people had managed with the early prototypes.

"We have a lot of debts to pay off," Kladds remarked, telling K'k'rt nothing he did not already know. "See that they keep coming."

Debts ... Yes, I have a debt to repay as well, K'k'rt thought.
K'k'rt nodded slowly in reply, not looking at Daimin Kladds at all.

* * * * * * * *

It was a cloudless night in Scar Harbor, the stars shining clear as the new moon gave them reign over the heavens for the evening. The lamp-lit streets muted the majesty of the night sky, but the side roads and byways bore no such hindrances. The carriage had been eschewed as well, in favor of a stroll through the brisk Seawatch air. It was a fleeting time of year, for by Greywatch, the nights would be too cold to enjoy at leisure.

"Do you think he will approve of me?" Abbiley asked, a note of doubt in her voice.

Tomas Harwick turned to face the girl whose arm was entwined with his, and smiled, finding her earnest self-consciousness endearing. He patted her arm with his free hand.

"I have had many an argument with my father over the years. I think he finds them to be an exercise of the mind more than a true quarrel. Lord Harwick has a keen mind, and widely acclaimed judgment and wisdom. He would put lie to all that, should he find anything to disapprove of about you," Tomas reassured her. She smiled back at him. "But if he does ... well, we shall have our quarrel at a later date about that, in private."

They continued their walk in companionable silence. Abbiley kept her gaze largely skyward, allowing Tomas to guide them along the roundabout route to his estate. Tomas had initially had doubts about the wisdom of allowing himself to become enamored of a tradesman's orphan. It was a trap for the heart, surely, for when the families became involved, and practical matters came into play, things were bound for ruin. He had been pleasantly astonished upon discovering that his father had no objection.

Tomas's home was modest by the standards of Acardian nobility. Tomas lived alone, except for his servants and the occasional guest. The two-story manor house of granite walls and slate-tile roof suited his needs. The gate was open when they arrived; the carriage they had ridden to dinner had preceded them back to the estate by nearly an hour.

Lord Harwick was awaiting them in the back drawing room when they arrived. His lordship had been passing the time in contemplation, smoking a pipe, and drinking some of Tomas's best brandy as he looked out into the darkness of the gardens. There was no mistaking that the two men were related. Though stouter of build, and with greying hair too short to tell if it would fall into curls like his son's did, the facial features were strikingly similar.

"Tomas," the elder Harwick bellowed upon noting their arrival. He extracted himself ponderously from the high-backed chair in which he sat. "Your letters do not do your lady justice, it seems. I am Lord Dunston Harwick."

"I am honored to meet you, your lordship. My name is Abbiley Tillman," Abbiley replied, curtseying with unpracticed grace. Tomas had schooled her on what to expect, but she had never dealt with nobility before meeting him.

"Indeed, you could be none other." Lord Harwick took her hand and kissed it. "Might I offer you a drink?"

Abbiley looked askance of Tomas, who gave a tiny nod of encouragement, smiling the whole time.

"Of course, your lordship," she said.

"Tomas, if you would be so good as to pour," Lord Harwick said, looking to his son. The younger Harwick went to the liquor cabinet, and retrieved an excellent vintage, pouring glasses for all three of them.

They chatted for a long while, plodding through the necessary banalities of making formal acquaintance. Tomas heard nothing from either of them that he had not already known, and his mind wandered. He knew his father's presence was only partly social. Abbiley's involvement in the witch scandal had been far more prominent in his father's letters than any concerns about her station or character. Thus it was no surprise when—

"Tomas, if you would be so good as to allow us a time in private. I am afraid that my duties to the king must intrude upon our social gathering. That whole nonsense about a witch, and the events that followed it were botched so badly that the records have been expunged, and I have taken it upon myself to set the official accounting in order," Lord Harwick said.

"Father, is this really the best time to have at this bone of yours? Gnaw on it come mid-morrow, if you must," Tomas replied.

"It's all right, Tomas. I have answered questions about those events enough times now to no longer take offense. I have nothing to hide," Abbiley said, putting a hand on Tomas's knee.

"Indeed, there is no aspersion at all directed toward Miss Tillman. Her involvement, however, is a matter of some speculation after the obvious incompetence of the previous magistrate was brought to light. It is an unfortunate matter, and I believe one that will get no more pleasant with aging."

Tomas knew that his objection had been noted and overruled. He could do no more. Despite being in his own home, he was very much subject to his father's jurisdiction. Tomas graciously bowed and took his leave, adjourning to his study.

Attempting to lose himself in literature proved not so effective a pastime. Tomas found himself checking his pocket watch, an heirloom from his grandfather. While of excellent repute in its day, the old Sterle & Forthwright piece lost minutes an hour. His inquiries to the Errol workshop to refit it with workings of their own make had been met with polite refusal—the master insisted his logo be prominent on any piece of his. Thus Tomas kept uncertain track of how long his belle had been under questioning.

While tempted to eavesdrop, it was below his station as a gentleman. Nearing distraction at having re-read the same two pages of *The Honor of Arghus* a dozen times without absorbing a word, he was finally granted a reprieve from his isolation.

When he escorted Abbiley to the carriage that would deliver her safely home, she seemed nearly asleep on her feet. Her eyes were glassy and focused poorly. She leaned against Tomas for support as he walked her out to the front gate, muttering sweet words of appreciation for the aid.

After the carriage departed his view, Tomas turned and stormed as politely as possible back into the house to find his father.

"What manner of treatment is that for a young lady?" Tomas demanded, finding Lord Harwick back in the same chair as when he and Abbiley had first arrived. "You would not have treated a highborn girl in such a way."

"Tomas, sit," Lord Dunston Harwick instructed, his voice flat, calm, even. "I am a progressive man, champion of the lower classes, overseer of His Majesty's reform movement. It is not often I am accused of bias against the lowborn, and tonight will be no exception."

"Well, you certainly—"

"I was not finished," Lord Harwick snapped, forestalling Tomas's fountain of spewed indignities before it even had a chance to begin. "While the girl seems pleasant enough, comely, and with a working mind between her ears, there will still be troubles if you pursue her seriously. I am of a mind to help considerably with cobbling over those difficulties, should you indulge me in a not-inconsiderable favor."

"What sort of favor?" Tomas asked in a huff, trying not to give ground against his father.

"There are things you do not understand. There are matters of witchcraft that ought not come to light, which, due to several recent and a few upcoming events, will require discretion. You are in line to learn of these matters, and your discretion is crucial."

"What are you trying to tell me, Father?"

"Tell you? I will do more than just tell you."

* * * * * * * *

The sounds of slippered feet on carpet and the wheezing breath of ancient lungs were periodically interrupted by a hollow clatter of steel. Though nearly blind, Axterion could hear well enough, and the echoes were leading him back to their point of origin. When he found his youngest grandson, Danilaesis was in Brannis's room, sparring with the Kadrin Imperial Grand Marshal's old, disused suit of plate. The steel armor hung in midair, wobbling from the latest blow of Danil's broom-handle sword.

"Cease that cacophony at once!" Axterion ordered, bringing the two masses of wrinkles that passed for hands up to cover his ears as Danil slammed the wooden dowel hard into the chest of his imaginary opponent.

Danil turned, looking at Axterion with wide-eyed innocence, as if nothing at all was amiss.

"Hello, Grandpa," Danil said, lowering his sword. "I have to practice if I am going to be a warlock someday."

"Is that so?" Axterion replied, his tone suggesting that the question was rhetorical. "Well, I seem to recall that warlocks need to know their arithmetic, and certainly their penmanship. It took me and three of the servants to get your tutor out of the storage closet."

"I am going to the Academy this autumn. I can learn all that stuff there, from sorcerers who are smarter than Challeigh," Danil said. "They won't teach me to sword-fight there, though, so I have to learn that on my own."

"Challeigh is a fine young man and smart as they come. We spare no expense in educating you, I trust you know."

"Not smart enough to get himself out of a closet," Danil muttered.

"Just because you can lock the door with a ward, and he cannot break it does not mean you are smarter than him," Axterion said. "He is a scholar, not a sorcerer. Now set all that rubbish aside, and we can get you back to your lessons."

Danil stared at his grandfather but did not move to obey. What might have begun as a look of defiance slid slowly into a sly grin.

"Make me."

"Hmm, what was that?" Axterion asked. "I may have misheard you just now."

"Challeigh isn't a sorcerer, Grandpa, but you are. Beat me in a draw, and I'll go back to my lessons."

"It appears that I did indeed mishear you," Axterion began, a note of menace creeping into his voice. "Because I thought I just heard you challenge the former High Sorcerer of the Imperial Circle to a draw. That cannot be true, of course, seeing as how you are a young, unblooded pup who has yet to even practice in draws against his peers, while I was once the strongest sorcerer in the Empire. It also cannot be true, because I am a feeble old man, using what I have left of my Source to hold onto the last few hours of life I have left in this creaky, old corpse I walk around in; it would not be sporting. One might question the valor of a warlock went around challenging greybeards in their twilight. But of course, I am certain I misheard you. Correct?"

Danilaesis nodded vigorously but said nothing.

Axterion took the boy by the hand. With a quick, masterful tug—about all the magic he could manage—he unraveled Danil's clumsy levitation construct. Brannis's armor clattered to the floor with a sound like a kitchen accident.

"Besides," Axterion said, "there is no one about to judge a draw at the moment. And let me assure you, I am just about enough of a competitive, stubborn, spiteful old bastard to accept. I would teach you a hard lesson about humility, and it would cost you a grandfather. Now ... let us get you back to your lessons, if Challeigh is in any fit state to teach for the remainder of the day."

"Can I practice more after lessons, at least?" Danil asked, sounding hopeful.

"I suppose. I do not know why you are so set on becoming a warlock, though. Your uncle Rashan is rather an exception. Few of them lived long enough to become old and feeble like me. Take my advice: aim to become High

Sorcerer one day, not Warlock. You get to work indoors, and the only people trying to kill you are friends and colleagues."

Danil nodded respectfully but made no comment.

* * * * * * * *

"The work is much the same, I suppose, but in all other respects, I can scarcely imagine a greater adventure," Davin Chartler replied between sips of wine.

"As it should be. As it should be," agreed his dinner companion, Oriedel Conniton. The elderly former scribe to King Gorden was naught but skin and bones. His body's only task left seemed to be the carrying about of fourscore years' wisdom locked up in a hairless, age-blotched head. "I must say I have missed it terribly. Once he warms to you a bit, you will find no better companion than His Majesty, you know."

"Indeed, I could only imagine," Davin replied. Expert Conniton had known the king since they were both much younger men. If such a bond were even possible between Davin and His Majesty, it would be years in the formation.

The elderly scribe chuckled. It sounded like a wheeze. The older man looked all about the small dining room in the servants' wing of the palace, taking in everything, and clearly lost in reminiscence.

"This was my home a long time, but I believe you cannot truly appreciate something until you lose it or discover you are about to," Expert Conniton observed. Sensing that Conniton was about to embark on a soliloquy, Davin did not step in to fill the gap in the conversation as Conniton paused. "I had the ear of a king, and I think I had no small part in His Majesty's reforms. King Gorden is a man of reason, and you can appeal to a man of reason with logic and sense. I see a fair bit of that in you, Davin, mind you, so do not withhold it from His Majesty. I had my little plans and intrigues on the side, of course, just like everyone at court, though my aims were at once both more humble and more noble. Disenfranchise the nobility, focus on the greater good above personal gain, let the smart folk run things. That was my advice."

"Sound advice, indeed," Davin murmured, drawing an approving nod from Expert Conniton.

"Yes, but I have one regret. One last task that I feel I need to pass along to you."

"What is that?" Davin asked.

"Your former apprentice …"

"Kyrus?"

"Yes, Kyrus Hinterdale," Expert Conniton said.

"What a mess that was." Davin shook his head. "I do not even know what to make of it all. Kyrus, accused of witchcraft, murdering guards and escaping a jail cell in Scar Harbor. They even think he was consorting with Denrik Zayne. It seems farfetched but everyone believed it at the time."

"Well, I had hoped to meet your Kyrus before that chaos swept him off to who knows where. If he were to return to Acardia, though, I suspect he would seek you out," Expert Conniton said, looking hard at Davin as he did so.

"I would hope the boy would have more sense than that, but I admit the possibility," Davin said, trying not to sound too hopeful. He missed Kyrus terribly, especially knowing that he had fled Acardia as a fugitive, and that his return was implausible.

"Well, as I said, I had hoped to meet him personally, and I still do. If he comes to you, have him seek me out. However, I know that I have not much time left. I find my health failing faster than I had accounted for in my planning," Expert Conniton said, snorting in self-derision. "If the day comes when Kyrus returns, and I have expired, have him seek out Lord Dunston Harwick in my stead."

"Lord Harwick?" Davin asked, perplexed. "The magistrate?"

"That is the one. We are ... kindred spirits, you might say. He will want to see Kyrus, I am sure."

"What make Kyrus so important to you ... if you do not mind my asking, of course?" Davin hastily amended, remembering to whom he spoke.

"I had certain suspicions about him after reading a book he copied. I have shared my suspicions with Lord Harwick, and he will look into them on my behalf if I am unable."

"What sort of suspicions?"

Expert Conniton paused for a moment, pursing his lips, before answering. "I suspect we might be ... distantly related. I suppose that would be my suspicion."

* * * * * * * *

On a moonless night in a secluded vale, a slim, fey figure knelt in the mud, heedless of the white gown she wore. Tiny hands pressed lightly into the muck to support her as she hung her face over a puddle. Light radiating from that puddle cast her features in harsh relief against the dark of night, colors dancing in patterns too muted by reflection to make any attempt at ascribing meaning to them.

With but a thought—half a thought even—she could have held herself aloft and clear of nature's grime, but the scenes she witnessed playing out before her held her rapt. She had not the thought to spare.

A splash in the water shocked her from her reverie. The image in the puddle wobbled and warped as the echoing ripples of a rock's passing spread. She glanced about, startled, unused to being approached unawares.

"Viyax!" Illiardra scolded when she noted the bronze-skinned intruder upon her privacy. "Why did you do that?"

"It seems you are becoming too attached to something you know will not last. You said yourself you expect him to fail," Viyax said.

"I may have, but I keep seeing signs of hope," Illiardra countered.

"Hope for which of them?" Viyax asked, smiling like a cat who had just trapped a mouse in a corner. "I thought you had given up on Rashan."

"Both. It is the same hope: redemption."

Viyax peered over her and into the vision in the puddle, a look of detached interest on his face. Illiardra watched him watch. A sudden look of disgust curled Viyax's features, and he cringed. Illiardra's eyes snapped wide as she spun about on her knees, and looked to see what had befallen.

"No!" she screamed when she saw.

She slammed a small fist into the puddle, splashing both of them with crystal-clear water as her hand hit the muddy bottom. The spell ended, and the water became just water again. Leaping to her feet, the mud on her hands, knees, and dress sloughing off to leave every bit of her pristine, she ran off into the night, sobbing.

Viyax watched her depart. He stood for a while staring at the ruin of the scrying puddle. After a time, he shook his head slowly, shrugged, and walked off in a different direction.

Chapter 26 - Pieces of the Past

It was an unusual book, and Kyrus was an expert on books. The script within it was sloppy, harsh, and if Kyrus could attribute emotion to lifeless ink on paper, it was angry. Flecks of ink were scattered here and there; Kyrus would have discarded and rewritten them had it been his own work. There were smudges as well. It contained empty pages in plenty; nearly the last half of the tome was blank. The book must have been created blank, and been written in as a bound volume. Kyrus assumed it had been written as a journal rather than compiled from notes.

Kyrus leafed through the pages, hardly stopping to make out words. He watched for changes in the character of the writing. At times, it grew slack, flowery, and lazy. Other pages were barely legible, looking as if they had been scratched out in great haste or with great anger, leaving scores where quill had gouged into paper. Likely there were ways to tell the age of ink or paper, but Kyrus did not know them, neither magical nor scientific. He suspected years might have passed between individual entries, though it was mere speculation on his part.

Kyrus sat with a readied quill, ink, and a stack of paper beside him when he began to read. He intended to copy the contents before finding a way to return the original to Rashan's possession.

The large majority of the passages were gibberish, or at least they were as he began. As he got farther along, he began to take note of themes, repeated imagery, and allusions to historical events that Brannis had learned of as a boy. It might take many readings, Kyrus knew, before he could understand the contents.

Kyrus read one of the more lucid passages:

Lion cub, copper crown
Grows but never grows father's claws
Purrs his orders, his pack grows wheat and worships scarecrows
His only hunter kills his cubs
His only hunter steals his cub
His only hunter waits and feasts on carrion

Another read:

Fallow field, fertile mind

Potato planted but grows into grape
The vintage will only tell with time
We sip the vintner's craft whether we choke or revel in it
A drunkard captains the ship we all sail on but does not steer it

These two passages Kyrus made a note of in his own copy, suggesting a link between them and the historical events they foretold. If he could find similar links elsewhere in the prophecies, he might be able to construct a rough chronology of the entries.

Kyrus could make no sense of any entry for a long while. They seemed to rage, making vague threats against uncertain foes. It was disturbing to read, knowing that it was Rashan who had written it all. The worst he found among them read:

Breathing blood
Thinking fire
Eating hope
Deaf to mercy
Blind to fear
Cities become tombs
The grateful chain held by no hand

Kyrus was tempted to give in to the lure of sleep, but he felt the need to see the task of copying the book through in a single night. Even if he did not understand everything he read—or even much of it—he needed to see it all.

Time started swimming in Kyrus's head. The drawn curtains of his window showed no fringe of light about them to suggest that sunlight dwelt outside, but that was the only clue he had as to how long he had read. His eyes burned with fatigue, making it hard to bring the scratchy text into focus. Kyrus noted that there seemed to be more consistency between passages later in the book, at least insomuch as it looked like it was written in a similar hand. He decided that the entries were being written with less time between them.

Kyrus noticed another trend as well. There seemed to be more specifics mentioned. He could not identify everything, but he strongly suspected a correlation to actual events that took place.

"If these are actual events, then what place would they have in prophecies?" Kyrus wondered aloud, a clear sign that he was overtired. "Who predicts events that have already taken place?"

Kyrus closed his eyes, and rubbed his temples, trying to think. He needed to find historical references to compare the prophetic texts to. If he could begin matching entries to Kadrin history, he might discover the reason. Tired as he was, he could not make the link solely within his own head.

He made note of three more entries:

Death fights the act of death
How many times must Death be killed
One more
One more
Never
To stop the rebirth of Death
First defeat death
Then Death

Followed by:

Broken vase spills blue-white blood
The missing pieces are keys that lock the final door
Patch the wholes that are only halves

And lastly:

One vase, filling fast, spilling faster
To see another, no mirror may reflect it
Where to find its shadow, an absence not a copy
Seek a way among the spirits

Piecing together the three of those seemed to be the key. They were not consecutive in the text but seemed related. He would need fresh eyes—and a fresh mind—to make any further progress. Kyrus set the book cover-down on his desk, with the spine facing the wall, then set two others atop it. His loose-sheet copy he rolled, and put into a case that had contained a report from Pevett.

He fell asleep in his clothes, atop the blankets.

* * * * * * * *

Rakashi found Soria breaking her fast on a meal of bacon and eggs in the common room. They had stayed overnight at an inn whose Takalish name translated to "Quiet Sea." The rocky outcroppings north of the port city of Daisha shielded the small, expensive establishment from the noise of the busy port. Soria and her companions had grown accustomed to the finest accommodations, and spared little expense in their choice of lodgings.

"Just you this morning?" Rakashi asked, pulling up a chair next to her.

"Brannis sleeps like a bear. Our ship won't leave until noontime, so I left him in our room. Figured it was easier than trying to wake him," Soria said, not bothering to wait between bites. She ate like a warrior, not a lady, Rakashi noted, not for the first time. She shoveled her food in until her cheeks bulged, washing it down with ale even in the morning hours. He wondered how much of her behavior was rebellion against the strictures of Kadrin life, and how much was just how she preferred to live. It was the hatred of those strictures that he needed.

"Has having him here, in Tellurak, made life in Kadrin easier?" Rakashi asked. "I remember how upset you were when you told me of your betrothal. Before your wedding day, you were worse. You seem happier now but what of Juliana?"

"Philosophical this morning?" Soria asked, casting a sidelong glance at Rakashi. "I am fine. I have Kyrus there now too, don't forget. Iridan didn't even stay long after the wedding. We had a fight." Soria stuffed another forkful of eggs into her mouth, forestalling any elaboration.

"What did you argue over?" Rakashi asked. "Was it something to do with Brannis?"

"You're starting to sounds like the House Archon lady-servants, you know. And I never said we argued. I made some jest about his manhood, and he took a swing at me, caught me off guard," Soria said, not looking in Rakashi's direction.

"How cowardly ..." Rakashi said, developing a stronger dislike for Iridan than he had known before. He preferred it, suspecting that he would face him soon in Munne as Tiiba. Just from talking with Soria, he knew that Rashan was still in Kadris, not making trouble in the newly conquered city. "You tell me much; why had I not heard of this? I would have offered solace, you know this."

"Spare me the maiden rescue, Rakashi," Soria replied. "You know my temper. I stopped myself just short of killing him with my bare hands."

"Juliana bested the new warlock?" Rakashi asked, a bemused grin spreading across his face, white teeth shining out from his dark features.

"Hey now! I might have bruised some knuckles and twisted a wrist, but I can fight," Soria said, vexing Rakashi with her persistent use of the first person for both herself and Juliana. She was the only twinborn he had known to suffer that particular foible. "For my coin, Kadrin still only has one warlock. Iridan panics when he's caught off guard ... aether-burned himself trying to raise a shield spell."

"Have you heard from him since he left?" Rakashi shifted the conversation slightly.

"Naw ..." Soria turned and gave Rakashi a long look. "I get it. He's not twinborn, so you're trying to sneak around our little pact, right? I might tell you about my marriage problems like you were the girl who helps me into festival-day dresses, but I'm not going to sell out my husband or Kadrin that easily." She winked, making it appear a jest. Rakashi shrugged with a little smile, because after all, he could not deny the charge.

"Is there really so much difference between Iridan and his father?" Rakashi asked, hoping Soria might find the question less invasive.

Soria bit into a strip of bacon, leaving only a morsel the size of her thumbnail. She held it out for Rakashi's inspection.

"The difference between this and a whole pig," she told him.

"What of Kyrus?" Rakashi asked. "He is one of us, and yours in particular. I am merely quite curious."

"Even in jest, I would stay well clear of Kyrus. I don't think Brannis trusts you yet, but he has enough self-control not to act rashly. Kyrus isn't like Iridan. When he panics, I wouldn't want to be anywhere near him; you saw Marker's Point. Even with the bit of magic he knows, I think Rashan's nervous around him."

Rakashi took her advice to heart. While Iridan was his problem in Munne, he would do all within his power to steer clear of the Acardian twinborn.

* * * * * * * *

Rakashi sought his own morning meal after that exchange, leaving Soria alone for a moment. She suspected that his interest in Iridan was something of a practical matter. If the reports of Iridan terrorizing Munne were accurate, it would not surprise her to hear that Rakashi's counterpart had been sent to deal with him. She was not certain how she felt about that. For all her claims that Iridan was no warlock, he was certainly powerful in his own way. She would be furious with him should anything happen to Rakashi, whom she loved like a brother.

The thought sobered her when she put it in those terms. Their years of conflict—much of it instigated by her—had never resulted in her hating Iridan, but despite the trappings of marriage, neither did she love him. He was always Brannis's little puppy, following Brannis around even when he was not wanted. He had been an annoyance but a familiar one. Yes, that was it: "familiar"—that was how she felt about Iridan.

The part about Kyrus worried her more. There had been two books she had thought to leave him. The book of prophecies was a warning; things went on inside the head of her oathfather that Kyrus might puzzle out better than she, and none of it seemed reassuring. The second book she had found in her room after receiving the first. She could only assume it was left by her fey oathmother as well. The title had read *The Peace of Tallax*. She knew the name, associated with ancient legends, but nothing of the story behind it. Having read the whole of it—more than she normally read in a season—she could not decide whether to share it with Kyrus as well.

Chapter 27 - Lone Warlock

Iridan navigated the back streets of Munne by aether-sight. The spring rains had let up sometime after midnight, leaving every surface wet, and a light fog hanging amid the stone buildings, but the skies had not cleared. There was scant light to avoid tripping by, and he was not foolish enough to create any for himself.

He was playing a game of hide-from-his-lordship with Megrenn's occupation forces, but during the nighttime hours, he was not the one who hid. Three nights running, he had hunted them, leaving corpses and fire-gutted buildings in his wake. It might take him half a season to cleanse the city of enemy troops, but he was determined to see it through.

He peered around an ivy-covered wall, using its scraggly Source to help conceal his own. There was a patrol on foot, a dozen infantry with one especially strong Source among them, which seemed like as not to be a sorcerer.

"It seems they are looking for me," Iridan muttered aloud, a habit that was growing the longer he spent alone. Folk who were intent on his demise made for poor conversation, and he could not abide the prolonged silences when he was alone. "Whether they mean to confront me or avoid me, it seems they have not noticed me." The newly regrown teeth felt strange in his mouth, but at least he could speak normally again.

Iridan began drawing aether very slowly. It was a simple trick, drawing just enough to offset the aether a Source gave off. It was not enough to appear invisible in the aether, but it made it much easier to hide a strong Source among weaker ones. For his sword, there was not much he could do, save hope that his adversaries were less vigilant; Dragon's Whisper showed up clearly in the aether, and he had not the talent in illusion to hide that.

The patrol was heading away from him, so Iridan slipped from behind his cover, blade drawn and held in one hand. His boots scraped on the cobbled roads, and made tiny, wet, sucking splashes where he stepped in the ubiquitous shallow puddles. The soldiers in the patrol were conversing among themselves, however, and were wearing metal armor. The noise Iridan made was drowned out. Iridan quickened his step, knowing it was only a matter of time before—

There was a shout, something in Megrenn that Iridan understood by context, and not by vocabulary. The soldiers turned, swords drawn. Iridan could only tell the latter by their stance, using aether-vision as he was. The patrol, rather than taking up a defensive stance or launching an attack, rushed sidelong, spreading out to either side as if to contain Iridan's escape.

"As if I planned to run," Iridan said, muttering to himself as he launched a spread of fiery darts at the Megrenn soldiers.

"Fire and steel, those are what you kill with. All else is vanity," Rashan had instructed him. "Strike to wound, to maim. Obliterating foes wastes aether. Conserve for your defenses." The lessons had been sinking in now that he had worn himself down over the course of his nightly raids, body and Source alike.

Many of the darts struck home. A few hit metal armor to little effect, but most caught cloak, hair, or skin. Men screamed, dropping to the wet ground for relief from the fires.

A pair of Iridan's magical projectiles had struck a shielding spell that had not been active when the attack was launched. The sorcerer among the Megrenn patrol had quick reflexes with his magic. Less concerned about the common soldiers, Iridan was about to launch a more focused attack on the sorcerer when he saw a blade spring to life in the aether.

Iridan switched his vision back to the light, seeing through the gap in the fog that his use of fire magic had created. It was still dark, but there was enough light from the burning men to get a view of his opponent. The man wore blue and gold. By his dark skin, he was Safschan. The blade that had drawn Iridan's attention enough to warrant a look in the light was a rune-blade—which meant his opponent was a blade-priest.

The blade-priest called out to Iridan. There were several foreign words, which Iridan's education failed to identify as either Megrenn or Safschan, but the last was a name: "Rashan." Iridan cocked his head to the side, confused. The blade-priest must have realized Iridan had not understood him, for he tried again in thickly accented Kadrin.

"I am honored by fighting you, Warlock Rashan," the blade-priest said, repeating his greeting.

Iridan shook his head. The blade-priest stiffened, straightening from the ready stance he had eased into after making his challenge. It seemed that Iridan had offended him. Some small, strange, misguided part of Iridan's mind could not allow him to cross blades with the misunderstanding hanging between them.

"I am Warlock Iridan Solaran. Rashan is my father," Iridan said by way of clarification.

The blade-priest's expression turned sour. "Then I will kill you instead, unworthy spawn of evil. I am Souka, and I will wash my blade in your blood," the blade-priest said, readying himself once more.

The soldiers who had survived Iridan's initial attack made no move to intervene. They had been bait for a trap, but had not caught the quarry they thought they were after.

With no further preamble, the blade-priest Souka charged Iridan. Souka held his rune-blade with a greatsword grip, both hands at the end of the elongated handle spaced just a bit apart. Iridan watched his opponent change from a fire-shadowed form obscured by fog to a distinctive blue-white Source wielding a blade that shone brightly as he switched back to the aether to ready himself for combat.

There was a temptation to unleash an aether blast, and see if he could end the fight at once, but Iridan reined in the thought. Tightening his grip on Dragon's Whisper, he strengthened his shielding spell, and prepared to meet the charge head-on. Souka's blade hit like thunder against Iridan's parry, sending a jolt through Iridan's arms. In the aether, he saw that the Safschan had put a bit of aether through his muscles just before the blades collided. If not for the magically enhanced speed behind his own sword, Iridan never would have generated enough power to stop the stronger fighter's initial attack.

There was no respite for Iridan to digest this information, and formulate a strategy. Souka's second slash followed close behind, forcing Iridan to retreat a step as he parried a somewhat less forceful blow, and deflected it wide. The blade-priest slid one hand up the hilt of his sword as he stepped in to follow Iridan's retreat, reversing the momentum of his weapon faster than Iridan had anticipated. Iridan felt the impact as his shield took a brutal strike that would have bisected his chest had he been wearing armor of steel instead of pure aether.

Thoughts of feeling out his opponent, and husbanding his aether flew from his mind like leaves before a gale. Instinct took over, and Iridan's aether bolt lifted the blade-priest from his feet, and deposited him supine on the cobblestones some dozen paces distant. Iridan took a moment to catch his breath, and renew his shielding spell as he walked over to where Souka had fallen. Iridan had seen the blade-priest's shielding spell fail when he hit the ground after it had done all it could just stopping Iridan's spell from killing him instantly.

With admirable willpower, the wounded Souka drew himself to his feet, using his blade as a crutch, before Iridan arrived. He still held the sword in a ready grip, but Iridan could see that he was merely preparing to give a last accounting of himself before he was defeated.

"You will die with a clean blade, my friend," Iridan told him, stopping just outside his reach.

The blade-priest was probably glaring lightning at him, but it was a hard thing to discern just by aether. He watched as Souka gathered a bit of aether using a draw that would not have gotten him past most of the fifteen-summer students on Ranking Day at the Imperial Academy. There was no reappearance of a shielding spell around him, though; the aether flowed to arms and legs.

Having seen the blade-priest's preparation so clearly in the aether, Iridan was not surprised when Souka leapt at him, taking one last desperate shot at killing him. Iridan suspected his shielding spell could turn the blow aside even if he missed the parry entirely, but he had crossed blades once already, and lost to the superior swordsman. Iridan's second aether bolt caught Souka mid leap, and hurled him against the stone wall of a nearby tavern with a crunch that had a note of finality to it.

The soldiers who had been watching the encounter saw that it was ended, and turned to flee. Iridan sent darts of flame after them, killing all but a pair, whom he did not bother pursuing. Instead he stalked over to examine the body of his adversary. Close examination was not needed to know the man was dead, but Iridan felt better having a look in the light to make certain.

Blood smeared the tavern wall, a place called The Happy Hog by its sign, though it had seen happier times to be sure. The body of Souka lay crumpled in the small herb garden that was adjacent to the tavern, surrounded by a shin-high brick retaining wall. The rune-blade lay just at the base of the wall, in the road, as blood from its former owner ran down the overflowing garden wall to soil it.

"I suppose it does not count if it is your blood, does it?" Iridan asked the corpse.

He regarded Souka's weapon for a moment, noting the exquisite workmanship, the detailed etching of runes and decorative scrollwork, the gems inlaid in the small cross-guard and pommel. The half-blade, half-handle weapon was versatile in the hands of a master, but it took many summers to gain proficiency. Even if Iridan had no better weapon—and he felt that he did—he knew no one who would be of any use with it.

Dragon's Whisper came down in a whistling blur, smashing against the rune-blade and into the cobblestones beneath it. The blade did not shatter, but it was bent beyond use, ruined.

Iridan slipped back to aether-vision, and scanned the area for signs of nearby foes, then set off, no particular destination in mind.

* * * * * * *

With the rush of adrenaline from the battle worn off, Iridan noticed that the blade-priest's blow had told. It hurt to take a deep breath, likely due to a cracked rib. It was yet another in a long series of minor hurts he had suffered, worse than the ache of an overused Source or a turned ankle, but not as bad as Juliana knocking his teeth out. The latter still rankled him.

"Some warlock I am, not even master over my own bed," Iridan said to himself. He was getting stronger, he knew. His instincts were being retrained to fight rather than flee or cower. There was no Brannis to save him, as there had been most of his life.

He ran his tongue over his new teeth, feeling the odd contours and unfamiliar shape of them in his mouth. He had grown them in too quickly, not taking the time to do a proper job of it. When he was done freeing Munne, barring another pressing task, he would see to reshaping them a bit until they felt right. It was an unmanly hobby, reshaping the body for aesthetic reasons, but he could find plenty of sorceresses who could advise him on it. Brannis's sister Aloisha—his cousin or niece or something, he supposed—was part of the Inner Circle, and could likely be trusted for some discretion on the matter. Her beauty was rather unlikely to all be natural. The thought of asking Juliana was out of the question twofold. Not only was she responsible for the ill-fitting teeth in the first place, but she seemed not to practice such magic herself. Surely that color hair was her own doing, but her mother had probably straightened her teeth as a girl, and she was sorely lacking in womanly curves. Iridan did not know if he had the courage to suggest she do something about the latter, else he might be starting over on another new set of teeth.

Wandering the foggy streets of Munne as he mused, he was startled from his reflections by the gathering of Sources in the area. He had been learning to ignore the unmoving, horizontal forms of the sleeping citizenry that he could make out within the buildings he passed, but the ones he noted now were approaching. They were spread out over a wide area, closing some sort of search pattern, not quite converging on his location, but aware that he had to be somewhere within.

"I should have chased down the survivors," Iridan said, cursing himself for laziness.

While he had planned to continue his killings, he greatly preferred striking from ambush. Not only was it safer, but it was much more efficient at eliminating large numbers of Megrenn troops quickly. He scanned about for stronger Sources among the searchers to see if they had any sorcerers or blade-priests among them. He also looked for large Sources that would indicate they had gone back to trying stripe-cats against him. He suspected not, since he had hardly seen any since his first night of raiding. The beasts were outrageously expensive to be thrown at Iridan to their near-certain demise—and by the winds did those things have a lot of blood in them!

There were indeed strong Sources to be found among those intent on surrounding him, three in fact. A fourth was borderline, either just an unusually aether-strong soldier or a weakling sorcerer. Iridan picked one of the strong ones at random, and quickened his pace, heading straight for it. It would be best for him to engage them before there was a chance for the strong ones to join forces against him.

A cry went up as Iridan's hellfire spell crashed into his chosen target and everything within a dozen paces of it. Those not consumed by flames shouted things Iridan could not understand. After a moment's confusion, he could see that the rest of the searchers had begun closing on his location. A scattering of dead Sources remained where his spell had hit, save for one that shone with the light of a shielding spell, and appeared to be stumbling around, either dazed or choking on the smoke from the corpses and two buildings that had been engulfed in the conflagration.

Iridan ran to close the distance before the sorcerer could recover, wincing at the pain in his ribs as his lungs expanded. The fires had burned away the fog in an instant, so Iridan was crossing open ground as he neared his opponent. Arrows stung against his shield as Megrenn archers among the patrols could now see him. Single arrows were little danger to him, but in the aggregate, they became a threat, wearing away at his shield, and requiring him to draw more aether to strengthen it.

The sorcerer straightened at Iridan's approach, and he could hear him choking on the first words to a spell. Dragon's Whisper put an end to that, though, carving the man in half neatly—at least as seen in the aether. Iridan ignored the spray of warm blood as he turned to seek out the archers who had harried his charge. Head-sized balls of flame shot from his hand in the direction of each he discovered. They were larger than the flaming darts he had used earlier, but he wanted to make sure that the bows were consumed in flame as well.

With immediate threats destroyed, and more on the way, Iridan paused a moment to catch his breath, and discovered his folly. The smoke from the many fires his magic had started was invisible in the aether, but he could feel the stinging in his eyes. When he tried to fill his lungs with air, he breathed it in. *Stupid,* he thought, unable to draw breath enough to berate himself aloud. *I heard that Megrenn coughing in it.* Dropping to the ground, and crawling away from the fires, his hacking, gasping coughs wracked his injured ribs with agony.

The onslaught began as the outlying members of the Megrenn search team arrived in numbers. Seeing Iridan stricken and debilitated, they tried to finish him much as he had done with the sorcerer. From his hands and knees, Iridan swatted ineffectually with Dragon's Whisper as he was set upon by swordsmen, whose blows wore at his shielding spell anew.

Iridan wished that it was Heavens Cry he carried instead of the gift from Brannis. He liked the idea of just purging the city with the greenish, acidic fumes of Rashan's weapon. It would be like smoking out a hive of vermin, purging the city of Megrenn and Kadrin alike, but allowing it to begin anew, fresh and clean of infestation.

Instead Iridan fought to his feet as he cleared his lungs. Dragon's Whisper took little effort to wield, and against such foes as he faced, he required only a fraction of his attention as he worried more about his breathing. It batted aside their parrying blades as it snapped through the air like a serpent's strike. The impacts against his shield grew infrequent as he finished off one opponent after another, until he was breathing heavily again, suffering the stabbing pain in his ribs as the price that had to be paid for the victory.

He had not had the presence of mind to keep lookout for the other two Sources he had identified initially. When he found all foes within arm's reach dead around him, he noticed them again at last, bracketing the length of road he was standing on. There were only ten paces or so between him and each of them: two more of the blade-priests. He might have been able to make it to one of the narrow alleys to one side or the other between the houses that lined the road, but he was in no shape for running.

Iridan stuck Dragon's Whisper into the ground at his feet, and collapsed to one knee, using the blade for support. Tears streamed from the corners of his eyes from the pain and from the smoke he had just escaped. If either of the blade-priests was aware of Iridan beginning to make a concerted draw upon the aether, neither showed a sign.

"This is not an honorable death, demon-spawn, to face you wounded and two against one," one of the blade-priests said by way of apology in advance of finishing him.

Iridan saw nothing but a Source and a weapon. "The light is filled with distraction," Rashan had told him. "Empathy worst of all. See a Source, destroy a Source." The voice might have been older, but the Safschan accent made guessing tricky. The Source of the voice's owner was the weaker of the two, but only by a hair.

"To slay Rashan in such a manner might be worthy of note, but to kill one such as you, we do our duty, and no more," the other blade-priest finished summing up their statement.

Iridan had realized his mistake with the first blade-priest, engaging him in parley to no advantage. The fleeing soldiers had obviously spread the word that it was not Rashan Solaran rampaging through the nighttime streets of Munne. Though there was nothing more he might give away in banter, he was not going to repeat the error. Iridan said nothing, just waited, and drew more aether as they wasted time explaining their motives to a man they intended to live only a moment longer.

They approached briskly, the middling ground between caution and a reckless charge. It seemed very professional by Iridan's estimation—good teamwork. It also showed a weakness of the blade-priests: a clear lack of awareness of the aether as they fought. It seemed that they were not suited to fighting warlocks.

Iridan let them get close, but not within reach of their rune-blades. Twin blasts of aether hit the two men in the chest as Iridan thrust his arms out to either side, releasing his grip on Dragon's Whisper. They were tighter, more focused blasts than he'd had time to form in his earlier engagement, when he was fighting in a panic. Iridan found a new moment of panic, however, when the bolts did not stop his adversaries' momentum. He threw himself backward to the ground as two corpses stumbled into one another with ragged, bloody holes through them.

The impact with the ground nearly made Iridan black out in pain from his ribs. He felt one of the rune-blades bounce off his shield, and another try to knife into his leg as it was caught between him and its former owner. Iridan felt a volley of arrows strike his shield, weakening it near the point of failing. The archers had no reason to hold their fire now that the blade-priests were not in danger.

Iridan drew more aether, realizing too late that the blade-priests' newly dead aether was closest at hand. He strengthened his shield and shot more balls of fire, both at the archers, and at any buildings within easy range. He needed time. The Megrenn occupiers had shown that they would stop pursuit of him to attend to fires in the city. The chaos of the frightened peasants who would be flushed into the streets would help as well.

Iridan pulled himself from beneath the pile of dead blade-priests, and retched. The feeling of the dead aether passing through his Source had disgusted him. It was a sensation his body had been unaware it could experience.

His stomach empty of its contents, Iridan wobbled to his feet, retrieved Dragon's Whisper, and set about to find his shelter for the daytime.

* * * * * * * *

"Very well, we will try your plan tomorrow night," General Rozen said, staring out into the night to watch the fires of Munne burning. "I am sorry for the loss of your brothers."

"A priest does not expect to die of age or sickness. To never be defeated is the wish of the vain, thinking that none is better, or luckier, or more worthy than they," Tiiba replied. He stood at the general's side, but did not look out at the burning city. His attention remained fixed on the general as a show of respect. "Do you really think it will work? You seem to assume much."

"I study. To spend hours each day in sparring and meditation, and think oneself adequately prepared, ignores half the equation of combat. The study of foes is the other half. Understanding his training, his motives, his fears, and his vanities—that is the other half. I have read books, including one about this new warlock's father. I have reports from the battles he has fought in the city, both his ambushes and in the attack that slew Souka. I will have reports of tonight's battle, if any survive to make one. I also have other sources of information that—with respect, General—are secret to my kind."

General Rozen nodded, satisfied that if the plan did not work, it was at least well thought out—and the planner was at greatest risk. Plans that were assembled by men who would be safely removed from battle were never as trustworthy as plans by men who would risk their own lives in trying them. General Rozen did not think to ask what those secret sources of information were. He assumed they were secrets of Tiiba's brotherhood of blade-priests.

They were not.

* * * * * * * *

Iridan stumbled into the wine cellar of a nobleman's estate. He did not know which, and could hardly have cared less. The Megrenn occupiers had leveled a great many of the wealthier estates, places that could have been used by generals, sorcerers, even the accursed blade-priests, who counted among their own elite. Part of the ceiling was caved in, but a comfortably large space remained, smelling of the grape.

Iridan had swept away the broken glass, and burned off the spilled wine, making it into a hideaway for the hours when Megrenn and peasant alike would be stalking the streets of Munne. He had brought in blankets and some pilfered foods to hold him over for a few days—he could always loot more from either the occupiers or the peasants. His aching body needed rest, and lots of it.

"Maybe I will rest tomorrow night as well," Iridan told himself. He knew that he would not. The drive to save the city kept him out on the streets each night, every death bringing the city closer to freedom.

Iridan uncorked a bottle of a vintage he had never heard of. Wine was all the same to him, whether it was of ancient vintage or last season's grape juice. He just needed to get drunk enough to fall into a dreamless sleep. He half-succeeded ...

He found himself stalking the streets as he had on his first nights in Munne. He dodged among the buildings, facing off against stripe-cats and infantry patrols. Nothing hurt in the dream, not when the headless stripe-cat collapsed atop him momentarily, not when he landed awkwardly jumping from a third-story rooftop to pursue a fleeing Megrenn captain. Every opponent he faced off against fell either by blade or by spell.

He found himself bereft of opposition, and decided to find shelter and respite. The dream fatigue felt real enough. Everything slowed to where he felt like he was wading through honey; he needed rest.

A peasant home caught his eye. It opened onto an unremarkable street and, from its look, likely had a loft where he could hide. Blade still in hand in case of ambush, he used a bit of telekinesis to flip the bar that held it firm against intruders. The dream was in the light, so Iridan could not see the occupants within, but he remembered them from when it happened to him in the waking world.

The husband and wife within had been awakened by the throwing of the bolt, and had both come to investigate. The man carried a wood axe, the woman a small knife.

"I am Warlock Iridan. You have nothing to fear from me. I seek shelter as I drive out the Megrenn soldiers," he said to them. They looked at him with fearful eyes, seeing a black-clad swordsman, dripping blood all over their floors, and with a readied blade in hand.

"Leave us alone! We want no trouble here!" the man shouted at him.

"Be quiet," Iridan ordered, trying to sound authoritative, but in the dream it came out with a savage growl.

"Mommy, what's goin' on?" a voice came from above. There had indeed been a loft in the house, and a young girl of perhaps six or seven winters leaned her head over the edge to see. When she did, she screamed. It was the shrill, piercing note that only the very young and very frightened can manage.

Iridan panicked. He needed stealth and refuge, safe from further discovery by the occupiers until he had rested. His hand acted before he could think enough to stop it.

A little girl's head dropped to the floor. In the dream, it kept screaming.

Chapter 28 - Found

Dingy light fell through the sewer grating to cast the passageway in a gradient of shadows, devoid of color. A trickle of water echoed in the dark recesses past that border of illumination. Sodden, filthy debris piled in the path of the flow dammed it off after a fashion, leaving a space that was merely damp, rather than awash in sewage.

Measured in the length of Anzik's foot, the area was twelve feet wide and thirty-one feet long, in the direction the flow would have gone, had he not stopped it. But he had stopped the flow. Sometimes it would leak, but he would stop it again. The Staff of Gehlen was nine feet long. He had to measure it so that he could find the height of the ceiling by pushing it against the top of the passageway, and seeing how many feet fit beneath it. The ceiling was thirteen feet tall, except where the grating was—it was sixteen there.

Anzik had checked his measurements fourteen times; he got the same results every time. It comforted him to get the same results every time. That was the way it was supposed to be. Counting kept his mind busy, and the voices away. He had refrained from using any magic at all since meeting Faolen.

It should be soon.

Anzik started another survey of his hideaway, pressing heel to toe, heel to toe across the passage. *One, two, three ...* A pang of hunger growled for his attention, but he was counting. There was food, stolen from the marketplace, in a cloth sack on the ground by the staff. He had dates, plums, apples, hard-crusted bread, and a cheese that smelled like he remembered from home. But he had started counting. It would be wrong to stop in the middle. *Four, five, six ...*

Anzik paced off the space, then double-checked himself by doing it again. Satisfied that everything was where it belonged, he sat himself down, and ate his meal. He had paid little attention to time since he had run away, so he decided that every meal was lunch. Lunch had no runny eggs that felt funny in his mouth. Lunch did not need a knife or someone to cook it—though soup might have been nice.

Faolen is going to get you now, voices. Just you wait. Any time now ...

* * * * * * * *

The wagon trundled along at a relaxed pace. The wooden rumbling of the wheels set a counterpoint to the rhythm of the horses' hooves. Five other wagons traveled alongside them as they made their way down the Tradeway, the east-west road that ran the length of Takalia. The caravan was a common means of traveling safely over long distances, providing safety in numbers as well as in paid guards. For their part, the Takalish guards cost little enough: food for the journey and a small stipend paid by each wagonload of passengers or goods.

Zellisan looked the four caravan guards over, and was impressed with what he saw. None was older than twenty-five years by his reckoning, but they had a polite, calm dignity about them. Left alone, they would ride in silence for hours; strike up a conversation, and they bantered like they knew you since childhood. They would answer any question like a proud host, showing off his new home to guests at a dinner party. They knew every inch of the Tradeway and a good ways to either side of it. They were passing through wine-making lands, with vineyards stretching as far as could be seen from hilltop to hilltop. The distinctive wide-brimmed hats they wore—large enough to cover an open barrel without risk of falling in—let brigands know the caravan was protected.

Should any brigand be foolish enough to attack the caravan, he was in for a rude welcome. Zell had seen Acardian muskets in his military days. They were scary to hear fire—louder than pistols even—but not terribly accurate. The long guns that the Takalish caravan guards wore slung over their shoulders were of fancier make: polished barrels gleaming down their length without a hint of a flaw in their straightness, dark-stained stocks padded in leather, and each carrying a small spyglass mounted to the top. He knew before he noticed the distinctive square-on-end *C.E.* logo on the stock that they had to have been from the Errol workshops. It stood to reason, since the Mad Tinker's island refuge was not far north of Takalia.

Zell found himself ill at ease with his new traveling companion. He knew that Wendell was a Kadrin sorcerer in Veydrus, which ought to have made him trustworthy. Being brought in to head the Imperial Palace's guards had given him too much insight into the goings on of the seat of imperial power of late, though. House Archon had its flaws, its malcontents, and, from time to time, its high sorcerers summarily executed for treason … but he trusted all of them. He had known Brannis since he was a lad, and knew that he had carved himself a separate path, but the rest of the Solarans were a scheming lot. Wendell seemed cut from the Solaran cloth rather than from the Archon.

"What is it you keep looking at me for?" Zellisan asked, noticing the magician's gaze wandering his way too often for comfort.

"I might ask you why you spend so much time looking at the caravan guards. I suppose it might be the same reason: I am curious about whose hands my protection lies in," Wendell replied. In his road-dusted gentleman's suit and hat, he looked the very image of the traveling neophyte—overdressed and underprepared.

"Not a bad life, if you don't mind the pay," Zellisan said, conceding the point. Wendell had already made clear that his power in Tellurak was limited. He would need Zell's protection should any danger find them once they were clear of the caravan's protection. "I could do the same back home. Know every road from Scar Harbor to Urdur like I put 'em down myself."

"So why don't you? Seems an easy living, seeing the land and meeting people, making a bit of coin for the trouble?"

"It's the 'bit of coin' part, really. Couldn't see docking myself pay. Couldn't see folk paying my typical rate just for some light guard duty," Zell answered, lacing his fingers behind his head, and leaning back on the bench seat of the wagon.

"You're paid that well, are you?"

"I don't need to pass a hat around at the end of a job, magician."

"The hat takes care of me. I don't expect to die a rich man."

* * * * * * * *

"Jinzan, a word, if I might?" Narsicann said, diverting Jinzan's attention from the farewell dinner he was enjoying with his wives and children—those who had not run away at least.

"Is this urgent, or can it wait until we have eaten?" Jinzan asked, setting down the slab of bacon he had been working on, and sucking the grease from his fingers.

"One bit of news could, I suppose. The other, no."

Jinzan regarded him a moment, looking for hints that he might be jesting, but he found no such indication. Narsicann's humor could be subtle at times, but he would not dare trifle with Jinzan just before he left to make war.

"If you would excuse me, everyone," Jinzan said to his family, making sure his gaze swept across each of them. He wanted to make sure he remembered them as they were, not the fading memories of the children as babes or his wives as when he had met them. He was home too infrequently, even when he was in Zorren—sleeping did not count for making memories.

"We have found a Kadrin sorcerer within the city," Narsicann told him once they were alone on Jinzan's balcony. Narsicann was back-lit by the low sun, making his expression hard to read. Jinzan wondered how the spy-sorcerer always kept such subtle tricks at hand, even when dealing with friends.

"Where? To what end?" Jinzan knew that if the Kadrin had been captured already, Narsicann would have said so first off.

"He and an accomplice seem to be closing down a business in the warehouse quarter. Checking on it, they set it up several days ago, fronting a half-season's rent, and claiming to be traders. The fact that they are leaving now—"

"You think they found the staff?" Jinzan said, interrupting Narsicann. He felt like a cold-blooded politician for asking first about the staff, and felt a pang of guilt.

Narsicann nodded.

"We think it quite likely, in fact. Their rented shop is surrounded—we even have the nearby sewer entrances watched. Everyone is keeping their distance until we arrive."

"You need my help in case the Kadrin uses the staff against us," Jinzan said, drawing another nod from the master of spies.

"Indeed. I have five other sorcerers already waiting for us, but none so strong as you. We need you," Narsicann stated, not quite asking it as a question, but Jinzan heard it that way.

"Of course, let us be off," Jinzan replied, wondering if his last look at his family truly would be the last. Jinzan knew the power that the staff granted its wielder. "Once I have it in hand, I will make for Munne, and deal with Rashan Solaran."

"Well ... that was the other thing, the one that could have waited until your dinner was ended. It seems that the trouble in Munne is not Rashan Solaran, but his son Iridan. The young demon-spawn styles himself a warlock now, and has slain three of the blade-priests you sent," Narsicann said.

"Was Tiiba among the fallen?"

"No, Master Tiiba has a plan for dealing with this 'warlock.' He intends to set a trap and—"

Jinzan waved off the explanation. "Tell me about it afterward, whether he succeeds or fails. We have more important matters to attend."

"Agreed."

* * * * * * *

"I see no Sources inside," Jinzan whispered, peering around the stone bricks of an adjacent building.

"Neither do I, but I trust the eyes of the men who said there are two Kadrins inside. I find it more likely they are concealed in magic than escaped by it," Narsicann replied, crouched low next to him.

"The two of us, then—prepared for whatever lies inside?" Jinzan asked.

"Aye, it's been too long since we last fought together. If we fail, it is unlikely that the perimeter guards will be able to stop them. We must not fail."

"If we do, it has been a pleasure knowing you, old friend."

"Likewise."

The shop door bore no visible ward upon it. A simple spell of telekinesis lifted the bar from inside. Jinzan pushed the door in, and was relieved that it did not squeak as it swung. It was dark within the building, the curtained windows permitting scant slivers of filtered starlight about their edges and little else. The only other illumination came from the newly opened door.

Jinzan conjured a tiny sphere of pale blue light, and sent it whizzing about the front room of the shop, finding nothing out of the ordinary. There were no spies and no staff, just a counter and a number of crates half-filled with useless bric-a-brac. Jinzan and Narsicann tiptoed into the room, and searched about from closer up, but found no sign of their quarry. The door to the storage area in back was unlocked, and opened easily, quiet as the first. The blue light led the way again, doing a circuit of the larger space, and showing nothing extraordinary. Jinzan turned to Narsicann, who only shrugged.

There was a set of stairs that led to an enclosed loft over the customer-oriented front half of the store. Jinzan crept up them, careful to ease onto each in turn, lest they—

Creeeeeeeeeeee ...

Jinzan mouthed a variety of curses without lending breath to them as the stair creaked loudly enough for someone to have heard from the shop's front door. He felt Narsicann grab his arm to stop him from going any farther. The two sorcerers waited, motionless, silent. Jinzan could hear his own breath, coming faster and deeper than he would have hoped. He swallowed, wondering if that sound really carried as far as it seemed to in his head.

Noises came from above, behind the door at the top of the stairs. A creaking of a floorboard—softer than his own misstep but unmistakable—followed by a rustling noise. Jinzan felt a tug at his arm, and turned to look Narsicann's way. He saw Narsicann's face by the ghostly light of his spell, the man's eyes wide. Narsicann jerked his head in the direction of the door they had entered by.

There is certainly time to run, Jinzan thought. *We could be gone before anyone came down the stairs.* Jinzan looked Narsicann in the eye, and shook his head. *If we give up now, we lose the staff.*

Jinzan pointed up the stairs, making certain his hand was visible in the scant light available. He held up his hand, fingers spread wide, watching to see Narsicann's eyes focus on it.

Jinzan pulled in his thumb, leaving just four fingers extended.

He put down his little finger, leaving just three. He watched Narsicann's head nod just enough to let on that he understood.

Two.

One.

The two men rushed up the stairs, all attempt at stealth abandoned. Soft-soled boots thudded heavily on the wooden treads. Jinzan leaned his shoulder against the door as he thrust it open, trusting to brute force over magic in his haste; he found it unbarred, unwarded, entirely unprotected against his advance.

Jinzan stumbled into the loft, Narsicann close on his heels, and the first words to a spell poised ready on his lips. There was nothing there.

While there was a bed, a scattering of blankets upon the floor, and various personal effects lying here and there, it amounted to nothing. There was no spy, no accomplice, and—after a cursory viewing in the aether to be sure—no Staff of Gehlen.

"Your informant was wrong, it appears," Jinzan said, casting an annoyed glare at Narsicann out of the corner of his eye, a gesture lost in the gloom of a single open window, whose light did not quite reach the doorway.

"At first glance, it would appear so," Narsicann said. He stalked past Jinzan into the room, and lit it with a spell of his own, banishing all semblance of nighttime. The master of spies made his way to the window, and stuck his head out, looking for signs that their prey had climbed out onto the roof or dropped to the ground below. "But I like to be thorough. We should burn the building to the ground." He pulled the shutters closed.

Narsicann picked up one of the blankets from the floor, giving it a look over as it began to smolder. As it caught fire, he tossed it into a corner of the room piled with soiled clothing.

A form slipped from under the bed, hooded cloak pulled low to shield the face from the view of both Megrenn sorcerers. Quick as a hare, the cloaked figure dashed to the window, and dove headlong through it, splintering the shutters. Narsicann raced to the window to see where the fugitive had gone.

"Look out! The Kadrin is on the move!" he shouted out to the sentries stationed all around the shop.

Jinzan knew that he was too old to be leaping out windows to pursue anyone. After recovering from his initial surprise, he made for the doorway. He bumped into something that he did not see, immediately realizing the ruse they had both just fallen for. He reached out, and grabbed what felt like an arm.

"I have him!" Jinzan shouted. He clawed at magic he could not see, hoping to unravel the aether construct that wrapped the Kadrin sorcerer in invisibility. The arm he held onto struggled; he felt a hand on his own, trying to pry loose his grip.

The invisibility spell gave way against Jinzan's efforts … and he saw that he was holding onto none other than Rashan Solaran! The vile demonic warlock stopped struggling, and just grinned at him, a look that promised a death at his own leisure. Jinzan let go and stumbled away, preparing to fight for his life.

Rashan turned and ran, vanishing again as he passed through the doorway.

Not the real Rashan …

Jinzan cursed his gullibility. He was about to give chase when he heard Narsicann's spell chant. The spymaster pushed past him mid spell, reaching the doorway just as he was finishing.

"… *daxgak sevdu wenlu.*" Narsicann pointed down the stairs, and forks of lightning flooded the way down. They caught something in their path just before reaching the foot of the stairway, adding a smell of cooked flesh to the heavy ozone scent that they created. Something invisible slumped to the ground, giving off wisps of visible smoke.

"Nicely done," Jinzan commented, nodding in appreciation of Narsicann's work.

"I am of a mind to let the place finish burning down. If the accomplice is here somewhere as well, he will either try to escape, or burn."

Jinzan worked to unravel yet another invisibility spell as they descended the stairs, finding the true visage of the man who might yet know the location of the Staff of Gehlen. Bereft of illusionary protection, Jinzan could see a living Source still within him.

"You do good work, Narsicann. He still breathes."

"He is going to need that breath soon. I am eager to test out this new theory of yours on restraining captive sorcerers."

* * * * * * *

The wagon bearing Zellisan and Wendell had parted from the caravan shortly after dawn, having spent the night in the group's protection. As they headed north into the low mountains, the trees to all sides were decked in vibrant red, orange, and yellow. Zellisan had a look on his face that could have been mistaken for homesickness, had he not been a hardened, black-hearted coinblade—his native Acardia looked much the same in autumn as the leaves turned. Wendell was Acardian born as well, but felt little attachment to his birthland, traveling all his life as he had. If the colored foliage held a place in his memories, the sight still would have been lost on him, his eyes remaining unfocused as he looked out into the woods they drove through.

Wendell had problems, Faolen's problems, weighing heavily on him. With problems beyond a certain level of severity, most men need to turn to someone for guidance, support ... empathy even. But the wagon driver was an elderly Takalish gentlemen who barely spoke Acardian, and Wendell was far from fluent in Takalish. As for Zellisan ...

Wendell sighed, and stared at the scenery, if only because he preferred to keep his eyes open, and they needed somewhere to face. Closing them, he might fall asleep with the gentle rolling of the wagon, and the pleasant, woodsy smell in the air. What he would see in his sleep was something he did not want to witness right about then.

He had not been able to eat. The first mouthful of jerky he had swallowed still sat disquieted in his stomach, threatening to come back up at any moment. He had not attempted a second bite.

The wagon driver whistled amiably as the morning wore on, tunes that struck no familiar chord in Wendell's mind. He tried to follow the melodies, but the driver was no musician, and the tunes were inconsistent. *I must set my mind to rights before we arrive,* Wendell chided himself. *My mission was crucial before but somehow is much more so now. I can make it all an act if I must but I have to prevail.*

Pious Grove Sanctuary sat nestled among the mountains, rather than far up the side of them. The road wound its way gradually up and through the low-lying foothills, and around the smallest of the mountains in the Sali Peaks range. Around one final bend, the woods overhanging the road parted, revealing an old but well-kept compound of stone buildings, the largest of which was four stories tall with gabled rooftops and creeping vines climbing the walls.

It was at that largest of buildings that their driver stopped the wagon, and let Zellisan and Wendell disembark. People bustled about the compound at various chores and errands, and the driver set off to find someone whose task was to tend to horses, leaving the two foreigners standing before the large double-doors that led inside the heart of the sanctuary.

One of the staff noticed them waiting outside, uncertain of what to do with the wide-open doors that would have allowed them free access to a facility they were entirely unfamiliar with. The middle-aged man in humble grey attire told them in slow, clear Takalish—the sort that one uses when speaking to someone they think cannot understand a word of what they are saying—to wait, gesturing with palms held outward to make clear his intent. He then scurried off down one of the side corridors.

Zellisan turned to Wendell, and shrugged. Wendell stared after the man, his heart quickening in his chest. *Relax. There will be no troubles here. These folk are healers, not monsters.*

They did not have long to wait before an elderly woman approached them, their initial greeter in tow. She was bone thin with wrinkled ebony skin hanging loosely about her cheeks and arms, but unbent by age. She had no hair at all, sunlight reflecting off her shiny scalp as she emerged into the daylight. Her pale blue eyes were alert and vibrant, making her broad smile seem warm and inviting.

"Welcome to Pious Grove, travelers. I am Nephanti," the old woman greeted them in Takalish.

"I Wendell. This man Zellisan," Wendell introduced them, his Takalish something he was less than boastful of.

"I speak Acardian as well, if it would be easier, Mr. Wendell," Nephanti said, chuckling softly. "Though I give you credit for trying. Many foreigners come here and babble away until they realize that the person they are talking to cannot understand a word of Acardian, or Kheshi, or whatever language they brought here from far away."

"Are you the translator, then?" Wendell asked, feeling much more at ease now that he would not be having to perform his act speaking in Takalish.

"It is one of my many tasks here. Mostly I oversee what everyone else does, though," Nephanti replied. Realization dawned on Wendell, but Zellisan recovered more quickly.

"I am sorry, my lady. We did not know," Zell said, hastily smoothing down his unruly hair.

"Nonsense, I am no 'lady.' I am no more important than any other here, just busier than most. I am too old to spend all day in the gardens or the woods, too weak to tend horses or the adult patients who cannot lift themselves from bed. So I spend days making sure folk remember their tasks, write letters to beg donations from men who have money to spare, and need their conscience cleansed; I help tend to the children when time allows, and I greet guests, whom we receive far too infrequently. You and your friend look in fine health generally, though you might do with some food by the look of you, Mr. Wendell."

"Thank you, Sister Nephanti." Wendell figured that was the best translation of her title into Acardian. "I am sure that having as few visitors as you do, you must be wondering as to the reason for our being here."

"I had supposed you would come to it in time. I am a busy woman, but not so busy that I need to badger our guests with questions upon their arrival," Nephanti responded.

"Well, professionally, I call myself Wendell the Wizard. I am a traveling magician," Wendell said.

"Oh, how delightful!" Nephanti said, her smile broadening. "We have not had an entertainer pass through in years."

"I would like to perform for your residents. Also, I find myself in search of a young boy who I believe may be here."

"Oh, what boy?" Nephanti asked, eyes narrowing a little, not giving the appearance of suspicion so much as a shrewd curiosity.

"I do not know yet myself," Wendell admitted, smiling in what he hoped was a self-deprecating manner. His stomach twisted itself in knots. "But I will know him if I see him."

"Some relation of yours, perhaps?"

"Nothing so straightforward as that. You see, I am advancing in my years, and I begin to realize that I only have so much time left to properly pass along my trade to the next generation. I seek an apprentice," Wendell stated, painting an earnest grin on his face to distract from his sweating.

"This seems an unlikely place to find one, but I will not begrudge you looking. We take care of the children as best we can, but learning proper trades is something we struggle to provide. They learn enough to earn their keep, and a few of the staff here grew up as orphans in our care. Most leave when they come of age, to make what they can from what fortune provides. Can you say, though, that yours is a proper trade, sir?"

"Proper as any that takes on orphan apprentices, I would say. No boy born of unknown parents is likely to be taken on by a barrister or a physician, but I would lay my stake upon mine being as good a life as any baker or cobbler can offer. A boy would have a roof over his head each night, though they may be many different roofs; but that is because he would also get to see the world. A butcher's boy might know a dozen men as brothers, but I know a thousand as friends. A boy apprenticed to a carpenter will learn to make chairs and tables, but I will show him how to make smiles appear on unfriendly faces." Wendell had rehearsed what he would say, but none of that came out. He spoke instead from the heart.

"How will you know the right boy when you see him?" Nephanti asked.

"Why ... using my magic, of course."

That afternoon, in a dining hall where the wooden tables and long benches had been pushed aside to leave a floor-level stage, Wendell was allowed to perform his act for the residents of the Pious Grove Sanctuary. It was filled with a bedraggled assemblage of discarded humans, orphans, and the very sickly. They wore homespun clothes that appeared threadbare, but well cared for. Patches were sewn in here and there; all had the look of being washed regularly for many years. Zellisan sat well off to the side, with Nephanti and the staff who could be spared for an afternoon's diversion. Wendell scanned the crowd, looking for a boy who might be Anzik's twin. There were too many faces, though, packed too close together. Wendell's eyesight was not so keen as it had been in his younger years, either.

Nephanti gave the crowd a brief introduction of the act, sparing Wendell the need to converse in Takalish. His Acardian would have been understood by many, at least; the residents of Pious Grove, unlike the staff, were a diverse bunch. A majority were still native Takalish, understandable since orphans are not the most well-traveled lot, but there were lighter-skinned peoples mixed among them as well. Takalia was renowned for their acceptance of foreigners in their charitable homes, and Pious Grove Sanctuary was among the best-known across the seas.

Wendell began his act as normal, with simple tricks using coins and cards. He pulled scarves from his sleeves, and had them dance about. He placed his hat on his head, and walked about, leaving the hat hanging in the air until he stopped beneath it once more. The crowd laughed and applauded.

As the show drew to a close, he performed one last trick, one that he'd had in mind since learning that Anzik Fehr was twinborn. He began his juggling doves trick, a variant of the one he had worked in Marker's Point. Doves rose and fell like cloth balls as he tossed them about, until they rebelled, and began flying about the room, still returning to his hands occasionally to be launched anew.

"If you would translate, please," said Wendell as he turned to Nephanti, who was enchanted with the whimsical display.

She nodded her agreement.

"If there is one among you who would like to learn magic, as my apprentice, first catch a dove," Wendell spoke loud enough for the whole room to hear him. Nephanti echoed his words in Takalish.

Wendell had used nonsensical magical gibberish amid his spells throughout the show, but he switched to Megrenn, which only one in the audience ought to have been able to understand: "If you are Anzik, you must catch a dove," Wendell said.

As if in response to a magical incantation, the doves broke off their pattern of flight. As a flock, they flew across the room just over the heads of the crowd. Boys, girls, men, and women all laughed as they jumped and grabbed, save for a few too sickly to make the attempt. There were jokes and teasing and cries of dismay as everyone failed to grab hold of one; they were mere illusion, and hands passed through them. One bird, however, bigger and slower than the rest, flew lazily over the crowd. It had a bit of substance to it. It was also invisible, but in the aether would stand out from the rest as a brighter bird among the paltry magics that formed the others.

It was a difficult spell for Wendell. It stretched him to the limits of his magic, but with the stakes as high as they were, he pushed himself to that limit. Wendell waited and watched, directing the invisible bird in a careful circuit of every part of the crowd amid the general chaos of the flapping flock.

"I got one!" exclaimed a thin, childish voice, speaking Megrenn. Wendell let the rest of the imaginary birds flutter up into the rafters and disappear. The invisible bird turned visible in the hands of a willowy stick of a boy, the very image of Anzik if he would have eaten like a mouse.

Everyone turned to see the bird nestled in the boy's hands. His fellows pushed and prodded, herding him to the front of the crowd.

"What is your name, boy?" Wendell asked in Acardian.

"His name is Jadon," Nephanti answered in the boy's place.

"Hello, Jadon. Do you know who I am?" Wendell asked.

Jadon frowned for a moment. Then his eyes lit up, and he nodded vigorously.

"Would you like to be my apprentice, Jadon?" Wendell asked.

"Yes," Jadon replied in Megrenn.

"Jadon, if you want to be a magician, you are going to have to remember to speak a real language, like Acardian or Takalish, not ones you hear in your head. Can you do that?"

Jadon looked puzzled, lost. With a moment to gather his thoughts, he replied, "Yes." This time, he spoke Acardian.

"How did you do that?" Nephanti asked. "He rarely deigns to speak anything other than gibberish, and we have had experts in many languages try to talk to him."

"I was afflicted much the same as a boy," Wendell said. "I was lost in the musings within my own head. It seemed more real than the world around me. Dreams can be more interesting than being awake, and he chooses to live in the dream world when awake as well as asleep. He knows this world is here, but ignores it. Magic helps, because it brings a sense of wonderment to the real world that can make it seem worth seeing. In time, he will learn to properly separate the real world from his imagined one. My master did the same for me, many long years past. I would like to do the same for Jadon."

It was highly irregular, but Nephanti apparently had seen such a change in Jadon that she could not in conscience deny him Wendell's help. There were forms to sign, and contracts promising that he would take proper care of the boy, but by the evening, Jadon sat in the same wagon that Wendell and Zellisan had ridden in on, prepared to depart for a new life. Wendell sat beside him, handing the boy a spare cloak to use against the evening breeze.

Zellisan paused just within the entryway. Wendell watched him turn to look back inside the main building. Zell started to take a step, then retracted it. He reached into his coinpurse, and pulled something out. Wendell saw his hand go somewhere out of sight behind the door; he had seen a donation box there when they had entered.

"Does your conscience feel cleaner?" Wendell asked once Zell had climbed into the wagon.

"S'pose it does," Zell said with a grunt, not looking right at him.

I wish my own felt a bit cleaner.

Chapter 29 - Ascension

Steel clanged against stone as Kyrus's sword bounced to a stop against the wall of his bedchamber, missing a bookshelf by a mere handsbreadth. He winced at the sound, reflexively bringing his hands—one of them smarting from where the sword was bashed free of his grasp—to cover his ears. Once the noise stopped, he hung his head and went to retrieve it.

"We have time for another go of it," Kyrus said, flexing and clenching his fingers to work the sting out of them.

"Suit yourself. I've got nothing to do today but show up to the coronation, and that's not till sunset," Tanner retorted, grinning.

The Veydran incarnation of the Tanner whom Brannis had met in Tellurak was, if possible, a smugger, cockier, less disciplined version than the one who led the free and easy life of a coinblade. He had a slouch about him, not of the hunched and self-conscious type, but rather the casual, relaxed posture of someone who does not feel the need to make any effort in order to excel. He could lean against a wall from the middle of a room.

"Might have picked a later hour for it," Varnus called out from Kyrus's desk chair, which creaked under the bulk of the giant guard captain as he leaned it back on two legs, watching the two men spar. "My stomach's craving dawn feast, but I couldn't very well miss this spectacle."

Kyrus brought his sword up to guard position, locking gazes with Tanner, or at least attempting to. Tanner's gaze wandered the room, his sword bared but resting across his shoulder in a loose grip.

"Whenever you're ready, boss," Tanner said, covering a yawn with his off hand.

Kyrus launched a probing thrust, but Tanner stepped aside and back, well out of reach. A follow-up thrust got Tanner to take the sword off his shoulder and the more expertly wielded blade picked off the attack with contemptuous ease. Three more attempts at attack were met with increasing levels of defense, until the parries themselves were putting Kyrus on the defensive, pulling his blade back to guard himself against a counterattack he knew would come as soon as Tanner grew bored of defense.

"You could at least make it look like you are trying," Kyrus complained, feeling the burning in the muscles of his arms that alerted him that his sword was slowing.

Tanner's sword whipped around in response, sliding past Kyrus's awkward attack, and slamming into the side of his neck.

"Dead," Tanner said with a shrug. "Or would be if you didn't have a shield spell like the walls of Raynesdark … from about two seasons ago, anyway."

"Aye, Brannis, give those little twigs dangling from your shoulders a rest," Varnus added. "Even dead men need a good dawn feast."

"It ought to be here soon," Kyrus said. "I arranged for a full dawn feast to be brought up. I have things to discuss with both of you besides swordplay."

A disturbance in his wards alerted Kyrus to the arrival of their meal. The servants had been taught the proper spot to knock where the wards would not suffocate any hint of noise from the outside. Two young cooks' assistants carried covered platters that smelled of fresh-cooked meats and citrus, a young serving girl brought a pitcher of ale and tankards, and a group of porters carried in a small table and chairs for them.

"I had half-expected field rations and last night's bread with a bit of water to wash it down with. Ale in the morning … my sort of dawn feast," Tanner said once the assemblage of servants had departed.

"We don't allow that dried leather you soldiers eat past the palace gates," Varnus said, tankard in hand already.

"Well, I meant that with the coronation tonight, I expected the servants to be too busy to make such a diversion for us."

"Well, I have a bit of a say in such things," Kyrus said with a sly grin. "As to the selection, I picked a few of the things that seem to taste close enough to Tellurak fare that it does not bother me. The spices are all wrong, the game fowl seem a bit … foul, many of the fruits here do not seem sweet enough, and I do not know what you do to the waters in Veydrus to make the fish taste too oily. The citrus is strong enough to overpower any strange flavors, though, and bacon … well, the bacon tastes just like home."

"And the ale? You prefer it over mulled wine, or even just plain water with breakfast?" Tanner asked, humoring Kyrus's treatise on the local cuisine.

"Well, it took a few days to realize the cause, but the drinking water was giving me the runs. The wines here feel grimy in my mouth, like they could have used a straining through a fine cloth. Do they leave the skins ground up in it or something of the like?" Kyrus asked.

"Gut me if I know," Varnus replied. "At least you've got ale, eh?"

"Well, the ale was merely the best among bad options," Kyrus replied, lifting his eyebrows and his tankard in unison.

Kyrus waited until they had settled in, and begun their meal in earnest, before deciding it was time to change to more delicate topics. The wards in the room ought to have given them privacy enough should anyone attempt to eavesdrop. Kyrus could only hope that he would be perceptive enough to notice should anyone test themselves against those wards.

"So how fare you two on the other side?" Kyrus asked, leaving the question open ended, lest he get an exact answer that left out details. If he was to set up his own private network of spies, he ought to at least act like a master of intrigue.

"Well, Captain Denrik Zayne wanted me to convey to you that this whole war was just a simple misunderstanding," Tanner said, causing Kyrus's eyes to widen in surprise. "You see, there were these detailed orders on how *not* to launch a war against us, and a splotch of ink happened to fall on the 'not' bit."

"Stow it, jester. Be serious," Varnus chided Tanner, giving him a backhanded slug in the shoulder. "Stalyart hasn't even got you to Zayne's ship yet, and we all know it."

"Hey now! I'm stuck for days on a ship in the middle of the Katamic with a bunch of pirates. I got nothing to do but swill rum, and gamble at dice and cards. Can't even properly enjoy it, though, worrying 'bout a knife in the back, shield or no shield. I think I'm entitled to piss in Brannis's ale a bit in return," Tanner said. Kyrus paused mid sip, giving Tanner a narrow-eyed glare. "Figure of speech, of course," Tanner said.

"Well, at least there you've got rum and cards," Varnus commented. "Did either of you hear that there were three bodies found last night? Separate incidents scattered about Kadris, but all three were sorcerers."

"No," Kyrus answered, Varnus having taken the entirety of his attention away from Tanner's jests. "I have not left these quarters yet today."

"City guards were handling it, but the Inner Circle pulled them off the job. Dolvaen assigned a bunch of sorcerers to look into it."

"Anyone important?" Tanner asked.

"No more so than a typical sorcerer, I would say. Two Sixth Circle I never heard of, and a Fourth Circle by the name of Kaman who tried courting one of Juliana's cousins a while back. Didn't know him well, but I knew his face well enough to find him in a crowd."

"Megrenn assassins, that'd be my guess," Tanner speculated. He mimed a dagger thrust to the back. "More of those invisible fellows like tried to snuff out Warlock Rashan and Mr. Tellurak here."

"No ..." Kyrus began, causing Varnus and Tanner to wait expectantly in the heavy pause he left as he gathered his thoughts. "I think not. The coronation is tonight. Not everyone has been enamored of the choice of successor to the throne. The city is packed to the rafters with visitors despite the war going on, meaning that there are likely many more sneak-blades about than usual, coming in with the noble guests."

"You think this is the start of a coup? They were no powerful or influential sorcerers, the three victims. It seems an unlikely first open move for one," Varnus said.

"Well, Megrenn's already tried twice, so why not assume it was them until you've got a better idea?" Tanner countered.

"I do have a better idea," Kyrus answered, his voice hollow, his gaze vacant, as if he were musing on his own thoughts, rather than conversing. "Rashan has said since before Raynesdark that he suspected plots against him. I have reason to believe that to be true. This could mean that, in the shadows, sides are being drawn among the Imperial Circle."

"Sides? What sides?" Tanner asked. His bean-shaped face scrunched up even farther in a look of confusion and concern.

"Those who support Rashan and those who would rather see him replaced as regent—by someone other than his handpicked bastard descendant of his old friend Emperor Liead."

Varnus cast Kyrus a wary glare.

"Which side are we on?"

"Mine, I am hoping," Kyrus replied. "As to which side I have picked, I have not picked at all yet. By rights, I ought to support Rashan, since he is the reason I am in this position at all ... grand marshal that is, not me being switched with Brannis; that was my own doing."

"So the dead sorcerers, which side were they on?" Tanner asked.

"If I knew that, I might be able to tell you which side I was on," Kyrus answered.

* * * * * * *

The corridors of the palace teemed with servants intent upon tasks they surely had been told were crucial to the coronation ceremony. *A misplaced tablecloth, or one pheasant too few for the banquet, and we would have to find a new emperor,* Juliana thought sourly as she wove her way through the press of bodies. A few who recognized her gave way, and allowed her to pass, but she was wearing a plain grey tunic and men's breeches, nothing that would single her out as a member of the Imperial Circle, let alone the regent's oathdaughter. Still, being caught up in the tide of busy humans was better than dwelling alone in her room or passing idle chatter with the folk who made a habit of lounging about the palace. If nothing else, her current circumstance was a temporary inconvenience until she could escape the confines of the palace grounds, and hide out by the waterfront until her duties required her back for the ceremony.

"Juli!" she heard a shout from behind her down the hall. It was a woman's voice, but not a very feminine one. Juliana slouched slightly, and continued walking, hoping her pursuer would lose track of her amid the throng. Being an Archon had its disadvantages, though. Even slouching, she was taller than most of the peasant folk about her, and her reddish-gold hair shone like a lighthouse beacon among the drab brunettes and pale blondes surrounding her.

"Juli, wait!" the voice came again, closer than the last time. Even if she had not recognized the timbre and tone, the use of the disused diminutive form of her name would have narrowed the list of suspects to a short list: classmates from the Academy who had been too much older or stronger than her to beat until they stopped calling her that. She gritted her teeth, paused, and waited for Brannis's older sister to catch up to her.

Aloisha Solaran was almost Juliana's height, but shaped nearer to Soria's more muscular frame, with a mannish jawline and wide blue eyes that offered a challenge wherever they looked. Those eyes swept up and down Juliana as she got close enough for the crowd to part between them.

"Washerwoman got your Circle garb? Rinsing the sweat stains and the smell of ale away before the coronation ceremony?" Aloisha asked with a smirk. "I am sure I could loan you a gown, if you would prefer, though it might hang a bit loose on you."

"You're one to talk," Juliana retorted, eyeing the elaborate nest of braids curled about Aloisha's head. "Last time I saw you primped like this was for your own wedding. You usually just go about like a man who grew his hair long, and stuffed a pair of melons into a gown. I have work to do, and I'm dressed for it."

"Work? You? I had thought your father got you that appointment as contraband inspector just so you had an excuse to hang about in disreputable ale-halls all day."

"I am good at my job. I just don't do it the way everyone would expect. At least I am suited to mine. You look like the serving maid, or the scribe for the Inner Circle when you're all gathered together," Juliana retorted. She would be gutted before she let Aloisha run her to ground verbally.

Aloisha Solaran fumed silently for a moment, lips pressed tight in an obvious effort to remain civil, or at least as civil as either of them had been to that point. She drew a deep, steady breath. She took Juliana by the arm and pulled her aside, dragging her into one of the guard rooms near where they had been standing.

"What do you think you're doing?" Juliana demanded, twisting free of Aloisha's grasp. It took a degree of self-control to keep from using a Tezuan technique to flip the elder sorceress to the ground, breaking her wrist in the process.

The door slammed shut behind them. Juliana knew Aloisha was holding it closed telekinetically, in lieu of warding it.

"We need to talk."

"We were talking out there," Juliana noted.

"Was it you?" Aloisha demanded.

"Was what me?"

"The three murders last night. Three dead sorcerers the night before the coronation. The Inner Circle are having fits over it."

"What would make you think that—"

"Raynesdark. I heard the stories, and pieced it together. Goblin assassin in the castle dead by your hand the night before the battle. A half dozen guards and Sorcerer Ruuglor Megaren dead by dagger, but no dagger found on the assassin's body. After the battle, Duke Pellaton found dead, same wounds, dagger left by his body."

"So why do you assume it was me?" Juliana asked, crossing her arms in front of herself defiantly.

"I brought my theory to Rashan, and he agreed. He had assumed it was you all along, but did not care enough to mention it. I got the impression he was not bereft over the duke's death, and I decided not to press him on it."

"If I did, you think that means I'm responsible for those murders last night?"

"You do not just hire any jack-blade out of the alleys, and set him off on a merry romp among the Circle. Whoever killed three in one night knew what they were doing around magic."

"Thanks ... I think. But I had nothing to do with them. And if I had, what had you planned to do about it?"

Aloisha's eyes unfocused for a moment. "You are carrying those daggers my brother gave you as a wedding gift," Aloisha said, making an accusation of it. "What would you have done if I had said I was going to tell Rashan it was you, attack me? You are Sixth Circle, and content to remain so. I am Inner Circle; I could crush you like a gnat if you tried it."

"Well, it is a very good thing that I had nothing to do with those murders, then, isn't it?" Juliana said. Faster than Aloisha could react, a pair of daggers appeared in Juliana's hands, blades poised beneath the startled sorceress's ears. Each of Aloisha's dangling earrings was delicately draped over a bared dragon-bone blade. "I would hate to have gotten hurt." Slowly, Juliana lowered the blades, and returned them to the recesses beneath her tunic. Aloisha had managed no more than a startled intake of breath.

Swallowing, and letting out a shuddering breath to calm herself, Aloisha broached the subject one further time: "There are forces at work to tear down Warlock Rashan, and return control of the Empire to the Circle. Which side are you on?" Aloisha asked, more politeness evident in her tone than before she had been frightened.

"I don't think I am quite the kind either side is interested in recruiting, if indeed there are sides at all. I've heard Rashan rant about conspiracies before, but I assumed he was paranoid. It's one of the perks of being important, as far as I can tell. I assume you have sided with Rashan, since he's the only reason you aren't still Third Circle."

"Yes, the whole family is with Rashan, but I am less certain of the Archons. The death of High Sorcerer Gravis sits ill with them."

"Yeah, I was never fond of my grandfather, but he was my blood. Still, even if I don't side *with* him, I'm certainly not fool enough to side *against* Rashan. Besides, I'd hate to have to get my oathsister's blood all over my nice new daggers. Now, if you'll excuse me, I have places to be." Juliana shouldered her way past Aloisha, and found the telekinesis spell that had held the door was no longer doing so.

She tried to gather her thoughts while she wove through the tangle of servants, headed for the palace gates. She had heard of the murders, of course—they were the talk of the city that morning, with rumors spreading like the morning sunlight—but had not thought it to be a fight within the Circle for control of the Empire.

* * * * * * * *

Kyrus arrived at Rashan's office to find Celia waiting there in his stead. She sat demurely, legs crossed, hands in her lap. She started to get up when Kyrus entered, but a look of disappointment crossed her features as she sat right back down again.

"I had thought Rashan was back," she said, by way of apology. She stifled a yawn.

"Glad to know where I rate," Kyrus commented with an amused grin. "I thought you were going to be working for Caladris now."

"I do, and he often has me running errands between the two of them. But I have personal business with the warlock." She raised her eyebrows, and turned her head a bit, as if challenging Kyrus to ask about it.

"Well, he had left word that he wanted to see me, so I assumed he would be here. Do you know where he is?"

"He is the busiest man in the Empire; he could be anywhere. He is even busier than you, Brannis, though I would wager you do not think so often. You can wait here with me, if you like," Celia offered.

"I suppose I will have to," Kyrus replied, blushing as he realized how that must have sounded. "I meant that I have a lot of things to do as well, as you mentioned. But I cannot just ignore Rashan's request."

Kyrus walked over behind the desk and sat down.

"You should not sit there," Celia said. "I would not want to see Rashan get angry."

"It is the only other chair here. It is not as if he would kill me for taking his seat anyway. He is not quite that temperamental." Kyrus was only partially certain on that last point.

Celia said nothing after that, just sat there looking nervous. She did not look directly at Kyrus, but as he sat at Rashan's desks, surrounded by confidential reports on troop movements and Kadrin political affairs, his eyes were drawn to her. *The hair does not quite match,* he thought, comparing her to his mental image of Abbiley. *The build is close ... very close, but Celia is a touch thinner, and her breasts are higher. The nose seems about right. The eyes are identical. Celia's teeth are perfectly straight and white, while Abbiley's are more natural looking. She sounds like Abbiley,* Kyrus added mentally, though he knew his ear for such things was poor. It seemed a horrible question, but he had to ask it of himself anyway: *If I was Abbiley, and had the magic to do so, what would I change about myself?* That was the crux of it.

"You keep looking over this way," Celia mentioned.

Kyrus turned his gaze away, and blushed anew. "There are not many places to look in here. It is a small office. I cannot help where my eyes are drawn," Kyrus said. He tried to focus his attention on a guest list for the reception after the ceremony.

"Had a change of heart perhaps?" Celia asked, a playful note sneaking into her voice, accompanied by a shy smile.

Kyrus's brow burrowed in genuine contemplation. *Have I?*

A change of heart would imply that he had not been attracted to her ever since noticing the resemblance she bore to Abbiley when he first saw her through Brannis's eyes. Or it would imply that he had been initially attracted to her, but was no longer.

"No." Kyrus's voice went hoarse on him. He cleared his throat, and tried again. "No, I have not." He smiled in her direction. She smiled back, showing those perfect teeth that reminded him that even if she was Abbiley in Tellurak, she was different here.

"There is nothing in our way, you know," Celia said, obviously having guessed at how Kyrus had meant his answer. She was smart, one of the things he admired in her.

"There are a great many things in the way. Again as you pointed out, I am busier than anyone except perhaps the warlock."

"No one is making you sketch up new runes to build airships with. You have no duties to the Circle. Just manage the army—which should be enough work for any man—and leave the rest to others. And ... well ... do not make yourself any more of a target than you already may be."

"What do you mean by that?" Kyrus asked.

"Brannis, think about it. There has already been one attempt on your life," Celia explained. "Now there is someone killing sorcerers right here in Kadris."

"What has Caladris heard?" Kyrus asked. She was his assistant now, so the idea that she might have special knowledge of the attacks was not unreasonable.

"Dolvaen is the one investigating it. He has said nothing to Caladris that I am aware of."

Kyrus was about to ask whether she knew of factions within the Circle, and which the victims might have belonged to, but Rashan chose that moment to arrive back at his office.

"Ahh, Brannis, good of you to wait for me. I hope you took care of a few of those annoying reports for me while I was delayed," Rashan jested, his mood better than Kyrus was accustomed to seeing it. "Celia my dear, your presence is a bit more of a surprise. What brings you to my offices on a frenetic day such as this?"

"It is the dreams again," she replied, casting a quick, sidelong glance at Kyrus as if deciding how much she ought to say in front of him. "I slept all night but woke exhausted. My mind was occupied all night as if stuck watching a play that ran from dawn to sunset."

"What is it that you would have me do for you?" Rashan asked. "End the dreams? Tell you what they mean? Reassure you that you are not losing your mind?"

"Well, maybe all three but in reverse order," Celia answered.

"Without knowing more of them, I would venture that there is little risk to your sanity. Folk have dreamed all manner of things, and if they say nothing of it upon awakening, it may as well never have happened. From kings to killers, warriors to lovers, all within the span of a night, all within the confines of the same head. You may do what you like within it. As to the meaning, you ought to search through them yourself for that. Dreams are an insight into your own life. If, as you mentioned to me once before, you are the same person in your dreams night after night, you ought to begin by learning more about this dream-self. As to ending them … there is only one way I know of to end dreams permanently: stop sleeping."

"Well, that is not much use to me, now is it?" Celia asked in a plaintive tone.

"I have many demands upon my time, else I would be willing to discuss your dreams with you at length. However, those demands are lessened greatly in the deep hours of the night when sensible folk are sleeping. You can come back then, and seek both refuge from dreaming, and maybe a more detailed insight, if you can put more details to your description. Now if you would allow, Brannis and I have matters to discuss that I would prefer my great-nephew to hear about when I am ready to tell him myself."

"Sorry to have bothered you, Warlock." Celia stood, gave a small curtsey to the warlock, and took her leave. She cast a hesitant glance over her shoulder at Kyrus just before closing the door behind her.

Ignoring what formal protocol would have dictated, Rashan slumped down into the chair Celia had vacated, leaving Kyrus seated at his desk.

"Interesting girl, is she not?" Rashan asked, lacing his fingers behind his head as he lounged, stretched out diagonally on the chair. "Did you ever ask her about that name you had? Abbiley?"

"Yes. She accused you of having revealed it to me. I am still not entirely certain she is Abbiley, but my suspicions are growing."

"Well, keep that attitude of suspicion. Easy trust is a bad habit to fall into. It is easy for me to be flippant about it, given my current condition, and lack of a direct link to Tellurak these days. You, on the other hand, do well to doubt. The girl you described to me from Tellurak sounded like a sweet, innocent thing, but Celia is a clever girl. If the two are one in the same, and she fully realizes it, their personalities will drift together over time. That sweet, young, innocent girl might find a way to get hold of you by the manhood in one world and own you in both. Positioned well, blackmail between worlds can be brutally effective."

"It is the look that makes me doubt. She is so close, but there are a number of small things that are off. I cannot tell how much could be explained by magic," Kyrus said, hands spread wide in a helpless gesture.

"Most sorceresses get around to hammering out any blemish they find in their appearance, though some are more vain about it than others. A few carry around some flaws as marks of pride that their looks are natural. The sensible ones come to realize that menfolk are not as picky as they imagine them to be. Celia I would place among the first group."

"Can you tell by looking what has changed?" Kyrus asked.

"Not if she is any good at it, no," Rashan responded. "I have more important matters to attend to today. Your little personal mystery can occupy some other chunk of time, separate from my day."

"So which shall it be then, coronation or murderous intrigue?" Kyrus asked.

"No one ever said we could not combine the two," Rashan joked. "But actually I wished to speak to you of what will be taking place *after* the coronation."

"The reception?" Kyrus ventured a guess.

"No, me leaving to go to war."

"Oh."

"And you taking my place overseeing affairs in Kadris."

Silence.

And silence in reply. Rashan only smiled.

"You are really going to leave me to run everything in your absence?" Kyrus asked.

"I could not leave Brannis in charge, even though he had the brains for it. You, though, 'Brannis,' are a bit of a different tale. Brannis would have had to worry about plots directed against him, magical manipulation, or someone just straightforwardly turning him to ash. You are raw, largely untrained, but potentially dangerous enough to give anyone pause. You can bully them into obeying you, if transferred authority is not enough to win their cooperation."

"But what about the new emperor? What if he wants you to remain? You have been protecting him all this time."

"I have hammered it into his head since I got him selected that once he is emperor, he should order me into the field to clean up the mess this war is becoming. We can protect him from Megrenn well enough. Once he is emperor, I will cease worrying so much about threats from within. Killing a crowned emperor is a whole different matter from disposing of an appointed heir who did not enjoy wide support."

"Speaking of threats from within, what about those murders last night?" Kyrus asked.

"A tantrum perhaps, by those who disliked my choice of emperor. None of the three who were killed were particularly important, but I counted them among my supporters. Had they managed to kill Caladris or Aloisha, maybe I would have taken them seriously, but I do not see a threat in this. Mistake me not, though, I will delve into the matter through other parties, and find out the culprit. Just because I do not feel a threat does not mean it ought to go unpunished."

"You think Dolvaen will discover the murderer or murderers?" Kyrus probed.

"No. If anything, Dolvaen would be among my suspects, though I doubt he would have done the deeds himself. No, I have my little guild of rats pursuing the matter through more oblique channels. They will find out the comings and goings around the sites of the murders, and narrow the list of who might have been in all three places."

"What if they cannot find out?"

"Then I will pick someone who has not been so cooperative with my regency, and make them the scapegoat," Rashan said, shrugging. Kyrus's eyes widened in surprise. "What? What is that look for? Why would I lie to you, if I expect you to carry on in my absence? You need to know these things."

"I suppose I am surprised to hear you admit it openly."

"The wards will make our conversation gibberish to anyone standing outside. It is just you and me here. You know me for what I am, and have had no qualms yet in working with me."

"There is a difference between brutal methods, and killing innocents to make a point," Kyrus argued.

"Who said anything about killing innocents? Any scrupulous ruler keeps a few guilty men dangling by a thread of hope. It is a form of clemency that is never openly granted, but remains contingent upon not needing to connect a crime and a perpetrator."

"Is that what happened with my father ... with Brannis's father?" Kyrus demanded. *My father is a kindly farmer with a bumpkin's accent, alive and well a half-day's ride from Scar Harbor. For a moment, though, I would have sworn Maruk Solaran was my sire.*

"No, quite the contrary. The rest of the Inner Circle are all on a form of parole, as far as I am concerned, Iridan and Aloisha aside. No, Maruk Solaran—as well as Stalia Gardarus and Gravis Archon—were very much guilty of their crimes. Quite a number outside the Inner Circle are paroled as well. Your traveling companion Faolen, for one, has earned his clemency in earnest, as has Caladris, without whom I do not think I would have kept a civil war from starting."

"What if that is what was started last night?"

"Well, since you will be in charge here come dawn, I would suggest averting it if possible, and winning it if not."

"You are not worried?" Kyrus asked.

"You are young. I have seen a lot in my time, so I trust that it will all work out in the end. I usually have a hand in ensuring that it does so. Once I crush Megrenn and their allies, I will return and deal with any trouble remaining," Rashan said.

"Is that the reason for the jovial mood?" Kyrus asked, suddenly piecing it together.

"Am I in a good mood? Hmm, I suppose I am."

* * * * * * *

Civil war. The thought haunted Kyrus as he rode down to the waterfront. He had not planned on making his inspection until the morning after the coronation, but ideas were sloshing around in his brain, attempting to coalesce into a plan. It bothered him that Rashan expressed so little concern for the prospect, shrugging responsibility onto Kyrus, and merrily heading off to war.

By the sound of it, Rashan and Dolvaen were going to be conducting parallel investigations into the murders. By Kyrus's reckoning, given Rashan's admission that the victims were supporters of his, the warlock would be seeking the identity of the murderer while Dolvaen acted to obscure it or cast suspicion on another. *But if Rashan suspected Dolvaen of involvement, why would he not just confront him? He has never seemed shy about such things before.*

Kyrus's own conversation with Dolvaen Lurien had left little room for misinterpretation. He knew that the house-less sorcerer was aiming to return Kadrin to the rule of the Inner Circle, and not an upstart emperor. He knew he could bring that information to Rashan, and have the demon deal with the matter as he saw fit. The problem was that Kyrus was not certain whom he wished to prevail in the struggle. Dolvaen was powerful in his own right, and entrenched in Kadrin politics. He had to be aware of the possibility of a confrontation should anyone betray him; Kyrus could not imagine that Dolvaen did not have a contingency in place. Whether it would be enough, he had no way to tell but he suspected not.

Kyrus's new sword belt chafed as it bounced against his hip. There was nothing noteworthy about the blade, but he felt he ought to get into the habit of carrying one. Of late, he felt much more at home among the sorcerers of the Circle. It would be best for him to maintain at least the illusion that he was still Sir Brannis, Knight of the Empire. Whichever side the sorcerers of the Imperial Circle fell on, he wanted the knighthood and the army to fall on his own ... whichever side he decided on.

The eastern end of the Kadrin waterfront was home to the shipwrights that built the vessels of the much-maligned Kadrin navy. With five berths, five vessels under construction, and nearly a thousand workers, it rivaled the palace in its orchestrated chaos. Greetings were called out to him from various quarters as he was recognized. It felt good to hear a friendly welcome without wondering about sub-context and ulterior motives. His workforce took pride in the airships, and admired him for designing them. When history looked back on the era, they would be the birthplace of the first aerial navy. That historical perspective might have been lost on the more grounded among the workers, but the palpable buzz of that energy pervaded the worksite.

"Sir Brannis," called out a familiar voice.

Kyrus turned to see Goloway, Brannis's personal armorer, striding down the gangplank of the newest of Kyrus's designs—the first actually, since Brannis's hand had described all the others. The *Daggerstrike* was the first of a new sort of airship; it was entirely unseaworthy. Built around a flat-bottomed ship's skeleton, the hull was plated in steel, slotted with arrow-slits, and devoid of sails and rigging of any sort. The latter was no oversight, but rather a change in locomotion.

The *Daggerstrike* was the first vessel that would be powered entirely by aether.

Kyrus climbed down from his horse in time to clasp wrists with Goloway when he arrived. Though taller than the armorsmith, Kyrus was nowhere near Goloway's girth, little of it anything but muscle; the man's grip was like the steel he worked.

"Is everything ready?" Kyrus asked.

"Just polishing door handles and the like now, makin' it pretty for inspection," Goloway replied, beaming with pride.

"Know anything about how the runework has been going?" Kyrus ventured.

There was no reason to expect Goloway to know anything about how the runes worked, but it was not unreasonable to suppose he might have heard how the work was going.

"All finished, near as I can tell. The Circle boys workin' at it took off 'fore dusk last night, and haven't been back. I can go find one of the superintendants if you'd like, Sir Brannis."

"No, that will be quite all right, Goloway. I would just like a look around," Kyrus informed him.

Armorsmith in tow, he climbed aboard and admired the craftsmanship. There was little wood used in the construction beyond the timbers that gave the vessel its shape. The shipwrights could not work in metal, and the metalworkers had no feel for shaping a hull. Future versions would be entirely of metal, once the metalsmiths could learn the ship-building trade well enough to get the shape right. Kyrus ran his fingers along the contours of the runes that covered most surfaces of the ship. It was the largest, most intricate pattern—no, system of interconnected patterns, he corrected himself—of any of the airships to date.

"I've heard 'em grumbling, sir. Some of them sorcerers don't think this one will get off the ground. Too heavy. Too many runes for anyone to activate. Not using the wind for power. So ... what do you say to that?"

"If you can keep a secret for a few hours," Kyrus said, pausing to wait for Goloway to nod in acknowledgement before continuing, "you can see for yourself."

"I thought it was going to be activated tomorrow."

"Was."

Kyrus grinned. Goloway found it contagious.

* * * * * * *

Juliana arrived back at her room with pockets heavier with gold than when she had left that morning. Festival days were always lucrative occasions for a port inspector, if they had the right frame of mind. There were always shipments arriving with critically demanded goods, and men willing to pay extra for theirs to make it through the process more quickly. *I would not want to trade places with Aloisha. More work and less coin at the end of it, plus a lot of folk poking around at your business.* Juliana was content working occasionally, and keeping her own endeavors quieter.

The ward on her door took an effort to disengage, which raised her hackles. *Someone has been in here.* Juliana was inexpert in her ward-crafting; it had been Iridan who had carved the runes for their bedchamber. With any luck, it was just Iridan who had been there in her absence, but the ward felt different. It was the same pattern of runes; it had not been recarved or anything so extreme as that. It was merely infused with more aether than she was accustomed to putting into it when it needed refreshing.

She entered the room with a hand under the back of her tunic, on the hilt of Adventure. A quick scan in the aether revealed nothing, but she was all too aware that assassins of late had managed to avoid such scrutiny. The space was as disheveled as she remembered leaving it, bedclothes rumpled, jewelry scattered on the bedside table, piles of soiled clothing on the rug. Her black silk formal Circle uniform had been laid out on the bed, folded clumsily. She relaxed a bit. *Someone let the servants in to set out my attire for the evening?* Stranger things had befallen of late, but she could not rule out the possibility that something was seriously amiss.

Having left herself little enough time as it was, she decided that she was safe enough to strip out of her working gear and bathe. She had spent the day consorting with the sort of folks who did so infrequently themselves, and hanging about in locales that smelled of fish and ale. She had long since become inured to the odors, but knew that they would stand her in poor company at the ceremony. She was not so important to the proceedings that her presence would be missed if she was a bit late, but coming in reeking of dockside swill would draw attention she preferred to avoid.

After an all-too-brief cleansing, she donned enough lavender perfume to cover any lingering odors. She did not use the little bottle of honeysuckle that she knew Brannis remembered, and loved from when they were both younger: that was only for special occasions, not mere coronations. When she picked up her evening attire, she heard a crinkling sound. Turning the garment about, she located the source of the noise, a note stuffed into one of the sleeves.

Skip the reception afterward.
Head to the drydocks. Ask for Daggerstrike.
I will keep an old promise.

The note was written in beautiful Acardian script, casually scrawled artwork that served as adequate identification for the unsigned note. Juliana pondered for a moment, but knew that she did not have the time right then to puzzle through it. She did, however, reconsider her decision to leave her daggers behind for the coronation. Half the sorcerers in the Empire would be there, ensuring that only suicidal violence would be possible. With the change in plans for immediately afterward, she decided that she would be better off finding a place for them under her formal attire. A quick check in the mirror revealed slight bulges where the harness held Adventure and Freedom against the small of her back. Brannis's daggers were far superior to the ones she had brought with her to Raynesdark, but they were also a bit bulkier.

It would be cold enough at the outdoor ceremony, she decided, that wearing a cloak would not seem inappropriate. Any sorceress worth the title ought to have been able to shield herself against a bit of chill—and Juliana was certainly capable of doing so—but she was enough maligned among the Circle for her idleness and lack of ambition that it would not surprise most folk.

Juliana made her way across the room, and opened the wardrobe. She found it half empty. Missing half her clothing would be a minor inconvenience, but the half that remained was Iridan's, not hers. She hurried to her dresser, and began pulling out the drawers. Empty. Empty. Empty. She looked under the bed and found her spare boots missing as well.

What have you got in mind, Kyrus? Are we making an escape tonight? If you were going to do it, I would have rather it been the wedding rather than an assassination that gave you the idea.

She went back to the wardrobe, and pulled out one of Iridan's cloaks. It did not hang quite low enough for her taste, but it would do. She posed in front of the mirror to be sure, then left for the coronation ceremony of Emperor Sommick.

* * * * * * *

There must have been thirty or forty thousand in attendance, Kyrus estimated. The tournament grounds in Kadris were used all too infrequently, but they had been refurbished in short order upon Rashan's orders. The structure itself was a stepped bowl shape of cut stone blocks, covered with an overhanging wooden roof supported by stone pillars. The roof only covered the outermost half of the seats; the sod field of roughly tended grass and the seats nearest it were exposed to the night sky. The stars themselves would bear witness to the crowning of a new emperor.

The grounds had been opened up to anyone in the Empire who wished to attend. The throng outside attested to how many more wished to witness history than were able to actually get seats. The commoners crowded together on bench seats, packed in so tightly they could scarcely move. Kyrus thought back to all the things that Denrik and Stalyart had told him about the lot of the peasantry of the Kadrin Empire as he watched them herded to their seats like cattle to market. *There is only so much room to be had. It is not as if anyone is forcing these conditions on them. They are at least allowed the privilege of attending. More can have that privilege if more are allowed to crowd in together,* Kyrus told himself from the Solaran section of the reserved seating. The nobles, the sorcerous houses, the Circle members whether they had a house or not, knights and officers of the army ... all those were allowed spacious seating, cordoned off from the rabble.

He searched the crowd for signs of Juliana. The arrangement of the seating made it difficult, with the Solarans and Archons seated on the same side of the bowl, but not so closely that there was an unobstructed view. His aether-vision was mostly useless as well, since the sorcerers of the various blooded houses had Sources that ran the full gamut: stronger, weaker, and similar in strength to Juliana's. Picking her out among the commoners would have been easy enough, but finding her among her own family was difficult. Everything that made her stand out in crowds happened to be traits that ran among the Archons, from her height to her Source; she even had cousins and older sisters who had their hair colored not so differently from hers.

"Uncle Brannis, I can't see what's going on," a small voice complained from beside him. Through some perversity of humor, it seemed that Axterion had arranged for Danilaesis to be seated next to him.

"There is nothing to see yet. Just wait," Kyrus told him.

"Can I sit up on your shoulders?" Danil asked, making it sound as easy at nearly eight summers as it would have been when he was four.

"You are too big for that now. Just settle in. There is not going to be much to see anyway."

"Then why are so many people here to watch it? They must be expecting to see something good," Danil said.

"When someone is made emperor, they want lots of people to see it. It helps give the emperor legitimacy. Everyone here can personally vouch for having seen him take the crown, and all the people accepting that fact. Most of the people here are just here to be able to tell people they were here. The rest of us are here because it is expected of us. You are old enough now that you are expected to be here as well."

"Who expects us to be here?"

"Everyone else who is expected here. It is sort of a mutual affair. By coming, we show that we support the new emperor. Anyone who did not come would, in a way, be saying that they did not."

"Why is grandpa not here, then? Will people think he doesn't support the emperor?"

"No. He is too old for anyone to expect him to travel, even if it is just halfway across Kadris by carriage," Kyrus said. "Try looking around to find all the people you know. Make a list in your head of the ones you do not see. Find them afterward, and ask why they were not here." *That ought to keep him occupied a while.*

Kyrus's plan worked well enough for him to watch what little of a show accompanied the ceremony. A mix of palace guards and an honor guard of soldiers marched into the stadium carrying torches. There was something primal and ancient about bared flames, accentuated by the lack of magical lights as dusk began to fade. After marching out in formation, they spread themselves, and lined both sides of a path out to the center of the tournament grounds, which yet more of them encircled in fire. There was a circular stone slab at the very center, which Kyrus could see glowing with runes around the outer edge.

A hush fell over the crowd. Emerging from the end of the torch-lit line was Sommick Highwater, who would shortly become Emperor of the Kadrin Empire. He was clad in red-and-gold velvet, accented in white. His head was bare, ready to receive a crown. Hard though it was to tell from so far away, Kyrus thought he looked nervous.

Behind him followed two of the most influential figures in the Empire, walking side by side. To his right was Dolvaen Lurien, dressed in his Inner Circle finery, black with red-and-gold trim. To his left was General Sir Hurald Chadreisson, his runed armor polished to a shine that glowed orange in the torchlight. Both men were choices of politics rather than true influence. Though Kyrus knew for certain that Dolvaen opposed the emperor's selection, Rashan had ceded the honor of issuing the Circle's blessing to his second in command to force Dolvaen to publicly endorse him. Kyrus had given his own honor over to his former commander as a peace offering. He knew that Rashan intended him to take over his regency in all but name, so the oversight of the army would fall to Sir Hurald anyway unless he chose to replace the man.

Lastly came the imperial regent, Warlock Rashan Solaran, bearing in his hands the crown that had been worn by the last twelve emperors. It was a golden circlet ringed in golden horns. Four gems were set equally spaced around it: emerald, ruby, sapphire, diamond. Kyrus knew the last fact from Brannis's history lessons; it was too far to make out what gems might have been set in it. It glowed in the aether as well, prompting him to wonder what powers the crown might possess—if the aether indicated anything more than just preservative magics, that is.

The four men came to a stop on the stone slab, the emperor at the center, the other three arrayed around him. The purpose of the runes became clear when Rashan began to speak. His voice carried throughout the tournament grounds, reverberating like the roar of a dragon. Kyrus could attest to that from Brannis's experience.

"People of Kadrin, we gather today to crown a new emperor, Sommick the First. I ask of you, Sommick, of House Highwater, are you prepared to accept the mantle of emperor, as is your birthright?" Rashan said for all to hear and bear witness.

"I am."

"Does this man have the support of the army?" Rashan asked.

"I give my support, and that of the Imperial Army, to the claim of Sommick, of House Highwater," Sir Hurald attested, swearing his fealty, and committing the military to back the new emperor.

"Does this man have the support of the sorcerers?" Rashan asked.

"I give my support, and that of the Imperial Circle, to the claim of Sommick, of House Highwater," Dolvaen Lurien attested.

Kyrus was impressed at the man's acting ability. He gave every indication of sincerity. Kyrus supposed it was how Dolvaen had kept his ruse from being accidentally exposed.

"From this day forth, let any who speak or act against Emperor Sommick be struck down by the might of the Imperial Army, acting as the left hand of the emperor, or by the might of the Imperial Circle, acting as the right hand of the emperor." Rashan paused. "As Imperial Regent, I have ruled over the Kadrin Empire this past season as we sought the rightful heir to the throne. As of this moment, I resign the position of regent, renounce all claim to rulership, and swear my fealty to Emperor Sommick, the First. I bestow upon you, my Emperor, the crown of the Kadrin Empire, and with it all rights and powers granted to her emperor."

Sommick Highwater knelt at Rashan's feet, and accepted the crown as it was placed upon his head. It was awkward and unwieldy upon Sommick's head, an ornament destined to the storage vaults until the next grand occasion, unless Sommick turned out to be exceedingly vain and insecure. As Sommick arose, Sir Hurald and Dolvaen knelt. All the torchbearers knelt as well. Of all the men standing below in the field, only Rashan did not kneel; the demon warlock merely bowed his head in acknowledgement.

The emperor turned his back on his entourage, and faced the crowded stands, specifically toward the commoners. He held out his arms to them, spread wide.

"My people! It fills me with pride to see what an empire I have inherited, what a fine people to have turned out in such numbers to see me take up the crown. We are an empire at war, beset by many enemies. I will see that this threat is ended. My first order as emperor is this: Warlock Rashan, I hereby command you that, on the morrow, you take personal action to bring war to Megrenn and her allies, that you use that terrible sword of yours to make them suffer for their transgressions against us."

"As you command," Rashan replied for all to hear. Kyrus wondered how much of that little speech was written for him by the warlock.

"But that is tomorrow. Tonight we celebrate!" Emperor Sommick proclaimed, signaling the official end of the ceremony. The crowd cheered. There was to be a grand procession of carriages across the city to the palace, where the revelry would stretch into the deep hours of the night. That procession was a time Kyrus had plans to make use of.

Pushing his way through the crowd, Kyrus muttered about having matters to attend to. For most who were able to make room, that vague excuse was cause enough to let Brannis Solaran pass. Warlock Rashan's lieutenants were not known for making their motives plain, and Brannis was known to be well above that rank in Rashan's personal hierarchy. By the time the crowd began filtering out into the streets to either join or watch the procession, Kyrus was already at the front of the pack. He disappeared from the crowd as quietly as he was able.

* * * * * * * *

Juliana had sat uneasily through the coronation. She saw Brannis searching the crowd for her, but could hardly find an inconspicuous method of drawing attention to herself without ... well, without drawing attention to herself. Brannis, of course, had been easy to spot. Just shifting into the aether, and looking for the blinding light was all it took. In fact, Juliana would not be surprised if many sorcerers had to forgo enjoying the view in the aether during the ceremony because of the distractingly painful glare from Brannis's Source.

A tiny voice in her head had reminded her that Brannis was now really Kyrus, and that Brannis was off in Tellurak with Soria, but she had hushed it, and told the voice that it did not matter.

Juliana had tried to keep her focus on the ceremony itself, which had been thankfully brief. There were too many thoughts bubbling in her head. Aloisha's accusation, or at least near-accusation, had been the first item to put her on edge. She had initially heard of the murders with a detached curiosity, the sort that comes easily when you can see no connection between an event and how it affects you. After the "chat" with Brannis's sister, she had been trying to find a motive for the killings that would fit with the intrigues Aloisha hinted at or the machinations of the Megrenn, who had already tried two assassinations previously. Down by the waterfront, her seafaring acquaintances were no help to her state of mind, having all manner of theories on the deaths of the three sorcerers. The cryptic note and the emptiness of her bedchamber had only served to add a layer to the mystery; she just did not know quite what it was.

The crowd carried Juliana along toward the exits. She made no effort to speed the process, allowing herself to blend in among the sorcerers, dressed nearly identically in black, save a few rank insignia and the differences between men's and women's attire. Once the crowd oozed her out into the streets, she flowed to the edges of the group and disappeared down a side street.

Feast nights drew thieves and cutthroats like flies to a corpse. They lurked at the edges of crowds, waiting for errant merrymakers to wander away from the safety of guards and numbers. Juliana activated a shield once she was well away from the bulk of the realm's sorcerers. After that, any cutthroat would merely pose a delay, a straightforward problem on a day where she had her fill of mysteries; an attack would have been a welcome diversion, a problem she knew exactly how to handle.

Despite her misgivings, the thieves and worse among the Kadris underworld were either lucky or smart that night. She arrived at the waterfront without incident, but was unfamiliar with the drydocks. Of all the parts of the waterfront, it was the place least in need of someone to oversee cargo arriving. There were only two places ships went where they never needed such an inspection: the drydocks where they originated, and the seafloor where they eventually all wound up.

There was more activity than she would have expected at so late an hour on a day of celebration. She would have expected the workers to be among the revelers drinking themselves stupid over the crowning of a new emperor. She did not know the names of any of the new ships that were being built, so she had to ask someone which the *Daggerstrike* was.

"The metal ship with no masts. You can't miss it, girl," one of them informed her.

When she found it, it looked even stranger than any airship she had seen so far. The modifications to most just involved a lot of runes, some extra rigging to keep crewmen from falling off as they pitched and rolled in the air, and a steering sail. The *Daggerstrike* looked like a ship dipped in molten metal, hot enough to burn away masts, rigging, and rudder. It looked incomplete, heavy, and unlikely to float either on water or in the air.

"There you are. Good. Quickly, get up here," she heard Brannis call down from above.

She looked up and saw him on the deck, leaning over the railing. Juliana looked around, and found the gangplank. She took Brannis's advice, and rushed up to meet him on the deck.

Brannis put his arm around her, and hurried her down belowdecks, lighting a soft blue light as they went. Juliana could not help but marvel at how nearly every metallic surface was covered in runes. Brannis pulled her into a room at the end of the corridor that turned out to be a bedchamber.

"Brannis, if this is what you wanted, you could—"

"No, it is not like that," Brannis replied. "These are your new quarters."

"My what?" Juliana shouted.

Brannis pantomimed quiet by patting his hands downward in the air. "Things here are going to get messy in Kadris very soon. You have seen a piece of the puzzle, unless you have been oblivious to the rumors about the murdered sorcerers. I am fairly certain that there is a civil war beginning. You are a perfect target for such intrigues," Brannis said, holding up a hand that forestalled an objection before she could voice it. "I know, you take care of yourself far better than anyone here credits you with. That said, I have a good, legitimate use for those same skills. I have it worked out perfectly."

"What perfect plan would that be?" Juliana asked. "I remember your 'plan' from Raynesdark, which—"

"No, that was Brannis's plan," Brannis said.

Kyrus! Juliana reminded herself. *I keep telling you they are not the same.*

"I have this thought through well enough. I want you to captain the *Daggerstrike*. I have no need of sailors on this ship, I have realized. This is a ship to be run by a sorcerer, or a sorceress in this particular case. I have written up all the appropriate orders to promote you to a naval captain, assign you a crew, and relieve you of your current Circle commitments."

"I'm not certain you are authorized for all that," Juliana replied, raising a skeptical eyebrow.

"That is the beauty of the plan. You are leaving tonight, not very long from now, in fact. By the time you are gone, you will be unreachable to rescind any orders. Before anyone can make any serious effort to recall you, I will have all the authority I need. Rashan arranged for Emperor Sommick to send him off to war; the bloodthirsty bastard cannot wait to free himself of the shackles of politics. He told me that he will arrange for me to be left in charge, to take his place tomorrow when he departs for Megrenn, or at least the parts of Kadrin that are under their control now."

"Wait, what about the emperor? Rashan is free to go because there is an emperor now to take care of all the politics."

"No, the emperor is a fool. Rashan wants *me* running things in his absence, not Emperor Sommick. I trust that he will arrange it so that happens."

"What about this ship, then? I know nothing about captaining a ship, and this thing doesn't look close to getting off the ground," Juliana protested, knowing that it would not change anything. She loved hearing Brannis's convoluted mental acrobatics. It was among her favorite things about him.

"The ship is ready to fly. It just needs aether to get it started. I will empower it momentarily. I just wanted to wait until you were ready to depart. I ... um ... think it may draw a small amount of attention. I will show you everything you need to command the ship; it is as simple to use as I could think to make it. As for the captaining part ... you already run a small crew of mercenaries in Tellurak, plus you have been aboard a number of ships; you have seen how captains act."

"But what do I do once I leave? I am not a battle commander."

"No, but you are a mercenary. I do not want the *Daggerstrike* within a cannon's range of a real battle. I want you to cause havoc. Ambush supply caravans, pick off scouting parties, strike remote garrisons, that sort of thing. I shall leave the details entirely to your judgment and discretion."

Juliana got a quick tutoring on everything she would need to know about the controls for the ship, how to steer it, how to make it climb or dive. Everything from the gangplanks to the hidden hatches in the sides to disgorge corsairs was all commanded by the captain from one of several points on the ship that would accept commands. When he felt she knew all she would need to get her started, Brannis shooed her off the ship.

"I will need to draw a lot of aether to get this monster started. Best not to be too close," Brannis warned.

Juliana retreated to the ground, where she found her crew gathered, awaiting orders. She met her new first mate and officers, all of whom were army, not navy. They made introductions as Juliana felt alarming amounts of aether flowing to the interior of the ship. The nearest sensation she had ever felt was being there in the mines of Raynesdark when Jinzan Fehr had used the Staff of Gehlen. As the draw ended, the ship began to crackle with energy, and a throbbing, pulsating hum emanated from the steel hull.

"Everything is ready. It took," Brannis called down to her as he descended the gangplank. He looked haggard. "You should all get aboard and get going. Head out to sea a bit before looping around out of sight of the city. I have to get back to the palace before my presence is too sorely missed."

"Brannis, you never promised me a ship of any sort, or a command of my own. What promise were you referring to keeping in your note?"

"Bran—I gave you Adventure and Freedom," he said, nodding in the direction of where she kept her dragon-tooth daggers. "It might have been a sweet gesture, but it was ultimately a hollow one. It was cheating. *Now* I am giving you adventure and freedom—the proper sort this time."

She did not care that it was in front of her entire new crew; she crushed Brannis—*Okay ... Kyrus*—in her arms and kissed him before she took her leave.

The *Daggerstrike* lifted effortlessly at her command, holding the ship's wheel just as Kyrus had shown her. The thrills of adventure and freedom awaited.

Chapter 30 - Intentions

The morning sun brightened the sky over the islands of Kapish, where the *Fair Trader* sat at anchor, but did nothing for the mood of her captain. Denrik Zayne was a patient man but he was being sorely tried. The *Sea Dragon* had already come and gone, paying their tribute to Zayne as the owner of the vessel and liege of her captain. That had been two days prior. Stalyart's *Merciful* had been due around the same time, but there had been no sign of him or his ship.

"Another day, Cap'n?" Holyoake asked, approaching Denrik as he stood at the ship's port railing, staring out into the northern sea.

"Aye, Mr. Holyoake. Another day," Denrik concurred. "Captain Stalyart stood by for three years, and got me off that miserable hunk of rock the Acardians stuck me on. The least I can do it pay him the courtesy of waiting three days."

"And tomorrow, sir?" Holyoake asked. "Men are grumblin'. Not me, mind you. The men. I'll handle 'em sure nuff, don't you worry. But you know … the men."

Marfin Holyoake finished saying his piece, and clamped his pipe between his jaws. He dug in the pockets of his jacket until he found a small cloth bag. Reaching in, he took a pinch of pipeweed, and stuffed the bowl of the pipe with it. When Denrik looked his way, Holyoake angled the pipe in his direction, and gave a wink.

Smiling, Denrik focused in the aether, managing to draw enough of the stuff to get the pipeweed to smolder. The first mate of the *Fair Trader* took a few quick puffs to get the flame burning properly, and returned the smile. It was reassuring to Denrik to find that sort of acceptance. Too few men knew of his powers, paltry though they might be. Holyoake would never understand what it was like to be twinborn—Denrik would never reveal *that* secret to anyone who was not twinborn himself—but him even knowing that he was some sort of witch or wizard or shaman, whatever he chose to perceive it as, was comforting.

"Round up a few of those men for me, Mr. Holyoake," Denrik said over his shoulder as he looked back out to sea. "Put together a game of Crackle. That ought to occupy their time."

"Aye, sir. Mind if I count myself among 'em?" Holyoake asked.

"Unless your eyes have gotten a fair sight better since you served on the *Honest Merchant*, you shall do no good out here, watching the horizon. Of course you may join in."

If there was anything that was likely to draw Stalyart back to him, it would be the presence of a game of Crackle. Fill that game with amateurs like Holyoake and the crewmen, and how would he be able to resist? Despite a thorough understanding of the workings of magic, there were still some forms of it that defied explanation.

Come now, Mr. Stalyart, you know you would not want to miss such a game.

* * * * * * * *

On another ship, in another part of the Katamic, a ship called the *Sand Piper* carved a line through the water. It was a Takalish vessel with a mostly Takalish crew, charting a course around the northern side of the small continent. It was similar in design to the Acardian galleon, but smaller and lighter in the water.

The *Sand Piper* was a passenger vessel, first and foremost. Any cargoes she carried were incidental. Most of the passengers were Takalish, with a number of light-skinned Acardians mixed in among them. In every direction, there was evidence of wealth, from finely tailored suits to jeweled necklaces; passage on board a vessel such as the *Piper* was not for the weak of purse. Brannis squirmed in his newly bought outfit, trying to keep the seams from rubbing in the wrong places. The sleeves were cut too narrow for his muscles to flex comfortably. Juliana—Soria—had insisted on outfitting him to match the cover story she had arranged for them.

"There you are," Soria called out.

Brannis turned to see her appearing more feminine than he had realized she could look. The Takalish were fine, by and large, with the concept of warrior women, but unwed couples traveling together was looked down upon. Soria had the playful idea to pose as husband and wife for the trip to avoid drawing both scorn and attention. She had decided to look the part of an idle kept-wife to some merchant, who in this case would be Mr. Brannis Hinterdale. A low-cut pink gown outlined her figure—gave her a figure, it seemed—distracting Brannis from all else he had been thinking about. Her hair seemed more golden and less reddish, curled into an elaborate knot at the back of her head, stabbed through with thin wooden skewers in a Kheshi fashion. Breaking up the expanse of bare skin from her chin to her bosoms was a gold chain and diamond pendant, flanked by emeralds; a pair of dangling diamond-strand earrings paired with it, each one appearing to drip from a single emerald. The jewels appeared so extravagant as to make one assume they were fakes. Brannis suspected they were real, stolen, and worth more than the *Sand Piper*.

"About time you woke up. I thought that was my exclusive purview," Brannis said, managing with effort to look her in the eye.

"I was having the most wonderful dream," Soria replied, unable to remove the grin from her face.

Brannis had overlooked it as he gawked at her, but she carried a spitted rabbit haunch, soaked in some sweet-smelling sauce that hinted at honey and ginger. She took a bite, leaning forward over the ship's railing to keep the oozing sauce from dribbling onto her dress. She wiped away the excess with a finger, and sucked it clean.

Brannis eyed the morsels until she held it up for him to try. He bit in, and savored the sweet, spicy flavor. He found his tastes to be more suited to Tellurak's food than Kyrus's had proven toward Veydran fare.

"So where did you end up taking it?" Brannis asked.

"Sure you want me to tell you?" Soria teased. "They can't torture you for my whereabouts if you don't know."

"You had fun with it, I take it?"

"Oh, how I wish this pretty little bucket we're bobbing along in could take wing, and soar like my *Daggerstrike!*" Soria exclaimed, looking up into the sky and twirling around once, billowing her dress out like he had seen Juliana do so many times. It had the same effect on him now as it had when she did it in their youth.

"How were the crew? They warming to you at all?"

"They seem like they'll be all right. I think once they get their air legs, it will be a bit better, with less vomiting. A few took to it right off, though. All those harnesses around made it seem a lot safer, being tethered to the decks and walls when it goes upside down."

"You ... flipped it over in midair?" Brannis asked, looking at her sidelong, eyes wide.

Soria nodded, her mouth occupied with tearing a chunk of rabbit meat from the skewer. With her free hand, she pantomimed a series of loops and rolls. "Made a mess of everyone's quarters, though," Soria replied with a gasp as she gulped down the bite. "We'll be keeping it a bit more level until I get someone to rig up a way to hold footlockers down to the floors."

A cold gust of wind caught them, speeding the ship by a hair, and causing Brannis to shiver.

"You warm enough out here?" Soria asked.

Brannis was dressed in a long-sleeved white shirt with ruffled shoulders and cuffs in current Takalish fashions. They were supposed to fit loosely, but without having something tailored, everything was tight around his arms. Pinkish skin showed beneath the fabric where it was taut, hinting at just how little protection it gave against the wind.

"I am using a bit of aether to cheat the cold," she said. "I would die from exposure in this thing elsewise."

"I should be fine," Brannis assured her. "Have you seen Rakashi this morning?"

"No, and I don't expect to see him much this voyage unless we try. Warrior-scholars are a pretty big deal around here. They'll have him telling stories to their children, and giving blessings. They'll ask him about health problems, and his opinion on just about everything from wheat prices to whether the peace will last with Khesh. The captain gave him a cabin nicer than ours, and didn't charge him a single darshi."

"You think he is the same in Veydrus?" Brannis asked her.

"You plotting again?" Soria chided, waggling a finger at him. "I told you, we have a deal worked out. We don't play politics between worlds. Speaking of which, would you care to elaborate on that whirlwind explanation for shipping me out of Kadris last night? Distracting me with my own airship was only going to get you out of explaining yourself for so long, you know?" Soria could not help but grin anew at the reminder of the *Daggerstrike*.

"Those murdered were supporters of Rashan. That means they were supporters of Emperor Sommick as well, whether because they believed in his claim or because they are obsequious bootlicks looking for personal gain, it matters little. If there are sides being taken in earnest—and if the fact all three victims were on one side was not simple coincidence—it very much looks like one side has started a war."

"Don't most folk support Rashan? I mean, maybe he isn't popular in the 'Let's name our firstborn after him' sense, but I would assume anyone would support him out of ... well ... laziness if nothing else. Just doing a job in the Empire and following orders from above is 'supporting,' isn't it?" Soria asked. "It takes some initiative to actually oppose a regent."

"Dolvaen. Dolvaen has taken that initiative," Brannis told her. "It is safe to know, now that you are out of the city, but he is the one leading the opposition."

"How do you know?" Soria wondered aloud. The last bit of rabbit dripped sweet sauce onto the *Sand Piper*'s polished deck as the skewer drooped limply in her hand.

"He tried to recruit me to his cause," Brannis replied.

There was a metallic clatter as the skewer dropped from Soria's neglectful grasp. With a warrior's instincts and a debutante's tenuous hold on newfound propriety, the skewer disappeared overboard before anyone could turn to see what had happened. All anyone might have seen was a slippered foot retreating beneath a frilly pink dress of a very innocent young bride as she spoke with her new husband by the railings.

"He really did that?" Soria asked in a loud whisper once bystanders had returned to their previous distractions.

"Yes, came right out and made his case, too. He left no doubt. He told me that Rashan and I would not be able to coexist in the long term, and that eventually he would grow wary of me, and find an excuse to kill me. He seemed to think I had the potential to swing the balance of power against Rashan."

"Well, you have all the power and control of an untrained monohorn. Sure, you ought to be able to hurt something if you got hold of it, but you're no warrior, at least not with aether. You're just a really, really impressively dangerous firehurler. Don't think you can fight someone like Rashan, or even Dolvaen, if it came down to it. I don't like how you're sounding like you're getting caught right in the middle of this."

"Well, if I wait it out, I might not have to choose sides. Rashan seems to suspect something is amiss, but is not concerned by it. Keep in mind, it is not just him; Caladris and my whole family seem solidly behind him, plus who knows how many others, not to mention the army seems to have warmed to him," Brannis said.

"Have you told Rashan about Dolvaen's offer?" Soria asked. "If you want to avoid a conflict, why not just let Rashan take care of the traitors?"

"I am not sure he is in the business of killing traitors," Brannis replied. "He may have killed my father and your grandfather for treason, but he has let many others walk free who he knows are guilty. He will wait until he has another reason for killing them. He told me of his cynical method for resolving mysterious crimes: let a few guilty ones run free, and cull them when you need a scapegoat. He might well hold onto the knowledge until he sees some better reason to kill Dolvaen, and in the meantime, I gain an enemy; I am sure word of it would get back to Dolvaen. He is too clever."

"Have you ever considered that maybe I was just the one you should have wanted to keep close by? This sort of thing is far closer to my domain than wars with cannons and dragons. Your sister tried to accuse me of those murders— stopped me in the middle of the palace and everything—but she wasn't far from the mark. I wasn't the killer but I certainly could have been. For the right reason, I could be."

"If you are looking for me to thank you for killing Duke Pellaton, then fine: thank you. I had assumed you wished that incident kept quiet, but here in Tellurak, I do not quite think any harm will come of saying it."

Soria's eyes widened. "You knew?" she asked. "Did Rashan say something about it?"

"I was the one who told him—and told him that he was better off with a younger, more pliable Duke Pellaton. The man threatened me, then the next thing we know, he wakes up dead, with a goblin dagger stuck in him. Really now … there was one dead goblin assassin with no dagger, and one goblin dagger in a dead duke. Not a lot of people got out into that hallway the morning before the battle, but if none of the others who were there picked up on that, shame on them."

"Oh. Well … you're welcome. It was probably not the wisest decision I've made, but I guess it all worked out, right?"

Another gust sucked the warmth from Brannis's core, and set him to shivering again before the blow passed. The ship was taking the northern route around the Takalish coast before heading out into the deep Katamic to make the crossing to Acardia. The southern route was shorter and warmer, but of late, it had been beset by pirates. The captain of the *Sand Piper* was a cautious man who was paid handsomely to ferry his passengers safely to their destination. If that meant a long, chilly voyage via the northern coast, so be it. The Mad Tinker kept the waters near his islands north of Takalia well clear of pirates.

"Well, pleasant as the sea air smells, I think I am going to retreat belowdecks. I rescind my previous boast," Brannis said, still shivering.

"Wait up!" Soria called after him as Brannis headed for the stairs that led down below, away from the winds. "I'll help you keep warm."

Without even having to turn back, he could hear the mischievous grin on her face.

* * * * * * *

"Why does he just stare like that?" Zellisan asked. "It isn't natural."

The wagon rumbled amiably along down the Tradeway, continuing westward. There was no sign of the caravan they had started out with. Even though they were likely outpacing it, the caravan had half a day's lead on them. It would be unlikely for them to close that sort of distance before reaching Naia, their destination by default, not by design; it was the next city along the Tradeway.

"It will take some time for him to get over his apathy toward this world. Anzik lives a much more engaging life. In Megrenn, his family is wealthy, and he is surrounded by magical wonders, including those he can work himself. He has little incentive to pay attention to this world, beyond the physical discomforts he suffers by ignoring it," Wendell explained. "I grew up much the same. It was not until my own master discovered me that I found something in Tellurak that I cared about enough to pull my attention away from Veydrus."

The two spoke openly in Kadrin. If either the driver or Jadon understood a word of it, they did not let on. The driver likely could not tell the difference between their otherworldly speech and any other of the more exotic tongues he knew not a word of. Of course, Jadon might have learned plenty of Kadrin through Anzik, if the boy was well educated, and still not given any hint that he understood them.

"How much time, you think?" Zell persisted. He looked at the boy like an unlucky uncle who had been pressed into child-watching duty, and could not be done with it quickly enough. He shifted in his seat, his aging back protesting both the hard wooden bench of the wagon, and lending support to his general irritation with the whole situation. "I want to get done with whatever business you and Brannis are up to."

"Oh, believe me ... I am more eager for a resolution to this than you are," Wendell promised, giving a tenuous little smile. Zell noticed that Wendell looked awful—he had not paid much attention to the magician's appearance before then, spending much of his time avoiding conversing with the street-performer.

"Are ... you all right, Wendell?" Zell ventured tentatively, trying to look concerned. "I know you and Brannis wanted to keep this whole business secret, but if there's something I need to know, tell me."

"Things are going better here than in Veydrus, shall we say?" Wendell allowed. He turned away from Zell after that, fixing his attention on the boy, Jadon. Zell watched one broken, spooky magical creature stare at another one.

"Is ... Naia ... nice?" Zell asked, trying his pidgin Takalish in an effort to strike up a conversation with their driver. The wizened old Takalish twisted in his seat to look back at his passengers, making an inquiring little noise, as if he had forgotten that his cargo could speak.

The driver garbled something in reply in the casual patois of one who does not realize how to soften his speech to the understanding of a non-native speaker. Zell imagined he caught enough to gather that indeed it was a nice place. He gave a satisfied grunt, and nodded sagely in lieu of continuing a verbal exchange.

Zell slumped back into his seat as the driver returned his attention to the road, which hardly needed it. The horses were the ones keeping the wagon from veering off the road, maintaining a steady pace they had learned over many such crossings of the Tradeway.

"Anything I could maybe ask Brannis about for you?" Zell offered.

"No. No, I do not think that would be helpful," Wendell replied, shaking himself from whatever musings were occupying his thoughts just long enough to form a reply before giving all appearance of heading right back to them.

That settled it in Zellisan's mind. His next opportunity, he would talk to Brannis about whatever mysterious problem Wendell did not want to discuss.

* * * * * * * *

Denrik did not enjoy taking his crew's coin. The easiest way to maintain loyalty among cutthroats had always been to establish a belief that you were the key to their future wealth, he had always believed. Distracted as he was, it was no trouble at all avoiding impoverishing his common sailors. Bad cards came his way in plenty, and saw more play than they probably should have. Good cards came his way occasionally, and earned him little, as he testily overplayed them, scaring away players before pots grew large.

He was beginning to wonder when he ought to call off the game, risking sounding like a sore loser if he did so when he still had a pile of coins on the table in front of him that were frequently heading to his men's piles. The decision was made easier by a shout from on deck. A ship had been sighted!

Denrik threw in cards that might have had some potential to win the hand, but he had mainly been biding his time. He gave his pile of coins, paltry though it had become, a meaningful look. He ran a finger over them, making it look like he was taking a count. He had no time to actually count the varying currencies in the pile to take a proper accounting of them, but the worry that he *might* have done so ought to have been enough to stay greedy hands.

Denrik took his hat from the back of his chair, and set it on his head slightly askew. The angle was just enough to make the Acardian captain's hat look less than properly naval. He felt more a proper pirate captain by the day, worry over Stalyart's absence excepted, looking the part played into it. He was no longer wearing the castoffs of the ship's previous captain, but had a full wardrobe of tailored clothes, new pistols, a jeweled sabre. He strode out onto the deck of the *Fair Trader* as a king of a small, floating kingdom, prepared to watch the return of his favored knight.

The ship on the horizon had been too far to identify when he first arrived on deck. He took his own personal spyglass from a case that hung at his side, and watched the ship approach. It was heading straight for their position—either a good sign or a very bad one. With just a head-on view, he could not get a full count of sails, but he could at least rule out—

Kthooom. Kthooom. Kthooom. Kthooom.

Both broadsides of the unidentified ship opened fire at once. Plumes of thin, grey smoke rose from either side of the ship. Denrik smiled, and a cheer went up from the *Fair Trader*'s crew. *A waste of munitions, to be sure, but the man has style.* The shots splashed harmlessly into the Katamic, launching cascades of water into the air.

The tension of the ship's approach immediately changed to eagerness and preparations to greet the returning *Merciful*. Captain Stalyart offered no further theatrics as he piloted his ship in, and slid it up next to the *Fair Trader*, then threw a pair of gangplanks between the two vessels. Stalyart himself was the first to cross the gap.

"Captain Stalyart, I was beginning to think you had gone and gotten yourself sunk," Denrik called out loudly enough for both crews to hear. It was a public event, and needed a public greeting to go with it.

"Ahh, Captain Zayne. I think my tale will put thoughts of lateness very much to the back of your mind. I have two little newses for you, and someone new whom you need to meet," Stalyart replied in a somewhat more reserved volume. From a showman like Stalyart, it boded ill.

"Let us talk it over in my cabin while the crews catch up on old times," Denrik told him, keeping the tone light until he could get his former first mate somewhere private. Stalyart followed him as he returned to his cabin.

"I see you have played Crackle without me. I am hurt." Stalyart feigned offense at the sight of the hastily adjourned game still occupying a table in Denrik's cabin.

"Worked like magic, getting you back here." Denrik smiled, his mood rather lighter than normal despite the foreboding he had picked up on from Stalyart upon his arrival. He was a good man to have around, and bad news from him was better than no news without him. "So what had you to tell me?"

"Well, I have determined that Mr. Hinterdale has departed Denku Appa, and seems to have no interest in pursuing any sort of vengeance against you. In fact, he has arranged for a replacement for himself as Kadrin ambassador aboard the *Fair Trader*, should your offer of such still stand. I have the man in question, who goes by the name of Tanner, on board the *Merciful* right now."

"Well, those were not such bad 'newses,' now, were they?" Denrik said, giving a chuckle to put Stalyart at ease. The man seemed to have had a rough go somewhere along the way that he had yet to detail, and Denrik did not want Stalyart to think him upset with the idea of another try at the "floating embassy" idea.

"Oh, my pardon, Captain. If you consider those separate bits of news, then I have three," Stalyart amended, his face grave.

"What is the third, then?" Denrik's eyes narrowed.

"By rather fantastical means, it appears that our Mr. Hinterdale has escaped

Denku Appa via Kadrin. He has traded places with Brannis Solaran."

"Could you repeat that please, Mr. Stalyart?" Denrik asked, declining to form a proper reaction until his mind wrapped that sentence up into a package it could digest. He pushed his hat up a bit so that it gave a clearer view, with no corner overhanging any part of his field of vision—as if that would somehow allow the information to make more sense as it reached him.

"Kyrus Hinterdale is in Kadrin. I dropped Brannis Solaran off in Takalia, Daisha to be precise. He travels with four other Kadrin twinborn," Stalyart said, speaking slowly and deliberately.

"That was not what you said the first time. That was worse!" Denrik snapped. He squeezed his eyes shut, and rubbed them with thumb and forefingers, willing the news to make sense, or to somehow be less awful. "Sit. I need to get through this, and I am going to have a lot of questions, I think." Stalyart obligingly pulled up a chair, straddling it backward with his arms crossed atop the back.

"Before you ask, I know your first question. It is *not* Kyrus I met. I do not see the aether well, but Mr. Hinterdale stood out quite clearly to me. Brannis Solaran is a ghost, as close to Sourceless as I can remember seeing."

"A trick. Some way to hide his Source," Denrik proposed.

Stalyart shook his head. "I think not. You said you met Brannis Solaran at Raynesdark. You described him in resplendent golden armor with a sword that practically radiated magic. When I encountered Mr. Solaran, he was on a ship the *Merciful* attacked, singlehandedly fighting off my crew in a golden suit of armor that shrugged off all blows, and wielding a sword that crushed all in its path. He is Mr. Hinterdale's height, and has his face, but he is built like Mr. Reggelend, perhaps a bit thinner." Stalyart drew the comparison to the largest of Captain Zayne's "crew" from his imprisonment on Rellis Island. Tawmund Reggelend was a street enforcer for a land-based gang of thieves; he was the sort who broke legs when debts went unpaid.

"Magic?" Denrik suggested, lamely, optimistically.

"Captain. You may ask me a thousand questions if you like, but I think Mr. Tanner would be more helpful," Stalyart suggested. He looked over at the cabin door. Denrik could not recall seeing the man seem so discomfited.

"Very well, but before you go fetch him, what sort of man is he?" Denrik asked. "Who am I going to be hosting as a Kadrin ambassador?" He had visions of a man of middle years to all appearances, but older than most toothless greybeards. Perhaps a sorcerer of the Imperial Circle, if not even the Inner Circle. Surely if there were as many twinborn among the Kadrin as Stalyart's claim of four in Kyrus's immediate company indicated, sorcerers would be prominent among them.

"He fits in well with the crew, I must admit. He is a coinblade and a quickblade. A saw a bit of him fighting during a boarding action he was, at the time, on the other side of. He is at least my equal with a sword. He knows a touch of magic, just enough that it makes him feel important. He can hold his drink, and pisses away his coin at Crackle like a merchant's son."

"Hmm." Denrik gave it some thought. "Could be worse, I suppose. Go along, then, and send him in."

Stalyart did not need goading. He was gone from the cabin as quickly as dignity allowed. *He is either nervous about this whole Kyrus business, or he has something he does not want to tell me. You are an excellent Crackle player, Robbono, but I know you too well.*

The man who entered Denrik's cabin looked like he had lost a fistfight, and never quite recovered his looks. A flattened nose hunkered between an overhanging brow and a jutting chin. He strutted in as if he was considering buying the ship from Denrik. He looked about at the decor before settling his gaze in Denrik's general direction.

"Nice ship. I guess it will look a bit more pirate once you've had it longer. Still smells navy to me," Tanner commented, rubbing his chin with one hand while the other rested on his hip.

"You must be the one Stalyart called Tanner," Denrik said by way of greeting. "I am Denrik Zayne, Captain of the *Fair Trader*."

"Wasn't just Stalyart; everyone calls me Tanner. Keeps it simpler. Looks like we're going to be stuck with each other a while."

"Stuck? Are you saying that you are here unwillingly?" Denrik thought that sounded promising.

A discontented ambassador? Could Kyrus have been such a fool as that?

"Well, it was a hasty plan that got me sent here. Lots of moving parts to it, I guess, and I was the misfit piece that got packed off with Captain Stalyart," Tanner said with a shrug. "I know spit about being an ambassador. I think in this case, though, I'm more of a go-between. I am with Kyrus in Kadrin, and with you here. If Brannis and Jinzan Fehr want to talk … here I am to bridge the two worlds. Just consider me a messenger pigeon, or a bottle to float notes across the aether in."

"So you have no initial greeting from Kyrus to start us off with?" Denrik asked, amused with the prospects that a careless, bored twinborn might pose.

"Way I figure, I'm mostly just going to hang about drinking your best rotgut until you give the word that Megrenn's had enough," Tanner said, his offhanded manner about something Denrik cared deeply about immediately souring his mood.

"You seem to have missed an essential briefing: Kadrin is losing this war. We are winning on every front, and more nations join us as we speak. They see our success, and believe in the downfall of the once mighty bully of Veydrus. Your warlock might have won you one battle a season ago, but he has hidden away ever since," Denrik boasted.

"Hey, he never told me *not* to tell you, so just to clear things up, we just crowned a new emperor last night. First thing he did? Ordered Rashan to go out and start killing your folks off, using that nasty piece of work of a sword of his. Plus I think if you ever got anywhere near Kadris, Kyrus would try to figure out which end of a hellfire spell is which, and set half the continent ablaze. Politics,

Cap'n, politics has been keeping Megrenn in one piece. Once we get our heads out of our backsides and fight back, it'll be messy."

"I see," Denrik said, his dry tone contradicting the spoken words. "Well, enjoy your stay here, and if I find myself needing to surrender, I will alert you without delay."

"Thanks. Nice to see we're seeing things the same way," Tanner said with a smile.

Oh, he is not so foolish as he acts, I see.

Tanner opened the door to leave, turning back to leave a final thought. "Oh, and if you find a missing warlock, please have him sent back. He isn't quite big enough to keep if you catch him."

* * * * * * * *

Rakashi strode through the small taproom on board the *Sand Piper*. His soft boots made muffled thumps on the carpeted floor, drawing Brannis's attention from his ale.

"I had not expected to see you without an entourage until we set foot in Acardia," Brannis called out to him.

The Takalish warrior smiled, but did not say anything until he had poured himself into a chair next to Brannis. "I told them that I was traveling with friends, and was neglecting them badly. It will not end the attentions they lavish upon me, but it buys me a small respite," Rakashi replied. "I had expected to find Soria with you. Have the two of you quarreled?"

"Far from it," Brannis answered, lifting his eyebrows suggestively as he lifted his tankard to his lips. "But I have no energy to keep pace with her. She found a game of Pak Chu in the social galley; it seems Kheshi parlor games are a fancy among rich Takalish women these days. I left her to it. She could not resist the lure to play, said she had not seen anyone play it in years."

"Good. I worry about her at times, especially in Kadrin, where I cannot look out for her. There I worry about her life, inhabiting a nest of dragons as she does. A misplaced word could bring down swift death if she treads wrongly. Here, I worry for her heart. Soria is always so full of anger. There is a Safschan expression that translates to 'hornets in the blood,' and it describes her aptly. She prefers to strike out at the target of her anger before considering alternatives. Since finding you, her mood has lightened like the sky after the passing of a storm. She laughs more in a day than I have seen in a year from her before."

Brannis studied Rakashi's expression, which he kept so carefully neutral most of the time. He could see something there that he had not expected. *He is in love with Soria*, Brannis realized. It might not have been the passionate love that Brannis felt for her, but he saw that Rakashi cared more for her than he had realized.

"She does not need a lot of looking after, even in Kadrin. Still, I am not blind to the treachery that has seeped into the streets of Kadris like weeds between the cobblestones. I cannot pull every weed—not quickly at least—but until they are cleared, I found a way to get her clear of the danger. I will let no harm come to her," Brannis assured Rakashi.

The Takalish warrior put a hand on Brannis's shoulder. The smile on his face relaxed with genuine warmth.

"With the troubles I hear of from Kadrin, I find your assurance a great comfort. Soria would never admit the need for help, or perhaps even notice such a need. I am glad she has you now." Rakashi stood. "I think I will go see how Soria's game of Pak Chu is proceeding."

Chapter 31 - Tangling Knots

Kyrus could hear the shouting as he approached Emperor Sommick's chambers. He was on his way to meet with the emperor and Warlock (no longer regent) Rashan, but it seemed that there was already a meeting in progress—a contentious one. The emperor's voice carried down the halls as Kyrus approached.

"... as of last night!" were the first words Kyrus made out.

"I am not some lackey to be ordered about. I do your bidding for the glory of the Empire, and the safety of her people. I am not a chamber-servant."

"I will not be made a puppet of. When I give a command, I expect—"

Suppressing an instinct of self-preservation that told him to wait outside, Kyrus approached the door. The two palace guards who flanked it stood too stiffly, as if afraid to move—no magic held them thus. Neither guard made a move to hinder him as he opened the door.

"I thought I saw the sunrise coming down the hall at us," Rashan greeted him, smiling as he turned his attention away from Emperor Sommick.

The emperor was clawing at Rashan's arm, trying futilely to remove the demon's hand from over his mouth. Muffled protests sounded from behind that hand. The emperor's face was bright red with rage.

"Please close the door behind you. Emperor Sommick and I were just hashing out the boundaries of power between the two of us."

The emperor went to his knees, using his weight as leverage to try to pry free from the warlock's grip.

"Oh, just let him go. This is no way to treat an emperor," Kyrus chided Rashan.

The warlock shrugged, and released Sommick, who fell forward onto his hands, gasping for breath after his exertions. Kyrus noticed that Celia was present, sitting at a desk in the corner of the room with quill and ink at the ready.

"Let me know if you change your mind about that," Rashan said. "He was getting rather tiresome, and I consider myself the model of patience."

"Sir Brannis," Emperor Sommick managed between sucking in lungfuls of air. "Arrest Warlock Rashan, and ... throw him in the dungeons. I understand that ... we have cells for sorcerers."

Kyrus looked over one shoulder, then the other. "I seem to have come alone. Had I known I was to be arresting warlocks, I ought to have brought a few from the Inner Circle along with me. Besides, those cells do not hold much of anything, in my experience. Warlock Rashan can break out of them any time he wishes," Kyrus replied. He had initially had every intention of politeness, but could not help his reply sounding sarcastic even to his own ears.

"Is this how it is to be?" Sommick asked. "Defied by my advisors and subjects at every turn?"

"It is not defiance, as such. I was merely pointing out that your orders were not going to have the effect you intended," Kyrus explained. "You no doubt envisioned me marching off to the dungeons with Rashan by the scruff of his neck, throwing him in a cell, then releasing him days later, much chastened and properly subservient. What was more likely to have happened would have been a magical struggle that would have left most of us dead, and Rashan once more in charge of an empire with no emperor."

"Emperor Sommick, you need to understand that we are neither wooden play-soldiers nor your personal handmaidens," Rashan explained, speaking as if to a small child. He helped the emperor to his feet, and brushed his royal robes off where they had touched the floor. "And you also need to understand that you are the offshoot of a wet little mistake a good friend of mine made a hundred and fourteen winters ago, when he was far from home and the company of his empress."

"None of that matters now. I am emperor. My word is law!"

"Celia, my dear, did you happen to write any of that down?" Rashan asked across the room, keeping his eyes fixed on the emperor as he did so.

"No, Warlock," came Celia's reply.

Rashan smiled. "You see? None of what was said or done actually happened. An emperor needs supporters, loyalists, obedient subjects. Without those, you are just a young man in expensive clothing, who happens to have some very noteworthy blood in his veins. Please understand that *we* are your supporters, your loyalists. If we are not the obedient servants you crave, then see for yourself how many of *those* you have if our support—my support—were withdrawn."

"Um, Warlock Rashan ... does this mean you have not gotten to the point of discussing the arrangements for your ... absence?" Kyrus asked.

"No, but I suppose we ought to. My sword hand itches to hold a blade, and I am not sure I trust myself with one in hand while our new emperor persists in vexing me. The sooner I am off to war, the better."

"What arrangements are you referring to?" Emperor Sommick demanded, having recovered enough of his dignity and ill-won egotism to resume demanding things.

"Sir Brannis will be running the Empire in my absence," Rashan began, holding up a hand to forestall the emperor's nascent interjection. "I know, I know, you had thought yourself clever in ordering me away. I let you grow that idea from seeds I planted in your head. You are not qualified to oversee the Empire's flower gardens, however."

"But it is my empire now. I rule it, not you, and certainly not Sir Brannis!"

"And you will continue to rule it. You will just not run it. You will sit a horse in parades, wave from balconies, throw feasts. But do not attempt to meddle in the affairs of the Circle or the army, and do not get involved in the wranglings among the nobles. Bring in jesters and musicians to amuse yourself, if you like. Get roaring drunk every day, and no man can gainsay you. Take the company of any—"

"But I would lose the respect of the people!" Emperor Sommick protested.

"No worse than you would by trying to control something you do not understand. Emperor Dharus did not even exist, and he was looked upon well enough by the commoners."

Kyrus was distracted from the exchange by a sound he was more sensitive to than most: the scratching of a quill. He looked over from the corner of his eye, and saw that Celia was writing something. He judged from the pacing, and lack of stops when the conversation broke, that she was not taking down the current, highly subversive, discussion between emperor and warlock.

"Think about whom you might wish for an empress, as well. You may as well aim high; no unwed girl in the Empire could refuse you," Rashan told Sommick.

Kyrus noticed that the warlock glanced sidelong at him as he said it, though. Brannis had heard a similar speech from Rashan, and had still not heeded the advice.

The scratching noises from the corner stopped, replaced by the sound of chair legs scraping on stone. Kyrus looked over to see Celia rising from her task. She sprinkled a bit of sand over the wet ink as an afterthought.

"I have finished, Warlock," Celia called over to Rashan.

"Ahh, excellent. Let us proceed with the formalities then. Emperor Sommick, if you would come this way."

Rashan put a hand to Sommick's back, and guided him over to the desk that Celia had just vacated. The emperor looked confused, but there was likely so much buzzing about in his head that he could mount no objection.

Kyrus followed just behind them, close enough that he could read over the emperor's shoulder—seeing over the diminutive warlock was no trouble at all.

I, Sommick the First, Emperor of the Kadrin Empire, do declare as follows:
I appoint, in all matters, Sir Brannis Solaran, as overseer of the Kadrin Empire and such decisions as require imperial consent …

Kyrus skimmed the rest of the single-page document, and found that it would be his official appointment. Celia's penmanship was labored. He could see it in the lack of fluidity in the looping letters, where she had moved her wrist in the formation of the curve rather than managing it strictly in the fingers. He realized a vague annoyance at not being able to write the document on his own behalf. With how long she had worked at it, he was amazed at how short it was in the end.

He watched the emperor take his seat, and peruse the document. Rashan stood over him like a disapproving tutor, waiting for some mistake to give him reason to berate his pupil. Emperor Sommick looked up at Rashan, saying nothing, but conveying a protest by eyes alone. He took up the quill, and signed his name to the document, his signature an atrocity of ink.

"If anyone requires me, I will be holding court in the throne room with a barrel of wine," Sommick informed the three who had just wrested his imperial authority from him. He pushed back away from the desk, and rose, shouldering his way between Kyrus and Rashan when they were not quick enough to clear a path for him. No one said a further word until the door had closed behind him.

"My, but did that not go well?" Rashan commented. To Celia, he said, "Take this over to the Sanctum. Oh ... Sir Brannis still needs to sign it."

Kyrus leaned over the desk, and took up the quill in his own hand. He was growing accustomed to the Kadrin goosefeather quills, though they still felt too light to him. After a quick dip in the ink, he touched the tip to the parchment.

Kyrus Hinterdale. His hand froze. A dollop of ink pooled where a "K" was poised to begin.

No. Kyrus breathed, the sound filling the silence of the room around him.

Sir Brannis Solaran, he wrote instead, as if he were signing a client's name in script more elegant than they could manage for themselves.

The ink was given a moment to dry before Rashan sealed it with wax, and an impression from the emperor's signet, which he then left on the table.

"I shall get this to the Inner Circle straightaway," Celia said, taking her leave.

Rashan watched her go; Kyrus followed suit, wondering if her walk was similar to Abbiley's or if he was just imagining it.

"It is about time I take my leave as well. I had initially thought to have you activate the *Daggerstrike* for my use, but I find that I am half a day too late for that," Rashan said once his attention was turned back to Kyrus.

"Well, I—"

"Well played, Brannis," Rashan interrupted him, smiling. "This is the other reason I feel I can leave the Empire in your hands. You can keep up with the game, ahead of it even, when you have a mind to. I have gathered that Juliana Solaran is aboard ..."

"Yes, I thought it was about time we used the ships for other than transportation duty. Munne showed the hazard of bringing them into battle against large forces, but I think that harrying tactics are ideally suited to them. The *Daggerstrike* will outrun anything we have made thus far."

"And you picked Juliana as captain, despite her lack of any naval experience, because...?"

"I like having more than one reason for something. The *other* reason is that in Tellurak she leads as good a group of coinblades as I have seen. She knows ambush tactics better than any of the garrison commanders we have running the army," Kyrus explained, thinking the jab at the passive army commanders would fit well with Rashan's view of them.

"So the gallant reason is to get her out of harm's way, and the practical reason is that she is suited to this assignment you have created just for her. Ahh, but there are at least two more that I can think of." Rashan grinned. It was the same grin he used when he taunted Gravis Archon upon his return to Kadrin. Kyrus waited to hear how much of his plan was already laid bare in the demon's mind. "You are also worried for her reputation. As murders pile up in the city, a select few wonder whether she might be involved. Rightly or wrongly—and I think she had no part in these—she has bits of her past and quirks of personality that make it seem plausible. The last reason is the clever one though: you cannot investigate Celia's link to Tellurak with her around. If Celia is your girl Abbiley, you can take no action on that knowledge with Juliana about. I truly hope for your sake that she is, for it will disentangle you nicely from Iridan and Juliana, and keep peace between you all—perhaps not between Celia and Juliana, though we can work on that over time."

"..."

Rashan smiled. "I have been at this a lot longer than you, Brannis. You are off to an excellent start, mind you, but you have ages to catch up on. I ran a network of spies from Acardia to Khesh, Kadrin to Safschan, and back again. Unravel the conspiracy against the throne in my absence, and see how it feels. You have it in you."

"Do you know who heads the conspiracy?" Kyrus asked.

"Not yet. Work that out, and the rest ought to fall in behind. Trust in Caladris for advice while I am gone. You can trust him and Aloisha among the Inner Circle, and Iridan when he returns. The rest are all suspect, either sitting on their hands or actively dirtying them against me."

"Will you go to Munne to find Iridan?"

"Reports are that Munne is stalled. Megrenn has been unable to remove forces from the garrison to continue an advance. That would indicate that Iridan is proving his worth after all. I will not steal his glory from him."

* * * * * * * *

"He has held out admirably. I could spare you this, possibly, with another day or two. He keeps asking for you, though, and I think it best if you indulge him in this," Narsicann told Jinzan.

They stood together in a level of the army headquarters that dated back to the Kadrin occupation of Zorren. Rough-cut stone blocks lined the walls and ceiling. Others of the same make—worn by the passages of a hundred winters' worth of feet—comprised the floor. Wooden beams provided structural support at intervals. Torches flickered and guttered in wrought-iron sconces all down the corridor. There was no natural light as far down as they were, and the air hung heavy with the burning scent of pitch-soaked wood.

"You know I prefer a clean death. This sort of business reminds me of the Kadrins. I will not presume to tell you your job, though. Yesterday was torment, waiting for word of the prisoner relenting," Jinzan said. He looked better rested than his claims would have led one to believe. He would not leave Zorren without an answer to the question of what the Kadrin spy knew of the Staff of

Gehlen … and of Anzik.

"It was your idea that even let us keep him captive this well. I have never questioned a sorcerer before. At least, not under such duress. It is amazing the difference in the sorcerous mind, compared with the mind of a soldier or a common sneak."

"Well, let us get on with this," Jinzan grumbled.

He followed Narsicann down the dungeon passageway, unused cell after unused cell. Iron doors, iron bars, a place for souls forged of iron, with hearts that were cold lumps of stone.

The Kadrin spy was in the last cell on the right. He hung limp in his chains, dangling from the wall by his wrists, his buttocks not reaching the floor to allow him to sit. His head lolled forward, but perked up at the sound of their approach. The Kadrin was naked, looked to be perhaps thirty or thirty-five winters in age if the age of a sorcerer was to be judged thus. Stripped of the illusions he had worn when they found him, he looked slovenly; his hair was flecked with grey, as was his unshaven scruff. Most notable about his appearance, though, were the runes covering most of his flesh, carved in shallow knife-cuts.

"What is his name?" Jinzan asked. He felt sick to his stomach. The prisoner's own filth pooled beneath him.

"He has not said. You will find him quite hungry and thirsty. I told him he would be fed when he gave me a name. He has not even tried to lie about one," Narsicann said, visibly less bothered by the conditions.

"Has he tried to use magic?"

"He figured that one out quickly. I brought some reports down to read while I waited for him to awaken. He tried to draw as soon as he woke. The sound alerted me that he was ready to interrogate."

A key hung in the lock, a convenience in a place where sorcerers could almost as easily manipulate the mechanism by magic. Narsicann turned it, and preceded Jinzan into the room.

The prisoner mumbled something, his voice weak, dry, incomprehensible.

Narsicann kicked him. After a grunt, the prisoner cleared his throat, spat, and tried again: "Just Jinzan. The other one can leave."

Narsicann looked to Jinzan, question clear in his eyes.

"Go ahead. I am in no danger from this one, even turned loose," Jinzan reassured him.

Narsicann's patronizing smile in reply assured Jinzan that such was not the question he was worried about. "Just give a yell if you need anything," Narsicann told Jinzan before exiting the cell.

"Food and water. Whether I give him either remains to be seen, but I want them at hand."

There was an awkward silence, broken only by receding footsteps. The prisoner looked up at him, bloodshot eyes judging him, weighing him.

"There, you have me all to yourself. Now where is the staff?"

"Not so simple as that," the prisoner replied. "Introductions first, I think."

"You already know my name. Give me yours."

"Ah, here is where we make it interesting. I know who *else* you are, Captain Denrik Zayne." The prisoner grinned with cracked, bleeding lips. Jinzan's heart quickened. "That torturer of yours ... I had no grasp on his throat. You, I can deal with."

"Deal? What sort of deal do you think you can make from that position, whatever knowledge you may possess?" Despite his bluster, Jinzan worried that there might be a true answer.

"Here, not much, maybe something. There? Everything."

"You will have to do better than that."

"Tanner, for starts," the prisoner said. "Kyrus set it all up. Brilliant. Has a sword at Denrik Zayne's throat. I can give the word."

Jinzan's expression turned from annoyed to fury instantly. He drew aether, and thrust it into the runes on the prisoner's chest, ignoring his revulsion at the man's condition. Lightning sparked and crackled along the prisoner's exposed skin. He screamed, thrashing convulsively in his chains.

"You Kadrin bastards! I shall have that wretched swordsman tossed over the side of the ship. We will see how he fights sharks with that blade of his. If that was your master plan, it will not work."

"Backup plan," the prisoner managed between coughs as he recovered control of his muscles. "Anzik is twinborn, too."

Jinzan's hot blood turned to ice. *No.* His mind fought to deny it, but the prisoner knew too much. Had he seen clues, and not known them for what they were? Anzik had always been odd, but had never shown any knowledge from Tellurak. He had just always been cursed by constantly seeing aether all around him.

"Where is he?" Jinzan demanded.

"Which one?"

Jinzan hesitated. "Both," he answered.

"Anzik is in hiding. I do not know quite where. His twin is asleep within arm's reach of mine."

"So is that it?" Jinzan asked, seething. "You would hold a young boy hostage? Where do you have him?"

"Well inland." The prisoner managed to make a joke of it.

"So is that the bargain you propose? Your life for Anzik's twin?"

"No," the prison replied. He tried to say something else, but the words failed him. With effort, he instead said, "Water."

Jinzan waited for a guard to fetch water and stew. He placed them well clear of the prisoner as he worked magic to loose him from his shackles, and deposit him gently on the cell floor away from the muck of his bodily excretions.

"Your name, now," Jinzan stated as if fulfilling Narsicann's bargain from the previous day.

The prisoner crawled over, and drank sparingly from the jug of water, seeming to lack the strength to tilt it back far enough to drink his fill.

"Faolen. Faolen Sarmon, Fourth Circle, personal agent of Warlock Rashan Solaran. We crossed draws briefly at Raynesdark, though you did not know it at the time. That is sort of my specialty, or was until you carved runes into me like that staff you want back so badly." Faolen picked up the bowl of stew, seeming surprised to find a wooden spoon in it. He began eating, poking at the steaming food before he took a bite.

"What deal do you propose then, Faolen Sarmon?"

"My life for the Staff of Gehlen."

"I thought you did not know where it was," Jinzan retorted, having caught Faolen in a lie.

"I do not. I have access to Anzik's twin, though. I can get messages through to Anzik. I can get you back both your son and the staff," Faolen replied.

"Were you not tasked with finding and retrieving the staff yourself?" Jinzan asked. "Would that not be a betrayal of your mission?"

"I would buy my own life with it, if I could. Had I not been caught, I would most certainly have taken the staff back. But I have my priorities."

"What of the other boy? If I find the staff on my own, what becomes of him?"

"I plan no harm to that boy in either case. He is to be my apprentice. Of course, I could not say what might happen if I were to die here, or go mad. But I *intend* no harm."

"Very well, have Anzik bring me the staff, and you may have your life, Kadrin traitor."

* * * * * * *

Rashan was gone. The *Ironspar* had borne him aloft with a crew of sailors from the navy and the ship's sea captain. Kyrus gave even odds of anyone besides the warlock surviving the trials he was sure to put them all through.

With the warlock gone, Kyrus was in charge of the top-level affairs of the Empire. Or rather, Brannis was in charge of those, and Kyrus was tasked with being Brannis. It was getting more complicated the more he thought about it. Without a complete picture of the state of the Empire, he took Rashan's final bit of advice, and sought out Brannis's uncle Caladris.

The Tower of Contemplation seemed deserted compared with the energy abounding in the days leading up to the coronation. Kyrus passed several junior sorcerers along the stairs, the sort who got their assignments and carried them out; no one who had a choice seemed to be about. *The murders. The Circle are more in tune to the politics of those killings than I had realized.* He exchanged perfunctory greetings with a few who recognized him, but the acquaintances were not mutual.

As he neared the top of the tower, he could hear voices. It sounded as if the Inner Circle were having a heated debate. It seemed like meeting with Caladris separately would have to wait. As he summited the mountainous stairway, he gave a salutatory nod to the two guards flanking the entrance, their trident-like weapons held at the ready. The guards returned the nod of the army's commander, though their own chain of command ran parallel to his, up through to the Inner Circle. Kyrus stood, and contented himself to wait out of the session, ready to take Caladris aside immediately afterward.

The conversation within involved too many people talking over one another for him to make out more than occasional words. All at once, it broke off.

"What ho! Sir Brannis, that Source of yours gives you away. Get in here!" he heard Caladris's voice bellow from within the Sanctum.

One of the guards held out an arm in the direction of the Inner Circle's meeting chamber, formally showing Kyrus the way. Kyrus met the man's amused expression with a wry smile of his own. *Done in by my own Source. I wonder which of them keeps an eye to the aether to have noticed me.*

Kyrus walked the few paces to the stairs that led up into the supplicants' floor of the Sanctum, the center of the Imperial Circle's power. He had been there before, but the last time he had attended a full (or as full as available sorcerers allowed) session, Gravis Archon had been High Sorcerer. The seating arrangements had moved since then, placing Caladris to one side of the vacant High Sorcerer's seat, and Dolvaen to the other.

"Brannis, my boy, come in, come in," Caladris beckoned.

Kyrus entered the chamber, and stood near to the center. It was far less intimidating than it had once been. With his aether-vision, he could see the sorcerers behind him, taking away from the feeling of being surrounded. He could also tell who were the powers among the Inner Circle, and he knew them much better than he had his last time before them all.

"We were just discussing you, Sir Brannis," Fenris added. The old man to Dolvaen's other side had a shrewd look to him that morning.

"What about? I take it that you have received Emperor Sommick's proclamation, then?" Kyrus ventured a guess. There was little else about him worth discussing, at least in an open council section.

"Yes, indeed. Are we to believe this document is legitimate?" Dolvaen asked, cutting to the quick. "I find it hard to believe the emperor would hand control of the Empire to you so shortly after having gained it back from Rashan."

"The emperor was under no compulsion. He read the proclamation over prior to signing it, and I witnessed the signing myself. My own signature below his is also authentic," Kyrus replied.

I ought to have expected them to raise a fuss over this.

"What threat did Warlock Rashan use to obtain this signature?" Fenris asked. "I do not doubt that it was the emperor's hand, but I wonder at his motivation for doing so."

"Warlock Rashan is quite persuasive. He made the emperor see reason behind appointing another to take on the daily duties of administering the Empire. The emperor still has ultimate authority, but he chooses not to be bothered by the intricacies of rulership. He will drink, and feast, and go about selecting an empress. He strikes me as well qualified for all three tasks."

"You are an admirable wordsmith, Sir Brannis, but you well admit that Rashan convinced him to leave you in charge of the Empire," Dolvaen said. "I would propose that you cede that authority to the Inner Circle. It is well established that we have kept the Empire operating smoothly for longer than anyone had realized until a season ago. In light of the likely coercion at hand, it would be prudent to know that the Empire is in experienced hands."

"As acting High Sorcerer, that would leave the Empire in yours, presumably?" Kyrus asked, directing his question solely at Dolvaen.

"In the Inner Circle's hands, yes. I merely lead them. Warlock Rashan hinted that he might forgo the title of High Sorcerer, which would leave me in that position."

"I thought that Rashan disliked using seniority as the means to promotion," Kyrus replied innocently. He knew the ages of the Inner Circle members well enough to know better.

"Indeed he had made clear as much," Dolvaen replied. "But as much as you may credit my life extension both Fenris and Caladris are my elders. I suppose I ought to take it as complimentary, though. But no, I am in line for High Sorcerer because of my strength of magic."

"Ahh, I see. Well, I think I have a solution that would satisfy both sides. We can allow the emperor's edict to stand, yet still allow the Inner Circle to retain charge of Kadrin affairs," Kyrus said, trying to keep a smirk from his features.

"You would write an edict of your own, further ceding power down to us?" Dolvaen asked.

"No."

"No?"

"Dolvaen Lurien, I challenge you to a draw, for the position of High Sorcerer, or acting High Sorcerer ... whatever post it is you hold. *That* will settle both issues to my satisfaction," Kyrus proclaimed.

So much for keeping out of politics. I suppose that document precluded that, though.

There was a stunned silence in the chamber.

"Brannis, what are you doing? You lost to Iridan," Aloisha broke the silence first.

"Anyone who did not see that he threw that match was not paying attention," Caladris shot back.

Fenris nodded his agreement with the sentiment.

"I am not Iridan, either," Dolvaen said softly.

Caladris tried from Dolvaen's peripheral vision to signal him to back down. Eye movements, head shaking, hand gestures, all failed to draw Dolvaen's attention from his would-be challenger.

"Dammit, man, snap out of it," Caladris relented, breaking with decorum. "I know you worked your way to the top with no help from a blooded house. Admirable. Do not let pride get in the way of sense. *Look* at that Source. It is not a matter of training or technique or trying hard—"

"It was a challenge. If I would still call myself High Sorcerer, I have to accept.

That is how it was meant to be, sorcerers ruling sorcerers by acknowledgement of might."

"I could withdraw the challenge, formally, if you agree to abide Emperor Sommick's decree," Kyrus offered. "I came here to seek counsel from my uncle, not to take control of the Imperial Circle. Carry on as you had, and you will have no quarrel with me."

"You would rethink your challenge, then?" Dolvaen caught hold of the thread he was offered, gave it a tug.

"My apologies, Sorcerer Dolvaen. I had meant the challenge as a figure of speech, a debate tactic, if you will. I regret if I led anyone to believe otherwise," Kyrus conceded.

"Well, you posed your point eloquently. I see no reason why we should contest the emperor's transfer of authority to Sir Brannis," Dolvaen stated. He eyed Kyrus dangerously, but no hint of that crept into his voice.

"If, as I have surmised, this session was called for the primary purpose of discussing Emperor Sommick's dispensation of authority, would that mean that this meeting might now be adjourned? I *do* have business to discuss with my uncle."

* * * * * * *

"Brannis, my boy, you have a knack for twisting words. I am glad to have you free of so much time in the warlock's company. You are honing that craft against a master of it," Caladris joked. They had adjourned to Caladris Solaran's office just beneath the Sanctum.

"He was like that before, near as I have gathered," Celia Mistfield commented. They had found her waiting there for her superior's return. She was busily making copies of the edict to distribute to the far-flung cities of the Empire. "After he got his Source freed up, though, he has been more bold about whose words he is willing to twist. Trust me, he twisted mine often enough when he was just a knight who had been promoted above his station."

"I prevented the subversion of Emperor Sommick's orders, and averted an embarrassing draw with Dolvaen Lurien. What is wrong with that?" Kyrus asked.

"Nothing on the surface of it. It is when those words twist a way I do not like. That is what I worry about: not being able to twist them back in my favor," Caladris replied, slumping down into his padded, high-backed chair. He tipped it back until it leaned against a bookcase. "What had you needed to speak to me about?"

"Well, for all that bluster in the Sanctum, I was left holding the reins of an empire with no idea how to ride one," Kyrus stated.

"You could always just do as Rashan does: put me in charge of anything you do not wish to deal with. He has already given me purview over his pet thieves and all the night-stabbing activities—which used to be more of a figurative term," Caladris said. He reached for a drawer that was *just* within arm's reach of his reclined position. He pulled out a pipe and a box, from which he took a pinch of crushed darweed. He stuffed the bowl of the pipe with the foul-scented herb, and set it alight, puffing to create little gouts of smoke.

"What do I do about the murders?" Kyrus asked. "Can Dolvaen be trusted to follow through on an investigation?"

"Why would he not be?" Celia asked.

Kyrus looked in her direction as she spoke, then quickly turned his attention back to Caladris.

"Brannis, you can drive yourself mad with such things. If you like, leave dealing with the murders and Dolvaen's investigation to me. You were already seeing to the army, now add the nobles and court matters to that, and consider yourself sufficiently burdened. It would take me half a season to get you caught up on all the conspiracies of every make and size that are going on among the Circle. It was Rashan's style to deal with every detail, but he is a demon. You need sleep. Learn to lean on folk whom you can trust."

"Can I trust you?" Kyrus asked.

"Brannis!" Celia chided, her tone indignant.

"It is all right, my dear. Brannis is showing wisdom, if not tact. We ward these rooms so that frank conversations are possible. I know that there are sides being drawn up. I have been drawing up one side of them. Warlock Rashan had little time to align supporters in his favor. I did all that work on his behalf. If you would align yourself with Rashan, you align yourself with me. Thus far, both sides have seen you as a wild card, Brannis. You think too independently to be thought of in Rashan's coinpurse, despite all that you owe him. I do not find that a fault; I feel confident you will see which side is right, not just follow along blindly."

"I should still be made aware of these conspiracies, even if I allow you to manage them," Kyrus said.

"Fair enough. Celia, if you would be so good, take a few evenings and give Brannis an understanding of what goes on when you peel back the layers of this rotten onion of an empire."

"Of course, Caladris," Celia said, perhaps a bit too eagerly.

Kyrus kept himself from objecting. He felt like he ought to, but really did not wish to. It was the opportunity he had arranged for himself, after all.

"Now you have other duties to attend," Caladris said to Celia. "Be about them, my dear, and leave Brannis and me to discuss some family matters."

Celia straightened up the papers she was working on, and stood to leave. Kyrus stepped aside to let her by.

"I will stop by your room this evening, around sunset," Celia whispered to him as she passed by. Kyrus nodded in reply. She opened the door, stepped halfway through, then leaned back. "See you tonight, then ... Kyrus." She disappeared as the door closed between them.

"Now, Brannis ..." Caladris continued to talk, but nothing registered with Kyrus. He babbled through replies. His brain needed time to recover as he sorted through the possibilities conveyed by that one spoken name.

* * * * * * *

A blackened timber held up a loose blanket of rubble in one corner of the basement of what had once been a store peddling imported goods. Burned wood, shattered pottery, various dented and fire-blackened metal curios had settled into a cooling, mushy mess within the foundation, like layers of sedimentary rock: basement, first floor, loft—all compressed to a knee-high refuse pile that scavengers would mine for treasures once it seemed safe enough.

Hidden beneath that lonely beam, sheltering under it like a lean-to, was Aelon Beff. When the Megrenn sorcerers burned their shop to the ground, he and Faolen reacted very differently. The illusionist had attempted a diversion and escape—and failed. Aelon had trusted to something different: dragonflesh.

Aelon Beff and Sanbin Colvern had caught Warlock Rashan's attentions after the battle of Raynesdark. Of all the feast-goers after the battle, the two of them were the ones who became most fond of the taste of dragonflesh. Of course, fondness is no crime, but stealing crates full of the cured, smoked flesh of the great reptilian goddess Jadefire (whose proper name was Nihaxtukali) was another matter. The two men gorged themselves in clandestine contests of gastric fortitude. The rarest of delicacies was washed down commoners' gullets by tankards of cheap ale.

The warlock's anger had been a capricious thing. One moment, it seemed as if they would be ripped open, and gutted to reclaim as much of the precious meat as possible. The next he was marveling at the uncanny resistance both men had developed to fire. Sanbin's work as a smith was well served by immunity to the effects of the forge's heat. Aelon had found little use for the gift aside from parlor tricks until he found himself within a burning building.

There is an instinct in all animals to flee from fire. Aelon fought that instinct once he saw what had become of Faolen. He knew in his head that the flames could not consume him, but there are organs in the human body that offer their thoughts as secretions, quickening the heart, clenching the gut, widening the eyes. It was the smoke that panicked him, nearly broke him. The heat from the flames was like the summer sunlight beating on his skin, noticeable but no threat. The smoke clouded his vision, displaced the air, threatened to fill his lungs.

Draped with Faolen's invisibility spell, Aelon had pressed himself flat to the floor, wondering if he dared flee as the illusionist had, taking his chances against being discovered. In the end, the fear of discovery won out, and he remained frozen in place as the smoke reached floor level. He pressed the cloth of his tunic over his face, and breathed through it, still smelling the disconcertingly pleasant smell of wood smoke despite his precaution. The cloth blocked too much air to his lungs, though, and in his panic, he was short of breath, and began feeling light-headed. He took a deep, sucking breath around the cloth, having the fool idea to fill his lungs as they demanded, then resume his filtered breathing.

He inhaled the smoke.

He exhaled.

Aelon nearly gave himself away by laughing aloud, exultant in his relief. He sat up, surrounded by fire and engulfed in smoke, a bemused, manic expression spreading across his face. He watched the room burn around him with a rather draconic sense of detachment. He reveled in the absurdity until the floors began to give way beneath him. Then practical concerns crashed back down around him. Checking that he was still invisible, he scrambled to the windows to see if anyone was still waiting outside; they were.

It was tense as Aelon dodged about the shop, seeking to keep ahead of the destruction, not trusting himself to flee while he could remain hidden within the safety of his private inferno. Eventually he wound up in the basement, cowering beneath a sturdy section of timber propped where it had fallen in a corner.

Something had fallen and knocked him cold. When he had awakened, it was daylight, although he knew not what day. He hid away until nightfall, weathering the spring rain that filled the foundation pit a fingersbreadth deep. By the starlight of the clearing sky, he found little scraps to shore up his hovel and provision it, unsure of where to go.

Now he awoke with a sense of purpose, but no clear direction. He had survived, against all odds, against all reason. He had three choices as far as he could figure them: he could seek out Faolen—should he still live—and rescue him; he could continue the mission, and try to contact Anzik Fehr to bargain for the staff; or he could sneak back to Kadrin-held territory with his tail between his legs, informing Rashan that the mission had failed.

Aelon propped a large shard of a shattered mirror against the stone wall. Huddling beneath the protective canopy offered by the beam, he took a sharp knife, and began carefully scraping away at the hair on his scalp. Someone had recognized them, had reported about them, knew about them. With no more of Faolen's magic to hide him, he needed to become someone else.

None of the three paths he saw would matter if he was identified and captured.

* * * * * * *

"Your plan was approved, Tiiba," General Rozen said. "Councilor Fehr has sent along two additional instructions, however."

The general and the blade-priest stood together on a balcony overlooking the central square of Munne. Foot traffic was brisk, both among Kadrin citizens and Megrenn occupiers. The general looked out over the city as he spoke, but Tiiba's attention was focused solely on Rozen.

"What conditions has the Councilor attached to the plan?" Tiiba asked. He stood with his feet spread, arms clasped behind his back.

"He will not honor the bargain, if it is accepted," General Rozen began.

"I am not concerned about that. It is the Council's prerogative, and I shall abide their decision. It will not change the plan."

"He also requests that, if at all possible, Warlock Iridan Solaran be captured alive."

"Does he give any indication of how he will accomplish the feat of caging a warlock?" Tiiba asked, a scholarly curiosity bubbling to the surface.

"You can ask Dembeck Drall, if you want to know. I did not delve into the details of the magic, but Councilor Fehr has instructed him on how to manage exactly that feat."

"Hmm, I may do just that."

* * * * * * * *

"Sir Brannis," Kyrus heard behind him. He was still in a haze of mental overflow, unable to put a name to that voice, perhaps able to put too many names to it. His mind threatened to rebel at the double thinking required of a twinborn; it would have preferred a nice game of chess.

"Sir Brannis," the voice persisted.

Kyrus was almost back to his own quarters. He could have easily made a dash to the safety of a well-warded room where he could collapse into his bed, and try to sort out everything that was going on.

Some sense of duty, stuffed away in a resilient corner of his mind, forced Kyrus's head to turn, and identify the speaker. It was Varnus. Varnus knew important things. *Blast it!* Varnus was someone he had to stop and talk to.

"What is it?" Kyrus said, no energy in his voice.

"Not for talking about out here. Too many ears. Let's get us behind those wards of yours," Varnus replied.

That was my plan. I would have had you out there, too, though, Kyrus thought wearily.

A few moments later, the two men were sealed up safely in Kyrus's chambers. It occurred to him, not for the first time, that he ought to have a separate office in the palace, apart from his bedchamber. It was growing unseemly the number of people who saw his soiled clothing and disheveled bed linens.

"What is it?" Kyrus asked again.

"It is Wendell. He's acting strange."

"Strange how? I hardly know him well enough to judge. What makes you say so?" Kyrus pressed.

"Well, he seems distracted. Not talking much. Usually he's looking around too much, talking constantly. He seems ... creepy."

"Could it be something related to his mission for Rashan?" Kyrus wondered. "Has he given any indications of his progress?"

"Well, we found a boy who speaks Megrenn, and can see aether. Wendell picked him up at the Pious Grove Sanctuary."

"Anzik Fehr," Kyrus said, drawing a surprised look from Varnus.

"So *that's* what we're up to?" Varnus fumed. "We're takin' twinborn boys hostage?"

"Calm yourself. No. We are bargaining with a twinborn runaway for a stolen staff. Find out what is going on in Megrenn. I do not care whether Wendell or Faolen wishes to divulge it. Wring it out of him somehow, preferably—and I mean preferably, not exclusively—without violence. Wendell and Faolen both seem too comfortable with dissembling. Both work at it professionally. He cannot keep such crucial information to himself, though. He should have already told you his plan once the two of you were alone and away from Rakashi."

"Wait, wait, wait, wait. Hold on now; Rakashi is one of us. Anything you say in front of me or Tanner, you can say in front of him. Er, and a fair portion of what you say to Juliana or Soria, but don't get carried away on that count. But what I mean is: you don't have to go sneaking about behind Rakashi's back. He has a knight's soul in him, and a scholar's eyes. He can keep his mouth shut about things that shouldn't go beyond Tellurak."

"Maybe one day, I, too, can trust him like you all do, but I do not know him yet. Tanner I barely know, but he is an officer in my army. You, I have known for summers, since Brannis was a young man. Rakashi's twin is Safschan, which means if he fights, he fights for Megrenn. I cannot let him in on the key to their undoing. The man would have to be made of stone to sit by for that."

"He is."

"No man is. He has a heart and a conscience. He will decide using those, like any man would. Perhaps he will make the decision that favors us, perhaps he will break the bargain you have made for the benefit of his people."

"You are a smart fellow, Kyrus. You've set it up so Tanner and I can't get to Rakashi and Soria doesn't know any better."

* * * * * * *

Kyrus was poring over written petitions from the nobles and merchants, tasks that had until recently been within Rashan's domain, when the knock came. It startled him from his glazed viewing of complaint after complaint, laying bare the pettiness of Kadrin's upper class.

Kyrus stood, leaving the papers scattered about his desk, and released the wards. The door opened by telekinesis, a spell he felt he was finally growing comfortable with silently.

Celia stood there outside, having dressed for the occasion. The simple black dress she wore for her official duties had been replaced with the dress he had first seen her in at Raynesdark. She had let down the tight, elaborate knots that kept her hair out of her way while she wrote. It fell loose about the bare skin of her shoulders and back.

"I suddenly feel underdressed," Kyrus greeted her, smiling without having to think about it.

"Nonsense. You are the most powerful man in Kadris at the moment, after the emperor, of course," Celia said, punctuating the last bit with a roll of the eye that none outside in the hallways could have seen.

She seemed about to enter when Kyrus waved her away, heading for the doorway himself. "I have had my fill of this room for a while. We can dine in the eastern sitting room."

"Will that be safe enough to talk?"

"Rashan held meetings there. It is warded, after a fashion. It allows servants in and out, but nothing can pass undetected. So long as we mind our tongues while our courses are brought, and our wine refilled, we may speak freely," Kyrus replied.

The eastern sitting room was cozy by palace standards. Twenty might have talked over drinks in the space it provided, but the lone table was set for two. They were surrounded by priceless heirlooms of the Empire, dating back hundreds of summers, a few possibly thousands. Celia sat in her chair as if afraid to touch anything beyond the confines of the table linens.

"Brannis, this is *too* nice. Emperors used to take tea here with their empresses or concubines. If I broke something here, I could not replace it with a lifetime's salary."

"I suppose that there is an emperor to take offense now, should we wreck the place," Kyrus replied. "No more of Rashan's inspirational acts of vandalism."

"How do you know about that?" Celia asked, her face scrunching up in a frown. Kyrus tried, unsuccessfully, not to find it adorable. "I thought I was supposed to be briefing *you* on the little background dealings of the Empire."

"You must either not be very much of a spy, or you must be continuing to act so, if you thought that was why we were dining together tonight," Kyrus replied.

"Oh, really? Why do *you* think we are having dinner tonight?" Celia asked, slathering on the sarcasm, lest Kyrus miss it.

"Two reasons. The other is that I need to know a few things about your dreams," Kyrus answered.

"'Other reason,' huh? Before I go any further with that, which of you started that annoying little word trick, you or Rashan?"

"I have not kept track. Him, I think."

"So what was the reason too obvious to name?" Celia demanded. "Pretend I am too dumb to guess it."

"You are not stupid. You are witty, beautiful, and resourceful. I find myself drawn to you for those reasons and more, despite my obstinate resistance due to having been prodded toward you at every turn. I dislike being manipulated, and I react poorly to it. I might ... *might* ... be able to get past all that, because for all the reasons I should push you away, none truly matter in the end. What if our meeting was all arranged, our times together plotted, your dogged pursuit of me according to orders? What of it, if in the end we would choose each other anyway?"

Celia was speechless for a moment, blushing from forehead to neckline.

"Just answer me one thing first, truthfully. You accidentally called me 'Kyrus' earlier, when you left Caladris's office. Where did you hear that name?"

"I remembered you from my dreams."

Chapter 32 - Freedom and Adventure

Nestled in the foothills of the Cloud Wall mountain range, on the eastern side, sat an unusual dwelling. It had a flat wooden roof and steel walls that echoed as the rain beat against them. The sides were slitted with narrow windows at regular intervals, too skinny to reach so much as an arm through. The two doors on each side opened downward into ramps, and lay open as the inhabitants busied themselves about putting the place in order. On the whole, it looked large enough to house twenty or more. In the right frame of mind, one might describe it as shaped like a sailing vessel that was missing its sails. The name on the side identified it as *Daggerstrike*.

The captain and crew of the *Daggerstrike* had set down in the rolling high hills of the Cloud Wall for the night after Captain Juliana's ill-fated attempts at aerial acrobatics made a shambles of the crew quarters. There were repairs to be made. It was nothing complicated, but they were in the wilderness with no shipwright among them, so the work would take time. Men also needed a good long feel of the ground beneath their feet once more, after a harrowing flight.

Captain Juliana had won herself few friends among the crew with her antics in testing out the *Daggerstrike*'s capabilities. Going off with a pair of crewmen, and killing a mountain goat for their dawn feast helped a ways toward making amends.

"Captain Juliana, is a fire wise? What if we are spotted by Megrenn forces?" Lieutenant Trosh Garrist asked. He was the senior member of the crew assigned to her. He might have been five winters older than Juliana, six at the most, with blond hair and dark eyes that accused when they looked at her.

"We should still be far enough south that they won't see us," Juliana replied, the title of "captain" before her name still echoing oddly in her ears. Owning no sort of military uniform, she was dressed in her riding leathers with a white tunic, with matching leather gloves and boots. She wore the harness for her dagger sheaths openly, outside her tunic, the blades having already been bloodied once in the appropriation of dawn feast. "Besides, how else would we cook our meat?"

"They might have scouts in the area," Lieutenant Garrist persisted, to all appearances unconvinced that his captain knew anything about what she was doing. Heads nodded along with him.

"Look around. See any roads here?" Juliana asked. A general grumbling of "No" answered her. "Does this look like easy terrain? If they manage to spot us, and sneak up for a look, so be it. They won't catch us off guard in any numbers. By the time scouts could make any report at all, we will be airborne again and long gone."

"Still—"

"Your name is Trosh, right? Look, Trosh, you boys are soldiers, not sailors, and I am a sorceress, not a ship's captain. We are all going to be learning as we go here," Juliana said to Garrist.

"I am properly addressed as Lieutenant Garrist, Captain." Trosh Garrist set his jaw and stared down Juliana, or attempted to. He was met with a smirk.

"Oh. I see how it is. New girl isn't good enough for you. You don't like being bossed around by a sorceress," she said, nodding to herself as she said it.

"You do not have any qualifications to captain a ship or lead a crew, a platoon, or any other assemblage of soldiers. If you would be so good as to keep the ship on course, I think it would be best if I took command," Lieutenant Garrist replied.

"Fine. I'll make you all a deal. Line up, any of you who think you'd rather have someone other than me as captain. I'll give you each a shot at me, bare fists, no magic. First one who bests me can decide who gets to captain the *Daggerstrike*. When everyone who wants a shot has had one, if I am still captain, everyone who tried to throw me off my own ship can walk home," Juliana offered. Though among the tallest of the *Daggerstrike*'s complement, Juliana gave up at least five gallons to the slimmest of them.

"No magic?" Trosh Garrist asked, skeptical. "How can we be sure?"

"How would any of you take me seriously if I cheated?" Juliana drew her daggers, and tossed Freedom and Adventure hilt-deep into a tree trunk, well out of casual reach.

Lieutenant Garrist removed his sword belt, along with the dagger sheath it also bore, and removed a concealed boot dagger as well, tossing it to the ground out of the way.

"I don't like the idea of hitting a woman, but everyone heard you ask for it, real clear," Garrist called out, pointing his finger, and sweeping it across the crew, making sure everyone heard him. He took up a brawler's pose, fists up, forearms framing his head as he tucked his chin low.

Juliana relaxed into a fencer's posture, one foot leading, turned sideways, but with her arms hanging loose at her sides. She flexed her fingers, clenching and stretching them alternately. She locked her gaze on Garrist's.

Trosh Garrist took a tentative step in, knowing better than to rush someone who clearly came prepared to fight. He threw a quick, probing jab, but provoked no flinch from Juliana. He threw another, long enough to land, but Juliana turned aside, and Garrist felt his world tilt as his feet did not follow him as he advanced with the punch.

"Hey, you all saw that," Garrist said from the ground, pushing himself to hands and knees, and scrambling to his feet as quick as he could manage. "She just used magic on me!"

"Haw, Lieutenant, she tripped ya!" someone called out. "You wasn't even lookin' at her feet."

Juliana shrugged and smiled.

Garrist gritted his teeth, and resumed his fighting stance, his face reddening. Whether it was anger or embarrassment, Juliana could not say. He rushed forward, not recklessly, but at least imprudently, pulling up short of bowling Juliana over to throw a hard overhand right.

A slim hand closed over his wrist, guiding it wide of Juliana's face. At the same moment, a delicate knee drove itself into the space just below the center of his rib cage. Juliana pulled the blow, putting no aether behind it; she could easily have ruptured his stomach, lungs, or both. Off balance, and with the wind knocked out of him, Trosh Garrist was in no position to defend himself when Juliana took her free hand to his shoulder, and pushed.

It was a hilltop they were fighting on. Though it was far from a sheer drop, it was a long way before Garrist stopped rolling and sliding through the underbrush. The crew rushed to the edge of the drop to see what had become of their lieutenant. Groans and far-off cursing wafted up from below, prompting jeers and laughter among the men.

"Someone throw down a rope," Juliana shouted over the cacophony.

Rope was a wonderful material, impervious to the damaging effects of being dropped to the ceiling when it and the floor switch places. There was rope aplenty in the stores, provisioners of ships having yet to grasp that the *Daggerstrike* had no rigging to repair, and little need for more than a token amount of the stuff.

Trosh Garrist could not meet Juliana's eye when he was finally hauled up from where he had fallen. The blow to his gut obviously still hurt him as well, keeping him from standing upright.

"What now?" he asked.

"What, indeed," Juliana replied unhelpfully. "Well, I cannot take Lieutenant Trosh Garrist back onto my ship. That was part of the deal. The lieutenant can make his own way back to Kadris, or whatever part of Kadrin he wishes to settle in."

There were mutters among the men but no one spoke up. Juliana walked over, and picked up Garrist's weapons, giving them an appraising look as she brought them over to return them. She stopped short, though, doing a circuit of the lieutenant, giving him an appraising look as well.

"Of course, I do see some potential here. It would be a shame to waste it. If only you were *not* Lieutenant Trosh Garrist anymore ..." Juliana took Garrist's dagger, slid it behind the golden lieutenant's emblem pinned to his uniform, and gave a flick of her wrist. The emblem fell to the ground, and disappeared among the weeds.

"In fact, I see a lot of potential in this crew, but I don't think this is a job for a bunch of infantrymen and archers, led by a sorceress. Do you know what our mission is?" Juliana waited as a lot of noncommittal answers were bandied. "No, our mission is to harry Megrenn supply wagons, to strike at weak garrisons, to pick off scouting parties. We are not planning to return to Kadris or any other friendly territory except rarely; we will live off what we take from Megrenn. Do you know what that makes us?"

She let them go longer at their guesses this time, hearing things like "thieves" and "soldiers," her favorite guess being "wolves," but that was not what she was looking for, either.

"That makes us *pirates*!" Juliana shouted. "It makes us privateers," she clarified, belatedly realizing that the more technically accurate term was also more confusing. "We have latitude to carry out our mission as I see fit. So from now until the time I release you from my command, you are all pirates ... *my* pirates. My crew. I can out-fight, out-drink, and probably out-gamble any of you, and I invite you to prove otherwise. We will not fight fair, we will not give quarter, and we will not lose. We will eat like kings on what we can steal, and we will drink like princes from our enemies' wine cellars." She looked over to see eager gleams in the eyes of her crew. She had gotten their attention.

"Trosh, I will take you back as part of my crew, but the lieutenant stays here."

"Aye aye, Captain Solaran," Trosh replied glumly.

Juliana wrinkled her nose. "Too stuffy, and I am not yet used to that name. Captain Juliana will do fine," she said.

"Captain Juliana it is, then," Trosh replied, managing a smile.

"Same goes for the rest of you; cut those rank emblems off. When we start raiding supply wagons, pick out anything you like to wear. Silks, leathers, furs, whatever strikes your fancy or suits your tastes. If anyone asks you, you are one of the *Daggerstrike* Corsairs."

* * * * * * * *

The straps fitted snugly around her waist and upper thighs, though the holes she used for the buckles were of her own making. Whoever had done the leatherworking for the *Daggerstrike* had not considered the possibility of someone so slender taking the helm. Juliana was tethered to a pair of posts that flanked her at the ship's wheel. She could not quite straighten her legs beneath her, allowing her to keep pressure against the deck even when flying inverted. The leather straps attached to the posts were pulled taut, keeping her hips from jostling to the sides as the ship banked and rolled.

The ship's wheel itself was fixed in place, unable to turn. Each handle around the wheel was inscribed with rune patterns that activated the various controls of the ship, from propulsion to steering, gangplank release to defensive shields. There were also controls for the glass panel that hung in her field of view, suspended in a steel frame just past the wheel. It allowed her to see what was hidden by the deck of the ships, mainly what was in front and below them.

"Well, I don't know that they trust me yet. Merciful One, if I have not yet used up all my favors, just see us safely through the insanity we are about to embark upon," Juliana said aloud, since she was the only one on deck. The crew was safely strapped into harnesses of their own, holding them fast to the walls of the outer hull, in reach of the arrow slits.

Juliana let aether flow into the proper runes on the wheel of the *Daggerstrike*, and the ship rose from the ground, fighting against the growing strength of the rainstorm. Higher and faster it rose, the clouds growing from a vast, theoretical ceiling to the sky into a bank of fog that they approached, and the scope of that vastness challenged the waking mind to grasp.

Through the clouds they shot, streaking at arrow speeds, and into the brilliant daylight. Juliana let out a whoop of delight, and heard it echoed from the crew below.

* * * * * * * *

The storm that had blown in from the Aliani Sea had dropped rain across half the continent of Koriah. It had let up around midday, but had run long enough to fill Iridan's empty wine barrel with enough water to wash in. Though he sloshed about in ankle-deep water in his wine-cellar hideaway, there were enough rat droppings, dirt, and who knew what else in there for him to dismiss it as possible bathwater.

Iridan shaved as well, thinking that the scant aether it took would hardly be noticed. He had come to feel like a vagabond, and the ritual of shaving helped make him feel civilized again. He tried to justify it to himself as presenting a formidable, intimidating visage to his foes but he knew it for vanity, and could not swallow his own lies.

It was nearly time for his nightly raid. Though sound military tactics would have had him vary the times from night to night, he preferred to get to his grim duties as quickly as the darkness allowed. With the advance of springtime, the days grew longer. Though he could not have noticed such tiny variances from day to day, he imagined that he could, and rankled at the increasing wait each evening.

"Soon," he told himself. "They are getting weaker by the day. Those blade-priests were a challenge, but how many more could they have? Once those run out, I am free to kill at will again."

"They could have a lot more," he answered himself. It was a habit that had begun to worry him. "They might send every priest in Safschan here for all I know." He noticed that his hands were shaking. "It's not nerves," he told his hands. "I just need a drink before I go."

The wine felt good as it poured down his throat. It steadied his hands, and washed away a headache he had not even noticed until it was gone. Iridan felt better, less irritable, more able to think. He briefly considered bringing a bottle with him, just in case he needed it. "No, that would be stupid. It's glass. It would get broken far too easily, and its weight would be awkward for fighting."

Iridan collected Dragon's Whisper, and set off to find his night's quarry. He took a quick surveillance of the vicinity of his hideaway for Sources, finding only a few animals about, nothing smart enough to pose a threat. "No nosy neighbors to kill tonight," he muttered to himself. He hated disposing of observers, since he had to move the bodies as well, lest they give clues to his lair's location.

The streets seemed quieter than usual as Iridan crept along the shadowed alleyways off the main thoroughfares. He caught glimpses of fire in the distance, more than just a torch or a signal beacon. He decided to take a better vantage to try to figure out what the cause was. Sheathing his blade at his back, he climbed a low wall, and leapt to a nearby window sill. He pulled himself up, and launched himself onto the roof of the building next door and from there to the roof of another building a story higher. He would have taken more pride in the acrobatics had aether not done nearly all the work.

There was firelight coming from the central square of Munne. If the square had a proper name, he knew it not. It looked like a gathering by torchlight, if he was to guess. It cast the Megrenn's headquarters in orangish light. He thought he could make out someone walking on a balcony.

"*Makto enfusi delgaja,*" Iridan intoned. He hated that there were still so many basic spells he could not perform silently. He touched his hands together thumb to thumb, forefinger to forefinger, drawing them slowly wider. A shimmering field formed between his hands, magnifying the distant scene.

Walking the balcony was a Megrenn general. Iridan knew little of their hierarchy, but by his position overlooking the gathering from the headquarters, he might well have been the commander of the whole occupying force of the city.

"HEAR ME, KADRIN WARLOCK!" A voice boomed through the city, obviously amplified by magic. It startled Iridan, his foot shifting on the slippery roof tiles on which he stood. His magnification spell ended as he caught himself.

"I OFFER A CHALLENGE." The voice spoke Kadrin with a strange accent. The amplification and the echoing from all the surrounding buildings made any further guesses about its owner pure speculation. "WE MAY END THIS TONIGHT. DEFEAT ME, AND OUR FORCES WILL WITHDRAW, RATHER THAN FORCE YOU TO SLAY US ALL. SINGLE COMBAT, UPON MY HONOR. I AM DENCHI, PRIEST OF THE BLADE."

"So another of the bastards wants to take my head off," Iridan mumbled. "What sort of fool do they take me for?"

"YOU HAVE TWO HOURS TO DECIDE."

"Well now. Two hours. There is a lot a fellow can do with two hours."

A plan began to form in Iridan's mind, none of it involving marching into a circle of Megrenn soldiers to engage in single combat. Instead his thoughts turned to the figure he had seen on the balcony.

* * * * * * * *

The sewers were cleaner than he had imagined they would be, which was the one saving grace of his chosen route to Megrenn headquarters. Iridan had gotten as close as he dared above ground before taking a detour to the waterways below.

Sewers were a boon to the health of a large city, keeping offal from clogging the streets. They were also a bane to guardsmen, generals, and anyone looking to maintain law and order. They were places respectable folk would not go, and places disreputable folk used as highways, be they thieves, fugitives, spies ... or assassins. The same measures used to keep those disreputables away also thwarted the civic efforts of the poor souls charged with maintenance, and the whining of civil servants was louder than the whisper-quiet passage of an illicit traveler.

Iridan kept a close eye to the aether as he went, chancing no surprise encounters. He went so far as to draw the Sources out of rats when he found them. Rat Sources were as weak as mammals came, but it still made him feel powerful wrenching the wretched little Sources clear out of them.

Rat-killing aside, Iridan's precautions paid off. Roughly where he expected to find his destination, he found a pair of guards stationed to protect the way up. Guarding the sewer exit of a building populated by military men was among the worst assignments Iridan could think of. He almost felt as if he were putting the two unlucky blighters out of their misery as he slew them. They died in confusion. Iridan's sound-deadening spell kept the brief struggle noiseless, and prevented the crash of armored bodies from raising an alarm.

As Iridan emerged into the keep, he scanned the aether yet again. The building was nearly deserted. He was able to avoid a few wandering servants, and find a window to get his bearing. He knew that the balcony faced the east, and was on the fourth floor. Once he found which side of the building faced the torchlight from the square, he rushed for the stairs leading up.

On the fourth floor landing, there was a large door to the east. It had to be the one. In the aether, he saw two Sources within—neither strong enough to be a threat.

Iridan tried the door gently, ready to hurl it back with telekinesis if he found it locked, but hoping to conserve both the aether and the element of surprise. It opened readily at his touch. "Cut off the head," Rashan had told him. It had been the key to Rashan's easy victory over Megrenn when he had first conquered them.

Iridan moved to make quick work of the Source nearer the door before making his way to the one nearer the balcony, which he assumed would be the leader of the occupation force. There was a problem, though.

Still watching in the aether, Iridan saw the weak Source he was about to attack strengthen tenfold. A second bit of aether separated from it, shaped like a blade, blocking the path of Dragon's Whisper. That Source grew a shield around it even before dragon bone had struck steel.

"Welcome, Iridan Korian, Sorcerer of the Fourth Circle," his intended victim greeted him in excellent Kadrin. The barest genteel hint of a Safschan accent told him his opponent was another blade-priest.

"By the winds! Just how many of you are there? And I am Warlock Iridan, not some Fourth Circle," Iridan replied. He realized he was being goaded when his response provoked a chuckle. Iridan shielded himself in preparation for a battle rather than the assassination he had intended.

"Myself and the one who issued the challenge, in the square below. We are the last two here; you slew the others. My name is Tiiba," the blade-priest introduced himself.

Iridan took a respite from the aether to view his opponent. He saw a man larger and more muscular than himself—though most taverns boasted a score each night fitting that description—dressed as his fellows had been. Tiiba's features were difficult to discern, dark flesh in a darkened room, the only light coming from the torches at street level below. What stood out to Iridan was the one mismatched eye, whiteness reflecting back at him in the paltry light. He switched back to aether-vision immediately thereafter.

"My name is Iridan Solaran now, but you knew that, I think."

"My thanks for that clarification," Tiiba said. "It will sound much better when my life's victories are read, to have the correct name for the warlock I slew, and not the name of some cowardly nobody from a peasant family who was only Fourth Circle."

The blade-priest launched a slash-thrust combination that had Iridan backpedaling, taking him sidelong across the room, rather than toward either the door or the balcony.

"You seem to know a lot about me. You have spies watching me or the like." Iridan tried to counterattack, making use of Dragon's Whisper's superior speed, but the blade-priest Tiiba seemed to anticipate each attack and have a parry in place and waiting by the time his blow arrived.

"You Kadrins are arrogant, brutish. You think strength of arms or strength of magic is enough for victory. I talk to people, *listen* to people. I keep company with travelers who know both lands. I study my opponents, when I know who they will be."

Tiiba launched a combination like nothing Iridan had seen before, even from two opponents. Tiiba slashed, reversed his grip, and slashed back the other direction, then brought a foot around to try to trip him, made a thrust that Iridan had to parry, and used the momentum of the parry to bring the long hilt of his weapon around to slam Iridan in the face.

Iridan's shield bore the blow well but it knocked him off balance. Iridan stumbled against something, discovering a bookshelf in the wall he had been driven back against.

As with the other blade-priests, Iridan found himself outmatched in skill at arms. He switched his attacks to the aether before he took too much punishment against his shielding spell. He gathered aether quickly, and launched an aether-bolt at Tiiba's midsection, hoping to blast him backward if not win the battle right then and there.

Tiiba parried.

Iridan's eyes widened in shock as the rune-blade turned aside his magical attack. He did not react in time to get his blade in the way of Tiiba's next attack.

The world spun as the blow hammered home against his shield. Again the shield held but Iridan was hurled to the ground.

Iridan gathered aether to him, drawing for all he was worth. A bit of it he directed into his fading shield spell, the rest he unleashed as hellfire. Tiiba did not attempt to parry that attack. Though his aether-vision was not detailed enough to reveal his foe's expression, Iridan imagined with glee the shocked look on Tiiba's face as he set the room aflame.

His own safe haven free of the blaze would not last long, he knew, but he could see by Tiiba's persistent shield that the battle was not yet over. Iridan tried to bolt for the door but Tiiba cut him off, holding his ground despite the conflagration.

"No escape for you this way, warlock pup," Tiiba quipped. It seemed the blade-priest was willing to let both of them die in the fires, or at least bring it down to a test of shield spells to see who would last long enough to escape.

"Stay in the flames if you like," Iridan shot back, bolting for the balcony. It was four stories down and into the teeth of the Megrenn army, including the last blade-priest, but Iridan still preferred his odds there. The Megrenn commanding officer was taking refuge in a corner of the balcony, away from the flames. Iridan cut him in two before hopping up onto the railing, and jumping down.

The impact on his shield spell was worse than Iridan anticipated. Despite the spell, he felt something crunch in his leg. He collapsed to the ground.

"Stay back!" a voice shouted.

Through the haze of pain, Iridan figured it to be the second blade-priest. *Blade-priest—Tiiba!*

The immediacy of his injured leg had distracted him from the thought of pursuit. He rolled in time to see Tiiba falling from the sky, heading straight for him, blade raised to strike. Iridan raised Dragon's Whisper, preparing to deflect the attack if he could. He drew aether like a madman, giving no consideration to his capacity. The abundance of idle Sources milling about had left the square awash in aether.

Tiiba's impact sent Dragon's Whisper skittering across the flagstones, broke down what remained of Iridan's shielding spell but did not finish him. Tiiba seemed to sense victory, holding his rune-blade high as he prepared for a decisive strike. Iridan's lips curled into a smile as he anticipated the wreckage of a man that would be left after he unleashed his spell.

"Juliana will never love you, monster," Tiiba said to him, venom in his voice.

Iridan's eyes widened in horror. His concentration broke for a moment, but that moment was too long. Through the searing pain of the drawn aether coursing unchecked through his body, he saw Tiiba's blade come down.

Chapter 33 - Reconnecting

The *Sand Piper* bobbed proudly in her berth, having delivered her passengers safely to Scar Harbor. Porters and longshoremen filed along the gangplanks, coming and going with supplies, cargo, and luggage. The onshore breeze reminded everyone that autumn had come to Acardia, and that unlike the tame lands of the south, bright blue skies did not guarantee balmy temperatures; there was a toothy edge to it that cut through thin cloth, and went straight to the skin.

Several of the gentlemen passengers made a show of carrying their own belongings, generally to fluff their egos in front of their ladies. In Brannis's case, he felt awful watching a man half his size attempting to wrangle a trunk filled with his armor, sword, and a collection of Kadrin books, not to mention the full wardrobe that Soria had acquired for him. The trunk seemed sized optimistically for future purchases, and was of unwieldy size as well as weight. Brannis took it by the handle on one end while the porter had both hands under the other. Soria allowed three trunks of hers to be carried by the dockhands and Rakashi's belongings were brought ashore by two young passengers who insisted that it was an honor to be of assistance to him.

A short while later, they were piled into a hired carriage, bound for The Little Manor. Soria paid for their transportation from her seemingly bottomless supply of coin.

"Where do you all make so much coin?" Brannis asked, baffled that Soria seemed to squander money at every opportunity without worry. "Have you taken my arrival as a special occasion, or is it typical for you to throw gold at every nicety that comes along?"

Soria laughed. "What brings this up all of a sudden? It isn't as if this carriage cost all that much," Soria replied. She wore a warmer woolen dress, trimmed in ermine, keeping up the appearance of being a highborn lady.

"Well, I knew you were spending a lot, but I *know* how much carriages cost in Scar Harbor. The other splurges passed quietly when I hardly knew what was going on. And hey now, when did you decide to take on a Kheshi accent?" Brannis switched trails, distracted by Soria's transition to another persona, one he had not seen yet, or more precisely, had not heard yet. This time, it was Rakashi who chuckled.

"She sounds like that most of the time," the Takalish warrior explained.

"Brannis," Soria said, "I grew up in Khesh. Until I started traveling more widely, I hardly remembered the Acardian I learned when I was a little girl. It was so bad for a while there that I could hardly get Zell to understand me. We spoke Kadrin together for the first year and more that we traveled together until I picked up enough Acardian. Of the three of them, only Rakashi could speak Kheshi worth spit."

"So what is this Little Manor like? I know of it, but I have never needed to take a room in the city before."

"It's nice but stop being so ... so 'Brannis' for a moment while we sort a few important things first." Soria's curt tone reminded him that Kyrus was a wanted fugitive in Scar Harbor, and that he bore an uncanny resemblance to the scrawny scrivener. "We need a name and a background for you while you're in Acardia."

"How about we just keep going with 'Brannis Hinterdale'?" Brannis said with a shrug.

"Doesn't that sound just a bit too Kadrin to you?" Soria asked, shaking her head.

"What if it does, a bit? Who is the wiser; my parents chose an odd name, perhaps? Do you go about wondering where odd names come from?"

"Yes," Soria and Rakashi answered in unison. Brannis was taken aback.

"Brannis," Soria said, "you're still so new at this. We are on guard constantly for twinborn. Whether they turn out to be potential allies, casual acquaintances, or deadly enemies, it all comes down to figuring out their connection before they figure out yours. There are signs to look for. If you get good at spotting them, you have a huge advantage."

"What if the carriage driver is one? If that is the case, you have just given all of us away," Brannis said.

"Well, since I plan on killing the carriage driver, I don't think he will be telling anyone else," Soria answered casually, not so much as lowering her voice. She paused, cocking her head. The carriage continued along uninterrupted. "Nothing. Carriage driver isn't listening to us or he has nerves like a dragon. Anyway, if we run across anyone from Veydrus here, that name will be a flag flying over your head with 'twinborn' written on it. Thanks to my oathfather, that name is known rather widely across Koriah, on both sides of the war."

"What about the Hinterdale part?" Brannis said. "Someone is bound to note the resemblance, and perhaps being a relative would be a suitable excuse."

"Yes," Soria said, "that works. We need a better name than Brannis, though. Got any ideas, Rakashi?"

"Do you speak any other Telluraki languages, Brannis? Perhaps you could have been raised abroad, much like Soria. She is as Acardian as you, but can pass for Kheshi easily with a bit of disguise. The language is key," Rakashi said.

"Well, that would be nice, but aside from picking up a bit of the Denku tongue, I have little to go on," Brannis said. "I left here with Denrik Zayne, stopped in Marker's Point, got stranded on Denku Appa for three months or so, then a tempest's swirl through Takalia with you two, and now I am home again."

"Well, how about we just say he grew up in Marker's Point? Hard to argue against that, unless anyone talks to him long enough to realize how naive he is.

No one as knightly as Brannis comes out of the Point," Soria said with a smirk. "How about 'Erund'? Erund Hinterdale ... you can plead ignorance of any relation if it comes up. Don't give the surname out unless asked, though; save the excuse for when you need it or it will be suspicious."

"Maybe grow a beard," Rakashi suggested.

Brannis shook his head. "Kyrus used to wear a beard, if it could be rightly called one. It would do little as a disguise. Fewer folk might know me without one."

"Well," Soria said, "I heard no objection—"

"Hey, wait!" Brannis tried to enter his opinion before the matter was deemed closed.

"—so Erund it is," Soria finished.

"I am not sure I care for that one," Brannis said.

"Sorry, what was that, Erund? I didn't quite hear you," Soria said.

Rakashi smiled.

* * * * * * *

Sleight of hand with coins. Silks from his sleeves. Conjured fire. Juggling doves. Everyone cheers. Hat fills with coins. Same as every day since they have been in Naia, a different street corner each time. Sooner or later, everyone who cared to would have seen the act, then the coin would dry up like a creek bed once the thaw has passed.

Zell stood off to the far side of the crowd, keeping a hand on Jadon lest the boy wander off. Discovering that tendency had led to a panicked search their first night in the city, but with more dutiful supervision, it had been limited to the single incident. As for the boy, he seemed better than when they had found him at the sanctuary. He spoke sometimes—only in Megrenn still—but it was more promising than just staring straight ahead with nary a blink as he so often had on the wagon ride.

Zell looked down at the boy, seeing if he was having any more reaction to this show than any of the others. It looked strange, seeing him dressed up like a Takalish boy. He was clearly Acardian in heritage—possibly mixed with a touch of Feru, if Zell had to hazard a guess—and seeing him in local garb seemed out of place. He ought to have been wearing trousers and a plain grey or brown woolen tunic, running around barefoot. Wendell had purchased him a proper Takalish wardrobe: wide-legged pants of shin length, tied at the waist with a cord; a two-layer pullover jacket, the outer, deep-blue layer parting in a large V in the center to reveal the white layer beneath; a pair of doeskin boots; and a puffy cap that kept falling off for Zell to retrieve.

As the show ended, Zell hooted and applauded, trying to work up the sentiments of the crowd. They needed little prodding, however. The show was still new and impressive; it ought to have been, what with Wendell working in real magic. Zell had watched it once with the magic-seeing helm, and it lost a lot of its appeal when you could see how it was being done. He looked down at

Jadon in his Takalish clothes, and gave him a gentle shake to get his attention. It was gratifying when the boy actually turned and looked up at him.

"Do like everyone else. It's what to do at a show," Zell told him, using Megrenn, which was not his strongest language. He clapped to demonstrate, filling in the gap in his vocabulary.

To his surprise, Jadon complied, clapping awkwardly but enthusiastically.

Wendell came over to them as soon as the crowd began to disperse. "Did I see what I think I saw?" Wendell asked, addressing Zell but looking at Jadon.

The boy looked back but his expression was blank.

"Aye, you did indeed," Zell said. "Not sure what got into him, but whatever it was, it got in somehow. Not sure whether he finally understood the show or just got caught up, and copied what I showed him," Zellisan replied, using Acardian, as Wendell had when speaking to him.

"Well, either way, that is wonderful, Jadon. Keep this up, and you will be better in no time. I went through the same thing. I know you can do it," Wendell told the boy, persisting in using Acardian when he did not urgently need the boy to understand him. The sooner they weaned him off of Veydran languages, the better.

* * * * * * *

Evening was setting in by the time they had settled into their rooms at The Little Manor. A turkey-and-capers dinner in the inn's renowned common room filled Brannis's stomach with familiar foods, even if they tasted somewhat different from how Kyrus had remembered them. Kyrus had been so long in Kadris that the differences between his tastes and Brannis's had been thoroughly explored. Brannis had been regularly exposed to foods that Kyrus found unfamiliar—even the fare on Denku Appa to an extent—and the return to Kyrus's hometown was turning over that packed soil.

Back in their rooms after their meal, signed under the names of Erund and Soria Hinterdale, Brannis and Soria relaxed, and began to plan their tasks for Brannis's homecoming trip. He had deftly avoided managing to commit to specifics during their passage from Takalia. Soria, as it turned out, could easily be distracted from boring conversations when need be.

"So what do we need to take care of while we are here? Once we take care of the business, I intend to have you show me around the city. I want to see where Kyrus grew up. See? I even remembered your name from here," Soria proclaimed proudly, clasping her hands behind her back, and rising up on her tiptoes. Brannis could not help wondering where she got all her energy, whether from some aspect of her Tezuan training or just a quirk of her nature.

"Well, I shall want to collect any personal effects from the shop that I can. That might involve sneaking around the place—actually it almost certainly will—and it may involve finding where the sheriff and magistrates keep evidence," Brannis said, sitting down on the edge of the bed. It squished with the telltale softness of down stuffing.

"If you let me know of any particulars you are interested in, it might be best for me to go off, and take care of that. After nightfall, I am far less conspicuous than you. What else?"

"I would like to check in on the well-being of some friends of mine. I do not know whether any of them may have taken partial blame in my escape. There was some ... unpleasantness involved," Brannis said, choosing his words with care.

"We know. How do you think we found you? We tracked you from the point you escaped. They put you in cahoots with Denrik Zayne. His involvement overshadowed any thought that locals might have been done up in the whole affair," Soria explained.

"Oh," Brannis replied. Soria watched him, waiting for him to continue. "Well, I should still like to check, all the same."

"Anyone in particular?" Soria asked, raising her eyebrows expectantly. A tiny smile curled the corner of her lip.

"Well, there is my friend Greuder—"

"The baker? Good sort. Seemed inclined to think you were innocent, from what Zell told us. Didn't hear a bad word about his bakery, so it doesn't seem he was in any difficulty due to your ordeal. By all means, though, check up on him. Who else?" Soria smiled as she waited for an answer. Brannis felt like a calf being led to slaughter. He began to see where she was goading him.

"Then there is ..."—Brannis cleared his throat—"... Expert Davin, my old employer. He lives—"

"Over in Golis. We can head there once we are done in Scar Harbor. I rather look forward to meeting him. Who else?"

"I suppose I should also go see—"

"Abbiley Tillman?" Soria asked, folding her arms across her chest, and watching with a smug look as Brannis felt his face flush.

"I ... um ... well, you know when ... you see it was not me ..."

Soria began chuckling, saving Brannis from further embarrassing himself.

"You are *so* new at this. And that's why I don't mind," Soria said. Brannis cocked his head to the side, not sure he had heard her correctly. It certainly *seemed* like the sort of thing he would have expected her to mind. "Go see her tomorrow, if you feel like you need to. She was Kyrus's first love, wasn't she ... before you realized Kyrus was even real?"

"Yes."

"Well then, what should it matter to me? You can check in for Kyrus's sake, then later on, I can remind you how much better you have it now." Soria's eyes gleamed lasciviously. "Now, is there any other business you have here in Scar Harbor that needs attending to?"

"Well, I do not know quite how to get into this, but since the part I was worried about appears to have gone well, I may as well venture it: I think there is a possibility that there is a conspiracy at work here," Brannis said. He found his heart still thumping in his chest, and suspected that his face was still pink, but he was beginning to feel his guts unclenching from the knot he had tied them in.

"Brannis, you already explained that one. Kadrin has been rife with conspiracies since long before either of us was born."

"No, *here.*"

"Here in Tellurak?" Soria asked.

"*Here!* Scar Harbor," Brannis said. "I think there may be twinborn at work that we do not know about."

"Who do you suspect?"

"I am not certain, but I think Rashan may be at the heart of it. He hinted that he once led a cabal of spies who passed information between worlds. I do not know who he has running this side of it, but I suspect Abbiley may be a pawn in this."

"Why her? It seems to be a bit of a convoluted plan, don't you think? I mean, what are the odds you would even head back here to find out about her? Coming back here—without backup like me and Rakashi at least—would be foolhardy. And how would they even know about her?"

"Rashan knows. We got to talking one night—he was in his cups, which seemed odd all to itself. He told me about his life in Acardia when he was young; we compared how Scar Harbor looked then and now. He told me about a girl he once loved, a long time ago—"

"And of course, you told him all about the artist girl," Soria finished for him.

"Yes, but showed him, too. He taught me an illusion spell that night. We used them to put pictures to our stories. I even gave him her name," Brannis said, shaking his head. "I could have accidentally put her in danger. There is this look Rashan gets in his eyes when he looks at me now, looks at Kyrus, that is. I think he is wary of me, and I think he might use Abbiley as a hostage to ensure his safety."

"Seems a bit paranoid, even for a twinborn. You're learning to think of this sort of thing at least. That's a start. Ever consider that you wouldn't know what became of her if you never checked, and that your ignorance would have protected her from becoming a hostage?"

"Oh, I did not need to come back here to find out about her, just to check on her, and possibly protect her. Abbiley seems to have been an even later bloom that I was."

"Wait. Are you saying she is twinborn too?" Soria seemed incredulous. She came over and sat beside Brannis on the bed. "Do you know who else she is?" Brannis said nothing, but a look of dawning realization widened Soria's eyes, quickly changing to a look of displeasure as she wrinkled her nose. "No. Not *her!*"

"You noticed the resemblance, too?" Brannis ventured, treading carefully.

"Oh, sure, cow's teats, hips wide enough to birth a monohorn, peasant teeth that whistle in the wind when she smiles. At least the one in Veydrus has magic enough to fix her teeth and complexion," Soria ranted, her speech accelerating and gaining momentum as she went. "It just figures that the little harlot was always sniffing after you like a hunting dog. No wonder! She was just following some leftover feeling from his artist girl. It's not like she ever had a real chance of—"

"Hey!" Brannis cut her off before she could get far enough with her slanders to truly anger him. "I need to protect her. I might be the one responsible for putting her in danger. I was able to get Juliana out of Kadris before things got out of hand. I might have done something to protect Celia as well, but for two things. Firstly, she is on a tight leash, working for Rashan, and now for Caladris. Secondly, I had only one airship to give that did not need a naval crew."

"I doubt she would have known which end was up on a ship," Soria said.

"That is not the point. Kyrus gave it to *you*, not her."

"So you are saying Kyrus chose me? Not you?" Soria smiled, but without her eyes lighting up the way they normally did.

"By the winds, Juliana, I chose you nine summers ago!"

Soria breathed a long sigh, releasing pent-up tension. The lascivious look returned to her eyes as she turned toward Brannis.

* * * * * * *

Their boarding-house room was small but clean. The dark wood floors shone with well-worn varnish. The lath and plaster walls were painted pale blue, giving the room an airy feel. A pair of bunk beds took up much of the available floor space, the rooms being rented primarily to laborers, migrants, and visitors to the city. It was not the sort of place to raise a family, cook meals, or sit around in playing cards and dice—though the latter had occurred far more often than the previous two activities.

Nevertheless, Wendell and Zellisan found themselves with a small family of sorts: a would-be master, his intended apprentice, and ... Zell, who did not quite fit in anywhere yet.

Jadon wheezed slightly in his sleep, the only sign he breathed at all, his thin chest moved so little as he slept, occupying the top bunk, above where Wendell slept. It was early yet, and neither of the two adults had any intention of slumber for some time yet. Wendell took occasional pulls at a bottle of wine from the region they had just passed through. Zellisan sipped a Takalish whiskey with too refined a flavor to it to waste on gulping it down.

"Kid sleeps. I'll credit him that much," Zellisan remarked, seated on the edge of his bunk. The wooden frame creaked at his every movement, protesting the over-large Acardian's heft.

"Just give him time. You cannot imagine what it ish like, living with two worlds before your eyes at the ... at the same ... at once. We need to help him sheparate the two in his mind. I think today was a good shign," Wendell replied. He thumped his fist against his chest, trying to quell the burning feeling as the strong wine scorched its way down his throat. The Takalish called it "partially distilled," but it was more a liquor than a wine to Faolen's sensibilities.

"So ... what? We wait for him to figure out which world is which, and then what?" Zell asked, speaking slowly though remarkably clearly for all the alcohol he had consumed.

"Anzik Fehr *has* the Staff of Gehlen. I just convince him to give it to me. Shimple as ... as that," Wendell replied, managing to snap his fingers. Being a magician had its advantages when drunk; certain muscles just coordinated themselves without needing much brain involved.

"Well spit on me!" said Zellisan. "So all we gotta do is get that one's head cleared of lint and cowflops and ... and ... and whatever else is up in there ... and we win? Hot biscuits!" Zell tilted back his expensive whiskey, and took a long swig of it.

Wendell did not reply, but joined the undeclared toast in honor of Kadrin victory, slinging back an eye-crossing amount of the distilled wine. Tears welled at the corners of his eyes. In his stupor, he could not quite settle on why.

It was not long before Zellisan was sprawled across his bed at an uncomfortable-looking angle, atop the blankets, snoring like a bellows. Wendell had an advantage that Zellisan could not compete with: a breezy wake-me-up in the form of aether. Just a few simple illusions were enough to freshen his mind temporarily. It was all he would need before collapsing in his own turn.

Wendell climbed the first small steps up to the top bunk, high enough that he could lean across the sleeping Jadon to whisper into his ear.

"Anzik. Can you hear me? This is Faolen. I am the only voice now. Give me the staff, and it will all be done."

Wendell waited but got no response. He began to feel the insistent pressure of the wine pitting its will against his own. He repeated the message. Jadon stirred in his sleep.

"Where are you, Faolen?" Jadon murmured, still asleep.

Wendell smiled in relief. "I am at the High Council chamber. Just go to the door, and ask for me. They will take the staff but it is all right."

Chapter 34 - Tides Turn

The morning dew was still wet upon the grassy hilltop as General Hellmock dismounted his horse. He noted, with the curious guilt of someone about to commit an act of desecration, just how beautiful the Kadrin countryside was in early springtime. He held a hand out to his side, upturned, not looking back as someone placed a farseeing lens in his grasp. His gaze was fixed out on the mass of troops positioned to block his army's advance.

Adjusting the tube until the blur sharpened into focus, he took a census of the enemy before him. Arrayed in red and gold, with plate armor gleaming where it peeked from beneath their uniforms, were real Kadrin infantry. They were not conscripts, he realized, but a knot of the standing army that Kadrin still kept. His practiced eye counted by thousands, coming to a conclusion that ten was as good a number as he was likely to assign them, milling about in preparation for an assault. Of course, not all of them were infantrymen, just the ones foremost. Mixed among them were archers, catapult crews, a smaller number of perhaps a hundred or so knight-led cavalry. No doubt as well, there would be sorcerers among them. Aside from the trap laid at Temble Hill, there had been members of the thrice-accursed Imperial Circle opposing them at every turn. The Ghelkan sorcerers helped a great deal, but always seemed outmatched. His troops always paid in blood to even the odds.

Still, the Kadrin numbers did not concern him. His forces outnumbered theirs fivefold, and with monohorns as well. A handful of stripe-cats would serve as flankers, mostly to keep the Kadrin force from repositioning freely, but the terrain made them less than essential for the coming battle.

The Kadrins had chosen the battlefield, a low-lying flatland alongside the Thadagar River, between the forest's thick tangle and the water's edge. It meant that the Kadrin generals were learning from their earlier defeats. Not content to sit behind the walls of Pevett while cannons worked to pound those same walls to dust, they had decided to meet Megrenn's forces in the open field—or at least in the field, for the battlefield was as narrow as Hellmock could remember encountering.

As Hellmock continued perusing the Kadrin assemblage, a few of his officers cried out. General Hellmock took the tube of the farseeing lens from his eye, and followed their gazes and pointed fingers. It was one of the Kadrin airships. It circled about, never coming near enough to the Megrenn forces for him to consider ordering archers or cannons to fire upon it. It landed in the midst of the

Kadrin host, soldiers scrambling out of the way to make room.

A cheer rose from the Kadrin camp, the sound carrying over the distance to where Hellmock and his officers stood. The ragged, disorganized cheer faded into a chant. There were two syllables to it, but between the distance and the language barrier, Hellmock could not tell what they were chanting. He looked to his officers, but was met with shrugs and shaking heads.

The Kadrin forces began furious activity, men shifting all about down in the floodplain of the Thadagar. Hellmock took up his lens once again, and saw that they were forming up ranks, infantry at the fore.

Hellmock was puzzled. The Kadrins would have plenty of time to set their defenses once they saw his own troops begin their advance. Had some high general been flown up from Kadris, and was now mucking about, making his troops wait in formation until the Megrenn decided to attack? Hellmock nearly considered making them stand there in armor for a few hours, just to tire their feet before the assault. But no ...

The Kadrin infantry began to move. They were launching an assault of their own! *Why would they take up a defensive position, only to give it up just before we attack?*

"Send down the orders for the monohorns to meet the Kadrin advance," Hellmock shouted. From his high vantage, he watched his own forces array themselves. The monohorn cavalry ought to be more than a match for the Kadrin infantry, with the Ghelkans countering whatever tricks of magic they no doubt had in mind.

The Kadrin line slowed when the monohorns began their own advance. The pause was noticeable but brief, as the troops—with admirable discipline—resumed their pace. Horse-mounted sorcerers rode at the ready behind the monohorns, on guard for deceit.

They were not enough.

Before the monohorns reached the Kadrin front line, the beasts, under full gallop, lifted into the air. The Kadrin advance halted. A lone figure walked out before all the infantrymen, small, clad in black. The two dozen monohorns held aloft by magic were hurled back, lobbed shrieking—beast and man alike—into the body of the Megrenn army. The ground shook. Panic spread. Men died.

What little Kadrin that Hellmock understood had a military bent to it. He understood every word when a magically enhanced voice boomed out over the battlefield:

"DEATH TO THE MEGRENN! NO SURVIVORS!"

The Kadrin infantry charged, full run, toward the suddenly exposed Ghelkan sorcerers. The sorcerers fired off spells of lightning and aether before turning their horses to flee. A magical barrier stopped each assault, leaving the Kadrin forces unscathed.

The black-clad figure was faster than all the rest, and brooked no comparison. He chased down the horses, butchering steed and rider with his sword, only a handful surviving to reach the Megrenn main force. Far from daunted by the prospect of being amid a host of fifty thousand enemy soldiers, the black-clad sorcerer plowed into their ranks, blade leading. Bodies fell and blood flew in sprays.

Kthoom. Kthoom. Kthoom. Kthoom.

The body of the Kadrin sorcerer was thrown like an angry child's doll, tumbling end over end through the air to land in a heap before the astonished Kadrin infantry. The soldiers stopped short of where their champion had fallen, unsure what the sorcerer's death boded for them.

Hellmock's mouth went dry; his throat tightened as if physically gripped by the fear he felt. The Kadrin sorcerer stood, unsteadily at first, and brushed himself off. Bereft of weapon, he raised his arms slowly, palms upturned. It seemed then that half the Megrenn army caught fire as flames rose up from the ground over a wide expanse of the riverside.

The men nearest the Thadagar sought refuge in its deep, slow currents, armor or no. The Kadrins nearest the sorcerer fell back as well, as a pair closest to him collapsed. Hellmock knew little enough about sorcerers and how they worked their magic, but he suspected the sorcerer to have affected their doom as collateral damage.

No, not sorcerer, Hellmock thought, *demon.* Warlock Rashan Solaran had come to personally destroy his army. He watched helplessly, passively, as the doom engulfed them all. It would be his turn soon enough, he realized.

* * * * * * * *

Donnel's Fort was a small township on the border of the ogrelands, with little strategic value. It would have been swept up eventually, along with all the other places that would be cut off from Kadrin support by the loss of the major cities and crossroads. It was walled in stone, high enough that ogres of the neighboring tribes could not just grab the top, and vault themselves over. There was a possibility of a sorcerer or two dwelling among the residents, depending on whom they had crossed among the upper echelons of the Imperial Circle.

Jinzan's transference spell had deposited him just outside the city gates, which stood open in the daylight hours as folk who worked outside the walls preferred easy access—primarily woodsmen and farmers. Scouts on the wooden towers just inside the wall were on constant alert for ogre raids, for the brutes hated Kadrin for encroaching on what they viewed as their own lands.

Those scouts spotted Jinzan appearing out of nothingness. No one knew what to make of him. Sorcerers usually brought ill tidings, not because they were enemies, but because they came with edicts from the Circle. To men who lived under the constant threat of ogre attack, the Circle was still more feared.

"Who goes there?" one of the scouts shouted down in Kadrin.

Jinzan looked up into the youthful, pale face of the spotter of ogres. He wore a plain brown tunic, not the heraldry of the Kadrin army, but that did not mean that he was not a soldier. Ogres saw the color red better than most others, and anyone hoping to avoid their notice took care to avoid it.

"…" Jinzan thought to reply, but wondered what he could possibly say that would be anything but lies or self-important bluster. He turned his attention to the staff in his hands. The white wood was smooth against his fingers, carved with runes thousands of summers old, with angular "wings" of wood sprouting from the top. It smelled incongruously of sewage, but that would not last, especially once Jinzan took the time to give it a thorough cleaning.

Jinzan drew.

The scouts clearly felt the effects, bracing themselves against the wooden railings of their tower as they felt an airless wind blowing past and through them. There was no physical force behind it, but most folk were unused to the feel of the aether, oblivious to it until it flowed like the waters of a burst dam around them.

"To arms! We are under attack!" the scout shouted, with every bit of breath in his lungs. His companion took hold of a rope and pulled, ringing a bell hidden up under the roof of the tower.

"*Eehu dolkavi esfenetor gelex pinudox,*" Jinzan chanted, holding the Staff of Gehlen in one hand while thrusting the other forth with a twisting motion.

Wind whipped about, scattering leaves and debris as a cyclone formed. Faster and faster the winds blew, sucking at Jinzan's clothing, and pulling his cloak out taut in front of him. He was not near enough to the tornado to feel the worst of its effects, though, and its movements obeyed his commands as he directed it through the watchtower. Wood splintered and split, chunks of the structure were wrenched off entirely. The two men in the tower screamed, but their voices were barely audible above the roar of the magical winds. The bell clanged a few final times as it was jerked about on its supports before being ripped free of the tower along with the roof, and devoured by the storm winds.

The rallying cry had prompted an admirably quick response among the Kadrin defenders. Men with leather armor and long spears rushed toward the town gates. Jinzan moved the twister into their path, a child's finger crushing and scattering ants as they emerged from their burrows. The survivors moved in too many different directions for Jinzan to bother chasing them all with the storm winds.

"*Fetru oglo daxgak sevdu wenlu,*" Jinzan spoke as he pointed at a cluster of the militiamen. Forks of lightning stabbed from his fingers, throwing the defenders of Donnel's Fort into helpless convulsions as they cooked.

By then, folk were fleeing the part of the town nearest to Jinzan's assault. A few hunters had taken shots at him with bows, but after disposing of them, there had been no further retaliation. He watched as people fled homes and workplaces, directing his spell over the vacated buildings, leaving the ones with basements as nothing but foundations. The ones with wooden or earthen floors were merely gone.

Jinzan allowed the women and any children of Anzik's age and younger to live, either to flee to other parts of Kadrin, into the ogrelands, or to remain behind to try to rebuild.

Anzik, Jinzan thought, distracting himself inadvertently, *I will find you, my son. I know not what Faolen's twin has been telling you but I will welcome you home if you return.*

The boy had left the Staff of Gehlen at the door to the High Council chambers but fled when told he would be taken to see Jinzan. Anyone who had been aware of the chase for the boy was wary of angering him, even without the staff. He had escaped for the time being, but without the staff, even the Kadrin illusionist's help from the other side would not be enough to hide him forever.

Jinzan left a message before he departed, burned into the ground outside the city gate.

"Megrenn is your friend." The message was written in ogreish.

* * * * * * * *

"Councilor Fehr," a messenger approached him at a run, panting for breath. "Word from the Pevett assault. Councilor Narsicann is waiting for you in the Council chambers." The messenger was a professional, gasping out his missive between breaths.

"Very well. I will be there directly," Jinzan replied. He had just returned from Donnel's Fort, and had not so much as changed out of the boots he had worn, caked with mud and dirt from the Kadrin outpost's destruction. He turned to his wives, Nakah, Frenna, and Zaischelle—the latter showing unmistakable signs of being with child—and made his farewell after so brief a return. "I will return tonight. I think that whatever needs my attention cannot take me from my home this night. With the Staff of Gehlen, I might return most nights, even out on a campaign. I swear I will not let these interruptions rule over our lives."

"Just go, Jinzan. They need you," Nakah said.

"If you do not, I swear I will name the babe after Narsicann when he is born," Zaischelle threatened, drawing a chuckle from Nakah and Jinzan. She was by far the youngest of his wives, and the only one likely to yet bear his children; this would be his first by her. He looked forward with curiosity to see how much the babe resembled him, and how much he took after Zaischelle's Safschan heritage.

"Do what you need to do. Once Kadrin is burned, you can lay about enjoying your victory," Frenna added, souring the mood once more.

One wife that always vexes me, mother of a son who vexes me all the more. If Anzik has children of his own one day, they will be the death of me.

While Jinzan could have transferred to the Council chambers, his Source was weary from all the aether it had channeled earlier in the day. Without having to actually use his Source to draw the aether, the strain had been lessened, but the forming of the magic still took considerable effort. He rode instead, taking the road along the shoreline so he could watch the Aliani Sea crash against the shores. He wondered for the hundredth time whether Denrik Zayne ought to take his retirement in Khesh when the time came. He could look into buying up the same piece of land that his own home was on in Veydrus, and have the same view in Tellurak.

The ride put Jinzan better at ease, though riding with a staff in hand was more awkward than he had envisioned. He was unlikely to leave it behind any time soon, after the trouble he had gone through to reclaim it.

"Jinzan, get your scrawny arse in here. Narsey's boy must have got to you an hour ago," Kaynnyn bellowed from the Council table, where only his own seat was vacant. On the table rested one of the Ghelkan-made speaking helms.

"Your messenger did not convey a sufficient need for haste for me to attempt a third transference spell today," Jinzan replied as he strode across the room to take his seat.

"So it is still fully functioning?" Narsicann asked, jumping straight to the magical concerns.

"Yes, it appears no worse for its wanderings."

"Good, because you are going to be needing it in earnest soon, I think," Narsicann said. He gestured to the helm on the table.

"What is this about?"

"General Hellmock's army carried one of the helms. We heard from that helm after a battle that took place this morning, along the Thadagar River, just north of Pevett," Kaynnyn replied.

"What news, then? Are they encountering difficulties?"

"*They* were not the ones who wore the other helm," Narsicann replied. "I was the one who took the message. It was—"

"It was *him*! Rashan Solaran," Kaynnyn interrupted. She shook her head in dismay, accompanied by a tinkling sound of dangling jewelry.

"He asked for you specifically," Narsicann followed up, nonplussed by the interruption, which was unusual all on its own. Narsicann was prickly at the best of times. He had a haunted look on his face.

"You expect me to pick it up, and find him waiting to speak to me?" Jinzan asked. He eyed the helm with trepidation. Long moments passed, he realized, without making a move toward it.

"So I see I am not the only one spooked by ghosts speaking to me from history, heard only within my own head," Narsicann joked lamely, trying to salvage a bit of pride. "Varduk has given me naught but grief for most of the time we have waited for you."

"Give me that," Jinzan said testily. He reached to the center of the table, and grabbed the helm, armoring himself with anger against the rising bile in his throat. He jammed the helm down onto his head before he could have second thoughts, keeping the Staff of Gehlen in hand, despite the fact that the helm could not harm him.

"*So which of you is it this time?*" a disembodied voice came through clearly in Jinzan's mind. Devoid of timbre, it was less fearsome than he had expected. It sounded ... flippant?

"*I am High Councilor Jinzan Fehr,*" Jinzan replied. "*Am I addressing Rashan Solaran?*"

"*Why yes, you are, Councilor. I just wanted to try this thing out. It is like our speaking stones but portable. The voices sound awful, I must say, but it is a fair price to pay for the convenience."*

"What do you want?" Jinzan asked. He had no time for idle banter. He knew that time passed strangely while conversing in the aether. He trusted that Narsicann or one of the others would prevent him being in the thrall of the helm for more than a few hours, but he did not want to waste that time, however much he had.

"Why ... a great many things. I have the patience to get them all, I think. I want Ghelk. I want the ogrelands. I want Safschan and Narrack, the Painu Islands ... and I want Megrenn. I want the Staff of Gehlen. I want your skull for a trophy."

"Oh, is that all? Well, demon, I have the Staff of Gehlen, and I think I have the power to destroy you with it," Jinzan boasted. It was all he could think to do besides tear the helm off his head, and throw it across the room.

"Oh, maybe you do, maybe you do not. What you do have, though, is a need to sleep. I could wait, find you defenseless in your own bed. I can slip past whatever wards you think to set up to prevent me. Or else ... perhaps I could come to where you go when you sleep. What would you think of that, Captain Zayne?"

Jinzan felt his breathing coming quick and shallow. What sort of monster was he talking to? He could think of no response. He heard a chuckling laughter through the helm, stripped of all humanity by the magic. It sounded demonic.

"Sleep well, Captain. We will meet ... soon enough."

* * * * * * * *

Rashan removed the magical helm from his head, still smiling and chuckling. He crushed it between his thin, delicate-looking hands, and tossed it into the Thadagar River.

Chapter 35 - Unlocking Secrets

Kadrin was a vivid map beneath them ... or perhaps it was Megrenn. For an aspiring ship's captain, Juliana's knowledge of geography translated poorly from old paper and ink maps to real trees, rivers, and mountains. There were no dotted lines denoting borders, no names scrawled in giant letters above cities and forests. From what little she had ever paid attention to maps, she was surprised by the number of tiny communities that existed where no map took the trouble to denote them.

Juliana had kept the *Daggerstrike* heading north by keeping the Cloud Wall to their left. Her ship was an airship, and her crew were soldiers, not sailors. She would be gutted before she had them all waste time learning what starboard, port, and all the other nautical nonsense meant. Left was called left, right was called right, and since they all spoke Kadrin, everyone knew what everyone else was talking about.

It was lonely on deck. Despite the two spotters on each side of the ship, tethered to the railings for safety, conversation needed to take place at a shout, and preferably from close range. Soria had spent enough time alone with her thoughts for the both of them, and now that Soria was ensconced with Brannis in Tellurak, Juliana hoped that the two of them had not exchanged roles; she did not wish to become the stoic one.

One of the spotters on the right side of the *Daggerstrike* shouted something that could not be made out over the rush of air. Juliana slowed the ship from "gale" to "breeze" speed.

"Horses, heading north," the spotter repeated, pointing down to the ground.

Juliana fiddled with the ship's wheel, trying to activate the proper runes to convince the illusory display to show her where her spotter was pointing. The scene shifted wildly at each touch. Finally she got it facing roughly forward and below them, and turned the ship instead, rotating it in the air until the viewer displayed the aforementioned horses.

There were five of the animals in all, pushing hard. Three bore humans, the other two went riderless. Juliana and her crew had found a battle farther south along the Thadagar and steered well clear of it. It seemed likely that these were either runners racing to Megrenn with news of their battle—which would account for the spare horses—or survivors fleeing for their lives—which would account for the missing riders.

Juliana looked over the runes on the many handles of the wheel. They were not labeled with their function, which meant she either had to look over the rune structures to figure out what they did, or she had to remember Kyrus's whirlwind tour of the ship and what he had told her of their purposes. It would be some time before she knew them all to use the ship without consciously thinking through every action.

"Now, one of these shouts inside the ship, the other to the outside …" she muttered to herself as she examined the handle that bore communication runes. She touched one, sneaking just a bit of aether into it as a test.

"Hello. Hello. Can you hear me?" she said, keeping her voice low. She heard her voice coming from over the side of the ship. She swore beneath her breath, heard that coming from over the side of the ship as well. She heard laughter from belowdecks, so they were at least hearing her, even if her words were being shouted into the sky. She tried the other rune.

"Fine. Laugh all you like, but we are going to be taking on our first enemy target, so I want straight faces and sharp eyes by the time we reach ground level. Bows to the ready, arrows nocked. Wait for my signal to fire unless you see a sorcerer begin casting," Captain Juliana ordered. There was a loose brotherhood at best among sorcerers, even within the Empire. If anything, knowledge of how their own kind thought made them *less* likely to be lenient, rather than more.

Juliana brought the *Daggerstrike* into a shallow, spiraling dive, still wary of repeating her initial mistake about flipping the ship on a whim. Her archers would be far more accurate if they were not busily retching out their dawn feast all about the hold. At least she was getting the hang of steering the ship, even if many of the other controls left her baffled.

It was near enough to noontime for the shadow of the *Daggerstrike* to alert the Megrenn to their presence overhead. They were caught, however. The flatland between the river and the surrounding forest was the only terrain suitable for horses. The flood banks of the Thadagar were chest height to a horse and, even if leapt, would only put them in dense forest, too thick for their mounts to navigate quickly. The Megrenn pressed on, hurrying their horses in a desperate hope of finding a breakaway to the east, some trail or road that led into navigable forest.

The *Daggerstrike* swooped low, coming alongside the frightened horses. Juliana banked them in gently, giving herself enough of an angle such that she could see them for herself without having to rely on the magical viewer and its convoluted workings. Two wore armor—bearing markings of Megrenn and Safschan between them, though helms hid their faces from easy view. The third was Ghelkan by both skin and dress, wearing the tan colors of his people's sorcerers beneath a Megrenn-blue cloak.

"SURRENDER!" Juliana called out in Megrenn, her voice echoing from the sides of the ship as she remembered the correct rune to touch.

Though she assumed the Megrenn had understood her, despite her Kadrin accent, and the distortion from the magical amplification, they nonetheless galloped away. Juliana fought with the viewer's controls to try to get the horsemen into the picture, rocking the ship side to side to give herself intermittent looks at them to keep apace.

At length, more through chance than practice, she was able to realign the view to her liking. She steadied the ship alongside the riders again. Even if they were to find an eastern escape route now, it was blocked off by the bulk of the *Daggerstrike*, flying too low to the ground for the horses to cross beneath, even were the riders to duck.

"LAST CHANCE! SURRENDER OR WE WILL FIRE!" Juliana warned. Had she anyone at hand to wager with, she would have bet against them complying. Still, it hardly seemed sporting not to offer.

The Ghelkan let go his reins, and attempted to cast a spell. Juliana never got a chance to figure out what it ought to have been, as a dozen arrows streaked out from the left side of the ship, three finding their mark. The sorcerer's shielding spell held, but his concentration was ruined. In the blink of an eye, the Ghelkan burst into flames, not even surviving long enough to scream, though his horse did enough to account for the dead man's share as the panicked beast threw its flaming rider, losing ground on its companions before falling into pace behind them.

Realizing that their attempt at escape was merely testing the ship's archers rather than saving themselves, the two survivors slowed their horses to a trot and surrendered. Juliana slowed the *Daggerstrike* to match them. The frightened steed whose rider had burned, seemingly the wisest among them, continued to run, leaving the rest to their fates as Juliana did not bother with pursuit.

"Who are you?" the Megrenn survivor shouted up. By his face, he appeared native Megrenn, a blank palette if ever a people were one, with skin not quite so pale as common in the Kadrin southlands, mid-brown eyes and hair, and a face neither flat nor particularly angular.

Juliana set the *Daggerstrike* down, the deck pitching a bit left as it settled on the uneven ground, and opened the side hatches. Then she unbuckled herself from the captain's harness, and made her way over to the railing to introduce herself in person.

"I am Captain Juliana of the *Daggerstrike*," she called down to him. "What are your names? If I find you cooperative, you may yet live through this day."

"I am Colonel Jaimes Arbret of the Free Megrenn Army. My companion is Puuna Tsaki, Third Highblade in the Safschan Army. What do you intend to do with us?"

Several of Juliana's crew, with swords drawn, made their way down the ramps that the hatches became when opened. They encircled the four horses, taking the reins both of the ones that were mounted and those saddled but riderless. From within the ship, archers still manned the arrow slits, ready to provide covering fire.

"For starters, to find out whether you speak any Kadrin. I would prefer my men be able to understand what you are saying," Juliana said over the railing.

"I do," Colonel Arbret conceded, demonstrating by replying in Kadrin. "I grew up in an occupied Megrenn. Puuna only speaks a few words, best as I know."

The dark-skinned Safschan shrugged, nodding.

Neither of the two looked to Juliana to be a great warrior. Colonel Arbret was thin of build, Puuna's hair was shot through with enough grey to suggest his best summers were long past. She gave no order to have them disarmed, so each of them sat their horse with a sheathed blade at hand.

"Good," Juliana said, switching to the language her crew understood best. "First things first, were you a part of that battle we saw, farther down the Thadagar?"

"Battle?" Arbret scoffed. "There was no 'battle.' That was a slaughter. We three were the only ones I am aware of who escaped, and your archers just killed Vaeldak."

"Warlock Rashan?" Juliana guessed.

"Who the bloody gravelands knows? One moment, we are getting ready to launch our assault on your forces, dug in betwixt the river and the forest; the next, your infantry is advancing. It got a bit hazy after that, what with the monohorns being flung in amongst us, and half our forces bursting into flame. I turned and fled before being properly introduced."

"Well, it certainly sounds like him," Juliana replied, trying to keep an even tone as she heard about the horrific destruction her oathfather had wrought. She knew he was powerful. History had told that he had swung the balance in every battle he had fought. But the succession of wars against Loramar and his undead legions had hinted at limits to his power, of a foe nearly his equal, a force that he had to strike at and retreat. "Where would you go now, if you had a choice?"

"Hah, to Azzat, if I could. As far away from here as I can imagine. I used to think the myths about a demon that secretly ruled there were just meant to keep outsiders from attacking, and give them an air of mystery. Now? I would go there, and hope that a few thousand years of never being conquered were more than a coincidence."

"Well, Azzat is a bit out of our way, but we could drop you at the next Megrenn settlement or force we find, for the cost of your weapons and a promise of good conduct," Juliana offered.

"Why would you?"

"Why not? You think it works against Kadrin to report what happened to one of your armies when it crossed paths with our warlock? If you ask me, history has not done him justice. It would be good for your people to hear about it firsthand from a survivor."

Colonel Arbret studied her a moment, weighing her offer. Having apparently made his decision, he unbuckled his sword belt. Third Highblade Puuna took his lead, and did likewise, handing down his weapon to the crewman nearest to him. The two officers then dismounted.

"What of the horses? If we are to set them wild, we should unsaddle them first," Arbret asked. Juliana frowned, not having considered the fate of the animals.

"Bring them aboard," she said. "But if they foul the hold, you two are cleaning it up."

* * * * * * *

"Not much of anything, really," Dolvaen said. He sat in his study, same as Kyrus had seen him the last time the two men met privately. He seemed to prefer it to working from his office in the Tower of Contemplation. "There is scant evidence to be found."

"Since we are alone, and I can see that you have the room sufficiently warded, I would like to be frank," Kyrus said, standing across the desk from Dolvaen with his arms crossed. He tried to keep a stern expression on his face, hoping it did not come across as comical. Kyrus had never been one to bully, so the posture was new to him. He hoped that bullying worked the same when it came to intimidating by magical might. There was a whole cultural rift that Brannis had been unable to prepare him for.

"Go right ahead. Be forewarned about frankness in return, though," Dolvaen both agreed and cautioned. He crossed his arms as well. Kyrus was not sure whether he was prepared for an arm-crossing contest. Dolvaen seemed more experienced at battles of will.

"The three murdered sorcerers were known to be supporters of Rashan. You have admitted to me that you are, if not the leader, then at least chief among his opponents," Kyrus said.

"I am the leader," Dolvaen interjected into a pause Kyrus had left open too long.

"Have you begun killing off his supporters, starting at the lower echelons?"

"Hmm, more frankness than I had even expected. You came right out and accused me of murder." Dolvaen sounded mildly surprised.

"I find that I am perhaps one of the few left the luxury of bluntness to the point of rudeness. It took me a while to realize, but I am growing to be widely feared," Kyrus said. "But no, I ask, not accuse. If I had meant accusation, I would have hauled you down to the palace dungeons first."

"You might have tried …" Dolvaen left the rest of his statement to Kyrus's imagination.

"If you will allow me a simple demonstration, and please construe this as no actual threat," Kyrus said, drawing a consternated look from Dolvaen. That look—lips pursed, brow knit—froze on the elder sorcerer's face as Kyrus's magic grabbed him, and held him from moving. Kyrus felt a thrashing at his aether construct, silent spells cast by Dolvaen to affect his release.

"This is not even taxing me," Kyrus said. "I have had little cause to test myself, but I have been putting little pieces together of late. The assassin who attempted to take the life of Emperor Sommick in the days leading up to his coronation—his Source was rather impressively strong. Yet on more than one occasion, I have seen evidence of others either claiming or being unable to secure hold of a strong-Sourced individual. I nearly crushed that assassin to death, nearly suffocated him from being unable to move his lungs. Before I release you, stop your fighting, or I will wait until you pass out from lack of air." Kyrus noted that the attacks against his construct ceased.

He took a moment to reinforce his own shielding spell, lest Dolvaen have taken things badly, and unraveled his own magic. Dolvaen collapsed back in his chair, gasping for breath. Kyrus allowed him a moment to gather himself.

"How did you do that? What spell did that demon teach you? I saw you cast nothing," Dolvaen blurted once he collected enough breath to do so.

"That was telekinesis. I know few spells well enough to cast them silently. It was either that or a light spell, or simple firehurling. Anything else, you would have seen me perform." Kyrus felt that his arm-crossing was perhaps carrying more weight than when he had first tried it.

"I had nothing to do with those murders. It would have been patently idiotic to do so. By striking at his lowest loyal underlings, it merely alerted him to a conspiracy, if he did not already have full knowledge of one."

"He knew. He has known from the first, though more by instinct than fact," Kyrus replied.

"You have not told him of my involvement, have you?" Dolvaen sounded sure of the answer when he asked it.

Kyrus humored the question anyway. "No. I have yet to decide what is best for the Empire. For the time being at least, the political sphere is free of his influence."

"Can you be so naive as to think so?" Dolvaen asked, raising his voice. "The emperor is his pet, he has agents throughout the Empire, and even you are appointed indirectly by his hand."

"The latter is his mistake, if he thinks to dominate politics via me. Let him play at war. I will see what I can do to sort out the rats' nest of double-dealing within the Circle and among the nobles. As such, I need to know as much as you are able to provide about those murders."

"There is little to tell; the servants are under the same oblivious compulsion as much of the palace staff. They remember what pertained directly to their jobs, and nothing else. The murders were daggerwork but no weapon was found."

"What of whoever was tasked with answering doors?"

"There was a visitor at one of the three, as far as the chamberlain remembered, but of course, no identity, nor even a clue as far as time."

Kyrus said nothing, but seemed to have discovered a clue that Dolvaen was either overlooking or refusing to share.

* * * * * * * *

The food was slop, but at least he was no longer chained naked to the walls. Faolen counted it as progress at least. His merchant disguise had been ruined during his capture. The clothing the jailors had provided was undyed wool, still smelling of the pasture by Faolen's reckoning. It itched against his bare skin, stung where it rubbed against raw wounds—which was pretty much everywhere on him. He was constantly putting up with scabs tearing loose and seeping blood. The latter, strange as it seemed even to him, proved to be a boon.

When Anzik Fehr has returned the Staff of Gehlen, Faolen had proven the truth of his end of the bargain; he had access and some degree of influence over Anzik's Tellurak counterpart. The return of the staff fulfilled his end of the deal he had made with Jinzan Fehr, but the boy's escape had forestalled any thought of release. After all, Faolen might be the only one still able to track the boy down.

Thus Faolen had been upgraded to the sort of prisoner who was fed and clothed, the sort who was not tortured for information. He was now in fine company along with killers, rapists, and thieves.

Why did the boy run? Faolen wondered. Jadon had been no help in answering that. Wendell got blank stares when he asked about Anzik. He got blank stares back from the boy when he asked about a great many things, but if it were possible, they grew blanker when the subject of his twin came up.

Faolen had not been idle in his waiting. Left alone for long hours in the deserted lowest level of the old Kadrin dungeon in what was once occupied Megrenn, he worked at the beginnings of a plan. His fingernails had grown long and ragged, sharp enough after a bit of careful filing against stone that he could cut skin with them. Far from an effective weapon to overpower jailors with, it was enough to begin altering the runes that the vile Megrenn spymaster had cut into his flesh. It would be a long time before the wounds healed enough on their own for him to try drawing aether, and there was no guarantee that there would not be scarring that might allow the runes to remain effective.

The effect of the runes on his own Source was impossible to judge. Allowed to actually use his Source, he could use magic to examine it, and determine how immediate his peril was. Day by day, though, as he was denied the ability to access the aether without triggering the lightning wards, he felt himself growing weaker. Painful though it was to deface himself with new cuts, he knew he had to fracture the wards' control over him.

That morning, Narsicann had come along with the jailor. Faolen had asked to speak with Jinzan Fehr again, but the presence of the spymaster told him that his request had been denied. He stood, pacing the small cell as his captors approached. He had a plan concocted for this contingency—one he had not been sure that he would get another chance to enact.

The jailor carried a tray with a bowl of stew and a mug of what Faolen knew would be ale, likely watered down with the jailor's own urine. He tried to put the thought from his mind as they neared his cell. The jailor balanced the tray in one hand as he fumbled a ring of keys free from his belt, and unlocked Faolen's cell.

"Fair morning. I understand you wished to see Councilor Fehr," Narsicann greeted him. The saccharine in his voice could have rotted a rat's teeth.

"I do."

"Well, Councilor Fehr is far too busy with other important matters, and this is really more of my little corner of Megrenn than his, anyway. You can say to me what you would have said to him."

As Narsicann spoke, the jailor handed the tray to Faolen, who set down the tray and mug to begin devouring the stew at a rate much quicker than his appetite demanded.

"I wanted to discuss the conditions of my release," Faolen managed, speaking without regard to the fullness óf his mouth. He tried to ignore the sour, spoiled taste of bad meat in the stew.

"There are no 'conditions' as you put it. When Councilor Fehr is satisfied with your side of the bargain, he will decide your fate. It is a family matter, and it would not be fitting for me to interfere with how he goes about getting Anzik back, were I even inclined to."

"Has it also possibly occurred to you that I might be interested in furthering my career among your people, rather than returning home?" Faolen suggested. He had thought long and hard, and decided it was the subject he felt most likely to prolong the conversation. He continued working at his stew as fast as his stomach would let him. The stew was leaving a foul, slimy feeling in the back of his throat the more of it he ate.

"Hah. I suppose that if they find you had access to the Staff of Gehlen, and traded it for your own worthless skin—no jest intended, I assure you," Narsicann said, glancing meaningfully down at Faolen's exposed forearms, and the carved runes they bore, "there might not be so welcome a return in store for you."

"You saw during my capture that I have useful skills. Had I not the misfortune of bumping into Councilor Fehr, you would never have known I had gone," Faolen said. He fought back the urge to vomit his stew, and forced down another mouthful.

"True, perhaps, but ultimately you failed. I might not be the one to boast to of those skills. After all, I got the best of you," Narsicann teased.

Faolen finished the last spoonful. His stomach felt the worse for it, but it seemed that the stew was content to merely protest its location in his stomach, not seek relocation to the floor.

"How many would it have worked on? I got Councilor Fehr to release me just for appearing as Rashan Solaran," Faolen bragged. He eyed the remains of the stew in the bowl, nothing but mushy trails left where the spoon could not get everything. Suppressing a sigh, he wiped up the last of the stew with a finger, sucking it clean.

"Well, I think it is a matter of more than just competence. You should have saved your offer for Jinzan; he is less cautious about things of this sort than I am. I deal in spies all day long. Trust is slow to earn, quick to lose. You are already betraying your own kind. What makes you less likely to do so with Megrenn?"

Narsicann meant the question rhetorically, Faolen knew, so he just shrugged in reply. The Megrenn spymaster took it as a sign that the usefulness of the encounter had reached an end.

Faolen picked up the mug of ale, the empty stew bowl held awkwardly in his other hand, spoon in danger of toppling over the edge.

"I will hang on to this for a while, if you do not mind," Faolen said, gesturing to indicate the ale. "You can take this away, though." Faolen said, leaning past Narsicann to push the bowl into the jailor's hands.

The spoon slipped …

There was a brief commotion as the spoon hit the floor. Faolen and the jailor both bent to retrieve it. In the process, Faolen spilled half his ale as he bumped shoulders with the jailor. When it was all resolved, Faolen backed meekly away, hands spread wide in contrition.

"Sorry," Faolen said, a wan smile on his face.

"Set that down, and search him," Narsicann ordered. "Check that he did not just sneak something from you."

The jailor set down the bowl outside the cell. Before searching Faolen, he checked his own pockets, seeming to find nothing amiss. Faolen spread his arms wide, careful to keep the ale from spilling, giving every indication of compliance. Finding nothing, the jailor gave a cursory examination of the rest of the cell. Given how little there was, it did not take long for him to conclude that there was no contraband present.

"Keep my offer in mind," Faolen told Narsicann as the jailor locked the door behind them.

"Patience. You will be of no use to anyone for a while yet," Narsicann replied, prompting a self-deprecating smile from Faolen.

He watched Narsicann and the jailor depart down the cell block. He stayed silent, listening for their footsteps to fade up the stairs.

Once he was sure they were well and gone, he fished Narsicann's set of keys from the ale mug, wondering idly if they had improved the taste of the beverage. It would not be long before Narsicann discovered the theft of his keys, Faolen suspected. He tried three keys before finding the one that unlocked his cell.

With the door open, the real key to his escape was at hand. He drew in aether, cautiously at first. He felt one of the wards kick to life, shocking him in the left side of his abdomen, but it did not intercept remotely enough aether to stop what he had in mind.

With a thought, Faolen used a spell he knew back to front. He vanished. With a few fumbling key twists along the way, he vanished from the Megrenn dungeon as well.

* * * * * * *

One additional perk of Rashan's absence in the city was that Kyrus felt free to pursue a research project of his own. Of course, that freedom involved visiting libraries in the Tower of Contemplation with a sack, and taking twelve additional books he did not need. It involved delegating a number of tasks that he likely ought to have overseen personally. Lastly that freedom also required that he ward himself up in his bedchamber, lest anyone see what he was doing. Strange though the freedom was, it felt far safer without the imminent threat of being summoned by the warlock.

"Dolvaen was right about one thing. One day I am likely to overstep my bounds with Rashan. I need to unravel his game before I do so. It might be that he is in the right. It would be so simple merely falling into the role he sets before me," Kyrus said aloud to himself, the freedom to voice that sentiment was a relief. He had not realized the tension he felt in the warlock's presence until it was removed. That presence Rashan had was the sort that lay over the whole of Kadris like a shroud.

Kyrus had filled his quota for poking hornets' nests for the day as well. Dolvaen had given him more information than he had realized. Kyrus had fresh insight into his standing with Dolvaen, as well as the elder sorcerer's investigation. But Kyrus was always unsettled by confrontation. Humiliating Dolvaen once more—in private this time, at least—took a major potential ally, and threatened to turn him against Kyrus.

Kyrus sat at his desk, quill in hand, cross-referencing a number of books, foremost among them *The Warlock Prophecies*. Against that schizophrenic mass of gloom and vengeance, he pitted the forces of Kadrin's historians. He had six books that chronicled various aspects of the Empire in the latter days of Rashan's first term as warlock—anything that covered roughly from the First Necromancer War to the Battle of the Dead Earth. He also had a copy of *The Diplomacy of Fire and Steel*. He hoped that, amongst all the references at hand, he would be able to assemble the prophecies into a timeline, and place them in context. It was the sort of thing that students found excruciating and tedious. Kyrus was finding it fascinating.

Brannis had always had a sort of general curiosity about history, but mostly as related to war and conquest. It was a phase many boys went through, especially those encouraged by the School of Arms. Kyrus was finding little tidbits about the lesser aspects of Kadrin history as he delved deeper into a particular era.

For long hours, Kyrus made little progress on the meat of his search. He got sidetracked, and read entire passages even after discovering straightaway that they were not germane to his search, at least at first. After a time, he realized that the whole era of history was wrapped around Rashan like a cloak. There was no aspect of either the Circle or the military that he had not insinuated himself into. Rashan had the emperor by the chin, pointing his head wherever he chose him to look. Of all the books, *The Diplomacy of Fire and Steel* was the only one written after his apparent death that cast the warlock in a positive light. Had the thought not been so implausible, Kyrus would have reasoned that the author knew Rashan would return one day and read it. Every other account immediately after the Battle of the Dead Earth seemed to thank Rashan for saving the Kadrin Empire from Loramar, and backhandedly thank Loramar for saving them from Rashan.

The picture he assembled of Rashan was both tragic and frightening. He had few friends over the hundred and forty or so winters he lived prior to his disappearance. While he got on well enough with many of his apprentices, there was always the implied dynamic of the master-apprentice relationship at work—they could not afford to get on poorly with him. The closest person to Rashan had seemed to be Emperor Liead the Only, to whom Rashan was friend, mentor, and surrogate father. Rashan's early writings, once Kyrus began to pick up enough clues to begin placing prophecies amid historical markers, showed occasional signs of irrational anger. His later writings, after the death of Liead, showed little else.

One interesting conclusion he drew was that there was a large gap in the entries. He had already taken note of a passage that read:

Fallow field, fertile mind
Potato planted but grows into grape
The vintage will only tell with time
We sip the vintner's craft whether we choke or revel in it
A drunkard captains the ship we all sail on, but does not steer it

Kyrus had learned from *And They Knelt Before Him,* a treatise on the lives of several Kadrin emperors around Rashan's time, that the warlock had gotten on poorly with Tameron the First. He had come to the conclusion that the passage was a reference to the birth of Liead. It showed a skeptical sort of optimism that his days serving a "potato" of an emperor were giving way to an era of a quality yet to be determined. Kyrus did not need histories to hear how Rashan spoke of his friend and emperor Liead. Throughout the rest of Liead's lifetime, there was not another entry in the book of prophecies.

Once he established a foothold in the timeline, Kyrus's work accelerated. The loss of Rashan's only true friend tore him apart. The prophecies darkened. By all accounts, Rashan had liked Merenon the Second well enough, but was always just a mentor to him. Merenon ordered the creation of the Red Riders, Rashan's sorcerers who trained as knights, and used their draws only to defend their own Sources against Loramar's powers. Rashan understood the decision. It was rational, logical, and cold-blooded. Merenon was not the one who had to train the sorcerers from adolescence, knowing that in the end their destiny was to be thrown against the undead legions until one side or the other was exhausted.

Kyrus found that the three passages he had marked previously as important were hinting at Rashan's developing plan to defeat Loramar by becoming immortal. He made his own copies of the passages, and pieced together what he could infer from both other prophecies and the happenings of that era.

Death fights the act of death—Loramar and himself, warlocks being bringers of death
How many times must Death be killed
One more—First Necromancer War
One more—Second Necromancer War

Never
To stop the rebirth of Death
First defeat death—He capitalized it when he meant Loramar; he meant "become immortal."
Then Death

Kyrus felt confident that he had the thrust of the prophecy correct, whether or not he had it exactly right in the details.

Broken vase spills blue-white blood—Aether? Is the vase the mortal Source?
The missing pieces are keys that lock the final door
Patch the wholes that are only halves
...
One vase, filling fast, spilling faster—Another Source reference? A leaking bucket?
To see another, no mirror may reflect it
Where to find its shadow, an absence not a copy
Seek a way among the spirits—Could there be spirits in the aether, as the Denku think?

The first of the three making some sense to him did not help decipher the other two. They seemed as important as ever, but the imagery was too vague. They seemed to say that the Source needed to be repaired, but did not give a clue as to how, aside from seeking an answer among the spirits.

Kyrus was disturbed from his research by a knock at the warded door. It surprised him only insomuch as he had not realized the time that had passed.

"Come," he called out, releasing the wards as he said it.

Celia was there when the door opened. Kyrus beckoned her inside.

"My, what an undertaking," Celia commented upon seeing Kyrus's pile of open and ready books, hovering open in midair when they were not in use. Kyrus was not worried that she would piece together his puzzle, since all the clues he had discovered were written in Acardian, as good a cipher as he was likely to come up with that was not a hindrance to his work. If she could read it, all the more evidence that she was really Abbiley.

Kyrus shut the door behind her, and re-warded it. Celia turned around as the door slammed a bit upon closing, startling her.

"Intent that I not leave?" Celia smiled coquettishly, tossing her hair.

Kyrus maintained a stern expression despite the rise of other feelings beneath the surface. *Curse all women, my brain stutters over the simplest of looks. How do they manage such aetherless magic?*

"That depends, in part, on why you are here," he said.

"Well, business first, I suppose. Caladris wanted to know how your meeting with Dolvaen went," Celia told him. She held her hands clasped in front of her, posture rigid with her chin straight out, as if she was reciting spell words before the whole class.

"I am closer to uncovering the mystery of the murders than Dolvaen is," Kyrus said, leaving vague whether he was closer because of some special insight or merely disparaging Dolvaen's progress sarcastically.

"He is doing that badly, is he?" Celia smiled, relaxing from her "business first" posture. Kyrus nodded. "So was that the 'why' that lets me stay a while or the one that gets me sent away?"

"Neither, yet. Answer me this if you can: who did Caladris get to kill those three sorcerers?" Kyrus asked.

"What has Dolvaen been telling you?" Celia demanded, her voice rising as her face reddened. "Brannis, do not tell me you let him convince you that Caladris killed three of his own sorcerers."

"I already told you, I know more than Dolvaen. Dolvaen was correct when he told me that murdering Rashan's least significant supporters was not in his interest. It got the whole Empire gossiping about conspiracies, which is the worst environment for such a conspiracy succeeding. That is Caladris's play, framing the conspiracy for murder. Sacrifice pawns, expose their king, protect your own."

Celia flushed, if possible, a deeper red. She turned and ran for the door, but Kyrus's wards might well have rendered the wall an unbroken cliff wall. The door gave no sign of even noticing her efforts to open it.

"It was you," Kyrus said aloud, just as the realization dawned on him.

"Please, just let me go!" Celia begged. She began to cry, slumping against the door, and sliding down until she was sitting with her back to it. "He said I had to …" Celia managed between sobs.

"I see now. Caladris is Rashan's agent on both sides of this. He gave me a choice. I either join his side or I have to see you pay for the murders he made you commit. Checkmate."

"What are you going to do with me?" Celia said, fear evident in her quavering voice.

Kyrus walked across the room to her, feeling a pang of guilt as she cowered at his approach. He put his arms around her.

"I am going to protect you."

Chapter 36 ~ Pulling the Chain

"Brannis," Soria whispered. She put her hand on his shoulder, giving a shove that bounced Brannis's limp body on the bed. There was no hint of response; Brannis continued to slumber on. The sun was up, and Soria was tired of waiting for him to arise. She was tempted to go find herself breakfast without him.

"Brannis," she called out again, this time not bothering to whisper. She shook him with hands on both shoulders, eliciting a rude grunt, and prompting Brannis to roll over, turning his back to her.

Soria climbed up onto the bed, kneeling next to him. With a great heave, she attempted to roll him onto his back once more, but Brannis's knees were tucked up enough that she could not get enough leverage to turn him. She briefly tried magic, but Brannis's Source might as well have been greased in pig fat.

"Merciful Tansha, forgive me," Soria prayed aloud, looking up at the ceiling. She took the washbasin, and tilted it above Brannis's head, letting a trickle of water pour down onto his face.

"Mpff," Brannis grunted, bringing his hands up to defend himself. Soria stopped the flow as Brannis wiped the water and the sleep from his eyes. He blinked several times, shook his head, then blinked a few more. "What is going on?"

"You are wasting away the morning is what."

"No, I mean I can still see Veydrus," Brannis clarified. He shook his head, and rubbed his fingers in his eyes.

"That's probably from me waking you unexpectedly. Sorry, but I would have thought you would have grown accustomed to it by now," Soria said. "I used to have it happen all the time when I was little, but I learned how to block it out easily enough. Once you're alert, it should go away on its own."

"Yes. It has mostly faded now," Brannis said. "What was so important that you needed me awake?" Brannis looked at her in earnest for the first time since awakening. She was wearing an outfit of all black, loose-fitted fabric. It had a certain stylishness to it, but was unflattering to Soria's figure—specifically in that it was hard to tell she had one. "And where did you get that ensemble?"

"Well, to answer both, I have been out scouting," Soria replied. She pulled the hood of the cloak down. It hung low, over her eyes. She reached both hands back within the hood, and tied something, pulling the hood close over her eyes. There were cutouts for her to see through, and the rest of the hood hung low over her nose and mouth. She took a pair of black leather gloves from where she had tucked them in her belt and pulled them on. Fully kitted out, it was hard to tell much of anything about her aside from her height—and the color of her eyes if one was truly observant. "I visited your old shop a little while ago, before the predawn light came and spoiled everything."

"Did you find anything interesting?" Brannis asked. He pushed himself up onto his elbows to be at less of a disadvantage in the conversation.

"Well, for starters, did you happen to live like there had been some sort of riot going on in your workroom?" Soria asked.

"Yes," Brannis replied, perfectly serious.

Soria laughed. "Well, then, it would appear nothing was put amiss. I took a few things I thought you might like to have back." She gestured to a knapsack in the corner of the room. "There was only so much I could carry when traveling by rooftops."

"Thank you," Brannis said, smiling at the mysterious masked figure in his room.

"We have a lot to do today, according to your plans. Let's get changed into some respectable attire, and be about our day."

"Why is my armor all laid out on the floor?" Brannis asked.

"Scar Harbor doesn't see too many knights these days, but that doesn't mean there aren't any. Besides, you're going to be foreign, remember, Erund? What could be more respectable—and less Kyrusy—than a knight? You look near to twice his size as it stands; you'll look thrice with the armor on. Mind you, leave the helm behind ... nasty thing."

* * * * * * *

Wendell sat bolt upright, hitting his head on the bunk above. Cursing himself, he rubbed at the sore spot on his head he had just created. He found himself breathing heavily, but quickly calmed himself with the knowledge that there was no immediate threat to *him*. It was Faolen who had just made a harrowing escape.

"You okay over there?" Zellisan asked. He was sitting, fully clothed, on his own bunk. He was watching Wendell with a concerned vulture's look.

"I am fine. Faolen less so. I need you to get a message to Sir Brannis."

"What's the message?" Zell asked. It was the first time Wendell had shown any interest in sending word back to Brannis for anything.

"I need passage out of Zorren—and quickly. I have heard rumors of flying ships that we have now. If those rumors are true, I need one sent to fetch me," Wendell said.

"They are true. Sir Brannis had a bunch of them made up. What kind of trouble are you in? They are going to ask before sending an airship for you, I would think."

"I have failed to obtain the Staff of Gehlen, but I should be able to escape with Anzik Fehr." Wendell chose his words carefully, lest the intermittently observant, slumbering boy overhear. Zellisan was an old coinblade; he could probably hear the words "hostage" and "kidnap" even without Wendell having given voice to them.

Zellisan fixed an unsteady, sleepy glare on Wendell.

"Fine," Zellisan agreed after a moment's contemplation. "I suppose it won't be the worst thing I've done. I'm still drunk enough to fall right back asleep, I think." The burly coinblade lay back down in his bunk, and began to snore before Wendell had time even to wonder whether he would remember the message, if he was as drunk as he claimed.

Dismissing the thought as a ship already sailed, he turned his attention to Jadon's bunk. The thin sliver of a boy slumbered peacefully, showing no sign that he had been aware of Wendell and Zellisan's conversation.

"Anzik," Wendell whispered. "Can you hear me?" He waited. There was no response. "Anzik, can you hear me? It is me, Faolen, the last of the voices you will hear. Tell me where you are."

"Go away." The voice came from Jadon, but it spoke Megrenn with more purpose and clarity than Jadon was wont to display. The boy rolled to face him, eyes heavy-lidded, but open.

"Yes, we can go away. I have an airship coming to take us away. A ship that flies in the sky."

"Will Father be on the ship?"

"No. He will stay behind, and you will not have to hide anymore. Nice beds, good food ..."

"Your store burned down."

The abrupt change in topic was jarring. Wendell was not sure what Anzik was driving at. The boy's motivations were simple on the surface, but what roiling waters lurked beneath he could only guess at.

"Yes, it did. I was there when it caught fire. I had to run away," Wendell explained.

"Your man lives there now," Anzik told him in Jadon's voice.

"That is good news. I had not found him after the fire. I am happy to hear he is doing well."

"He lives in a basement in a burned building. Why?"

"He is probably hiding, just like you. How about we all stop hiding, and go together on the airship? Go find him there, after dark. I will meet you there as well."

* * * * * * * *

Varnus stalked down the hallways of the palace, garnering occasional salutes as he passed the guardsmen under his command. The imperial uniform felt the same as his House Archon regalia, mainly due to it lying atop the same suit of armor he had worn for many summers. The effect it had on others was remarkable, though. While the guard captain of a highborn house might have some large degree of influence within his lord's or sorcerer's realm, visitors always took him for, but the foremost among many lowborn, insignificant men.

Captain of the Palace Guard was a real position of authority, though, speaking for the safety of the emperor. Folk moved when he came by.

It was thus with a certain degree of humbling consternation that he stood outside Kyrus's door with no means of entry. He had tried knocking in the usual spot, a place the servants and other non-sorcerers had been shown where Sir Brannis could be alerted to their presence outside. There had been no sound at all. Magic was something Varnus only understood in bits and pieces, and he had no experience with it at all personally. Though he understood there were wards and aether at work, it was still unsettling rapping your knuckles against something, and not hearing so much as a finger's tap for the effort.

He could not fetch someone to open the door for him, nor even ask that Brannis be alerted by some magical means. He had no official business that he could give as justification for such a request, and folk were wary of Sir Brannis since his Source had torn itself loose of whatever shackles that once held it. Of course, Varnus knew it was Kyrus Hinterdale's Source they were all in awe of, not Sir Brannis's, but there was no way to make use of that knowledge, either. Juliana might have been of some use in gaining entrance, but she was off on her own airship somewhere. Tanner knew a bit more magic than he did, but Varnus knew his skills would not be enough; if Tanner was a sorry sorcerer in Tellurak, he was a mule's whisker short of useless in Veydrus.

Varnus waited.

After how long, he had no idea, the door to the grand marshal's chamber opened, startling three people.

"Sorceress Celia." Varnus nodded in her direction. "My pardon for startling you. I have business with Sir Brannis of an urgent nature. I was unable to alert you to my presence, so I waited without."

"It is all right, Captain Varnus," Kyrus replied on her behalf. He turned to the sorceress. "Celia, just do as I told you, and everything will be fine."

Celia nodded, her reddened eyes speaking volumes about her state of mind as she hastened down the hallway, her destination unknown to Varnus.

Varnus stepped into the room as Kyrus made way for him. The door shut behind him, presumably warded as well. Kyrus seemed to be getting the hang of a few basics of sorcery, at least.

"What did you need to see me about?" Kyrus asked. Varnus made no immediate attempt to reply, he just looked askance of Kyrus. A sly little smile worked its way to the corner of his mouth. "You want to know what she was doing here? Fine. We will discuss that first. I think you best to tell anyway, I suppose.

"Celia Mistfield is twinborn. I was skeptical at first, since it seemed entirely too convenient, but the evidence has piled high on just one side of the scales; I can ignore it no longer. She has been caught up in the murder conspiracy."

"She's one of ours?" Varnus asked. "Who would have guessed ..."

"Certainly not her. She is not entirely certain of herself. I have just taken my attempt at explaining it to her, but her dreams are still scattered recollections at this point. Caladris and Rashan figured her out before I caught on. One or both—and if just one, I suspect Caladris—is likely working on securing her twin. If Rashan is involved, he is either the oldest man in Tellurak, or he has additional agents at his disposal."

"Caladris, too? I had suspected the warlock, frankly, but that chubby, drunkard uncle of yours? Nah." Varnus had never minced words when it came to Brannis's relatives. Despite intermarriage between houses dulling the worst of the rivalry, they took their shots at one another often enough, especially among the household servants. Varnus had nicknames and unflattering descriptions for all of them—though he had ceased disparaging Brannis a long while ago, about the time Juliana got to the point of being a bit dangerous when angered.

Varnus listened as Kyrus outlined all he knew of the plot between worlds, the connection between Abbiley and Celia, and Caladris's role in the murders, using Celia as his pawn.

"If you think she might be in danger, why not let her stay here, with you?" Varnus asked. "Everyone thinks this place is locked up tighter than a dragon's ..." Varnus trailed off, realizing the turn of phrase he was about to use was less than appropriate for polite company—and he did not know Kyrus quite well enough to be sure how he would take to being spoken to like a tavern regular.

"Because I want her safe, period. I do not want her safe just long enough for Juliana to return, and find out—via whatever feminine network of spies keeps track of such things—where Celia has been spending nights."

"Good point."

"By the by, what had you come here for, initially?"

"Oh, that. Faolen just needs an airship ..."

* * * * * * * *

Darkness negated much of the need for invisibility, but Faolen was past the point of taking chances. It was just past dusk, and folk were still milling about the streets, enjoying a fine springtime night, even in the midst of war, as they set about finishing their day's business. In a city the size and diversity of Zorren, a lone figure clad in little more than rags might have been unusual, but not so much as to draw extraordinary attention. Of course, all it took was for one person to realize that the roughspun garments he wore marked him as an escaped prisoner, and he would be on the run again in a hurry.

He peeked above the tops of the two barrels he had hidden between, wary even while invisible, as he turned his consciousness fully to Wendell's world. Seeing that there was no one likely to bump into him, he stood. He was still wobbly of leg after his ordeal—wobbly of stomach as well. The sudden change in his equilibrium was the final indignity his guts would suffer. He vomited the stew he had tried for so long to keep down, hiding his head between the barrels that had been his haven, hoping to keep the sound from carrying far enough to draw attention.

Stomach emptied thrice over, he set about gathering Aelon and Anzik for their escape from the city. The rest was up to the convoluted communications system that Brannis had created between worlds. If there was no airship that could be dispatched in time, his escape might result in nothing more than all three of them being taken captive, instead of just himself.

In his exploration of the city when they were still looking out for Anzik, Faolen had avoided the city center—a calculated risk but a conservative one. The closer to the seat of the High Council, the greater the chance had been of encountering someone strong enough in aether to potentially see through his illusions or cunning enough to spot someone who did not belong in the city. He had counted on Anzik avoiding the area for similar reasons. Unfortunately it meant that he was navigating unfamiliar streets after dark, and was in no position to ask directions. He briefly considered trading in his invisibility for an illusory disguise, but he was feeling simply awful. He did not trust his acting abilities just then to pull off both a convincing non-Kadrin accent, and not act as if he had been used like one of the clay tablets that Academy students practiced rune-carving on.

For a time, Faolen tried to keep to the side streets, but he was no explorer. His sense of direction, at best, relied on the commonly known fact of the sun rising east and setting west. Sun gone from the skies, he was at the mercy of the madmen who had laid out the city's streets. Built on the hills surrounding a prime inlet on the Aliani Sea, Zorren had molded itself around the uneven terrain much the way weeds and vines grew around ruined stonework: they filled in the easiest spots first, and worked from there, resulting in a jumble of intersections and irregular buildings fitted between non-orthogonal roads. Faolen resigned himself to following a main thoroughfare until he found himself on familiar ground once more.

Over the sleepy sounds of a city slowly shutting itself up for the night, a roar split the air; a shouted curse in a quiet library would have sounded less out of place. Faolen had no experience with stripe-cats, but he could guess no other creature that might be loose upon the Zorren streets. The timing was too inconvenient, as well. A series of answering roars gave the impression that there were a number of the beasts scattered about. Narsicann appeared not to have taken his escape well.

There were a great many parts of Faolen's stripe-cat education that were lacking, but the one he presently regretted the most was not knowing how keen was their sense of smell. *If they were as good as bloodhounds, I would have to think they would have used them to look for Anzik by now. No, they must not realize that I am able to use my magic a bit. They expect to see me.*

It was his own mind he was trying to convince. His empty stomach was threatening to retch up contents it did not even possess. His heart was pumping fast enough to suit a sprinting pace, throbbing in his eardrums. His hands were shaking, both from a lack of food and from nerves. He quickened his pace, liking his odds against curious bystanders, should he rouse any, over his odds against a stripe-cat with his magic still greatly hindered.

The shop was nothing but a burnt-out foundation when he found it. The low stone wall that kept the ground floor above the level of rainwater came only to his knee. He peered down into the refuse pit the basement had become, looking for signs of occupation, had Anzik's claim about Aelon been more than fanciful imaginings. There were heavy structural beams that had survived somewhat, charred and cracked, but still largely whole. They made a number of little sheltered areas that rats would no doubt take over in time, should the place remain abandoned. Faolen saw no signs of a human about, but he had no intention of letting the paltry moonlight be his only means of searching.

Into the aether Faolen sent his vision, losing the details of their former hideout as everything faded into a blue-white haze—his aether-vision had never been among his greatest assets. He had been prepared to scan about for a Source that could have been Aelon's, but was startled immediately upon his switch in vision by a Source *right behind him*!

"Hello," Anzik Fehr said to him. It was the simple, casual greeting he might have offered to one of his father's dinner guests. A jolt of panic shot through Faolen. He checked immediately in the light to see if he had turned visible, but found himself perfectly transparent to his own eyes.

"Hello, Anzik. It is I, Faolen. I am invisible. You need to hide; people can see you," Faolen whispered to the boy.

"I thought we were going to go in an airship now."

"We have to wait. It has to get here. I am looking for my friend Aelon, and the three of us will wait together for the airship."

"He is right there," Anzik said, pointing down into a corner of the basement.

Faolen turned to follow the boy's gaze, which was rather unfocused, but clearly directed along the way he was pointing.

"Anzik, are the voices still bothering you?" Faolen asked. It was the most lucid he could recall either Anzik or Jadon being. Anzik frowned a bit.

"It is better but I still hear yours too much."

"Let us help Aelon out of that basement, and find a place to hide, shall we?"

Faolen was liking their odds of getting safely away much better if Anzik was aware enough to use any part of his magic to help them. Even without the Staff of Gehlen, the boy had to have had some useful talent.

* * * * * * * *

Arm in arm, Brannis walked the streets of Scar Harbor with Soria. It was a long way from The Little Manor to the part of the city where Kyrus had dwelt, but Soria had insisted on seeing the sights on foot to better get a feel for the place. Brannis showed her the courthouse where he had been tried for witchcraft, the clock tower that rang out the hour of eight o'clock even as they passed by it, the Brown Elk Tavern where he had bought the scriveners' shop from Davin on the night he announced he had been hired by the king.

They were making their way to Greuder's Pastries for a late breakfast. Brannis wanted her to try some of the spiced crescents that he had always preferred.

There was some incongruous worry in Brannis's head when he realized that the crescents were Kyrus's favorite, and not his own; he had never had one before, might not even like them. Kyrus was certainly unused to the finer fare of Veydrus, and had taken poorly to it.

"Well, that is good news at least, I suppose," Brannis said. They had been discussing Juliana's capture and interrogation of a pair of Megrenn officers. There was something private about a walking conversation that he could just not pin down. Had they been seated at a table in a noisy tavern, he would have kept his voice down when discussing otherworldly military affairs. At best, it made them sound quite mad; at worst, some twinborn would pick up on the information. Ambling along looking at the notable places of Scar Harbor, they talked openly of Kadrin news, subduing their conversation when they passed close to other pedestrians, but otherwise making no concessions to secrecy.

"I plan to let them go in the morning. For now, we're all sleeping with the ship floating up above cloud level. You're *sure* that thing has enough aether to be idling away the night up there, right?"

"Of course," Brannis replied. "You know me, expert on all things magical."

Soria elbowed him in the ribs, or at least tried to. She had overlooked the fact that he was wearing armor beneath his tabard, though its bulk was obvious when she was paying attention. Soria had to admit, he cut a dashing figure in the gold-and-silver regalia, with Avalanche swinging from his hip.

"Hey, if it starts drifting down, recharge the runes yourself. It is not like doing it the first time, overcoming the resistance of new, inert runes. Your Source should be plenty strong ... I think."

They spoke of Juliana's opinions about the controls of the *Daggerstrike*, and how Kyrus and he were both idiots when it came to making things easy to use.

"Fine, fine. It was my first try at building a ship to run on aether alone; of course it is a bit clumsy. More importantly, though, how does it feel to fly?" Brannis asked.

"You know that feeling you get when out riding, with the wind blowing through your hair?" Soria asked. Brannis nodded. "Well, even that trip we made with the runed horseshoes can't compare to the rush of wind among the clouds. My cloak snapped about like a pennant in a storm, the air tore at my clothes, but nothing could stop me; it was all according to my whim as the deck swayed, and the *Daggerstrike* banked. When I did that loop in the air, I could see the whole world up above my head, played out like someone had made one of your little illusion maps, but life sized."

"Less use as a map at that scale," Brannis noted.

"And nothing to tell you the names of the mountains and rivers," Soria agreed. "And I imagine that the soldiers of the full-sized map aren't perched atop the cities and fields, taller than mountains, either. Maybe that map of yours could use some improvements."

"Well, I could try—" Brannis stopped short. With her arm looped through his, and a dozen or more gallons lighter, Soria jerked to a stop as well.

"What?" Soria asked.

Brannis blinked his eyes hard, and slow several times, as it trying to work something out of them. "Kyrus is still awake. It is ... unsettling ... being aware of it. I am sure we have both been awake at the same time before—neither of us sleeps half the day—but I cannot recall. I can see Varnus if I close my eyes. Kyrus is talking to him right now."

"Say 'hello' to Zell for me then, would you?" Soria asked, smiling.

"Stop that," Brannis chided her, trying to concentrate on Veydrus. Kyrus was trying to convey something to him. He knew it more than he heard or saw anything that told him.

* * * * * * *

"She agreed to take the *Daggerstrike*, and head to Zorren. This is not what I had in mind when I sent her away from Kadris, but I cannot deny that Faolen sounds like he needs rescuing," Kyrus said. "I had to let her be the one to decide, or she would never have let me forget it if she found out."

I wonder if I ought to have defied Rashan, and sent her to Munne straightaway, to retrieve Iridan first.

"Good. Should I tell Wendell anything?"

"Try to find out where they will be. I have no way to calculate the travel time for the ship. Everything is new, and I do not even know quite where Juliana and her ship are. She does not even know herself. If possible, convince them to get outside the city. I do not relish the thought of them being on the ground in Zorren. Even with the element of surprise, they might get in trouble."

"Will do. You going to be able to keep relaying messages to Soria?"

"We can send for some tea to keep awake as long as this takes. Soria and Brannis will find a place to settle in to wait for instructions," Kyrus said. He shook his head, fighting the onset of fatigue already. "I need to cross-reference some maps one day, and find where Krangan is in Veydrus ... see if they make tea there."

* * * * * * *

"Well, if we do not get eaten by stripe-cats, I will see if I can oblige you. For now, we are going to see what we can do about living long enough to see a rescue at all," Wendell said upon hearing of Kyrus's request.

"Hey, just passing it along," Zell said. "Get angry at Kyrus if anyone; just keep in mind it's him sending Juliana to fetch you. She's got the newest ship, and Kyrus says it's the best one yet. No way to tell how long it will be, but it's the quickest rescue you're likely to get."

"I would be willing to chance a transference spell, if it comes to it."

"Kyrus missed Tellurak entirely the last time he tried one, mind you. I think I'd take my chances waiting for a flying boat, myself, and I'm not keen on trusting my life in the hands of runes that just got carved a couple days ago."

"Well, let him know that I have fewer qualms about the nature of my rescue.

If there ends up being two of me in Tellurak, I will learn to adapt."

* * * * * * *

"Wake up everyone!" Juliana's voice echoed through the ship. The crew and their guests felt a momentary queasiness in their stomachs, and felt the floor press less strongly against them as the ship began a sudden descent. "Get those horses ready to ride. Sorry, but we have new orders, and you are on your own the rest of your way home. Just remember: fearsome warlock on the loose, surrender is always a nice option. Tell everyone you meet."

Juliana set the ship down in a small clearing. The two Megrenn prisoners were shooed off the ship with all practical haste, even giving them back their weapons to forestall objections to being abandoned unarmed in the wilderness. The *Daggerstrike* then took to the air once more, a sleek steel blade catching the moonlight as it rose.

"Everyone strap into those harnesses. We are heading for Zorren for a rescue mission," Juliana's voice sounded in the hold. "You have about a ten-count before I find out how fast this thing goes."

There were frantic sounds of jostling and thumps of men dropping to the deck to get hold of the ends of the harness straps that would keep them from being thrown about the interior of the ship.

Comfortably above tree height, and hearing the sounds below die down, Juliana rechecked that her own harness was secure. Finding everything to her liking, she flooded the rune responsible for accelerating the ship with aether. She held tight as she could to the ship's wheel as the *Daggerstrike* sprang forward, her grip and the leather harness all that kept her from tumbling off the ship as it tried to speed out from beneath her.

It was time for Captain Juliana to figure out how to find Zorren.

* * * * * * *

Brannis blinked his eyes several times until they were able to focus in Tellurak again. He sat across the table from Soria in a small restaurant they had found on the way to Greuder's, a trip that would be delayed now due to more pressing concerns.

"There is a lighthouse, yes. Just follow the Cloud Wall north, then turn west when you reach the sea. It should not be hard to find. Only a handful of Kadrin cities are larger than Zorren. It is no Kadris, but I doubt anywhere in Veydrus or Tellurak has a city quite the size of Kadris."

"Probably not. Kadris uses magic to keep the sewage from overflowing the place. Khesh has enough people to support a city that size, but they have more cities, and spread them more widely. How is Kyrus holding up? Juliana and I are always keeping odd hours, but I imagine like the dual awareness, you're probably not used to being off your sleep routine. It's harder for our kind usually."

"I think he will be okay. He and Varnus just got a hot pot of tea sent up."

"Oh, tea. I am sure you are all sorts of endearing yourself to Varnus," Soria

396

said, teasing Brannis about the choice of beverage for the hard-drinking guard captain.

"I will allow him free rein of the emperor's wine cellar if he stays awake with me long enough to get this done."

"I'll tell him you said that," Soria promised, still smiling.

* * * * * * * *

"I never expected I would be seeing you again alive, let alone finding both you and the boy, with a rescue on the way," Aelon said, his voice echoing from the stone ceiling overhead. Three sloshing sets of footsteps kept him from attempting to whisper; if the noises they made were heard from above, at least they had the advantage of an expert guide if it became a game of hide-from-his-lordship in the sewers.

"Well, let us just say that this plan is little more than optimism and running at the moment. Anzik, where are we right now?" Faolen asked, following close behind Councilor Fehr's evasive child.

The boy had taken the lead without being asked. Faolen had trusted the instincts that had kept Anzik ahead of half the city's efforts to find and capture him. Of course, the boy had not gone unnoticed. With the Staff of Gehlen, he had solved his problems with force when cornered.

"Up there is a stable with a door that is easy to open. The horse in the third stall died eighteen days ago, and they have not gotten a new one to replace her yet. The stable boy came once right before dusk, and then not again until morning. The hay was—"

"That is good enough, Anzik. Thank you. Which way will get us outside the city fastest, either to the east or south?" Faolen asked.

"None. The sewers do not go outside the city at all."

"Well, I mean what will get us closest to outside the city? We can go up to the streets before we actually leave the walls of Zorren."

Anzik's gaze went glassy, staring at nothing in particular a moment as Faolen and Aelon watched the boy by the magical light emanating from Faolen's finger, which was all the light they had with them.

"This way." Anzik pointed down a side passageway.

"Lead on," Faolen told him.

* * * * * * * *

The night sky was darker than Juliana had expected when the *Daggerstrike* entered a passing rainstorm. The moonlight that had showed the snow-capped peaks of the Cloud Wall as Juliana steered her ship by them was blocked by a wall of actual clouds—well, more of a ceiling than a wall, but its opacity was of more concern than its orientation.

She tried taking the ship above the clouds. The view was breathtaking, a three-quarter moon nestled among a dazzling array of stars, with the moonlight making the clouds below them glow with a ghostly light. It was as if there was an ocean of luminescence that they sailed. It was all very poetic, and in less pressing times, she hoped to see such sights again. In the meantime, it blocked her view of the ground. It was a significant detriment to her ability to navigate by following Koriah's geography.

With some reluctance, she dropped the ship back below the clouds, cursing Brannis, Kyrus and whoever else he might be for not providing some shelter against the weather for the poor sorceress forced to stand out on the exposed deck to operate the controls. Figuring she could afford a momentary lapse, she unfocused her attention.

Somewhere in Tellurak, Soria kicked Brannis under the table where they were sharing an early luncheon. Juliana blinked back to her present situation, content to let Soria explain what he had done to warrant the kick.

Resigned that she could see as little beneath the clouds as above, she took the *Daggerstrike* up once more, hoping that they would pass the storm before reaching the sea. At least above, she would not be getting wet.

* * * * * * *

Anzik jogged along, panting for breath with the mild exertion. Despite being a young boy, and despite being out on his own for more than a tenday, he was unused to long exertion. The sounds of pursuit in the tunnels had prompted Faolen to prod the boy along. Anzik had gamely complied, understanding that whoever was behind them was going to take him back to his father if they were caught.

"Soon enough, they will get ahead of us on the surface, you know," Aelon said.

Aside from having to duck a little in spots where the sewer grew shorter, Aelon was faring by far the best of all of them. As little demand as the life of a merchant placed on the body, it seemed he was in better condition than either of the sorcerers, younger or older.

"What do you suggest?" Faolen asked. "I do not think our chances of outrunning them are any better above."

"They know we are down here. There are only so many passages to take, especially if they guess we are trying to get outside the city. We have more directions to travel above ground."

"And more eyes seeking us out," Faolen countered.

"Eyes are your specialty, are they not?" Aelon argued. "Hide us from view with your illusions."

"I do not know that I trust my magic to keep three of us safe. I am still quite weakened."

"I have an idea," Anzik said, stopping and turning to look at the two adults. "Why not go back to the middle of the city?"

"Anzik, we are trying to escape the city, not keep hiding in it. Hiding one small boy is impressive. Hiding two grown men along with him is asking too much."

"I thought it was an airship that was coming to rescue us. Can it not just come over the city to get us?"

Faolen and Aelon looked to one another. Aelon shrugged. Faolen spread his hands, inviting an argument against the idea but there was none to be had.

* * * * * * * *

"No. Tell them to find a way to sneak outside the city walls."

"Brannis, they are desperate," Varnus said, his voice soft.

"I gave Juliana that ship to get her safely away from Kadris and all the daggerwork the Circle is planning. You make it sound as if they have alerted the whole city with their escape thus far. I am not sending her into a mess like that. Picking them up outside the city is risky enough," Kyrus argued. He stifled a yawn, taking another sip of tea while still angry, and burning his mouth on it.

"Juliana is Soria. Soria has been in and out of tighter places than that a hundred times. If you want her to be yours, you are going to have to let her be herself. She's a warrior, skinny thing that she is. Juliana, same as Soria. It's in the heart more than the muscles or the Source. Besides, if you do not tell her, she will search the city for them when she doesn't find them waiting outside." Varnus locked gazes with Kyrus, who sat fuming until he satisfied himself that he had no proper argument to turn against Varnus's final thrust.

"I do not like this one bit," Kyrus said, folding his arms across his chest, and trying to slip his mind back into Brannis's to convey the message.

* * * * * * * *

Faolen searched above first, in the aether. Finding nothing immediately threatening, he poked his head up through the open sewer grating that Anzik's magic held open. It was strange relying on the magic of one so young, but the boy seemed innately talented. His magic was silent and artful; Faolen felt no wasted aether as was common when around Source-strong children first feeling out the process of learning magic. The boy's magic was as fluid as a Fourth Circle adept.

The three fugitives clambered out of the sewers, dripping fetid water from their ankle-deep trek through the muck. Taking stock of their surroundings, Faolen found that they were in a low-lying portion of the city, in between two of the major hills. The night had grown cloudy, but there were fires aplenty in the city, kept for the nightly activities of the harbor and the military, which kept some amount of activity going throughout all the hours of the day. It was enough to make out the larger towers that dominated the skyline of Zorren.

"Too bad we cannot climb one of those, eh?" Aelon said, noting Faolen's gaze.

Faolen nodded his assent but did not comment on it. "For now, I will conserve my magic. If we get cornered, I will buy us what time we can. The most important thing is for Anzik to get aboard. If you two can get away, do not risk staying too long waiting for me. I will fend for myself if needs be."

"Is that the airship?" Anzik asked, pointing up.

A tiny shape glinted in the fires from the city, circling high above Zorren.

* * * * * * * *

"Anyone see them yet?" Captain Juliana shouted out, realizing they were too high for them to be heard. Likely they had already been spotted. The city swarmed with troops carrying torches or magical lights. It seemed that Faolen had kicked a wasps' nest.

"Nothing yet, Captain," one of the spotters called out. She had summoned them up on deck when she first spotted the city by its lights on the coastline. It was either Zorren or she had gone well off course.

"All right, I'm bringing us in lower. Shout out if you see them *or* if you see anyone getting ready to shoot at us, especially sorcerers," Juliana ordered. She shifted her hold on the wheel, and angled the ship's nose downward, banking a left turn as she did so. The controls were still awkward to her, but she was growing more familiar with them, at least.

"All rain and cloud cover, Captain. Can't see a bleeding thing down there," another of the spotters shouted.

Juliana gritted her teeth in frustration, knowing they were right. Any efforts Faolen and his companions took to conceal themselves from their pursuers would keep them hidden from the *Daggerstrike*'s crew as well. Any signal they gave would be seen by both as well—if they were lucky enough for her crew to see it at all. The city was large enough for sure, not the size of Kadris, but large enough that it was inconvenient to see all at once. She spared a moment's concentration yet again to start a chain of messages back and forth between the worlds.

"Watch for a plume of fire," Juliana called out. "That will be our beacon."

She kept the ship moving fast in circles above the city, hoping that any ambitious archer or gunner would be hard pressed to lead their target by enough to hit the *Daggerstrike*. It was only a matter of time now, unless her request proved too much for Faolen, if what Brannis reported of his current condition was understated.

"Captain, arse-left. I saw a plume of fire, just like you said."

Juliana turned her head quickly to look off the ship's arse-left side. She had also done away with the nautical terms bow and stern. Her ship had a left, a right, a nose, a belly, and an arse end. The term "deck" had unfortunately stuck when she could think of none better on short notice.

Captain Juliana slowed the ship, twisting it about in air in a manner that neither sea vessel nor the wind-catching airships could manage. The arse of the ship swung about, waggling back and forth a bit as the front darted off in their intended direction: toward the flame.

"Captain, it looks like the Megrenn saw that too," one of the spotters yelled.

"I see them, " Juliana replied. "It is going to be a race." She accelerated the ship, hoping fervently that it could stop just as quickly. They were aimed at a down angle, straight for a crash landing if they did not have that ability.

Buildings whisked by beneath them, growing closer to the belly of the ship as they crossed half of Zorren to reach their target. Juliana and the spotters lost the citywide view of the overall Megrenn search effort as the height of the buildings obscured the far reaches of Zorren from them.

There were glimpses of roving infantry patrols, seen between buildings as they crossed over the streets that were being combed for Faolen. Most disturbing were sightings of stripe-cats among the searchers. Faster and more dangerous than infantry, the huge felines were to be Juliana's largest worry until she took note of any cannons or sorcerers. Should Jinzan Fehr be in the city, and join the search using the Staff of Gehlen, there was a good chance that they would not escape, airship or no airship.

"Found them, Captain. They are off to the left-nose side; they are waving us down."

Juliana looked through the viewer, having toyed with it a bit en route until she had gotten the controls figured out. There they were, three of them, looking bedraggled but whole, standing in an emptied market square, two adults and a scrawny child. The two adults were waving their arms overhead, frantically signaling to the *Daggerstrike*.

Juliana brought the ship low, hitting the rune that dropped the left-nose hatch. The ship lurched as it bumped down against the flagstones of the marketplace. She saw a stripe-cat enter the marketplace, a rider with someone seated behind her. Behind them, trailing a bit, were a number of infantry.

"GET IN, QUICKLY!" Juliana's voice boomed outside the ship. The time for even the barest pretense of stealth was now passed. Faolen and his two companions rushed for the ship.

"Stop them!" the passenger on the stripe-cat called out in Megrenn as he slipped from the beast's back, and quickly cast a spell.

"*Eket jimagu denpek wanapi,*" the Megrenn sorcerer chanted hurriedly. Bolts of flame shot from his outstretched fingers. He had the control to avoid aiming any at Anzik, but the two other fugitives were clearly his targets.

Aelon turned to look over his shoulder as the spell was cast. Hopping to the side, he threw his body between himself and Faolen, taking the sorcerer's share of the flaming missiles. The searing bolts of fire scorched his clothing, setting him aflame. His dragon-like skin felt none of it, though. He continued onward to the ship.

"Why is Uncle Narsicann shooting flame bolts at us?" Anzik asked, looking over his shoulder while Faolen pulled him by the arm aboard the *Daggerstrike*. Despite the distraction, Anzik kept his feet moving in the proper direction.

Seeing that her charges had made it aboard before the Megrenn sorcerer could manage another spell, Juliana touched the rune to raise the hatch, and got the *Daggerstrike* moving upward, hoping to get a bit of air between them and the ground while her new passengers settled themselves in, and found something to hold onto. That reminded her …

"Grab hold of something," Captain Juliana said, voice projecting down into the ship's interior. "We are about to—"

"Captain, look out!" one of the spotters cried out, terror in his voice.

They were well up off the ground, the belly of the ship level with the shorter buildings already. Incredibly, though, the stripe-cat had made the leap, claws hooking arrow slits and the ship's railing. The rider was pressed tight in against the scruff of the beast's neck as it scrambled onto the deck. It took a swipe at the left-arse spotter, snapping his safety harness, and sending him tumbling overboard, likely dead before the straps broke.

Juliana swore loudly when she realized that the beast was heading straight for her. She fought back her first instinct, which was to draw forth her daggers, and fight the thing off. Instead she looked to the ship's wheel. The actions were not instinctive yet; she had to search the runes, frantic, as the stripe-cat was a bound away from reaching her.

The beast's claws slammed into Juliana at the same moment she found the rune to put the ship into a right-over-left roll. The ship lurched as her shielding spell took the impact, forcing her awkwardly against the ship's wheel. The deck tilted beneath her feet. She felt the strap attached at her right hip pull taut against the support pillar that was there just to keep her in place in such orientations of the ship.

The one thing she had not accounted for was the stripe-cat's claws. Her shielding spell had kept her skin from being shredded by the stripe-cat's claws, but the harness was just sturdy leather. As the huge cat panicked and scrambled for purchase on the tilting ship, it caught the straps that tethered Captain Juliana to her ship. Stripe-cat, rider, and ship's captain all plummeted to the ground.

Juliana knew well enough what to do in a fall. Trusting to her shielding spell, she pushed the stripe-cat away—or rather pushed against it, and thrust herself away, given the size difference. She hit the ground lightly, cushioned by magics she knew well enough to perform while drunk if she needed to. Unlike their domesticated relatives, stripe-cats did not always land on their feet. If not dead, the beast was at least critically injured. The rider did not appear to have survived the fall.

The lack of a stripe-cat to fight was scant comfort. Overhead, the *Daggerstrike* lay on its side, no longer spinning but continuing to drift upward, well out of reach of any spell she knew. In the marketplace there was a Megrenn sorcerer, a platoon of infantry, and half the city likely heading her way. There was only one thing she could think to do.

* * * * * * * *

A hand reached across the table, and grabbed Brannis by the wrist, shaking him from a daydream. It was a confusing day, and Brannis had been losing track of himself as he shifted his consciousness to Veydrus and back. He snapped to alertness, looking to the owner of the grabbing hand, seeing a desperate look in Soria's eyes when his gaze met them.

"Send Kyrus. I need help," Soria said. There was no brooking an argument. "Now."

Brannis nodded, not even responding verbally before he closed his eyes.

* * * * * * * *

"Get out," Kyrus said to Varnus. "I have to use a transference spell. You do not want to be nearby."

"Brannis, are you sure about that. I mean, you said that last—"

"GO!" Kyrus shouted. He broke the wards that sealed his bedchamber, scavenging their wreckage for any salvageable aether, and drawing yet more from whatever was available within the palace.

Varnus realized they were past the point of arguing the matter. He paused only long enough for one final message before rushing off down the hall to find shelter: "Good luck. Bring her back safe."

"*Doxlo intuvae menep gahalixviu junumar tequalix ferendak uzganmanni dekdardon vesvata eho,*" Kyrus chanted, still having the spell well committed to memory. He had no time for self-doubt, no time to wonder how he was going to find Juliana, presumably somewhere in Zorren. He had to go, and there was no time to wait.

A sphere of aether obscured Kyrus, and his consciousness was catapulted into the vast nighttime of the deep aether once more.

Chapter 37 – Once More into the Aether

"Well now, look what we have," the Megrenn sorcerer remarked. "A Kadrin sorceress who has lost her ship. Surrender, and you will be treated well."

Juliana looked at the man she had heard the Megrenn boy call "Uncle Narsicann," who had flung bolts of fire aimed not a pace from the boy. There was something about his demeanor, mocking, flippant ... cold. She knew that his words were meaningless. Rashan's Bargain was an ironic tool in the hands of a Megrenn, but that was her guess—easier to take her by guile than by force.

The Megrenn ground forces were beginning to arrive in numbers. Juliana glanced down one street, then another. The marketplace was a crossroads of sorts, but wherever she looked, infantry were either already entering the market square or could be seen approaching. Horns sounded, calling for even more forces to congregate on the area.

"There is nowhere to run. It would be a shame to have to kill you, but that is the alternative you face," Narsicann called out to her, drawing Juliana's gaze back to him. She noted that he was making no move to approach her. Cautious. Cowardly? It seemed to matter little, since Juliana was no match for an army, even if she might take her odds against just the sorcerer. She looked up at the *Daggerstrike*, still continuing a lazy drifting upward, lying on its side like a wounded animal.

A few paces from Juliana, an actual wounded animal whimpered. The huge stripe-cat was trying to pull itself along the ground toward her, dragging both the limp body of its rider as well as its hindquarters. She glanced all around, edging away from the beast as she considered her options.

Her breathing quickened with a rising panic. She was not liking any of them.

* * * * * * * *

The world of light vanished once more, as it had on Kyrus's journey from Tellurak. He knew that his perception of time was altered, that he had the ability to consider his course. Nevertheless, he felt a pressing need to make all haste. He drifted up and out of the vicinity of the palace and the Tower of Contemplation. There were too many wards about, too much aether for him to see through. He felt nothing as he passed through barriers that would have stopped most physical and magical assaults.

He remembered his mistakes on Denku Appa. He had relied on the physical placement of stones to mark his course. Whether through his own error or—as he rather suspected—the intervention of Tippu and Kahli, that method had failed him. Kyrus gave brief consideration to the advice he had just given Juliana a short time ago: follow the Cloud Wall to the sea, and turn left along the coast. That was all well and good for the world of light, but mountains were not known for having Sources, nor did they have any noticeable effect on aether. The sea would be rife with aether along the coasts where sea creatures abounded. That made a better landmark—seamark?—but it seemed like there must be a better method, but he had little time for introspection. He needed to go.

Kyrus stretched his vision out, roughly the direction he believed Zorren to be. He tried to quiet his mind, remembering the feeling of being around Juliana. There was a sense of motionless vertigo; the universe shifted around him. There was no physical sensation to accompany the purely mental motion, but his mind insisted on trying to insert one on his behalf.

Trees, grass, birds ... Sources in numbers his eyes could not count as they whisked by him. The eddies in the aether seemed like the currents of a river, but the aethership *Kyrus* plowed through, tacking against the wind, defying the forces of nature that sought to impede him.

Fields of fresh-planted crops, vast grids of nascent Sources as germinating seeds began their lives as vegetables ... schools of fish, packed tightly along a narrow ribbon of river ... people, pockets here and there: villages ... more fish, vastly more as the sea showed itself ... people again, a coastal city, far more populous than the villages ... one person ... one Source ... Juliana.

He knew her Source by its look, its *feel*. With thousands of human Sources all about, hers stood out, unique as her face and easier to pick from among those teeming multitudes of weakling Sources. He felt drawn to it, associated it with *her*, not just the abstract look of a blue-white humanoid form against the backdrop of the lighter aetherial winds. It evoked feelings of being near her, of her smell and her feel, the warmth of her skin against his own. It dredged up old, shared memories of Brannis's as well, of her as an adolescent girl, tugging Brannis about like a fish on a hook. Kyrus smiled in his mind, not knowing whether his body mimicked the thought, way back in Kadris. It was time to arrive in Zorren.

Kyrus fought his first instinct, which would have had him protect her against all harm by exchanging places with her, letting the spell deposit her safely in Kadris. Kyrus tried to shake his head, mentally shaking the universe instead—his view of everything swung wildly, disorienting him. His view of Juliana's Source gave him something to keep his bearings by. He remembered Varnus's admonishment; he could keep neither Juliana nor Soria locked away safely somewhere if he ever hoped to understand her ... both of her.

The world snapped back into the light. Kyrus found himself a few paces short of a running Juliana. He had seen the Sources all about before ending his spell but, Zorren being a city of tens of thousands, thought little of them. He realized that Juliana's predicament was every bit as dire as she had let on.

Juliana stumbled, startled by the massive disruption in the aether that marked

Kyrus's arrival. What must have been a hundred or more foot soldiers skidded to a halt, not daring approach the apparition who had just appeared before them.

"Brannis!" Juliana shouted. "Merciful One, thank you!" she called out to the sky.

A hail of arrows sought Kyrus as the Megrenn soldiers gathered wits enough to decide to attack first, and figure out what had befallen later. Juliana had been a target for capture, but the newcomer apparently bore no such restrictive orders. The tiny, fletched insects were nothing to Kyrus. The paranoid shielding spell he had been keeping while going about his daily routine in Kadris turned them aside without any noticeable effort. Dragons do not bother to swat mosquitoes.

"Are you all right?" Kyrus asked, walking over to her, gathering her in his arms. She slumped against him, drawing a shuddering breath.

"Now I am. If you hadn't come, I don't know how long I would have lasted against them," she admitted. "This is why I stay away from all-out wars." She punched him playfully in the chest in remonstration.

"What happened to the *Daggerstrike*?" Kyrus asked, now that he was sure Juliana was physically unharmed.

"Up there still," Juliana said. "Crazed stripe-cat pulled me free of the ship."

She raised up the broken leather strap from the harness that still dangled from her midsection. Kyrus then followed her gaze upward. The *Daggerstrike* continued to float away, the way chimney smoke wafts from the rooftops of cities. Kyrus frowned up at it. Arrows continued to brush against his shield, which enveloped Juliana as she nestled against him, her feeling of safety more than romantic illusion.

Kyrus reached a hand out in the direction of the airship. Slowly, with the deliberate care of the craftsmen who make ships in bottles, he righted the *Daggerstrike*. Once he judged it to be level, he started it on a gradual descent down toward the marketplace once more.

"Brannis." Juliana got his attention, pointing to the stripe-cat, still trying valiantly to chase down its prey: a certain Kadrin sorceress.

Kyrus blinked, distracted from his telekinesis, to see the beast approaching them. It was obviously mortally wounded and in pain. Its mewling whimpers made it seem especially feline and piteous.

A blast of aether against his shields diverted Kyrus's attention in a third, possibly fourth different direction, annoying him. He turned to see the Megrenn sorcerer who had just attacked him. *I am too tired to deal with all this.* Kyrus sighed mentally. He fixed the sorcerer with his best withering glare, and unleashed a jet of hurled fire.

The Megrenn sorcerer flinched, a reaction to the shock wave in the aether that accompanied the blast. The stripe-cat's misery was ended. There was a scattering of shattered bones and melted scraps of ruined armor from both the creature and its rider, nothing else. There was a furrow of molten flagstones where Kyrus's attack had cut into the marketplace ground.

His glare still fixed on the sorcerer, Kyrus cocked his head to the side, and raised his eyebrows. The Megrenn sorcerer froze in place, eyes wide in awe and fear.

Kthoom.

A cannon's report shattered the air. A hollow bell sound rang out as the shot slammed against the hull of the *Daggerstrike.* Some enterprising Megrenn artillerist was apparently an excellent shot. Kyrus saw a dent in the armor plating of the airship.

Kthoom.

A second shot never reached its target.

There was a rumbling noise of displaced earth and stone as a massive, translucent barrier grew, encircling Kyrus, Juliana, and the spot where the *Daggerstrike* was being steered to set down. The barrier rose up into the sky, shielding the airship from further target practice. As it formed, it shoved all in its path out of the way, cutting a pace or more into the ground, and carving its way through stone buildings, pieces of which crumbled into the streets where insufficient structure was left to support them. It was the same spell Kyrus had once used to hold back a Katamic Sea storm. It seemed like a lifetime ago.

"Stop that," Kyrus ordered. He did not raise his voice. He had not, he realized, used his voice at all in erecting the barrier.

"Cease fire!" Narsicann ordered. The sorcerer backed away from Kyrus and the cylindrical wall that glowed with a soft yellow light. The soldiers followed his lead, withdrawing to positions that offered cover in case Kyrus tried some sort of attack. A handful who had been trapped on the inside cowered together near the wall, as far from Kyrus as they could get.

"We are leaving," Kyrus informed anyone within earshot, shouting as loudly as he could. Juliana covered her ears. "Do not give me any reason to change my mind and remain!" The *Daggerstrike* settled a handspan from the ground. Kyrus lifted Juliana gently up onto the deck. "Open the hatch, if you would not mind," he called up to her.

Kyrus stepped into the *Daggerstrike,* looking about at the crew he had hastily assigned to the ship. He also saw the three escapees from Zorren that Juliana had been sent to rescue. Faolen's Source was a tattered mess, fraying and spilling aether irregularly, but he seemed physically sound enough. Aelon was bare chested, with his head shaven; Kyrus was sure there was a story there somewhere that would bear hearing at a later time. The most interesting, though, was a young boy who bore a notable resemblance to Denrik Zayne—and Jinzan Fehr, he supposed.

"Are you Tallax from the storybooks?" Anzik Fehr asked. Seeing Kyrus's puzzled look, he clarified: "Tallax has a really, really bright Source and so do you. Are you him?"

"No." Kyrus shook his head. "Those are just old stories about a sorcerer who died a long time ago."

"I like your airship, whoever you are. Faolen just told me that it was you who made it. Where are we going?"

"Home."

The *Daggerstrike*, with Captain Juliana once more at the helm, headed off for Kadris.

* * * * * * *

A yellowish glow lit the airship as it floated up from the middle of Zorren. Jinzan watched from the open balcony door of his study as it turned slowly in the air, bow to the southeast as it shot off, and vanished into the distant darkness. He stared after it for a time, wondering whether the clenched fist gripping his heart was just his imagination or some subtle magic at work upon him. He felt trapped, helpless to make a move; he knew he ought to, but no action proceeded from that knowledge.

"What are you doing out here? It is too cold to be in just your nightclothes," Nakah chided him.

His wife sidled up next to him, huddling against him for warmth as she wore only a nightgown herself. Jinzan put an arm around her by habit and reflex, continuing to stare out at the magical glow over his city. In his other hand, he clutched the Staff of Gehlen, his boon and curse. Word had reached Zorren of vicious attacks by Rashan Solaran against Megrenn forces. Now, if he did not miss his guess, Kyrus Hinterdale had just used a transference spell, followed by several other magics that had wrenched and torn at the aether around the city, awakening him from a deep slumber.

He should have been out there with the Staff of Gehlen, the only with who could stand in confrontation against either Kyrus or the demon. He was the only hope against either of them, and he was Megrenn's only hope of victory. Yet he stood watching, unsure of what he could do in the face of the power he saw, content to let the question rest unanswered for one night longer.

"Do you see that light out there?" Jinzan asked, nodding in the direction of the glow. The question was rhetorical of course, since it outshone the moonlight. "One of our enemies has come and gone tonight. I am spared having to face him for now."

"Jinzan Fehr came to our bed tonight. Councilor Jinzan awoke and left us. Zaischelle is worried, but I made her stay inside and warm. Come back, but leave Councilor Jinzan watching out here if you must. Our husband needs his rest."

"Very well," Jinzan relented. It was such nights that made him grateful he did not dream, as others did. It kept nightmares away as well.

Chapter 38 - Introductions

"I swear I told you all about it," Brannis protested. He held his hands up as if to ward off thrown cutlery. Soria still sat across from him at the same table they had occupied since first settling there to deal with Faolen's emergency summons.

"No. No, you missed mentioning that there was a shielding spell for the entire deck of the ship. I spent hours in the rain, soaked through to my ..." Soria began, but she must have noticed that her voice was rising. She caught herself, and continued as a harsh whisper: "... soaked through to my nether-garments."

"You forgot," Brannis insisted. "I am sure I told you."

"You know, Erund, a sensible man learns to lose this argument, admit he was wrong, and move on."

Somewhere above Veydrus, the two of them were sleeping in shared quarters on board the *Daggerstrike*. As captain, Juliana had her own, and as commander of all Kadrin military forces, no one objected when Kyrus joined her. Still shaken from her close encounter with the Megrenn military, and being dragged bodily from her own ship, Juliana had been rather more forgiving of her earlier discomforts than Soria seemed to be.

"I suppose sensible men are liars, then. I would admit it if I did not remember telling you about the shield," Brannis said, smiling to diffuse the rising anger Soria was showing.

Soria muttered something under her breath in Kheshi as she turned her head to look anywhere but at Brannis.

"What was that?" he asked. Brannis had some guesses but none were flattering. It was his curse that he felt compelled to ask anyway.

"Nothing. Just a little mantra they made us recite at the temple. It's supposed to be calming, but I don't know if it's working."

"Maybe when we are done in Acardia, we can visit Khesh. You can show me where you grew up."

"Maybe." Soria did not sound enthusiastic, so Brannis did not press the issue.

Soria looked down, and began fishing about in her coin purse, the metallic clattering drawing the attention of the proprietor. Brannis felt a pang of guilt, since they had been occupying a corner table of his establishment for hours. Soria assuaged that guilt easily enough with a pile of eckle coins whose value was difficult to count, spilled haphazardly across the table, but there was at least ten times what they owed for their meal.

"Let's go," Soria said, standing up. "We had a day planned."

Greuder's Pastries was closed for the day when they arrived. Their interworld distraction had delayed them into mid afternoon, while Greuder closed up shop shortly after noontime. The handle of the door jiggled a little when Brannis gave it a pull, but it held fast.

"We can try again tomorrow," Soria suggested. "I cannot imagine that such a problem will come up twice in two days."

"No. I think he is still in there. Follow me," Brannis said.

He walked around the building, down a narrow space between the bakery and the silversmith who owned the shop next door, and around to the back of the building. There was another door there in the alleyway. Brannis knocked.

"We are closed on this side as well, sir," Greuder's familiar voice called out from inside. "Come back in the morn."

Brannis knocked again.

"Still closed."

Brannis knocked a third time. He heard footsteps from inside the bakery. There was a noise of some bar being drawn. The door swung open.

"Now listen here—" Greuder began, but stopped, mouth agape.

"Can we come in?" Brannis asked.

Greuder nodded, stepping aside to allow Brannis and Soria to get by him.

"Kyrus, what are you *doing* here?" Greuder asked, once he had herded them inside, and secured the door once more.

The back of the bakery was packed with shelves full of ingredients and tables for mixing, rolling, and kneading. Dominating the whole of it, though, was the large stone oven from whence came spiced crescents. Alas, the oven was cold, and Greuder had been cleaning up after the day's work when Brannis's knocking had interrupted him.

"Well, first off, do not call me Kyrus. I am going by the name Sir Erund Hinterdale, and I came from Marker's Point. I figured I could not ignore the resemblance to a certain fugitive, but I can explain it as a distant relation. As for why I am here, I wanted to see how you had been faring in my absence."

"Well, spiced crescents do not sell like they once did, but otherwise I have fared well enough. You seem unusually hale and hearty, though I imagine a suit of armor can hide a lot," Greuder said with a wink. "Are you going to introduce me?"

"Soria Hinterdale," Soria stepped in and introduced herself. Brannis cringed, remembering the talks that Kyrus had with Greuder about Abbiley. He also noticed that she was playing up her Kheshi accent.

"Another distant relation?" Greuder ventured a guess.

Brannis relaxed a bit as Greuder did not attempt to make the more obvious—

"Wife," Soria replied, tossing Brannis's hopes of avoiding an awkward conversation right overboard.

"Congratulations!" Greuder cried out, beaming. "Kyrus, you've done well for yourself, picked a real beauty."

"Well, this is all sort of unofficial—"

"Yes, as fugitives, Kyrus and I have not had the chance to have a proper ceremony," Soria clarified.

"Well, of course. I can understand that, certainly. My congratulations to the both of you, though, in the hope that you can settle down somewhere nice, where you can leave your troubles here behind you."

"I think once I have seen to some business here in Acardia, we will take ourselves off to Khesh. Soria is Acardian, but she traveled down there with her family as a young girl, and was raised there," Brannis said. It seemed better to tell Greuder their actual plans, and let the information be known, rather than spend a few seconds coming up with a lie, and having Soria beat him to the storytelling.

Brannis itched to ask about Abbiley, but Soria seemed intent on thwarting his efforts, making sure Greuder knew that he was hers. Greuder also seemed complicit, even though it was out of politeness in his case, not mentioning Kyrus's sweetheart in front of Soria.

They talked a long while, snacking on tarts that were left over from the day's sales. Kyrus heard bits and pieces of the aftermath of his escape, and the reemergence of Denrik Zayne as the Scourge of the Katamic once more. Brannis filled Greuder in on the missing portion of Kyrus's story, leaving out the more fantastical ones, like the explosion on Marker's Point. They left the bakery by early evening, taking the back way again. Soria left Greuder with a trade bar, for use in any emergency that might come up due to their meeting. It was a cryptic warning, but Brannis knew that if his suspicions about a conspiracy were right, there might be bystanders who got pulled into it as well.

"It ought to be time to find ourselves dinner, but I stuffed myself with enough blackberry tarts to last me the night," Soria commented as she strolled down the wide cobblestone avenues of Scar Harbor alongside Brannis.

"I could have done with a spiced crescent, to see if they were all that Kyrus made them out to be. We ought to go back before we leave the city."

"Bra—Erund, you have to know that isn't a good idea. I know this all feels like a homecoming lark, but you are the one who thinks that something nefarious is going on here. Anyone you talk to is endangered, if only a little, just by speaking to you," Soria told him.

"Yes, I know why you gave Greuder a whole trade bar, just for interrupting his daily cleaning of the bakery. He might need to flee Scar Harbor if people start coming after him to get leverage over me."

Soria wrapped herself around Brannis's arm as they walked, squeezing it in lieu of a full hug.

"At least you understand that much. I was getting worried that I would have to do all the underhanded thinking for both of us."

"Well, I am still not comfortable with calling myself 'Sir' Erund. Impersonating a knight is an actual crime in Acardia."

"You are *not* impersonating a knight. There is no Erund Hinterdale to take offense. We made him up," Soria said cheerfully, smiling up at Brannis. She seemed to be enjoying playing at being the knight's lady. Soria was such a warrior all the time, from what he had gathered from Varnus and Tanner.

How much does she envy Juliana her life of parties, fashions, and idleness? Juliana certainly seemed hungry for a taste of the warrior life.

"Yes, but I am not a knight at all. Whether I take the name of a real knight or just make one up, it is still just as criminal."

"I am sorry, Sir Brannis Solaran, but I seem to rather strongly recollect that you *are* a knight. The ones around here are hereditary knights and bootlicks who get the title handed to them for 'meritorious distinction' and such nonsense. If anything, they're the ones impersonating knights, not you."

* * * * * * *

In the small hours of the morning, shortly before dawn, a small crowd still occupied one of the innumerable portside taverns along Kadris's waterfront. Work in the port continued round the clock, though it ebbed and flowed, slowest in the wee hours, but never quite stopping. The taverns mirrored the pattern, with one or more always open, come sun or moon.

Tanner awoke to the sound of monohorns thundering across the table in front of him. The huge, savage beasts had already trampled his head flat, and were proceeding to run in loops just to vex him. Three empty bottles lay on the table in front of him but, with effort, they turned into just a single bottle, lying on its side, a leftover splash of whiskey pooled shallow within.

He started trying to trace back his evening. He had been kidnapped by a worried Varnus, forced at drink-point to listen to a convoluted tale about messages being ferried every which way from Veydrus to Tellurak and back. The burly old guard captain had matched him drink for drink, but Tanner had never had the head for it that Zellisan did, and that went for Varnus as well.

"I was beginning to think I would have to find you another time," a voice called in his direction. It sounded familiar but he could not place it. He raised his head from where it had laid, pressed flat against the wood grain of the table, for how long he could not tell. The side of his face was sore, and a line of drool clung to the corner of his mouth. He wiped it away with his sleeve as he looked for the one who had addressed him.

Tanner blinked in confusion when he saw Captain Stalyart walking over from a nearby table to join him. It was the same man, there was no mistaking him. The bronzed skin, dark hair, the amused expression permanently carved into the features of his face—there could never be two such as him, except as twinborn.

"Just to be on the safe side here … where are we?" Tanner asked, wincing and putting a hand to his eyes to shield them from the lantern light.

"Kadris," Stalyart's twin replied. "You are not imagining. Like you, I try to keep myselves easy to remember. I do not play at games of disguises and layer upon layer of selves."

"So what's your name here, then?" Tanner asked.

"Hmm, perhaps some other time I will tell you, once I know you can be trusted with it. For now, I will answer to Stalyart if you call me such," Stalyart's twin said, pulling up a chair with a shrieking noise of wood scraping against wood that made Tanner's head resonate like a struck chime. Stalyart sighed, plunking down a bottle on the table that looked like a more reputable version of his own. Stalyart's had a cork in it, appeared to be full, and had not lain for the better part of the night in a pool of spilt liquor and drool. "The cure that sickens." Stalyart pulled the cork, and offered it to Tanner, then took a seat, straddling the chair with his arms propped up on the back.

Tanner gave the bottle a skeptical look for just long enough to realize that looking hard at anything hurt. He sat up, slouched back in his chair, eyes half closed to ward away the worst of the light. He took a long pull at the bottle, tasting nothing but the welcome burning sensation as he swallowed.

"So you're here," Tanner observed, once he had a few swallows to stop the worst of his pains.

"So I am."

"Why?"

"Ahh, so now you are awake. Excellent. Yes, 'why' is a very good question," Stalyart's twin said. "You see, I am a cautious man. One may not think it from the occupations I choose, but given that each man must work, I am cautious when you consider all things."

"That clears that up," Tanner replied. "Clear as ... as ..."

"Yes, yes, something not very clear at all. Your wits are, regrettably, a lost cause this morning. Please listen, though, because I come on behalf of a friend. There may come a time when we two might stop a war."

"Oh, you some hot-as-hobnails sorcerer around here? You got the ear of those Megrenn bastards and their High Council?" Tanner asked, overplaying his sarcasm to the point of self-mockery.

"No, but consider this. Brannis and Councilor Jinzan Fehr are both relying on you to relay messages," Stalyart said, talking as if to a young child, slowly and clearly.

"Yep, that's me, message boy to the twinborn and the powerful."

"Ahh, but consider that they have only your memory to rely on, not wax seals and warded parchments. You not only carry each message, held open in your hands, but you must read it, remember it, and recite it."

"Oh yeah. I'm a talented guy. A regular talking parrot."

"Have you considered that perhaps, with a bit of help, those messages could be ... rewritten—perhaps a few words here and there," Stalyart's twin suggested.

"And do what?"

"Bring two sides closer together. Arrange a truce, before we are all consumed by the war."

* * * * * * * *

Brannis had hated the idea the moment he thought of it, Soria knew, yet he suggested it anyway. *I am sure he had dreamed of some sweet little reunion, but he's gotten smarter than that. He might still have his chance to talk to the peasant girl, but not until I have made certain she is safe.* The trust Brannis showed in her was more valuable than all the coin in the purse she had left behind in their room, the caches she had hidden across Tellurak, and everything House Archon owned.

Soria skulked along the streets of Scar Harbor, clad once more in the dark, hooded ensemble. Even though there was nothing unsavory about being out late at night and Scar Harbor was likely safe enough for an unescorted young lady who was *not* a trained Tezuan warrior, she preferred to remain unseen. Whoever might be involved in Kyrus's conspiracy—and somehow she thought that it was Kyrus at work here, not Brannis—she wanted to give them as little knowledge about her and Brannis as possible. The fact that she was starting to see differences between Brannis and Kyrus—beyond the obvious physical differences—was irksome to her.

Soria remembered the way to the peasant girl's studio, which doubled as her home. The route she took to get there avoided the lamp-lit main thoroughfares, and took her through alleys, and over estate walls. She envied Faolen's illusions right then, since she could have made the trip in half the time, a tenth the effort, and with no chance of being seen, had she the ability to turn invisible.

There was a light in one of the upper-story windows. It was faint, orange, small. It had to have been a single candle. A few fools were reckless enough and scared enough of the dark to keep a lit candle by the bedside, but the peasant girl did not seem to be the type. Tooth-rotting saccharine optimism did not fit with being frightened of the dark of one's own bedchamber. *It does not fit with being Celia Mistfield, either,* Soria thought bitterly.

Was it even possible for nascent twinborn to be so different in demeanor? Soria could not conceive of it. She and Juliana had been joined for so long that the line between them was naught but a smudge. Kyrus and Brannis had been aware of one another a few months, but aside from superficial traits, they were mostly the same: a scholar with a heart of a hero, stubbornly naive, too clever to twist except by womanly charms. She smiled, knowing that hers were the charms that worked best on him, or rather that hers and Juliana's worked the best on them. Sourly, she reminded herself that they were not the *only* charms that worked at all.

It was time to meet Abbiley Tillman once again, this time knowing that she was Celia on the other side.

Soria edged her way up the side of the studio, finding a few handholds, and making them work for the whole of the climb. Her long limbs and strong fingers made it easy work; once she reached and took hold of the sill, it was child's play. A quick check of the aether showed a single Source inside, lying down. She pulled herself up to see inside in the light.

There were two bedrolls laid out on the floor, not even proper beds with posts and frame. One was vacant, the other held a sleeper, camped near the candle, possibly awake, possibly asleep. With great care to remain silent, Soria edged her grip on the sill until she could push herself through the window. She was glad that the night was warm enough that the window had been left open.

Creeeeeaaak.

Her undoing was the old woodwork. Thin as she was, Soria's weight was plenty to set the sill to creaking. The sleeper rolled over, startled by the noise. Soria took no time to think, but vaulted into the room, rushing to prevent a cry of alarm.

Soria's hand clamped over a mouth. Even through her gloves, she knew it was not the peasant girl. The sleeper had been male, with a wide jaw and a nose bigger than Celia's, for certain. Soria conjured a tiny light, counting on her mask to hide her identity, and reveal that of the man she had just assaulted.

Boy.

Soria corrected herself immediately on seeing the youthful features. He had unwrinkled skin marked with reddish blemishes, and a paltry scruff of beard that reminded her of Iridan. His hands came up to fend her off, and she quickly realized that, boy or not, he was nearly full grown and physically stronger than her. Soria changed tactics.

While she could not manage illusions like Faolen, there were a few tricks that came close. She let her light spell end, and conjured two soft, red lights, locating them on her own eyes. It made it dreadfully hard to see, so she let her vision switch to aether. Of course, aside from the scant candlelight, all the boy would see would be the illumination of two red eyes.

"Don't kill me. Don't kill me. Pleeeease don't kill me. I'll have the money soon, I swear," the boy said as soon as he was able to push Soria's hand free of his face.

"Your name," Soria said, making her voice as gravelly as she could. It was difficult sounding intimidating with a naturally high voice. She kept her words to a minimum.

"Uh, uh, Neelan."

"Where's Abbiley?"

"I ain't tellin' you where my sister's at."

"Stupid boy," Soria said. "I am not going to hurt her. You? Maybe."

"Well, you can't get her anyway," Neelan said. "Tomas Harkwick's courtin' her now. You give her trouble, you'll deal with him and Lord Harwick. Even you lot ain't fer havin' that kind of trouble as what they can make for you."

"How long?"

"How long what?" Neelan asked, starting to get the impression he was not the object of the red-eyed shadowy figure who had invaded his home.

"Courting her for how long?"

"Months? I dunno. She barely comes home at all most nights. They done made up a room for her at the lord's estate. Just … Just leave her alone, all right? Even if she's got a lord to protect her now, don't mean I can't look after her too, right?"

"She loves him?"

"How would I know? Yeah, sure, I guess. She thinks he's gonna marry her."

Soria gave Neelan a shove as she turned all the lights went out, two red, one orangish candle glow. In a ruffle of cloaks and a few quick, quiet footsteps, she vanished out the window.

Chapter 39 ~ Crossroads of War

The city of Kanem sat at the border of Kadrin and Megrenn. In more cordial times, it served as the first Megrenn settlement along the most heavily traveled land route between Kadris and Zorren. Being a trade city had given them coin to spare, and like the rest of Megrenn, they had prepared for war. The city wall was new, and in pristine order, tall and thick, with high towers outfitted with catapults. It was a city poised on the border of their enemy, and expected to be the first to feel the brunt of any counteroffensive.

Ever since the first day of springtime, the city had been on guard for signs of Kadrin troop movement. As Megrenn forces pushed ever farther into Kadrin territory, fears of the Empire's reprisals lessened. Trade within Megrenn still carried on apace; fears of war plied themselves against the scent of gold and lost, as they always seemed to in the end.

When a Kadrin airship was spotted flying past in the north, within Megrenn territory, the lax attitude snapped back into its proper shape. With no enemy ground forces in sight, the soldiers patrolling the walls called for the gates to be partially closed. Horsemen rode out to herd the traders inside the city with all haste, convincing caravan leaders to quicken their plodding pace lest they arrive at Kanem to find the city shut tight against invasion.

Amid the chaos of merchants and horse cavalry mixing upon the roads, no one thought much of a lone traveler in homespun clothes, leading his gelding afoot. He was part of no caravan, carried nothing but the clothes he wore and a few packs slung across the back of his equine companion. When the horsemen told him to hurry, he did, quickening his pace, and falling in amid the myriad travelers whose days had been compressed by the urgency the Megrenn outriders were conveying.

Cursory checks were made by the gate guards, but contraband was low on their priorities with the thought that Kadrin forces might have landed nearby. The wooden sailing ships had been harassing Megrenn forces of late, ferrying reinforcements about to head off assaults. It seemed to them that it had come time for them to land troops inside Megrenn and add a new chapter to the war.

The lone traveler took note of this, opinions of their state of mind and all, as he was ushered through the Kanem gates. He looked upon the walls, studied the armaments of the guards, and critiqued their search techniques as they interviewed caravaneers. He did this silently of course, for no impoverished wanderer ought to be a connoisseur of well-run armies. No old mule-drover ought to remember Kanem as a simple border outpost with wooden palisades and a dusty marketplace, a mere stopover on the journey from the Kadrin heartlands to Zorren and the foreign ports her ships sailed to.

But Rashan Solaran did.

The airship *Ironspar* had left him on the plains north of Kanem, on a lightly traveled road between one of the little hamlets of rural Megrenn and the main tradeway. There had been a father and son making a trip to Kanem. Rashan had slain them both, and taken their mule as a lark, deciding on the spot to sneak inside the city in disguise. It had been too long since he had been free to indulge such whims.

Now that he was inside, Rashan began looking around for weaknesses. The city was of modern design, built up with newfound Megrenn wealth. The walls bore Ghelkan wards, glowing uniformly in the aether, little tested by weather, and never having seen war. There were troops in plenty, though it was a mere curiosity to the demon; nothing without the means to attack him in the aether was of any true concern to him. While it was never a precise art, he singled out a few Sources that might be strong enough to indicate sorcerers about. None worried him; only the strongest were worth worrying about. To all appearances, he was clear of such impediments.

Satisfied that he had free rein, Rashan looked up at the fortified towers. He idly counted the men up on the walls as he did so, but he was looking for something else. He spotted it along the wall, built into a modest wooden frame with a slat roof above: an alarm bell. A malevolent grin spread across his face as he reached out with a simple telekinesis spell, and shoved the bell, reveling in the sound of chaos about to spread.

The ringing of the alarm bell, too sheltered and too heavy to have been sounded accidentally or by wind, signaled that the enemy had been sighted. The guards rushed the last of the road travelers they could manage to get within the city walls as they made ready to close and bar the gates. Rashan watched them work, noting that they were doing quite a remarkable job under the circumstances. Whether they were seasoned in combat or not, he could do with having soldiers like those of the Kanem garrison.

As Rashan stood admiring the fruits of his mischief, one of the many fresh arrivals to the city crossed too close to him. The man, stocky and with a wobbling gait, jostled into Rashan, shoulder to shoulder, sending the warlock stumbling a pace. With an annoyed pique, Rashan held him in place with magic. Allowing his illusory disguise to fade, he spun the man about like a wooden soldier in a child's playtime march, allowing the man to watch as Rashan drew Heavens Cry, and slid it through his belly.

Rashan left the man to spill his innards out onto the dirt streets of Kanem, still held upright, and strode over to the city gate. His action had not gone unnoticed. Dozens had watched in horror as he murdered a helpless traveler. A handful had taken note when an old man in careworn clothes faded, only to be replaced by a sword-wielding Kadrin sorcerer. Screams and pointing had eliminated everyone else from the ranks of the oblivious, and word of his presence sparked a general panic on the streets.

Rashan continued onward, unfazed. Kanem was a new city, with all the latest fortifications. The city gates opened inward, with a portcullis able to drop down behind. It was an excellent defense against rams, and made the gates nearly as impregnable as the outer walls. However …

With a metallic snap, and a clatter of chains, Rashan's magic broke the portcullis free, dropping it into place behind the city gate with no ready means for the garrison soldiers to lift it again. Satisfied that one of the two city gates was unusable for the time being, Rashan jogged across Kanem, herding terrified peasants in his path, to the southern gate. Having outpaced any coherent account of what he had done in the north, the guards at the southern gate had lowered the portcullis on their side themselves. Rashan had but to snap the chains to render that gate useless as well.

Rashan knew that any city, even one as new as Kanem, must have other means of egress. That was less of a concern than allowing a mass exodus, however.

Rashan attempted to count as he killed, but it was a hopeless task. He found five who opposed him with some form of sorcery, but the common soldiers died by the hundreds, the peasants by the thousands. When Rashan finally blasted down the southern city gate, he had found threescore and more Kadrins among those within Kanem. He gave them free rein of the city, and leave to take whatever they wished as they headed home to the Empire.

* * * * * * * *

"Well, it is not as if I wanted to let them escape!" Narsicann shouted. The Council was holding one of their few closed sessions in the aftermath of the escape of the prisoner Faolen Sarmon and his hostage, Anzik Fehr. "That thing wasn't human, whatever it was." The rest of the Council members kept to their assigned seats, but Narsicann stood up from his as he spoke, and Jinzan paced, clutching the Staff of Gehlen.

"What did this demon look like?" Jinzan asked, trying to focus his thoughts along practical paths. Denrik Zayne had spent most of an irritable day pondering the nighttime raid on Zorren and what it meant. It was the nearest most twinborn came to having nightmares. Little had he known upon Jinzan retiring for the night that Anzik had been found and lost in the span of that frantic chase.

"It looked young," Narsicann began.

Jinzan nodded slightly, knowing that Rashan Solaran appeared as little more than adolescent. Still, he suspected it to be Kyrus, as he had guessed during the night.

"Tall, light hair, dressed in black, though all the Kadrin sorcerers seem to favor the dark. I did not note the color of his eyes or whether he had a pretty smile. If you want such detail, you can go find him yourself. That is what you got *that* thing for, after all." Narsicann pointed to the staff.

"Not small, not white haired. Are you certain?" Jinzan asked. He had been worried, but was not sure which adversary was worse. The demon would oppose them, he knew that with absolute certainly; Rashan Solaran was the living embodiment of aggression, the avatar of war incarnate. Kyrus Hinterdale was a thinker. Somewhere within the boy, paired opposite him world for world, was the heart of a knight. He was not battle shy, but seemed to have more sense than to rush off blithely into the lair of his enemy.

"I could not judge exactly but he appeared tall enough. The hair was most certainly not white. Of course, he could have used any of a number of simple tricks to change his hair color if you saw him differently," Narsicann conceded.

"His Source. Did you get a look at his Source?"

"No," Narsicann admitted. "There was too much magic about. It was blinding the second I tried to shift my vision. I know the Kadrins have some strong sorcerers, but I cannot fathom there being another of such power that we did not know about."

"Explain from the beginning," Jinzan said. "Leave out no detail."

The Council sat and listened as Narsicann gave his account of the events of the previous night. The spymaster was no great storyteller, but his profession had given him a keen eye for detail, and a habit of remembering those details. His tale was dry and professorial. From his telling, you could almost imagine that he had not been there at all, merely reading from reports of those who were. By the end, they knew the name of the dead stripe-cat rider who had carried Narsicann to the scene of the escape, the size and estimated complement of the Kadrin airship, and had descriptions of the mystery sorcerer, the airship captain, and the two Kadrins who had absconded with Anzik, one of whom they already knew was Faolen Sarmon.

Jinzan could say little enough in open Council, but as he heard bits here and there, they clicked into place like the tumblers in a lock. It was most certainly Kyrus Hinterdale who had transferred into Zorren. Denrik's conversations with Tanner and Stalyart over the past few days had given him enough background to know that the airship captain was Juliana Archon, the same slip of a sorceress that Brannis Solaran had thrown himself atop to save in the mines of Raynesdark. That Faolen was telling the truth about his connections through Tellurak was obvious; between him and Kyrus, they had devised the escape plan, sending the airship once he was able to free himself from his cell. When Juliana Archon was pulled from her ship, she must have turned to Brannis in Tellurak— her counterpart had to be with him. Kyrus came almost immediately thereafter, by Narsicann's timeline.

Much of the information was merely interesting. He had no way to get to either Brannis or Soria Coinblade, but felt better for understanding how he had been bested. It was simpler than his own escape from Rellis Island had been, but it was better than having a mystery on his hands. The best news of all, though, was that Kyrus had arranged for Tanner to be his ambassador. In Kyrus's hands,

Anzik might become a commodity, but he could make a deal. Had it been Rashan Solaran, he knew it would merely be a matter of how much torment the demon would inflict on him before realizing that the boy's peril could not get him to betray Megrenn.

"Jinzan?" Kaynnyn asked.

Jinzan blinked a few times, realizing that he had been staring out the window as he pondered. "My apologies. My mind turns over the possibilities." It sounded like a poor excuse to his own ears, but he had his supporters.

"Just remember that sort of concentration when you fight Rashan Solaran," Narsicann said. "You are the only one who can stop him. I am sorry your son was taken, but better that you have the Staff of Gehlen. With that, there is hope that anything can be salvaged from this."

"Yes."

"Jinzan," Kaynnyn said to him, "we have troops ready to take Illard's Glen. It is a small force, and could well use a practiced hand at sacking the city." The old general smiled at him, her teeth as white as her close-cropped hair. Jinzan was supposed to be above such trivial feelings, but he felt his spirits buoyed by her support. She had inspired Megrenn armies in the Freedom War, and he finally felt what it was like to be the one needing morale. He found himself nodding without realizing he was doing so.

"Very well," he said. "I shall go there and lend what aid they need. The defenses were a shambles last I saw them; it should not take overmuch force to see the city toppled again. I will return afterward with no delay. We have seen that Zorren is vulnerable. I should be here to defend it as much as is feasible."

"I will see about contacting the Ghelkans for more of the speaking helms. A dedicated pair of them could leave you with one while its mate remains here with the Council," Narsicann suggested. The others voiced their consent, and by common accord, they considered the meeting adjourned. Councilor Feron Dar-Jak stayed behind to conduct another meeting with the Interior Ministry as the rest made their way to the exit.

As the two men passed through the doorway side by side, Varduk took Jinzan aside briefly.

"We will get Anzik back. Do not think that with all else that goes on, that he has been overlooked. There are just ... so many things that demand attention. Anzik ... well, he never did demand much attention, did he?"

* * * * * * *

Jinzan's head was filled with more maps than he ever would have believed possible when he was a boy. He knew the reefs of every major port in Tellurak, tradeways on land and sea. He knew the terrain of Koriah and its nations: the goblin and ogre homelands, Megrenn, Ghelk, and Kadrin. He had committed maps of Safschan, Narrack, Gar-Danel, Painu, and what little was known of Elok to memory. Despite few maps ever being made of the place, Jinzan even suspected he knew the layout of the secretive kingdom of Azzat, given that it was

Acardia in Tellurak.

All his knowledge was put to the test when rivers and mountains faded from view, and he saw nothing but aether as he transferred himself to the large cluster of humanoid Sources gathered outside Illard's Glen.

The startled troops nearly attacked him before he identified himself and took command. He allowed the major in charge of the smallish force of seven hundred to retain his functional command over his men's deployment, but Jinzan was the one who would order the attack. He had plans to make before he did so.

Surveying the city from a hill not so far from where he had camped with G'thk's goblins a season or so earlier, he found it to be rather better repaired than he expected. The walls looked good as new; the only sign of work having been done was the different color of the new stonework. On a hunch, Jinzan looked at the wall in the aether. He had seen it briefly as he arrived from his transference spell, but he had been concentrating on finding his troops, not on the city. The wall shone with aether. *How many sorcerers does Kadrin have that they can rebuild that whole wall, complete with wards, in so short a time?*

The assault force had not brought any cannons. They had traveled lightly, thinking to find the city still crippled from the goblin attack Jinzan had taken part in. Instead they found a city more formidable, perhaps, than the one that Jinzan and his goblin allies had sacked last autumn.

"No matter the wall. It slows us; it will not stop us," Jinzan called out for all his troops to hear. Whatever reservations he might have about what the improved fortifications boded, he could afford nothing but utter confidence in front of the common soldiers.

"Haru bedaessi leoki kwatuan gelora." With a supreme effort of aether, Jinzan tore loose a chunk of rock from the hillside the size of a small inn. His Source burned with the effort, but he hurled the boulder. The Megrenn swordsmen who watched in awe as the rock had slowly lifted airborne now cheered wildly as it smashed into the wall of Illard's Glen.

In the charge that followed, Jinzan hung back, neither out of reluctance nor fear, but simple age. The men all about him were young and fit. Jinzan conserved his breath for spellcasting, keeping up a swift walk, and not worrying about pacing his men.

Archers from the walls fired down at them. It seemed that their numbers were not great, but Kadrin had re-garrisoned the city at least. Shaken by the knowledge that incredible magic was at work—and not on their side in this battle—the defenders seemed demoralized. There were no catapults raining gravel, horseshoes, or the like down on them, nor were their spells being cast back at them from the city.

As the Megrenn swordsmen neared the breach in the wall, Kadrin spearmen rushed to fill the gap. There were also a few … creatures.

Jinzan had not seen their like before. Human in general shape, but thicker and stockier, perhaps twice as wide at the shoulder. He saw no armor on the creatures unless it covered them so completely as to resemble greyish-brown skin. Unlike their human counterparts, these few standing amid their defensive lines carried hammers. *The stone folk—the daruu. Kadrin must have bargained with them to have rebuilt their walls so fast. These may just be stoneworkers, not warriors.*

Jinzan's cautious optimism about the occupation of the stone folk mixed in with Illard's Glen's defenders was short lived. As soon as the two forces engaged, he saw that these were not simple laborers. While the Megrenn swordsmen batted aside spear-tips to press their Kadrin foes, the hammer-wielding daruu batted whole soldiers aside. Jinzan knew he needed to lend his aid at the wall. He quickened his pace, and ran through in his mind the spells he knew that he could use with his own men in close combat with his targets.

"Fetru oglo daxgak sevdu wenlu," Jinzan mumbled, having decided on one that he could aim finely enough for his purposes. Lightning forked from the Staff of Gehlen as Jinzan managed to use it to conduct much of the needed aether, sparing his Source the full force of channeling that much power.

The first daruu hit by the bolt was felled instantly, smoke rising from his flesh. As the lightning continued onward, raking across the line of defenders, human and daruu alike, it became clear that the stone folk lived up to the stories of their hardiness. Though every human struck by Jinzan's spell was slain, only the first of the daruu, hit by the very strongest of the blast, was fatally wounded. The others looked the worse for it but fought on. Fortunately the advantage of numbers gained by the loss of the Kadrin spearmen allowed Jinzan's swordmen to overwhelm the remaining daruu.

The defense was paltry beyond what had hastened to the stricken wall's defenses. Reinforcements from other parts of the city continued to arrive, but in no numbers to hope to drive back the Megrenn force.

The ground beneath Jinzan's feet began to rumble. He could sense the aether without having to switch his vision over to see it. His head snapped to one side, then the other, searching for any sign of Kadrin sorcerers. Instead, huddled behind a chunk of the boulder he had hurled to sunder the city wall, was another of the daruu. This one was unarmed, and was on his hands and knees, head bowed. Jinzan did not have to be able to hear the spell-words to know that it was likely the aethersmith who had carved the wall's new wards.

Before he had a chance to applaud himself for the deduction, Jinzan found that claws of rock were rising from the earth all about him. Jinzan rushed to draw aether to counter the threat as the tips of the claws grew taller than his head. They reached up and over him, began curling around and down to interlock, and crush the life from him with a stony embrace. Jinzan had not the time to form a proper spell; he kept his mind as calm as he could, and sent a blast of aether all about himself.

Rock rained down across the vicinity of the breached wall as the stone claws exploded. Kadrin and Megrenn alike dodged the debris or were injured by it—the rock did not care. The one who commanded the rock looked up from his spell, pale eyes glaring with a hatred that transcended language. Jinzan saw that a yellowish gem was embedded in the daruu's forehead. It had to mean something, but Jinzan knew next to nothing of the stone folk's culture. With neither word nor gesture, the daruu aethersmith sank into the ground as if it were quicksand.

I cannot let him escape me. The risk of suffering ambush attacks from beneath the ground worried Jinzan, for he knew not the limits of the stoneman's power. To head off any such worries, he repeated the spell from the hilltop, tearing loose a small section of Illard's Glen from the rest. Presumably, Jinzan thought, it held the stoneman as well.

Jinzan raised the chunk of earth as high as he might have been able to throw a small rock, then brought it back down ... hard. He drove the section of ground into ... more ground, as hard as he could. He waited a few moments, ignoring the rout that was going on all about him as he focused on making certain that his foe was no longer a threat. When those moments passed without incident, he sifted through the shattered rock until he found the daruu's body, telekinetically lifting it free, and laying it out on the street.

He looked from the daruu to the Staff of Gehlen in his hands. Whomever he had just killed was likely well respected among the stone folk. Though he knew little of their ways, their reverence of stonework was their hallmark. Unless the stone folk were fools, they would know that Megrenn had been responsible for the death of their workers—and their aethersmith.

Allies ... Kadrin has never before taken allies. It is likely that these were just hirelings, paid blood-price for a quick repair of the city wall. Now, though ... whether Kadrin gained an ally, we have likely made an enemy today.

Jinzan returned leadership of the invasion force to its former commander. Drawing once more on the vast power of the staff, he transferred himself back to Zorren.

* * * * * * * *

Jinzan's journey back was much easier. He had returned home via that same spell several times, and had begun to learn the look of Zorren in the aether. His sphere popped back into existence in a little-used courtyard off to the seaward side of the Council building. The double-doors leading inside were left open, unguarded. Jinzan clutched the Staff of Gehlen tightly in his hands, put on his guard by the unusual desertion of even so insignificant a post as a back garden.

Jinzan peeked through the open door before proceeding inside. He saw nothing unusual, except that he saw very little at all. There ought to have been people about. The hour was not yet so late, and there was no event in the city that would draw the functionaries from their posts—or the guards for that matter.

Jinzan looked about and found nothing. Looking into the aether, he saw folk gathered outside the front entrance of the building but nothing in sight within. He wandered the foyer, looking for signs of what might have driven everyone out of doors. He was nearly ready to go out, and ask among the crowd, when he noticed the first body.

Crumpled on the first landing of the stairway up to the first mezzanine level, one of the guards had been torn in half. Jinzan had just come from a sight far more horrific. Bodies were strewn about Illard's Glen like a child's dolls after a tantrum. The single dead guard knotted Jinzan's stomach.

I am the guardian of Megrenn, Jinzan thought as he approached the stairs, placing first one foot then another upon them as he crept upward. *So long as I wield this staff, whatever may threaten Zorren will ultimately fall to me. I cannot go out and show them that I am as fearful as they are.*

As he ascended the levels of the headquarters of Megrenn's High Council, Jinzan found more bodies. He began to imagine that a stripe-cat had gone berserk, so savage was the carnage. Men were not merely killed but lay in pieces, scattered down stairways and corridors. As he got higher, he began to hear something as well. As first, he thought he imagined it, but as he advanced, it became clear that it was singing. When he got to the landing halfway up to the top level where the Council chamber was, he paused to listen to a somewhat off-key tenor sing an old Megrenn folk song:

"Rains fall, marking the springtime,
Flowers bloom, colors so bright,
Fireflies herald the nighttime,
Dance in the meadows tonight."

Jinzan knew the words, listening to a few more familiar verses before gathering his nerve to finish his ascent. The stairs seemed farther apart than Jinzan remembered them, his feet heavier; he forced them to move.

The doors to the Council chamber were a shambles. One lay near the top of the landing, forcing Jinzan to step over it. The other hung askew, dangling by a single, battered hinge. The floor was slick with blood, and littered with the bodies of men. Jinzan recognized a few as members of the Interior Ministry.

Jinzan's breath caught in his throat as he saw into the Council chambers. It was a slaughterhouse, appearing as if everyone who had been meeting with Councilor Feron and the Interior Ministry had been butchered, along with a large contingent from the city guard and a number of regular infantry. Jinzan could only imagine the scene that had befallen in his absence.

As for Feron Dar-Jak, the interior minister was impaled through the chest, staked to the Council table by a wickedly serrated sword, which had cracked the heavy stone table. Seated right next to the dead Councilor, slouched across the arms of Jinzan's own chair at the Council table, and indolently popping grapes into his mouth from the Council's refreshments, was Rashan Solaran.

"About time you got here. I only know a few Megrenn songs. I was going to have to start breaking in to Acardian sea chanties if you had dallied much longer on those stairs," Rashan called out casually, choosing to speak in Kadrin now that he was done singing.

"You think yourself clever, demon?" Jinzan snapped, anger helping him find a voice that had thickened, and clogged his throat just a moment before.

"Not as clever as I thought myself before your cannons sank my airship when I arrived. I would not have expected them to aim so well at an airborne target," Rashan replied.

"We learn quickly. One airship over the city was enough for us. Two was brash and foolish, and now you will pay for that."

"Oh, there was another one here?" Rashan mused aloud. "Hmm, I suppose I must know which one *that* was. *Hah!* I shall certainly hear of it when I return without mine, then."

The demon seemed amused and completely at ease. Jinzan could barely convince his reluctant legs to move, but he forced himself to advance. Jinzan knew well the lessons of history. His forebears had parleyed with Rashan Solaran to their own destruction. He was not about to concede the initiative.

"Kanethio mandraxae." Jinzan thrust the Staff of Gehlen in Rashan's direction, aiming a blast of aether his way. The blast tore through the corpse of Councilor Feron and slammed into a shielding spell that protected the demon.

"Not a talker, I see," replied the nonplussed demon. Twisting about in the chair, Rashan Solaran got his feet beneath him, and hopped up onto the Council table, yanking Heavens Cry free of the table, further cracking it.

"Eket jimagu denpek wanapi." Jinzan called forth bolts of flame, but again his attack struck an impenetrable defense.

Rashan examined his sword, giving it a flick of the wrist to clean it of Feron's blood. He began stalking toward Jinzan with a hungry look in his eyes.

"Once I have that staff away from you, this little war will be at an end," Rashan promised.

Jinzan heard the lie, though, clear as if Rashan had said it aloud. It would merely turn into a one-sided slaughter once there was no one left to oppose the demon.

Jinzan needed no words to use telekinesis. He used that to his advantage.

"You know what you must do to—" Jinzan said as he lifted two of the heavy chairs from behind the demon, "—TAKE IT!"

The two chairs slammed together, crushing Rashan Solaran from both sides. But the attack caught the demon by not the slightest surprise. The chairs passed through him to strike one another as he stepped through them, briefly incorporeal.

"I really have been at this a lot longer than you have. I read up a bit about you. Excellent student but a bit of an irritable sort. First on Ranking Day your last two years at the Academy ... quite admirable. Fought in the little rebellion that freed Megrenn from Kadrin rule—with distinction, it seems. You are even twinborn. Please understand that I *hate* having to kill twinborn. It is a tragic waste, but *that* is how much I want that staff."

Jinzan swallowed. He had imagined the encounter differently. He thought he would be trading spells with the demon like a pair of bare-knuckle pit fighters. Instead he was finding his attacks ineffective, and the demon more interested in lecturing than fighting back.

"What are you doing, trying to frighten me into bargaining the staff for my life?" Jinzan demanded. His mind spun. He shook his thoughts, angrily demanding an answer to how he could hurt the demon, but no answer came readily to mind.

"No. Once I realized your limitations, I knew I was in no real danger from you. You ought to have bargained with more dragons. *Those* are dangerous. They have a draw like that staff gives you, but they know what to do with it. Blah, blah, blah, spell comes out. It is like fighting an Academy student. You do not even see your folly; because you know I am a demon, you are not watching the aether as you attack me."

Jinzan frowned. *What am I missing?* He switched to aether-vision. He could locate the demon by the shielding spell around him and the rune-forged sword in his hand. The demon himself was a ghost in the aether.

"Fetru oglo daxgak sevdu wenlu." Jinzan pointed the Staff of Gehlen at Rashan, striking him with the same lightning spell that he had just used in Illard's Glen. Just before he finished his spell, though, he noticed a change in the shielding spell.

Jinzan snapped his eyes back into the light. He glared at Rashan, incredulous.

"You changed your shield spell!"

"Blah, blah, warlock recognizes your spell, blah, blah, shield is ready when you finish. Try your little telekinesis tricks all you like, but I do not see how you can keep pace with me."

"I will find a way, you monster!" Jinzan shouted, blustering to keep despair from engulfing him.

"People call me that, but really, what have I done but wage war?" Rashan asked. "I enjoy my work, but so does many a general. I may be guilty of hubris, I admit, but nothing worse."

"Kidnapping children is nothing worse to you?" Jinzan screamed, finally striking a telling blow when the demon's eyes widened in surprise.

"I did what?"

"You would have me believe that you know nothing of my son's kidnapping by your pet Acardian?" Jinzan demanded.

"Ahh, I think I begin to see now. You are accusing me of Brannis's crimes? Still, I suppose I gave him leave to do as he liked, so I bear some amount of blame. I think I was enjoying this more when I was firmly on the moral high ground, fighting off an aggressor in defense of my homeland." Rashan brandished Heavens Cry, and leapt toward Jinzan.

Jinzan was caught off guard by the demonic madman's abrupt shift of mood. He stumbled back, tentative on the slick footing of the bloody floor. He drew frantically, piling aether into his own shielding spell. Heavens Cry was turned aside, but the demon was unrelenting.

I have to get away somehow, Jinzan realized. *I cannot win this day. I am no match head-on against Rashan Solaran.*

Jinzan tried to use the Staff of Gehlen as a weapon, and noticed quickly that the demon was mindful of damaging it. Twice Jinzan moved to block slashing strikes, only to have Rashan pull his attack at the last moment. Still, Jinzan was no young man, and he would tire soon from the exertion of the combat, whereas the demon could conceivably keep up his assault indefinitely. He needed to buy himself the time to make his escape.

"At least I care enough about my son that I will seek to save him," Jinzan said, beginning to grow short of breath.

"What is that supposed to mean?" Rashan asked, not pausing in his assault.

Curse him, Jinzan swore, *he is too focused.*

"If you return to Kadris in time, you may just find out," Jinzan answered, trying to give as cryptic an answer as he might, while still leaving enough to pique the demon's curiosity. This time, it worked. Rashan cocked his head to the side, looking puzzled.

"What are you going on about?" the demon asked.

Jinzan had little experience with silent casting of battle spells. It was, by common agreement of every sorcerer he had studied under, quite a bad idea. However, since he had never studied with anyone who had defeated a demon or a warlock, let alone both in one body, he was inclined to venture outside the realm of commonly agreed upon teachings.

A blast of aether caught Rashan in the chest, launching the diminutive demon across the length of the Council chamber to slam heavily against the far wall.

"See you in Kadris!" Jinzan shouted. He took the time only for that one parting barb before beginning his next spell, drawing for all he was worth, and with all the might the Staff of Gehlen lent him. *"Doxlo intuvae menep gahalixviu junumar tequalix ferendak uzganmanni dekdardon vesvata eho."*

A sphere of aether formed around him. Jinzan had no intention of heading into the heart of the Kadrin Empire, but he needed something to convince the demon to leave Zorren once he was no longer there to at least put up a token defense. All Jinzan could do, as he popped into the aether, was hope that he had given enough cause for Rashan Solaran to worry.

Chapter 40 - Noble Goals

Wind rustled the leaves of the ash and maple trees, yellow, orange, and red fluttering like uncounted thousands of tiny pennants. Booted and slippered feet walked side by side along well-worn footpaths that wended their way through Darrow Park. It was not along their way, but afforded Brannis and Soria some peace and a tranquil setting to talk.

"It may be 'cold,' Brannis, but it makes sense. If this girl isn't Celia, and you don't fall for their trick, then the conspirators have no reason to harm her. If you do try to help her, Celia or not, then she is valuable to them," Soria reasoned. She was dressed against the cold, in a long fur coat that looked either brown or black depending which way the light caught it.

"And if she is Celia, and we do nothing?" Brannis asked.

"Then she fends for herself. If she is Celia, she has it in her to do whatever it takes to get by," Soria replied.

"Would it make you happy if she got herself killed because you left her to her good fortune?" Brannis rather suspected it would, but he wanted to hear it from her.

"Maybe. Maybe not. I don't see why I ought to stick my head in the noose for her, though."

"You just hate that everyone in Kadrin seems to be pushing her and Kyrus together. With you married off now, it had to be someone, you know. Kyrus cannot stay a bachelor forever, not with sorcerous blood like that. The Inner Circle would never stand for it."

"You could have picked someone who was not a lying, murdering ... manipulative ..." Soria stopped her litany of derogatory adjectives when she noticed Brannis smiling.

"Seems to be the type of girl who is drawn to me," he commented, grinning.

Soria's jaw clenched, her lips pursed tight—she looked ready to hit him for a moment. She glanced at Brannis in his armor, and he found himself thankful that he was rather well protected from physical chastisement.

Soria took hold of his arm for the rest of their walk through Darrow Park, a possessive gesture to be certain. Brannis shook his head when she was not looking his way. It was as if they were schoolchildren again, and she was waiting to hear if they were to be betrothed. Such bald jealously was unbecoming, but given her recent brush with death—Juliana's at least—he could understand her need to cling to him.

When they arrived at Abbiley's studio home, Brannis hesitated. The two of them stood at the door, Brannis staring dumbly at it, unable to move, with Soria still clutching his arm. *It is just a door. She is just a girl. This is nothing to be nervous about.* Brannis managed to knock.

They waited again, hearing voices from inside, then footsteps.

"Hullo, what have we here?" a man greeted them as the door opened. He was dressed in a gentleman's manner, with an embroidered red doublet and black hose, with a gold chain about his neck, bearing a heraldry Brannis did not recognize. He was not certain by his face, but between Kyrus's half-remembered knowledge of the man and Soria's report, he had to be Tomas Harwick.

"Hello, might we speak with Abbiley Tillman?" Brannis managed to ask. He worried that the awkward pause before speaking to the man was not mistaken for rudeness.

"Of course, of course," Tomas assured him. "Abby, dearest, you simply must come here, and meet your guests. You will see why, I promise," he called across the studio. There was a sound of something wooden being set down. A moment later, Abbiley appeared at the door.

A gust of memory extinguished Brannis's thoughts, leaving him mute and blank faced while he sought to relight the wick. Luckily Abbiley seemed similarly afflicted.

"My good sir, I mean no rudeness, but you must come inside, and see this," Tomas said, then ushered Brannis and Soria into the studio before either Brannis or Abbiley recovered their power of speech.

And Brannis saw it. Propped on Abbiley's easel was … him. Mirrors had occasionally shown him a better resemblance but just barely. He was dressed in armor, plainer than Liead's that he wore, but similar in style to what he had worn upon his first adventure with Rashan, when they had met in Kelvie Forest. He was sitting on a log in the middle of a woodland scene, resting one hand on the pommel of Massacre—the serrated blade of Heavens Cry and the whimsical sculpted dragon hilt-and-crossguard and all. In his other hand, upraised, he held a ball of flame. He did not think it was Kyrus in the picture, but himself. Soria and Juliana swore to the resemblance, but Brannis knew his own face and Kyrus's; more importantly, he knew them apart from one another.

"I say, it is uncanny, do you not agree?" Tomas asked.

"Aye, it is," Abbiley managed to reply. She sounded just as Kyrus's memory would have her, though perhaps a bit more confused.

"Indeed," Brannis agreed. He looked to Soria, whose eyes were wide, staring at the nearly finished painting.

"You had said this was a painting of Kyrus Hinterdale someone commissioned," the gentleman said. "It certainly looked enough like the fellow I saw at trial that I would never have spoken a word against it, but it is strikingly like this fine gentleman before us. Oh, but pardon me, my manners … My name is Tomas Harwick."

"Sir Erund Hinterdale. This is my lady, Soria," Brannis presented Soria, preferring to leave their exact relationship vague.

"Oh, I was not aware of any Hinterdales in the knighthood," Tomas commented.

"My husband's title was bestowed in Khesh, by Lord Khazen. He uses the Acardian term to prevent having to explain the intricacies of the Kheshi Order of Fallen Stars to everyone he meets," Soria explained, allowing her Kheshi accent to come through clearly in her Acardian.

"Oh, you have traveled?" Abbiley asked, displaying her curiosity about the wider world. It was rather unlike Celia, Brannis thought, but he could still not deny the resemblance, nor the inexplicable ability to paint a picture of him.

"To come here, yes. I was raised in northern Khesh by Acardian parents. Sir Erund grew up in Marker's Point as a merchant's son, and lived for a time in Khesh, where we met," Soria said. Brannis wondered how much of that she had prepared ahead of time, and how much she was making up as she went.

"This is simply fascinating. I must admit that I had a bet going with my father. I am losing a thousand eckles for someone showing up looking like this painting. You simply must join us for dinner this evening. My father, Lord Harwick, would be equally interested to meet you, I am sure. It is one of his 'causes,' to see the Hinterdale family compensated for the false claims of witchcraft, and see Kyrus Hinterdale's name cleared. His kidnapping by pirates made the thing a right mess, but seeing as how you must be some sort of relation, I am sure he would want to speak with you as well."

"That—"

"That would be wonderful," Soria cut Brannis off before he could respond. "We shall give you back the remains of your day, then, and continue making acquaintances this evening."

"Yes, yes. If you have any troubles finding Harwick Manor, just hire a carriage, and it will be taken care of," Tomas said.

"It was very nice to meet you, Sir Erund," Abbiley said.

Brannis felt Soria's grip on his arm tighten as she spoke.

"Until tonight, then," Brannis concurred.

* * * * * * *

"Three kings," Tanner announced, spreading his cards face up in front of him, drawing groans from the crewmen he played against as he gathered a pile of coins to add to his own.

Someone scooped up the discarded Talis cards, and began to shuffle them when the tenor down in the hold changed. The sailors began to straighten up, laughs were cut short, eyes turned their attention toward the approaching Captain Zayne.

"At ease, men," Captain Zayne called out ahead of him. "Mr. Tanner, come with me. We have things to discuss."

Tanner scraped his coins into a pouch, and hung it about his neck, tucking it safely inside his tunic. *Maybe with luck, he is ready to surrender*, Tanner thought. *These boys of his don't have the coin to keep these games interesting.*

He followed Captain Zayne back to his cabin, where the twinborn pirate closed the door, leaving just the two of them to converse privately.

"So, had enough yet? I can let Kyrus know straightaway," Tanner offered.

"Stow it, Mr. Tanner," Captain Zayne said. "You dance a bit close to the railings as it is. If you had any idea how many times I considered having you thrown to the sharks, you would not sleep nights."

"'No' would have been fine," Tanner said, offering a lopsided grin in exchange for the threat.

"How well do you know Kyrus Hinterdale, Mr. Tanner?" Captain Zayne asked.

"Barely at all, personally. Heard stories about him for years, though, from Soria. Well, those stories were about Brannis, but, you know, spuds 'n' potatoes," Tanner said with a shrug.

"Would it surprise you to know that he is now in the business of kidnapping children?" Captain Zayne pressed.

Tanner was not sure he liked how the conversation was going. It sounded like he was having his boots polished. He wondered if Captain Zayne was going to try some sort of bribe.

"Hey, I'm a coinblade. I'm a hard guy to surprise with the sticky, red side of human nature. I haven't seen it all, but I've seen most of it, ya know?"

"Kidnapping *my* child, my children ... sometimes this twinborn thing confuses even me," Zayne said, shaking his head as he blew out a sigh that spoke to his frustration. "I may sound like the thieving preacher for saying so, but you are working with monsters, Mr. Tanner. Mr. Hinterdale possibly only figuratively so, but Rashan Solaran is inhuman of mind and body."

"Yup," Tanner agreed.

"'Yup' what?" Captain Zayne pressed Tanner to clarify.

"You sound like the thieving preacher. Far as I can tell, you went out of your way to get your reputation, Captain Scourge of the Katamic. Can't rightly complain when someone ignores all the nice bits of civilized life, and does a better job at it than you," Tanner explained. He saw a dangerous look come over Denrik Zayne's eyes. Tanner held his arms wide in a universal gesture of helpless innocence. "Hey, who am I to judge? I just say what I'm seeing; can't claim I'm any better, I just don't complain about it."

"What have you got to complain about ?" Zayne asked. "You laze about my ship, drinking rum, and keeping my men gambling at cards when they should be working. In Veydrus, you are Kyrus's lapdog, cozy and safe from the war."

"Hey, boats are great; they get you places. They're no place to *live*, though."

"Hah! And here I thought you might make a fair pirate, if you lifted a finger to work," Zayne scoffed.

"No, thanks. I could buy this ship. I don't need to steal shipments of wine and spices, and divvy it eighty ways to try to make my fortune."

"I think you underestimate what a ship costs, Mr. Tanner," Captain Zayne said with a look Tanner found patronizing.

"Hundred fifty, two hundred trade bars?" Tanner guessed.

Captain Zayne frowned, and said nothing for a breath. "No. Not quite that much."

"Really, if you aren't ready to surrender, what did you want to talk to me about?" Tanner asked, tiring of trading barbs with Denrik Zayne. "You need me to get some message to Kyrus or not?"

"Not a surrender, but an offer. A ... trade. Possibly a peace."

"What ya offering?"

"I will give him the Staff of Gehlen ... in return for the head of Rashan Solaran," Captain Zayne said.

"Oh, is that all?"

"No. I want my son back, too."

* * * * * * *

The coin flipped end over end, making its way across the backs of Wendell's fingers. Jadon had his hands up on the common-room table as he leaned well across to watch intently. Twice already he had watched the coin disappear, unable to figure out where it had gone. The Acardian five-eckle that Wendell was using reached his index finger, and tumbled over between his finger and thumb. He turned his hand over, and there was nothing there.

"How?" Jadon asked, using Acardian.

It was a good sign as far as Wendell was concerned. Jadon climbed up onto the table, and took Wendell's hand in two of his own, turning it over, prying the fingers apart to check between them. Wendell allowed the boy to conduct his search. Showing interest in Tellurak was what he really needed, much more so than he needed him to find the coin. He almost felt guilty deceiving the boy, but if using magic to hide the coin in both the light and the aether was what it took to pique his curiosity, it was worth suffering a bit of guilt over.

Heavy footsteps from the upper floors heralded the waking of Zellisan. The big man had trouble recovering from the wakeful night, and Wendell had preferred to wait for him to awaken rather than take Jadon out by himself to perform.

"You still here? Thought you would have gone off, and left me the boy, or at least gone to do your tricks, and take him with you. I think he's past the point of running off, by now," Zellisan said once he reached the common room. His greasy black beard and hair looked just as slovenly as ever, his recent awakening detracting little from his typically disreputable appearance.

"I thought this morning I might make an exception," Wendell said. He drew Jadon's attention to his other hand, producing the coin, and handing it to the boy, prompting a whole new examination, this time directed at the mischievous currency.

"Well, under the circumstances, I can understand that," Zell said. "You're welcome."

Wendell smiled at Zellisan's presumption.

"Well, yes, there is that. But more than that, I think your assignment has been completed. I have Jadon, safe and recovering, and we are in the middle of Takalia. No place is perfect but Takalia is a fair sight safer than most lands. Jadon even has a bit of a Source in him, so he will be able to learn real magic, not just the paltry tricks I can manage. In a year or two, he might not even need me to defend him."

"Hey now," Zell said. "Remember, I was the one passing those messages back and forth. I know that this is far from over. You have one of the most dangerous men in Tellurak riled, and likely wondering how he can track you down. I don't think I'm done protecting you by a half measure."

"I might need a lot less protection if we could just hide. You stand out a bit, my friend," Wendell argued.

"Yeah, that whole standing on street corners and in marketplaces and making magic birds appear ... really bad habit of mine. Draws a lot of attention," Zellisan countered.

Wendell wondered if his own sarcasm was rubbing off. "I do not *have* to perform, you know."

"I'm not sure about that. It seems to be in your blood. I have coin enough to hide us all somewhere out of the way. You don't need to perform to eat."

"I need to wake him up," Wendell said.

"And when it winds up with hired blades sniffing around for us on Denrik Zayne's coin, I'll be here to do something about it."

* * * * * * * *

After trying to find the manor first by Brannis's memories of what Kyrus knew of Scar Harbor, then of Soria's best guess as to where it ought to have been, the two eventually relented, and took a carriage to the gates of the small manor home where Tomas Harwick abided with his father, at least while Lord Harwick was staying in the city. Despite Tomas's promise to cover the expense of their transport, Sir Erund and Mrs. Soria Hinterdale were world travelers, and not without the means of affording their own conveyance. There was a way of acquitting oneself in society that Soria knew well: Tomas making the offer was good form; accepting it would have been poor form, as would either party mentioning the matter again.

Tomas and Abbiley greeted them at the door. Brannis felt odd being in her presence. It was like spying on Celia without her knowing. Abbiley gave him queer looks, but he suspected the matter of the painting was at issue; she thought he looked like Kyrus. He got no sense that she realized who Soria was, and if Celia was lurking just behind those innocent blue eyes, Juliana's twin ought to have looked nearly as familiar as Brannis.

"Dinner will be set out shortly. My father will be down shortly thereafter. I believe my butler is helping him preen," Tomas joked. "He can be quite vain, our Lord Harwick."

"Tomas!" Abbiley chided, smiling despite her tone. "Lord Harwick isn't even here to defend himself. You should at least give your father the courtesy of poking your fun at him when he is here."

Brannis found himself smiling as well, until he caught Soria's gaze, frowning slightly at him. He smoothed his features once more into dignified politeness.

"He seemed quite eager to meet you. Once my father puts his mind in a certain frame, it consumes him. You have the fortune of being named Hinterdale at a time when my father is quite interested in the Hinterdale name. The whole 'witch trial' business reflected poorly on the kingdom, and he is rather intent on patching up the holes it left."

"Well, I am eager to meet him as well," Brannis said in reply. He did well to keep his apprehension in check. He and Soria were both unarmored, and she unarmed. As a knight, it was socially acceptable for him to be armed with Avalanche even at a polite dinner. Depending on the scope of the conspiracy, he hoped that it would be enough. More than that, he hoped it would not be needed at all.

Servants brought out a course of soups for them to occupy themselves as they awaited the lord. Wine was poured for them as well, a Takalish vintage some twenty years old. Brannis found himself trying to piece together the contents of the soup and the origins of the wine, and make some prejudgment of the lord, find some small thing he could deduce that could be of use. He took a calming breath. He resolved to wait, and observe with a clear mind instead.

Lord Dunston Harwick arrived just before the first course of dinner. He was older than Brannis had expected by Tomas's age, which he had guessed at perhaps thirty summers—years, he reminded himself. The lord's hair was gone to grey nearly completely, with a few black strands to be seen among them. His face was wrinkled and sagged, but there was something too familiar about it to dismiss out of hand—something more than the rough resemblance to his son.

"Tomas, you were not wrong," Lord Harwick bellowed jovially. "Sir Erund here is the very image of Miss Abbiley's painting. It would almost seem as if the painting had called him to her."

"Father, allow me to introduce Sir Erund Hinterdale and his wife, Lady Soria," Tomas said.

Soria extended her hand, which Lord Harwick took delicately in his own, but did not make the old-fashioned gesture of kissing it. Brannis offered his own, and shook the lord's hand, feeling a grip that he suspected had never been crushing, even in the lord's younger years. He met Lord Harwick's gaze straight on as he did so, looking for some spark, some flinch, some sign of recognition, but found nothing.

Introductions passed, they took their seats for dinner. After some tiny meat pastries, they were served a meal of roasted duck in a sauce made with Kheshi spices. The servants refilled their wines, prompting Lord Harwick to rise from his seat.

"I would like to propose a toast," he called out. Everyone else rose and took up their own glasses. "As they said in ancient Garnevia, 'Play along, and we shall speak later.'"

The latter was not Garnevian at all, Brannis knew, unless the ancient Garnevians spoke Kadrin. *Well, the conspiracy is real*, Brannis realized. *I hate being right at times.*

"Hear, hear," all mumbled in rough unison. Brannis exchanged a quick look with his "wife," and her expression told him that she had been paying attention as well. *Drat. I should have been looking for a reaction from Abbiley, not Soria.*

Brannis fumed at himself a moment, careful to keep any hint of his turbulent thoughts out of his expression as the conversation turned to pleasantries and amusing stories—the sort of things that people talked about when they were not part of inter-world power struggles. Brannis played along, as he had been told to do, but found himself fidgeting at the table as the meal wore on.

At long last, after four courses and a dessert of pumpkin pie, the meal was called to a close.

"Tomas, perhaps tonight would be a nice night for a carriage ride. There is a clear sky, and I know how Miss Abbiley loves stargazing. It will allow me to have some time to interview our guests," Lord Harwick said.

"Father ... always working," Tomas mused with a slow shake of his head. Still, the younger Harwick took his father's advice, and departed with Abbiley.

"We can speak in my study," Lord Harwick said to Brannis and Soria once Tomas and Abbiley were beyond hearing. With no further explanation, Lord Harwick led them upstairs.

Up one flight and down a short hallway, Lord Harwick opened a door. Soria, who had been walking with her arm twined with Brannis's, pulled up short. Lord Harwick, more observant that one might have expected of a man of advancing years, took note.

"Yes, it is warded. I can explain inside."

Soria glanced up at Brannis, her look telling him to be on guard ... or that she was suspicious ... possibly that they were making a mistake—Brannis had never quite gotten the hang of all the things he was supposed to be able to infer from her various looks. He shrugged in reply, too far committed to turn back, even if they might be walking into a trap. He followed Lord Harwick into the study.

"Tomas does no real work, so the study in his home is mainly for my use when I visit. Close the door, and we might converse without minding our voices," Lord Harwick instructed Brannis, who complied.

Lord Harwick seated himself behind the dark-stained oak desk, and rummaged in the drawers as Brannis and Soria found chairs to pull up across from him. Lord Harwick pulled out a pipe, and some pipeweed; it lit with no need for tinder, to the surprise of neither twinborn. The lord also pulled out three small glasses and a crystal decanter filled with an amber liquid.

"I never quite expected this day would come, Brannis," Lord Harwick said in Kadrin, not looking Brannis's way as he poured them all drinks. He slid two across the desk, and Brannis and Soria took one apiece, neither drinking as they waited for the little drama Lord Harwick was playing out. "I went to quite a bit of trouble getting you here, playing both sides, holding the knife by the blade." He looked up at Brannis, pipe clamped in his mouth, drink in hand, and smiled.

"Caladris!" Brannis exclaimed. He had seen that same expression on his uncle's face, looking twenty summers younger than Lord Harwick, and thicker of both face and gut than the somewhat stout lord.

"You?" Soria asked.

"Yes, me," Harwick replied. "And *you* ..." He took the pipe from his mouth, and pointed the stem at Brannis's chest. "... really are Brannis Solaran. Fit me for a saddle if that boy Kyrus is not something unnatural!"

"Wait, so *you* are behind this conspiracy? To what end?" Brannis demanded.

"Conspiracy? Hah! Pick one!" Harwick scoffed. "Brannis, I have petty schemes, wrapped around minor plots, disguising treasons. Where would you like me to start?"

"Can you tell him whether his peasant girl here is Celia or not? He's been insufferable about it of late," Soria requested.

Brannis turned to give her a scowl, but saw such an earnest plea in her eyes that he nodded his agreement, and waited for his uncle to answer her.

"Not. There are a few twists around that particular mystery, but before you blame me for it, I must tell you it was the warlock's idea. He is wary of Kyrus, Brannis. The boy is raw as pheasant on the wing, but no one has seen power like that, bottled up in just one body. He figured if Kyrus has a sweetheart, he'd make a twinborn of her, and keep the Kadrin version close when you were about."

"But there were so many little details, things I never told him," Brannis said. "All I gave him that he could have used was her name and likeness. How did he get Celia that information?"

"Well, *that*, I am afraid, I must confess to. A name was all I needed, the likeness was just what Rashan needed to pick a girl out to match. The fact that Celia looked so much like her was good fortune for Rashan, but those tiny little flames you keep stamping on that you have for Celia ... that, I believe, was Kyrus's influence on you."

"Too convenient," Soria said, crossing her arms and frowning.

"Lucky, perhaps, but had Abbiley and Celia not shared a close enough resemblance as to perhaps be explained by those vain cosmetic magics you ladies fancy—and I must heartily voice my support of them, Acardia could use their like—well, Rashan would have found someone else," Harwick explained.

"Did she know?" Brannis asked. It was his turn to show anger. Kyrus had promised to protect her. Had she been playing him for the fool?

"Abbiley, no. I planted images in her mind that led her to paint that portrait of you. Celia, yes," Lord Harwick said, somberly at the last. He knew that he might be condemning Celia, Brannis realized. He turned to see Soria's reaction. She stared ahead, not showing a response. "We could have tried planting simple ideas in her mind, like I did with Abbiley, but Celia is a sorceress; strong as I am, she still might have slipped free of the false memories. Instead we took her into our confidence, and trusted that if she could fool Jinzan Fehr when she was captured, she could keep up the act with you as well."

"Do I have to wake Kyrus up to keep you from killing her?" Brannis asked Soria.

"You cannot kill her, Juliana," Harwick said, choosing to call her by the name he had long known her. "Rashan can know nothing of this. He must believe that Celia is a deterrent to violence near him. If he does not think that you would be hesitant to use strong magics near her, he will look to some other method to leash you. Valuable as you are, he is likely to find a way to kill you, or have you killed, if he thinks you are a threat. There is a terrifying madness that lies just beneath that veneer of control."

"Wait, I thought you were Rashan's indispensible man, his most trusted ally?" Soria asked, bewildered. She took a swig of the brandy in her glass, blinking momentarily as the drink was stronger than she expected.

"He has to believe that. We lost three of our strongest sorcerers in a fit of his rage. The rest of us he trusts like boys outside the virgin cloister. He watched us, waiting for any of the others who had worked closely with Gravis and Maruk to slip, and betray themselves. I made myself valuable enough that I was able to take over that watch."

"You mentioned Gravis and my father; what of Stalia Gardarus?" Brannis asked, picking up on the omission.

"She was aware but not nearly so guilty as they. He killed her as an example, since otherwise House Gardarus might have gotten ideas that they were above Solaran and Archon. The heart of the emperor conspiracy were Gravis, Maruk, Dolvaen, and myself," Harwick explained.

"But why? Why are you going to all this trouble? If everyone opposed Rashan, why not all unite against him?" Soria asked.

"They were scared," Brannis said.

Lord Harwick closed his eyes and sighed. He nodded his admission as he took a drink from his own glass.

"Dolvaen is resourceful. He has stayed out of trouble with Rashan despite openly opposing him *and* secretly working against him. It is the openness that has fooled Rashan thus far. The warlock is devilishly clever, but admitting his opposition has made Dolvaen a known threat, a mere political adversary. I think Rashan even admires him, after a fashion—the principled stand against his stewardship and the purity of the imperial line ... all quite admirable."

"But then, what about the murders?" Brannis said. "Celia told me you arranged them, had her carry them out."

"That was for your benefit, I am afraid. Dolvaen's support was growing, threatening to expand beyond the point where it could be hidden."

"How does that benefit *me?*" Brannis asked.

"Kyrus was going to be forced to take sides. There could not be an open rebellion in Kadris with you remaining neutral. If you sided with Rashan, then Dolvaen's faction would have been crushed. If you sided with Dolvaen, you would have been pitted against Rashan directly. Strong as you are, I do not think that would bode well for you, or for our chances of eventually putting the fire to that demon."

"So what now?" Soria asked.

"We wait for the time to be right. Brannis, you must make sure Kyrus takes no overt interest in battle magic or anything else that makes you a more immediate concern for Rashan. He likes you, values you, but at the same time, one misstep might be all it takes for him to decide you are no longer worth the risk of keeping alive. If luck plays into our hands, we might secure the Staff of Gehlen, which might give Kyrus enough of an advantage to risk a confrontation, but I think it may be more prudent to slowly master magic until your control matches your Source."

"So in the meantime, we just do—"

"One moment," Harwick interrupted. His eyes stared past them with heavy lids, unblinking. Brannis and Soria waited, recognizing that far-off look as either aether-vision, or more likely attention paid to Veydrus. "You two should awaken in Kadris. We can continue our discussion another time."

Chapter 41 - A Wagon's Burden

A steady wooden rumble and the clop of hooves were the only sounds for hours at a time as a lonely wagon made its way across the countryside. Its driver, an elderly Kadrin man with stooped shoulders and a shriveled face, guided it along the trade road toward the city of Kadris. It was wartime, so soldiers were wont to stop stray merchants to check for smugglers and spies. The old wagon driver had been stopped thrice thus far, climbing down from his seat, throwing back the blankets that covered his cargo, and waiting as the soldiers came to look. Each time, the Kadrin soldiers had hurried him along on his way, wanting nothing further to do with him.

His journey was nearly at an end, he saw. The great towers of Kadris could be seen in the distance, peeking over the low rolls of the uneven landscape. To his left, as he drove, lay Podawei Wood. A moment's dark whimsy took hold of the driver, and he wondered if the old stories were true about there being spirits deep within the ancient forest. He could leave the wagon, and disappear deep into Podawei, never to be seen by men again. The driver shook his head, dismissing such folly; the horse had never so much as slowed during his musing. No, he preferred to accept his fate, and meet it with some dignity.

Upon his arrival at the outskirts of Kadris, he was stopped once more. The guards at the city limits were of more use than the soldiers he had encountered on the roads. They directed him to the Imperial Palace, where Warlock Rashan Solaran had recently returned. Cargo covered once more, the driver climbed up onto the seat of his wagon, and took the reins in shaking hands. He drove his little wagon across Kadris as the sun set, darkening the streets and his fears. Each step of his horse's gait was like a grain of sand falling through an hourglass, counting the time until he reached the palace, and his doom.

* * * * * * *

Kyrus rubbed the sleep from his eyes as he strode down the palace hallways. He had yet to ascertain the reason for Caladris's warning, but noted that there was more activity than there ought to have been in the palace. Certainly the servants worked round the clock at small tasks, cleaning and preparing while the common areas of the palace were deserted, but nothing on the scale he was seeing.

"You there." He stopped one of the porters who was passing him in the opposite direction. "What is this ruckus about?"

"Out in the courtyard, your lordship," the man replied, botching Kyrus's title in his haste to be free of the conversation. The porter continued on past Kyrus, disappearing down a side hallway.

Kyrus's mind began puzzling as he walked. There were too many possibilities to even venture a guess. The *Daggerstrike* had been landed in the gardens behind the palace; the porter might have confused which outdoor venue from whence the disturbance originated. It could also have had something to do with their new charge, Anzik Fehr. Kyrus had heard about the trouble the boy had been in Zorren, and wondered if perhaps he was now causing mischief in Kadris on a scale that would warrant such frenzied activity. Kyrus's feet kept moving as he thought, guiding him toward his answer, whether he could work it out before he got there or not.

"Brannis!"

The shout came from behind him. He turned to see Celia hastening to catch up with him. A bile rose in Kyrus's throat as the thought of her betrayal came foremost to his mind. Tempting as it was to confront her about her role in impersonating Abbiley as a twinborn, he knew he had to follow Caladris's advice. *You are a fine actress, Celia, but it is your turn to play the fool.*

"Celia! Are you all right?" Kyrus called back, pausing to wait for her. The primitive parts of Kyrus warred within him, one side continuing the belief that she was either Abbiley or at least close enough that it did not matter; the other side screamed for him to slay her where she stood for toying with his feelings.

"Yes, but what is going on here?" Celia reached him, huffing for breath.

"Something outside in the courtyard," Kyrus replied.

* * * * * * * *

A crowd had gathered, and not the usual rabble that gawked at every little thing of interest. Much of the palace staff had gathered outside in the middle of the night. Courtiers that stayed near the palace were present, and Kyrus saw many of the Empire's sorcerers in attendance as well. A few had cast balls of light in the air overhead, pushing back the gloom of night, but also casting the crowd in eerie pallor of washed-out light and harsh shadow.

Kyrus pushed his way through. Though he lacked the size to force folk out of his way, the press of bodies parted before him when they realized who was trying to get by. Celia had ventured down to the courtyard with him, taking him by the arm, but he left her behind at the outskirts of the throng.

A horse-drawn wagon was at the center of the mass of gawkers. Rashan was standing in the back of it, looking downward, the demon's expression revealing nothing of his thoughts. He saw Juliana nearby as well; she had apparently had a quicker time of it than Kyrus had of getting down to investigate. She was pressed against Caladris, not looking at Kyrus as he approached, her face buried against his shoulder. Caladris said something to her, and she turned to see Kyrus.

"Oh, Brannis," she sobbed, releasing Caladris, and rushing over to Kyrus. "I'm sorry. I'm so sorry. It's all my fault. If I hadn't teased him and shown him up, he would never have gone."

"Juliana, what's wrong? What happened?" Kyrus asked, gathering her in his arms, and pulling her close, careless of who saw them together, even with Rashan looming.

"Iridan," she said simply, turning her head to the wagon.

Kyrus's blood froze in his chest. He eased himself away from Juliana, walking over to the back of the wagon. Looking inside, he saw the body.

Iridan was laid out inside, wrapped in white linen except for his head. His friend's face was a greying blue, pocked with small wounds that would now never heal. He saw a bit of discolored flesh around the neck, and surmised the cause of death. Someone had used magic—a bit still lingered about Iridan's neck in the aether—to reattach the head. The joining had been imperfect, but was more respectful than returning the body in pieces.

Kyrus looked up at Rashan Solaran, who had not moved since he had arrived. The warlock's head turned slightly, acknowledging Kyrus.

"My legacy ..."—Rashan spoke softly; Kyrus could barely hear him—"... snatched away from me yet again."

* * * * * * * *

By sunset of the following night, all the arrangements had been made. On the grassy grounds behind the Solaran Estate, folk from all over Kadris had gathered. Airships had spent the day delivering nobles and sorcerers from the nearby parts of the surrounding empire as well. No one wished to risk the warlock's ire by refusing the invitation in his hour of grief.

A pyre of carefully stacked wood stood chest high to Kyrus, covering an area the size of two trellis tables set side by side. Iridan's body lay atop the pile, dressed in clean, new warlock regalia, with Sleeping Dragon resting on his chest, its hilt beneath Iridan's crossed hands. The smells of wood chips and pitch overpowered the scent of death that clung to Iridan despite the oils and unguents that had been used to make him look less gruesome in death.

Guards in imperial livery surrounded the pyre, keeping back all but a select few. Emperor Sommick was among those who were permitted near the pyre, as were Juliana, Rashan, Kyrus, and Iridan's foster parents. Kyrus had made a point to seek them out, personally flying the *Daggerstrike* out to their home to fetch them, and to tell them the news of Iridan's death personally. They had taken it better than he had imagined, proud that their son had died fighting for the folk in Munne. Kyrus wished he could have shared their peace of spirit.

One guest whose arrival had caused no small amount of surprise, and whose presence within the guarded area went unchallenged despite receiving no permission to be there, was Illiardra. She arrived accompanied by a disturbance Kyrus felt in the aether that he could only describe as something like the passing of a swarm of butterflies; he saw it more than felt it, and had he not been looking at the time, never would have noticed it. She was dressed in a full-length gown of black silk and matching black cloak, hood pulled low.

"I am sorry for the loss of your friend," Kyrus heard in his mind. He knew that it was Iridan's demonic mother who had addressed him.

"How did you know to come here?" Kyrus asked in kind.

"I watched. I saw him fall. I saw him brought here."

"If you were watching, why did you not save him?" Kyrus demanded, his anger flowing clearly in a medium of nothing but thought.

"He could have been saved, but not by me. Had I intervened, I might have spared his life for a time, but he would have suffered more greatly in the end."

"If you could not have saved him, who could have?"

"Two who, each for their own reasons, could not bring themselves to."

"Do you mean me and Juliana? Were we what stood between Iridan and death? What could I have done?"

"No. You, perhaps, are the one who had saved him for far too long already. But enough for now, twin of Brannis, the ceremony is beginning."

Kyrus shook himself from his magical conversation, and reacquainted himself with his surroundings. He stepped up to the pyre as he saw the others doing.

"We commit this hero to the fire," Rashan spoke, his voice carrying through the crowd as if he personally stood next to each man, woman, and child. Rashan released a tiny lick of flame that sparked a fire in the kindling packed in and around the logs of the piled wood. Juliana, Kyrus, and even Illiardra did likewise, setting flames at points roughly spaced out around Iridan's pyre.

A small stone slab, inlaid with runes, had been placed in the ground at the head of the pyre. Emperor Sommick walked over, and stood upon it. When he spoke, his voice was amplified throughout the estate grounds.

"We gather this night to honor Iridan Solaran, Warlock of the Kadrin Empire. Though he never spoke his pledge before me, he was pledged to the service of the Kadrin Empire at the time of my coronation, and he will henceforth be considered to be the first warlock of my reign. Though we have not gathered the entire circumstance of his death, we know that he fell in battle, and that his death was bought at the price of many Megrenn lives. I honor him, and wish that I could have had a dozen more like him, that we might never face an enemy willing to contest against us."

Emperor Sommick left the slab amid a respectful hush, and the soft crackle of four small fires as they began to spread. Rashan took the emperor's place next on the slab. Though he did not need the magical aid it provided, he allowed it to amplify his voice as well.

"I was gone from the Empire a very long time. In that time, I fathered Iridan, and left him to the fosterage of these kindly folk who have joined us this evening. They raised a fine young man, and sent him to the Imperial Academy when his magical talent became evident. As a child of an unknown bloodline, he fought for everything he got, earning his way to the top of his class. Upon my return to Kadrin, I sought to mold that boy into my own image. I saw the potential of a warlock within him, and indeed he became a warlock. But tonight I beg forgiveness for not doing enough to prepare him, for allowing him to go off alone when he might have been better served by more training. Twice before, in winters long past, I have said good-bye to sons who failed to walk the path I blazed for them. I find my curse in the repetition of mistakes I knew better than to make. I was blinded by the potential I saw, the visions of glory, of the legacy I would be able to pass on. Now I consign those dreams to ash."

To oblivion with you, demon, this is your fault.

Taking small steps, seeming unsure of her balance, Juliana took her turn next upon the speakers' slab. The magic made clear not only the words she spoke, but the sniffling between words as she struggled to maintain her composure.

"Iridan, I am sorry. We have quarreled since long before we were wed, and the childish torments I once inflicted on you ... I never outgrew them in time. You deserved much better than I gave you, and I cannot help wondering how much better your life would have been if not for mine. We would have grown together, in time, but I pushed you away. I made you feel like you needed to prove your worth. It was my fault you went off alone to Munne. It is my fault that you now lie before us, instead of standing alongside us." Juliana stepped off the slab just before she burst into tears.

Standing in the front row of spectators, just behind the halberds of the guards, Axterion stood with his hand on Danilaesis's shoulder for support. He leaned down, close to the boy's ear, and whispered, "Do you still want to be a warlock now? This is what happens to all of them, eventually."

Danil stared at the spreading fires but did not answer.

Illiardra took an unanticipated turn upon the slab herself, though only metaphorically. She chose to float above it, letting the crowd see her clearly as she threw back the hood of her cloak. She had done nothing to hide her inhuman appearance. Her thin, delicate horns framed her face, and her long ears poked from beneath her hair. Her voice echoed with her own magic as she shunned the stone runes.

"Iridan Solaran was born of my body, but was Rashan Solaran reborn. Every bit of power and potential that a young Rashan possessed, so too did Iridan. Raised with no knowledge of his lineage, Iridan developed kindness, compassion, and humility. This gave me hope that his father might learn these traits himself. Instead, within little more than a season of their meeting, Rashan destroyed Iridan, shattering a blade he believed himself to be tempering. Arrogance, wantonness, cruelty, a quickness to violence—all lurked beneath, exposed as the rest was stripped away. Today I mourn the death of everything that was good within Rashan Solaran."

With no further explanation, Illiardra was gone. Even paying attention that time, Kyrus could not see the magic she used.

Kyrus watched the flames for a moment, smelling the wood smoke, noting the subtle exchange of the fading twilight for the growing firelight. He made his way over, and took his turn upon the runed slab.

"The day I met Iridan, we were eight summers old, and at the Academy together. He was shy and quiet, peasant born and wary of all the highborn children about. I spent much of the winters that followed protecting him, helping him, watching over him, as would an older brother, though he was older than I by a turn of the moon," Kyrus said, noticing that his voice was wavering. *He was Brannis's friend, not mine. I barely knew him.* Kyrus wiped at his eyes. "We became the best of friends, constant companions. He was the only one from the Academy who did not shun me after I left there.

"Once our paths diverged, he carved a place for himself. He had a true talent for wardkeeping, and a bright future before him in the Circle. I looked on with pride at his accomplishments, knowing that because I had been there when he needed me, he could now stand on his own. He had become the stronger of the two of us. But ..." Kyrus found himself needing a pause to collect himself. *But I remember everything so clearly. It is as if I was there with them, with Brannis and Iridan as they grew up together.* He wiped his eyes dry again on the end of his sleeve. "But he did still need me. I was not there when he died. I could not save him.

"No, instead, all alone in some forsaken corner of a Megrenn-occupied city, Iridan was overcome. Some bastard cut his head off, and no amount of magic is going to undo that."

The crowd began to grow nervous as the sorcerers present began backing away from the pyre. There was a strong draw in Kyrus's direction, and the flow of aether was growing in strength.

"Iridan, I am sorry. I would do anything in my power to bring you back to life, but I cannot. All I have to offer is vengeance, and a proper farewell. I will not let this paltry fire be all the tribute you receive. Let the heavens themselves mark your passing!"

The crowd scattered, pushing back to a safer distance as the pyre erupted. A pillar of flame reached up into the night sky. A torrent of aether flooded through Kyrus's body, purging all the guilt, all the sorrows, all the regrets ... at least for a little while. The only thing it failed to burn clean of him was anger.

When the fires subsided several moments later, when the beacon trailed off into the starry sky, and faded away, Kyrus was left staring across the glowing embers of a crater where once a pyre had been. He saw Rashan Solaran, the only one who had remained unmoved, witnessing the awesome display of power in his son's name.

You are the one who killed him, you bastard! You may as well have wielded the blade yourself!

About The Author

Born in New Hampshire in 1977, J.S. Morin found himself captivated by the wonders of fantasy novels at a young age. He was introduced to the genre via the works of R.A. Salvatore, Ed Greenwood, and Margaret Weiss and Tracy Hickman. He loved exploring other people's worlds, from Shadowdale to Hyrule. He also quickly found Dungeons and Dragons to be a creative outlet for stories, characters, and new worlds of his own creation.

His other passion was for building and designing things, and when it came time to choose a career, he went down that road. A Mechanical Engineer by day, he spends his evenings with his wife in their New Hampshire home, enjoying the simplicity of life in a quiet state.

By night he dreams elaborate dreams of visiting fanciful worlds, performing acts of heroism, and solving intriguing puzzles, which inspire him to craft stories that he hopes will help shape the lives of the next generation of fantasy readers. He hopes to avoid finishing growing up.

42843413R00276